The Oxford Dictionary of
Nursery Rhymes

Page from Walter Crane's *Baby's Own Alphabet*, 1874, one of Routledge's 'New Sixpenny Toy Books'

The Oxford
Dictionary of
Nursery
Rhymes

Edited by IONA *and* PETER OPIE

Oxford New York

OXFORD UNIVERSITY PRESS

1997

Oxford University Press, Great Clarendon Street, Oxford OX2 6DP

Oxford New York

Athens Auckland Bangkok Bogota Bombay
Buenos Aires Calcutta Cape Town Dar es Salaam
Delhi Florence Hong Kong Istanbul Karachi
Kuala Lumpur Madras Madrid Melbourne
Mexico City Nairobi Paris Singapore
Taipei Tokyo Toronto Warsaw

and associated companies in
Berlin Ibadan

Oxford is a trade mark of Oxford University Press

First published 1951
New Edition published 1997

British Library Cataloguing in Publication Data
Data available

Library of Congress Cataloging in Publication Data
Data available

ISBN 0-19-860088-7

1 3 5 7 9 10 8 6 4 2

Typeset by Pure Tech India Ltd., Pondicherry
Printed in Great Britain
on acid-free paper by
Bookcraft (Bath) Ltd
Midsomer Norton, Somerset

Preface to the Second Edition

I T is forty-six years since the *Oxford Dictionary of Nursery Rhymes* was first published. During this time we ourselves made some further discoveries, and many people kindly wrote to us with additions to the histories of the rhymes, sometimes even providing a previously unknown source in, for instance, a medieval manuscript or seventeenth-century play. I would here like to thank all those valuable contributors, and in particular Lawrence Darton, historian of his family's famous firm; Pat Garrett, collector of alphabet books; Cecily Hancock, scholar and musicologist, of Portsmouth, New Hampshire; David Hounslow, student of street cries; Andrea Immel, Curator of the Cotsen Collection at Princeton University; the late Marjorie Moon, bibliographer and collector of children's books; Roy Palmer, who generously shared his wide knowledge of folk songs and ballads; Justin Schiller of New York; and that eminent collector of children's books, Robert Scott. Now that the *Dictionary* is being reset I am glad to be able to incorporate this important new material. My renewed thanks are due to the courteous and friendly staffs of the British Library and the Bodleian Library, and especially to Clive Hurst and Sylvia Gardner of the Bodleian. I owe a particular debt of gratitude to Brian Alderson, who has checked the work throughout, and has, especially, brought the bibliographical references into line with present-day knowledge.

Nursery rhyme books since 1951

WE followed *The Oxford Dictionary of Nursery Rhymes* with *The Oxford Nursery Rhyme Book*, 1955, in which we presented 800 rhymes and ditties, making it the largest nursery rhyme book and one of the biggest anthologies of traditional English verse. Deliberately we sometimes gave more than one version of a rhyme, and deliberately we sometimes gave versions different from the text rhymes appearing in *ODNR*. Having had the benefit of a further four years' collecting, we were able to include a number of rhymes or versions of rhymes which had not been in print before. This in turn was followed by *The Puffin Book of Nursery Rhymes*, 1963. Although 150 of the rhymes are those we considered essential for anyone setting forth in life, nearly as many again are either additional to those in the Oxford books, or in a distinctly different version.

There have been a number of notable nursery rhyme books since 1951. I thought it important to give some post-1951 references in the apparatus, perhaps less to record the appearances of rhymes than to show that the publishing of nursery rhyme books, many of them superbly illustrated, went on from strength to strength. The problem has been that the contents of many of them were taken from the Oxford books. The more civilized editors or artists applied for permission to use texts; others did not, but had clearly used the Oxford books rather than going to original sources. An honourable exception is Brian Alderson's *Cakes and Custard* (Heinemann), 1974, in which every rhyme was selected from a primary source.

Preface

A HUNDRED years have passed since the first publication of *The Nursery Rhymes of England*, 'collected principally from oral tradition' by James Orchard Halliwell. This little volume, by the young man of 22 who was later to become world-renowned as a Shakespearian scholar, has been reprinted (in various guises) more times than any of his numerous later, and more ambitious studies. The collection, interspersed with notes about the age and origins of the nursery rhymes, was the outcome of much random delving and is a treasure store of curious information. It was the first work to draw attention to the antiquity of the rhymes with any conviction, and the first collection which attempted to be comprehensive. For a century its authority as the standard work has been unchallenged. Together with his *Popular Rhymes and Nursery Tales*, published in 1849, it is the basis (whether acknowledged or not) of almost every nursery anthology, and it has been the principal English source, often the sole source other than the fertile imaginations of the 'happy guessers', of every essay and paragraph on the origin of nursery rhymes which has been published since.

Halliwell opened the gate to a fascinating field of research and it is strange that little attempt has been made to continue his work. The extent of his reading and his erudition were such that a superstition arose, persisting to this day, that there was nothing more to be learnt about the rhymes. In all these years no attempt has been made to verify his statements; his inaccuracies have been repeated with monotonous regularity, and no attempt has been made even to consolidate the new facts which have come to light in the past three generations. Yet Halliwell himself knew more than he ever cared to publish. Although it may be true that he collected 'principally from oral tradition', there were a number of contemporary rhyme books available to him, and there were others which might have been considered antique when he himself was a child.

In the introduction to his first edition he acknowledges having seen *Infant Institutes*, published in 1797. In subsequent editions he refers to three other books: *Gammer Gurton's Garland or the Nursery*

Preface

Parnassus (1810), *The Popular Rhymes of Scotland* (1824 and 1842), and Bellenden Ker's fanciful *Essay on the Archaeology of Nursery Rhymes* (1834). It is also clear that he made use of some of the juvenile books at the Bodleian, especially *Songs for the Nursery*, an excellent seventy-six page booklet which first appeared in 1805. Mention of these collections is not meant to belittle Halliwell's work, but it is to be regretted that he did not always manage to say exactly where he found his material. Also, if one is to make a study of these rhymes, it is helpful to compare the first collections which were made, and note which pieces were included in them. This has been done for the present volume.

In a work of this kind, as the compilers of such dictionaries as those of Proverbs and of Christian Names have already found, the difficulty is to know where to start and where to draw the line, and, having decided on the scope, to know how the material should be presented. The compiler after a number of years' work is confronted with a table-load of manuscript notes, recording, if he has been conscientious, every laborious detail and every speculation however improbable. He must decide how technical and how selective he should be. In the present work we have attempted to be detailed, without, we hope, being tedious. We have not thought it necessary to set down endless variations of a rhyme unless these variations, in themselves, have a particular interest. Not the least of our difficulties has been to know what to adopt as the standard text. Should it be the version which happens to be the earliest recorded? Or the version which is the most euphonious? Or the one we ourselves remember from our childhood? Our answer has been a compromise. We have chosen the version which seems to us the fullest, while bearing in mind how the rhyme is commonly known today.

For the first time nursery rhymes have been arranged alphabetically to facilitate easy reference. Halliwell's attempt to classify the rhymes was to divide them into fourteen (later eighteen) sections under such headings as 'Natural History', 'Love and Matrimony', 'Historical', 'Paradoxes', 'Gaffers and Gammers'. This system, on account of its quaintness, has been imitated by many of the anthologists, but, as Halliwell himself admitted, it was open to criticism. Nursery rhymes may be gathered but they defy regimentation, and we cannot claim complete orderliness for our system either. Arrangement by the most prominent word (where possible a proper noun) has a number of advantages. Thus, 'This

Preface

little pig went to market' will be found under *Pig*, 'A frog he would a-wooing go' under *Frog*, 'Ride a cock-horse to Banbury Cross' under *Banbury Cross*. The better-known nonsense jingles, such as 'Hey diddle diddle' and 'Eena, meena, mina, mo', are listed under their opening phrases. Where a nursery character has more than one name the arrangement is by the first name, *Jack* Horner, *Humpty* Dumpty, *Cock* Robin; and this applies equally to nick-names, as *Mother* Hubbard, and *Boy* Blue, though the formal titles, Mr., Dr., General, and so on, are ignored.

Most of the rhymes will, we believe, be readily located; while reference to the index at the end which lists the first lines of both the standard text and all variations quoted, should lead the way to any pieces proving elusive.

In scope this dictionary is intended to embrace those verses which are traditionally passed on to a child while he is still of nursery age. As well as the nonsense jingles, humorous songs, and character rhymes, it includes the more common lullabies, infant amusements, nursery counting-out formulas, baby puzzles and riddles, rhyming alphabets, tongue twisters, nursery prayers, and a few singing games, the words of which have an independent existence in the nursery.[1] The collection does not, however, include a number of pieces which, though sometimes appearing in 'Nursery Rhyme' books, belong, strictly speaking, to older children. For instance, the dialogues of dramatic games (as 'We are three brethren out of Spain'), and the rhymes bandied between school-children.[2] Nor, with a few exceptions, are there included local, dialect,[3] and other folk rhymes,[4] rhymes of divination, magic spells, and fairy tales in verse. Further, it has not been our object to resurrect pieces long forgotten, and when the contrary might be supposed we have been careful to supply evidence of contemporary or recent vitality.

---

[1] Whole books could be (indeed have been and still need to be again) devoted to several of these categories individually. Counting-out formulas, for instance, come only on the fringe of nursery rhyme lore. This dictionary cannot pretend to be exhaustive under these sub-headings.

[2] See I. and P. Opie, *Lore and Language of Schoolchildren*, 1951; *The Singing Game*, 1985; and *Children's Games with Things*, 1997.

[3] Except as variations to rhymes in standard English.

[4] These are often, of course, learnt in childhood, e.g.

> A swarm of bees in May
> Is worth a load of hay,

but are clearly adult in character.

Preface

This brings us to the notes on the rhymes which are, we believe, of a comprehensiveness not previously attempted. Our aim has been to find the earliest recording of each piece no matter in what kind of literature it appeared; to offer the possible circumstances of its origin, to illustrate changes in the wording through the years, and to set it beside its forebears or companion pieces from other lands. It has been our intention to build up a picture of the surroundings in which the rhymes have thrived, and of the effect they have had upon their hearers; to tell of the poets who have been warmed by them, the children who have delighted in them, and the customs, superstitions, and amusements which have become associated with them. Our belief is (for this has been our own experience) that a knowledge of their past adds to the pleasure of them in the present.

In our references we set out with the ambitious plan of consulting the original sources wherever possible; on important occasions when this has not been possible, the source has been indicated in a bracket succeeding the quotation. In the case of undated anonymous and pseudonymous literature the name of the publisher, where it is of moment, appears in brackets after the title.[1] When the publisher has been American, the place of origin has also been given. It should be noted that we have not, except in special cases, given references to rhyme appearances where they have merely been unedited copyings from an earlier work. This accounts for the comparatively small number of references subsequent to Halliwell, and is why those which are given are drawn mostly from *Notes and Queries*, publications of Folk-Song and Folk-Lore Societies, from personal collection, or from our noble band of helpers. Correspondents were asked to send rhymes or versions of rhymes which they had 'never seen in print'. This has made their contributions of particular value, for they give a picture of how the rhymes are known today in oral tradition.

We believe that we have assembled here almost everything so far known about nursery rhymes together with a considerable amount of material hitherto unpublished. We are, nevertheless, keenly aware how necessary it is for us to add a note of diffidence.

---

[1] This is particularly necessary with such ephemeral literature as the juvenile chapbooks. There is much uncertainty about when some of the publishers were working and our estimation of the dates of their productions does not always agree with those given by the Copyright Libraries.

Preface

We dare not hope that we have discovered every early reference to a nursery rhyme, nor that those who follow will find no gaps or inaccuracies; we can only hope that however patently they have been caused by our lack of diligence or of erudition, they will be brought to our notice with gentleness.

I.O. and P.O.

Alton in Hampshire
1944–51

Acknowledgements

THE present work embodies the personal recollections, knowledge, and collectings of many friends and friendly correspondents, and it gives us pleasure to make the following acknowledgements:

To those who have come forward with rhymes and information, among them: Mrs. E. Louie Acres; Mr. Victor G. Alexander; Mr. Robert D'O. Aplin; Lady Archibald; Mr. L. G. D. Arland; Sister M. Ayres; Mrs. C. C. Baines; Lady Balfour; Mr. Richard Bell; Mr. Howard Biddlestone; The Rev. Peter B. G. Binnall; Mrs. Alicia E. Bourne; Miss M. Bremner; Mrs. William W. Brockwell, with a generous gift in aid of Dr. Barnardo's; Miss C. Campbell Thomson; Miss Cartmell; Miss Emily Chisholm, who has in preparation *Nursery Rhymes for Nursery Reasons*; Miss Pat Challis; Mrs. R. W. Christy; Miss Ethel E. Coath; Mrs. M. D. Collingham; Miss C. Crawford; Miss A. F. M. Cuppage; Mrs. Joan Cutsforth; Mrs. Jane Dawson; Mr. Desmond H. Dickson; Miss Ruth Duffin; Mr. J. R. S. Duncan; Mr. Oliver Edwards; Mrs. E. Eripper; Mrs. M. E. Evans; Mrs. Awrea Farmer; Miss Joan Ford; Mr. Donald A. Foster; Mr. John L. Gilbert; Mr. F. Grice, author of *Folk Tales of the North Country*; Miss F. Doreen Gullen, compiler of *Traditional Number Rhymes and Games*; Mrs. E. F. Hall; Miss Innes Hart; Mrs. A. F. Hay, donor of some of Caldecott's hand-coloured proofs, two of which are reproduced here; Miss Renée Haynes; Major F. E. Hill; Mrs. Valerie Hills; Mrs. F. W. Chant Hobrow, donor of *Food for the Mind: or, A New Riddle Book*, 1787; Mr. Clifford L. B. Hubbard, compiler of the forthcoming *Bibliography of British Dog Books*; Mrs. Hunt-Lewis; The Rev. E. Clafton Illingsworth; Miss Carrol Jenkins, who has given much time to collecting; Lady Knight; Mr. N. Lincoln; Miss L. M. Littlewood; Nurse Lloyd; Miss K. E. Lloyd; Mrs. Eleanor M. Macqueen; Mrs. Margaret Miller; Mr. and Mrs. William Montgomerie, compilers of the delightful *Scottish Nursery Rhymes* and *Sandy Candy*; Mrs. B. Monypenny; Mrs. Vaughan Nash; The Rev. and Mrs. Colin Opie; Masters James and Bobby Opie, who dutifully submitted to early training as collectors; Mrs. H. R. Page; Mrs. S. Dauncey Pearce; Miss F. P. Plant; Mrs. S. A. Pope; Canon Prideaux, D.D.; Mr. Hugh Reid; Miss Jean V. Robinson; Mr. R. D. Rudwick; Miss A. Russell; The Hon. Miss

Acknowledgements

Maud Russell; The Hon. Miss V. Sackville-West, C.H., who passed on material additional to that used in her *Nursery Rhymes* (1947); Miss Beatrice Saunders; Mrs. M. Scaife; Mr. W. K. Scudamore; Mrs. S. Stuart; Mrs. P. Tatlow; N. D. Alessandra Tinelli di Gorla; Mrs. Jane Toller; Mr. H. Tyson; Miss Florence C. Urquhart; Mrs. R. St. J. Walker; Mr. L. Warner; Mr. R. C. Warner, whose entertaining recollections have added a number of light touches to this work; Miss Maureen Wells; Mrs. W. Wells; Mrs. Agnes Whitworth; Miss Flora L. Willoughby; Mrs. D. Woodfine; Mrs. D. Wormald; Miss Dorothy Wright; Miss M. A. Yorker.

To specialists and others who, when applied to, readily came to our aid, including: Mr. J. Leslie Abbott, of Messrs. Francis, Day & Hunter, Ltd., for the original words of the song, 'Jeremiah, blow the fire'; Miss Dorothy Mary Armitage, great-great niece of and authority on Ann and Jane Taylor; Dr. A. A. Barb, of the Warburg Institute, who loaned us his valuable paper 'Animula Vagula Blandula' and directed our attention to Köhler's *Kleinere Schriften*; Mrs. H. A. Lake Barnett, the active Hon. Secretary of the Folk-Lore Society; Colonel Reginald Bastard, D.S.O., who read and commented upon the article on 'Old Mother Hubbard', and passed on to us his family's traditions about Sarah Catherine Martin; The Rev. Dr. Henry Bett, author of *Nursery Rhymes and Tales* and *The Games of Children*; Mr. Ernest Bletcher, Librarian, County Borough of Derby, for additional information about 'The Derby Ram'; Mrs. John Boon, who generously gave time to translating; Mr. E. Kenneth Brown; Lt.-Col. A. H. Burne, D.S.O., author of *The Noble Duke of York*, quoted in the article, 'Oh, the brave old Duke of York'; Mrs. Raymond Burrell, who generously gave time to translating; Mr. Charles Chilton, of the B.B.C., for information and guidance about songs popularized by the nigger minstrels; Mr. Walter de la Mare, C.H., whose letters, reminiscent of the delights in *Come Hither*, reminded us that what our notes say is scarcely more important than the way they say it; Miss Ann Driver, of the Schools Dept., B.B.C.; Mr. Charles P. Finlayson, Keeper of MSS., the Library of Edinburgh University; Miss A. G. Gilchrist, O.B.E., with whom we have been privileged to have an unending correspondence, as enjoyable as it has been valuable, and whose reading of the manuscript was unhappily interrupted by a fall in her eighty-sixth year, when she broke her leg—her remarks warm and illuminate many of our pages; Mr. Robert Graves, for annotations to his beautiful anthology, *Less Familiar Nursery Rhymes*;

Acknowledgements

Mr. Duncan Gray, City Librarian, Nottingham, for information about Gotham; Mr. W. Claud Hamilton, County Librarian, Durham, for additional information about the song 'Elsie Marley'; the late Rev. F. P. Harris, authority on the works of Beatrix Potter; Mr. Reginald Hart; Miss Joan Hassall; Mr. E. Austin Hinton, City Librarian, Newcastle-upon-Tyne, for verifying facts about the life of Elsie Marley; Dr. R. W. Hunt, Keeper of Western Manuscripts, Bodleian Library, who directed our attention to several MSS. in his keeping, and has afforded us other kindnesses; Mr. F. M. C. Johnson, late Hon. Librarian, The Folk-Lore Society; Mr. Richard Kelly, of the B.B.C., Newcastle-upon-Tyne; Mr. Allan M. Laing; Mr. Raymond Mander and Mr. Joe Mitchenson; Miss Enid Marx, compiler and illustrator of *The Zodiac Book of Nursery Rhymes*; The Earl of Oxford and Asquith, who read and commented upon the article on 'Little Jack Horner'; Mrs. Margarita Peel for translations from the Spanish; Dr. Elfriede Rath; Dr. Cecil Roth; Miss Elsie A. Russ, Deputy Director, Victoria Art Gallery and Municipal Libraries, Bath; the late Lord Saye and Sele, an early member of whose family may or may not have ridden a cock-horse to Banbury; the late Mr. George Bernard Shaw, by a couple of years the contributor to this work with the longest memory, for the MS. 'Bernard Shaw's Nursery Rhymes', and other reminiscences; Mr. L. F. Shenfield; Professor J. Simmons, biographer of Southey; Professor Archer Taylor; Mr. T. Todd; Mr. Herbert van Thal, whose advice at an early stage proved invaluable; Dr. Arthur Waley, for some literal translations of the Chinese in J. T. Headland's *Chinese Mother Goose Rhymes*; Mr. Harold Williams; Miss Dora E. Yates, Hon. Secretary, The Gypsy Lore Society.

To private collectors of children's books who have allowed us to examine their collections: Mr. Charles W. Traylen; The National Magazine Co. and the National Book League, who gave special facilities in respect of the collection formed by the late F. R. Bussell; Miss Elisabeth Ball, of Muncie, Indiana, who did not allow distance to come in the way of our knowing everything we wanted to about her superb collection; Dr. d'Alté A. Welch, of Ohio, who similarly allowed us to view the highlights of his collection by microfilm; and Mr. Roland Knaster, whose fabulous collection is blessed with a generous and knowledgeable custodian.

To kindly members of the antiquarian book trade (a part of whose nature it seems to be to go out of their way to be helpful),

Acknowledgements

especially Mr. L. W. Bondy; Mr. J. Burke; Dr. Ettinghausen; Mr. Ifan Kyrle Fletcher; Mr. David Low; the late Mr. Henry M. Lyon, with whom we have spent many a pleasant day, not only searching through every volume and broadsheet in his Dickensian repository of juvenilia and curiosa—the like of which we shall probably never see again—but also drawing upon his wide knowledge of the ephemeral printers; Mr. Waldo Maas; Mr. C. D. Massey; Mr. P. H. Muir; Mr. Kenneth Mummery; Mr. Colin Richardson; Mr. Arthur Rogers; Mr. G. P. Romer; and Mr. T. D. Webster.

To various libraries, whose staffs we have found ever-willing to do their utmost to help us: The British Museum, where we have done most of our original research; The Bodleian Library, especially Miss G. M. Briggs, Assistant Secretary, who has also done copying for us; The London Library, where Mr. Cox remembers the days when J. O. Halliwell, 'a tall and always courteous gentleman', used to call for his books; The Victoria and Albert Museum; The Saint Bride Foundation; Kensington Public Library, where Mr. Boxall and Mr. Young have frequently assisted us; Chelsea Public Library.

To Miss E. G. Withycombe, compiler of *The Oxford Dictionary of Christian Names*, who patiently read our MS as it was prepared, and who by advice and strenuous criticism attempted to indoctrinate us with her own high standards.

Finally, to Mr. W. W. Collett-Mason, for very acceptable assistance; and to Mrs. Margaret Opie, without whose realistic aid the commencement of the work would have been impracticable and its completion impossible.

Acknowledgements of the material loaned for the illustrations, and of permission granted to reproduce copyright material, will be found in the List of Illustrations. We would like, however, to mention here our particular gratitude to Messrs. Frederick Warne & Co. Ltd. for permission to reproduce the page from Kate Greenaway's *Mother Goose* (plate XV *a*); the panel from Walter Crane's *The Baby's Opera* (plate XXI *a*); and the illustration by L. Leslie Brooke (plate XXIII *a*). And we think it interesting to record that Messrs. Warne have also long been the publishers of Randolph Caldecott's 'Picture Books' (plates III *b* and XI); they are the publishers of *Squirrel Nutkin* (plate XVI *b*); while *Aunt Louisa's Sing a Song of Sixpence* (plate XVII *a*) was published in their second year of business.

Contents

List of Illustrations

List of Illustrations

List of Illustrations

List of Illustrations

List of Illustrations

Illustrations in the text

List of Illustrations

List of Illustrations

Abbreviations

advt.	advertised	illus.	illustrated by
biblio.	bibliography	MS	manuscript
c.	*circa*, about	n.d.	not dated
cf.	*confer*, compare	*NR*	*Nursery Rhymes* (in book titles)
ed.	edition, or edited by	p.p. ed.	privately printed edition
e.g.	*exempli gratia*, for example	q.v.	*quod vide*, which see

Authors and Books

American Folk-Lore	Journal of American Folk-Lore, 1888–1950.
Baby's Bouquet	*The Baby's Bouquet*, 'A Fresh Bunch of Old Rhymes and Tunes', arranged and decorated by Walter Crane, 1879.
Baby's Opera	*The Baby's Opera* 'A Book of Old Rhymes With New Dresses. The Music by the Earliest Masters', by Walter Crane, 1877.
Baring-Gould	Sabine Baring-Gould, *A Book of Nursery Songs and Rhymes*, 1895.
Bett	Henry Bett, *Nursery Rhymes and Tales*, 1924; *The Games of Children*, 1929.
Bolton	Henry Carrington Bolton, *The Counting-out Rhymes of Children*, 1888.
Chambers	Robert Chambers, *The Popular Rhymes of Scotland*, 1826. Revised and enlarged 1842, 1847, and 1870.
Christmas Box	*Christmas Box* (A. Bland and Weller). Tunes by James Hook, 1797. Vols. ii and iii, 1798.
Crofton MS	Addison Crofton, 'Children's Rhymes', 2 MS vols., completed 1901. (Bodleian Library MS Eng. misc. e 39–40.)
DNB	*Dictionary of National Biography.*
Douce MS	Francis Douce and another, MS additions to *Gammer Gurton's Garland* (1784), c. 1800–c. 1820 (Douce R 227).
Douce MS II	? Member of Douce family, MS additions to *Gammer Gurton's Garland* (1810), c. 1820 (Douce Adds. 134 (8)).
Eckenstein	Lina Eckenstein, *Comparative Studies in Nursery Rhymes*, 1906.
Folk-Lore	*The Folk-Lore Record*, 1878–82; *The Folk-Lore Journal*, 1883–9; *Folk-Lore*, 1890–1950.

Abbreviations

Folk-Song	*Journal of the Folk-Song Society*, 1899–1931; *Journal of the English Folk Dance and Song Society*, 1932–50.
Ford	Robert Ford, *Children's Rhymes*, 1903, 1904.
FT Thumb's LSB	*The Famous Tommy Thumb's Little Story-Book* (S. Crowder and B. Collins), c. 1760.
GG's Garland	*Gammer Gurton's Garland or The Nursery Parnassus* (R. Christopher), 1784. Enlarged editions (Christopher and Jennett), c. 1799; (R. Triphook), 1810.
Gomme	Alice Bertha Gomme, *The Traditional Games of England, Scotland, and Ireland*, 2 vols., 1894–8.
Gosset	Adelaide L. J. Gosset, *Lullabies of the Four Nations*, 1915.
Gumuchian	Gumuchian et Cie, *Les Livres de l'enfance du XVe au XIXe siècle*, 2 vols., 1930.
Herd MS	David Herd, *Scots Songs and Ballads*, 2 MS vols., completed 1776, subsequently partially printed same year. (British Museum MS Adds. 22311–2.)
Hindley	Charles Hindley, *Life of James Catnach*, 1878; *History of the Cries of London*, 1881; *History of the Catnach Press*, 1887.
Holme MS	?Randle Holme, MS Riddle Book, c. 1645 (MS Harley, 1960).
Hugo	Thomas Hugo, *The Bewick Collector*, 1866; *Supplement*, 1868.
Infant Institutes	*Infant Institutes, part the first: or a Nruserical Essay on the Poetry, Lyric and Allegorical, of the Earliest Ages*, &c., 1797 [*N & Q*, 5th s., iii, p. 441].
JOH	James Orchard Halliwell, *The Nursery Rhymes of England*, 1842. Revised and enlarged, 1843, 1844, 1846, 1853, and c. 1860. *Popular Rhymes and Nursery Tales*, 1849 and c. 1860.
Juvenile Amusements	*Juvenile Amusements* (Dr. Samuel Arnold, Duke Street, Westminster), 1796–1797 [or 1798].
Kidson	Frank Kidson, *75 British Nursery Rhymes*, 'with the melodies which have always been associated with them', 1904.
Maclagan	Robert Craig Maclagan, *The Games and Diversions of Argyleshire*, 1901.
Mason	M. H. Mason, *Nursery Rhymes and Country Songs*, 'Both tunes and words from tradition', 1877.
MG's Melody	*Mother Goose's Melody; or Sonnets for the Cradle. In two parts. Part I. Contains the most celebrated songs and lullabies of the old British nurses; calculated to amuse children, and to excite them to sleep. Part II.*

Abbreviations

Those of that sweet songster and nurse of wit and humour Master William Shakespeare; adorned with cuts, and illustrated with notes and maxims historical, philosophical, and critical, probably being compiled in manuscript c. 1765, but not registered at the Stationers' Company as a published book until the entry by T. Carnan (bookselling partner of John Newbery's son Francis) in 1780. The earliest known English edition however is that published by Francis Power (see below p. 32). Endorsing, however tentatively, the argument for an early compilation we have given c. 1765 throughout as date for MGM.

MG's Quarto	*Mother Goose's Quarto: or Melodies Complete* (Munroe and Francis, Boston, Massachusetts), c. 1825 [Whitmore].
Musical Museum	*The Scots Musical Museum,* 'Consisting of Six hundred Scots Songs with proper Bases for the Pianoforte, &c.'. Edited James Johnson, vol. i, 1787; vol. ii, 1788; vol. iii, 1790; vol. iv, 1792; vol. v, 1797; vol. vi, 1803.
Nancy Cock's PSB	*Nancy Cock's Pretty Song Book for all Little Misses and Masters* (John Marshall), c. 1780.
N & Q	*Notes and Queries,* 1849–1950.
Newell	William Wells Newell, *Games and Songs of American Children,* 1883; revised and enlarged 1903.
Newest Christmas Box	*The Newest Christmas Box* (Longman and Broderip). Tunes by Reginald Spofforth, c. 1797.
Northall	G. F. Northall, *English Folk-Rhymes,* 1892.
Nurse Lovechild's DFN	*Nurse Lovechild's Ditties for the Nursery* (D. Carvalho), c. 1830.
OED	*Oxford English Dictionary.*
Only True MG Melodies	*The Only True Mother Goose Melodies* (Munroe and Francis, Boston, Massachusetts), c. 1843 (reprinted 1905; date of original incorrectly given as 1833).
Peter Puzzlewell	*A Choice Collection of Riddles, Charades, Rebusses, &c.,* by Peter Puzzlewell, Esq. (E. Newbery), 1792 [1794].
Prideaux	W. F. Prideaux, *Mother Goose's Melody,* 1904.
Rimbault	Edward F. Rimbault, *Nursery Rhymes with the tunes to which they are still sung,* 1846.
Rosenbach	A. S. W. Rosenbach, *Early American Children's Books,* 1933.
Rymour Club	*Miscellanea of the Rymour Club,* Edinburgh, 1906–28.

Abbreviations

Songs for the Nursery	*Songs for the Nursery collected from the Works of the Most Renowned Poets* (Tabart and Co.), 1805; (William Darton), 1818.
Top Book	*The Top Book of All, for Little Masters and Misses* (R. Baldwin, &c.), c. 1760.
T Thumb's PSB	*Tommy Thumb's Pretty Song Book* (M. Cooper), vol. ii, c. 1744.
T Thumb's SB	*Tommy Thumb's Song Book for all little Masters and Misses* (Isaiah Thomas, Worcester, Massachusetts), 1788.
T Tit's SB	*The Tom Tit's Song Book* (C. D. Piguenit), c. 1790.
Vocal Harmony	*Vocal Harmony, or No Song, No Supper* (no imprint), c. 1806.
Whitmore	William H. Whitmore, *The Original Mother Goose's Melody*, 1892.
Williams	Alfred Williams, *Folk-Songs of the Upper Thames*, 1923.

Introduction

In Britain and America, and wherever the English word is spoken, the children become joyful and wise listening to the same traditional verses. In the New World as in the Old their first poetic memory is of 'Four and twenty blackbirds baked in a pie', 'A slipkin, a slopkin, a pipkin, a popkin', 'Pat-a-cake, pat-a-cake, baker's man', and 'Over the hills and far away'. Almost the only point of difference is that in England the verses are known as 'nursery rhymes', and in America as 'Mother Goose songs'. The term 'nursery rhyme' seems to have become current in the second decade of the nineteenth century (see e.g. *British Review* (Aug. 1815), 55), probably promoted by Ann and Jane Taylor's immensely successful *Rhymes for the Nursery* (1806), which was actually labelled 'Nursery Rhymes' in gilt on its spine; and James Kendrew plundered this volume for some of his chapbooks. Previously the rhymes had been known as 'songs' or 'ditties', and in the eighteenth century usually as 'Tommy Thumb's' songs, or 'Mother Goose's', the title retained in America.

The problem of where nursery rhymes come from is perhaps of minor importance to literature. Yet these trivial verses have endured where newer and more ambitious compositions have become dated and forgotten. They have endured often for nine or ten generations, sometimes for considerably more, and scarcely altered in their journey. 'Pat-a-cake, pat-a-cake, baker's man', to take an everyday example, is shown in D'Urfey's comedy *The Campaigners* to have been waiting to greet infant ears two-and-a-half centuries ago. It was undoubtedly already old in 1698 when Fardell, the 'affected, tattling, nurse', crooned to her charge,

Ah Doddy blesse dat pitty face of myn Sylds, and his pitty, pitty hands, and his pitty, pitty foots, and all his pitty things, and pat a cake, pat a cake Bakers man, so I will master as I can, and prick it, and prick it, and prick it, and prick it, and prick it, and throw't into the Oven.

1

Introduction

Quality

What kind of verses are they to have become the best known in the world? Individual examination shows that not all are the doggerel they are popularly taken to be. 'The best of the older ones', says Robert Graves, 'are nearer to poetry than the greater part of *The Oxford Book of English Verse*.' 'They have', says Walter de la Mare, 'their own complete little beauty if looked at closely.' 'The nursery rhyme', says Professor Cammaerts, 'is essentially poetical because essentially musical.' They do not fail to satisfy the ear. 'G. K. Chesterton', writes Ivor Brown, 'observed that so simple a line from the nursery as "Over the hills and far away" is one of the most beautiful in all English poetry', and, as if in confirmation, Gay, Swift, Burns, Tennyson, Stevenson, and Henley thought well enough of the line to make it their own.

The themes of the nursery rhymes are so diverse that it does not seem to matter what they are. In some there are no two words together which make sense ('... Pin, pan, musky, dan, tweedle-um, twoddle-um, twenty-wan', which delighted Scott); in others there are as lively incidents and keenly drawn characters as are to be found in the language, and the tremulous Miss Muffet, the heroic Priest of Felton, the earnest and subservient Mother Hubbard may live, as Clifton Fadiman has suggested, as long as the plays of Shakespeare.

They contain wild extravagances, as 'the cow jumped over the moon', invitations to irresponsibility, as 'Hannah Bantry in the pantry', and illustrations of violence, like 'cut off their tails with a carving knife'.[1] Yet alongside these are love ballads, among the most pleasant we possess, 'Lavender's blue, diddle, diddle, lavender's green', 'Curly locks, Curly locks, wilt thou be mine?', and Sir Charles Sedley's 'There was a little man and he woo'd a little maid'.

Nor should the critic be surprised when verses now preserved solely for the amusement of the young are discovered to have come from such an accomplished hand as Sedley's. Here is not the place to dwell upon the realization, which folk-lorists in the twentieth century are reluctantly having to admit, that the folk 'had neither part nor lot in the making of folk-lore', that the

[1] Because of their nonsense, or the sadistic tendencies some of the rhymes are alleged to arouse in children, there have been several attempts to suppress or alter them, notably by George Wither (1641), Sarah Trimmer (beginning of nineteenth century), Samuel Goodrich (first half of nineteenth century), Geoffrey Hall (1948 onwards).

Introduction

early ballads were the concern of the 'upper classes', that the dancers on the village green were but imitating those who danced at court, and that the picturesque peasant costumes of today are simply survivals of the fashionable apparel of yesterday.[1] We will remark merely that our own excursions in nursery rhyme bibliography appear to support this view. We believe that if all the authors were known, many more of these 'unconsidered trifles' would be found to be of distinguished birth, a birth commensurate with their long and influential lives.

Sources of the Rhymes

The nursery rhyme, which by tacit and universal consent may be either said or sung, is resorted to by the mother for the soothing and amusement of her child without thought of its origin, except in that usually she remembers it from her own childhood.

The beginning of 'Tom, he was a piper's son', whose only tune was 'Over the hills and far away', may be traced to a song attributed to Motteux, while the magic tune which pleased both girls and boys figures in a ballad collected by Pepys, which appears to be alluded to in 1549. Here is an example of a nursery rhyme which was not in the first place intended for the nursery. Chesterton would have been more exact if he had said 'preserved by the nursery' rather than coming 'from the nursery'. Indeed, the farther one goes back into the history of the rhymes, the farther one finds oneself being led from the cot-side.

It can be safely stated that the overwhelming majority of nursery rhymes were not in the first place composed for children; in fact many are survivals of an adult code of joviality, and in their original wording were, by present standards, strikingly unsuitable for those of tender years. They are fragments of ballads or of folk songs ('One misty moisty morning' and 'Old woman, old woman, shall we go a-shearing?'). They are remnants of ancient custom and ritual ('Ladybird, ladybird', and 'We'll go to the wood'), and may hold the last echoes of long-forgotten evil ('Where have you been all day?' and 'London Bridge'). Some are memories of street cry and mummers' play ('Young lambs to

---

[1] See the two admirable Presidential Addresses delivered by Lord Raglan to the Folk-Lore Society, 20 Mar. 1946, and 5 Mar. 1947.

sell! young lambs to sell!' and 'On Christmas night I turned the spit'). One at least ('Jack Sprat') has long been proverbial. Others ('If wishes were horses', and 'A man of words') are based on proverbs. One ('Matthew, Mark, Luke, and John') is a prayer of Popish days, another ('Go to bed, Tom') was a barrack room refrain. They have come out of taverns and mug houses. ('Nose, nose, jolly red nose' still flaunts the nature of its early environment.) They are the legacy of war and rebellion ('At the siege of Belle Isle' and 'What is the rhyme for porringer?'). They have poked fun at religious practices ('Good morning, Father Francis') and laughed at the rulers of the day ('William and Mary, George and Anne'). They were the diversions of the scholarly, the erudite, and the wits (as Dr. Wallis on a 'Twister', Dr. Johnson on a 'Turnip seller', and Tom Brown on 'Dr. Fell'). They were first made popular on the stage (Jack Cussans's 'Robinson Crusoe') or in London streets (Jacob Beuler's 'If I had a donkey'). They were rude jests (like 'Little Robin Redbreast sat upon a rail'), or romantic lyrics of a decidedly free nature (as 'Where are you going to my pretty maid?'), which were carefully rewritten to suit the new discrimination at the turn of the last century. We can say almost without hesitation that, of those pieces which date from before 1800, the only true nursery rhymes (i.e. rhymes composed especially for the nursery) are the rhyming alphabets, the infant amusements (verses which accompany a game), and the lullabies. Even the riddles were in the first place designed for adult perplexity.

Their Possession by the Nursery

The circumstances which gave rise to this curious state of affairs throw an interesting light on our social history. It is only when we remember the attitude towards children in Stuart and early Hanoverian days, that we see how they came to be familiar with bawdy jokes and drinking songs. We read that in the seventeenth and eighteenth centuries children were treated as 'grown-ups in miniature'. In paintings we see them wearing clothes which were replicas of those worn by their elders. The conduct and the power of understanding we find expected of them were those of an adult. Many parents saw nothing unusual in their children hearing strong language or savouring strong drink. The spectacle of their fathers asleep under the table and in other 'even more

Introduction

lamentable positions' would not be unfamiliar to them. The Puritans had good cause for some of their objections, as the popular literature of the time is vivid witness. And this very literature often passed into youthful hands, for before 1740 there were few juvenile publications as we know them today. Steele, in the *Tatler* (1709), relates how familiar his godson is with the chapbook histories, and Ben Jonson in *Bartholomew Fair* (1614) makes Squire Cokes recall 'the ballads over the nursery chimney at home of my owne pasting up'. Probably only the Jews, whose ideas about children have always been enlightened, may be excepted. The two rhymes towards the end of the *Haggadah* which are included for the special entertainment of children during the long Passover service, 'Ehod Mi Yode'a' and 'Had Gadyo', are probably the earliest nursery pieces to have received official approbation.

However, the process of a particular poem or snatch of song making a place for itself in the nursery's permanent repertoire may be watched even in recent times. The tale of 'Willie Winkie' is an example of a poem being truncated, simplified, and so severed from its original context by the nursery, that writers are already telling stories of its fame 150 years before it was written. Septimus Winner's 'Der Deitcher's Dog', published in 1864, though originally intended as an adult song, has similarly had its tail cut off and been adopted by the nursery. 'Twinkle, twinkle, little star', 'Mary had a little lamb', 'There was a little girl, and she had a little curl', and 'Ten little nigger boys', are other pieces composed in the nineteenth century which are assured of immortality. Some fragments of Edward Lear, particularly the refrain of 'The Jumblies', are now finding their way into oral tradition. Mary Howitt's 'The Spider and the Fly', Alfred Scott Gatty's 'Three little pigs', Harry Graham's 'Billy in one of his nice new sashes', and A. A. Milne's 'Isn't it funny how a bear likes honey?' may confidently be expected to follow. It must be remembered that rhymes enter the nursery through the pre-disposition of the adults in charge of it. The mother or nurse does not employ a jingle because it is a nursery rhyme *per se*, but because in the pleasantness (or desperation) of the moment it is the first thing which comes to her mind. In a future age scholars may be delving into the origins of 'Chick, chick, chick, chick, chicken, lay a little egg for me' and 'Horsey, keep your tail up', popular commercial songs of the 1920's which are beginning to take root in the nursery, but are already near-forgotten by the rest of the world.

Age

On the whole, fewer of the nursery rhymes come from antiquity than seems to be popularly supposed. Because there is said to have been a Prince Cole in the third century A.D., 'a gode man and welbeloved among the Brytonnes', it does not follow that the song 'Old (or Good) King Cole' dates back to that period, even in the unlikely event of it referring to this chieftain. A large number of our rhymes have not been found recorded before the nineteenth century, while some, as has been pointed out in the previous section, are actually of recent manufacture. It is, we feel, from the beginning of the seventeenth century onwards that the majority of the rhymes must be dated.

However, from the little sample of children's song quoted in the gospels (Matthew xi. 17; Luke vii. 32), from the Roman nurses' lullaby *Lalla, lalla, lalla, aut dormi, aut lacta*, in a scholium on Persius, and from Horace's *puerorum nenia* recited by children, possibly while playing 'King of the Castle', it is clear that nursery lore 2,000 years ago was not really different from that which maintains today. The earliest pieces still surviving are the unrhymed folk chants with their numerous equivalents throughout Europe, the counting-out formulas hardly even of onomatopoeic sense, the simpler infant amusements, and a number of the riddles. Haphazard references in the Middle Ages confirm the existence of some of them. A phrase of 'Infir taris' is recorded about 1450; 'White bird featherless' appears (in Latin) in the tenth century; the germ of 'Two legs sat on three legs' may be seen in the works of Bede. Agricola (b. 1492) learnt the German version of 'Matthew, Mark, Luke, and John' from his parents. The whole of 'I have a ȝong suster fer beȝondyn the se' had been set down by 1450. A French version of 'Thirty days hath September' belongs to the thirteenth century. A game of 'falling bridges', on the lines of 'London Bridge', seems to have been known to Meister Altswert.

The following table may perhaps help to give an over-all picture of the age of the rhymes. The first and second rows of percentages are based exclusively on evidence provided by contemporary documentation, and show, in some measure, the success or other-

Introduction

wise of present research. The third row is based on internal evidence in the rhymes, and other relevant factors.

	1599 and before	1600–49	1650–99	1700–49	1750–99	1800–24	1825 and after
Per cent. definitely found recorded	2.3	6.9	4.2	8.8	22.2	21.7	33.9
Per cent. probably identified	4.2	8.2	4.7	11.3	21.1	20.6	29.9
Per cent. believed to date.	27.1	11.8	9.3	20.2	16.8	10.7	4.4

From this it will be seen that almost certainly 12.4 per cent of the rhymes, and certainly 9.2 per cent., were known when Charles I was executed in 1649. Nearly 50 per cent, and very likely 85 per cent of the rhymes are more than 200 years old. It may further be remarked that nearly one in four of all the rhymes are believed to have been known while Shakespeare was still a young man.

It should be noted, however, with reference to the last statement, that despite much searching and many claims little *positive* evidence can be brought forward to show that Shakespeare was familiar with any one of the nursery rhymes (unless, that is, we admit the Giant's slogan 'Fie, foh, and fumme, I smell the blood of a Brittish man', in *King Lear*, III. iv). However, while positive evidence may be wanting, there are reasons for supposing that he refers to two rhymes known in the present nursery, and to one other now obsolete; that he knew six others, at least in embryo, and was familiar with a book which contains several popular riddles.[1]

Oral Transmission

An oft-doubted fact attested by the study of nursery rhymes is the vitality of oral tradition. This vitality is particularly noticeable where children are concerned, for, as Jane Austen shows in *Emma*, and as V. Sackville-West has put it, children say 'tell it again, tell it just the same', and will tenaciously correct the teller who varies in the slightest particular from the original recital. It is this trait in children which makes their lore such a profitable subject for research.

[1] See under Shakespeare in the index of literary references, and also the section on Riddles hereafter.

Introduction

The infrequency with which the rhymes were recorded before the nineteenth century establishes that the written word can have had little to do with their survival. The song 'The King of France', said in 1649 to be one which 'good fellowes often sing', was familiar to Victorian nurses, although it does not seem to have been once written down in 180 years. Similarly, 'If all the world were paper', found tucked away at the end of an adult anthology of 1641, next makes an appearance in a nursery anthology of 1810. 'As soft as silk' and 'Riddle me ree, a little man in a tree' after being noted about 1645 disappear altogether, so far as literature is concerned, for the space of nearly two centuries. 'A—Apple pie' would have been thought to belong to the eighteenth century were it not for a chance analogy in 1671. 'When I was a little boy', twice quoted in the seventeenth century, is not seen again till the end of the eighteenth century. 'The hart he loves the high wood' and 'Whose little pigs are these?', both set down in 1632, were then apparently carried solely in men's minds for six or more generations. 'I have four sisters beyond the sea' played will-o'-the-wisp for four centuries before it was caught in the printing press. 'There was a lady loved a swine', first recorded in full in 1784, is found to have been already well known 160 years earlier. 'The carrion crow sat on an oak', which was not set down in full till even later (1798), is also known to have been current in Charles I's reign. There are many such examples. Nor does a rhyme necessarily cease to be passed on by word of mouth when it is written down. Very many recordings of 'Brow bender' have been made since 1788 when it appeared in a toy book, but none of them have been exactly the same as the first. Then, in 1944, we heard a nanny reciting to one of our children the whole 1788 version together with five additional lines not previously recorded.[1]

---

[1] That there are instances of rhymes being resuscitated by appearing in print cannot be denied. There is the temptation to the pedant to select verses from old works and speak of them as if they were still current in the language. Several of the rhymes in Halliwell's collection are suspect on this count. We do not believe that he ever heard 'The white dove sat on a castle wall' in the nineteenth century, but took it direct from *The Longer thou livest* (c. 1559). Others of his which we have excluded as not being genuinely traditional include, 'See-saw, sack-a-day' (from Douce MS 357); 'We make no spare of John Hunkes' mare' ('Bib. Reg. MS 8 A. v.'); 'Hush, hush, hush, hush' (*Patient Grissill*, 1603). This is not to say, however, that, through Halliwell, these rhymes may not now be read in nursery books. We recently saw 'The white dove sat on a castle wall' in a cheap production on sale at the bookstalls.

Introduction

Germanic Equivalents

It was Jamieson (1814) who first pointed out, and Halliwell who publicized it, that in Scandinavia there are rhymes which are equivalent to ours. 'We find', says Halliwell (1849), 'the same trifles which erewhile lulled or amused the English infant are current in slightly varied forms throughout the North of Europe; we know that they have been sung in the northern countries for centuries, and there has been no modern outlet for their dissemination across the German Ocean. The most natural inference is to adopt the theory of a Teutonic origin, and thus give to every child rhyme found in England and Sweden an immense antiquity.' In this class may be put 'Humpty Dumpty', 'Handy dandy', 'Brow bender', 'Four stiff standers', 'Where have you been today, Billy, my son?', 'Hitty pitty within the wall', 'A girl in the army', 'There was an old man and he had a calf', 'This pig got in the barn', 'Ladybird, ladybird, fly away home', and 'Snail, snail, put out your horns'. Lina Eckenstein, pursuing the theme,[1] quotes collections of rhymes published in Germany and France. 'The comparison of these collections with ours', she says, 'yields surprising results. Often the same thought is expressed in the same form of verse. Frequently the same proper name reappears in the same connection.' Calls such as those addressed to the ladybird and the snail, and riddle rhymes such as that on 'Humpty Dumpty', have numerous and close parallels half across Europe. 'In many cases rhymes, that seem senseless taken by themselves, acquire a definite meaning when taken in conjunction with their foreign parallels. Judging from what we know of nursery rhymes and their appearance in print, the thought of a direct translation of rhyme in the bulk cannot be entertained.' How close the parallels are may be seen from 'Humpty Dumpty'. In England children are told,

> Humpty Dumpty sat on a wall,
> Humpty Dumpty had a great fall.
>   All the king's horses,
>   And all the king's men,
> Couldn't put Humpty together again.

In Saxony,

> Hümpelken-Pümpelken sat op de Bank,
> Hümpelken-Pümpelken fêl von de Bank,

---

[1] *Comparative Studies in Nursery Rhymes*, 1906.

Introduction

Do is kên Dokter in Engelland
De Hümpelken-Pümpelken kuräre kann.

And in Denmark,

> Lille Trille
> Laae paa Hylde;
> Lille Trille
> Faldt ned af Hylde.
> Ingen Mand
> I hele Land
> Lille Trille curere kan.

The rhyme is also known in Sweden, France, Switzerland, and Finland. In a German version of 'Ladybird, ladybird' the name Ann is preserved, which in England is the name of the child saved from the fire. In the Swedish version of 'The girl in the army' the creature in the cradle is described as having 'long legs', exactly as in England and Scotland. In 'There was an old man and he had a calf' precisely the same joke is perpetuated both sides of the North Sea. The English 'Four stiff standers' is almost word for word as it is known in France, Germany, Italy, Norway, Moravia, and Lithuania; while 'What God never sees', recorded in Germany four-and-a-half centuries ago, is also common in the Dutch, French, Swedish, and Norwegian tongues. Versions of 'London Bridge' are found in France, Italy, Spain, Germany, Denmark, Hungary, and Slovakia. The nursery prayer seeking the protection of the four evangelists Matthew, Mark, Luke, and John, or similar figures, is common to almost every European country. Other rhymes with European equivalents include 'Robert Barnes, fellow fine', 'Who killed Cock Robin?', 'The twelve days of Christmas', 'Here goes my lord', 'Good morning, Father Francis', and 'Round about there sat a little hare'; the riddles 'As black as ink', 'As soft as silk', 'White bird featherless', 'Twelve pears hanging high', 'Two legs sat upon three legs', and 'As I was going to St. Ives'. The possibility of direct translation, however, in some of these latter instances, or of the rhyme crossing at a comparatively recent date, cannot altogether be overlooked.[1] 'Good morning, Father Francis', for instance, is not likely to be old, and is found

---

[1] An example of an English rhyme becoming a part of the oral tradition of another language is supplied by Henry Baerlein in *Landfalls and Farewell* (1949). In Anholt,

Introduction

only in French and English; as also is the riddle 'Twelve pears hanging high'. Riddle collections were made at an early date on the Continent, and some translations from French prose enigmas are known to have been made at the beginning of Henry VIII's reign.

Special Classes of Rhymes

1. *Counting-out rhymes*

When children wish to play a game in which one of their number must take a part different from, and therefore usually disliked by, the rest, they employ a formula such as,

> Eena, meena, mona, my,
> Barcelona, bona, stry,
> Air, ware, frum, dy,
> Araca, baraca, wee, wo, wack.

This is repeated by the leader as he points at the players in turn, one accented syllable to each child, and the child on whom the last word falls is the one chosen. These formulas, though often gibberish, have recognizable metrical shapes; versions collected in widely separated regions have remarkable similarity. The example above may be compared with,

> Eeny, meeny, mony, my,
> Barcelona, bona, stry,

from Wisconsin;

> Ena, mena, mona, mite,
> Basca, lora, hora, bite,

from Cornwall;

> Hana, mana, mona, mike,
> Barcelona, bona, strike,

the Danish island in the Kattegat, the children sing what is to them a nonsense rhyme,

> Jeck og Jill
> Vent op de hill
> Og Jell kom tombling efter.

It transpires that this is one of the last discernible relics of the British occupation of the island during the Napoleonic wars.

11

Introduction

> Hare, ware, frown, venac,
> Harrico, warrico, we, wo, wac,

from New York 130 years ago; and,

> Ene, tene, mone, mei,
> Pastor, lone, bone, strei,
> Ene, fune, herke, berke,
> Wer? Wie? Wo? Was?

from Germany.

Great antiquity was attached to these pieces well before 1820. The tradition in England was that counting-out rhymes were remnants of formulas used by the Druids for choosing human sacrifices. Charles Taylor mentions it in *The Chatterings of the Pica*, and seventy years later Gomme gave credence to it. How the idea arose it is impossible to say, though the practice of selection by counting, e.g. the decimation of enemy armies, is certainly apposite.

Since the rhymes are concerned with counting, it is natural to look at the early Celtic numerals:

Welsh	(Pronounced)	Cornish (recorded 1542)	Irish	Breton
un	*een*	ouyn	aon	unan
dau	*daay*	dow	do	daou
tri	*tree*	tray	tri	trî
pedwar	*pai'dwaar*	peswar	ceathair	pévar (*fem.* peder)
pump	*pimp*	pimp	cuig	pemp

Little connexion with the rhymes is immediately apparent, though in relation to the Welsh numerals a 'chappin' out' rhyme, collected in 1881 from north of the Tweed, might be considered:

> Eetern, feetern, peeny, pump,
> A' the laddies in a lump...

There exist, however, in oral tradition some other sets of counting words, reaching to twenty, and used by shepherds for counting sheep, fishermen for reckoning their catch, and old knitting-women for their stitches. These scores were named by A. J. Ellis, in 1877, the 'Anglo-Cymric Score', leaving it open whether Cymric was to mean simply Welsh, or both Welsh and Cumbrian. It is

Introduction

from the north country and East Anglia that they are mostly obtained.

High Furness	West Riding, Yorks.	Yar- mouth	Northum- berland	Westmor- land	North Riding, Yorks.
aina	eina	ina	eën	yan	yan
peina	peina	mina	tean	tyan	tean
para	paira	tethera	tether	tethera	tithera
peddera	puttera	methera	mether	methera	mithera
pimp	pith	pin	pimp	pimp	mimph
ithy	ith	sithera	citer	sethera	hitter
mithy	awith	lithera	liter	lethera	litter
owera	air-a	cothra	ōva	hevera	over
lowera	dickala	hothra	dōva	devera	dover
dig	dick	dic	dic	dick	dick

It is apparent that there is a connexion between these scores (here given to ten) and the Celtic numerals, and similarly a link may be discerned with the children's rhymes, corrupted though they are, e.g. between the north Yorks. score and a rhyme from Edinburgh:

> Inty, tinty, tethera, methery,
> Bank for over, dover, ding;

between the Westmorland score and that of a twelve-year-old reader of the *Daily Mirror* children's page (1948):

> Ya, ta, tethera, pethera, pip,
> Slata, lata, covera, dovera, dick;

and between the Northumberland score and an American rhyme collected by Carl Withers (1946) known as 'Indian counting' and popularly believed to be in the language of the Red Indians:

> Een, teen, tether, fether, fip,
> Sather, lather, gother, dather, dix.

Such assemblages of words (very many examples could be given) belong mostly to school-children, and as such are not part of the present inquiry. But the beginning of 'Eena, meena, mina, mo', on which Kipling was so eloquent, may be seen in the Yarmouth score; and 'Ziccoty, diccoty, dock' (or 'Hickory, dickory, dock'), another nursery favourite, is reminiscent of 8, 9, and 10 of the

Introduction

Westmorland score. It seems certain that if further sets of early numerals were known, more children's rhymes could be identified as coming from them.[1] The theory is that, when the Romans and then the Saxons invaded and occupied Britain, it was in Scotland, in Wales, and in the west country that the Celts managed to retain their language and customs. The rest, in the course of years, came more and more completely under the influence of their conquerors. An exception was those whose work was lonely and who were left unmolested, particularly by the Romans, because of their value to the garrisons in supplying provisions: such were the stock-breeders. This is demonstrated by the snatches of language preserved through almost two millenniums by (i) people living in mountainous and outlandish parts, (ii) shepherds, (iii) children in their games. For children, as has been noted, are conservative and exact, and tend to be in touch with the non-working (oldest) members of the family, who themselves delight in recounting their earliest memories.

2. Riddles

Rhyming riddles have been out of fashion with adults (other than newspaper racing tipsters) for three centuries; they owe their survival almost entirely to their adherents in the nursery. Some of them are found embedded in early ballads, in which a girl wins a husband or a suitor his lady's hand by solving them (as in 'Captain Wedderburn's Courtship') or by successfully evading them (as in 'The Elphin Knight').[2] The hey-day of rhyming riddles, however, the Elizabethan age, came when the ancient prose enigmas were extended and versified, often with most attractive results. The short prose riddles had been popular since remote times, and the Renaissance, in conjunction with the printing press, had hardly become active in England before there was a collection of them in circulation. *Demaundes Joyous* was printed in 1511 by Wynkyn de Worde, Caxton's apprentice and successor. 'Whiche was fyrst ye henne or ye egge?' is a riddle familiar in every household, and the riddle of the bee, 'What is it that is a wryte and is no man, and he dothe that no man can . . . ?', is a question of which a poetical version ('Little bird of Paradise') was collected only recently.

---

[1] Bibliographies of printed collections appear in *Transactions of the Philological Society*, 1878; *The Counting-Out Rhymes of Children*, H. C. Bolton, 1888; *Notes & Queries*, vol. 180, 1941. See also, as a corrective to Ellis, Henry Bradley in *The Academy*, 17 May 1879.

[2] See under 'I have four sisters beyond the sea' and 'Can you make me a cambric shirt?'

Introduction

A problem intriguing alike to the riddle collector and to the Shakespearian student is the identity of the 'Book of Riddles' lent by Master Slender to Alice Shortcake (*Merry Wives*, I. i). It is almost undoubtedly that listed by Laneham in his letter from Kenilworth (1575) and by *The English Courtier* (c. 1579) as *The book of Riddels*. Whether it was the same as *The Booke of Meery Riddles* as is presumed by Furnivall, Brandl, and other scholars is not proven, though it is probable. The collection is extant in an edition of 1600, and from internal evidence seems to belong to one of the previous decades. Among the seventy-seven riddles are seven rhymes still known to children: 'He went to the wood and caught it', 'Two legs sat upon three legs', 'What is that as high as a hall?', 'What is they which be full all day?', 'I came to a tree', 'What is it that is higher then a house?', and 'What is that as white as milke?' Even if Shakespeare was referring to another book it would not be unreasonable to suppose that he was familiar with these problems. Further editions of the *Meery Riddles* were printed in 1617, 1629, 1660, 1672, and 1685, a collection similarly styled appeared in 1631, and *A New Booke of Merry Riddles* (in two parts) was issued in 1665. Many of the riddles of 1600 reappear in the 1631 collection, though they had obtained a more literary flavour; others are noted for the first time, e.g. ''Tis black without and black within', 'I am cald by name of man', and the renowned 'Hitty pitty within the wall', later to become a favourite of the impertinent Squirrel Nutkin. Indeed, the riddles were already termed 'Very meete and delightfull for Youth to try their wits' (1631) and 'No lesse vsefull then behoouefull for any yong man or child, to know if he be quick-witted, or no' (1629). The remaining important collection of the seventeenth-century underlines what has been said. It is a manuscript collection (Harley 1960), apparently of youthful composition, for the spelling is vile even for the period (c. 1645). It was made by the Holme family of Chester, principally (?) by the Randle Holme (1627–99) who later wrote *The Academy of Armory*. The manuscript is one of the most valuable of all English riddle collections. Its very imperfections are of interest, for they show, in contrast to the complete forms of the riddle-books, the manner in which the rhymes were orally transmitted three centuries ago. It contains fourteen rhymes still commonly remembered, including, 'j have a little boy in a whit cote' (Nancy Etticoat), 'What is y^t that is rond as a cup?', 'On yonder hill ther stand a Knight' (Gray Grizzle), 'Four & twenty white

Bulls', 'There was a King met a King', and most of those already mentioned.

A number of the riddles, even metrical ones, may further be traced to European collections. Some of these were printed earlier than any in English, and it should be remarked that *Demaundes Joyous* (1511) was itself largely a discreet reprint of a French collection of similar title, published about 1490. There was, for example, a collection published at Strasbourg in 1505, and there was *Les Adeuineaux amoureux*, which was published in Bruges about 1478. In the former may be seen the old Alsatian rendering of 'What God never sees'; in the latter a close equivalent to 'Twelve pears hanging high', providing, incidentally, the solution, which in England had been lost.

3. *Infant Amusements*

Often a verse emerged as an accompaniment to certain actions. Some early ballads and folk-songs are said to have accompanied dances. Dramatic singing games (e.g. 'How many miles to Babylon?', 'Here we go round the mulberry bush') used to be, and still are, a feature of the play of school-children. Words and phrases of children's sports tend in time to become formalized and versified. (Petronius Arbiter about A.D. 50 tells of a small boy saying 'Bucca, bucca, quot sunt hic?'; children today demand 'Buck she, buck she, buck, How many fingers do I hold up?' or even, as in New York, 'Buck, buck, you lousy muck, How many fists have I got up?') Rhymes which accompany infant amusements are probably among the oldest verses there are. The game of Handy-dandy, in which a small object is juggled from hand to hand, is mentioned by Miege (1688), Mabb (1622), Shakespeare (1608), Florio (1598), Robert Browne (c. 1585), and Skelton (1529). Langland (1362) wrote, 'Wrong þenne vppon Wisdom wepte to helpe Him for his handidandi Rediliche he payede'. On this the *OED* comments, 'the transferred use... implies that the child's play was known before this date'. When the rhyme itself started it is impossible to say, but Chapman quoted it in 1598, 'handy dandy prickly prandy, which hand will you haue?', and it exists in Germany,

> Windle, wandle,
> in welchen Handle,
> oben oder unt.

Introduction

The small game of Bo-peep, peek-bo, or peep-bo, is referred to by Urquhart (1653), Herrick (1648), Fletcher (c. 1620), Florio (1611), Shakespeare (1608), Warner (1606), Jonson (1599), Joye (1535), Tindale (1528), and in a manuscript of about 1364. Most of these rhymes, as is only to be expected, have parallels in other countries, for instance, the face-tapping formula 'Brow bender' is known in Germany as 'Kinne Wippchen'; the palm-tickling 'Little Hare' is exactly matched in Italy by 'Una Lepre Pazza'. Poking and tickling, it may be noted, often play as big a part as the rhymes in infant distracting. The face is further touched when reciting 'Here sits the Lord Mayor', the palm again tickled in 'If you be a gentleman'. The nose is 'chopped' in 'My mother and your mother'. The foot is slapped in 'Shoe a little horse' and the toes tweaked in 'This little pig went to market', 'This pig got in the barn', and 'Let's go to the wood, says this pig'. More enterprising are the illustrative games such as 'Here's the church' and 'Here are the lady's knives and forks', or the games that mystify, like Goldsmith's 'Two little dicky birds'. And if all else fails there are the jog-along knee songs, 'A farmer went trotting upon his gray mare', 'Here comes my lord with his trusty sword', and, one which has numerous Continental parallels, 'This is the way the ladies ride'.

4. *Lullabies*

Little has been written about the lullaby, though it is a most natural form of song and has been declared to be the genesis of all song. As Sir Edmund Chambers has said: 'It must be remembered that the dance was not the only primitive activity, the rhythm of which evoked that of song. The rocking of the cradle was another.' In England the lullaby has been a recognized literary form for six centuries, ever since, in the reign of Edward II, an Anglo-Irish friar wrote,

> Lollai, lollai, litil child,
>   Whi wepistou so sore?
> Nedis mostou wepe,
>   Hit was iyarkid[1] the yore...

There was necessarily an established folk tradition in being when this was penned, and undoubtedly long before. As John de Trevisa put it in 1398, 'Nouryces vse lullynges and other cradyl songes to

---

[1] *iyarkid*, ordained.

pleyse the wyttes of the chylde'. The interest of the Roman lullaby already quoted (p. 6) is that it reveals the existence of a folk tradition utterly independent of the literature of the time. It has, in fact, more in common with the songs sung by the Italian peasantry of today than it has with the productions of the contemporary Latin poets of classical times.

Whether any of the lullabies sung to England's present generation have made their way from long ago is, with one exception, doubtful. 'Hush-a-bye, baby, on the tree top', the best-known lullaby, is probably not older than the sixteenth century, and legend associates it with the seventeenth. Indeed, the word *hushaby* is not found in use before 1700, though *hush*, as in 'Hush thee, my babby, lie still with thy daddy', is apparently a back-formation of *husht* and belongs to the sixteenth century. *Babby*, incidentally, retains the old pronunciation of *baby*; Shakespeare rhymed *babe* with drab and slab. *Rockaby*, the alternative reading in some lullabies, e.g. 'Rock-a-bye, baby, thy cradle is green', seems to be a comparatively recent innovation (first recorded in 1805), though *rock* is ancient, even in association with rocking the cradle. *Bye*, meaning sleep, as in 'Bye, baby bunting', 'Bye, baby bumpkin', and 'Bye, O my baby' dates at least from the fifteenth century, and is still retained in the nursery word *bye-byes*. The earliest quiescence word in cradle songs is the lulla of *lullaby*. *Lollai, lollai,* will have been noted in the Anglo-Irish song (c. 1315); *lullay* may be seen in John de Grimstone's manuscript of 1372,

> Lullay, lullay, litel child,
> Softë slep and faste.

Particular Sources of Rhymes

1. *Printed Ballads*

Some of the rhymes are found to be stanzas from ballads printed in the seventeenth century. These ballads, issued on broadsides, usually in black-letter and surmounted by crude woodcuts, were sold by the hawkers in street and market place. Sometimes they treated of heroes long gone by, and their very wording belonged to tradition. More often they were new writings; they were humorous, or pornographic, or concerned with the news of the day. They were churned out by literary hacks. When bought they were stuck on cottage and alehouse walls, or folded many

Introduction

times and carried in the pouch. 'I love a ballad in print a-life' says the shepherdess Mopsa in *The Winter's Tale*.

It is usually the ballad's first stanza to which the nurses have given immortality. Thus a ballad *The Wiltshire Wedding* (c. 1680) begins with the lines,

> All in a misty Morning,
>> So cloudy was the Weather,
> I meeting with an old Man,
>> Who was cloathed all in Leather.

The Old Pudding-Pye Woman set forth in her colours (c. 1670, possibly by John Lookes) starts 'There was an old woman sold puddings and pies'. The first stanza of *The Happy Husbandman: Or, Country Innocence* (c. 1686) is found to be the favourite verse 'My maid Mary', and another of Arcadian sentiment, *Diddle, Diddle, Or, The Kind Country Lovers*, begins 'Lavenders green, diddle, diddle, Lavenders blue'. In *Choice of Inuentions* (1632) the first stanza and the refrain are remembered independently: 'There were three men of Gotam' (now, 'There were three jovial Welshmen'), and 'There was a man had three sonnes' (now, 'There was an old woman had three sons'). In *The Lamentations of a Bad Market*, however, it is the twelfth, eighteenth, and nineteenth stanzas which are known to the world; they tell of 'Three children sliding on the ice'. Occasionally a rhyme is only part quoted in a ballad, or the ballad merely helps to date a rhyme by its phraseology. In *The Unconstant Maiden* (c. 1690) the third stanza begins,

> Bad news is come to Town, bad news is carry'd,
> Bad news is come to Town, my Love is Marry'd,

lines which bear comparison with the nursery 'Jemmy Dawson'. In *New Mad Tom of Bedlam* (c. 1673) the nursery 'Man in the moon' is echoed in the subtitle, *The Man in the Moon drinks Clarret, With Powder-beef, Turnep and Carret*. In *Tom Tell-Truth* (c. 1676) is the curious conjunction of 'Moorfields' and 'Paul's steeple running upon wheels' which appears in the rhyme 'As I was walking o'er little Moorfields'. A study of the ballad sheets thus becomes valuable over and above the number of rhyme origins discovered.

2. *Song Books*

Sometimes ballads were extended songs, sometimes a song was the condensation of a ballad. An example of a ballad later

19

included in a song book, and now a nursery epic, is *A moste Strange weddinge of the ffrogge and the mowse* (registered 1580). This was almost certainly a forerunner of 'The Marriage of the Frogge and the Mouse', ancestor of 'The frog who would a-wooing go', and one of the 'covntry pastimes' given with music in *Melismata* (1611). An example of the opposite, a song being extended to fill the requirements of the broadsheet, is that of the eighteenth-century 'Alice Marley'. The earliest printing known is on a broadside but it is clear that this was not the original form, nor the most popular. There are fourteen verses as opposed to eight and nine in the versions collected not long afterwards by Ritson, Bell, and Sharp, and the additional six verses are crude and of general application, they in no wise carry the story forward, and may indeed have come from another ballad.

The song books of the seventeenth century were finely printed, their words and music set together, sometimes having the part of the third voice inverted so that three singers could use the book at once. *Melismata Musicall Phansies, Fitting the Court, Citie, and Countrey Humours. To 3, 4, and 5 Voyces* was one of three collections produced by Thomas Ravenscroft (b. c. 1590). They were made up of roundelays, catches, and (in *Melismata*) short madrigals, many of them being folk-songs, others probably of Ravenscroft's own composition. *Pammelia* (1609) the first volume, and the first collection of rounds ever published, contains 'Iacke boy, ho boy newes', alluded to in *The Taming of the Shrew* and the possible starting-point of 'Ding, dong, bell, pussy's in the well'; also 'Birch and greene holly', sometimes found in nursery collections (e.g. L. E. Walter's, 1924), but strictly speaking a school rhyme (*vide* our *I saw Esau*, No. 172). *Deuteromelia or the Seconde part of Musicks melodie* (also 1609) contains the renowned 'Three blinde Mice', also 'Of all the birds that euer I see' with its refrain, now known independently, 'Nose, nose, nose, nose, and who gave mee this jolly red nose'. Thus of 152 songs printed by Ravenscroft in Shakespeare's lifetime the beginning may be seen of six pieces prized by children in the present century.

These three collections had to satisfy the needs of singers for forty years until the publication of *The Musical Banquet* (1651). In the spate of song books which followed (particularly after the Restoration) to meet the predominantly English love of catch and round singing, are found further verses which have descended to the nursery, 'Wilt thou lend me thy mare to ride but a mile', written by Nelham, appears in *Catch that Catch can* (1652). 'When I was young, I then had no wit', described as 'a New Catch', is in *Wit and Mirth* (1684). 'Peter White that never goes right', written and composed by Richard Brown, is included in *The Second Book of the Pleasant Musical Companion* (4th edn. 1701), and by the same hand is "Tis pitty poor Barnet a Vigilant, Vigilant Curr' (now, 'Barnaby Bright he was a sharp cur') in *The Jovial Companions* (1709). 'When V and I together meet' and 'Aron thus propos'd to Moses', included in Halliwell's nursery rhymes but of pleasure rather to school-children, may be found in *The Pleasant Musical Companion* (1686) and *Vinculum Societas* (1688) respectively. 'All in a misty morning' and 'There was an old Man had three Sons' from the ballad sheets, appear in *Wit and Mirth* (1700) and *A New Academy of Compliments* (1715). And from the stage 'Buz, quoth the blue fly' is in *Catch that Catch can* and 'Jockey was a Piper's Son' ('Tom, he was a piper's son' in embryo) is in *Wit and Mirth* (1706).

3. *Stage Productions*

In the sixteenth, seventeenth, and eighteenth centuries comedies were enlivened with songs introduced, as in the present day, on the mildest pretext. In the part of Shakespeare's *The Two Noble Kinsmen* completed by Fletcher, the jailor's daughter enters singing 'There were three fooles, fell out about an howlet'. In Ben Jonson's *The Masque of Oberon* (1616) the Satyrs, on the excuse of working a charm, sing 'Buz, quoth the blue fly', lines which, three centuries later, the bats in *The Tailor of Gloucester* murmured in their sleep. In Jonson's *The Masque of Queens* (1609) the eleventh hag sings 'I went to the toad', a verse which is also found in nursery books. In Beaumont and Fletcher's *Knight of the Burning Pestle* (1609), Merrythought, in a happy state, enters singing 'Nose, nose, jolly red nose'. And earlier, in *The longer thou livest* (registered 1569) among the ditties sung by Moros are 'Tom a lin and his wife, and his wiues mother', and a fragment of 'John Cook's mare'. As a source for research the scripts of early plays are of extreme value. Not only are new songs introduced but the popularity is shown of others already established. To the students who wrote *Grobiana's Nuptialls* (c. 1620) 'There was a lady loved a swine' seems to have been so well known that there was no need to write it in full, and it is quoted again in a familiar manner in Brome's *The English Moor* (1658), and in Edward Ravenscroft's

Introduction

London Cuckolds (1682). Other students (those of St. John's College, Cambridge) were clearly familiar with 'Thirty days hath September', which appears in *The Retvrne from Pernassvs*, 'publiquely acted' about 1602. In Penkethman's *Love without Interest* (1699) a character quotes 'When I was a little boy, I washed my mammy's dishes' which Aubrey twelve years previously had described as 'an old filthy Rhythme used by base people'. In *Love in a Village* (1762) Isaac Bickerstaffe incorporated 'There was a jolly miller' and it became one of the most popular songs in the country. 'A master I have, and I am his man' by O'Keeffe (the father, incidentally, of Adelaide, part author of *Original Poems for Infant Minds*) became well known after being sung in *The Castle of Andalusia* (1782). Often the alleged enthusiasm with which a song was received is described in the song sheets. 'There was a mad man' was sung by Mrs. Massey in *The Devil to Pay* 'with great Applause'. Jack Cussans's rendering of 'Poor old Robinson Crusoe!', to a pantomime tune of 1781, was sung 'with unbounded applause' by Russell in his revival of *The Mayor of Garret*. The titles of pantomimes themselves indicate the popularity of certain rhymes in the nineteenth century. *Harlequin Horner or the Christmas Pie* was performed at Drury Lane in 1816. *Harlequin and Poor Robin; or The House that Jack Built* was at Covent Garden in 1823; *Old Mother Hubbard and her Dog* was presented ten years later. *Harlequin and Little Tom Tucker* was at Queen's in 1845, *The Old Woman Tossed in a Blanket* at the City of London in 1847, and *Lady-Bird, Lady-Bird, Fly Away Home* at the Pavilion in 1853. At Drury Lane *Hey Diddle Diddle and the Seven Ages of Man* was performed in 1855, and *See-saw, Margery Daw, or, Harlequin Holiday and the Island of UPS and SNMOC* in the next year. At Astley's, which went in for even longer titles, the Christmas production in 1864 was *Harlequin Jack Sprat or the Three Blind Mice, and Great A, Little A, and Bouncing B*, and in 1865 *Harlequin Tom, Tom, the Piper's Son, Pope Joan and Little Bo-Peep*. Not to be outdone, the young W. S. Gilbert the succeeding year called one of his early dramatic attempts *Harlequin Cock Robin and Jenny Wren; or, Fortunatus and the Waters of Life, the Three Bears, the Three Gifts, the Three Wishes and the Little Man Who Woo'd a Little Maid*.

4. Folk-Songs

The history of folk-song collecting is brief. Bishop Percy in 1765 published his *Reliques of English Poetry* which, though it contained few folk-songs, was symptomatic of the growing interest in all traditional verse. In Scotland and the north country, David Herd, a Glasgow solicitor's clerk, Ritson, Thomson, James Johnson, the friend of Burns, and, indeed, Burns himself, were active collectors in the latter half of the century. Buchan, Hogg, Bell, Cunningham, Chambers, Scott, and Mactaggart, followed in the early nineteenth century. But so far as southern England was concerned it was thought that few folk-songs existed, and it was not until shortly before the formation of the Folk-Song Society in 1898 that collecting properly commenced. There is thus little information about the age of the songs. The slight contribution which the present work makes to folk-song study is through the fact that it was for the nursery that some of the best-known songs were first recorded. Several of the songs discovered in the twentieth century through the oral collection of Baring-Gould, Frank Kidson, Cecil Sharp, Vaughan Williams, and Alfred Williams, were among the 'Pretty Songs for Little Masters and Misses' printed in the eighteenth century. 'When I was a little boy, I lived by myself' was recorded about 1744 (170 years before Cecil Sharp found it in North Carolina). 'We will go to the wood, says Robin to Bobbin' and 'We're all dry with drinking on't' were printed at the same time. 'Trip upon trenchers', 'Little Betty Pringle', and 'There were two birds sat on a stone' appeared in *Mother Goose's Melody* (c. 1765). A verse of 'Jackey come give me your fiddle' is in the first edition of *Gammer Gurton's Garland* (1784), as is a verse of 'I am a pretty wench'; and 'When good King Arthur ruled this land' appeared in the second edition (c. 1799), thirty years before Peter Buchan recorded it. The earliest version of 'The Twelve days of Christmas' is in a minute nursery book *Mirth without Mischief* (c. 1780). 'I shall be married on Monday morning' is taken back to 1805 by a verse in *Songs for the Nursery*. 'My father he died but I can't tell you how' is yet another song first known through juvenile literature, and so is 'I love sixpence' (negativing the claim that it was written by Moncrieff). The song 'The cuckoo is a merry bird' was said in 1796 to have already appeared in a children's book which had been published 'for years, if not many generations'. The nursery, too, upholds the fact, seldom appreciated outside specialist circles, that English folk-songs treat more with maids and courting than with hounds and the chase. 'It's once I courted as pretty a lass, as ever your eyes did see', 'Little maid, pretty maid, whither goest thou?', 'Where are you going to my pretty maid?', and 'Lavender blue and Rosemary green, when I am king you shall be queen' are examples in point. To place against them there is only 'There were three jovial Welshmen as I have heard men say' and 'There was a little man and he had a little gun', both of which make fun of hunters. Folk-songs, in and out of the nursery, most often describe homely and everyday events. For instance 'Old woman, old woman, shall we go a-shearing?', 'A carrion crow sat on an oak', 'Whistle, daughter, whistle', 'Oh, what have you got for dinner, Mrs. Bond?', and 'There was a little woman as I have heard tell', all of which are known in the nursery, and for all of them children's literature provides either early recordings or valuable variations.

5. *The Mummers' Play*

The folk-play lingered into the twentieth century, even less noticed than the folk-song. When Sir Edmund Chambers, after long and diligent search, published his findings, he had located in England, Scotland, Ireland, and Wales, little more than 100 texts (of very varying merit), mostly of the late nineteenth century.[1] This does not mean that the folk-play was infrequently performed; rather, the scarcity of texts shows that it was so regularly performed (usually each year at Christmas time) that there was no need for written prompts. It is, perhaps, inevitable that an entertainment so embedded in the life of the country should have left traces of its existence in the nursery. Even if the mummers had left no texts one would suspect that some of the rhymes were a legacy of their fooling. The mummers, in their strange costumes, calling at one house after another, must often have been the first actors a young child knew, and the only ones a nurse ever saw. Indeed, Mrs. Ewing has written of the effect their visit had on one young family.[2]

Fragments of the mummers' play, as of folk-song, appeared in books for children long before they were collected by the folklorists. The mad sequence beginning 'Last Xmas day I turned the spit' which was a part of the Robin Hood play written down in Gloucestershire in 1868, had appeared in *The Famous Tommy Thumb's Little Story Book* (c. 1760), in a version probably much closer to the original speech of the mummers than that collected in the rarefied air of the nineteenth century. Further lines of this

---

[1] *The English Folk-Play*, E. K. Chambers, 1933.
[2] Juliana Horatia Ewing, 'The Peace Egg', in *Aunt Judy's Magazine*, Dec. 1871.

Introduction

sequence were collected from the nursery by Halliwell in 1844, who also included the verse 'Here comes I, little David Doubt' as a nursery rhyme. The introductory lines to the performance, as might be expected, and the closing lines, are the best remembered. 'Bounce, buckram, velvet's dear', sometimes opened the play; 'This poor old man is dead and gone' were the exit lines. The nursery preserves early or alternative versions of songs which the mummers incorporated, such as 'Old King Cole', 'My father died a month ago', and 'When good King Arthur ruled this land', and an array of lines, names, and allusions, as 'ekee-okee, adama pokee', 'mince pies hot, mince pies cold', 'black puddings enough to choke our dog', and 'my poor father, Abram Brown', which will have a familiar ring to those who know their nursery lore.

It is very probable that if earlier texts of the mummers' play existed we would find in them yet more nursery nonsense jingles, such as 'Here am I, little Jumping Joan', 'Rowsty dowt, my fire is out', and 'I'll sing you a song, the days are long', rhymes which are much in the idiom of the mummers.

6. *Political Squibs*

Much ingenuity has been exercised to show that certain nursery rhymes have had greater significance than is now apparent. They have been vested with mystic symbolism, linked with social and political events, and numerous attempts have been made to identify the nursery characters with real persons. It should be stated straightway that the bulk of these speculations are worthless. Fortunately the theories are so numerous they tend to cancel each other out. The story of 'Sing a song of sixpence', for instance, has been described as alluding to the choirs of Tudor monasteries, the printing of the English Bible, the malpractices of the Romish clergy, and the infinite workings of the solar system. The baby rocked on a tree top has been recognized as the Egyptian child Horus, the Old Pretender, and a New England Red Indian. Even when, by chance, the same conclusions are reached by two writers the reasons given are, as likely as not, antithetical. This game of 'interpreting' the nursery rhymes has not been confined to the twentieth century, though it is curious that it has never been so overplayed as in the age which claims to believe in realism. Dr. William King was probably reflecting the talk of his day when, nearly two and a half centuries ago, he speculated on

Introduction

the identity of 'Good King Cole'. Sixty years later the jesting editor of *Mother Goose's Melody* gave birth to a new set of propositions, still sometimes taken seriously, and subsequent eighteenth-century writers added to the confusion. The most remarkable attempt, however, to read significance into nursery verses was made by John Bellenden Ker (formerly Gawler) who in 1834 published *An Essay on the Archaeology of Popular English Phrases and Nursery Rhymes*. This volume is probably the most extraordinary example of misdirected labour in the history of English letters. With infinite patience and elaboration the author set out to show that English phrases and nursery rhymes were transmogrified from an early form of Dutch (the invention of Mr. Ker) and that the rhymes had originally been 'popular Pasquinades, illicited by the soreness felt by the population at the intrusion of a foreign and onerous church-sway'. One example will suffice. 'Ding dong bell', he says, derives from,

> Ding d'honig-beld,
> Die kaetst in de weld.
> Hwa put heer in?
> Lyt 'el Je haen, Je Grijn.
> Wat! er nauwt je boei-wo aes dat?
> Te draa! hone puur boose guit.
> Wo nijver dijdt ene arme
> Bat ghild hem eys in 'es vaders baen.

Meaning:

'It is the honey-bearing image that brings this revenue, it is this that affords all this wealth. Who is it takes it out? That curse to us all, the sneering bully (the monk). What hav'nt you always a pair of handcuffs ready for such a carrion-rogue as that? At once! make an example of this thorough-paced villain. While industry and hard work can alone avail the vassal-peasant, the idle pick-pocket-career of the monk affords him abundance.'

This is followed by a detailed glossary justifying the interpretation, and thirty-four rhymes are treated in this way. Nor did the 1834 volume suffice. By 1837 he had extended the work to two volumes, and after a further three years' labour he produced a third. Ker has given delight to students of mania ever since.

Halliwell struck a saner note (1842) but greedily copied down as facts any theories related to him, and, though he lambasted Ker, he was not above speculation himself. Lucy Locket and Kitty Fisher are baldly stated to be 'two celebrated courtezans of the time of Charles II'; 'I had a little nut tree'...'perhaps refers to Joanna of Castile'; 'I had a little husband'...'may probably commemorate a part of Tom Thumb's history, extant in a little Danish work...'. And he emulates Ker when he gives 'Hey diddle diddle' as a corruption of $\overset{?}{A}\delta'$ $\mathring{a}\delta\eta\lambda\alpha$, $\delta\tilde{\eta}\lambda\alpha$ δ' $\mathring{\underset{\iota}{a}}\delta\epsilon$.

Another ingenious essay on the rhymes, probably a leg-pull, appeared in 1872, when a gentleman who signed himself A. M. Nitramof, of Warsaw, claimed that he had heard peasants in the neighbourhood of the Bocage repeating the French originals of most of the better-known English rhymes: 'Jack Sprat', for example,

> Jaques Spras
> N'aimoit pas le gras,
>   Sa femme le maigre détestoit:
> Ainsi, que ses deux
> Rien au monde n'alloit mieux,
>   Et rien sur la table ne restait.

Fortunately this pamphlet does not seem to have come the way of the popular folk-lorists. The same cannot be said of *The Real Personages of Mother Goose*. This lavishly produced book written by Katherine Elwes Thomas and published in Boston in 1930, is a curious mixture of fact and fable, and a cheerful determination to prove that the nursery characters were real persons regardless of what the sources quoted say. Thus 'Bo-peep' becomes Mary, Queen of Scots; 'Jack Sprat', Charles I; 'Curlylocks', Charles II; 'Simple Simon', James I; 'Old Mother Hubbard', Cardinal Wolsey; 'Tommy Tucker', also Cardinal Wolsey; the lady who rode to Banbury, Queen Elizabeth; the cat in 'Hey diddle diddle', also Queen Elizabeth; the pussy in 'I love little pussy', Queen Elizabeth again; and so on. As Scott said, 'Nothing so easy as to make a tradition'. *The Real Personages* has received both circulation and credence, and has even had a film based on it.

The foregoing remarks, however, should not be read as a complete rejection of the idea that some of the rhymes originally referred to actual people. The present century seems to be the first in which it is a rarity for popular songs to be written about the heroes of the day.[1] There is, for instance, fair evidence for

---

[1] Popular songs reflecting the conditions of the times, especially in war time, are abundant ('The last time I saw Paris', 'Forty million Churchills', and 'We're going to hang out

Introduction

identifying the cast of five northern ditties of the seventeenth and eighteenth centuries, 'Elsie Marley' (a Picktree alewife), 'Jacky, the fiddler' (Rattlin' Roarin' Willie), 'What is the rhyme for porringer' (the Prince of Orange), 'Charley over the water' (Bonnie Prince Charlie), and 'Bessy Bell and Mary Grey' (two ladies of Perth). It is well known, too, from the numerous examples which have been preserved, that political lampoons have been common in every previous period of history. 'Little General Monk', 'Hector Protector', and 'Little Jack Horner' are possible examples of such doggerel now retired on nursery pension; 'There was a monkey climbed a tree', 'The Parliament soldiers', and 'William and Mary, George and Anne' certainly are. 'Old Sir Simon the King' is generally supposed to have been Simon Wadloe of the 'Devil' Tavern in Fleet Street (c. 1621). 'Jack Sprat' appears (at latest in 1659) to have ridiculed an Archdeacon Pratt. 'As I walked by myself' was placed on record about 1720 as referring to William III. 'The brave old Duke of York' was probably Frederick, George III's son. And we have the evidence of a future Historiographer Royal, James Howell, writing only a few years after the event, that the 340-year-old song 'The King of France and forty thousand men' refers to Henri IV and his last dubious enterprise.

Emergence of Nursery Rhyme Literature

References in the sixteenth and seventeenth centuries to verses now known in the nursery have been shown to exist in some number. But there are few descriptions of the rhymes actually being in the possession of children. John Aubrey (1687) is almost the only early writer to have gone out of his way to quote a song sung by young girls ('The Tailor of Bisiter'). This, as we know, does not mean that children had not acquired their own peculiar lore; it means that nobody, other than Aubrey, had thought it interesting enough to perpetuate. The glimpses we get of its existence are by the way; a clergyman (1671), wishing to illustrate a theological point, quotes 'A apple pie'; an ageing lexicographer (1611), attempting to define the Italian word *abomba*, recalls part of a rhyme from his childhood, 'as we use

the washing on the Siegfried Line'), but the writers can only think of two songs about specific persons in recent years, 'Amy, wonderful Amy' (Amy Johnson) and 'Oh, Mr. Gable' (Clark Gable).

28

Introduction

to say Home againe home againe market is done'; a pamphleteer (1606), reporting a murder trial, reveals that children regularly repeated a 'Cock a doodle doo' couplet; and a playwright (c. 1559) introducing a clown singing old songs ('Tom a lin' amongst them) makes him admit they were learnt from his fond mother 'As I war wont in her lappe to sit'.

At the beginning of the eighteenth century, in the reign of Queen Anne, appeared the first book expressly designed for the young which had traditional rhymes in it. Whoever was its modest author, 'T. W.', was thirty or forty years before his time. *A Little Book for Little Children* (like several other primers printed in Little Britain) was produced, as its sub-title says, in a 'plain and pleasant way'. It contains two rhymes still rightly celebrated, 'A was an Archer' and 'I saw a Peacock with a fiery tail', and three well-known riddle verses.

The next events of note took place in 1709, 1725, and c. 1728. In 1709 Dr. William King produced his *Useful Transactions in Philosophy*, in 1725 the poet Henry Carey wrote *Namby Pamby or A Panegyric on the New Versification*, and about 1728 the still unidentified author of 'The Nurse's Song' was realistically regretting some characteristics of the very young. All these works were satires, and as happened several times during the century, it is satirical writing which gives us the first intimation that a children's rhyme is current. The satirists profess to find great depths in the rhymes of children, or compare each other's verse with the familiar jingles. In so doing William King quotes 'Boys and Girls come out to play', 'Good King Cole', and 'The Lion and the Unicorn'; Carey refers to no less than eleven jingles including 'Jacky Horner' and 'See-and-Saw and Sacch'ry-down'; and 'The Nurse's Song', opening with 'Hey! my kitten', mentions 'Shoe, shoe, shoe the wild colt' and 'This pig went to market'.

Just over 200 years ago, probably in 1744, was printed the first considerable (though it measures but $3 \times 1\frac{3}{4}$ in.) nursery rhyme book. This was *Tommy Thumb's Pretty Song Book* in two volumes, 'Sold by M. Cooper, According to Act of Parliam[ent]'. It probably cost its original purchaser 4*d*.; but the value of the one surviving copy (in the British Museum) must be many pieces of gold. Even so, it is only 'Voll.II', a crudely printed little relic from a Georgian toy cupboard, but with contents (with three exceptions) as happy and familiar for the child of today as they undoubtedly were for the young Boswells and Cowpers and Gibbons, its readers at the

Introduction

time. 'There was a little Man, And he had a little Gun', 'Who did kill Cock Robbin?', 'Bah, Bah, a black sheep', and thirty-six other songs crowd the pages, most of them illustrated with pleasant and appropriate little engravings. How these rhymes came to be collected, what were the rhymes in the first volume, and who was the editor who chose to be styled 'N. Lovechild', are things which, it seems, we are never likely to know. Perhaps the publisher herself compiled it, the enterprising Mary Cooper whose imprint also appears on works by Gray, Fielding, and Pope. And perhaps she may be pictured asking her distinguished authors, after the more serious affairs of the day had been settled, if they knew any songs appropriate for Tommy Thumb's collection.

Not very much, either, is known about *The Famous Tommy Thumb's Little Story-Book*. On the title-page it says it was 'Printed for S. Crowder in Pater-Noster-Row; and sold by B. Collins, at the Printing-Office, Salisbury.' Stanley Crowder moved to the Golden Ball in Paternoster-row in 1760, and was concerned with Benjamin Collins (printer of *The Vicar of Wakefield*) in a number of ventures. *The Little Story-Book* is not dated, but must have been printed some time between 1760 and 1768 when it had reached America.[1] The booklet, opening with the 'Life and Surprising Adventures of Tom Thumb', and following with fables, concludes with Tommy Thumb's 'pretty stories that may be sung or told'. These are nine in number, and include the first recordings of 'This pig went to market' and 'Little Boy Blue'.

Probably contemporary with *The Little Story-Book*, and produced by the same publishers, with the addition of R. Baldwin, is *The Top Book of All, for Little Masters and Misses*. Its price was 2d. Its date, 1760, is again a conjecture, the clue being a cut of a George II shilling of that date, which is described as a 'new shilling'. This was the prize offered to any child who learnt by heart a longish poem at the end of the book, and many of the sixty-four pages are taken up with this and the questions and answers game of 'The Wide Mouth waddling Frog'. Nevertheless, there are eight well-known rhymes: amongst them 'Jack Nory', 'The three jovial Welshmen', and 'The Man of Thistleworth'.

---

[1] It was advertised 'price two coppers' by John Mein in *The Boston Chronicle* for 29 Aug. 1768. John Boyle, also of Boston, printed another edition (1771) which is in the Boston Public Library. A comparison of this with the English edition, which is in the writers' collection, shows nearly complete identity except for rearrangement necessitated by the move of one illustration.

PLATE II

THE
TOP BOOK of ALL,
FOR
Little *Masters* and *Misses.*
CONTAINING
The choiceft Stories, prettieft
Poems and moft diverting Riddles; all
wrote by *Nurfe Lovechild, Mother Goose,*
Jacky Nory, Tommy Thumb, and other
eminent Authors.

To which is added,
A NEW PLAY of the
Wide Mouth waddling FROG,
And a PRIZE POEM, to be learnt by
Heart, with a Shilling at the End for
every one that fhall fay it prettily
without Book, and not mifs a Word.
This Book is alfo enriched with curious
lively Pictures, done by the top
Hands; and is fold only at R. Bald-
win's, and S. Crowder's, Bookfellers
in Pater-nofter-Row, London; and
at Benj. Collins's, in Salifbury,
[Price Two-pence.]

a. Title-page, actual size, of
The Top Book of All, c. 1760.
British Museum

THE FAMOUS
TOMMY THUMB's
LITTLE STORY-BOOK:
CONTAINING
His Life and furprifing Adventures.
To which are added,
Tommy Thumb's Fables, with Morals:
and at the End, pretty Stories, that may
be either fung or told.

Adorned with many curious Pictures.

LONDON: Printed for S. CROWDER,
in Pater-Nofter-Row; and fold by B.
COLLINS, at the Printing-Office, in Salifbury, and by moft eminent Bookfellers.

b. Title-page, actual size, of
The Famous Tommy Thumb's
Little Story-Book, c. 1760.
Opie collection

Introduction

1760 has also been given as the date of *Mother Goose's Melody, or Sonnets for the Cradle*, though it is more likely to have been compiled in 1765 or 1766.[1] If either of these dates is correct, it must have been compiled for John Newbery whose stepson and successor Thomas Carnan entered it at Stationers' Hall on 28 December 1780. The delay in publication is explained by an advertisement in the *London Chronicle* for 30 December 1780 to 2 January 1781 (repeated for 16–18 January 1781):

> *This Day was published*, Price 3d.
> MOTHER GOOSE's MELODY;
> or Sonnets for the Cradle. In two parts.
> Part I. Contains the most celebrated songs and
> lullabies of the old British nurses; calculated to
> amuse children, and to excite them to sleep.
> Part II. Those of that sweet songster and nurse
> of wit and humour Master William Shakespeare; adorn-
> ed with cuts, and illustrated with notes and maxims
> historical, philosophical, and critical.
> Now first published from the papers of that very
> great writer of very little books the late Mr. John
> Newbery, and sold by T. Carnan in St. Paul's
> Church-yard.
> Of whom only can be had,
> All the late Mr. John Newbery's useful and enter-
> taining works for children, with the greatest allow-
> ance to those who retail them.[2]

The earliest surviving copy (albeit fragmentary) is an American piracy by the Massachusetts printer and publisher Isaiah Thomas, who put out an edition in 1786. The earliest known edition in England is that published by Newbery's grandson, Francis Power, in 1791, after which the book was transferred to John Marshall who continued to print it for twenty years or so. (There has also survived a pirated edition published by Simmons and Kirby of Canterbury in 1796.) The name John Newbery, as all who care for the history of juvenile literature must know, recalls some of the most celebrated children's books of the eighteenth century. John Newbery was, in fact, the first man to make the publication of

---

[1] One of the rhymes in it, 'There was a little Man, and he woo'd a little Maid', was not published, it is believed, until 1764.

[2] See M. J. P. Weedon, *The Library*, vol. 6, 1951–2, pp. 216–18.

Introduction

books for children a special line of business, and he issued them with some regularity. He came to London in 1744 and produced a juvenile of merit, *A Little Pretty Pocket-Book*, the same year. In doggerel verse it describes a number of children's games (listing 'Boys and Girls come out to Play' as one of them) and contains a popular rhyming alphabet ('Great A, B, and C'). Newbery, however, though a close associate of Benjamin Collins, one of the sponsors of *The Little Story-Book*, does not seem to have appreciated the value of nursery rhymes as a matter for commerce until the closing years of his life (1765–7). Then, at about the same time as he may have been working on *The Melody*, he brought out *The Fairing: or a Golden Toy for Children*, and *The History of Little Goody Two-Shoes*, both containing items of rhyme still commonly remembered. A pleasant tradition associates the latter story with the hand of Newbery's friend and sometime employee, Oliver Goldsmith, and there seems to be some historical and literary basis for the assertion. Certainly Goldsmith was constantly employed in hackwork for Newbery between 1762 and 1767. There is also an attractive amount of evidence, circumstantial though it is, to suggest that the other two works, particularly *The Melody*, are from the same pen. That Goldsmith loved children and was familiar with nursery rhymes is shown in a childhood reminiscence of Lætitia-Matilda Hawkins, where she says 'I little thought what I should have to boast, when Goldsmith taught me to play *Jack and Jill*, by two bits of paper on his fingers.'[1] The rhyme—

> There were two blackbirds
> Sat upon a hill,
> The one nam'd Jack,
> The other nam'd Gill.

—which accompanies this amusement, is to be found in *The Melody*. More curious, as will be seen, is the inclusion of 'There was an old woman toss'd in a blanket'. *Mother Goose's Melody* is a ninety-six-page toy-book divided into two parts: the first part contains 'the most celebrated Songs and Lullabies of the old British Nurses', fifty-one pieces in all; the second is made up of the lullabies of that 'Nurse of Art and Humours, Master William Shakespeare'. The songs are often titled, have facetious footnotes, and

---

[1] *Anecdotes, Biographical Sketches and Memoirs*, L.-M. Hawkins, 1822.

are preceded by a scholastically improbable preface 'By a very Great Writer of very Little Books'. This could have been Newbery himself, or Giles Jones, another of the hirelings. It is more likely to have been Goldsmith. On 29 January 1768 Goldsmith's play *The Good Natur'd Man* was produced. It was a failure and its best scene was hissed off the stage. Nevertheless, Goldsmith, at the Literary Club that night, pretended to his friends that nothing was amiss, and, as Johnson told Mrs. Thrale, 'to impress them still more forcibly with an idea of his magnanimity, he even sung his favourite song about *An old Woman tossed in a Blanket seventeen times as high as the Moon*'.[1] This song, with identical wording (though many versions existed) is dragged into the preface of *The Melody* without any excuse, but evidently because it was familiar to the writer. It is elaborately made out to be a song dating from the Hundred Years War, composed in derision of Henry V when he conceived new designs against the French. It has been suggested that the editing of *The Melody* was intended to parody one of the pretentious volumes of the period. Indeed, it looks as if it is aimed at Bishop Percy's *Reliques*, published in 1765, and this was a work, it may be remarked, the appearance of which pained the author of *The Vicar of Wakefield*.

From the point of view of the nursery, *Mother Goose's Melody* is important not only for the number of rhymes it contains, but because of the number of times it has been reprinted. Its influence may be noted in almost all subsequent collections. Editions of it were particularly popular in America; that of Isaiah Thomas has already been noted. Further important editions, with a greatly increased number of rhymes, were published in Boston and New York about 1825 and in 1833; and no doubt it is a sign of the influence of these collections that in America the rhymes continue to be thought of as belonging to 'Mother Goose'.

The first collector to be inspired by *The Melody* was Joseph Ritson. Ritson was a literary antiquary of some repute, a collector of old songs who did not feel that he had to 'improve' upon them, and therefore another critic of the *Reliques*. He had bought a copy of *The Melody* in 1781, and soon afterwards was urging his nephew to collect verses. Altogether there are seventy-nine pieces in his *Gammer Gurton's Garland, or, the Nursery Parnassus*, 1784.[2]

[1] *Anecdotes of the late Samuel Johnson*, Hester Lynch Piozzi, 1786.

[2] The date of this collection seems to be certain. Ritson himself, in another work, refers to it as being 1784.

Introduction

This collection was reprinted, with some small alterations, perhaps in 1799, and then lay unnoticed until seven years after his death when, in 1810, one of Ritson's publishers produced a much enlarged edition, arranged in four parts; parts I and II being identical with the first edition (not the second), while parts III and IV formed valuable supplements.

A contributor to this third edition, and probably the moving spirit in its production was the ex-Keeper of Manuscripts in the British Museum, Francis Douce, though it may have been Joseph Haslewood, Ritson's biographer. Douce seems to have bought (for 6s. 6d.) a parcel of juvenile books at the sale of Ritson's effects in 1803, and during the next few years he added to the collection extensively.[1] A pamphlet he also drew upon in 1810 was *Infant Institutes* (1797), another satire, this time on the Shakespearian commentators. In a small way this book is valuable because the Revd B. N. Turner, close friend of Dr. Johnson and its undoubted author, does not seem to have possessed a source-book for his rhymes, but to have relied on his memory. His wording of many of them is not found in any earlier collection.

In the meantime John Marshall of Aldermary Church Yard had produced *Nancy Cock's Pretty Song Book* (*ante* 1781), and C. D. Piguenit had published *The Tom Tit's Song Book being a Collection of Old Songs, with which most Young Wits have been delighted* (c. 1790). The music collections of Bland and Weller, and Longman and Broderip, had been issued (1797–8). Also *Songs for the Nursery collected from the Works of the Most Renowned Poets* had appeared (1805); succeeded by *Vocal Harmony, or No Song, No Supper*, a story interlarded with rhymes (c. 1806), *Pretty Tales*, published by T. Hughes (1808), and *Nursery Songs*, published by G. Ross (c. 1812). Of these the most important is *Songs for the Nursery*. This was originally issued by Tabart, a good-class publisher and one of the chief trade rivals of John Harris, successor to the Newbery firm. The collection, as well as being one of the corner-stones of Halliwell's work, was the chief additional source of the American *Mother Goose's Quarto* (c. 1825), and it was reprinted a number of times, notably in a finely illustrated edition by Darton, junior, in 1818.

Harris, however, who had been Elizabeth Newbery's general

---

[1] Douce Adds., Bodleian Library, Oxford.

manager, was not lacking in perception of the financial significance of verse in the nursery tradition. His beautiful hand-coloured decorations to nursery verses were equalled in the first decades of the nineteenth century only by those of John Marshall, who himself brought out an edition of *The Melody* about 1795 (and, in new format, about 1803 and in 1816). It is true that Harris published no extensive collection of the established favourites, but a number of the titles he brought out included them, as *Original Ditties for the Nursery* (1805),[1] or were based on single rhymes, as *Peter Piper's Practical Principles of Plain and Perfect Pronunciation* and *Cock Robin* (both 1819), and he will always be remembered—whether or not the verses were already known—for his production of *The Comic Adventures of Old Mother Hubbard* in 1805.[2]

Mother Goose in America

The bibliographical history of nursery rhyme books in America is complicated by a legend which arose in Boston in the middle of the nineteenth century to the effect that *Mother Goose's Melody*, or a book very like it, was first printed there in 1719, that many of the rhymes contained in it were of American origin, and that, in fact, Mother Goose herself was an American lady.

According to this story the fountain-head of the rhymes was a Mistress Elizabeth Goose (*née* Foster) widow of Isaac Goose (Vergoose or Vertigoose) of Boston, Massachusetts. Born in 1665, she had married when twenty-seven, had become in so doing the stepmother of ten children, and subsequently had a further six of her own. One of the latter, a daughter Elizabeth, married Thomas Fleet, a printer in Pudding Lane of the same town. Here in Pudding Lane a book called *Songs for the Nursery or Mother Goose's Melodies for Children* is alleged to have been printed. Its contents are said to have been collected by Fleet, for the most part from the lips of his wonderful mother-in-law, as she crooned the immortal verses—until Fleet was almost driven distracted by them—over first one, and then another (there were eventually

---

[1] Reprinted with introductory note by Iona Opie (1954). It was possibly intended to rival *Original Poems for Infant Minds*.

[2] See I. and P. Opie, *A Nursery Companion* (1980) in which sixteen Harris colour books are reproduced, together with ten others from rival firms.

six) of her grandchildren. It was to stem this babbling, and in deri-sion of Mistress Goose, that Fleet is said to have styled the rhymes 'Mother Goose's Melodies', and to have arranged a goose-like creature with long neck and mouth wide open on the title-page. The date of this publication, which has been described as 'the most elusive "ghost" volume in the history of American letters', is given as 1719.

This story, possibly because with its attendant details it is such an entertaining story, continues to have wide circulation. It has found its way into most works of reference, and so much study has been devoted to it that it has been made to seem consequen-tial.[1] Only the genealogical details, however, are verifiable. The story of the printing and existence of the book owes its warranty, if not its origin, entirely to one man, John Fleet Eliot, a great-grandson of Thomas Fleet. He launched the tale under the pseud-onym 'Requiescat' in *The Boston Transcript* for 14 January 1860. According to him it was well known to antiquarians that there was a small book in circulation in London before 1633 with the title *Rhymes for the Nursery: or Lulla-Byes for Children* which contained many pieces identical with those in *Mother Goose's Mel-ody*. Further, he stated, there was a book *Songs for the Nursery; or Mother Goose's Melodies for Children*, as already described, which had been printed by his great-grandfather. It later transpired that his authority for the first statement was one in the introduc-tion to the 1833 New York and Boston *Mother Goose's Melodies*, for which no confirmation will ever be found; his authority for the second statement was one he said was made to him by Edward A. Crowninshield, a literary gentleman (then 24 years old), who said he had seen a copy of Fleet's book in the Library of the Amer-ican Antiquarian Society at Worcester. The contents of the Mun-roe and Francis *Mother Goose's Quarto* of c. 1825 was supposed to derive from this. Unhappily (or perhaps happily for the fable) Crowninshield died eleven months before Eliot brought himself to refer to the discovery, though he said he had known of it for seventeen years. And, since repeated searches in the Library of the American Antiquarian Society failed to locate the book, it was generously accepted by the ardent publicist William Wheeler that it must have been 'mislaid, or overlooked, or lost, or destroyed'. Such a slender tale is largely kept alive by attack. The

---

[1] See especially *All about Mother Goose*, Vincent Starrett, 1930; *Colophon*, Oct. 1935 and Sept. 1938.

supporters demand, if Elizabeth Goose (or Vergoose or Vertigoose) was not Mother Goose, who was? They argue that it cannot be shown that Perrault's *Histoires ou contes du temps passé* or, as it was styled on a plaque in the frontispiece, 'CONTES DE MA MERE LOYE', had any connexion with the American Mother Goose. This, nevertheless, appears to be the case. Perrault's *Contes* were first printed in 1696–7. The term *conte de la Mère Oye* was already old. In Loret's *La Mvze historique* (Lettre Cinqvième, du douze Iuin, 1650) occur the lines,

> Pauvres, riches, mâles, femelles,
> Gueuzes, Bourgeoizes, Demoizelles,
> Petits & Grands, jeunes & vieux
> Paroissoient tout-à-fait joyeux:
> Mais le cher motif de leur joye,
> Comme vn conte de la Mer-oye
> Se trouvant fabuleux & faux,
> Ils devindrent tous bien penauts.

La Mère Oie may well be a lineal descendant of *La Reine Pédauque*, otherwise *Berthe au grand pied*, and there may also be a relationship to *Fru Gode* or *Fru Gosen* of German folklore. Perrault's tales were first published in English by J. Pote and R. Montagu (London, 1729), with the title *Histories, or Tales of Past Times. By M. Perrault. Translated by Mr. Samber.*[1] The placard on the wall, in the frontispiece, reads 'Mother Goose's Tales', and despite a long-standing claim to the contrary, this is the earliest known use in the English language of the term 'Mother Goose'.[2] So far as has been ascertained, her name did not become a household word either in England or America until the second half of the eighteenth century, when, for instance, it is found bracketed with Nurse Lovechild, Jacky Nory, Tommy Thumb, 'and other

[1] It was once believed that an earlier translation existed. An edition entitled *Histories or Tales of Past Times . . . Englished by G. M. Gent* was published with the date 1719 on the title page. However, in the first edition of *The Oxford Dictionary of Nursery Rhymes* we were able to show that this was a misprint for 1799. Also, it is now known that 'G. M. Gent' was invented by the publishers, Collins and Newbery, to disguise the fact that they had pirated Robert Samber's translation.

[2] John Payne Collier in *Punch and Judy*, 1828, p. 41, Robert Chambers in *The Book of Days*, vol. ii, 1864, p. 168, and other authorities following them, state that in *A Second Tale of a Tub: or, The History of Robert Powel the Puppet-Show-Man* published in 1715, a play of *Mother Goose* is bracketed with the traditional stories of *Whittington and his Cat*, *The Children in the Wood*, *Dr. Faustus*, *Friar Bacon and Friar Bungay*, *Robin Hood and Little John*, and *Mother Shipton*. In fact the play is of *Mother Lowse*.

Introduction

eminent Authors,' on the title-page of *The Top Book of All* (c. 1760). The earliness of undated chapbooks containing Perrault's tales has been greatly exaggerated. It seems fairly certain that it was the genius of John Newbery and his associates that spread Mother Goose's fame throughout Britain.

In 1763 Benjamin Collins of Salisbury published a third edition of *Mother Goose's Tales* (G. M. Gent edition), in conjunction with W. Bristow of London. This excellent Salisbury *Mother Goose* was unlike the productions of earlier publishers in that there was no French text alongside the English. It was a publication wholly designed for childish delight, and it had a sale which continued past the turn of the century. It is clear from where John Newbery had the title *Mother Goose's Melody*; if there were 'Mother Goose' tales, there could also be 'Mother Goose' songs. It is also clear that Isaiah Thomas of Massachusetts got the text for his *Mother Goose's Melody* from Newbery. His 'Worcester' editions are almost exact facsimiles of the London issues. The pagination is exactly the same, and the arrangement of matter very nearly so. It is from this book, and from Tabart's *Songs for the Nursery* (1805), that the *Mother Goose Quarto* is derived. Thomas, as it happened, was a young friend of Fleet's. If Fleet had in reality printed a book of rhymes, one feels certain that Thomas, who had antiquarian inclinations, would have reprinted it rather than the new collection from London. In fact, although he printed many such books, including the valuable *Tommy Thumb's Song Book for all little Masters and Misses* in 1788 (possibly a selection from the two volumes of *Tommy Thumb's Pretty Song Book*, c. 1744), he never seems to have been aware of Fleet's supposed *Songs for the Nursery*.

This is not to say that nursery rhymes both of English and American origin did not exist in puritan New England of the early eighteenth century. In the *Boston News Letter*, 12 April 1739, for instance, in a review of Tate and Brady's version of the Psalms, the critic complains of the phrase 'a wretch forlorn', chiefly because "twill be apt to make our Children think of the Line in their vulgar Play Song, so much like it, *This is the Man all forlorn, etc.*' This looks like a reference to 'The House that Jack built'. Nor need Thomas Fleet himself be entirely dissociated with the propagation of children's rhymes. His edition of *The New-England Primer* (1737) was the first to contain the renowned evening prayer 'Now I lay me down to sleep'. It is not known to have been printed in England for another forty-four years. Colonial printers were not

Introduction

so slow in adapting the minor literature of London to their profit. In 1761 A. Barclay of Boston issued *Tom Thumb's Play Book* which contained 'A was an Archer' and 'A Apple Pye'. This was presumably taken from the English *Tommy Thumb's Play Book*, registered at Stationers' Hall by M. Unwin in 1747, of which later editions were published by J. Warren in Birmingham [1750 advertisement] and A. Robertson in c. 1768 (complete with 'A was an Archer' and 'A Apple Pie'). John Mein, another Boston printer, reproduced Benjamin Collins's *The Famous Tommy Thumb's Little Story Book*, already referred to, in 1768. Later, Isaiah Thomas of Worcester and E. Battelle of Boston, in 1787, were not only advertising *Mother Goose's Melody*, but *Nurse Truelove's New Year's Gift* (containing 'The House that Jack built') and *The Fairing* (with 'There was a little man'), all of which were Newbery titles. The following year Thomas published *Tommy Thumb's Song Book*, containing thirty-three rhymes, and advertised numerous books for children including *Jack Dandy's Delight*, *The tragic Death of A, Apple Pye*, and *The big Puzzling Cap; or, a Collection of Riddles*, reprints of John Marshall's books.

Of rhymes which are essentially American, the War of Independence saw the popularizing of 'Yankee Doodle', a song now firmly ensconced in the nurseries of both countries; and a century later Longfellow's (?) 'There was a little girl and she had a little curl' was making a permanent niche for itself in Tradition's great memory. This last rhyme, and Sarah Hale's 'Mary had a little lamb' (concerning which there has been almost as much controversy as about Mother Goose herself), are America's two outstanding contributions to children's lore. Most Englishmen would probably be as ready to swear that they were English rhymes, as would many Americans that 'Mother Hubbard' and 'Twinkle, twinkle, little star' were genuinely American. Indeed, most English nursery rhymes are better known in the States, and in the case of the older ones, often known in versions nearer the original, than they are in their home country. The publication of 'Mother Goose' rhyme books of every shape and price is so extensive that a recent observer in a Chicago store counted thirty-five different editions on sale. How much a part of American home life are the rhymes may be gauged from the fact that William Wrigley thought it worth while distributing, over a two-year period, 14,000,000 'Mother Goose' books rewritten to tie chewing-gum into nursery jingles.

Introduction

Present-day Universality

'There is no surer sign of the oral knowledge of a people being on the wane than the attempt to secure it from oblivion by collecting its fragments and printing them in books.' This may, unfortunately, be applied to ballads and folk-songs, to folk-plays and dialect, and already in 1832 to the proverbs which William Motherwell introduced with these words. It cannot apply to nursery rhymes.

Most of the old rhymes seem to be better known today than they have ever been. References to them in literature are more common now than at any period in the past, and we seldom go a train journey without hearing some small child being kept quiet with a recitation of them. Indeed, the very railway stations are frequently placarded with parodies, and to be parodied is a measure of fame.

> Solomon Grundy
> Rich on a Monday
> Spent some on Tuesday
> More on Wednesday
> Poor on Thursday
> Worse on Friday
> Broke on Saturday
> Where will he end
> Old Solomon Grundy?

carries the legend 'Issued by the National Savings Committee'.

> Jack Sprat
> Would eat no fat
> BUT . . .

appears under the auspices of the Ministry of Food, while 'His Majesty's Government' displayed in the newspapers a 'Report to the Nation' (28 Mar. 1948),

> WHO'LL KILL INFLATION?
> I says John Bull,
> I speak for the nation—
> We'll work with a will
> And we'll thus kill inflation.

Private advertisers, too, are aware of the attraction of nursery rhymes. During 1947 a huge sum must have been expended in telling the public,

Introduction

There was a little man,
And he felt a little glum,
He thought that a Guinness was due, due, due.
So he went to 'The Plough' . . .
And he's feeling better now,
For a Guinness is good for you, you, you.

And,

Mary, Mary, quite contrary,
How does your romance go?
A boy, a girl, a Bravington ring,
And bridesmaids all in a row.

These two are but examples of many. Rewritten nursery rhymes are to be found everywhere. Now and then they form the basis of the unwritten jokes which go the rounds of saloon bars and the Stock Exchange. For instance, this commentary on the times was current during the Second World War and for several years afterwards—

The Queen was in the parlour,
Polishing the grate;
The King was in the kitchen
Washing up a plate;
The maid was in the garden,
Eating bread and honey,
Listening to the neighbours
Offering her more money.

In translation the English nursery rhyme has probably been carried into every country in the world. Приключение в карточном домике (The Queen of Hearts) and дом, который построил Джск (House that Jack built) are provided for the child of Russia (1936). In Hindustan the entertainment is *Humti Dumti char gia jhat* (Humpty Dumpty) and *Mafti Mai* (Little Miss Muffet). In Malaya the child is bidden to read *Hadji's Book of Malayan Nursery Rhymes* (with the English originals beside the translations). In Iraq the British Council reports (1947) that it has taught children to give nursery rhyme performances on percussion instruments.

It is probably a fact that every one of us could recite a string of nursery rhymes before we knew the meaning of the words which form them. And they stay with us throughout our lives, remem-

Introduction

bered even in the heat of parliamentary debate, so that the Chancellor of the Exchequer finds himself compared with 'Little Jack Horner', the Minister of Supply is likened to 'Little Bo-peep', and Mr. Churchill's fall is unkindly placed with Humpty Dumpty's.[1]

All of which is in the right tradition. For in the stress of battle three centuries earlier, when the Roundheads demanded the surrender of Hume Castle, Thomas Cockburn, the governor, retorted with a version of 'I'm the king of the castle', whereupon Fenwick, in command of the Parliamentarians, immediately placed a battery against the castle, and as the chronicler assures us, 'returns him Heroick Verse for his resolute Rhymes'.

[1] Respectively by the Member for Farnham, 22 Apr. 1947; by the Member for Aldershot, 29 May 1946; by the Attorney-General, 2 Apr. 1946.

The Singing Tradition of Nursery Rhymes

CECILY RAYSOR HANCOCK

Not all but a great many nursery rhymes are or have been songs, or fragments of songs, besides those that were collected or written as rhymes and acquired tunes later, either by adoption or by composition expressly for them. More of these tunes are available with very moderate searching than many people realize. There are also tunes that were printed with the words before the collection of nursery rhymes—some still in circulation, others dormant, the rhyme having perpetuated itself only as a rhyme rather than as both rhyme and song.

Before giving advice to people looking for tunes it may be worth saying that most books of nursery songs are intended for use with young children. They are quite short and limited to the youngest songs, and often contain other material for the same age, sometimes including copyrighted contributions by the editors, often new tunes to rhymes that already have good tunes. One can thus get a false first impression of the number of surviving tunes. Sir Percy Buck's *The Oxford Nursery Song Book* (1933) and Walter Crane's *The Baby's Bouquet* (1877) and *The Baby's Opera* (1879) are good places to start. (*The Baby's Opera* has been in print for a long time and is beginning to be reprinted or partially reprinted under titles that do not sound infantile to children, who cannot be expected to recognize a reference to *The Beggar's Opera*. Look under Walter Crane, the name of the illustrator. The musical editor, Walter's sister Lucy Crane, is acknowledged only in her brother's article on her in the *Dictionary of National Biography*.) More recent large collections that may be found in the children's section of a public library are useful too. Most of them are heavily, but not entirely, dependent on the Cranes or, in the United States, on the original compositions of J. W. Elliott. Alison McMorland's *The Funny Family* (1976) is a newer collection from people who sang the songs, with two exceptions; the sources are given.

The titles of many early nursery-rhyme books call the rhymes songs or suggest singing but give only rhymes, and many books that do have tunes do not make this clear in their titles. Any of

44

The Singing Tradition of Nursery Rhymes

the *Oxford Dictionary of Nursery Rhymes* references to M. H. Mason and to E. F. Rimbault, Frank Kidson, and Alfred Moffat will be tune-bearing, if they can be found—only Mason has been reprinted recently—and *ODNR* references to older tune-bearing sources such as the Ravenscroft books, the *Dancing Masters*, Gay's *Beggar's Opera*, *The Scots Musical Museum*, and W. Chappell's *Popular Music of the Olden Time* can be looked up—all of these have been reprinted and may be found in university libraries. Ballad operas less famous than *The Beggar's Opera* may or may not have the tunes printed in the edition on microfiche, and old sheet music is very chancy indeed, unless you can find a reference to a library that has it. Try the British Library's printed index of their music collection if you wish to find the oldest tune, or simply to find out if a current tune has a long history.

If the *ODNR* identifies the rhyme as words to a round, it may still be active in collections of rounds. The original music is likely to be hard to get at, but books of rounds often give composers and dates. Rhymes that go with singing games may have tunes in books of singing games, usually without references. Songs that have been or have become folk-songs may be found in folk-song collections and periodicals, either through *ODNR* references or by looking through tables of contents and indexes. (There is a great deal of American material untapped in *ODNR*, besides later publications.) The library song indexes are worth checking; many of the longer nursery rhymes were still printed in song-books for general use up to the middle of this century and still are, along with some of the products of the folk-song revival, in books of songs for older children. Most of the first sort are also in the Crane and Kidson collections, but some, like 'The Fox's Foray', which has medieval ancestry, are newer in song-books. (One version of 'The Fox' is in Thomas Wood, *The Oxford Song Book II* (1927 and constant reprints); several of the longer nursery rhymes appear here as songs for general singing.) Tunes in general collections are more likely to represent a singing tradition than those in large nursery-rhyme collections that are mainly reprints. The word 'traditional' over a nursery tune often seems to represent a reluctance to clutter a children's book with references. Even books that are almost entirely reprints, however, may contain a song or so collected from the user.

Songs that have been passed along orally develop variations in words and tune—not only folk-songs but convivial songs ('I Love

The Singing Tradition of Nursery Rhymes

Sixpence' and 'Old King Cole', for example) and other songs that have persisted in use. 'Oh, dear, what can the matter be?' is quite exceptional in having accurately maintained itself by constant reprinting just as it was printed at the end of the eighteenth century.

It may be puzzling to choose between variants. I stick to the first one I found, unless a change is worth the effort; for instance, the Scottish 'Aiken Drum' tunes (Robert Chambers, *Popular Rhymes of Scotland* (1870 edn.), and Alfred Moffat, *Fifty Traditional Scottish Nursery Rhymes* (1933)) have a livelier rhythm than Crane's. Variants are proof of a life outside the printed page, and people who are interested in old tunes will find that many nursery songs have more than one musical tradition. The familiar tunes are often old ones, but there is no obligation to change a tune if it proves to be a newcomer, made up or adopted by someone in the family. The American 'Rock-a-bye Baby' was made up by a baby-sitter, and published after she grew up (James S. Fuld, *The Book of World-Famous Music* (3rd edn., 1985)). The old tune 'Lilliburlero' is still attached to 'Old woman, old woman, whither so high?', and sometimes to 'See-saw, Margery Daw'.

Bertrand Bronson has traced a consistent singing tradition for 'Perry merry dixi domine' ('The Four Presents'; 'I have four sisters beyond the sea' in *ODNR*) through many variants back to the seventeenth century, in *The Traditional Tunes of the Child Ballads*, vol. I (1959), *The Riddle Song*. On the other hand, 'The Frog's Courtship' has several different families of tunes, usually associated with a different refrain pattern. The Cranes set a modernized form of the Ravenscroft words to the 'Rowley, powley, gammon and spinach' tune of 'The Frog in the Cocked Hat' (1809 and popular through the nineteenth century and beyond). Rimbault has a good 'Kitty Alone' tune to Ritson's 1784 version (supported by at least one other variant tune, though not by the Scottish tunes with forms of this refrain). This is in Rimbault's *Nursery Rhymes* [1846], and the subtitle reveals that the rhymes are 'with the Tunes to which they are Still Sung in the Nurseries of England. Obtained Principally from Oral Tradition.' In his *A Collection of Old Nursery Rhymes* [1864], subtitled 'With Familiar Tunes for Voice and Pianoforte...', Rimbault's 'The Frog and the Mouse' is a different version, words and tune, with a 'Fal la la (etc.)' tune. This second collection, by the way, is also referred to as 'Chappell's Nursery Rhymes', the title on the cover. There are many

The Singing Tradition of Nursery Rhymes

'Hmm hmm, hmm hmm' variants of a 'Frog's Courtship' tune established especially in the Southern United States but quite generally known. There is the 'Frog and Mouse' tune that was either adopted by or adapted from the eighteenth-century 'Amo Amas, I Love a Lass' (Mason), and several in the same format that may or may not be descended from it. And that is not all the tunes that have been picked up from singers of this venerable tale, besides the 'Humble-dum' tune printed by Ravenscroft in 1611 and reprinted in the *ODNR* and *The Oxford Song Book II*.

'London Bridge' has a song tune with a 'Dance Over My Lady Lee' refrain (given as 'the old tune' by Dr Arnold in his *Juvenile Amusements*, in print by 1797), and a game tune, with 'My Fair Lady', not recorded for nearly another century, but traditional then. 'Simple Simon', on the other hand, seems not to have a firm title to any tune; it appears in different collections with a variety of popular singable tunes that fit its very common broadside metre, and 'I Had A Little Pony' seems never to have the same tune twice, though 'I Had A Little Nutmeg', much more often printed as a song, has a tune with at least a strong song-book tradition.

Scottish and English versions of nursery songs have different words and tunes, and the same is true of English and American nursery songs, and the words and tunes of those that have had mainly oral transmission. 'Mary Had a Little Lamb' apparently crossed to England as a song, for the tune in *The Oxford Nursery Song Book* is a slightly used form of the tune written for it by Lowell Mason soon after its first publication; in the United States it was a schoolbook poem and allied itself with the tune of 'Merrily We Roll Along' only after an irreverent flirtation with the Civil War song, 'Shouting Out the Battle-Cry of Freedom' and a nursery song-book appearance with 'Auld Lang Syne'.

'Twinkle, twinkle, little star' was set to many tunes before settling down mainly to a French nursery tune, 'Ah! Vous dirai-je, Maman', but with a minority support for a less twinkly, more soporific hymn tune, 'The Spanish Chant'. (Both tunes are older than the poem.) 'Tom, he was a piper's son' still goes to the seventeenth-century 'Over the Hills and Far Away' for which it was written, and 'Lavender's Blue' to what surely must be its original seventeenth-century tune, not printed till the end of the eighteenth century (variants in *Juvenile Amusement* 24, in print by 1797, and *The Fairing*, c. 1799, supported by several nineteenth-century

The Singing Tradition of Nursery Rhymes

variants.) The current version, from Rimbault and Crane, was accepted by Claude Simpson in *The British Broadside Ballads and Their Tunes* on its character, without further confirmation. Jeremy Barlow notes in his Broadside Band record 'Old English Nursery Rhymes' (Saydisc CSDL 419, 1996) that 'A tune with a similar opening was known as the "Battle Galliard" in the late sixteenth/early seventeenth century, and was set by Byrd and Dowland.'

Many nursery rhymes, like 'Twinkle twinkle' and 'Mary Had a Little Lamb', and like current schoolyard verses, develop sturdy attachments to popular tunes, usually tunes that have been popular for several generations. The nursery mixture of different sorts and sources of songs includes a few schoolyard types—old jeers ('Barber, barber, shave a pig' and 'Georgie Porgie') and a few take-offs, with or without the tune of the song adapted. 'There was a little man and he wooed a little maid' shares its tune (older than the song itself—see Simpson) with 'There was a little man and he had a little gun'. The *Baby's Opera* tune of 'Tom, Tom, the Piper's Son' (the pig-stealing Tom) is a worn down skeleton form of 'Over the Hills and Far Away', the old tune of the longer nursery song in which Tom himself is a piper, which had one nineteenth-century printing with the decayed form of its tune but generally appears with much the same tune as on its first appearance in the seventeenth century. 'The Miller of Dee' was written to an older tune which it has kept alive in singing tradition (Chappell, Simpson), and so was 'Robinson Crusoe' (Kidson). 'Oh where, oh where has my little dog gone?' still goes to the older folk tune to which its comic-song original was set, a German import, 'In Lauterbach' (*Songs along the Mahantongo* (1951)).

Old nursery attachments are usually to tunes popular at the end of the eighteenth century, often tunes that were old in the eighteenth century. 'Greensleeves' ('Dame what makes your ducks to die?') is Elizabethan; 'Lilliburlero' and 'Over the Hills and Far Away' seventeenth century. 'Old King Cole' is often given a seventeenth-century date on the strength of Kidson's note that the name 'Old Cole' was several times mentioned in the seventeenth century and 'the tune is a fine specimen of 17th century melody', which it may be—Kidson's judgement in such matters deserves respect. 'Yankee Doodle' (mid-eighteenth century) has both nursery and schoolyard uses. 'King Arthur' and 'Three children sliding on the ice' go to one of the Chevy Chase tunes—'Now Ponder Well' or 'The Children in the Wood'—in nursery tradition.

The Singing Tradition of Nursery Rhymes

'King Arthur' also has other folk tunes; and 'Three children sliding on the ice' comes from a long seventeenth-century broadside
which was directed to be sung to another tune (although it
included take-offs of 'John Dory', 'The Children in the Wood',
and 'Chevy Chase'), and even the long broadside was printed
with 'Chevy Chase' tunes or tune directions in the eighteenth
century (Simpson, p. 105). Other songs seem to go to their 'own
tunes', in the broadside ballad phrase. 'The North Wind Doth
Blow' and 'Little Bo Peep' (in England, and in a sense in America,
where it is generally sung to a tune written for it by J. W. Elliott),
which both sound as if they were written for children, have their
own tunes. So do many adoptions from convivial or romantic
songs originally popular with all ages: 'Old King Cole,' 'I Love
Sixpence' (but Chappell gives a possible older source), 'O dear,
what can the matter be?', 'Lavender's Blue', and 'Where are you
going, my pretty maid?' ('The Milkmaid Song').

'Where are you going, my pretty little dear?', which is another
version of the milkmaid song in which the girl's charms are specified and she maintains that 'It's dabbling in the dew makes the
milkmaids fair', has a different good tune, considered by Sabine
Baring-Gould to be the proper traditional tune and the other an
eighteenth-century stage innovation, though nineteenth-century
variations show that the familiar tune was or became thoroughly
traditional in the nursery. 'Dabbling in the Dew' is in *English Folk-
Songs for Schools*, Collected and Arranged by S. Baring-Gould and
Cecil J. Sharp (1916). The Crane tune to the other version, with its
curtsying ' "Sir", she said', had been previously printed in *100
Comic Songs* (Boston, 1856). If E. S. Biggs was the original composer, the version he printed in 1800 had been improved by 1856.

The American tune for 'Billy Boy' is, or derives from (it has
begun to vary), sheet music printed in 1847 (Lester S. Levy, *Flashes
of Merriment* (1973)); the song has several variants with good folk
tunes in Great Britain. The introduction of the French nursery
tune 'Ah! Vous dirai-je, Maman' to the nursery was probably
from a popular song 'The Schoolmaster' (1834), which had the
alphabet sung to this tune as a chorus (Levy, also Fuld), though
Fuld gives a previous history for the tune outside of France. It is
now established for singing the alphabet as well as being the
tune for 'Twinkle, Twinkle', and is often used for 'Baa, Baa,
Black Sheep', an easy transfer from the somewhat similar Crane
tune.

The Singing Tradition of Nursery Rhymes

A fair number of songs popular with children and grown-ups (aside from lullabies and other songs used with children) turn up in American folk-song collections with words and tunes clearly akin to nineteenth-century nursery versions: 'There was an old woman and she had a little pig' ('Betty Pringle's Pig'), 'Over the Water to Charlie', 'The Three Huntsmen' and its cousin 'The Fox Hunter's Chorus', and, of course, 'Frog went a-courting'. Jean Ritchie sang a good American variant of the Crane 'What Are Little Boys Made Of' on a Riverside Folklore Series record, 'Riddle Me This' (1957). 'Robinson Crusoe' (Ira W. Ford, *Traditional Music of America*) (1940)) and 'Old King Cole' and 'I've Got Sixpence', which also turn up in American as well as in English collections, are long-lived convivial songs, old popular songs rather than what are usually considered folk-songs.

Old rhymes are sometimes associated with fiddle tunes. (Ford's *Traditional Music of America* is a collection of this sort.) Some of the short rhymes that are associated with fiddle tunes may be floaters, used with more than one tune, but others have quite well-established associations. 'Polly put the kettle on' and numbers of others are fragments of songs still with their own tunes. 'Sandy he belongs to the mill', which makes only occasional appearances as a rhyme (Opie, *The Oxford Nursery Rhyme Book* (1955); with tune in Edith Fowke, *Ring Around the Moon* (1987)), was collected at the beginning of this century with the same Scots tune that Herd said it was sung to in the eighteenth century.

Some of the marriages of old rhymes to old tunes have been made late in the life of both. We owe William Chappell a debt of gratitude for setting 'Golden Slumbers' to 'May Fair'. More such pairings have been made in print than have had permanent success. Many appear to have been made simply in use. 'Roberty Boberty' ('We will go to the wood, says Robin to Bobbin') turns up in Marie Boette's *Singa Hipsy Doodle* (1971), collected in West Virginia with a dance tune that is recognizably the sixteenth-century 'Dargason' (Chappell, Simpson, Fuld for the persistent survival of the tune). Other versions of the song go to other tunes—words and tunes have been wandering round the world separately.

Tunes can be written to any rhyme, and nursery riddles and proverbs and other instructive rhymes can be found with tunes in books for children—'Humpty Dumpty' and 'Early to bed, and early to rise' and 'Thirty Days Hath September', the last two as rounds. A few of the tunes set in impressive sheet music for chil-

The Singing Tradition of Nursery Rhymes

dren in the eighteenth century by popular composers Samuel Arnold, James Hook, and Reginald Spofforth, have turned up in simpler form in later tradition. 'Lavender's Blue' had different versions set by Arnold and Spofforth, and others may be settings of traditional tunes, but the survival of so few seems to suggest that many of them, perhaps even of the ones that survived, were original compositions, as Rimbault thought. (He said 'except for a very few': he has a 'Lavender's Blue' too, and his 'Curly Locks' tune is the same as Spofforth's. This 'Curly Locks' tune had also appeared, with 'Little Bo Peep' and its tune, in *Twelve Little Ballads and A Favorite Lesson: Arranged In a familiar Manner for Juvenile Performers: on the Piano Forte*, published and republished in Philadelphia and New York between 1810 and 1826.)

A lavishly illustrated book, *National Nursery Rhymes and Nursery Songs, Set to Original Music by J. W. Elliott* (1870)—*Mother Goose's Nursery Rhymes Set to Music by J. W. Elliott* in the American editions—has contributed several new tunes to American tradition (Fuld lists nine). They are beginning to show variation from transmission, though they are also still reprinted from the source—occasionally, but not often, with the composer's name. Two of them (Elliott's 'Hey Diddle Diddle' and 'See-saw, Marjorie Daw') have established themselves well enough in England to enter *The Oxford Nursery Song Book*.

It is fortunate that Walter Crane's illustrations have meant that his books, with his sister Lucy's good music in them, have continued to be available in libraries. Song-books in general have a tendency not to be kept on library shelves or, if they are bought by librarians, to be discarded when newer ones come along. When they go out of print they are hard to find. Rimbault's collections and the more-recent publications of Moffat and Kidson are now not easily come by, and recently Moffat's nursery song-books, with handsome illustrations by Willabeek LeMair, have been reprinted as picture books without the tunes, only the verses, as have the nursery song-books illustrated by Walter Crane.

Even people who sing to and with their children can use many more rhymes than songs, and certainly not every rhyme is or was a song. Not every song that children like is a children's song, or so many that were made for general use would not have contributed to the nursery tradition. But it is pleasant to think that old tunes as well as old rhymes are still entertaining children, along with more-recent additions to the nursery canon.

51

M   N

M mourned for it.

N nodded for it.

Page from *The History of an Apple Pie* published by Darton and Clark, c. 1840. Opie collection

Nursery Rhymes

1

A was an apple-pie;
B bit it,
C cut it,
D dealt it,
E eat it,
F fought for it,
G got it,
H had it,
I inspected it,
J jumped for it,
K kept it,
L longed for it,
M mourned for it,
N nodded at it,
O opened it,
P peeped in it,
Q quartered it,
R ran for it,
S stole it,
T took it,
U upset it,
V viewed it,
W wanted it,
X, Y, Z, and ampersand
All wished for a piece in hand.

It would appear that this rhyme was well known in the reign of Charles II. In 1671 John Eachard, an outspoken divine, quoted it in *Some Observations upon the Answer to an Enquiry into the Grounds & Occasions of the Contempt of the Clergy*, 'And why not, Repent rarely, evenly, prettily, elegantly, neatly, tightly? And also why not A Apple-pasty, B bak'd it, C cut it, D divided it, E eat it, F fought for it, G got it, &c. I had not time, Sir, to look any further into their way of Preaching.' In 1742 it figured in the Coopers' enlightened spelling book *The Child's New Play-thing*, and it was common in the latter half of the century in the chapbook series,

A

the usual title being *The Tragical Death of A, APPLE PYE Who was Cut in Pieces and Eat by Twenty-Five Gentlemen with whom All Little People Ought to be Very well acquainted*. The rhyme was a favourite for ABC instruction in the nineteenth century. Kate Greenaway made a book of it, *A Apple Pie*, which is still reprinted.

Some Observations, John Eachard, 1671 / *Child's New Play-thing* (T. Cooper), 2nd ed. 1742 / *Tom Thumb's Play-Book*, entered M. Unwin 6 August 1747; US ed. A. Barclay, Boston, 1764 [Welch's emendation of Rosenbach] / *Tragical Death of A Apple Pye* (R. Marshall), c. 1770; (John Evans), c. 1791 / With *Cock Robin*, editions: R. Christopher, c. 1782; Isaiah Thomas, Worcester, Mass. 1787 [Worcester biblio.]; Samuel Hall, Boston, Mass. 1791; John Adams, Philadelphia, 1805 [Rosenbach]; J. Catnach, c. 1805 [Hugo]; T. Batchelar, c. 1810; E. and E. Horsford, Albany, 1813 [Rosenbach] / *History of the Apple Pie*, 'Written by Z' (J. Harris), 1808, 'e Eyed it, f Fiddled for it, g Gobbled it, h Hid it, i Inspected it, j Jumped over it, k Kicked it, l Laughed at it' / *Royal Primer* (William Jones), 1818 / *History of Master Watkins, to which is added The Tragical Death of an Apple Pie* (I. Marsden), c. 1820 (T. Batchelar), c. 1820 (J. Paul and Co.), c. 1835 / *Life and History of A, Apple-Pie* (Dean and Munday), c. 1822 [Gumuchian] / *Sugar Plum* (J. Roberts), c. 1825 / *Picture Alphabet* (T. Richardson), c. 1830 / *History of an Apple Pie* (Darton and Clark), c. 1840, partially rewritten, e.g. 'Q quaked for it, R rode for it, S skipped for it' / JOH, 1844 / *A Apple Pie* (Darton's Indestructible Toy Books), c. 1860 / *A Apple Pie*, Kate Greenaway, 1886, 'J jumped for it, K knelt for it ... S sang for it, T took it, U V W X Y Z all had a large slice and went off to bed' / *A Apple Pie*, Gordon Browne, 1890 / *Baby's A.B.C.*, illus. Mary Tourtel, 1910, miniature book $1\frac{7}{8} \times 1\frac{1}{4}$ ins / *A was an Apple Pie* [a panorama], Tracey Campbell Pearson, 1986.

Parody: *Political A Apple-Pie*, William Hone, illus. George Cruikshank, 1820.

***In the earlier recordings the letters I and J, U and V, in common with other alphabets, are not differentiated.

2

A was an archer, who shot at a frog,
B was a butcher, and had a great dog.
C was a captain, all covered with lace,
D was a drunkard, and had a red face.
E was an esquire, with pride on his brow,
F was a farmer, and followed the plough.
G was a gamester, who had but ill-luck,
H was a hunter and hunted a buck.
I an innkeeper, who loved to carouse,
J was a joiner, and built up a house.
K was King William, once governed this land,
L was a lady, who had a white hand.
M was a miser, and hoarded up gold,

N was a nobleman, gallant and bold.
O was an oyster girl, and went about town,
P was a parson, and wore a black gown.
Q was a queen, who wore a silk slip,
R was a robber, and wanted a whip.
S was a sailor, and spent all he got,
T was a tinker, and mended a pot.
U was a usurer, a miserable elf,
V was a vintner, who drank all himself.
W was a watchman, and guarded the door,
X was expensive, and so became poor.
Y was a youth, that did not love school,
Z was a zany, a poor harmless fool.

This version of the noted rhyming alphabet, sometimes called 'Tom Thumb's Alphabet', is the one usually heard today but does not seem to be much more than a hundred years old. A second version is given in *A Little Book for Little Children*, by T. W. (sold at the Ring in Little Britain) which was published during the reign of Queen Anne:

A was an Archer, and shot at a Frog;
B was a Blind-man, and led by a Dog:
C was a Cutpurse, and liv'd in disgrace;
D was a Drunkard, and had a red Face:
E was an Eater, a Glutton was he;
F was a fighter, and fought with a Flea:
G was a Gyant, and pul'd down a House;
H was a Hunter, and hunted a Mouse:
I was an ill Man, and hated by all;
K was a Knave, and he rob'd great and small:
L was a Liar, and told many Lies;
M was a Madman, and beat out his Eyes:
N was a Nobleman, nobly born;
O was an Ostler, and stole Horses' Corn:
P was a Pedlar, and sold many Pins;
Q was a Quarreller, and broke both his Shins:
R was a Rogue, and ran about Town;
S was a Sailor, a Man of Renown:
T was a Taylor, and Knavishly bent;
U was a Usurer took Ten *per Cent*:
W was a Writer, and Money he earn'd;
X was one *Xenophon*, prudent and learn'd:
Y was a Yeoman, and work'd for his Bread;
Z was one Zeno the Great, but he's dead.

In America the rhyme was printed in Boston as early as 1750. An expanded version, with a couplet for each letter, appeared in a pirated Glasgow printing of *Nurse Truelove's Christmas Box*, 1795 [Justin Schiller, New York, cat. 29: 1222, 1973]. The words may have been the same as early nineteenth-century examples, e.g. in Catnach's *Easter Gift* (c. 1820):

> A was an Archer and shot at a frog,
> But missing his mark shot into a bog;
> B was a Butcher and had a great dog,
> Who always went round the streets with a clog;
> C was a Captain so brave and so grand,
> He headed in buff the stately trained band;
> D was a Drunkard and lov'd a full pot,
> His face and his belly shew'd him a great sot...

In 1820 John Harris issued *The Hobby-Horse*, 'being a revival of the favourite Alphabet, A was an Archer and shot at a frog' and he reproduced it, with clever hand-coloured illustrations, in its traditional form again. The alphabet was a dramatic feature of Blanchard's pantomime *Little Jack Horner; or, Harlequin A.B.C. and the Enchanted Region of Nursery Rhymes*, performed at Drury Lane in 1857, and, today, it may be seen in the Ladbrooke Grove Children's Clinic, London, where it is the subject of a decorative frieze.

Little Book for Little Children, T. W. c. 1712, as quote / *Child's New Play-thing* (T. Cooper), 1742, 'I was a Joiner, and built up a House. K Was a King, and he govern'd a Mouse. L Was a Lady, and had a white Hand. M Was a Merchant, to each foreign Land. N Was a Nobleman, gallant and bold. O Was an Oyster-wench, and a sad Scold. P Was a Parson, and wore a black Gown. Q Was a Quaker, and would not bow down. R Was a Robber, and wanted a Whip. S Was a Sailor, and liv'd in a Ship. T Was a Tinker, and mended a Pot. V Was a Vintner, a very great Sot...' / *The Child's New Plaything* (J. Draper for J. Edwards, Boston, Mass.) 4th edn., 1750 / *Tom Thumb's Play-Thing* (J. Marshall), advt. 1781; (Howard and Evans), c. 1800; (John Evans), c. 1805 / *Royal Primer* (William Jones), 1818, 'An Enticing Alphabet', 'I was a Join-er, a wor-ker in wood, K was a King, by his subjects stil'd good....M was a Man that had store of land. N was a Nobleman gallant and gay, O was an Owl that could not see day.... R was a Rob-ber that died by the rope, S was a Sultan as great as the pope.... Y was a Young-ster that drove a ho-gee, Z was a Za-ny that climb'd up a tree' / *Hobby-Horse* (J. Harris), 1820 / *A was an Archer* (Henry Mozley and Sons), c. 1825; (London: sold by the booksellers), c. 1840 / *Amusing Ditties* (D. Carvalho), c. 1830 / *Good Little Child's First A.B.C.* (Bishop and Co.), c. 1830 [Gumuchian] / *Good Child's Illustrated Alphabet* (Ryle and Paul), c. 1843 [Hindley, 1887] / JOH, 1844 / *Prince Arthur's Alphabet* (Dean), c. 1860, moveable book / *Tom Thumb's Alphabet*, illus. W. McConnell, c. 1855.

There were many imitations of 'A was an Archer' in the eighteenth century, e.g.: 'A was an Admiral over the Main, B was a Bomb by which thousands were slain...', 'A Set of Squares' (B. Collins, Salisbury), c. 1740?; 7th edn. Newbery and Collins, c. 1743 / 'A was an angler and he caught a Fish, B was a Brazier and he made a

A

Dish...', *Pretty Book for Children*, c. 1743?; 'A was an Alderman in a fine gown, B was a Barber that shaved his Crown...' and 'A was an Ass hard ladened with Goods, B was a Bear liv'd in the Woods...' Jane Johnson MS, 'Nursery Library, c. 1744 / 'A was an Ape you may easily tell, B was a Bird that sung very well...', *Tom Thumb's Alphabet* (J. Denham, Milborne Port), c. 1780.

3

> Here's A, B, and C,
> D, E, F, and G,
> H, I, K, L, M, N, O, P, Q,
> R, S, T, and U,
> W, X, Y, and Z;
> And here's the child's Dad,
> Who is sagacious and discerning,
> And knows this is the Fount of Learning.

Appears in *Mother Goose's Melody* (c. 1765) with the note: 'This is the most learned Ditty in the World; for indeed there is no Song can be made without the Aid of this, it being the *Gamut* and Ground Work of them all.' Rhyming alphabets of this kind were common in the eighteenth century, for instance one beginning:

> Here's A, B, and C,
> D, E, F, and G,
> And great H and I,
> And pretty Magpye,

in *Nurse Truelove's New Year's Gift* printed for John Newbery in 1750.

MG's Melody, c. 1765 / *Rhymes for the Fireside* (Thomas Richardson), c. 1828 / *Mother Goose's NR*, L. E. Walter, 1924.

4

> Great A, little a,
> Bouncing B,
> The cat's in the cupboard
> And she can't see.

The sign AaB, 'Great A, little a, and a big bouncing B', was displayed by some of the early printers of juveniles. Thomas Bailey of Bishopsgate was one, and another was probably John Marshall, for his shop became known as the 'Great A, and bouncing B Toy Factory'. Canning in the *Microcosm* (a weekly produced by Etonians), 11 June 1787, refers to the

'Bouncing B, Shoe Lane' as a place where histories of Tom Thumb could be bought. The rhyme appears in several early children's books and the sign was probably derived from it. Newbery's *A Little Pretty Pocket-Book* (1744) has a rather different version, beginning:

> Great A, B, and C,
>   and tumble down D,
> The cat's a blind Buff,
> And she cannot see.

In ten verses it runs through the alphabet. But this type of tuition does not seem to have found favour in the nineteenth century. Sir Francis Palgrave in 1819 was already regretting that nurses had become strangely fastidious in their literary taste as compared with the days when they 'took such desperate pains in leading us onwards from great A and little a, and bouncing B, even down to Empersand and Izzard'.

T Thumb's PSB, c. 1744 / *Pocket-Book*, 1744 [1767] / *Top Book*, c. 1760, as *Pocket-Book* / *MG's Melody*, c. 1765 / *GG's Garland*, 1784 / *T Tit's SB*, c. 1790 / Letter to Bernard Barton from Charles Lamb, 30 Apr. 1831, 'Felis in abaco est, et aegrè videt' [1905] / *Poetic Trifles* (J. G. Rusher), c. 1840 / JOH, 1842, 'A, B, C, tumble down dee, The cat's in the cupboard, and can't see me' / Bolton, 1888, two counting-out versions / *Folk-Lore*, 1889.

5

> Great A was alarmed at B's bad behaviour,
> Because C, D, E, F, denied G a favour,
> H had a husband with I, J, K, and L,
> M married Mary and taught her scholars how to spell;
> A, B, C, D, E, F, G, H, I, J, K, L, M, N,
> O, P, Q, R, S, T, U, V, W, X, Y, Z.

Recorded by a correspondent to *Notes & Queries*, in 1856, as 'known forty years ago'; it appeared again, in 1870, together with five other verses.

6

> Old Abram Brown is dead and gone,
> You'll never see him more;
> He used to wear a long brown coat
> That buttoned down before.

The rhyme was already being sung by children in 1849. M. A. Denham came upon 'more than half a dozen bairns' singing it 'in not very doleful measure' in August, that year. 'I must premise,' he said, 'that the children were playing the ceremonies attendant on a funeral, and the eldest of the little group, who could not be more than eight years of age, gave it a right clerk-like style, time by time, as follows:

> Poor Johnny's deed that nice young man,
> That nice young man, that nice young man,
> He used to wear a fustian coat,
> A fustian coat, a fustian coat,
> That buttoned up before!'

'Old Abram Brown is dead and gone', with varying names for the deceased, has often done duty on funereal occasions. It was traditionally sung in the folk play when the champion had been slain and had to be carried out of the arena. For instance, in the play performed at Camborne, near Redruth in Cornwall, Father Christmas and two Merrymen carry the Turk out, singing:

> This poor old man is dead and gone,
> We shall never see him more,
> He used to wear an old gray coat
> All buttoned down before.

The song is particularly popular in the form of a folksong in America, which may partly be due to the popularity of Albert Gorton Greene's humorous song 'Old Grimes', published anonymously in the *Providence Gazette* for 16 January 1822. Greene 'acknowledged authorship of all but the first stanza' in a letter to the *Manufacturers' and Farmers' Journal* in 1833. The tune adopted is usually 'Auld Lang Syne', but Benjamin Britten made a haunting original setting of it as a round for boys' voices in 'Friday Afternoons' (1935), with the text given by De la Mare in *Tom Tiddler's Ground* (1932).

JOH, 1853 / *The Mummers' Play*, R. J. E. Tiddy, 1923, as quote / *Big Book of Mother Goose* (James and Jonathan Co., Wisconsin), 1946 / *Cakes and Custard*, Brian Alderson, illus. Helen Oxenbury, 1974.

7

There was a man lived in the moon, lived in the moon, lived in
    the moon,
There was a man lived in the moon,
And his name was Aiken Drum;
> And he played upon a ladle, a ladle, a ladle,
> And he played upon a ladle,
> And his name was Aiken Drum.

Aiken Drum

And his hat was made of good cream cheese, good cream cheese,
    good cream cheese,
And his hat was made of good cream cheese,
And his name was Aiken Drum.

And his coat was made of good roast beef, good roast beef, good
    roast beef,
And his coat was made of good roast beef,
And his name was Aiken Drum.

And his buttons were made of penny loaves, penny loaves, penny
    loaves,
And his buttons were made of penny loaves,
And his name was Aiken Drum.

His waistcoat was made of crust of pies, crust of pies, crust of
    pies,
His waistcoat was made of crust of pies,
And his name was Aiken Drum.

His breeches were made of haggis bags, haggis bags, haggis bags,
His breeches were made of haggis bags,
And his name was Aiken Drum.

There was a man in another town, another town, another town,
There was a man in another town,
And his name was Willy Wood;
    And he played upon a razor, a razor, a razor,
    And he played upon a razor,
    And his name was Willy Wood.

And he ate up all the good cream cheese, good cream cheese,
    good cream cheese,
And he ate up all the good cream cheese,
And his name was Willy Wood.

And he ate up all the good roast beef, good roast beef, good roast
    beef,
And he ate up all the good roast beef,
And his name was Willy Wood.

And he ate up all the penny loaves, penny loaves, penny loaves,
And he ate up all the penny loaves,
And his name was Willy Wood.

Aiken Drum

And he ate up all the good pie crust, good pie crust, good pie
    crust,
And he ate up all the good pie crust,
And his name was Willy Wood.

But he choked upon the haggis bags, haggis bags, haggis bags,
But he choked upon the haggis bags,
And that ended Willy Wood.

Nothing is known about this song except that it was current in Scotland
in 1821, and that the name Aikendrum appears in a ballad about the
opposing armies before the battle of Sheriffmuir (1715):

> Ken you how a Whig can fight,
> Aikendrum, Aikendrum?
> Ken you how a Whig can fight,
> Aikendrum?

Aikendrum also appears in a poem in *The Dumfries Magazine* (Oct. 1825) as
the name of a strange little Brownie. In *The Antiquary* (1816), ch. 4, Scott
gives the name 'Aiken Drum', for no apparent reason, to the bridegroom
in Edie Ochiltree's story.

Jacobite Relics, James Hogg, 1821, 'There was a man cam frae the moon, Cam frae the
moon, cam frae the moon. There was a man cam frae the moon, An' they ca'ed him
Aikendrum' / JOH, 1842, 'There was a man in our toone, in our toone, in our toone,
There was a man in our toone, and his name was Billy Pod; And he played upon an
old razor, an old razor, an old razor, And he played upon an old razor, with my
fiddle, fiddle fe fum fo. And his hat it was made of the good roast beef, etc. And
his coat it was made of the good fat tripe, etc. And his breeks they were made of
the bawbie baps, etc. And there was a man in tither toone, in tither toone, in tither
toone. And there was a man in tither toone, and his name was Edrin Drum; And he
played upon an old laadle, an old laadle, an old laadle, And he played upon an old
laadle, with my fiddle, fiddle fe fum fo. And he eat up all the good fat tripe etc. And
he eat up all the bawbie baps, etc.' / Chambers, 1870 / *Baby's Bouquet*, 1879, as text,
with tune / Baring-Gould, 1895 / *Tailor of Gloucester*, Beatrix Potter (p.p. ed.), 1902 /
Oral collection, 1945.

8

> American jump, American jump,
> One—two—three.
> Under the water, under the sea,
> Catching fishes for my tea,
>   —Dead or alive?

American Jump

In this nursery game the grown-up holds the child's hands and jumps him up and down until the word 'three', when she gives him an extra big jump up so that he can twist his legs around her waist. While she says 'Under the water, under the sea, catching fishes for my tea', she lets the child slowly fall backwards until he is hanging head downwards. The grown-up asks, 'Dead or alive?' If the child answers 'Alive' he is pulled upright again, if 'Dead' he is allowed to fall on the floor. This game, preserved in the family of one of the editors, is also known in France. In another version, also orally collected, the child is offered a third choice of 'round the world', often a favourite choice, for the child is then whirled round and round.

Family traditional, from c. 1900 / *Saint Anne's Soho Monthly Paper*, June 1907, 'Very common (for skipping) is, "American jump, American jump; one, two, three"' / Correspondent, 1949, 'Down at the bottom of the deep blue sea, Catching fishes for my tea, How many fishes does he bring me?' for skipping / Oral collection several occasions, 1950, 'Down at the bottom of the deep blue sea, Catching tiddlers one, two, three'. Sometimes played with child astride knee.
Cf. Oral collection, 1948, 'Bateau va sur l'eau; La rivière est au bord de l'eau. Voulez-vous payer, Monsieur? Non. A l'eau, à l'eau!'

9

Anna Elise, she jumped with surprise;
The surprise was so quick, it played her a trick;
The trick was so rare, she jumped in a chair;
The chair was so frail, she jumped in a pail;
The pail was so wet, she jumped in a net;
The net was so small, she jumped on the ball;
The ball was so round, she jumped on the ground;
And ever since then she's been turning around.

A rhyme with structure and story much like 'I went down the garden' and 'There was a man, he went mad' (qq.v.). Boyd Smith in his *Mother Goose* (1919) writes 'This jingle is said to have pleased the children of Edward III', but he fails to add where he heard the suggestion.

Correspondents, 1951–66, 'Anna Maria, She sat on (or, 'peed on') the fire, The fire was too hot, She sat on the pot, The pot was too round, She sat on the ground, The ground was too flat, She sat on the cat, The cat ran away with Maria on her back'.

Apple

10

As round as an apple,
As deep as a cup,
And all the king's horses
Cannot pull it up.

RIDDLE. *Solution*: a well. An early style of 'demande' having many variants, and equivalents in French and German. It was first noted by Randle Holme in the seventeenth century, 'What is y^t that is rond as a cup yet all my lord oxen canot draw it up?'

Holme MS, c. 1645 / *Sir Gregory Guess's Present* (T. Batchelar), c. 1815, 'As round as a hoop' / JOH, 1842 / N & Q, 1865 / *Rymour Club*, 1911, 'As deep as a house' / *Folk-Lore*, 1923.

Cf. JOH, 1849, 'As high as a castle, As weak as a wastle; And all the king's horses Cannot pull it down' (smoke) / Also *Kinderreime aus Schwaben*, E. Meir, 1851, 'Es ist etwas in meinem Haus, Es ziehen es hundert tausend Gäule nicht naus' / *Devinettes ou énigmes populaires*, E. Rolland, 1877, 'Qu'est-ce qui est rond comme un dé, Et que des chevaux ne peuvent porter?'

11

When good King Arthur ruled this land,
    He was a goodly king;
He stole three pecks of barley-meal
    To make a bag-pudding.

A bag-pudding the king did make,
    And stuffed it well with plums;
And in it put great lumps of fat,
    As big as my two thumbs.

The king and queen did eat thereof,
    And noblemen beside;
And what they could not eat that night,
    The queen next morning fried.

This seems to have been an old song or part of a ballad, though exactly what was its original form is difficult to say. The first two verses are part of Buchan's version of the Scottish song 'Johnny Lad', a version which he described as 'very old' and 'the original of all other songs of this name'. The verses in question, however, appear to have been incorporated from another song. 'There was a man of Ninevah' (q.v.) is similarly embodied. The earliest version may well be the one which Halliwell says is introduced in an old play and instead of King Arthur features King Stephen; while another version which may have a history has been preserved in dialect:

> Our good Quane Bess she maayde a pudden,
> An' stuffed 'un vull o' plums.
> An' in she put gurt dabs o' vat,
> As big as my two thumbs.

GG's Garland, c. 1799 / *Ancient Ballads and Songs*, Peter Buchan, 1828, 'When auld Prince Arthur ruled this land, He was a thievish king; He stole three bolls o' barley meal, To make a white pudding. (chorus) The pudding it was sweet and good, And stored well wi' plums; The lumps o' suet into it, Were big as baith my thumbs' / *Nurse Lovechild's DFN*, c. 1830 / *NR from the Royal Collections* (J. G. Rusher), c. 1840 / JOH, 1842 / *Only True MG Melodies*, c. 1843 / Rimbault, 1846, 'King Stephen was a worthy king, As ancient bards do sing; He bought three pecks of barley-meal, To make a bag-pudding' / *Baby's Opera*, 1877 / *Berkshire Words*, B. Lowsley, 1888, as quote / Kidson, 1904 / *Arthur of Britain*, Sir Edmund Chambers, 1927, 'garnered from the mouth of an innkeeper at Tarn Wadling' in Cumbria, 'When as King Arthur ruled this land, He ruled it like a swine; He bought three pecks of barleymeal To make a pudding fine. His pudding it was nodden well, And stuffed right full of plums; And lumps of suet he put in As big as my two thumbs' / *The English Folk-Play*, Sir Edmund Chambers, 1933, psalm sung by the clown in the sword dance at Ampleforth collected by Cecil Sharp, 'When first King Henry ruled this land, He was a right generous King', &c., three verses / *Lark Rise*, Flora Thompson, 1939, described as 'a favourite for singing in chorus'.

Parody. *The Christening Cake* (John Lea), 1842, ballad on the reception after the christening of the Prince of Wales, begins: 'When great Victoria ruled the land, She ruled it like a Queen; She had a Princess and a Prince Not very far between.'

12

> Arthur O'Bower has broken his band
> And he comes roaring up the land;
> The King of Scots with all his power
> Cannot stop Arthur of the Bower.

Lines 'to be sung in a high wind'. A conjecture made by Lewis Spence (*Myth and Ritual*, 1947) is that Arthur O'Bower preserves the name of the old British hero Arthur. This mythological figure has been thought of as a god of the sun and the firmament, and possibly is the Wild Huntsman described in *The Complaynt of Scotlande* (1549):

> Arthour knycht he raid on nycht,
> vitht gyltin spur and candil lycht.

Arthur O'Bower

The word *Bower* may well be a corruption of the Scottish *bowder*, a blast or squall of wind. Further to this there are two curious parallels to the nursery rhyme offering evidence of its antiquity. One is from among Scott's materials for the *Border Minstrelsy*, a verse (MS 877) collected about 1815:

> The great Bull of Bendy-law
> Has broken his band and run awa,
> And the king and a' his court
> Canna turn that bull about.

The other is the opening of the ballad *Robin Hood and the Tanner* (Pepys, II. III), printed about 1650:

> In Nottingham there lives a jolly Tanner,
> His name is Arthur a Bland:
> There is ne're a 'Squire in Nottinghamshire
> Dare bid bold Arthur stand.

The earliest recording of the rhyme appears to be in a now lost letter from Dorothy Wordsworth, which Lamb acknowledged 2 June 1804.

Songs for the Nursery, 1805 / *MG's Quarto*, c. 1825 / Chambers, 1842 / JOH, 1846 / *Squirrel Nutkin*, Beatrix Potter, 1903 / *Works of Charles and Mary Lamb*, ed. E. V. Lucas, 1905, the rhyme Dorothy Wordsworth sent Lamb is said to be, 'Arthur's bower has broke his band, He comes riding up the land, The King of Scots with all his power Cannot build up Arthur's bower.'

13

> Hush-a-bye a baa-lamb,
> Hush-a-bye a milk cow,
> We'll find a little stick
> To beat the barking bow-wow.

Poetic Trifles for Young Gentlemen and Ladies (J. G. Rusher), c. 1840 / JOH, 1842 'You shall have a little stick, to beat the naughty bow-wow' / *NR Tales and Jingles*, 1844.

14

> Hush thee, my babby,
> Lie still with thy daddy,
> Thy mammy has gone to the mill,

Baby

To grind thee some wheat
To make thee some meat,
Oh, my dear babby, lie still.

Songs for the Nursery, 1805 / Douce MS II, c. 1820, 'Rock a bye baby—puss is a lady, Mousey is gone to the mill; And if you don't cry She'll come by and by So hush a bye baby lie still' / *MG's Quarto*, c. 1825 / *NR for Children* (J. Fairburn), c. 1825, 'To get some meal to bake a cake' / JOH, 1842 / Chambers, 1847, 'Hush a ba, babie, lie still, lie still; Your mammie's awa to the mill, the mill; Baby is greeting for want of good keeping—Hush a ba, baby, lie still, lie still' (with which cf. 'Bye, O my baby') / Mason, 1877, similar to c. 1820 / *Scottish NR*, R. J. MacLennan, 1909, 'Hush-a-bye baby, lie still an sleep soun', Your Mammie's awa tae the mill, An' she'll no' be hame, till the licht o' the mune, Sae hush-a-bye baby, lie still.'

15

Baby and I
Were baked in a pie,
The gravy was wonderful hot.
We had nothing to pay
To the baker that day
And so we crept out of the pot.

JOH, 1843. Whence often reprinted.

16

Baby, baby, naughty baby,
Hush, you squalling thing, I say.
Peace this moment, peace, or maybe
Bonaparte will pass this way.

Baby, baby, he's a giant,
Tall and black as Rouen steeple,
And he breakfasts, dines, rely on't,
Every day on naughty people.

Baby, baby, if he hears you,
As he gallops past the house,
Limb from limb at once he'll tear you,
Just as pussy tears a mouse.

Baby

And he'll beat you, beat you, beat you,
And he'll beat you all to pap,
And he'll eat you, eat you, eat you,
Every morsel snap, snap, snap.

A type of lullaby which hopes to obtain peace by intimidation. The bogeys who have been named in this song at one time or another would probably cover several chapters of British history. As well as Bonaparte in the above (sent by a correspondent who knew it from her grandmother), recorded versions include Menshikov, Russian Commander in the Crimean War, 'Black Old Knoll' (Oliver Cromwell), and Wellington. A writer in *Notes & Queries* remembered hearing some of the verses in 1836.

N & Q, 1877, Cromwell 'tall as Lincoln steeple' / *County Folk-Lore, Lincolnshire*, Mabel Peacock, 1908 / Gosset, 1915 / Correspondent, 1946.

17

Bye, O my baby,
When I was a lady,
O then my baby didn't cry;
But my baby is weeping
For want of good keeping,
O I fear my poor baby will die.

GG's Garland, 1784 / JOH, 1842 / *Traditional Nursery Songs*, Felix Summerly, 1843, illustration by R. Redgrave, R.A.

18

Dance a baby, diddy,
What can mammy do wid'e,
But sit in her lap,
And give 'un some pap,
And dance a baby diddy?

This was included in the performance of an 'old Italian way-faring puppet-showman of the name of Piccini' who began giving Punch and Judy shows in England about 1780. In 1828, when his script was transcribed, it was called 'the common nursery ditty'.

Baby

Infant Institutes, 1797, 'What shall Mama do wid ye, Set in her lap, And give ye some pap, And dance a Baby, diddy' / Douce MS, c. 1805, 'Danty baby diddy' / *GG's Garland*, 1810 / *Punch and Judy*, J. P. Collier, 1828, as text, also 'Dancy, baby, dancy, How it shall gallop and prancy! Sit on my knee; Now kissy me; Dancy, baby, dancy' / JOH, 1843 / Rimbault, 1846, three additional verses, probably apocryphal / Crofton MS, 1901.

19

Dance, little baby, dance up high:
Never mind, baby, mother is by;
Crow and caper, caper and crow,
There, little baby, there you go;
Up to the ceiling, down to the ground,
Backwards and forwards, round and round:
Dance, little baby, and mother shall sing,
With the merry gay coral, ding, ding-a-ding, ding.

This is one of the pieces in *Rhymes for the Nursery*, 'by the authors of *Original Poems*' i.e. (chiefly) Ann and Jane Taylor, first published in 1806. JOH included it as a traditional rhyme of unknown origin in 1842. 'Twinkle, twinkle, little star' (q.v.) is a rhyme from the same book which has similarly entered oral tradition. The baby's bell-bedecked rattle from which juts a sprig of coral, referred to in the last line, is not so common today as it was in the nineteenth century.

20

How many days has my baby to play?
Saturday, Sunday, Monday,
Tuesday, Wednesday, Thursday, Friday,
Saturday, Sunday, Monday.
Hop away, skip away,
My baby wants to play,
My baby wants to play every day.

This song travelled a long way before it reached the nursery. A catch by Arne (1710–78), in *Appollonian Harmony*, c. 1790, ran:

Baby

Which is the properest day to drink,
 Saturday, Sunday, Monday?
Each is the properest day I think,
 Why should I name but one day?
Tell me but yours I'll mention my day,
 let us but fix on some day...
Bravo, Bravo,
Tuesday, Wednesday, Thursday, Friday,
Saturday, Sunday, Monday.

Arne won a prize for this at a meeting of the Noblemen and Gentlemen's Catch Club (founded 1761).

In Lady Fenn's *School Dialogues* (1783), the schoolboy Frisk 'runs off singing, "How many days have I to play? Saturday, Sunday, Monday"'. A version in *School Boys' Diversions* (1820), returns to the form of the drinking song, beginning 'Which is the properest day to play?' and ending with the moral, 'We'll play six days in the week; But on the *seventh*,—Oh! never; Since He who made the world, decreed, *That* should be hallowed ever.'

Songs for the Nursery, 1805, first four lines of text, as also *MG's Quarto*, c. 1825; *Traditional Nursery Songs*, Felix Summerly, 1843; JOH, 1844 / Oral collection, 1945.

21

Hush-a-bye, baby,
 Daddy is near,
Mammy's a lady,
 And that's very clear.

A lullaby, probably only a fragment, given by 'Felix Summerly' (Sir Henry Cole) in *Traditional Nursery Songs* (1843). It seems to have been parodied by the old Italian puppet-showman, whose script was transcribed in 1828 by J. P. Collier:

Oh, rest thee, my baby,
 Thy daddy is here:
Thy mammy's a gaby,
 And that is quite clear.
Oh rest thee, my darling,
 Thy mother will come,
With voice like a starling:—
 I wish she was dumb.

22

> Hush-a-bye, baby, on the tree top,
> When the wind blows the cradle will rock;
> When the bough breaks the cradle will fall,
> Down will come baby, cradle, and all.

The best-known lullaby both in England and America, it is regularly crooned in hundreds of thousands of homes at nightfall. The age of both the rhyme and the melody, which is a variant of 'Lilliburlero', is uncertain. The words are first found in *Mother Goose's Melody* (c. 1765) with the footnote, 'This may serve as a Warning to the Proud and Ambitious, who climb so high that they generally fall at last'. Imaginations have been stretched to give the rhyme significance. Gerald Massey in *Ancient Egypt* suggests that the babe is the child Horus. Joseph Ritson states that the opening phrase of his version, 'Bee baw babby lou, on a tree top', is a corruption of the French nurse's threat in the fable, *He bas! la le loup!* Gosset says, 'On a tree-top—or green boh (bough)'. Note that boh rhymes with rock, and top fails to do so.' (Boh is a Saxon word.) The authorship has been attributed to a Pilgrim youth who went over in the *Mayflower* and who was influenced by the way the Red Indian hung his birch-bark cradle on the branch of a tree. It has been said to be 'the first poem produced on American soil' (*Book Lover*, 1904). Other American authorities, including Metro Goldwyn Mayer (1944) have seen it as a lampoon on the British royal line in James II's time. In *The Scots Musical Museum* (1797) appears a nursery song 'O can ye sew cushions?', which Burns submitted. In his second edition of the *Scotish Minstrel* (1823, IV) R. A. Smith gives, as the second stanza of 'O can ye sew cushions?':

> I biggit the cradle on the tree top,
> And the wind it did blow, and the cradle did rock,
> And hee and baw, birdie, &c.

and William Stenhouse produced a similar second verse to the song in 1839. This seems to be another hint that long ago, in Britain, as in other countries, cradles were rocked by wind power. (Cf. also the 1915 quote of 'Bye, baby bunting'.)

MG's Melody, c. 1765 / *GG's Garland*, 1784, 'When the wind ceases the cradle will fall' / *T Thumb's SB*, 1788 / *Hushaby Baby upon the Tree Top*, 'A Favourite Duet or Trio' (J. Dale), c. 1797, sheet music / *Songs for the Nursery*, 1805 / *Vocal Harmony*, c. 1806 / *Blackwood's*, ?John Wilson, July 1824 / *NR for Children* (J. Fairburn), c. 1825 / JOH, 1842 / Gosset, 1915, 'Hush a bee bo on a tree-top.'

Baby

23

Rock-a-bye, baby,
   Thy cradle is green,
Father's a nobleman,
   Mother's a queen;
And Betty's a lady,
   And wears a gold ring;
And Johnny's a drummer,
   And drums for the king.

Songs for the Nursery, 1805 / *MG's Quarto*, c. 1825 / *Cradle Rhymes for Infants* (J. & C. Mozley), c. 1840, 'Rock-a-bye, baby, thy cradle is clean; Father's a nobleman, mother's a queen, And Betty's a lady, her gown is pea green; And Johnny's a drummer and drums for the queen' / JOH, 1842 / *Mother Goose*, Kate Greenaway, 1881 / *Lavender's Blue*, Kathleen Lines, illus. Harold Jones, 1954.

Cf. Scott's 'Lullaby of an Infant Chief', 1816, 'O, hush thee, my babie, thy sire was a knight, Thy mother a lady both lovely and bright.'

Cf. also, oral collection, 1949, 'Schlaf, Kindlein, schlaf, Deine Mutter ist eine Edelfrau, Schlaf Kindlein, Schlaf.' Also see *Des Knaben Wunderhorn*, L. Achim von Arnim und C. Brentano, 3 vols, 1806–8.

24

Bye, baby bumpkin,
Where's Tony Lumpkin?
My lady's on her death-bed,
With eating half a pumpkin.

Blackwood's,? John Wilson, July 1824 / JOH, 1844.
***Tony Lumpkin is first heard of in Goldsmith's *She Stoops to Conquer*, 1773.

25

Bye, baby bunting,
Daddy's gone a-hunting,
Gone to get a rabbit skin
To wrap the baby bunting in.

A favourite song with nurses. 'Bunting', an old form of endearment, if it means anything probably means 'short and thick ... as a plump child', for

PLATE III

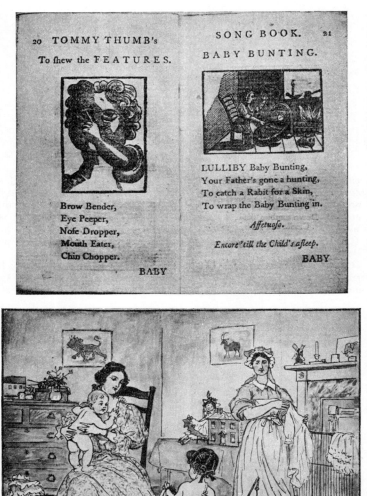

A CENTURY OF CHILDREN'S BOOK ILLUSTRATION

a. 'Brow Bender' and 'Baby Bunting' in *Tommy Thumb's Song Book*,
1788. British Museum. *b.* 'Bye, Baby Bunting!' in Caldecott's *Hey
Diddle Diddle and Baby Bunting*, 1882. Reproduced from the artist's
hand-coloured proof. Opie collection

Baby Bunting

which the only dated quotation in *OED* is 1665. As well as a rabbit skin, Daddy (or Mammie) has also set out to wrap the baby in 'a hare's skin', 'a bullie's skin', 'a sturdy lion's skin' (c. 1790), and 'a lammie's skin', as in the notable Scottish variation:

> Hushie ba, burdie beeton,
> Your Mammie's gane to Seaton,
> For to buy a lammie's skin
> To wrap your bonnie boukie in.

GG's Garland, 1784 / *T Thumb's SB*, 1788, 'Lulliby Baby Bunting' / *T Tit's SB*, c. 1790 / *Songs for the Nursery*, 1805, 'Bye, baby bunting, Father's gone a hunting, Mother's gone a milking, Sister's gone a silking, Brother's gone to buy a skin To wrap the baby bunting in' / Douce MS, c. 1805 / *Mother's Gift* (N. Coverly, Jun., Boston, Mass.), 1812, 'Rock a-by baby bunting, My father's gone a hunting, My mother's at home making a skin, To wrap up little baby bunting in' / JOH, 1842 / Chambers, 1842, as quote / *Changing Panoramic Toy Book* (Dean and Son), 1880 / *Hey, Diddle, Diddle, and Baby Bunting*, Randolph Caldecott, 1882 / Maclagan, 1901, 'Ba lamb, ba lamb, beattie O, Your mamy's away to the city O, To buy a wee bit croby's skin, To row about your feety O' / *Folk-Lore*, 1902, 'By, by, Baby Bunting, Your Daddy gone a-hunting, Your Mammy gone the other way To beg a jug of sour whey For little Baby Bunting', collected near Dean Forest / *Rymour Club*, 1911 / Gosset, 1915, 'Baloo, lillie beetie, Mammie's at the creetie, For tae plick an' tae pu', For tae gather lammie's woo', For tae buy a bullie's skin, Tae rock wir bonnie bairnie in', from Orkney, probably referring to the old custom of swinging the baby in a hammock of 'bullie' or calf skin.

Cf. Gosset, 1915, 'Father's gone a-flailing, Brother's gone a-nailing, Mother's gone a-leasing, Granny's come a-pleasing, Sister's gone to Llantwit fair, Baby, baby will go there.' Still heard in the Vale of Glamorgan.

Cf. also *Pesenki Baiki*, L. Diakonov (Moskow), 1942, 'Baiu-baiu, Otez ushel za riboiu, Mat ushla korov doit, Dedushka—uhu varit Nianechka—pelenki mit. Luli, luli, lulenki' (Hush, hush, Father has gone fishing, Mother went to milk the cows, Grandfather—to cook some soup, Nurse—to wash your clothes).

26

> How many miles to Babylon?
> Three score miles and ten.
> Can I get there by candle-light?
> Yes, and back again.
> If your heels are nimble and light,
> You may get there by candle-light.

In a Latin sermon of the late thirteenth century, the progress of Christians towards Heaven is compared to a boys' game, in which the dialogue runs: 'How many miles to Beverleyham?' 'Eight'. 'Can I get there in

Babylon

daylight?' 'Yes, indeed you can' (Balliol MS 230). Similar words for the same side-to-side catching game were still being used centuries later (see Opie, *Children's Games in Street and Playground*, pp. 124–6); and also for a thread-the-needle singing game (see Opie, *The Singing Game*, pp. 44–6). The words are now commonly a straightforward nursery rhyme. The inherent mystery of the lines has appealed to many, as Stevenson:

> Our phantom voices haunt the air
> As we were still at play,
> And I can hear them call and say:
> *How far is it to Babylon?*

Babylon, it has been suggested, is a corruption of *Babyland*. More probably it is the far-away luxurious city of early seventeenth-century usage. Kipling, too, seems to have felt that the words belonged to the long ago. Sir Huon of Bordeaux, Puck explains to Dan, succeeded King Oberon, but he was lost on the road to Babylon.

> 'Have you ever heard, "How many miles to Babylon"?'
> 'Of course,' says Dan flushing.
> 'Well, Sir Huon was young when that song was new.'

In Scotland they know an attractive longer version:

> King and Queen of Cantelon,
> How many miles to Babylon?
> Eight and eight, and other eight.
> Will I get there by candle-light?
> If your horse be good and your spurs be bright.
> How many men have ye?
> Mae nor ye daur come and see.

Mactaggart thought this likely to be 'a pantomime on some scenes played off in the time of the Crusades', Cantelon being a corruption of *Caledon*.

In the context of this song, 'by candle-light' does not, as usually thought, mean 'by the light of a candle', but 'by the time at which the candles are lit', as in the preface to Bentley's *Phalaris* (1699), 'The Whole might be done . . . twice over before Candle-light'.

Introduction to The Complaynt of Scotland, John Leyden, 1801, 'a nursery tale of which I only recollect the following ridiculous verses, Chick my naggie, chick my naggie! How mony miles to Aberdeagie? 'Tis eight, and eight, and other eight, We'll no win there wi' candle light' / *Songs for the Nursery*, 1805 / *Gallovidian Encyclopedia*, J. Mactaggart, 1824 / *MG's Quarto*, c. 1825 / Chambers, 1826, similar to first four lines of Scottish quote, above / JOH, 1842 / Chambers, 1847, as quote / Newell, 1883, 'Marlow, marlow, marlow bright, How many miles to Babylon?', words perhaps related to the Tudor game Barley Break / *Arbroath: Past and Present*, J. M. McBain, 1887, 'How many miles is it to Glasca-Lea?' / Gomme, 1894, collected nineteen versions / *100 Singing Games*, F. Kidson, 1916 / As well as Babylon places named include Bethlehem,

Babylon

Burslem, Banbury, Barney Bridge, Barley-bridge, Curriglass, Gandigo, Hebron, and Wimbledon.
Cf. JOH, 1853, 'Fox a fox, a brummalary, How many miles to Lummaflary? Lummabary. Eight and eight, and a hundred and eight. How shall I get home to night? Spin your legs and run fast'; described as 'A game of the fox'.

27

As I was going to Banbury,
Upon a summer's day,
My dame had butter, eggs, and fruit,
And I had corn and hay;
Joe drove the ox, and Tom the swine,
Dick took the foal and mare,
I sold them all—then home to dine,
From famous Banbury fair.

This comes in *The Cries of Banbury and London*. The fact that so many nursery pieces mention Banbury may, in part, be due to the energy of the printer, Rusher. Working at Banbury he often altered the wording to suit local patronage, but his influence was more than local. His juvenile publications are among the commonest chapbooks surviving today.

However, the verse seems to have been plucked from a widely-known folksong. Baring-Gould collected it from a labourer on Dartmoor, in a version beginning:

As I went down to Salisbury,
'Twas on a market day,
By chance I met a fair pretty maid,
By chance all on the way.
Her business it to market was,
With butter, eggs, and whey.
So we both jog on together my boys
With Derry-down weeday.

He and Fleetwood Sheppard used the tune for 'The Saucy Ploughboy', in *Songs of the West*, part IV (1889), but, he said, 'we could not employ the words'.

Cries of Banbury and London (J. G. Rusher), c. 1840 / *Land of NR*, Ernest Rhys, 1932 / *Puffin Rhymes*, illus. John Harwood, 1944, 'As I was going to Banbury All on a summer day, My wife had butter, eggs and cheese, And I had corn and hay...'

28

Ride a cock-horse to Banbury Cross,
To buy little Johnny a galloping horse;
It trots behind and it ambles before,
And Johnny shall ride till he can ride no more.

Sung while 'galloping' a baby on the knee.

Nancy Cock's PSB, c. 1780, 'Ride a cock-horse To Banbury Cross [To buy little Nancy] An ambling horse, It gallops before, And trots behind, So Nancy may ride it 'Till it is blind'—first song in the book and obviously rewritten for the occasion / *Songs for the Nursery*, 1805 / *MG's Quarto*, c. 1825 / JOH, 1842 / *Only True MG Melodies*, c. 1843, 'to Shrewsbury-cross' / *Northamptonshire Glossary*, A. E. Baker, 1854, 'Hight O cock-horse, to Banbury Cross, To buy a new nag, and nimble horse.'
    Cf. succeeding rhymes.

29

Ride a cock-horse to Banbury Cross,
To see a fine lady upon a white horse;
Rings on her fingers and bells on her toes,
And she shall have music wherever she goes.

The above wording is that commonly known today but early versions do not agree in their descriptions of the lady. She is 'an old woman' (1784), and has later (c. 1790) 'a ring on her finger, A bonnet of straw, The strangest old woman that ever you saw'. In *Infant Institutes* the rhyme commences:

Hight-a-cock horse to Banbury Cross,
To see a fine lady upon a fine horse.

But in *Songs for the Nursery* she is again 'old', and the horse 'black', facts repeated in *Mother Goose's Quarto* (c. 1825), and *Mother Goose's Melodies* (1833), though in the latter edition she 'jumps' on to the horse. In some nineteenth-century books the destination is said to be Coventry Cross. The problem of determining the likely age of the rhyme and the identity of the lady is most difficult. The rhyme is possibly referred to by Carey (1725), 'Now on *Cock-horse* does he ride', though this may equally be refer-ring to the shopper, Tommy (in the next rhyme). It has been suggested that the 'bells on her toes' points to the fifteenth century, when a bell was worn on the long tapering toe of each shoe. The 'goodly Crosse' at

Banbury Cross

Banbury was destroyed at the turn of the sixteenth century. A Jesuit priest wrote in January 1601: 'The inhabitants of Banbury being far gone in Puritanism, in a furious zeal tumultuously assailed the Cross that stood in the market place, and so defaced it that they scarcely left one stone upon another.' The inhabitants were much satirized by contemporary dramatists for their bigotry. Again, although it would seem unlikely that the rhyme originated very long after the cross was destroyed, there were, in fact, other, inferior crosses at Banbury, and the memory of the big cross always lingered. A modern cross now stands in its place. The term 'cock-horse' has been used to describe a proud, high-spirited horse, and also the additional coach-horse attached when going up a hill. A writer in the *Sunday Times* (2 Nov. 1930) said: 'It was a customary sight during the latter half of the 18th century for travellers to Banbury and Birmingham to observe a group of children clustered at the foot of Stanmore Hill to witness the be-ribboned and rosetted fifth horse attached to the coach. As the gaily caparisoned jockey flourished his gilt-staff the boys and girls would chant "Ride a cock-horse to Banbury Cross".' On what authority this statement is made is not known. 'To ride a cock-horse' is usually taken to refer to straddling a toy horse (or grown-up's knee) and is found used in this sense since 1540. Katherine Thomas in *The Real Personages of Mother Goose* describes 'a never to be forgotten incident . . . when, standing beside my mother as she sang "Ride a cock horse to Banbury Cross" she smilingly remarked "The Old Woman on the white horse was Queen Elizabeth". This comment [was] made with the certainty of one who repeats a wellknown fact.' Another story, however, equally prevalent in popular tradition and enhanced by the (? comparatively recent) 'Coventry Cross' version, is that the rider referred to is the famous wife of the Earl of Mercia, Lady Godiva; while a third sporting lady who merits attention is Celia Fiennes. Daughter of a Parliamentarian officer and sister of the third Viscount Saye and Sele of Broughton Castle, Banbury, she made many rides on horseback throughout England from about 1697. The story has got about that the original wording of the rhyme was 'Ride a cock-horse to Banbury Cross, To see a *Fiennes* lady'. However, the nineteenth Baron Saye and Sele, whose family seat is still Broughton Castle, suspected that his father, a noted wit (author of an autobiography *Hear Saye*) himself invented the 'Fiennes lady' version.

GG's Garland, 1784 / *T Thumb's SB*, 1788 / *T Tit's SB*, c. 1790 / *Infant Institutes*, 1797 / MS addition to Bussell copy of *MG's Melody*, c. 1803 / *Songs for the Nursery*, 1805 / *Blackwood's*, ? John Wilson, July 1824, 'To Bamborough Cross' / *MG's Quarto*, c. 1825 / *Mother Goose's Melodies*, 1833 / JOH, 1842 / *Ride a Cock Horse to Banbury Cross*, Randolph Caldecott, 1884.

Pantomime, *The Witch and the White Horse, or the Old Woman of Banbury Cross*, by Andrew Ducrow, performed at Astley's Royal Amphitheatre, 1833.

Banbury Cross

30

Ride a cock-horse
To Banbury Cross,
To see what Tommy can buy;
A penny white loaf,
A penny white cake,
And a two-penny apple-pie.

The pastry cake of Banbury has been renowned for several centuries. 'Banberie cakes' are referred to in 1586. Their ingredients are mixed peel, biscuit crumbs, currants, allspice, eggs, and butter, folded into a circle of puff pastry. And very good they are too. When in Banbury it was well worth visiting 12 Parson's Street, 'the original Banbury Cake shop', to try one.

T Thumb's PSB, c. 1744, last line, 'And a Hugegy penny pye' / *MG's Melody*, c. 1765 / *Nancy Cock's PSB*, c. 1780 / *GG's Garland*, 1784 / *Vocal Harmony*, c. 1806 / *NR* (T. Richardson), c. 1830 / JOH, 1842, 'Ride a cock-horse to Coventry cross; To see what Emma can buy; A penny white cake I'll buy for her sake, And a twopenny tart or a pie' / *Only True MG Melodies*, c. 1843.

*** For remarks on 'Cock horse' and 'Banbury Cross' see previous article.

31

Barber, barber, shave a pig,
How many hairs will make a wig?
Four and twenty, that's enough.
Give the barber a pinch of snuff.

Possibly this jingle was known about 1805 to the author of *Jerry Diddle and his Fiddle* (J. P., Great St. Andrew Street):

> He next met a barber,
>   With powder and wig,
> He play'd him a tune
>   And he shav'd an old pig.

The profitableness of shaving a pig appears to have been an old joke, perhaps similar to that of shaving an egg. In his *Table Book* Hone wrote (19 Mar. 1827), 'Carrying on the [toy] lamb business is scarcely better than pig shaving.'

JOH, 1842 / Maclagan, 1901 / Correspondent, 1946.

Barber

32

The barber shaved the mason,
  As I suppose,
  Cut off his nose,
And popped it in a basin.

This is given by JOH (1844), and seems to have a common origin with the following collected by M. A. Denham in *Folk-Lore in the North of England* (1858):

As I suppose, and as I suppose,
  The barber shaved the Quaker,
And as I suppose, he cut off his nose,
  And lap't it up in a paper.

A song 'The barber and his bason' is mentioned by Ritson in a letter to George Paton, 19 May 1795.

33

Barnaby Bright he was a sharp cur,
He always would bark if a mouse did but stir,
But now he's grown old, and can no longer bark,
He's condemned by the parson to be hanged by the clerk.

Described in Walsh's *The Jovial Companions* (1709), as 'A 3 Voc. Catch on a Parson's decriped old Dog call'd Barnet', by Mr. R. Brown, it appears as follows:

'Tis pitty poor Barnet a Vigilant, Vigilant Curr,
that us'd for to bark, if a mouse, if a mouse did but stirr,
should being grown old, and unable, unable to bark,
be doom'd by a Priest, be doom'd by a Priest, to be hang'd by his clark,
I pray good S^r therefore, weigh right well, right well his Case,
and save us poor Barnet, Hang cleric, hang cleric, hang cleric in 's
      place.

This was reprinted in *The Catch Club* (1733) and in *The Pleasant Musical Companion* (c. 1740). The version known today is from *Gammer Gurton's Garland* (1810).

34

> Barney Bodkin broke his nose,
> Without feet we can't have toes;
> Crazy folks are always mad,
> Want of money makes us sad.

These are the opening lines of a song called 'A Bundle of Truths' preserved in the Johnson collection in the Bodleian Library, the remainder of the first stanza being:

> A farthing rush-light's very small,
> Doctors wear large bushy wigs.
> One that's dumb can never bawl,
> Prickled pork is made of pigs.

The refrain of this song is also remembered in the nursery ('Hyder iddle diddle dell') (q.v.).

A Bundle of Truths (Laurie & Whittle), c. 1811 / *Universal Songster*, 1825, part-quoted in a comic medley / *Oliver's Comic Songs* (Oliver and Boyd), c. 1830 / JOH, 1846 / *Mother Goose's NR*, L. E. Walter, 1924.

35

> Go to bed first,
> A golden purse;
> Go to bed second,
> A golden pheasant;
> Go to bed third,
> A golden bird.

JOH, 1844 / *Favourite Rhymes for the Nursery*, 1892 / *Land of NR*, Ernest Rhys, 1932.

36

> Bell horses, bell horses,
>   What time of day?
> One o'clock, two o'clock,
>   Time to away.

Bell Horses

A rhyme common in the nineteenth century for starting children's races. Exactly what bell horses are in this context is undetermined. Bells used to be hung on the leading pack-horse, called the 'bell horse', and on festive occasions, particularly May Day, the wagoners' horses were, and still are, decked with bells. Denham tells how bells were used on coach horses up to the beginning of the nineteenth century. A New Zealand correspondent, stating that the rhyme was in use for race-starting in his childhood, explained 'bell horses' as meaning race horses, the term deriving from Stuart times when, instead of having cups as trophies, races were sometimes run for silver bells.

Douce MS, c. 1805 / *GG's Garland*, 1810 / *New Year's Gift* (J. Catnach), c. 1830 [Hindley, 1878] / JOH, 1842, 'Good horses, bad horses, What is the time of day? Three o'clock, four o'clock, Now fare you away' / *Folk-Lore in N. England*, M. A. Denham, 1858, 'Bellasy, Bellasy [and 'Coach horses, Coach horses'], what time o' day? One o'clock, two o'clock, three and away' / Gomme, 1894 / N & Q, 1907, 'Bell horses, bell horses, all in a row, How many fine bells I want to know?' / N & Q, 1922, additional couplet, 'The master is coming and what will he say? He'll whip them, and drive them, and send them away' / Correspondent, 1946; and 1949, repeated when blowing dandelion seed, 'Field Horses, Field Horses, What time of day? One o'clock (puff), two o'clock (puff), three (a tremendous puff), and away.'

37

> At the siege of Belle Isle
> I was there all the while—
> All the while,
> All the while,
> At the siege of Belle Isle.

A joke response to a request for a song or a story. 'How often in my youth', writes a correspondent, 'was I annoyed, when asking an elder to tell me a story, to be fobbed off with the insufferable:

> At the siege of Belleisle I was there all the while,
> I was there all the while at the siege of Belleisle,
> At the siege of Belleisle I was there all the while,

and so on, and so on, repeated until my infant temper could brook no more.' Probably these lines were the refrain of a song. Belle Isle (Belle-Île-en-Mer), dominating the west coast of France, was one of the British objectives in the Seven Years War. The siege, which lasted from April to June 1761, caught the popular imagination. Three years after the action, Mrs. Sneak, in Foote's *Mayor of Garret*, flatters the militia major, 'he is the very Broglio and Belleisle of the army'. In a song book printed at

Belle Isle

Stirling (1817) there is a song called 'The Siege of Belisle' but bearing no resemblance to the above. From Connecticut Bolton in 1888 reported:

> At the battle of the Nile
> I was there all the while,
> I was there all the while
> So you hop over that stile.

Punch, vol. iii, 1842, p. 156 / JOH, 1844 / *Look! the Sun*, Edith Sitwell, 1941 / Correspondent, 1949.

38

> Ring the bells, ring!
> Hip, hurrah for the King!
> The dunce fell into the pool, oh!
> The dunce was going to school, oh!
> The groom and the cook
> Fished him out with a hook,
> And he piped his eye like a fool, oh!

Under the Window, Kate Greenaway, 1878 / Oral collection, 1945.
*** 'To pipe one's eye', to weep. Originally nautical slang.

39

> Bessy Bell and Mary Gray,
> They were two bonny lasses;
> They built their house upon the lea,
> And covered it with rushes.
>
> Bessy kept the garden gate,
> And Mary kept the pantry;
> Bessy always had to wait,
> While Mary lived in plenty.

This is an adaptation of a pathetic little Scottish ballad:

> O Bessie Bell and Mary Gray,
> They war twa bonnie lasses;
> They bigget a bower on yon burn-brae
> And theekit it o'er wi' rashes.

Bessy Bell

They theekit it o'er wi' rashes green,
    They theekit it o'er wi' heather;
But the pest cam' frae the burrows-town,
    And slew them baith thegither.

They thocht to lye in Methven kirk-yard,
    Amang their noble kin;
But they maun lie on Lynedoch-brae,
    To biek forenent the sin.

The local tradition (first written down c. 1773) about these two girls is that Mary Gray was the daughter of the Laird of Lednock (also known as Lynedoch) and Bessy Bell of the Laird of Kinvaid, a place near by. They were both very handsome and an intimate friendship subsisted between them. While Bessy was on a visit to Mary the plague broke out at Perth (seven miles distant), and in order to escape it they built themselves a bower about three-quarters of a mile west from Lednock House, in a retired and romantic place called Burn-braes. Here they lived for some time; but, the plague raging with great fury, they caught the infection from a young man who was in love with them both and used to bring them their provisions. They died in this bower, and since, according to the rule in cases of plague, they could not be buried in a churchyard (verse 3), they were interred in the Dranoch-haugh, at the foot of a brae of the same name, near the bank of the river Almond. The burial place (which may still be seen) lies about three-quarters of a mile west from the house called Lynedoch Cottage. The date of this episode would be about 1645. In that year, and the year or two following, Perth and its neighbourhood was ravaged by plague; 3,000 people are believed to have perished. In spite of the tenor of the ballad it is likely that the girls had already caught the infection when they removed to their bower. It is written in an account of the plague, made soon afterwards, that 'it was thought proper to put those out of the town at some distance who were sick. Accordingly, they went out and builded huts for themselves in different places around the town, particularly in... the grounds near the river Almond.' The ballad was known in the late seventeenth century since there was a squib on the birth of the Old Pretender (1688), beginning:

> Bessy Bell and Mary Grey,
>   Those famous bonny lasses.

The ballad was later (1719) converted into a drawing-room song by Allan Ramsay, who, nevertheless, retained the first verse.

Ramsay's version, first printed in a pamphlet (Edinburgh, 1720), appears frequently in the 18th century, e.g. *Orpheus Caledonius*, 1725, 'set to music by W. Thomson'; *The Musical Miscellany* (John Watts), 1729; *O Bessy Bell & Mary Gray*, c. 1730, 'A Scotch

Bessy Bell

song, Sung by Mrs. Robinson at the King's Theatre in the Haymarket'; *Muses Threnodie*, James Cart, 1774; *The Pirate*, Walter Scott, 1821 (two verses). The tune is also in *The Beggar's Opera*, 'A curse attends the woman's love'. The ballad is given in *A Ballad Book*, C. Kirkpatrick Sharpe, 1824; *The Songs of Scotland*, A. Cunningham, 1825, as recited by Sir Walter Scott; *Ancient Ballads and Songs*, Thomas Lyle, 1827, two verses. As a nursery rhyme it appears in *The Cheerful Warbler* (J. Kendrew), c. 1820, first verse only, 'They built their house with walls of clay'; JOH, 1842; *Rymour Club*, 1911.

*** 'Bessy Bell' is possibly a traditional name. Martin Parker wrote a ballad 'Four-pence-halfe-penney Farthing' registered 9 Nov. 1629, which was to the tune 'Bessy Bell; or, A Health to Betty', and there is a poem on 'Bessy Bell' attached to *Barnabee's Journal*. Ritson wrote as if there were already more than one song about 'Bessy Bell and Mary Gray' in 1795.

40

Little Betty Blue
Lost her holiday shoe,
What can little Betty do?
Give her another
To match the other,
And then she may walk out in two.

Douce MS, c. 1815, 'Old Betty Blue . . . and then she may swagger in two' / JOH, 1844 / *Mother Goose*, Kate Greenaway, 1881 / *Hilda Boswell's Treasury of Nursery Rhymes*, 1960.

41

Betty Botter bought some butter,
But, she said, the butter's bitter;
If I put it in my batter
It will make my batter bitter,
But a bit of better butter
Will make my batter better.
So she bought a bit of butter
Better than her bitter butter,
And she put it in her batter
And the batter was not bitter.
So t'was better Betty Botter bought a bit of better butter.

Tongue twister, preferably to be recited without the *t*s.

Betty Botter

The Jingle Book, Carolyn Wells (Macmillan, New York), 1899, 'Betty Botta bought some butter' / *N & Q*, 1934 / *Reader's Digest*, 1944.

42

Little Betty Pringle she had a pig,
It was not very little and not very big;
When he was alive he lived in clover,
But now he's dead and that's all over.
Johnny Pringle he sat down and cried,
Betty Pringle she lay down and died;
So there was an end of one, two, three,
 Johnny Pringle he,
 Betty Pringle she,
 And Piggy Wiggy.

'Betty Pringle' is perhaps a traditional name, for it appears independently in a song 'I've lost my heart to Betty Pringle' composed by John Moulds and sung by him in *The Phisiognomist*, c. 1795. Southey relates that at two years old the sadness of 'Billy Pringle's Pig' was more than he could bear.

MG's Melody, c. 1765, 'Betty Winkle' / *GG's Garland*, 1784, 'Did you hear of Betty Pringle's Pig? It was not very little, not yet very big; The pig sat down upon a dung-hill, And then poor piggy he made his will. Betty Pringle came to see this pretty pig, That was not very little, nor yet very big; This little piggy it lay down and died, And Betty Pringle sat down and cried. Then Johnny Pringle buried this very pretty pig, That was not very little, nor yet very big; So here's an end of the song of all three, Johnny Pringle, Betty Pringle, and the little Piggie' / *Companion for the Nursery*, Goody Prattle (J. Hodson), c. 1795, as 1784 / *Infant Institutes*, 1797, 'It was alive and lay upon the muck-hill; And in half an hour's time it was as dead as a scuttle' / *Songs for the Nursery*, 1805, 'Johnny Pringle had a little pig' / *Vocal Harmony*, c. 1806 / *Oliver's Comic Songs* (Oliver and Boyd), c. 1830, 'Billy Pringle had von very pig' as part of the entertainment 'The Nightingale Club' / *Nursery Poems* (J. G. Rusher), c. 1840, 'Billy Pringle' / JOH, 1842 / Mason, 1877 / *Baby's Bouquet*, 1879 / The rhyme is also incorporated in chapbook histories of *The Life of Jack Sprat* (q.v.).

 Cf. *Nursery Songs from the Appalachian Mountains*, Cecil Sharp, 1921, song beginning 'There was an old woman who had a little pig, It didn't cost much for it wasn't very big.'

43

When shall we be married,
Billy, my pretty lad?

Billy

We'll be married tomorrow,
　If you think it good.
Shall we be married no sooner,
　Billy, my pretty lad?
Would you be married tonight?
　I think the girl is mad.

The earliest rendering of this is in Herd's MS. of Scottish songs:

Whan'll we be marry'd,
My ain dear Nicol o'Cod?
We'll be marry'd o' Monday,
An' is na the reason gude?
Will we be marry'd nae sooner,
My own dear Nicol o'Cod?
Wad ye be marry'd o' Sunday?
I think the auld runt be gane mad.

Whae'll we hae at the wadding,
My own dear Nicol o'Cod?
We'll hae father and mother,
An' is na the reason gude?
Will we na hae nae mae,
My ain dear Nicol o'Cod?
Wad ye hae a' the hail warld?
I think the auld runt be gane mad.

What'll we hae to the wadding,
My ain dear Nicol o'Cod?
We'll hae cheese and bread,
An' is na the reason gude?
Will we na hae nae mae,
My ain dear Nicol o'Cod?
Wad ye hae sack and canary?
I think the auld runt be gane mad.

Whan'll we gang to our bed,
My ain dear Nicol o'Cod?
We'll gang whan other folk gang,
An' is nae the reason gude?
Will we na gang nae sooner,
My ain dear Nicol o'Cod?
Wad ye gang at the sunsetting?
I think the auld runt be gane mad.

What will we do i' our bed,
My ain dear Nicol o'Cod?

Billy

We will kiss and clap,
An' is nae the reason gude?
Will we na do nae mae,
My ain dear Nicol o'Cod?
Wad ye do 't a' the night o'er?
I think the auld runt be gane mad.

This song dates from the seventeenth century, for the ballad *Joan's Victory Over her Fellow Servants*, as printed on a broadside about 1683, is given to the tune of 'My own sweet Nichol a Cod'.

Herd MS, 1776 / *Vocal Harmony*, c. 1806 / *The Comedy of Billy & Betty* (T. Batchelar), c. 1820, four verses / JOH, 1846, 'When shall we be married, My dear Nicholas Wood?' &c., three verses / Williams, 1923 / *Word Lore*, 1926, Somerset song, seventeen verses long, beginning, 'When shall we be married, dear John, Johnny me own true luve? We'll be marred nex Zundy vortnight, Wats ont bettur then that? Cant we be married sooner, dear John, Johnny me own true luve? Wats waant—tu be marred termorrer? Whoy zhurely ther wench be mad!' / *Folk-Song*, 1931.
   Cf. other rural courtship songs of the same genre, in which the eager one of the pair can be a simple-minded yokel or, as here, an over-enthusiastic maiden: 'I mun be married a Sunday', in Udall's *Ralph Roister Doister*, 1550s; *Melismata*, 1611, 'I have a house and land in Kent'; *Mock Songs*, 1675, 'The Suddain Wedding', beginning 'I'me in Love says Noll, Indeed says Doll'.

44

Where have you been today, Billy, my son?
Where have you been today my only man?
I've been a wooing, mother, make my bed soon,
For I'm sick at heart, and fain would lay down.

What have you ate today, Billy, my son?
What have you ate today, my only man?
I've ate eel-pie, mother, make my bed soon,
For I'm sick at heart, and shall die before noon.

The nursery here preserves in short and simple form what is perhaps the last living (i.e. still orally transmitted) link with a tale possibly terrible in origin and certainly mysterious in its subsequent history. It is indubitable that the lines are descended from the ballad 'Lord Randal', which has been found as far east as Czechoslovakia and Hungary, as far north as Sweden and Iceland, and as far south as Calabria. In Scott's *Minstrelsy of the Scottish Border* (1803), the ballad begins:

O where hae ye been, Lord Randal, my son?
O where hae ye been, my handsome young man?

Billy

I hae been to the wild wood; mother make my bed soon,
For I'm weary wi hunting, and fain wald lie down.

Where gat ye your dinner, Lord Randal, my son?
Where gat ye your dinner, my handsome young man?
I din'd wi my true-love; mother, make my bed soon,
For I'm weary wi hunting, and fain wald lie down.

What gat ye to your dinner, Lord Randal, my son?
What gat ye to your dinner, my handsome young man?
I gat eels boild in broo; mother, make my bed soon,
For I'm weary wi hunting, and fain wald lie down.

'More than three hundred years ago', writes Professor Gerould in *The Ballad of Tradition* (1932), 'an Italian professional singer, advertising his wares in easy verse on a broadside printed in Verona, quoted three lines which unmistakably belong to *L'Avvelenato* (*The Poisoned One*), as that ballad has been found in circulation up and down the peninsula within the last half-century; and *L'Avvelenato* is so close in form and content to "Lord Randal" that certain versions might be taken as paraphrases of one another.

> Where supped you yestereve,
> Dear son mine, noble and wise?
> > Oh, I am dying,
> > Ohimè!
> Where supped you yestereve,
> My noble knight?
> I was at my lady's,
> > I am sick at the heart,
> > How sick am I!
> I was at my lady's,
> My life's at an end.
> What supper did she give you,
> Dear son mine, noble and wise?
> > Oh, I am dying,
> > Ohimè!
> What supper did she give you,
> My gentle knight?
> An eel that was roasted,
> > Mother, dear mother;
> > I am sick at the heart,
> > How sick am I!
> An eel that was roasted,
> My life's at an end.

'The lines roughly translated above were taken down by D'Ancona (*Poesia popolare italiana*) in the country near Pisa some sixty years ago; and the

Billy

opening is almost identical with that quoted in the Veronese broadside of 1629. It is not a question of different songs with the same theme, but of the same ballad in circulation over wide areas.' 'It need occasion no surprise', continues Professor Gerould, '... that the migrations of "Lord Randal" cannot be traced as it has passed from land to land.' Only, perhaps, is its preservation accountable. 'It has had the good fortune', wrote Dr. Jamieson in 1814, 'in every country to get possession of the nursery, a circumstance which, from the enthusiasm and curiosity of young imaginations, and the communicative volubility of little tongues, has insured its preservation.' Certainly it was a well-known nursery song in his day. Burns knew two verses. Scott knew six, and his daughter used to sing them to him at Abbotsford:

> Where hae ye been a' the day,
> My bonny wee croodin doo?
> O I hae been to my stepmother's house;
> Make my bed, mammie, now!
> Make my bed, mammie, now!

> Where did you get your dinner,
> My bonny wee croodin doo?
> I got it in my stepmother's;
> Make my bed, mammie, now, now, now!
> Make my bed, mammie, now!

> What did she gie ye to your dinner,
> My bonny wee croodin doo?
> She ga'e me a four-footed fish;
> Make my bed, mammie, now, now, now!
> Make my bed, mammie, now!

> Where got she the four-footed fish,
> My bonny wee croodin doo?
> She got it down in yon well strand;
> O make my bed, mammie, now, now, now!
> Make my bed, mammie, now!

> What did she do wi' the banes o 't,
> My bonny wee croodin doo?
> She ga'e them to the little dog;
> Make my bed, mammie, now, now, now!
> Make my bed, mammie, now!

> O what became o' the little dog,
> My bonny wee croodin doo?
> O it shot out its feet and died!
> O make my bed, mammie, now, now, now!
> O make my bed, mammie, now!

Billy

Of this version Scott remarked that apparently 'to excite greater interest in the nursery, the handsome young hunter is exchanged for a little child, poisoned by his false stepmother'. Similar juvenile verses were known to Peter Buchan, Motherwell, Chambers, and Kirkpatrick Sharpe. Sharpe said 'The nurse, or nursery-maid, who sung these verses (to a very plaintive air), always informed her juvenile audience that the stepmother was a rank witch, and that the fish was an ask (i.e. newt) which was in Scotland formerly deemed a most poisonous reptile.' Scott's theory was that the ballad originally regarded the death of Thomas Randolph or Randal, Earl of Murray, nephew to Robert Bruce, and governor of Scotland, a great warrior who died at Musselburgh in 1332. Another theory is that it is a reminiscence either of Randal, sixth Earl of Chester (d. 1232), about whom there are known to have been songs as early as 1377, or of his nephew and successor, John the Scot, whose wife 'was infamous for plotting to take away the life of her husband by poison'. The ballad may well, however, be much older, and, as has been seen, it is not exclusive to Scotland. The father and mother of John Clare, the Northamptonshire poet (b. 1793), used to sing it to him to while away the long winter evenings. Baring-Gould tells of a west-country nurse who sang it in 1835. In America Professor Child (c. 1880) knew of several Massachusetts ladies who had learnt it in childhood.

F. J. Child in his monumental *English and Scottish Ballads*, 1883–98, gives fifteen recordings of 'Lord Randal' and references to continental versions. The following are appearances of the juvenile song: *Musical Museum*, 1792, contributed by Burns / *Illustrations of the Northern Antiquities*, R. Jamieson, &c., 1814 / Motherwell's MS, c. 1825 / Chambers, 1826 / Kinloch MS, c. 1826 / Buchan MS, c. 1828 / *Scottish Ballads*, R. Chambers, 1829, version differs from 1826 / *Lyric Poetry of Scotland*, William Stenhouse, 1839 [1853] / JOH, 1846 / Chambers, 1847 / Mason, 1877 / N & Q, 1894, 'What will you have for supper, King Henry my son?' (The name 'King Henry' may conceivably have been inserted after Henry I's death from eating a dish of lampreys) / Baring-Gould, 1895 / *Folk-Song*, 1905, five versions with tunes, including 'O where have you been, Randal my son?' and 'Henery, my son'; also 1908, 'King Henry', and 1915 'Oh, where have you been this live-long day, My little wee croodin' doo', and from Ireland 'Where were you all day, my own purtee boy?' / *Folk Songs from S. Appalachians*, Cecil Sharp, 1917 / *Shetland Traditional Lore*, J. M. E. Saxby, 1932, 'Whaur has du been a' the day, Bonnie Tammy'.

Cf. 'Where have you been all the day, My boy Billy', and Carl Loewe's ballad 'Edward'. There are references to continental versions additional to Child in *Folk-Song* (1915).

45

Where have you been all the day,
My boy Billy?

Billy

Where have you been all the day,
    My boy Billy?
I have been all the day
Courting of a lady gay;
Although she is a young thing,
And just come from her mammy.

Is she fit to be thy love,
    My boy Billy?
Is she fit to be thy love,
    My boy Billy?
She's as fit to be my love
As my hand is for my glove,
Although she is a young thing,
And just come from her mammy.

Is she fit to be thy wife,
    My boy Billy?
Is she fit to be thy wife,
    My boy Billy?
She's as fit to be my wife,
As my blade is for my knife;
Although she is a young thing,
And just come from her mammy.

How old may she be,
    My boy Billy?
How old may she be,
    My boy Billy?
Twice six, twice seven,
Twice twenty and eleven,
Although she is a young thing,
And just come from her mammy.

Halliwell collected two versions of this song in mid-nineteenth century, one from Suffolk, and one, as above, from Yorkshire. Stenhouse (b. 1773?) said that as a boy in Scotland he often heard it sung by old people. He considered the words to be 'quite puerile' but described the melody as 'very ancient and uncommonly pretty'. The melody is printed in *The Scots Musical Museum* (1797) where the words have been rewritten by the Scottish poet Hector Macneill. His version was first printed in 1791 in an Edinburgh periodical *The Bee*. It begins:

Billy

Whar hae ye been a' day,
　　my boy, Tammy?
Whar hae ye been a' day,
　　my boy, Tammy?
I've been by burn and flow'ry brae,
Meadow green and mountain grey,
Courting o' this young thing
　　Just come frae her mammy.

These lines were highly esteemed at the time. Stenhouse says 'Miss Duncan, the celebrated actress, used frequently to sing this ballad on the stage with great applause'. Baring-Gould collected the traditional words as sung about 1835 by a west-country nurse. He considered that it was the first part of the old ballad 'Lord Randal' and printed it like this in *A Garland of Country Songs*. Although the song bears comparison with 'Where have you been today, Billy, my son?' (q.v.) which stems from 'Lord Randal', it is not found connected elsewhere. The longest version, and perhaps the earliest, although it has partially been Americanized, may be that which was collected by Cecil Sharp among the unlettered hill folk of North Carolina.

Herd MS, 1776, 'I am to court a wife, And I'll love her as my life, But she is a young thing And new come frae her minnie. She's twice six, twice seven, twice twenty and eleven, Alack, she's but a young thing, And new come frae her minnie!' / *Lyric Poetry of Scotland*, William Stenhouse, 1839, 'Is she fit to soop the house, My boy, Tammy? (*bis*) She's just as fit to soop the house As the cat to tak' a mouse; And yet she's but a young thing New come frae her mammy. How auld's the bonnie young thing?' &c. [1853] / JOH, 1844, 'Where have you been all the day, My boy Willy? I've been all the day, Courting of a lady gay: But oh! she's too young To be taken from her mammy. What can she do, Can she bake and can she brew? She can brew and she can bake, And she can make our wedding cake. What age may she be?' &c. / *A Garland of Country Songs*, S. Baring-Gould, 1894; also *Nursery Songs*, 1895 / *Folk Songs from S. Appalachians*, Cecil Sharp, 1917, two versions: (*a*) 'O where have you been Billy boy, Billy boy, O where have you been charming Billy? I have been to seek a wife For the pleasures of my life; She's a young girl and cannot leave her mammy', five verses; (*b*) verse 1. 'Where have you been, &c. 2. She asked me to come in; she had a dimple in her chin. 3. She set me in a chair; she had wrinkles in her ear. 4. She asked me for to eat, She had plenty bread and meat. 5. She can card and she can spin, And she can do most anything. 6. She can sew and she can fell, She can use her needle well. 7. She can make a cherry pie, Quick as a cat can wink his eye. 8. She's twice six, twice seven, Twenty-eight and eleven' / *Four Old Nursery Songs*, tunes arranged by Adam Carse, 1928 / Oral collection, 1945, the song still has adult life as a folk-song and sea-shanty, 'Billy boy, Billy boy'.

Cf. With the Herd MS copy above, Burns's 'I am my mammy's ae bairn', the chorus of which he acknowledged was old.

Bird

46

Once I saw a little bird
Come hop, hop, hop,
And I cried, Little bird,
Will you stop, stop, stop?

I was going to the window
To say, How do you do?
But he shook his little tail
And away he flew.

Little Rhymes for Little Folks (By a Lady), 1823 / *First Lessons for Children* (Henry Mozley and Sons), c. 1825 / *NR Tales and Jingles*, 1844 / JOH, 1844 / *Cries of London and Banbury* (J. G. Rusher), c. 1843 / *Tailor of Gloucester*, Beatrix Potter (p.p. ed.), 1902.

47

White bird featherless
Flew from Paradise,
Pitched on the castle wall;
Along came Lord Landless,
Took it up handless,
And rode away horseless to the King's white hall.

This riddle of the snow and the sun was well known to readers of *Notes & Queries* in 1855, when one of them said his little girl had been taught it by an old servant. They, likewise, had learnt it in childhood. Some years later (1872) it was pointed out that Lydius in his *Sermones Conviviales* (1643) had recorded versions in Greek and Latin; while Kircher in 1653 had repeated a German rendering. Müllenhoff, the German folk-lorist, collected the riddle in Schleswig-Holstein in the middle of the nineteenth century:

> Da köem en Vagel fedderlos,
> Un sett sik op'n Boem blattlos.
> Da köem de Jungfru mundelos
> Un freet den Vagel fedderlos,
> Van den Boem blattlos.

The riddle is especially popular in Germanic lands, and Baesecke quotes a Latin translation found in a Reichenauer MS of the late tenth century:

Bird

Volavit volucer sine plumis,
sedit in arbore sine folis,
venit homo absque manibus,
conscendit illum sine pedibus,
assavit eum sine igne,
comedit eum sine ore.

N & Q, 1855 and 1872 / Folk-Lore of N. E. Scotland, W. Gregor, 1881 / Gentleman's Magazine, 1881 / Rymour Club, 1914, 'White doo featherless cam' doon frae Paradise, And lichtit on yon castle wa'; By cam' Laird Landless and took it up handless, Syne rain cam' and washed it awa' / Land of NR, Ernest Rhys, 1932, '...Poor Lord Landless, Came in a fine dress, And went away without a dress at all' / Shetland Traditional Lore, J. M. E. Saxby, 1932, 'Fleein' far but featherless, New come oot o' Paradise; Fleein' ower de sea and laund Deein' imme haund.'
    Cf. Sermones Conviviales, Jacobus Lydius, 1643, '"Απτερον ἐς δένδρον πτηνόν ποτ' ἄφυλλον ἐσέπτη, Καύθοθ' ἐφίζανον κατ' ἄρ' ἄστομον αὐτὸ πέπωκε, "Αστομος ἐξυπρόσωπος, ἐρυθρογένειος ἄναυδος; Non habuit pennas volucris, tamen ipsa volavit Desuper in quercus, exutas frondibus altis. Ore carens aliquis, de coetu (ut credo) Gigantum, Venit, et hanc consumpsit avem, licet ore careret.' Œdipus Ægyptiacus, Athanasius Kircher, 1653, 'Es flog ein vogel federlosz, Auff einen Baumb blattlosz, Da kam die Fraw mundtlosz, Vnd frasz den vogel federlosz' / Sagen... der Herzogthümer Schleswig-holstein, K. Müllenhoff, 1845 / Deutsche Kinder-Reime, E. Meier, 1851 / Deutsches Kinderlied, F. M. Böhme, 1897 [1924].
    Cf. also the traditional riddle 'A white bird floats down through the air, And never a tree but he lights there.'
    See G. Baesecke, 'Das lateinisch-althochdeutsche Reimgebet und das Rätsel vom Vogel federlos', Probleme der Wissenschaft und Gegenwart, 1 (Berlin), 1948; and A. Taylor, English Riddles from Oral Tradition (Berkeley), 1951.

48

Little bird of paradise,
She works her work both neat and nice;
She pleases God, she pleases man,
She does the work that no man can.

The sentiment and main phrasing of this riddle may be traced to the beginning of Henry VIII's reign. In Demaundes Joyous, printed by Wynkyn de Worde in 1511, the question is posed:

What is it that is a wryte and is no man, and he dothe that no man can, and yet it serueth both god and man.

Charles Butler, in 1609, speaks of 'The little smith of Nottingham (whose art is thought to excel al art of man).' How easily the learned may be led astray in simple things is demonstrated by Fuller (1662), who, referring to Butler, gives it as a metrical proverb:

Bird of Paradise

The little smith of Nottingham,
who doth the work that no man can,

and adopts the absurd rationalizing explanation that the lines are 'a peri-
phrasis of *Nemo, Οὔτις*, or a person who never was'. This explanation was
blindly followed by Ray in his *English Proverbs* (1670) and by subsequent
proverb-collectors, despite the subject of Butler's work, which was *Bees*.
Such sententiousness might have been avoided by consulting a riddle-
minded child. One of the 'divers prettie Riddles' printed 'for Youth to
try their wits' in 1631 was:

I haue a Smith without a hand,
He workes the worke that no man can:
He serues our God, and doth man ease,
without any fire in his furnace.

'Solution: It is a Bee that makes hony and waxe.' Further, this was known
to the young Randle Holme, Ray's contemporary:

There is a Bird of great renown, usefull in citty & in town, none work
like unto him can doe: hes yellow black & green a very pretty Bird j
mean, yet he is both firce & fell, j count hin wise that can this tell.

'A[nswer] the painfull bee.' For the past three centuries the riddle has
been retained in the storehouse of popular memory, for the pleasing
text version was collected for a book of folk-lore published in 1939.

Demaundes Joyous, 1511 / *Feminine Monarchie, Or a Treatise concerning bees*, C. Butler,
1609 / *Book of merrie Riddles*, 1631 / *Holme MS*, c. 1645 / *New Help to Discourse*, William
Winstanley, 1669, as previous / *Weardale*, J. J. Graham, 1939 / Randle Holme's version was reprinted by JOH, 1849, and has entered some present-day collections.

49

Away, birds, away,
Take a little, and leave a little,
And do not come again;
For if you do,
I will shoot you through,
And there is an end of you.

In past centuries village boys and young members of the farmer's family
used to be employed at seed time as bird scarers ('crow-keepers', 'crow-
herds', or 'bird boys'). It was proverbially a child's first employment,
much as delivering newspapers is today, and references to the occupation
are common in literature. Thomas Wilson (1553), for instance, speaks of

Birds

'Plaie as young boyes or scarre crowes do, which showte in the open and plaine feldes at all aventures hittie missie', and Shakespeare (in *Romeo and Juliet*) of 'Skaring the Ladies like a Crow-keeper'. The bird scarers seem to have sung special songs right to the end of the nineteenth century. A writer in *Folk-Lore* (1889) remarked, 'It is the custom in agricultural districts for boys and men to keep birds off cornfields until the seeds are up, and the stalks high enough for protection.... At such times songs or rhymes in a loud voice are frequently indulged in.' In *The History of Little King Pippin* (c. 1786) Peter was sent to keep the crows from Farmer Giles's corn, and sang:

> Away, away, John Carrion Crow!
> Your master hath enow
> Down in his barley mow.

In *The Boy's Country Book* (1839) William Howitt tells how in Sherwood one February he heard 'a faint, shrill cry, as of a child's voice, that alternating with the sound of a wooden clapper, sung these words:

> We've ploughed our land, we've sown our seed,
>   We've made all neat and gay;
> So take a bit, and leave a bit,
>   Away, birds, away!

He looked over the hedge, and saw a little rustic lad; about seven years old, in a blue carter-frock, with his clapper in his hand. The child was still there, 'with his melancholy song', when Howitt returned in the evening. Harriet Martineau's description of the little crow-minder in *Society in America* (1837) can be appreciated when she says he came in 'hoarse from his late occupation'.

Numerous scaring songs are known. Whether they were considered to be nursery rhymes before JOH included some of them in his collection is doubtful, though they would have been repeated to children at an early age / *History of Little King Pippin* (F. Newbery, advert. 1775), (E. Newbery), c. 1786, as quote / *Boy's Country Book*, William Howitt, 1839, as quote / JOH, 1842, as text / Rimbault, 1846, 'O all you little blackey-tops, Pray don't you eat my father's crops, While I lie down to take a nap, Shu-a-O! Shu-a-O! If father he by chance should come With his cock'd hat and his long gun, Then you must fly and I must run, Shu-a-O! Shu-a-O!' / JOH, 1849, 'Awa', birds, awa', Take a peck And leave a seck, And come no more today' / JOH, 1853, 'Eat birds, eat, and make no waste, I lie here and make no haste; If my master chance to come, You must fly and I must run' / *Northamptonshire Glossary*, A. E. Baker, 1854, 'Away, away, away birds; Take a little bit and come another day birds; Great birds, little birds, pigeons and crows, I'll up with my clackers and down she goes' / *N & Q*, 1859 / *Baby's Bouquet*, 1879, as 1846 / Northall, 1892, 'How dar' you, How dar' you Steal the master's wheat, While I'm so near you?' and many other versions / *Folk-Song*, 1905, with tune 'Shoo all 'er birds you be so black, When I lay down to have a nap. Shoo arl-o arl-o arl-o arl-o arl-o arl-o arl-o arl-o birds. Hi shoo all 'er birds. Out of master's ground into Tom Tucker's ground' / *Folk-Song*, 1944, 'Away you black devils away. . . . Away you black devils away. . . . You eat too much you drink too much you carry too much away' / *Big Book of Mother Goose* (James and Jonathan Co., Wisconsin), 1946.

***The leniency to the birds apparent in some of these rhymes finds collusion in the sowing-proverb 'One for the pigeon, one for the crow, one to rot, and one to grow.'

50

Of all the gay birds that e'er I did see,
The owl is the fairest by far to me,
For all day long she sits on a tree,
And when the night comes away flies she.

These lines form the opening of a song in Ravenscroft's *Deuteromelia or The Seconde part of Musicks melodie*, published in 1609. JOH (1842) collected the text version in Lincolnshire and as he remarks 'it is singular that it should have come down to us from oral tradition'. A writer in *Notes & Queries* (1915) inquired after 'an amusing old Yorkshire song, believed to be called "The Owl", containing a line—"Of all the gay birds that e'er I did see"'; and Williams found the song still being sung beside the upper reaches of the Thames. Furthermore, the burden of the song, 'Nose, nose, jolly red nose' (q.v.), which already by 1632 was sung independently, has also survived to the present day.

Deuteromelia, 1609, 'Of all the birds that euer I see, The Owle is the fayrest in her degree: Te whit te whow, For all the day long she sits in a tree, and when the night comes away flies she' / *The Pinder of Wakefield*, 1632, ends 'To whit to whooe, To whom drinke you' / *Antidote against Melancholy*, 1661 / *Windsor Drollery*, 1672 / JOH, 1842 / Williams, 1923, whole song / *The Little Piggy* (Juvenile Productions), c. 1945.

51

There were two birds sat on a stone,
    Fa, la, la, la, lal, de;
One flew away, and then there was one,
    Fa, la, la, la, lal, de;
The other flew after, and then there was none,
    Fa, la, la, la, lal, de;
And so the poor stone was left all alone,
    Fa, la, la, la, lal, de.

Birds

In Charles Kingsley's *The Water Babies* (1863) the last of the Gairfowl 'kept on crooning an old song to herself, which she learned when she was a little baby-bird, long ago:

> Two little birds, they sat on a stone,
> One swam away, and then there was one;
> > With a fal-lal-la-lady.
> The other swam after, and then there was none,
> And so the poor stone was left all alone;
> > With a fal-lal-la-lady.

'It was "flew" away, properly, and not "swam" away; but, as she could not fly, she had a right to alter it.'

MG's Melody, c. 1765 / Herd MS, 1776, 'There was Two Craws sat on a stane, Fal de ral &c. Ane flew awa & there remain'd ane, Fal de ral, &c. The other seeing his neibour gane, Fal de ral &c. Then he flew awa & there was nane, Fal de ral &c.' / *Nancy Cock's PSB*, c. 1780 / *GG's Garland*, 1784 / *Newest Christmas Box*, c. 1797 / *Vocal Harmony*, c. 1806 / *Nursery Songs* (G. Ross), c. 1812 / *London Jingles* (J. G. Rusher), c. 1840, additional verse, 'One of the birds then back again flew, T'other came after, then there were two: Said one to t'other—How do you do? Very well, thank you, and How are you?' / JOH, 1842 / *Only True MG's Melodies*, c. 1843, also with the (probably spurious) additional verse of c. 1840 / *Rymour Club*, 1911.

Cf. 'There was a monkey climbed a tree'.

52

> The tailor of Bicester,
> He has but one eye;
> He cannot cut a pair of green galligaskins,
> If he were to die.

Aubrey, writing in 1687, gives this rhyme, and explains: 'The young Girls in and about Oxford have a Sport called Leap Candle, for which they set a candle in the middle of the room in a candlestick, and then draw up their coats into the form of breeches, and dance over the candle back and forth, with these words.' He added that this game in other parts was called 'Dancing the candle rush'. Galligaskins were a type of wide breeches worn in the sixteenth and seventeenth centuries, and it is probable that the girls, aping men's costume, were perpetuating a custom they had seen performed on feast days (cf. 'Jack be nimble'). Northall, in 1892, knew a similar game in Warwickshire called 'Cock and Breeches'.

Lansdowne MS 231, 1686–7 / JOH, 1842 / *Mother Goose NR*, L. E. Walter, 1924.

a

b

c

d

e

f

g

h

Woodcuts from J. Marshall's edition of *Mother Goose's Melody*, c. 1795, depicting (*a*) I won't be my father's Jack; (*b*) There was an old man in a velvet coat; (*c*) Jack and Gill; (*d*) Hush-a-by baby; (*e*) What care I how black I be; (*f*) When I was a little boy; (*g*) O my kitten a kitten; (*h*) Bah, bah, black sheep. Bodleian Library.

Black

53

Black I am and much admired,
Men may seek me till they're tired;
I weary horse and weary man,
Tell me this riddle if you can.

RIDDLE. *Solution:* coal.

A Collection of Curious and Entertaining Enigmas (J. and C. Evans), c. 1815 / JOH, 1843 / N & Q, 1865 / *Rymour Club*, 1914 / Correspondent, 1949, 'I weary horse and comfort man'. Correspondent, 1951, family version from grandfather, born 1829, ends, 'When they find me, break my head, And take me from my resting bed'.

54

What care I how black I be?
Twenty pounds will marry me;
If twenty won't, forty shall,
For I'm my mother's bouncing girl.

The phrasing of the first line dates back to the beginning of the seventeenth century; thus, in Jonson's *Description of Love* (c. 1618):

If she be not so to me,
What care I how black she be?

Although the dark-haired were then often viewed with disfavour, the black lass's boast was probably no idle one. The masculine singer of a ballad printed about 1630 describes a most repugnant maiden 'a yard and a halfe in the waste', and yet she was pretty because 'to her portion, she hath thirty pound'. In 1833 a parody of the rhyme was addressed to Zachary Macaulay, then pressing for the abolition of slavery:

What though now opposed I be?
Twenty peers will carry me;
If twenty won't, thirty will,
For I'm His Majesty's bouncing Bill.

MG's Melody, c. 1765 / *GG's Garland*, 1784 / *Songs for the Nursery*, 1805 / *Vocal Harmony*, c. 1806 / *Rhymes for the Fireside* (Thomas Richardson), c. 1828 / JOH, 1842 / *Only True MG Melodies*, c. 1843 / *Book of NR*, Enid Marx, 1939, 'I am my mother's bouncing gal'.

Black Sheep

55

Baa, baa, black sheep,
  Have you any wool?
Yes, sir, yes, sir,
  Three bags full;
One for the master,
  And one for the dame,
And one for the little boy
  Who lives down the lane.

The words of this favourite rhyme have scarcely altered in 250 years:

Bah, Bah, a black Sheep,
Have you any Wool,
Yes merry have I,
Three Bags full,
One for my Master,
One for my Dame,
One for my Little Boy
That lives in the lane.

In the wool trade the division of the bags is said to refer to the export tax on wool imposed in 1275. The words are sung to the old French tune 'Ah vous dirai je.'

T Thumb's PSB, c. 1744 / *MG's Melody*, c. 1765, 'But none for the little boy who cries in the lane' / *GG's Garland*, 1784, and *Christmas Box*, vol. iii, 1798, as 1765 / *Songs for the Nursery*, 1805 / *Mother's Gift* (N. Coverly Jun., Boston, Mass.), 1812, 'Bah! Nanny black sheep' / *GG's Garland*, illus. T. Bewick, c. 1814, 'Yes, Mary, have I' / *Grandmamma's NR* (J. Fairburn), c. 1825 / *NR for Children* (J. Fairburn), c. 1825 / *London Jingles* (J. G. Rusher), c. 1840 / JOH, 1843 / *Mr. Sponge's Sporting Tour*, R. S. Surtees, 1849, 'The child [Gustavus James] who had been wound up like a musical snuff-box, then went off as follows:—"Bah, bah, back sheep, have 'ou any 'ool? Ess, marry, have I, three bags full; Un for ye master, un for ye dame, Un for ye 'ittle boy 'ot 'uns about ye 'ane"' / Rudyard Kipling used the rhyme as framework for his story *Baa, Baa, Black-Sheep*, 1888.

56

I had a little dog, and his name was Blue Bell,
I gave him some work, and he did it very well;
I sent him up stairs to pick up a pin,
He stepped in the coal-scuttle up to his chin;

Blue Bell

I sent him to the garden to pick some sage,
He tumbled down and fell in a rage;
I sent him to the cellar, to draw a pot of beer,
He came up again and said there was none there.

JOH, 1842 / *Children's Encyclopaedia*, 1908, 'I had a little boy'.
Cf. 'I had a little dog and they called him Buff.'

57

Little Blue Betty lived in a den,
She sold good ale to gentlemen;
Gentlemen came every day,
And little Blue Betty hopped away.
She hopped upstairs to make her bed,
And she tumbled down and broke her head.

Little Blue Betty appears to have been a member of the same profession as Elsie Marley (q.v.). She worked, according to the earliest record, at the sign of *The Golden Can*.

GG's Garland, 1810 / JOH, 1842 / JOH, 1843, 'Little Brown Betty liv'd under a pan, She brew'd good ale for a gentleman: A gentleman came every day, So little Brown Betty hopp'd away' / *Mill Hill Magazine*, 1877, 'Nancy Pansy lived in a well' / *N & Q*, 1884, 'Mary Carey, quite contrary, Baked a cake for gentlemen . . .' / *Folk-Lore*, 1900, 'Cicely Parsely lived in a den, She brewed good ale for gentlemen, Gentlemen came every day, Yet Cicely Parsely ran away' / *Cecily Parsley's Nursery Rhymes*, Beatrix Potter, 1922.

Cf. 'Hickety, pickety, my black hen.' Also the second line with Burns's 'There was a wife wonn'd in Cockpen, Scroggam! She brew'd guid ale for gentlemen', in the *Musical Museum*, 1803, which in turn was based on an older song 'There wonned a wife in Whistle-cockpen—Will ye no, can ye no, let me be! She brewed guid ale for gentlemen, And ay she waggit it wantonly.'

58

Buzz, quoth the blue fly,
Hum, quoth the bee,
Buzz and hum they cry,
And so do we:

Blue Fly

In his ear, in his nose,
Thus do you see,
He ate the dormouse,
Else it was thee.

In Ben Jonson's *Masque of Oberon* (first performed 1 Jan. 1611) the Satyrs were trying to wake the two Sylvian guards. Silenus says, 'Strike a charme into their eares', upon which they 'fell sodainely into this catch'. In John Playford's *Catch that Catch can: or the Musical Companion* (1667) with 'musick by Mr. Edmund Nelham', the opportunity was taken to add an inexcusably wicked couplet at the end. In 1805 the original verse appeared in *Songs for the Nursery*, and in 1842 JOH described it as 'a most common nursery song at the present time'. In Beatrix Potter's story *The Tailor of Gloucester* (1903) it is the 'something mysterious' which the bats said in their sleep.

59

Little Bob Robin,
Where do you live?
Up in yonder wood, sir,
On a hazel twig.

JOH, 1853 / *Young England's NR*, C. Haslewood, c. 1885.

60

Bobby Shafto's gone to sea,
    Silver buckles at his knee;
He'll come back and marry me,
    Bonny Bobby Shafto!

Bobby Shafto's fat and fair,
    Combing down his yellow hair;
He's my love for evermore,
    Bonny Bobby Shafto!

Bobby Shafto

The Shafto family took their name from the village of Shaftoe in North-umberland, and over the generations there were no fewer than seven Robert Shaftos. Most of the stories, however, centre around the Parliamentary election of 1761, when the song was used in support of Robert Shafto of Whitworth, of the County Durham branch of the family; his portrait shows him as young and handsome, and with yellow hair. An additional verse which seems to have been composed for this occasion is:

> Bobby Shafto's looking out,
> All his ribbons flew about,
> All the ladies gave a shout,
> Hey for Bobby Shafto!

Such was his beauty that Miss Bellasyse, the heiress of Brancepeth, is said to have died for love of him (1774).

Songs for the Nursery, 1805 / *Rhymes of Northern Bards*, John Bell, 1812, additional verse 'Bobby Shafto's getten a bairn, For to dandle in his arm; In his arm and on his knee, Bobby Shafto loves me' / *Redgauntlet*, Sir Walter Scott, 1824, 'Old Northumbrian ditty', 'Willy Foster's gone to sea, siller buckles at his knee, He'll come back and marry me—Canny Willie Foster' / *Bishoprick Garland*, Sir Cuthbert Sharp, 1834 / *Archaeology of NR*, J. B. Ker, 1834, 'Bobby Shaft' / JOH, 1842 / Rimbault, 1846 / Mason, 1877, 'Billy Button' / Kidson, 1904.

61

> As a little fat man of Bombay
> Was smoking one very hot day,
>   A bird called a snipe
>   Flew away with his pipe,
> Which vexed the fat man of Bombay.

This stands as above in *Anecdotes and Adventures of Fifteen Gentlemen*, possibly written by R. S. Sharpe, and published by John Marshall in 1821. Others of the 'Fifteen Gentlemen' who continue to find a place in nursery collections are 'a Tailor who sail'd from Quebec', 'a poor man of Jamaica', and 'a sick man of Tobago' (qq.v.). All are cast in limerick form and preceded Edward Lear's verses by a quarter of a century; in fact, 'There was a sick man of Tobago' (q.v. especially) was Lear's direct inspiration. JOH, in 1846, knew 'There was a fat man of Bombay' and 'There was an old man of Tobago'. He also printed the stories of three old women, those of Surrey, Leeds, and Norwich (qq.v.), which come from Harris's publication, *The History of Sixteen Wonderful Old Women* (1820).

Bond

62

Oh, what have you got for dinner, Mrs. Bond?
There's beef in the larder, and ducks in the pond;
Dilly, dilly, dilly, dilly, come to be killed,
For you must be stuffed and my customers filled!

Send us the beef first, good Mrs. Bond,
And get us some ducks dressed out of the pond,
Cry, Dilly, dilly, dilly, dilly, come to be killed,
For you must be stuffed and my customers filled!

John Ostler, go fetch me a duckling or two,
Ma'am, says John Ostler, I'll try what I can do,
Cry, Dilly, dilly, dilly, dilly, come to be killed,
For you must be stuffed and my customers filled!

I have been to the ducks that swim in the pond,
But I found they won't come to be killed, Mrs. Bond;
I cried, Dilly, dilly, dilly, dilly, come to be killed,
For you must be stuffed and my customers filled!

Mrs. Bond she flew down to the pond in a rage,
With plenty of onions and plenty of sage;
She cried, Dilly, dilly, dilly, dilly, come to be killed,
For you must be stuffed and my customers filled!

She cried, Little wag-tails, come and be killed,
For you must be stuffed and my customers filled!
Dilly, dilly, dilly, dilly, come to be killed,
For you must be stuffed and my customers filled!

'Mrs. Bond' was originally 'introduced and sung by Mr Bannister Junior in the character of Jerry Sneak', in Foote's 'The Mayor of Garret' (1763). The song was popular, and was immediately issued by rival music publishers such as Preston & Son, in the Strand, and Longman and Broderip in the Haymarket.

Juvenile Amusements, 1797, No. 48 / *The Nightingale*, 1831, with tune / *Sam Cowell's 120 Comic Songs*, c. 1850, stated to be from a version of *The Mayor of Garret* [*Folk-Song*, 1929] / *Baby's Opera*, 1877 / *Berkshire Words*, B. Lowsley, 1888, 'Pray what have you for supper, Mrs. Bond? Ge-us in the larder an' ducks in the pond. Dilly, dilly, dilly, dilly, come an' be killed, Passengers around us an' thaay must be villed' / Baring-Gould, 1895 / Kidson, 1904, to the air 'Will you come to the bower I have shaded for you.'

63

Old Boniface he loved good cheer,
And took his glass of Burton,
And when the nights grew sultry hot
He slept without a shirt on.

Boniface was the name of the jovial innkeeper in Farquhar's *Beaux' Strata-gem* (1707) whence it became a generic name for publicans.

JOH, 1844 / *Redicula Rediviva*, illus. J. E. Rodgers, 1876 / Correspondent, 1949.

64

As I went to Bonner,
I met a pig
Without a wig,
Upon my word and honour.

New Year's Gift (J. Catnach), c. 1830 [Hindley, 1878] / JOH, 1844 / *Folk-Lore*, 1889, ''Pon my life an' honner! As I was gowine to Toller, I met a pig a' thout a wig, 'Pon my life an' honner!' / *Rymour Club*, 1911 / *Mother Goose*, Arthur Rackham, 1913, 'Upon my word and honour, As I was going to Stonor.'

65

Bo-peep, Little Bo-peep,
Now 's the time for hide and seek.

JOH (1849) gives these as the words repeated by children when playing bo-peep. Whether the game was once a form of hide-and-seek, or never more than a baby amusement of covering the head and peeping out, as the early quotations suggest, is uncertain. Johnson (1755) defined bo-peep as 'The act of looking out and then drawing back as if frightened, or with the purpose to fright some other', and Herrick (1648) used it in the same sense:

> Her pretty feet
> Like snailes did creep
>   A little out, and then,
> As if they started at Bo-Peep,
>   Did soon draw in agen.

Bo-peep

The earliest reference to the game appears to be in 1364 when Alice Causton had to 'play bo-pepe thorowe a pillory' for giving a short measure of ale.

66

Little Bo-peep has lost her sheep,
  And can't tell where to find them;
Leave them alone, and they'll come home,
  And bring their tails behind them.

Little Bo-peep fell fast asleep,
  And dreamt she heard them bleating;
But when she awoke, she found it a joke,
  For they were still all fleeting.

Then up she took her little crook,
  Determined for to find them;
She found them indeed, but it made her heart bleed,
  For they'd left their tails behind them.

It happened one day, as Bo-peep did stray
  Into a meadow hard by,
There she espied their tails side by side,
  All hung on a tree to dry.

She heaved a sigh, and wiped her eye,
  And over the hillocks went rambling,
And tried what she could, as a shepherdess should,
  To tack again each to its lambkin.

That 'Little Bo-peep' was known in the eighteenth century seems certain from a version of the song 'Yankee Doodle' printed in London in or about 1777, and written, it seems, some years previously. Several of the verses are based on pieces that seem to have been current in the 1760s, amongst them:

> Our Jemima's lost her Mare
>   And can't tell where to find her,
> But she'll come trotting by and by
>   And bring her Tail behind her.

(S. Foster Damon, *Yankee Doodle*, 1959.)

Bo-peep

Attempts which have been made to give the rhyme a longer history have met with a notable lack of success; although certainly there has been, from early times, a baby-game called 'Bo-peep' (q.v.), and bo-peep is to be found rhymed with sheep, e.g. in a ballad of the time of Queen Elizabeth,

> Halfe England ys nowght now but shepe,
> In everye corner thay playe boe-pepe;

During the past 150 years the rhyme has often given its name to panto-mime productions, and it is on record that in his early days Irving played the part of the wolf in Little Bo-peep at Edinburgh.

Douce MS, c. 1805 / 'Critical Comments on the Bo-peepeid. An Epic-pastoral Poem', *Monthly Literary Recreations*, 1806, 'Little Bo-peep' used to ridicule the literary criti-cism of the day / *GG's Garland*, 1810, as text, except in last verse where rhyming words are 'stump-o' and 'rump-o' / JOH, 1842 / *History of Little Bo-peep*, John Abso-lon, 1853 / *Baby's Opera*, 1877 / Mason, 1877 / Kidson, 1904 / *Little Bo-Peep*, L. Leslie Brooke, 1922. Bo-peep is also met with in A. A. Milne's *When We Were Very Young*, 1924.

67

> Little boy, little boy, where wast thou born?
> Far away in Lancashire under a thorn,
> Where they sup sour milk in a ram's horn.

GG's Garland, 1784, 'Little boy, pretty boy, where was you born? In Lincolnshire, master: come blow the cow's horn. A halfpenny pudding, a penny pye, A shoulder of mutton, and that love I' / *Songs for the Nursery*, 1805, 'Little lad, little lad' / *MG's Quarto*, c. 1825 / MS addition, c. 1835, by John Bell, to his augmented *GG's Garland*, 'Heelandman, Highlandman where were ye born, Up in the Heelands amang the long Corn. And what grows there, Pray! why sibees and leeks, And lang legged Hee-landmen wanting their breeks' / JOH, 1842 / *Only True MG Melodies*, c. 1843, 'Little lad, little lad, where were you born? Far off in Lancashire, under a thorn, Where they sup butter-milk With a ram's horn; And a pumpkin scoop'd, With a yellow rim, Is the bonny bowl they breakfast in' / *Mother Goose*, Kate Greenaway, 1881 / *Fairy Caravan*, Beatrix Potter, 1929.

68

> There was a little boy and a little girl,
>   Lived in an alley;
> Says the little boy to the little girl,
>   Shall I, oh, shall I?

Boy

Says the little girl to the little boy,
What shall we do?
Says the little boy to the little girl,
I will kiss you!

GG's Garland, 1810 / JOH, 1842 / *Mother Goose*, Kate Greenaway, 1881 / *Nursery Rhymes for Certain Times*, Elinor Darwin, 1946.

69

There was a little boy went into a barn,
And lay down on some hay;
An owl came out and flew about,
And the little boy ran away.

Either an off-shoot of this, or a garbled version of a longer original, is known in America:

Jemmy Jed
Went into a shed
And made of a ted
Of straw his bed;
When a mousing owl
That about did prowl
Set up a yowl
And Jemmy Jed
Up stakes and fled.
Wasn't Jemmy Jed a pretty little fool,
Born in the woods, to be scared of an owl?

Songs for the Nursery, 1805 / *GG's Garland* (Lumsden) c. 1815 / *MG's Quarto*, c. 1825, as quote / *NR for Children* (J. Fairburn), c. 1825 / *New Riddles* (Henry Mozley and Sons), c. 1830 / JOH, 1846 / *N & Q*, 1921, as quote, 'familiar in my Connecticut home in the 1850's'.

70

When I was a little boy
I had but little wit;
'Tis a long time ago,
And I have no more yet;

Boy

Nor ever, ever shall
Until that I die,
For the longer I live
The more fool am I.

Wit and Mirth, an antidote against Melancholy (Henry Playford), 1684, 'a New Catch',
'When I was young, I then had no wit: 'Tis a great while a-goe, and I have none yet;
I think I shall ne're have none till I dye, For the longer I live, the more fool am I' /
MG's Melody, c. 1765 / *NR for Children* (J. Fairburn), c. 1825 / *Sugar Plum* (J. Roberts), c.
1825 / JOH, 1842 / *Mother Goose* (T. Nelson), c. 1945 / Correspondent, 1971, chorus of
folksong about a series of bad bargains, 'When I was young I had no wits, I've travelled far and I've got noan yit; No, nor I never shall till the day I die, The older I get
the bigger fool am I'.
    ***Some commentators have thought it worth comparing these lines with the
Clown's song in *Twelfth Night* (v) and the Fool's in *King Lear* (III. ii).

71

When I was a little boy I lived by myself,
And all the bread and cheese I got I laid upon a shelf;
The rats and the mice they made such a strife,
I had to go to London town and buy me a wife.

The streets were so broad and the lanes were so narrow,
I was forced to bring my wife home in a wheelbarrow.
The wheelbarrow broke and my wife had a fall,
Farewell wheelbarrow, little wife and all.

Known in England since the eighteenth century, this may come from a
Scots song, sung to the tune 'John Anderson my Jo',

> When I was a wee thing
> And just like an elf,
> A' the meat that e'er I gat,
> I laid upon the shelf.
> The rottens and the mice
> They fell into a strife,
> They wadnae let my meat alane,
> Till I gat a wife.
>
> And when I gat a wife,
> She wadnae bide therein,
> Till I gat a hurl-barrow
> To hurl her out and in:

Boy

The hurl-barrow brake,
My wife she gat a fa',
And the foul fa' the hurl-barrow,
Cripple wife and a'.

She wadnae eat nae bacon,
She wadnae eat nae beef,
She wadnae eat nae lang kale
For fyling o' her teeth,
But she wad eat the bonie bird,
That sits upon the tree:
Gang down the burn, Davie love,
And I sall follow thee.

T Thumb's PSB, c. 1744 / *F T Thumb's LSB*, c. 1760, 'The deuce take Wheelbarrow, wife and all' / *MG's Melody*, c. 1765, '—Farewell Wheelbarrow, wife and all' / Herd MS, 1776, as quote / *Nancy Cock's PSB*, c. 1780 / *GG's Garland*, 1784 / *T Thumb's SB*, 1788 / *T Tit's SB*, c. 1790, 'When I was a Batchelor' / *Songs for the Nursery*, 1805 / Douce MS, c. 1805, 'There was a little pretty lad' who 'went to Ireland to get himself a wife', and 'The wheelbarrow broke, My wife she got a keck, The deuce take the wheelbarrow that spared my wife's neck' / *Vocal Harmony*, c. 1806 / JOH, 1842 / Also incorporated in the chapbook story of *Jack Sprat* (q.v.), 'But no coach would take her The Lane was so narrow, Said Jack, Then I'll take her Home in a wheelbarrow'.

Cf. long version with chorus in Cecil Sharp's *English Folk-Songs from the Southern Appalachians*, 1917.

72

When I was a little boy,
I washed my mammy's dishes;
I put my finger in my eye,
And pulled out golden fishes.

John Aubrey quotes 'An old filthy Rhythme used by base people, viz.:

When I was a young Maid, and
wash't my Mothers dishes,
I putt my finger in my—and
pluck't-out little Fishes.'

This reappears in the seventeenth-century play *Love without Interest, or The Man too hard for the Master*, by Will Penkethman, and in the next century (c. 1780) in a longer version:

When I was a little boy,
I washed my mother's dishes;

111

Boy

I put my finger in my eye,
  And pulled out little fishes:

My mother called me good boy,
  And bid me do't again;
I put my finger in my eye,
  And got threescore and ten.

That 'fishing' was a bawdy metaphor for coition is made clear in the trick
played on the princess in the chapbook *History of Four Kings*, Tom Hodge,
c. 1750. The young shepherd pretends to draw a fish from his backside,
and she asks him, 'Do you think you could catch one in mine
too?...Then she laying according to his directions, he fell to fishing.'

Lansdowne MS 231, 1686–7 / *Love without Interest*, 1699, 'I put my finger in the pail' /
Nancy Cock's PSB, c. 1780 / *T Tit's SB*, c. 1790, with second verse '...I put my finger in
my ear And pulled out four score' / *Christmas Box*, vol. ii, 1798 / *Vocal Harmony*,
c. 1806 / *Songs for the Nursery*, 1818 / *Nurse Lovechild's DFN*, c. 1830 / JOH, 1842 /
Only True MG Melodies, c. 1843, 'When I was a little boy, I washed my mammy's
dishes, Now I am a great big boy I roll in golden riches' / *Mother Goose Comes to
Cable Street*, R. Stones and A. Mann, illus. Dan Jones, 1977.

73

When I was a little boy
  My mammy kept me in,
But now I am a great boy
  I'm fit to serve the king;
I can hand a musket,
  And I can smoke a pipe,
And I can kiss a pretty girl
  At twelve o'clock at night.

Probably the fragment of a song. The theme can be adapted to many
situations, as in the lines recorded by a Sutherland schoolgirl:

I've a lad in Golspie,
I've a lad at sea,
I've a lad at Golspie
And his number is twenty-three.
I can wash a sailor's shirt,
And I can wash it clean;
I can wash a sailor's shirt,
And bleach it on the green.

Boy

I can chew tobacco,
I can smoke a pipe,
I can kiss a bonny lad
At ten o'clock at night.

In Scotland the middle four lines of this conglomeration are traditionally sung to a child's first tune on the piano, in question-and-answer form: 'O can you wash a sailor's shirt? etc.', followed by 'Yes, I can wash a sailor's shirt, etc.' Similar lines appear in a song, 'The Ploughman', in John Bell's *Rhymes of Northern Bards* (1812); the second verse runs 'I will wash the ploughman's clothes, I will wash them clean, O, etc.'; but in Johnson's *Scots Musical Museum*, vol. ii (1788), the equivalent verse in 'The Plough-man' is, 'I will wash my Ploughman's hose, And I will dress his o'erlay; I will make my Ploughman's bed, And chear him late and early'.

Douce MS, c. 1815, 'My daddy kept me in ... but now I am a stout man ...' / *MG's Quarto*, c. 1825 / JOH, 1842 / Bodley MS Eng. misc. C 58, 1892, as quote / Maclagan, 1901, 'Hullie go lee, go lee, Hullie go lee, go lo, Upon a winter's night, I can chew tobacco. Hullie go lee, go lee, And I can smoke a pipe; I can kiss a bonnie lad At ten o'clock at night.' Words for a circling game.

74

Little Boy Blue,
    Come blow your horn,
The sheep's in the meadow,
    The cow's in the corn;
But where is the boy
    Who looks after the sheep?
He's under a haycock,
    Fast asleep.
Will you wake him?
    No, not I,
For if I do,
    He's sure to cry.

It has been asserted that Little Boy Blue was intended to represent Cardinal Wolsey. It is pointed out that Wolsey was the son of an Ipswich butcher and, as a boy, undoubtedly looked after his father's livestock. As proof, the second couplet of the rhyme has been quoted as being incorporated in *The Tragedy of Cardinal Wolsey* (1587) by Thomas Church-yard; a careful search of the original edition, however, has failed to pro-duce anything more resembling the rhyme than,

PLATE IV

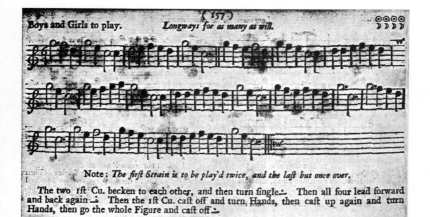

a. 'Boys and Girls to play', from *The Second Book of the Compleat Country Dancing-Master*, 1719. British Museum

b. One of Mulready's illustrations for Charles Lamb's first book for children, *The King and Queen of Hearts*, 1805. Opie collection

Boy Blue

> O fie on wolves, that march in masking-clothes,
> For to devour the lambs, when shepherd sleeps.

A more likely allusion occurs in *King Lear* (III. vi), when Edgar, talking in his character of mad Tom, in a confusion of rhyme, cries:

> Sleepest or wakest thou, jolly shepheard?
> Thy sheepe bee in the corne;
> And for one blast of thy minikin mouth
> Thy sheepe shall take no harme.

FT Thumb's LSB, c. 1760 / *Nancy Cock's PSB*, c. 1780 / *History of a Little Boy Found under a Haycock*, Richard Johnson, 1786 [c. 1820] / *Little Boy Blue* (L. Lavenu), c. 1795, 'A Favourite Glee for three Voices composed by Miss Abrams' / *Infant Institutes*, 1797, 'Little boy Bluet, come blow me your horn; the cow's in the meadow, the sheep in the corn, But where is the little boy tenting the sheep? He's under the haycock fast asleep' / *Christmas Box*, 1798 / *Songs for the Nursery*, 1805 / Douce MS, c. 1805, and *GG's Garland*, 1810, as 1797 / *MG's Melody* (Jesse Cochran, Windsor), 1814 [Rosenbach] / JOH, 1842 / Kidson, 1904. Boy Blue is also met with in A. A. Milne's *When We Were Very Young*, 1924, but Eugene Field's poem 'Little Boy Blue' has no connexion with the nursery rhyme.

75

> Boys and girls come out to play,
> The moon doth shine as bright as day.
> Leave your supper and leave your sleep,
> And join your playfellows in the street.
> Come with a whoop and come with a call,
> Come with a good will or not at all.
> Up the ladder and down the wall,
> A half-penny loaf will serve us all;
> You find milk, and I'll find flour,
> And we'll have a pudding in half an hour.

A favourite nursery song of the present time, formally repeated as a general call to players. The American folk-lorist Newell wrote (1883): 'In the last generation children still sang in our towns the ancient summons to the evening sports,

> Boys and girls, come out to play,
> The moon it shines as bright as day;

and similarly in Provence, the girls who conducted their ring-dances in the public squares, at the stroke of ten sang,

Boys

Ten hours said,
Maids to bed.

But the usage has departed in the quiet cities of Southern France, as in the busy marts of America.' The only game the song is now occasionally associated with is skipping, when 'We'll have a pudding in half an hour' is succeeded by 'with salt, mustard, vinegar, pepper'. Although the earliest references to the song are in adult literature, in dance books of 1708, 1719, and 1728, in satires of 1709 and 1725, and in a political broadside of 1711, the verse seems already, in Queen Anne's reign, to have belonged to children, and it is probable that it dates from the middle of the previous century. The verse has figured in juvenile literature more regularly perhaps than any other, and is mentioned in the first of Newbery's books for children, where 'Boys and Girls come out to play' is the caption to an illustration of children playing by moonlight. Once when Mrs Thrale was down in Brighton, Dr Johnson wrote (21 Nov. 1778) urging her to come home and added:

> Come with a whoop, come with a call,
> Come with a good will, or come not at all.

Useful Transactions in Philosophy, William King, 1708–9 / *All's come out*, 1711 [Chambers] / *Namby Pamby*, Henry Carey, 1725 [1726] / *A Little Pretty Pocket-Book* (J. Newbery), 1744 [1767] / *T Thumb's PSB*, c. 1744 / *FT Thumb's LSB*, c. 1760 / *MG's Melody*, c. 1765, additional couplet 'But when the Loaf is gone, what will you do? Those who would eat must work 'tis true' / *Nancy Cock's PSB*, c. 1780 / *T Thumb's SB*, 1788 / *T Tit's SB*, c. 1790 / *Infant Institutes*, 1797 / *GG's Garland*, c. 1799 / *Songs for the Nursery*, 1805 / *Vocal Harmony*, c. 1806 / *Pretty Tales* (T. Hughes), 1808 / *GG's Garland*, 1810, slight variations from c. 1799 / *GG's Garland* (Lumsden) c. 1815, 'Little boys come out to play...' / *Juvenile Pastimes, in Verse* (Mahlon Day, New York), c. 1830 [Rosenbach] / *London Jingles* (J. G. Rusher), c. 1840 / JOH, 1842 / Rimbault, 1846 / '*N & Q*, 1868, Tweedside, a call to play, known in childhood, 'Boys and girls come out and play, Here's a night like any day; Leave your supper, leave your sleep, And come and play in the High Street' / Kidson, 1904 / In Walsh's *Country Dances*, 1708 [Kidson] and in *The Compleat Country Dancing-Master*, vol. ii, 1719, the tune 'Boys and Girls to Play' is given with directions for the dance. Note: sometimes the opening line is 'Girls and boys come out to play'.

Cf. Chambers, 1847: 'Lazy deuks, that sit i' the coal-neuks, And winna come out to play; Leave your supper, and leave your sleep, Come out and play at hide-and-seek.'

76

What are little boys made of?
What are little boys made of?
    Frogs and snails
    And puppy-dogs' tails,
That's what little boys are made of.

Boys

What are little girls made of?
What are little girls made of?
  Sugar and spice
  And all that's nice,
That's what little girls are made of.

In c. 1820 the poet Robert Southey wrote these verses out, added ten other stanzas—probably of his own composition—and entitled the whole, 'What all the World is made of'. His version of the traditional lines is:

> What are little boys made of made of
> What are little boys made of
> Snips & snails & puppy dogs tails
> And such are little boys made of.
>
> What are young women made of, &c.
> Sugar & spice & all things nice

At the end of the MS he added, uncharitably:

> What are some women made of?
> Bell metal mouths and leathern lungs
> Goose's brains and parrot's tongues.'

The MS is in the collection of Carroll A. Wilson, see *Thirteen Author Collections of the Nineteenth Century AND Five Centuries of Familiar Quotations*, ed. J. C. S. Wilson and D. A. Randall (New York, 1950).

JOH, 1844 / Rimbault, 1846, two additional verses 'What are young men made of? Sighs and leers and crocodile tears. What are young women made of? Ribbons and laces, and sweet pretty faces' / Northall, 1892, 'What are old women made of? Bushes and thorns and old cow's horns' / *Children's Songs of Long Ago*, c. 1905, 'What are our sailors made of, made of? Pitch and tar, pig-tail and scar. What are our soldiers made of, made of? Pipeclay and drill, the foeman to kill.'

***'What are little boys made of' is said (in W. S. Kennedy's biography) to be one of the poems which Longfellow used to recite.

77

As I went up the Brandy hill,
I met my father with good will;
He had jewels, he had rings,
He had many pretty things;
He'd a cat with nine tails,
He'd a hammer wanting nails.

Brandy Hill

Up Jock!
Down Tom!
Blow the bellows old man.

This is 'another old rhyme repeated often for the amusement of children; it is unaccountable how these old sayings are so popular', as Charles Taylor wrote in 1820. At the same period it was also known across the Atlantic, in Massachusetts. Its general use is for counting-out, but Green reports it as going with 'the great and alluring exercise of "Through the needle-e-e'e, boys"'.

Chatterings of the Pica, Charles Taylor, 1820, additional couplet, 'Half a pudden half a pie, Stand ye out by' / *Blackwood's Magazine*, 1821 / Chambers, 1847 / Newell, 1883, also subjoined to 'Intery, mintery, cutery corn': 'Over yonder steep hills, Where my father he dwells...' / Bolton, 1888, three American versions, one as tail of the rhyme beginning 'Hinty, minty, cuty, corn', given as 'Mass., 1806' / *History of NR*, P. B. Green, 1899 / Ford, 1904 / *Rymour Club*, 1911, 'Far awa' amang yon hills, That's where my faither dwells; He has jewels...' &c. / *Counting Out*, Carl Withers, 1946, as Newell.

78

At Brill on the hill
The wind blows shrill,
The cook no meat can dress;
At Stow-on-the-Wold
The wind blows cold,
I know no more than this.

A local rhyme which has gained a more than local reputation with children, possibly through inclusion in JOH'S collection (1844). Brill and Stow-on-the-Wold are both near Oxford, as are Noke, Thame, Stokenchurch (where 'Mother Niddity Nod' was going) and Banbury (qq.v.), all of nursery fame.

JOH, 1844 / *N & Q*, 1852 / *Look! the Sun*, Edith Sitwell, 1941.

79

Two brothers we are, great burdens we bear,
By which we are bitterly pressed;
The truth is to say, we are full all the day,
And empty when we go to rest.

Brothers

A problem which has teased its way through three and a half centuries. In *The Booke of meery Riddles* (1600) it appears simply as, 'What be they which be full all day, and empty at night? Solution. It is a payre of shooes; for in the day they be full of mans feete; but at night, when he goes to bed, they be empty, & it may be assoyled by any other part of mans raiment' [1629].

Child's New Year's Gift (I. Hodges), c. 1748 / *Little Polite Tales, Fables & Riddles* (R. Baldwin), 1749 / *A Whetstone for Dull Wits* (J. White), c. 1765 / *Royal Riddle Book*, 1820 / *Sir Gregory Guess's Present* (T. Batchelar), c. 1820 / *N & Q*, 1865 / *Folk-Lore*, 1923.

Cf. *Riddles, Charades, & Conundrums*, 1824, 'Two brothers we are, yet can't hope to be sav'd; From our very first day to our last we're enslav'd; Our office the hardest, and food sure the worst, Being cramm'd with warm flesh till we're ready to burst; Though low in our state, even kings we support, And at balls have the principal share in the sport.'

80

> Brow bender,
> Eye peeper,
> Nose dreeper,
> Mouth eater,
> Chin chopper,
> Knock at the door,
> Ring the bell,
> Lift up the latch,
> Walk in ...
> Take a chair,
> Sit by there,
> How d'you do this morning?

Infant amusement. As the words are repeated, a finger is laid successively on the baby's forehead, eyes, nose, mouth, and chin. While saying 'knock at the door', the chin is tickled; 'ring the bell', the hair or ear pulled; 'lift up the latch and walk in', the baby's nose is raised and a finger is popped in the mouth. The fullest version found is the Scottish one which starts with the toe and ends at the top of the head:

> Tae titly,
> Little fitty,
> Shin sharpy,
> Knee knapy,
> Hinchie pinchy,
> Wymie bulgy,

Brow Bender

Breast berry,
Chin cherry,
Moo merry,
Nose nappy,
Ee winky,
Broo brinky,
Ower the croon,
And awa' wi' it.

Very many variations have been collected of this rhyme but it is notable
that the earliest version (c. 1746) is similar to the first five lines of the text
version, which was orally collected in 1944.

A Little Play-Book (G. Bickham), c. 1746 / *T Thumb's SB*, 1788 / *Nurse Lovechild's DFN*,
c. 1830, 'Forehead frowner, eye winker, Nose smeller, cherry cheek her, Mouth eater,
and chin chopper, Peter Van, Pea' / Chambers, 1842, 'Brow, brow, brenty, Ee, ee,
winkey, Nose, nose, nebbie, Cheek, cheek, cherry, Mouth, mouth, merrie, Chin,
chin, chackie, Catch a flee, catch a flee' / JOH, 1844, 'Eye winker, Tom Tinker,
Nose dropper, Mouth eater, Chin chopper, Chin Chopper' / *Old Nurse's Book*,
Charles Bennett, 1858 / *Shropshire Folk-Lore*, C. S. Burne, 1883, 'Knock at the door
(forehead), Ring the bell (ear), Peep through the keyhole (eye), Lift up the latch
(nose), Wipe your shoes (on upper lip), Walk in, Chin, chin, chin, chocker' / *Folk-
Lore*, 1886, 1887, and 1889, gives numerous variants / *N & Q*, 1910, 'Tom Thumper,
Ben Bumper, Long'nation, Tem'tation, Little man o' war, war, war', remembered
from c. 1845 / Oral collection, 1944.

   Cf. *Danske Folkesagn*, J. M. Thiele, 1820–3, 'Pandebeen, Oisteen, Næsebeen, Mun-
delip, Hagetip, Dikke, dikke, dik' ('Brow-bone, Eye-stone, Nose-bone, Mouth-lip,
Chin-tip, Dikke, dikke, dik', nurse tickles child under chin) [JOH, 1849] / *Das
deutsche Kinderbuch*, Karl Simrock, 1848, 'Kinne Wippenchen, Roth Lippchen, Nup-
pelnäsichen, Augenbrämichen, Zupp, zupp Härichen' / *Das Englische Kinderlied*, L.
Böckheler, 1935 / *Rimes et jeux de l'enfance*, E. Rolland, 1883, 'Nez cancan, Bouche
d'argent, Menton de buis, Joue brûlée, Joue rôtie, Petit euyet, Grand euyet, Toc,
toc, maillet'; seven versions / *Chinese Mother Goose Rhymes*, I. T. Headland, 1900,
'Knock at the door, See a face, Smell an odor, Hear a voice, Eat your dinner, Pull
your chin, or Ke chih, ke chih'. (In the original Chinese given the last two lines
are perhaps only nonsense.)

81

Bounce, buckram, velvet's dear,
Christmas comes but once a year;
And when it comes, it brings good cheer,
But when it's gone it's never near.

In the seventeenth century this was a proverb of scorn, and was co-opted
by the mummers for their Christmas entertainment. The second and
third lines were, and are, particularly popular, and often appear alone,
as in the 1573 edition of Tusser's *Five hundreth good pointes of husbandrie*:

Buckram

> At Christmas play and make good cheere,
> for Christmas comes but once a yeere.

It also heads the greeting rhymes of carol singers today:

> Christmas comes but once a year
> And when it comes it brings good cheer,
> A pocketful of money, and a cellar full of beer,
> And a good fat pig to last you all the year.

In Clarke's proverb collection (1639), and in JOH's nursery rhymes, only the first two lines of the rhyme appear, which made Hazlitt, who in 1862 knew it simply as a 'nursery jingle', believe that it was made up of two two-line proverbs.

Paroemiologia Latina, John Clarke, 1639, first couplet / *English Proverbs*, John Ray, 1670, complete rhyme / *Alexander and the King of Egypt*, 1788, at end of mummers' play 'Bouncer Buckler, Velvet's dear' / *North Country Words*, J. T. Brockett, 1825 / *Every Day Book*, William Hone, 1827 / JOH, 1843 / *English Proverbs*, W. C. Hazlitt, 1862.

Cf. the typically Irish 'Christmas comes but wanst a year, And when it comes it brings good cheer, And when it goes it laves us here, And what'll we do for the rest o' the year'? [Stevenson's Quotations].

82

> Buff says Buff to all his men,
> And I say Buff to you again;
> Buff neither laughs nor smiles,
> But carries his face,
> With a very good grace,
> And passes the stick to the very next place.

An old forfeits game. The players seat themselves in a circle, and one, taking a wand, points it at his neighbour repeating the rhyme with mock solemnity. The player pointed at then becomes the one who points, and so on round the circle. 'It is a game', remarks Chambers, 'in which the only art consists in keeping one's gravity while saying absurd things.' Those who laugh or smile must pay a forfeit. Sometimes, to increase the difficulty, the one pointed at is made to take a more active part, and the following dialogue takes place:

1. 'Knock, knock!' (*Thumping floor with stick.*)
2. 'Who's there?'
1. 'Buff.'
2. 'What says Buff?'

Buff

1. 'Buff says Buff to all his men,
   And I say Buff to you again.'
2. 'Methinks Buff smiles.'
1. 'Buff neither laughs nor smiles,
   But looks in your face [*or*, strokes his face]
   With a comical grace
   And delivers the staff to you, sir.'

OED quotes Cotgrave's French-English dictionary (1611), '*Esclaffer*, to buff, or burst out into a laughter.'

Girl's Own Book, Mrs. Child, 1831 [1831] / *NR from the Royal Collections* (J. G. Rusher), c. 1840 / JOH, 1842 / *Shropshire Folk-Lore*, C. S. Burne, 1883, similar to quote; also *Folklore*, 1888, and *Riddles and Rhymes* (T. Nelson), 1892. Newell, 1883, 'My father sent me here with a staff, To speak to you and not to laugh—Methinks you smile—Methinks I don't, I smooth my face with ease and grace, And set my staff in its proper place' / Gomme, 1894.

Cf. *Das deutsche Kinderbuch*, Karl Simrock, 1848, the child in the middle of the circle says: 'Ich gieng einmal über den Kirchhof, Da begegnet mir ein Bischof. Der Bischof der war jung und fein, Er wollt nicht gern alleine sein, Der Bischof, der Bischof, der Bischof.' He strikes with a stick in front of one of the children in the circle, who steps forward saying, 'Vater Eberhard, Ich fasse dich an deinen ehrwürdigen Bart. Wenn du mich wirst sehen lachen, Werd ich an deiner Stelle wachen.' Also, 'Ich bin der Herr von Rech, Verbiete Lach und Sprech: Wer lacht und spricht Ein Pfand verbricht.'

83

I had a little dog and they called him Buff,
I sent him to a shop to buy me snuff,
But he lost the bag and spilt the stuff;
I sent him no more but gave him a cuff,
For coming from the mart without any snuff.

NR from the Royal Collections (J. G. Rusher), c. 1840 / *NR, Tales and Jingles*, 1844, and JOH, 1844, four lines only, fourth line 'So take a cuff and that's enough' / Gomme, 1894, as words for the game 'Drop Handkerchief' / *Rymour Club*, 1913. 'Bufe' as a name for a dog occurs from 1567 onwards.

Cf. 'I had a little dog and his name was Blue Bell.'

84

Hot cross buns!
Hot cross buns!

London Cries for Children, 1806

Old Nurse's Book of Rhymes, 1858

'Young lambs to sell'. Engraving of William Liston, toy lamb
seller, for which he specially posed in 1826

Buns

One a penny, two a penny,
Hot cross buns!
If your daughters do not like them
Give them to your sons;
But if you haven't any of these pretty little elves
You cannot do better than eat them yourselves.

This was formerly a street cry, as mentioned, for instance, in *Poor Robin's Almanack* for 1733:

Good Friday comes this month, the old woman runs
With one or two a penny hot cross buns.

Hence it became a calendar folk-chant, customarily sung by children on Good Friday, when the hot cross buns are eaten for breakfast. The song is now remembered in the nursery throughout the year, and often accompanies the game in which the hands are placed flat in a pile, and the lowest removed and placed on the top, and so on.

Christmas Box, 1797 / *No. 2 of the Flowers of Harmony* (G. Walker), c. 1800, sheet music / *London Cries for Children* (Darton and Harvey), 1806, as illustration, p. 106 / *The Moving Market: or Cries of London* (G. Ross), 1815, as 1806 / *Blackwood's*,? John Wilson, July 1824 / *Cries of London* (J. Catnach), c. 1830, abridged version [Hindley, 1881] / JOH, 1846 / *Baby's Bouquet*, 1879 / Oral collection, 1946, 'One a penny poker, Two a penny tongs, Three a penny fire shovel, Hot cross buns' / A Latin rendering is in L.-M. Hawkins's *Anecdotes*, 1822.

85

Come, butter, come,
Come, butter, come;
Peter stands at the gate
Waiting for a butter cake.
Come, butter, come.

Although this centuries-old charm was still in superstitious use at the time, it was set to music in 1798 as a 'Bagatelle for Juvenile Amusement'. Indeed its supernatural aid has been consistently called upon through more than 400 years of Protestantism. Thomas Ady, writing in 1656, knew an old woman who said the butter would come straight away if it was repeated three times, 'for it was taught my Mother by a learned Church-man in Queen Maries days, when as Churchmen had more cunning and could teach people many a trick, that our Ministers now a days know not'. A writer in *Folk-Lore* in 1878 said, 'I have often heard our cook repeating [this rhyme] over her churn when the butter was slow in forming'. Crofton says it was 'well known in Reddish Vale, on the borders of Lancashire and Cheshire in 1880'. Another writer, in 1936, heard it recited in Southern Indiana 'to the accompanying splash of the old-fashioned churn when the butter was slow in coming'. It is indeed easy to believe that the pixies have got into the churn when the cream will not clot, although one has been steadily turning the handle for twice as long as usual. The strange line 'Peter stands at the gate' is found in other charms, as in one for toothache beginning 'When Peter sat at Jerusalem's gate', and may be traced back to the old story of St. Peter, when our Lord relieved him of his troubles 'Ad portam Galylee iacebat Petrus. Venit dominus et interrogavit eum. . . .' It may be compared with a Spanish charm 'Appollonia was at the gate of heaven', and perhaps be traced back ultimately to the prayer of Seth the son of Adam at the gates of Paradise in the apocryphal *Gospel of Nicodemus*.

A Candle in the Dark, Thomas Ady, 1656 / *Satan's Invisible World Discovered*, George Sinclair, 1685, probably quoting Ady / *Christmas Box*, vol. iii, 1798 / JOH, 1842 / *Northamptonshire Words*, A. E. Baker, 1854, 'Churn, butter, churn, In a cow's horn; I never see'd such butter, Sin' I was born. Peter's waiting at the gate', &c. Also 'Churn, butter, churn, Come, butter, come, A little good butter Is better than none' / *Folk-Lore*, 1878 and 1936 / *Lincolnshire Glossary*, Edward Peacock, 1877, 'Churn, butter, dash, Cow's gone to the marsh, Peter stands at the toll gate Begging butter for his cake; Come, butter, come!' / Crofton MS, 1901 / *Mother Goose's NR*, L. E. Walter, 1924.

86

Can you make me a cambric shirt,
　　Parsley, sage, rosemary, and thyme,
Without any seam or needlework?
　　And you shall be a true lover of mine.

Can you wash it in yonder well,
　　Parsley, sage, rosemary, and thyme,
Where never sprung water, nor rain ever fell?
　　And you shall be a true lover of mine.

Can you dry it on yonder thorn,
　　Parsley, sage, rosemary, and thyme,
Which never bore blossom since Adam was born?
　　And you shall be a true lover of mine.

Cambric Shirt

Now you've asked me questions three,
    Parsley, sage, rosemary, and thyme,
I hope you'll answer as many for me,
    And you shall be a true lover of mine.

Can you find me an acre of land,
    Parsley, sage, rosemary, and thyme,
Between the salt water and the sea sand?
    And you shall be a true lover of mine.

Can you plough it with a ram's horn,
    Parsley, sage, rosemary, and thyme,
And sow it all over with one peppercorn?
    And you shall be a true lover of mine.

Can you reap it with a sickle of leather,
    Parsley, sage, rosemary, and thyme,
And bind it up with a peacock's feather?
    And you shall be a true lover of mine.

When you have done and finished your work,
    Parsley, sage, rosemary, and thyme,
Then come to me for your cambric shirt,
    And you shall be a true lover of mine.

Ritson described this (1794) as 'a little English song sung by children and maids'. He had already set it down, ten years earlier, in *Gammer Gurton's Garland or The Nursery Parnassus*, and his version (as above) is still the best known. The story of a maid being asked to do the seemingly impossible task of making a shirt from a piece of linen 3 inches square may be traced to the Middle Ages. There was once a king who was stronger, wiser, and more handsome than any man, but he had no wife. His friends, when they urged him to marry, received the reply: 'You know I am rich enough and powerful enough as I am; find me a maid who is good looking and sensible, and I will take her to wife, though she be poor.' A maid was found whom his friends thought both beautiful and intelligent, and was of royal blood besides. The king, however, wished to make a trial of her sagacity and sent her a bit of linen 3 inches square, with the promise that he would marry her if she would make him a shirt from it of proper length and width. The girl replied that if the king would send her an implement in which she could work the shirt, she would make it for him. So the king sent her 'vas debitum et precosium', the shirt was made, and the king married her. This is one of the tales in the fourteenth century *Gesta Romanorum*, a tale which may be linked with oriental stories of great age. It is known also in Germany, where it was set down by the

Cambric Shirt

Grimms. Whatever variations there are in the tasks demanded in different renderings of the song, it is noticeable that one of them is always the making of a shirt. Professor Child says, 'A man asking a maid to sew him a shirt is equivalent to asking for her love, and her consent to sew the shirt is equivalent to an acceptance of the suitor'. The earliest appearance of the verses is in the black-letter broadside ballad *The Wind hath blown my Plaid away, or, A Discourse betwixt a young Woman and the Elphin Knight*, printed about 1670. The young woman wishes the knight would marry her though the knight says she is over young. The girl says she has a younger sister who was married the previous day. Whereupon the knight says:

> Married with me if thou wouldst be,
> A courtesie thou must do to me.
>
> For thou must shape a sark to me,
> Without any cut or heme, quoth he.
>
> Thou must shape it knife-and-sheerlesse,
> And also sue it needle-threedlesse.

To which the maid replies:

> If that piece of courtesie I do to thee,
> Another thou must do to me.
>
> I have an aiker of good ley-land,
> Which lyeth low by yon sea-strand.
>
> For thou must eare it with thy horn,
> So thou must sow it with thy corn.
>
> And bigg a cart of stone and lyme,
> Robin Redbreast he must trail it hame.
>
> Thou must barn it in a mouse-holl,
> And thrash it into thy shoes soll.
>
> And thou must winnow it in thy looff,
> And also seck it in thy glove.
>
> For thou must bring it over the sea,
> And thou must bring it dry home to me.
>
> When thou hast gotten thy turns well done,
> Then come to me and get thy sark then.

This ballad has been attributed to James I of Scotland. In later versions the setting is changed, and it is an old sweetheart who is challenged to prove her love with the tasks, and answers in the same strain. It is to this group that Ritson's 'Parsley, sage, rosemary, and thyme' belongs.

Cambric Shirt

Later, in the nineteenth century, the second series of tasks is found transposed into the light-hearted nursery nonsense song 'My father left me three acres of land' (q.v.) in which the riddle theme is completely lost.

The Wind hath blown my Plaid away, c. 1670 / *GG's Garland*, 1784 / *Songs of N. Scotland*, Peter Buchan, 1825 / *Ancient Scottish Ballads*, G. R. Kinloch, 1827 / Kinloch MSS, c. 1827, 'Did ye ever travel twixt Berwick and Lyne? Sober and grave grows merry in time. There ye'll meet wi a handsome young dame, Ance she was a true love o'mine. Tell her to sew me a holland sark, And sew it all without needle-wark: And syne we'll be true lovers again. Tell her to wash it at yon spring-well, Where neer wind blew, nor yet rain fell. Tell her to dry it on yon hawthorn, That neer sprang up sin Adam was born. Tell her to iron it wi a hot iron, And plait it a' in ae plait round' [Child] / Motherwell MS, c. 1827, 'Come, pretty Nelly, and sit thee down by me, Every rose grows merry wi thyme And I will ask thee questions three, And then thou wilt be a true lover of mine. Thou must buy me a cambrick smock...' [Child] / JOH, 1843, from *GG's Garland / English and Scottish Popular Ballads*, F. J. Child, 1882 / *Traditional Tunes*, Frank Kidson, 1891, 'Oh where are you going? To Scarborough fair, Savoury, sage, rosemary, and thyme' / *English County Songs*, L. E. Broadwood and J. A. Fuller-Maitland, 1893, 'Is any of you going to Scarborough Fair? Remember me to the lad as lives there, (*bis*) For once he was a true lover of mine...' / Baring-Gould, 1895, 'Will you buy me, my lady, a cambric shirt? Whilst every grove rings with a merry antine (antienne); And stitch it without any needle-work? O and then you shall be a true lover of mine.' 'In Cornwall formerly it formed a portion of a sort of play, and was sung by a young man and a young woman. The story was that she was engaged to him, he died, and his ghost came to claim her. She escapes through setting the ghost tasks, after he has set her others, which are impossible of accomplishment' / *Songs of Norfolk*, W. Rye, 1897, sixth and last verse, 'And pick it up with a cobbler's awl...And stow it all into the mousen's hall' / *Tailor of Gloucester*, Beatrix Potter (p.p. ed.), 1902 / *Folk-Song*, 1907, with tune 'As I roved out by the sea side, Ev'ry rose grows merry in time, I met a little girl, And I gave her my hand, And I says Will you be a true lover of mine? If you are to be a true lover of mine, Every rose grows merry in time, You must make me a shirt without needle or seam, And it's then you will be a true lover of mine', nine verses in all / Correspondent, 1949, 'Can you make me a sable shirt?'

Cf. 'I have four sisters beyond the sea.' It may be that the problems in the present version of the song are not impossible of solution: a shirt without seam might be a cobweb; a well where rain never fell, a dew pond. Allan Cunningham wove the song into a lengthy piece called 'The Bridegroom's Darg' which appears in Cromek's *Remains of Galloway Song*, 1810.

*** The refrain of this song, and the related 'My father left me three acres of land', list a number of plants, parsley, sage, rosemary, thyme, holly, ivy, and broom, to which magical properties were ascribed. It is quite possible that the refrains are the survival of an incantation.

87

A carrion crow sat on an oak,
Watching a tailor shape his cloak;

Carrion Crow

Wife, cried he, bring me my bow,
That I may shoot yon carrion crow.

The tailor shot and missed his mark,
And shot his own sow through the heart;
Wife, bring brandy in a spoon,
For our poor sow is in a swoon.

Amongst riddles, jokes, and epitaphs in a small commonplace book of
Charles I's time, the rhyme appears in this form:

Hie hoe the carryon crow for I have shot something too low I have
quite missed my mark, & shot the poore sow to the harte Wyfe bring
treakel in a spoone, or else the poore sowes harte wil downe.

In the papers of Francis Grose, published in 1796 after his death, it is
described as 'a silly vulgar ballad':

The carrion crow sat upon an oak,
And spied a taylor cutting out a cloak;
   With a heigh ho! the carrion crow!
   Sing tol de rol, de riddle row!

The carrion crow he began for to rave,
And call'd the taylor a lousy knave;
   With a heigh ho! &c.

Oh wife, fetch me my arrow and my bow,
That I may shoot this carrion crow;
   With a heigh ho! &c.

The taylor he shot, and he miss'd his mark,
And shot the old sow through the heart;
   With a heigh ho! &c.

Oh wife, fetch me some treacle in a spoon,
For the old sow is in a terrible swoon;
   With a heigh ho! &c.

The old sow died, and the bells they did toll,
And the little pigs pray'd for the old sow's soul;
   With a heigh ho! &c.

Zooks! quoth the taylor, I care not a louse,
For we shall have black puddings, chitterlings, and souse;
   With a heigh ho! &c.

Sloane MS 1489, c. 1627 / *The Olio*, Francis Grose, 1796 / *Grandmamma's NR* (J. Fairburn), c. 1825 / *Rhymes for the Fireside* (Thomas Richardson), c. 1828 / *Collection of NR*
(Oliver and Boyd), c. 1830 / JOH, 1842, as text, also similar, with refrain 'Sing heigho,

Carrion Crow

the carrion crow, Fol de rol, de rol, de rhino' / *The Carrion Crow*, Marcus Ward, c. 1875 / *Baby's Bouquet*, 1879, with refrain 'Derry, derry, derry, decco' / *A Garland of Country Song*, S. Baring-Gould, 1895, version taken down from Cornishman, 1844 / Kidson, 1904 / *The Tailor and the Crow*, Leslie Brooke, 1911 / Williams, 1923, similar to Grose's ballad, with refrain 'Rogue, go back! The carrion crow cried "Pork"' / *Nursery Songs from the Appalachian Mountains*, Cecil Sharp, 1923 / *Folk-Song*, 1934.

88

A cat came fiddling out of a barn,
With a pair of bag-pipes under her arm;
She could sing nothing but, Fiddle cum fee,
The mouse has married the humble-bee.
Pipe, cat; dance, mouse;
We'll have a wedding at our good house.

Rhyme found in a variety of forms, the earliest recorded appearing to be that in a Wiltshire manuscript dated 1740:

Fiddle-de-dee, fiddle-de-dee!
The wasp has married the humble bee!
Puss came dancing out of the barn
With a pair of bagpipes under her arm.
One for Johnnie and one for me,
Fiddle-de-dee, fiddle-de-dee!

It is very possible that the ditty sung by the cat is 'The Fly and the Humble Bee' (q.v.) also known in nursery circles. A tune called 'Fiddle-de-dee' is in *The Second Book of the Compleat Country Dancing Master* (1719).

A Wiltshire MS, 1740 [*Folk-Lore*, 1901] / *Nursery Songs* and *London Jingles* (J. G. Rusher), both c. 1840, 'A cat came singing out of a barn, With a pair of bagpipes under her arm, She sang nothing but fiddle-de-dee, Worried a mouse and a humble bee, Puss began purring, mouse ran away, And off the bee flew with a wild huzza!' / JOH, 1842 / *Baby's Bouquet*, 1879, 'Pussy-cat high, Pussy-cat low, Pussy-cat was a fine teazer of tow. Pussy-cat she came into the barn, With her bag-pipes under her arm. And then she told a tale to me, How Mousey had married a humble bee. Then was I ever so glad, That Mousey had married so clever a lad.'

89

The cat sat asleep by the side of the fire,
The mistress snored loud as a pig;

Cat

Jack took up his fiddle by Jenny's desire,
And struck up a bit of a jig.

This verse, usually found alone, is the first of the fifteen in *Whimsical Incidents, or, The Power of Music, a Poetic Tale by a near Relation of Old Mother Hubbard*, published by J. Harris, 25 October 1805. The lines, though, were not necessarily new at this date. In 'A Medley, Composed out of several Songs' in *Pills to Purge Melancholy* (1707) there is a possible reference to them ('The old Woman and her Cat sat by the Fire').

Whimsical Incidents, 1805; (Wm. Charles, Philadelphia), 1811 / *GG's Garland*, 1810 / JOH, 1842 / *Traditional Nursery Songs*, Felix Summerly, 1843, illustration by John Linnell / *Cakes and Custard*, Brian Alderson, illus. Helen Oxenbury, 1974.

90

Diddlety, diddlety, dumpty,
The cat ran up the plum tree;
Half a crown
To fetch her down,
Diddlety, diddlety, dumpty.

For some reason cats, in song, frequently take refuge in plum trees, e.g. 'Lady come down and see the Cat sits in the Plum-tree' in *Pammelia, Musicks Miscellanie* (1609).

Douce MS, c. 1815, 'Feedum fiddledum fee, the cat's got into the tree. Pussy come down, Or I'll crack your crown, And toss you into the sea' / *London Jingles* (J. G. Rusher), c. 1840 / JOH, 1853 / *Mother Goose*, Kate Greenaway, 1881 / Bolton, 1888, 'Iddlety, diddlety, dumpty, The cat ran up the plum-tree, Send a hack to fetch her down, Iddlety, diddlety, dumpty.'

91

Sing, sing, what shall I sing?
The cat's run away with the pudding string!
Do, do, what shall I do?
The cat has bitten it quite in two!

Formerly a performer's appeal for what to sing next; more recently a child's rhyme in place of a song.

Cat

Songs for the Nursery, 1805 / *Koningsmarke*, J. K. Paulding, 1823 / *Gallovidian Encyclopedia*, J. Mactaggart, 1824 [1876], and *MG's Quarto*, c. 1825, first couplet only / *London Jingles* (J. G. Rusher), c. 1840 / JOH, 1843 / *Cumberland Glossary*, W. Dickinson, 1879, 'Sing, sing, what mun I sing? Cat's run away wi' t' puddin pwoke string. Some get puddin' and some gat prick: They war n't warst off 'at gat clout to lick' / *Mother Goose*, Arthur Rackham, 1913 / Correspondent, 1952, 2nd couplet, 'Do, do, what shall I do? Cat's run away with the pudding too!'.

92

Old chairs to mend! Old chairs to mend!
I never would cry old chairs to mend,
If I'd as much money as I could spend,
I never would cry old chairs to mend.

Old clothes to sell! Old clothes to sell!
I never would cry old clothes to sell,
If I'd as much money as I could tell,
I never would cry old clothes to sell.

Charles Dibdin wrote a song, 'Old chairs to mend'—presumably based on the traditional street cry—which was sung by Miss Romanzini in the pantomime of 'The Lancashire Witches', performed at the Royal Circus in 1793.

GG's Garland, 1810, order of lines, 3, 2, 1, 4 / *NR from the Royal Collections* (J. G. Rusher), c. 1840 / JOH, 1843 / Baring-Gould, 1895 / *Mother Goose*, Arthur Rackham, 1913. A tune 'Old Chairs to Mend' appears in *Riley's Flute Melodies* (New York), 1814–16 [1973].
   Cf. 'Young lambs to sell'.

93

As I was going by Charing Cross,
I saw a black man upon a black horse;
They told me it was King Charles the First—
Oh dear, my heart was ready to burst!

In a ballad preserved in a Stuart manuscript at Oxford appear two lines reminiscent of the second couplet:

But because I cood not a vine Charlles the furste
By my troth my hart was readdy to burst.

Charing Cross

Black, in the seventeenth-century manner employed here, usually refers to the colour of the hair, but may in this instance be describing the blackness of tarnished brass. It is likely that this Puritan jingle satirizing the uninhibited emotions of the Royalists was not composed until the Restoration. In 1675 the statue of Charles I, which had originally been erected in King Street (and may today be seen at the top of Whitehall), was re-erected on the site of the old Charing Cross, and amongst London cries was:

> I cry my matches at Charing Cross,
> Where sits a black man on a black horse.

Ashmole MS 36, c. 1660 / *Pretty Tales*, 1808, 'Ride a Cock Horse, To Charing Cross, To see a Black Man Upon a Black Horse' / JOH, 1843 / *Look! the Sun*, Edith Sitwell, 1941. It also appears to be referred to by Charles Lamb, Feb. 1801, in a letter to Thomas Manning.

94

> King Charles the First walked and talked
> Half an hour after his head was cut off.

Peter Puzzlewell, 1792, 'King Charles walked and talked seven years after his head was cut off' / *I Saw Esau*, Iona and Peter Opie, 1947.

95

> Charley, Charley,
> Stole the barley
> Out of the baker's shop.
> The baker came out
> And gave him a clout,
> Which made poor Charley hop.

Mother Goose's NR, 1877 / *Rymour Club*, 1911 / Correspondent, 1949, for skipping. Cf. 'Handy spandy, Jack-a-Dandy'.

96

> Over the water and over the lea,
> And over the water to Charley.

Charley

Charley loves good ale and wine,
    And Charley loves good brandy,
And Charley loves a pretty girl
    As sweet as sugar candy.

Over the water and over the lea,
    And over the water to Charley.
I'll have none of your nasty beef,
    Nor I'll have none of your barley;
But I'll have some of your very best flour
    To make a white cake for my Charley.

According to Andrew Lang this is a parody of a Jacobite ditty of 1748. Probably it was one like that in *The True Loyalist*, surreptitiously printed in 1779:

The K—g he has been long from home;
    The P—ce he has sent over
To kick the Usurper off the throne
    And send him to Hannover.
        O'er the water, o'er the sea,
            O'er the water to C—lie:
        Go the world as it will
            We'll hazard our lives for C—lie.

Or 'Come boat me o'er', which was refurbished by Burns, and has a similar refrain:

We'll o'er the water and o'er the sea,
    We'll o'er the water to Charlie;
Come weal, come woe, we'll gather and go,
    And live or die wi' Charlie.

The song is referred to in *The Old Curiosity Shop* (1841) where some of the handbills for Jarley's Wax-Work Show were 'couched in the form of parodies on popular melodies, as "...Over the water to Jarley"'. And Charles Lamb is said to have had a liking for the tune, feeling that the lines (3–6 of the text) had a personal application.

Juvenile Amusements, 1797, as text, line 3–6, as also *Songs for the Nursery*, 1805, Douce MS, c. 1815, and *MG's Quarto*, c. 1825 / JOH, 1842 / *Only True MG Melodies*, c. 1843, 'Charley loves good cake and ale, Charley loves good candy, Charley loves to kiss the girls, When they are clean and handy' / *Baby's Bouquet*, 1879 / Crofton MS, 1901, 'Charley over the water, Charley over the sea; Charley caught a pretty bird, Can't catch me'—formula for a game of catch. The air 'O'er the Water to Charlie' is in James Oswald's *Pocket Companion*, ante 1750.

97

> Charley Wag, Charley Wag,
> Ate the pudding and left the bag.

This is, properly, a derisive call after persons named Charles, but by the middle of the nineteenth century it had also gained admittance to the nurseries of both England and America. 'Wag', in some places, is a nickname for Charles. To 'play the Charlie Wag' meant to 'play the truant', from c. 1865. At about the same period 'Charlie Wag' seems to have been an epithet for a thief, to judge from that 'least defensible of "penny dreadfuls"', *Charlie Wag, the Boy Burglar* (c. 1860), and the play *Charley Wag, the Outcast of the Thames*, by 'Pictum', performed at the Britania, Hoxton, (19 December, 1860), in which Charlie was a highwayman in a top hat.

Only True MG Melodies, c. 1843 / JOH, 1844 / Northall, 1892, 'Charley Wag, Charley Wag! Ate the pudding and swallowed the bag' / *Lark Rise*, Flora Thompson, 1939, 'Old Charley-wag! Old Charley-wag! Ate the pudden and gnawed the bag!'

98

> Charley Warlie had a cow,
> Black and white about the brow;
> Open the gate and let her through,
> Charley Warlie's old cow.

'In Galloway', said Mactaggart in 1824, 'now slumbers a singular old song and dance, called *Dolly Beardy*. After going through a world of trouble with great pleasure, I got a hint respecting the song, and here is the result of that:

> Dolly Beardy was a lass,
> De'il the like o'r on the grass,
> Her lad was but a moidert ass,
>   Hey, Dolly Beardy.'

Altogether he gave eight verses, of which the third was:

> Dolly Beardy had a cow,
> Black and white about the mou',
> She keeped her ay rifting fu',
>   Smock, Dolly Beardy.

Charley Warlie

There is tolerable proof that this song is more than three centuries old. 'Katherine Bairdie' is one of the tunes given 'for kissing, for clapping, for loving, for proving' in a manuscript of the Scottish poet Sir William Mure, believed to have been written not later than 1628; the same tune (called 'Kette Bairdie') appears in the Skene MS., of about 1700, and (called 'Simon Brodie') in the McFarlan MS. of about 1743. So certain was Scott that this was a popular dance in the reign of James IV that he introduces it ('Chrichty Bairdie') in *The Fortunes of Nigel*. When it was first given into children's keeping is uncertain, but William Dauney, born in 1800, said ' "Kitty Bairdie" is the heroine of a nursery rhyme in the recollection of most people'.

Herd MS, 1776, 'Symon Brodie had a cow: The cow was lost, and he cou'd na find her; When he had done what man could do, The cow came hame, and her tail behind her' (two verses) / *Gallovidian Encyclopedia*, J. Mactaggart, 1824 [1876] / Chambers, 1842, 'Katie Beardie had a coo, Black and white about the mou'; Wasna that a dentie coo? Dance, Katie Beardie!' (four verses) / JOH, 1844, 'Wooley Foster has a cow, Black and white about the mow, Open the gates and let her through, Wooley Foster's ain cow' / JOH, 1853, as text / *Rymour Club*, 1911, additional verses / Correspondent, 1948, 'Wiley, Wiley, had a cow, Black and white upon his brow'.

99

Three children sliding on the ice,
  Upon a summer's day,
As it fell out, they all fell in,
  The rest they ran away.

Now had these children been at home,
  Or sliding on dry ground,
Ten thousand pounds to one penny
  They had not all been drowned.

You parents all that children have,
  And you that have got none,
If you would have them safe abroad,
  Pray keep them safe at home.

These stanzas are similar to three appearing in a ballad *The Lamentation of a Bad Market; or, the Drowning of three Children in the Thames*, which first appears in *The Loves of Hero and Leander*, 1651. If the word of the publisher may be accepted, this was, more than 300 years ago, one of the 'choice Peices of Drollery' which was 'Got by heart, and often repeated by divers

PLATE V

'Three children sliding on the ice', as it appeared (stanzas 12, 18, and 19) in the ballad *The lamentation of a bad Market*, c. 1680. British Museum

Children

witty Gentlemen and Ladies, that use to walke in the *New Exchange*, and at their Recreations in *Hide Park*.' The ballad begins:

> Some Christian people all give eare,
>> Unto the greife of us,
> Caus'd by the death of three Children deare,
>> The which it happened thus.

It describes the burning of 'a bridge of London town' and was probably occasioned by the fire which, in February 1633, destroyed much of London Bridge. Stanzas 12, 18, and 19, run:

> Three Children sliding there abouts,
>> Upon a place too thin,
> That so at last it did fall out,
>> That they did all fall in.

> Yee Parents all that *Children have*.
>> And yee that have none yet;
> Preserve your Children from the Grave,
>> And teach them at home to sit.

> For had these at a Sermon been,
>> Or else upon dry ground,
> Why then I would never have been seen,
>> If that they had been drown'd.

This is undoubtedly a burlesque of the pious ballad-mongers whose 'Providential Warning and Goodly Counsels' wearied the Cavalier aristocracy. The modern condensed version is first noted in the writings of Dr. Wagstaffe at the latter end of Queen Anne's reign (one verse) and in a song collection of 1744 (the three verses). The subsequent popularity of the piece among children may be gauged by the number of its appearances in juvenile collections, though Southey, at two years old, could not bear it. JOH in 1843 described it as 'very popular'. The ballad was sung to the tune 'Chevy Chase' or 'Lady's Fall' and was printed with music in *Pills to Purge Melancholy*. The condensed version has been attributed to Gay, and also to Goldsmith, but the possibility of it being the latter's work is precluded by the earliness of its appearance in print.

The Loves of Hero and Leander, 1651 / *Merry Drollery*, W. N. &c., 1661, ballad entitled 'The Fire on London Bridge' / *The Lamentation of a Bad Market* (F. Coles, &c.), c. 1680 / *Pills to Purge Melancholy*, 1700 / *Character of Richard St—le, Esq.*, W. Wagstaffe, c. 1712 (one verse) / *Philomel* (M. Cooper), 1744 / *The Robin* (C. Hitch), 1749 / *FT Thumb's LSB*, c. 1760, one verse / *Pretty Book of Pictures*, Tommy Trip (J. Newbery), 1762 [1767] / *MG's Melody*, c. 1765 / *GG's Garland*, 1784 / *T Tit's SB*, c. 1790 / *Christmas Box*, 1797 / *Songs for the Nursery*, 1805 / *Vocal Harmony*, c. 1806 / *Nurse Lovechild's DFN*, c. 1830 / *London Jingles* (J. G. Rusher), c. 1840 / JOH, 1842 / *Harry's Ladder of*

Children

Learning (David Bogue), c. 1850 [*N & Q*, 13th s.] / *My ABC of NR Friends* (R. Tuck), 1947.
The tune 'Three Children Sliding on the Thames' is in *Songs Compleat*, 1719.

100

The first day of Christmas,
My true love sent to me
A partridge in a pear tree.

The second day of Christmas,
My true love sent to me
Two turtle doves, and
A partridge in a pear tree.

The third day of Christmas,
My true love sent to me
Three French hens,
Two turtle doves, and
A partridge in a pear tree.

The fourth day of Christmas,
My true love sent to me
Four colly birds,
Three French hens,
Two turtle doves, and
A partridge in a pear tree.

The fifth day of Christmas,
My true love sent to me
Five gold rings,
Four colly birds,
Three French hens,
Two turtle doves, and
A partridge in a pear tree.

The sixth day of Christmas,
My true love sent to me
Six geese a-laying,
Five gold rings,
Four colly birds,
Three French hens,

Christmas

Two turtle doves, and
A partridge in a pear tree.

The seventh day of Christmas,
My true love sent to me
Seven swans a-swimming,
Six geese a-laying,
Five gold rings,
Four colly birds,
Three French hens,
Two turtle doves, and
A partridge in a pear tree.

The eighth day of Christmas,
My true love sent to me
Eight maids a-milking,
Seven swans a-swimming,
Six geese a-laying,
Five gold rings,
Four colly birds,
Three French hens,
Two turtle doves, and
A partridge in a pear tree.

The ninth day of Christmas,
My true love sent to me
Nine drummers drumming,
Eight maids a-milking,
Seven swans a-swimming,
Six geese a-laying,
Five gold rings,
Four colly birds,
Three French hens,
Two turtle doves, and
A partridge in a pear tree.

The tenth day of Christmas,
My true love sent to me
Ten pipers piping,
Nine drummers drumming,
Eight maids a-milking,
Seven swans a-swimming,
Six geese a-laying,

Christmas

Five gold rings,
Four colly birds,
Three French hens,
Two turtle doves, and
A partridge in a pear tree.

The eleventh day of Christmas,
My true love sent to me
Eleven ladies dancing,
Ten pipers piping,
Nine drummers drumming,
Eight maids a-milking,
Seven swans a-swimming,
Six geese a-laying,
Five gold rings,
Four colly birds,
Three French hens,
Two turtle doves, and
A partridge in a pear tree.

The twelfth day of Christmas,
My true love sent to me
Twelve lords a-leaping,
Eleven ladies dancing,
Ten pipers piping,
Nine drummers drumming,
Eight maids a-milking,
Seven swans a-swimming,
Six geese a-laying,
Five gold rings,
Four colly birds,
Three French hens,
Two turtle doves, and
A partridge in a pear tree.

A rhyme or chant, also known in France, the meaning of which, if it has
any, has yet to be satisfactorily explained. The lines are first found in a
diminutive children's book *Mirth without Mischief*, published in London
about 1780. They are there the words of a fireside memory-and-forfeits
game, 'The Twelve Days of Christmas', which 100 years later Lady
Gomme described playing every Twelfth Day night before eating mince
pies and twelfth cake. The leader of the game commenced by saying the
lines of the 'first day', and they were repeated by each member of the

company in turn, then the leader said the 'second' and the 'first' days together, which were similarly repeated round the circle. This was continued until the lines for the 'twelve days' were said by every player. For each mistake a forfeit was demanded in the manner of 'The Play of the Wide-mouth waddling Frog' (q.v.). In Scotland, early in the nineteenth century, the recitation began:

> The king sent his lady on the first Yule day,
> A popingo-aye [parrot];
> Wha learns my carol and carries it away?

The succeeding gifts were three partridges, three plovers, a goose that was grey, three starlings, three goldspinks, a bull that was brown, three ducks a-merry laying, three swans a-merry swimming, an Arabian baboon, three hinds a-merry hunting, three maids a-merry dancing, three stalks o' merry corn. In the Cambrésis, in the north of France, the game is called 'Les dons de l'an', and the sequence is one partridge, two turtle doves, three wood-pigeons, four ducks flying, five rabbits trotting, six hares a-field, seven hounds running, eight shorn sheep, nine horned oxen, ten good turkeys, eleven good hams, twelve small cheeses. In the west of France the piece is known as a song, 'La foi de la loi', and is sung 'avec solennité', the sequence being: a good stuffing without bones, two breasts of veal, three joints of beef, four pigs' trotters, five legs of mutton, six partridges with cabbage, seven spitted rabbits, eight plates of salad, nine dishes for a chapter of canons, ten full casks, eleven beautiful full-breasted maidens, and twelve musketeers with their swords. A Languedoc chant is similar, but the gifts are made on the first fifteen days of May. A partridge that flies is followed by two doves, three white pigeons, four ducks flying in the air, five rabbits, six hares, seven hunting dogs, eight white horses, nine horned oxen, ten bleating sheep, eleven soldiers coming from war, twelve maidens, thirteen white nosegays, fourteen white loaves, fifteen casks of wine. Suggestions have been made that the gifts have significance, as representing the food or sport for each month of the year. Importance has certainly long been attached to the Twelve Days, when, for instance, the weather on each day was carefully observed to see what it would be in the corresponding month of the coming year. Nevertheless, whatever the ultimate origin of the chant, it seems probable that the lines which survive today both in England and France are merely an irreligious travesty, possibly of a chant like 'Dic mihi quid unus?', or of a carol like that in Sloane MS 2593, and in Wright's MS (printed 1847) of the fifteenth century:

> The fyrst day of ȝole have we in mynd,
> How God was man born of our kynd;
> For he the bondes wold onbynd
>   Of all owre synnes and wykednes.

Christmas

The secund day we syng of Stevene,
That stoned and steyyd up even
To God that he saw stond in hevyn,
And crounned was for hys prouesse.

The iij. day longeth to sent Johan, &c.

Mirth without Mischief (C. Sheppard), c. 1780, as text / Buchan MS, c. 1828, as quote /
Chambers, 1842, as 1828 / JOH, 1842, 'My mother sent to me... four canary birds
...eight ladies dancing... nine lords a leaping, ten ships a sailing, eleven ladies
spinning, twelve bells ringing' / Rimbault, 1846, as JOH / Gomme, 1898 / *Folk
Songs from Somerset*, Cecil Sharp, 1905 / *Folk-Song*, 1916, five versions noted by Cecil
Sharp in which singer begins with the 'twelfth day' and omits a day at a time until
'second day' when process is reversed. Thus one version begins 'The twelfth day of
Christmas my true love sent to me: Twelve bulls a-roaring, Eleven bears a-baiting,
Ten lords a-leaping, [no 'nine'], Eight hares a-running, Seven swans a-swimming,
Six geese a-laying, Five golden rings, Four colley birds, Three French hens, Two
turtle-doves And a part of a juniper tree' / *Come Hither*, Walter de la Mare, 1923 /
The 12 days of Christmas, Margaret Levetus, c. 1946.
  *** If 'The partridge in the peartree' of the English version is to be taken literally it
looks as if the chant comes from France, since the Red Leg partridge, which perches
in trees more frequently than the common partridge, was not successfully introduced into England until about 1770. 'Colly birds' are blackbirds, as in Shakespeare's
'collied night' (*Midsummer Night's Dream*, I. i).
  Cf. *Chants et chansons populaires du Cambrésis*, A. Durieux and A. Bruyelle, 1864,
'Le douzièm' mois de l'an, que donner à ma mie? Douz' bons larrons, Onze bons
jambons, Dix bons dindons, Neuf bœufs cornus, Huit moutons tondus, Sept chiens
courants, Six lièvres aux champs, Cinq lapins trottant par terre, Quatre canards
volant en l'air, Trois ramiers des bois, Deux tourterelles, Une pertriolle, Une pertriolle, Qui vole et vole et vole, Une pertriolle Qui vole Du bois au champ' / *Chants
et chansons populaires des provinces de l'ouest*, J. Bujeaud, 1866, begins, '(Le Prieur:) La
premièr' parti' d'la foi d'la loi, Dit'-la-moi, frère Grégoire? (Frère Grégoire:) Un bon
farci sans os'. Ends, 'Douze mousquetaires, Avec leurs rapières; Onze demoiselles,
Fort gentill's et belles, Garni's de tétons, Voilà qui est bon; Dix futailles pleines,
Qui feront merveille; Neuf plats de chapitre, Pour servir de suite; Huit plats de sal-
ade, Pour garnir la table; Sept lapins en broche, Rôtis à la sauce; Six perdrix aux
choux, Voilà tout; Cinq pieds de mouton, Voilà qui est bon; Quatre, quatre pieds
de porcs; Trois aloyaux rôtis au maluraux; Deux ventres de veau; Un bon farci
sans os' / *Chants populaires du Languedoc*, A. Montel and L. Lambert, 1880, 'Le pru-
miè del més de mai, Qu' embouiarei à mai mio. Uno perdic que bolo, que bolo', &c.

101

On Christmas Eve I turned the spit,
I burnt my fingers, I feel it yet;
The cock sparrow flew over the table;
The pot began to play with the ladle.

Christmas

These lines are traditional in some versions of the mummers' Christmas play, as performed, for instance, at Weston-sub-Edge, in Gloucestershire, about 1864, and at Kempsford, in the same county, about 1868. At Weston-sub-Edge, Beelzebub (it should, perhaps, have been John Finney) says:

'I went up a straight crooked lane, I met a bark and he dogged at me. I went to the stick and cut a hedge, gave him a rallier over the yud jud killed him round stout stiff and bold from Lancashire I came, if Doctor hasn't done his part, John Finney wins the game.

> Last Christmas night I turned the spit,
> I burnt me finger and felt it itch,
> The sparks flew over the table,
> The pot-lid kicked the ladle,
> Up jumped spit jack
> Like a mansion man
> Swore he'd fight the dripping pan
> With his long tail,
> Swore he'd send them all to jail.
> In comes the grid iron, if you can't agree
> I'm the justice, bring um to me.'

The last two lines, together with the second couplet of the text, form part of another rhyme preserved in the nursery, 'The sow came in with the saddle' (q.v.), which was recorded in the latter half of the eighteenth century. Both rhymes clearly emanate from the mummers' play, although printed before any performance in which they appear was recorded. Chambers, in 1842, scouring the Lowlands of Scotland for remnants of the idea of Christmas as a holiday and day of feasting, could find only the rhyme 'the boys have':

> On Christmas night I turned the spit,
> I burnt my fingers—I find it yet.

Chambers, 1842, as quote / JOH, 1844 / *Songs for the Nursery*, 2nd series, c. 1847, version continues 'The ladle stood up like an angry man, And vowed he'd fight the frying-pan; The frying-pan behind the door Said he never saw the like before; And the kitchen clock I was going to wind said he never saw the like behind' / *The Mummers' Play*, R. J. E. Tiddy, 1923, as quote, also 'Last Xmas day I turned the spit I burnt my fingers and felt it hit—The spark jumped over the table And the frying pan beat the ladle'.

102

> Here is the church, and here is the steeple;
> Open the door and here are the people.

Church

> Here is the parson going upstairs,
> And here he is a-saying his prayers.

Finger-game. As the words are repeated the fingers are interlocked with knuckles outwards, the two little fingers are raised to represent a steeple, and the hands turned inside out to reveal a congregation of digits. As the parson 'goes upstairs' the crossed hands are placed back to back, the fingers being inter-twined one by one. Finally, the palms are brought together and the thumb appears in a pulpit of the knotted hands. School-children then make the parson deliver an oration on potato peeling:

> Dearly beloved brethren, is it not a sin,
> When you peel potatoes to throw away the skin?
> For the skin feeds pigs, and pigs feed you.
> Dearly beloved brethren, is this not true?

The finger game was known at least as early as the beginning of the nineteenth century. It can be seen in Raeburn's portrait 'The Leslie Boy' (c. 1810), and was described by Madame Celnart, in *Nouveau Manuel Complet des Jeux de Société* (1827) [1846], under the name of 'Petit Bonhomme dans le puits'. Newell (1883) collected the first two lines of the text verse in the U.S.A. The mock sermon was written by Joseph Tabrar as the chorus to his popular music-hall song 'Dearly Beloved Brethren' (1881), unless—as often happened—he borrowed a verse already current in oral tradition.

103

> Cobbler, cobbler, mend my shoe.
> Yes, good master, that I'll do;
> Here's my awl and wax and thread,
> And now your shoe is quite mended.

Possibly for use in 'Hunt the Slipper', though the common formula for the game is:

> Cobbler, cobbler, mend my shoe,
> Get it done by half-past two;
> Half-past two is much too late,
> Get it done by half-past eight.

Original Ditties for the Nursery (J. Harris), c. 1805 [1807] / *Mother Goose's NR*, L. E. Walter, 1924, two variants / Oral collection, 1945, as quote; 1948, 'Stitch it up and stitch it down, And then I'll give you half a crown'.
  Cf. 'Robert Barnes, fellow fine'.

Cock

104

Cock:
Lock the dairy door,
Lock the dairy door!

Hen:
Chickle, chackle, chee,
I haven't got the key!

Lines mimicking the cock crowing, and the hen's clucking reply.

JOH, 1846 / *Mother Goose's NR*, L. E. Walter, 1924.
    Cf. 'Cock, cock, cock, cock'.

105

Cock, cock, cock, cock,
I've laid an egg,
Am I to go ba-are foot?

Hen, hen, hen, hen,
I've been up and down,
To every shop in town,
And cannot find a shoe
To fit your foot,
If I'd crow my hea-art out.

This imitation of a cock and hen is spoken rapidly on one note, rising to a scream at the end of each verse. It is one of two traditional pieces which the American children's writer Mrs. Follen included in *New Nursery Songs for All Good Children*. Her version ('Am I to gang bā-āre foot?') seems to have Scottish ancestry. The children's custom of putting words to the cock's music was remarked on three centuries ago (*vide* 'Cock-a-doodle-doo').

New Nursery Songs, Mrs. Follen, c. 1843 / *Only True MG Melodies*, c. 1843 / Chambers, 1847, '*Hen*. Every day, An egg I lay, And yet I aye gang barefit, barefit. *Cock*. I've been through a' the toun, Seeking you a pair of shoon; Wad ye hae my heart out, heart out?'; also this 'hen's song', 'The cock gaed to Rome, seeking shoon, seeking shoon, The cock gaed to Rome, seeking shoon. And yet I aye gang barefit, barefit!' / JOH, 1849, '*Hen*. Cock, cock, I have la-a-yed! *Cock*. Hen, hen, that's well sa-a-yed. *Hen*. Although I have to go bare-footed every da-ay. *Cock*. Sell your eggs, and buy shoes! Sell your eggs, and buy shoes!' / *Tale of Mrs Tiggy- Winkle*, Beatrix Potter, 1905, 'The speckled hen . . . clucking—"I go barefoot, barefoot, barefoot!"'

106

The cock crows in the morn
To tell us to rise,
And he that lies late
Will never be wise:
For early to bed,
And early to rise,
Is the way to be healthy
And wealthy and wise.

Probably composed early in the nineteenth century, this pleasant jingle is formed from two old proverbs. The sayings were and are very common, and have at all times been principally addressed to the young. Sir Anthony Fitzherbert (b. 1470) wrote 'At grāmer scole I lerned a verse & that is this: *Sanat, sanctificat et ditat surgere mane.* That is to say, erly rysynge maketh a man hole in body, holer in soule, & rycher in goodes.' Hugh Rhodes (c. 1545) wrote:

Ryse you earely in the morning, for it hath propertyes three:
Holynesse, health, and happy welth, as my Father taught mee.

The proverb 'Early to bed, early to rise', &c., appears in seventeenth-century Latin grammars and reading primers, and in children's literature in the eighteenth century, including *Goody Two-Shoes*, where it is said to be a verse composed by Ralph, the raven, 'which every little good Boy and Girl should get by Heart'.

The proverb 'Early to bed and early to rise, makes a man healthy, wealthy and wise' was first collected in *Paroemiologia*, John Clarke, 1639. In juvenile literature: *The Fairing: or a Golden Toy for Children* (J. Newbery), 1765, '. . . Is the way to be healthy, wealthy and wise' [1767]; *The History of Little Goody Two-Shoes* (J. Newbery), ? Oliver Goldsmith, 1765, as previous [1766]; *Favourite Rhymes for the Nursery* (T. Nelson), 1892. The proverb 'The cock doth crow, To let you know, If you be wise, What time to rise', is in *The Road to Learning* (B. Hobday), 1818; *NR* (J. Catnach), c. 1830, ''Tis time to rise' [Hindley, 1878]; *A Short History of Birds and Beasts for the Amusement and Instruction of Children* (F. Houlston and Son), c. 1830; JOH, 1844; *Proverbs*, M. A. Denham, 1846. The nursery rhyme is in *Little Rhymes for Little Folks* (J. Harris), 1823, 'The cock crows in the morn, To tell us to rise, And that he who lies late Will never be wise: For heavy and stupid, He can't learn his book; so as long as he lives, Like a Dunce he must look'; *Children's Encyclopaedia*, 1908, 'Cocks crow in the morn', &c.; *Big Book of Mother Goose* (James and Jonathan Co., Wisconsin), 1946.

147

Cock

Cf. the German proverb 'Früh zu Bett und früh wieder auf, Macht gesund und reich in Kauf'; the French 'Se coucher et se lever tôt Rend sage, riche et dispos.' The Latin proverb learnt by Fitzherbert may also be found in *A Health to the Gentle Profession of Serving men*, 1598. Cf. also *Marginalia*, Gabriel Harvey, c. 1590, 'He that will thrive must rise at five; He that hath thriven may lie till seven; He that will never thriven may lie till eleven.' This is also in the *Countryman's New Commonwealth*, 1647, and was the first lesson taught by Goody Two-Shoes.

Parodies. The rhyme invites sophisticated mockery, e.g. George Ade, c. 1900, 'Early to bed and early to rise Will make you miss all the regular guys'; Dorothy Parker, c. 1936, 'Early to bed, and you will wish you were dead, Bed before eleven, nuts before seven'; James Thurber, 1939, 'Early to rise and early to bed makes a male healthy and wealthy and dead' [Stevenson's *Proverbs*, 1949].

107

> The cock's on the wood pile a-blowing his horn,
> The bull's in the barn a-threshing of corn,
> The maids in the meadows are making of hay,
> The ducks in the river are swimming away.

Two lines are found in a Wiltshire manuscript dated 1740:

> The bull in the barn, thrashing the corn,
> The cock on the dunghill is blowing his horn.
> I never saw such a sight since I was born!

In *The History of A Little Child Found under a Haycock*, printed by N. Coverly in Boston (1794), appears a much longer song:

> The girl's in the garden
> Cropping the leeks,
> The cat's in the cream-pot
> Up to her cheeks,
> The maid's in the kitchen
> Frying the fish,
> The dog's in the cubbard
> Licking the dish,
> The Duck's in the water
> Swimming away,
> The girl's in the meadow
> Raking the hay,
> The bull's in the barn
> Threshing the corn,
> Did you ever see the like
> Since you were born.

Cock

A Wiltshire MS, 1740 [*Folk-Lore*, 1901] / *GG's Garland*, 1810 / *March's Nursery Tales*, c. 1860 / *Children's Encyclopedia*, 1908, 'The cock's on the housetop'.

108

Cock a doodle doo!
My dame has lost her shoe,
My master's lost his fiddlestick,
And knows not what to do.

Almost three and a half centuries ago, when Elizabeth was Queen, this rhyme was the first miraculous utterance of a little girl who had no tongue. The story is told in a black-letter pamphlet entitled *The Most Crvell And Bloody Mvrther committed by an Inkeepers Wife, called Annis Dell, and her Sonne George Dell, Foure yeeres since*. The murder was of a three-year-old boy, Anthony James, at Bishop's Hatfield, in Hertfordshire. The deed appears to have been seen by his sister, then 'not much aboue foure', and the perpetrators, to disembarrass themselves of the witness, cut her tongue out of her head 'hard by the rootes'. What happened thereafter is obscure, but three years later she reappeared at Bishop's Hatfield on her own, was recognized as the sister of the murdered boy (whose body had been found), and was put in the charge of a foster mother. The contemporary account continues:

'This wench (as before is reported) being by the direction placed where she had reliefe; one day, some month before Christmasse last, going to play with the Goodwifes daughter where she soiourned in a Parke ioyning to Hatfield (commonly called the Kings Parke) as they were in sport together, a Cocke harde by them, fell a crowing, when the other Girle mocking the Cocke with these words,

Cocka doodle dooe,
Peggy hath lost her shooe,

and called to her, Besse, canst not thou doe so? When presently the Girle in the like manner did so; which, drawing the child into amazement, she presently left her, and ran home crying out as she went, the dumbe Girle Besse can speake, the dumbe Girle Besse can speake.'

This wonder, continues the account, 'caused all the towne to gather in flocks, & ran to meet her'. Finding the truth of it, the girl was straightway taken before the Justice, Sir Henry Butler, and she was able to recount the story of her brother's murder by Annis Dell and her son. At the subsequent trial there was much marvelling 'how it pleased God to reueale the offenders, by giuing speech to the tongueles Childe' and it was noted that when the jury looked into her mouth they saw nothing but a cavity. Apropos the rhyme, it is pertinent to add that a second contemporary account of the affair shows that to 'mocke the cockes' by giving words to their crowing was a common game with children at that time. JOH, who was unaware of the age of the rhyme, described

> Cock a doodle doo,
> My dame has lost her shoe,

as 'a very common nursery rhyme', which, indeed, it still is today.

The Most Crvell And Bloody Mvrther, 1606, two lines / *MG's Melody*, c. 1765 / *GG's Garland*, 1784 / *T Thumb's SB*, 1788 / *Juvenile Amusements*, 1797, 'My Master has lost his Fud'ling Cup' / *Vocal Harmony*, c. 1806 / *GG's Garland* (Lumsden), c. 1815, 'The Cat has lost her Fiddle-stick' / *NR for Children* (J. Fairburn), c. 1825 / *Rhymes for the Fireside* (T. Richardson), c. 1828 / *Nursery Poems* (J. G. Rusher), c. 1840 / JOH, 1842, three additional verses probably of more recent date, 'Cock a doodle doo, What is my dame to do? Till master finds his fiddling stick She'll dance without her shoe. Cock a doodle doo, My dame has found her shoe, And master's found his fiddling stick, Sing doodle doodle doo. Cock a doodle doo, My dame will dance with you, While master fiddles his fiddling stick, For dame and doodle doo' / JOH, 1853, fifth verse 'Cock a doodle doo! Dame has lost her shoe; Gone to bed and scratch'd her head, And can't tell what to do.' Also, from Yorkshire, 'Cock-a-doodle-do, My dad's gane to ploo; Mummy's lost her pudding-poke, And knows not what to do.'

Cf. 'Lock the dairy door', 'Cock, cock, cock, cock'.

*** The version in JOH, 1846, 'Cock a doodle do, The princess lost her shoe, Her Highness hopped, The fiddler stopped, Not knowing what to do,' is from a 'piece of ingenious levity' printed in *The European Magazine*, 18 Jan. 1782, after the Princess Royal had lost her shoe while dancing at Court.

109

> Cock Robin got up early
>   At the break of day,
> And went to Jenny's window
>   To sing a roundelay.
> He sang Cock Robin's love
>   To little Jenny Wren,
> And when he got unto the end
>   Then he began again.

These lines form the first and second verses, or sometimes the seventh and eighth, of the eleven in the tale of Cock Robin's marriage to Jenny

Cock Robin

Wren. It has been said that the publisher John Harris commissioned the writing of the story with the idea of making it a forerunner to the already well-established rhyme 'The death and burial of Cock Robin' (q.v.). Under his imprint *The Happy Courtship, Merry Marriage and Pic-nic Dinner, of Cock Robin and Jenny Wren. To which is added, Alas! The Doleful Death of the Bridegroom* was published 20 May 1806. The mating of the Robin with the Wren is in accordance with a centuries-old tradition. A manuscript of about 1400 contains an anonymous poem in which 'Robert redbreast and þe wrenne' are represented as lovers (Cambridge MS G. 4, 27); and the traditional saying, 'A robin and a wren, Are God Almighty's cock and hen', must be far older than its first recording in Grose's *Provincial Glossary* (1787).

The Happy Courtship ... (J. Harris), 1806. Story begins, "Twas once upon a time When Jenny Wren was young'. Other editions include: J. Kendrew, c. 1820; Grant and Griffith, c. 1845; Addey and Co., illus. Harrison Weir, c. 1860; M. Ward and Co., illus. Jessie Watkins, 1892 / JOH, 1853 / Correspondent, 1946.

110

Who killed Cock Robin?
I, said the Sparrow,
With my bow and arrow,
I killed Cock Robin.

Who saw him die?
I, said the Fly,
With my little eye,
I saw him die.

Who caught his blood?
I, said the Fish,
With my little dish,
I caught his blood.

Who'll make the shroud?
I, said the Beetle,
With my thread and needle,
I'll make the shroud.

Who'll dig his grave?
I, said the Owl,
With my pick and shovel,
I'll dig his grave.

Cock Robin

Who'll be the parson?
I, said the Rook,
With my little book,
I'll be the parson.

Who'll be the clerk?
I, said the Lark,
If it's not in the dark,
I'll be the clerk.

Who'll carry the link?
I, said the Linnet,
I'll fetch it in a minute,
I'll carry the link.

Who'll be chief mourner?
I, said the Dove,
I mourn for my love,
I'll be chief mourner.

Who'll carry the coffin?
I, said the Kite,
If it's not through the night,
I'll carry the coffin.

Who'll bear the pall?
We, said the Wren,
Both the cock and the hen,
We'll bear the pall.

Who'll sing a psalm?
I, said the Thrush,
As she sat on a bush,
I'll sing a psalm.

Who'll toll the bell?
I, said the Bull,
Because I can pull,
I'll toll the bell.

All the birds of the air
Fell a-sighing and a-sobbing,
When they heard the bell toll
For poor Cock Robin.

PLATE VI

a. 'The timid hare' in Darton's *Death and Burial of Cock Robin,* 1806

b. 'The cock crows in the morn' from Harris's *Little Rhymes for Little Folks,* c. 1824. Both Opie collection

Cock Robin

Two theories prevail about this rhyme. One is that it originates with the intrigues attending the downfall of Robert Walpole's ministry (1742); the other is that it is related to similar metrical pieces known in Europe and emanates from some early myth, the Norse tale of the death of Balder being suggested. Although unnoted by its advocates, the possibility that Walpole is portrayed is enhanced by the almost contemporaneous date of the rhyme's earliest known recording (c. 1744). On the other hand, indications, internal and external, suggest that the rhyme has some antiquity. In verse five *Owl* is rhymed with *shovel*. This looks as if the fourteenth-century *shouell*, *shoul*, or *showl* (still retained in dialect) was the correct reading. It has been mooted (*British Archaeological Association Journal*, 1944) that the rhyme is depicted in a fifteenth-century stained-glass window at Buckland Rectory, Gloucester. A bird is there shown pierced through the heart with an arrow, and the painter has given the bird the markings of a robin. The story is in the same vein as John Skelton's 'Phyllyp Sparowe' written about 1508, which was possibly suggested by Catullus' *Luctus in morte Passeris*. Equivalent rhymes current in Germany are not clear about whose death is lamented, but feature birds prominently as the mourners:

> Wer is dod?—Sporbrod.
> Wenn ehr ward begraben?
> Oerwermorgen abend, mit schüffeln un spaden
> Kukuk is de kulengräver,
> Adebor is de klokkentreder,
> Kiwitt is de schäuler,
> Mit all sin schwester un bräuder.

('Who is dead?—Breadless. When will he be buried?—On the eve of the day after tomorrow, with spades and with shovels. The Cuckoo is the gravedigger, the Stork is the bell-ringer, the Pee-wit acts as scholar, with all his sisters and brothers.') It may be taken as certain that in the thirteenth verse of the English rhyme the word *bull* does not mean the bovine creature depicted today, but is a shortened form of bullfinch (as Cowper's 'Bully'). This is in keeping with the other small creatures in the story, and it is depicted thus in some of the early *Cock Robin* chapbooks (of which there were very many). The two theories about this rhyme are by no means incompatible. It may well have been an old rhyme which was resurrected, or perhaps rewritten, in Walpole's time. In the following century (1821) it was returned to by Byron, mourning the death of Keats:

> Who kill'd John Keats?
> I says the Quarterly,
> So savage and Tartarly;
> 'Twas one of my feats.

Cock Robin

First four verses only: *T Thumb's PSB*, c. 1744; *A Little Play-Book*, c. 1746; *FT Thumb's LSB*, c. 1760; *T Thumb's SB*, 1788. Entire rhyme hereafter. *Cock Robin. A pretty gilded toy for either girl or boy. Suited to children of all ages* (R. Marshall), c. 1770 / *The Life, Death, and Burial of Cock Robin* (J. Marshall), advt. 1780 / *Cock Robin* (R. Christopher), c. 1782 / *The Death and Burial of Cock Robin* (Isaiah Thomas, Worcester, Mass.), 1787 [Worcester biblio.]; (Samuel Hall, Boston, Mass.), 1791 / *T Tit's SB*, c. 1790 / *The Death and Burial of Cock Robin; as taken from the original manuscript in the possession of Master Meanwell* (M. Morgan), c. 1797 / *An Elegy on the Death and Burial of Cock Robin* (H. and G. Mozley), 1800. Other early chap-book editions: John Evans, c. 1800; T. Evans, c. 1800; Broadbent, c. 1800; John Adams, Philadelphia, 1805 [Rosenbach]; J. Catnach, c. 1805, illus. T. Bewick [Hugo]; G. Martin, c. 1810; T. Batchelar, c. 1810; G. Ross, 1815. Toy books with coloured illus.: *Death and Burial of Cock Robin* (W. Darton), 1806; (D. Carvalho), c. 1825; *Cock Robin. A pretty painted toy* (J. Harris), 1819; *Life and Death of Cock Robin* (J. Bysh), c. 1820; *The Tragical History of the Death and Burial of Cock Robin* (E. Marshall), c. 1821. Later chapbooks: J. E. Evans, c. 1820; J. Kendrew, c. 1820; J. G. Rusher, c. 1820 and c. 1840; T. Brandard, c. 1820; Hodgson and Co., 1822; J. Ross, c. 1825; T. Richardson, c. 1830; W. Walker, c. 1830; Orlando Hodgson, c. 1835; J. S. Publishing, c. 1840; 'For the Booksellers', c. 1840 / *The Cocco-Robinad*, ? J. J. A. Boase, c. 1840 / JOH, 1849 / *Dean's Moveable Cock Robin*, c. 1850 / *Death of Cock Robin*, illus. Harrison Weir, c. 1853; (Darton and Co.), c. 1860, in oil colours, also 'Moveable' and 'Indestructible' editions [advts.]; illus. H. L. Stephens, 1864 / *Cock Robin*, Walter Crane, 1870 [Massé biblio.]; illus. E. Morant Cox, 1888 / *Who killed Cock Robin?*, illus. J. A. Shepherd, 1900 / *An Elegy on the Death and Burial of Cock Robin*, S. and M. Gutherie, 1932 / *Who killed Cock Robin?*, illus. Arnrid Johnstone, 1944; illus. colour photographs, Paul Henning, 1945.

***Some of the versions introduce animal mourners, deer, fox, toad, ass, lamb, goat, and a human in the person of a beadle.

Cf. *Volksthümliches aus Mecklenburg*, R. Wossidlo, 1885, as quote [Eckenstein] / *Chants populaires du Languedoc*, A. Montel et L. Lambert, 1880, 'Balalin, balalan, La campana de Sant Jan Quau la sona? Quau la dis?—Lou curat de Sant-Denis. Quau sona lous classes?—Lous quatre courpatrasses. Quau porta la caissa?—Lou cat ambe sa maissa. Quau porta lou doù?—Lou pèirou' (Ding, dong, the bell of St. John.—Who tolls it and who says [mass]?—The priest of St. Denis.—Who sounds the knell?—The four ravens—Who bears the coffin?—The cat in its maw.—Who wears mourning?—The partridge) [Eckenstein] / *Rimas Infantils*, Rodríguez Marín, 1882, 'Quién s'ha muerto?—Juan el tuerto. Quién lo llora?—La señora. Quién le canta?—Su garganta. Quién lo chilla?—La chiquilla' (Who has died? John the one eyed. Who bewails him? His lady love. Who sings for him? Her throat. Who cries for him? His child). 'En Italia—"Gianandrea [John Andrew]. Chi è morto? Beccotorto. Chi ha sonato la campanella? Quel birbon de pulcinella"' (Who has died? Beccotorto. Who has sounded the bell? That mischievous clown).

Parodies: *The Trial and Execution of the Sparrow for Killing Cock Robin* (S. Lingham), c. 1744 / *The Doleful Death of Poor Old Robin* (J. Harris), 1814 / *Who killed Cock Robin? A satirical tragedy or hieroglyphic prophecy on the Manchester Blot!!!* (John Cahuac), 1819.

Individual rhymes: 'Who killed John Keats?', Lord Byron, July 1821 / 'Who'll teach the Prince?' (Prince of Wales), *Punch*, 1843 / 'Who killed the Arabs?', *Weekly Dispatch*, 1884 / 'Who killed Home Rule?', *The People*, 1886 / 'Who killed Gladstone?', *Pall Mall Gazette*, 1886 / 'Who mashed Stella?', George Bernard Shaw to Mrs. Patrick Campbell, 1913 / 'Who'll kill inflation?', issued by His Majesty's Government, 1948.

Cock Robin

Curiosa: The Death and Burial of Cock Robin, set piece of 100 stuffed birds, made 1844–51 by Walter Potter, Bramber Museum, Sussex.

111

A little cock sparrow sat on a green tree,
And he chirruped, he chirruped, so merry was he.
A naughty boy came with his wee bow and arrow,
Says he, I will shoot this little cock sparrow;
His body will make me a nice little stew,
And his giblets will make me a little pie too.
Oh, no, said the sparrow, I won't make a stew,
So he clapped his wings and away he flew.

This appears to have been a popular song. In *The Manchester Iris* (25 October 1823), a London dandy was reported to have sung the following 'new song', although he could not recollect the tune:

A little cock sparrow sat up in a tree,
As merry, as merry, as merry could be;
A little boy came with his bow and arrow,
And said he would shoot this little cock sparrow.
Says the little cock sparrow you sh'ant shoot me,
He fluttereth his wings and away flew he.

NR from the Royal Collections (J. G. Rusher), c. 1840, version beginning 'Little Tom Twig bought A fine bow and arrow' / JOH, 1846 / *Baby's Bouquet*, 1879 / Baring-Gould, 1895 / *Big Book of Mother Goose* (James and Jonathan Co., Wisconsin), 1946.

112

Old King Cole
Was a merry old soul,
And a merry old soul was he;
He called for his pipe,
And he called for his bowl,
And he called for his fiddlers three.

Every fiddler, he had a fiddle,
And a very fine fiddle had he;

Cole

Twee tweedle dee, tweedle dee, went the fiddlers.
   Oh, there's none so rare
   As can compare
With King Cole and his fiddlers three.

One of the most popular nursery rhymes, sometimes being used as the title-rhyme of a collection, e.g. Byam Shaw's *Old King Cole's Book of Nursery Rhymes* (1901). The question of this merry monarch's identity was already a subject for speculation in the reign of Queen Anne. William King quoting the rhyme in his satire *Useful Transactions in Philosophy* (1708–9) mentions the 'Prince that Built Colchester', and a clothier of Reading named Cole-brook, and favours the Essex candidate. The words Dr. King knew were:

> Good King Cole,
> And he call'd for his Bowle,
> And he call'd for Fidler's three;
> And there was Fiddle, Fiddle,
> And twice Fiddle, Fiddle,
> For 'twas my Lady's Birth-day,
> Therefore we keep Holy-day
> And come to be merry.

The prince after whom Colchester is incorrectly supposed to have been named, is said to have lived in the third century, and to have ascended the throne of Britain on the death of Asclepiod. If the old chronicler Geoffrey of Monmouth (1147) could be trusted, which he cannot be, King Cole had a daughter who was well skilled in music, but we are not informed whether her father appreciated her art. William Chappell, the nineteenth-century authority on popular music, believed that the subject of the rhyme was the Reading clothier. He points out that Cole-brook was familiarly known as 'Old Cole'. His name became proverbial in the seventeenth century through Deloney's best-seller *The pleasant Historie of Thomas of Reading: or, The Sixe worthie Yeomen of the West* (c. 1598). The merchant, according to this story, was a man of vast wealth, maintaining 140 menial servants in his house as well as 300 poor people who worked for him. In a song 'Kingship' might well be bestowed on such a man. Among Elizabethan dramatists there was some special significance, now difficult to recover, in the name 'Old Cole'; it figures, for example, in Dekker's *Satiro-mastix* (1602) and John Marston's *The Malcontent* (1604). The song appears to have been popular throughout the eighteenth century. Burns, who contributed the version in the *Musical Museum*, wrote to Johnson, 'I have met with many different sets of the tune & words'. The popularity of the song in Scotland may be accounted for by Sir Walter

Scott's theory that 'Auld King Coul' was the fabled father of the giant Fyn M'Coule.

Useful Transactions in Philosophy, William King, 1708–9 / Herd MS, 1776, 'Old King Cowl was a jolly old soul, And a jolly old soul was he, Old King Coul he had a brown bowl, And they brought him in fidlers three, And every fiddler was a very good fiddler, And a very good fiddler was he. Fidell-didell, fidell-didell, with the fidlers three: And there's no a lass in all Scotland Compared to our sweet Margarie'; four verses follow / *Musical Museum*, 1797, 'Our auld King Coul' / *Vocal Harmony*, c. 1806, 'Old King Cole was a merry old soul, And a merry old soul was he; He called for his bottle and he called for his pipe, And he called for his music masters three: There was tootle, tootle, tootle, says the piper, Drum, a drum, a drum, says the drummer, Feedle, feedle, feedle, says the fidler; There never was a man in merry Scotland, That was half so happy as he' / *Old King Cole or Harlequin and Fidlers Three* (Ducombe), c. 1820 [Gumuchian] / *Universal Songster*, 1825 / JOH, 1842 / Mason, 1877 / *Mother Goose*, Arthur Rackham, 1913. In Gay's opera *Achilles*, 1733, a song is directed to be sung to the air 'Old King Cole'.

Cf. 'Four-and-twenty Fiddlers all in a Row' in *Wit and Mirth*, 1699, which has much in common.

Parodies of 'Old King Cole' are fairly common, particularly with puns on 'Cole', e.g. Charles Mackay's fine song 'Old King Coal' in *Songs for Music*, 1856. During the 1914–18 War 'There's none so rare as can compare with Kitchener's New Armee' was popular with British troops.

*** William Oldisworth's *The Delightful Adventures of Honest John Cole, That Merry Old Soul*, 1732, has no connexion with the rhyme.

113

There were three cooks of Colebrook,
And they fell out with our cook;
And all was for a pudding he took
From the three cooks of Colebrook.

This possible inspiration to the Knave of Hearts was 'collected and published' by John Hilton, who also wrote the tune, in 1658. Originally there were twelve lines, not altogether graceful. The last four went:

And they fell all on our Cook,
And beat him sore that he did look
As black as did the pudding he took
From one of the Cooks of Colebrook.

Catch that Catch can, John Hilton, 1658 / *Merry Drollery*, 1661 / *Windsor Drollery*, J. M., 1672 / *Musical Companion*, 1673 / JOH, 1849 / Correspondent, 1947.
Colebrook, now Colnbrook.

114

> Come when you're called,
> Do as you're bid,
> Shut the door after you,
> Never be chid.

The advice seems originally to have been directed at servants. James Howell, recommending a footman in 1628, wrote, 'There be some things in him that answers for his Waggeries; he will come when you call him, go when you bid him, and Shut the Door after him'. Swift, in *Polite Conversation* a century later, enjoined, 'A good servant must always come when he's called, do what he's bid, and shut the door after him.' James Kelly in Scotland (1721) who knew the rhyme-form, gave it a like application:

> Speak when you're spoken to, do what you're bidden,
> Come when you're called, and you'll not be chidden.

He describes this as 'A cant of mistresses to their maid servants.' The exhortation first seems to have been directed at children in *A Pretty Book for Children*, published by Benjamin Collins of Salisbury c. 1743: 'Master Meanwell comes when he is called, does as he is bid, and shuts the door after him, and by that means has gained the good will of everybody.'

Scottish Proverbs, James Kelly, 1721, as quote, and apparently still known in Scotland (it is in, for example, *Sandy Candy and other Scottish Nursery Rhymes*, 1948) / *Early Lessons*, 1801, and *The Contrast*, 1804, both by Maria Edgeworth, versions differ slightly from each other / *The Royal Fabulist* (G. Ross), 1815, is described as 'A present for all those good Boys and Girls who behave according to the following Rules—That is Do as they are Bid, Come when they are Called, and Shut the door after them' / JOH, 1853, 'Speak when you're spoken to, Come when one call, Shut the door after you, And turn to the wall' / *Mother Goose*, Arthur Rackham, 1913.

115

> A cow and a calf,
> An ox and a half,
> Forty good shillings and three;
> Is that not enough tocher
> For a shoemaker's daughter,
> A bonny lass with a black e'e?

Cow

This is one of two verses of a humorous old song 'Jumpin' John' which Burns dressed up and contributed to *The Scot's Musical Museum*:

> Her Daddie forbad, her Minnie forbad,
>   Forbidden she wadna be:
> She wadna trow't, the browst she brew'd
>   Wad taste sae bitterlie.

>   The lang lad they ca' jumpin John
>   Beguil'd the bonie lassie,
>   The lang lad they ca' jumpin John
>   Beguil'd the bonie lassie.

> A cow and a cauf, a yowe and a hauf,
>   And thretty gude shillins and three;
> A vera gude tocher, a cotter-man's dochter,
>   The lass wi' the bonie black e'e.
>   The lang lad &c.

The tune 'Jumpin' John; or Joan's Placket' was printed in Playford's *Dancing Master* (1698), and is probably that referred to by Pepys (22 June 1667) as 'Joan's placket is torn'. The line 'A cow and a calf, an ox and a half' also occurs in the rhyme 'Robin the Bobbin, the big-bellied Ben' (q.v.).

Musical Museum, 1788 / *Songs for the Nursery*, 1805 / *Only True MG Melodies*, c. 1843 / JOH, 1853 / *Mother Goose's NR*, L. E. Walter, 1924.

116

> Cushy cow, bonny, let down thy milk,
> And I will give thee a gown of silk;
> A gown of silk and a silver tee,
> If thou wilt let down thy milk to me.

This charm used by milkmaids to induce refractory or bewitched cows to give their milk had degenerated into a nursery rhyme by the beginning of the nineteenth century. Cushy (sometimes pronounced *cuoshy*) is a pet name for a cow, and the tee is a cow-tie. That country women employed charms to make the cow they were milking 'let down her milk' is referred to by a writer in 1631.

Songs for the Nursery, 1805 / *Collection of Nursery Songs* (J. Fairburn), c. 1825 / Chambers, 1826, 'Bonnie ladye, let doon yere milk, And I'll gi'e you a goon o' silk; A goon o'silk and a ball o' twine,—Bonnie ladye, yere milk's no mine' / JOH, 1843 / *Folk-Lore*, 1886 / Baring-Gould, 1895 / *Book of NR*, Enid Marx, 1939, 'Cush cow, beauty, let down thy milk.'

117

Make three-fourths of a cross,
And a circle complete,
And let two semi-circles
On a perpendicular meet;
Next add a triangle
That stands on two feet;
Next two semi-circles
And a circle complete.

RIDDLE. The solution is definitely T-O-B-A-C-C-O, although an ingenious reader of the *Daily Mirror* (1945) managed to make the answer a picture of a bicycle.

A New Collection of Enigmas, 1791 / *Mince Pies for Christmas* (Tabart and Co.), 1804 / MS collection, 'Riddles, Jokes and Charades', c. 1810 (Opie collection) / *Riddles, Charades, & Conundrums*, 1824 / JOH, 1846 / *Folk-Lore from Nova Scotia*, A. H. Fauset, 1931.

118

Cross-patch,
Draw the latch,
Sit by the fire and spin;
Take a cup,
And drink it up,
Then call your neighbours in.

Lines to conciliate a sulky child, also common as a taunt. *Cross-patch*, originally 'peevish fool'.

MG's Melody, c. 1765 / *GG's Garland*, 1784 / *Vocal Harmony*, c. 1806 / NR (T. Richardson), c. 1830 / JOH, 1842 / *Only True MG Melodies*, c. 1843 / In *Favourite Rhymes and Riddles*, 1892, last line is moralized, 'And let good temper in'.

119

Catch him, crow! carry him, kite!
Take him away till the apples are ripe;

Crow

When they are ripe and ready to fall,
Here comes baby, apples, and all.

Sung when playing with baby in arms.

JOH, 1844 / *Mother Goose's NR*, L. E. Walter, 1924, 'Home comes Johnny, apples
and all'.

120

There was an old crow
Sat upon a clod;
That's the end of my song.
That's odd.

Words for the ungifted singer when asked to perform in company. JOH
(1844) describes it as 'an ancient Suffolk song'. A rather more forceful version was collected by a contributor to *Folk-Lore* (1924):

There was a crow sat on a clod,
And now I've finished my sermon, thank God!

121

The cuckoo is a merry bird,
She sings as she flies;
She brings us good tidings,
And tells us no lies.

She sucks little birds' eggs
To make her voice clear,
That she may sing Cuckoo!
Three months in the year.

Williams, at the beginning of the present century, collected four further
verses:

The cuckoo is a lazy bird,
She never builds a nest,
She makes herself busy
By singing to the rest.

Cuckoo

She never hatches her own young,
  And that we all know,
But leaves it for some other bird
  While she cries 'Cuckoo'.

And when her time is come
  Her voice we no longer hear,
And where she goes we do not know
  Until another year.

The cuckoo comes in April,
  She sings a song in May,
In June she beats upon the drum,
  And then she'll fly away.

The cuckoo is said to 'beat the drum' when it falters and cries 'Cuck-cuck-cuck' without the final syllable.

The text lines appear as a verse in a song, 'The Forsaken Lover', which was printed in *The Merry Gentleman's Companion: being a choice Collection of the newest and most favourite Songs: Sung this Season at the Play-houses, Public-Gardens and other Places of Diversion, in and about the City of London* (c. 1780):

A walking, a talking, and a walking was I,
To meet my sweet Billy, he'll come by and by
To meet him in the meadows is all my delight
A walking and a talking from morning till night.

Meeting is a pleasure but parting is a grief,
And an inconstant lover is worse than a thief
A thief can but rob me and take what I have,
But an inconstant lover sends me to my grave.

The grave it will rot me and turn me to dust,
But an inconstant lover no maiden can trust
They'll kiss you and they'll court you, poor girls to deceive,
There's not one in twenty that you can believe.

The Cuckoo's a fine bird, she sings where she flies,
She brings us good tidings and tells me no lies,
She sucks of sweet flowers to make her voice clear,
The more she sings cuckoo, the summer draws near.

Come all ye pretty maidens whatever ye be,
Don't settle your love on a sycamore tree,
The leaf it will wither, and the root it will die,
And if I'm forsaken I know not for why.

Cuckoo

This song, which may *not* have been new in c. 1780, has had a long life as a folk-song, usually under the title of 'The Cuckoo'. Some verses from it are found in the American folk song 'The Top of Old Smokey' (see A. L. Lloyd, *Corn on the Cob*, 1945).

Gentleman's Magazine, 1796 / *Songs for the Nursery*, 1805 / *GG's Garland* (Lumsden), c. 1815 / *NR for Children* (J. Fairburn), c. 1825, 'And never cries Cuckoo! Till spring time of the year' / Chambers, 1842, 'The cuckoo's a fine bird, He sings as he flies ... And when he sings cuckoo! The summer is near' / JOH, 1844 / Chambers, 1847, differs from previous edition, 'He drinks the cold water To keep his voice clear; And he'll come again in the spring of the year' / *Garland of Country Songs*, S. Baring-Gould, 1895 / *Folk-Songs from Somerset*, Cecil Sharp, 1906, 'O the cuckoo is a pretty bird', four verses / *Folk-Song*, 1907 and 1918 / *Folk-Lore*, 1909, learnt from a manservant born 1752 / Williams, 1923 / Correspondent, 1949, '... And when he sings cuckoo summer is here. Cuckoo in April, Cuckoo in May, Cuckoo in June, and then he flies away.'

122

Curly locks, Curly locks,
  Wilt thou be mine?
Thou shalt not wash dishes
  Nor yet feed the swine,
But sit on a cushion
  And sew a fine seam,
And feed upon strawberries,
  Sugar and cream.

According to an M.G.M. 'documentary' the original Curly locks of this rhyme was Charles II. No documentation brought forward however.

Infant Institutes, 1797, 'Pussy cat, pussy cat, Wilt thou be mine?' / *Newest Christmas Box*, c. 1797 / *Songs for the Nursery*, 1805, 'Bonny lass! Bonny lass!' / Douce MS, c. 1805 / *GG's Garland*, 1810 / Rimbault, 1846 / JOH, 1853, 'Cumberland courtship', 'Bonny lass, canny lass, wilta be mine?' / *Folk-Lore*, 1893 / Gomme, 1894, gives as a dramatic singing game.

123

Dance to your daddy,
  My little babby,
Dance to your daddy, my little lamb;

Daddy

You shall have a fishy
In a little dishy,
You shall have a fishy when the boat comes in.

A dandling song known particularly in Scotland and the north country,
sometimes (as in 1842) with the additional verse,

And ye'll get a coatie,
And a pair o' breekies—
Ye'll get a whippie and a supple Tam!

The last line has also been heard as,

An' a *whirligiggie* an' a supple Tam.

A 'supple Tam' is the jointed toy, worked with strings, which in England
is known as a Jumping Jack. JOH adds,

Baby shall have an apple,
Baby shall have a plum,
Baby shall have a rattle,
When Daddy comes home.

In Fordyce's *Newcastle Song Book* it is given, to a delightful tune, as the
refrain of a five-verse ditty 'The Little Fishy' by William Watson.

Vocal Harmony, c. 1806, begins 'Sing to your mammy, my pretty lammy' / *Fordyce's
Newcastle Song Book*, 1842, William Watson's song begins, 'Come here my little
Jackey, Now I've smoked my backey, Let's have a bit of crackey Till the boat
comes in. Dance to thy daddy, sing to thy mammy, Dance to thy daddy, to thy
mammy sing; Thou shalt have a fishy on a little dishy, Thou shalt have a fishy
when the boat comes in' / Chambers, 1842 / JOH, 1844; and 1846 as quote, also similar verse, as separate rhyme, 'You shall have an apple, You shall have a plum, You
shall have a rattle-basket, When your dad comes home' / Mason, 1877, 'Dance to
thy minnie, My bonnie hinnie' / *Folk-Lore*, 1886, two Scottish versions; 1914, a
third version / Kidson, 1904 / *Rymour Club*, 1928, 'An' ye'll get a slicie o' a dishie
nicey, An' a sweetie wiggie, an' a mutton ham' / *My Very First Mother Goose*, Iona
Opie, illus. Rosemary Wells, 1996.

124

I'll tell my own daddy, when he comes home,
What little good work my mammy has done;
She has earned a penny and spent a groat,
And burnt a hole in the child's new coat.

GG's Garland, 1784 / *Songs for the Nursery*, 1805 / JOH, 1843 / *Olney and the
Lacemakers*, E. Wilson, 1864, remembered from childhood by an old lacemaker,

Daddy

'I'll tell my mother when I get home What a sad thing my father's done; He earned a penny and spent a groat, Burned a hole in his holiday coat.' The English groat coined in 1351–2 was made equal to four pence. It ceased to be issued for circulation in 1662.

125

Daffy-down-dilly is new come to town,
With a yellow petticoat, and a green gown.

'Daffy-down-dilly', a playful expansion of daffadilly or daffodil, used by Tusser (1573), is still a name for the yellow daffodil in dialect forms.

Songs for the Nursery, 1805 / *Mother Goose's Melodies*, 1833, '... with a petticoat green, and a bright yellow gown, And her white blossoms are peeping around' / JOH, 1844 / *Mother Goose*, Kate Greenaway, 1881.

126

Dame, get up and bake your pies,
Bake your pies, bake your pies;
Dame, get up and bake your pies,
On Christmas day in the morning.

Dame, what makes your maidens lie,
Maidens lie, maidens lie;
Dame, what makes your maidens lie,
On Christmas day in the morning?

Dame, what makes your ducks to die,
Ducks to die, ducks to die;
Dame, what makes your ducks to die,
On Christmas day in the morning?

Their wings are cut and they cannot fly,
Cannot fly, cannot fly;
Their wings are cut and they cannot fly,
On Christmas day in the morning.

By the late eighteenth century this song was widely scattered and had been cast in several local moulds. The Shakespearian commentator Whiter (1794) in a note on Jacques's song,

Dame

Ducdame, ducdame, ducdame;
Here shall he see
Gross fools as he
An if he will come to me,

submits that the ambiguous 'Ducdame' is 'the usual cry of the Dame to gather her ducks about her'. He quotes George Steevens (1778) who recalled the occasion when the Shakespearian scholar Dr. Farmer heard a stanza having 'an odd coincidence with the ditty of Jacques'. Dr. Farmer told him that, being at a house not far from Cambridge when news was brought of a hen-roost being robbed, a facetious old squire who was present immediately sang the following lines:

Dame, what makes your Ducks to die?
duck, duck, duck.
Dame, what makes your chicks to cry?
chuck, chuck, chuck.

Whiter added two further verses, which he said were common in Cambridgeshire and Norfolk:

Dame, what makes your Ducks to die?
What the pize ails 'em, what the pize ails 'em,
They kick up their heels and there they lie,
What the pize ails 'em now?

Heigh, Ho! Heigh, Ho!
Dame, what ails your Ducks to die?
What a pize ails 'em, what a pize ails 'em?
Heigh, Ho! Heigh, Ho!
Dame, what ails your Ducks to die?
Eating o' Pollywigs, eating o' Pollywigs (i.e. Tadpoles)
Heigh, Ho! Heigh, Ho!

A writer to the *Gentleman's Magazine* in 1823 remembered a Christmas carol beginning,

Dame, get up and bake your pies,
On Christmas day in the morning,

to which the response was,

London Bridge is fallen down
On Christmas day in the morning.

'Why the falling of London Bridge should form part of a Christmas Carol at Newcastle-upon-Tyne', wrote the correspondent, 'I am at a loss to know'.

Dame

Notes on Shakespeare, George Steevens, 1778 [1821] / *Specimen of a Commentary on Shakespeare*, Walter Whiter, 1794 / *Suffolk Garland* (John Raw), 1818, augmented version of Whiter's dialect verses, five verses in all / *Gentleman's Magazine*, 1823 / *Bishoprick Garland*, Sir Cuthbert Sharp, 1834, two verses from Durham, beginning 'Maids get up and bake your pies' and 'See the ships all sailing by'; two other verses, 'Dame what makes your ducks to die?' and 'You let your lazy maidens lie' he considered old, though only a paraphrase of the former / JOH, 1842 / *Baby's Opera*, 1877 / Baring-Gould, 1895 / *Tailor of Gloucester*, Beatrix Potter, 1903, On Christmas morning, 'first and loudest the cocks cried out: "Dame, get up, and bake your pies!" "Oh, dilly, dilly, dilly!" sighed Simpkin' / Kidson, 1904, given to a version of the Elizabethan air 'Greensleeves' mentioned by Shakespeare / *Folk-Song*, 1907 and 1924 / *Big Book of Mother Goose* (James and Jonathan Co., Wisconsin), 1946.
    Cf. 'I saw three ships come sailing by'.

127

I had a little pony,
  His name was Dapple Gray;
I lent him to a lady
  To ride a mile away.
She whipped him, she slashed him,
  She rode him through the mire;
I would not lend my pony now,
  For all the lady's hire.

In a manuscript written about 1630 JOH says he found:

I had a little bonny nagg
  His name was Dapple Gray;
And he would bring me to an ale-house
  A mile out of my way.

The present rhyme may be stemmed from this.

Poetical Alphabet (Henry Mozley and Sons), c. 1825 / *NR for Children* (J. Fairburn), c. 1825, 'Apple Gray' / *NR* (T. Richardson), c. 1830; (no imprint? W. Walker), c. 1830 / *Nursery Poems* (J. G. Rusher), c. 1840 / Chambers, 1842 / JOH, 1842 and 1849.
    Cf. 'I had a little hobby-horse'.

128

Whistle, daughter, whistle,
  And you shall have a sheep.

Daughter

Mother, I cannot whistle,
  Neither can I sleep.

Whistle, daughter, whistle,
  And you shall have a cow.
Mother, I cannot whistle,
  Neither know I how.

Whistle, daughter, whistle,
  And you shall have a man.
Mother, I cannot whistle,
  But I'll do the best I can.

The above is reported in *Notes & Queries* (1868). In *Folk-Lore* (1901) the following is stated to be from a manuscript dated 1740:

I prithee, Molly, whistle,
  And you shall have a cow.
I fear I cannot whistle,
  I cannot whistle now.

I prithee, Molly, whistle,
  And you shall have a man.
I fear I cannot whistle,
  But I'll whistle as well as I can.

Newell (1883) gives an American rendering:

Whistle, daughter, whistle,
And I'll give you a sheep.
—Mother, I'm asleep.

Whistle, daughter, whistle,
And I'll give you a cow.
—Mother, I don't know how.

Whistle, daughter, whistle,
And I'll give you a man.
—Mother, now I can!

This is probably nearer the original than the two previous versions. Newell says that the song must be ancient, 'for it is identical with a German, Flemish, and French round of the 15th and 16th century, in which a nun (or monk) is tempted to dance by similar offers'.

A Wiltshire MS, 1740 [*Folk-Lore*, 1901] / Chambers, 1826, three verses, the third being 'Whistle, whistle, auld wife, And ye'se get a man. Wheep, whaup, quo' the wife; I'll whistle as I can' / JOH, 1846 / *N & Q*, 1868 / Newell, 1883 / *Folk Songs from Somerset*, Cecil Sharp, 1906, six verses: verse 3, 'Whistle, daughter, whistle, And you shall have

Daughter

a sleep, I cannot whistle, mother, But sadly I can weep. My single life does grieve me, That fills my heart with fear; For it is a burden, a heavy burden, 'Tis more than I can bear'; verse 6, 'Whistle, daughter, whistle, And I'll wed you to a man. (she whistles) You see how well I can, Fye, fye, you saucy jade, I will bring your courage down; Take off your silk and satin Put on your working gown' / *Scottish NR*, R. T. MacLennan, 1909 / *Rymour Club*, 1911.

129

As I was going to Derby,
　　Upon a market day,
I met the finest ram, sir,
　　That ever was fed on hay.

This ram was fat behind, sir,
　　This ram was fat before,
This ram was ten yards high, sir,
　　Indeed he was no more.

The wool upon his back, sir,
　　Reached up unto the sky,
The eagles build their nests there,
　　For I heard the young ones cry.

The space between the horns, sir,
　　Was as far as man could reach,
And there they built a pulpit,
　　But no-one in it preached.

This ram had four legs to walk upon,
　　This ram had four legs to stand,
And every leg he had, sir,
　　Stood on an acre of land.

Now the man that fed the ram, sir,
　　He fed him twice a day,
And each time that he fed him, sir,
　　He ate a rick of hay.

The man that killed this ram, sir,
　　Was up to his knees in blood,
And the boy that held the pail, sir,
　　Was carried away in the flood.

Derby

Indeed, sir, it's the truth, sir,
For I never was taught to lie,
And if you go to Derby, sir,
You may eat a bit of the pie.

This extravagant chronicle, which has been current for certainly two centuries, is capable of infinite expansion, each new verse being an attempt to outdo the last. Apparently the song has always had many verses, for the Rev. Henry Cantrill, vicar of St. Alkmund's Church, Derby, said at the end of a letter to his son (June, 1739), 'And thus I conclude this long story; almost as long a tale as that of the Derby Ram'. Rams have become closely associated with Derby; a ram is incorporated in the Borough coat-of-arms, and in 1855 a fine ram was attached to the staff of the first Regiment of Derbyshire Militia. Extolling the Great Derby Ram, however, is by no means confined to the county limits. The Manchester raconteur, 'Geoffry Gimcrack', set down thirteen verses in 1833 from his great-grandmother's recitation. 'The Ram of Diram' was one of the ballads sung by 'Mussel mou'd Charlie', the celebrated peripatetic ballad-singer of Aberdeen, who lived to be 105. The song is also well established in Canada and the United States. A version has been handed down from a Cape Cod sailor who learnt it when serving in the 1812–15 War. George Washington is said to have known it. Cecil Sharp collected it in the Appalachian mountains. And it was in the Boston *Mother Goose's Melodies* (c. 1843) that the song was first acknowledged to be nursery property.

Ballad Book, the ballads of Charles Lesly ['Mussel mou'd Charlie'], ed. G. R. Kinloch, 1827, six verses, the first being 'As I cam in by Diram, Upon a sunshine day, I there did meet a ram, Sir, He was baith gallant and gay'; chorus 'And a hech, hey, a-Diram, A-Diram, a-Dandalee; He was the gallantest ram, Sir, That ere mine eyes did see' / *Gimcrackiana*, 'Geoffry Gimcrack' [J. S. Gregson], 1833, thirteen verses similar to text and continuing the story beyond the ram's death, e.g. 'The little boys of Darby They came to beg his eyes, To roll about the streets Sir, They being of football's size' / *Only True MG Melodies*, c. 1843, 'As I was going to Derby upon a market day, I met the finest ram, sir, that ever fed on hay; On hay, on hay, on hay— I met the finest ram, sir, that ever fed on hay', and three more verses, beginning 'This ram was fat behind, sir, this ram was fat before', 'The horns grew on his head, sir, they were so wondrous high', and 'The tail grew on his back, sir, was six yards and an ell' / *N & Q*, 1850, 'very popular in my school-boy days' / *Popular Nursery Tales and Rhymes* (Routledge), 1859, similar to c. 1843 / *Ballads and Songs of Derbyshire*, L. Jewitt, 1867, similar to text, fifteen verses with chorus, 'Daddle-i-day, daddle-i-day, Fal-de-ral, fal-de-ral, daddle-i-day' / *N & Q*, 1891, many variants / *English County Songs*, L. E. Broadwood, 1893, three versions / *Household Tales*, S. O. Addy, 1895, sung by Mummers / *N & Q*, 1904, correspondent obtained a full-blooded version from the nephew of a Cape Cod sailor; includes 'The horns upon this ram, sir, they reached up to the moon; A man went up them in January and didn't come down till June', and last verse 'The man that owned this ram, sir, was counted very rich, But the one that made this song was a lying son of a bitch' / *Nursery Songs from the Appalachian Mountains*, Cecil Sharp, 1923, seven verses, including

Derby

'The wool upon this ram's tail Was very fine and thin, Took all the girls in Derby Town Full seven years to spin', and refrain 'Riddle to my rye, riddle to my rye' / Williams, 1923, chorus, 'That's a lie, that's a lie, That's a tid i fa la lie' / *Derby N & Q*, 1932.

130

A little old man of Derby,
How do you think he served me?
He took away my bread and cheese,
And that is how he served me.

Douce MS, c. 1815 / JOH, 1844.

131

Dickery, dickery, dare,
The pig flew up in the air;
The man in brown soon brought him down,
Dickery, dickery, dare.

Second Royal Infant Opera, O. B. Dussek, 1842, 'Clickety, Clickety clare, The pig he flew in the air, The man in brown, soon fetch'd him down, Clickety, Clickety clare' / JOH, 1844 / Bolton, 1888, from Connecticut / *Counting Out*, Carl Withers, 1946.

132

Two little dicky birds,
Sitting on a wall;
One named Peter,
The other named Paul.
Fly away, Peter!
Fly away, Paul!
Come back, Peter!
Come back, Paul!

Infant amusement. A piece of stamp paper is stuck on to each index finger, one being dubbed 'Peter', the other 'Paul'. The two fingers are placed at the edge of a table. On the command 'fly away' the appropriate hand is whipped over the shoulder and instantly returned with the middle finger substituted for the index so that the stamp paper is concealed. On the command 'come back' the reverse operation takes place, and the stamp paper reappears. This sleight of hand has been mystifying the very young for at least two centuries. It is on record that Goldsmith used to amuse Lætitia-Matilda Hawkins with it when she was small. Originally the birds' names were Jack and Jill; they are given thus c. 1765:

> There were two blackbirds
> Sat upon a hill,
> The one was nam'd Jack,
> The other nam'd Gill;
> Fly away Jack,
> Fly away Gill,
> Come again Jack,
> Come again Gill.

It seems probable that the pagan 'Jack and Jill' were replaced by the names of the two apostles during the nineteenth century when people were very conscious of such things. Of the remoter history of this rhyme, both Eckenstein and S. O. Addy believe that it had supernatural significance.

MG's Melody, c. 1765 / *Nancy Cock's PSB*, c. 1780 / *Christmas Box*, vol. ii, 1798 / *Vocal Harmony*, c. 1806 / *GG's Garland*, 1810 / *Nurse Lovechild's DFN*, c. 1830 / *Girl's Own Book*, Mrs. Child, 1831, game 'Fly away Jack' described [1832] / *Cries of Banbury and London* (J. G. Rusher), c. 1843, first four lines, then, 'When Jack flew away, Around the mill, Then Jack did return to Mistress Jill' / *Household Tales*, S. O. Addy, 1895 / *Rymour Club*, 1911.

133

> Little Dicky Dilver
> Had a wife of silver;
> He took a stick and broke her back
> And sold her to the miller;
> The miller wouldn't have her
> So he threw her in the river.

The brief story of Dicky Dilver and his wife, collected by JOH in 1844, would always have seemed to be a straightforward, if violent, nursery rhyme, had it not been that the American poet James Russell Lowell, shortly before he died, obtained the following ballad in Maine:

Dicky Dilver

Little Dickey Diller
Had a wife of siller;
He took a stick and broke her back,
And sent her to the miller.

The miller with his stone dish
Sent her unto Uncle Fish.

Uncle Fish, the good shoemaker,
Sent her unto John the baker.

John the baker, with his ten men,
Sent her unto Mistress Wren.

Mistress Wren, with grief and pain,
Sent her to the Queen of Spain.

The Queen of Spain, that woman of sin
Opened the door and let her in.

This appears to relate to the fortunes of a grain of wheat, personified as the wife of the farmer.

JOH, 1844 / *American Folk-Lore*, 1890 / *Mother Goose's NR*, L. E. Walter, 1924 / The pantomime *Little Dicky Dilver with his Stick of Silver; or, Harlequin Pretty Prince Pretty Boy and the Three Comical Cats* by E. L. Blanchard and T. L. Greenwood, was performed in 1871.

134

Ding, dong, bell,
Pussy's in the well.
Who put her in?
Little Johnny Green.
Who pulled her out?
Little Tommy Stout.
What a naughty boy was that,
To try to drown poor pussy cat,
Who never did him any harm,
And killed the mice in his father's barn.

Very common in the present day, this rhyme appears to have had a long history. In 1580 John Lant, an organist of Winchester Cathedral, collected:

Ding, Dong, Bell

Jacke boy, ho boy newes,
the cat is in the well,
let us ring now for her Knell,
ding dong ding dong Bell.

This canon was later printed in *Pammelia, Musicks Miscellanie*, 1609, and appears to be alluded to in *The Taming of the Shrew* (IV. i), while 'Ding, dong, bell' is the burden of songs in *The Merchant of Venice* (III. ii) and *The Tempest* (I. ii). Alternative names for the malevolent Johnny Green (c. 1765) are Tommy o'Linne (1797) and Tommy Quin (c. 1840). The name Tommy o'Linne may come from Tom a lin or Tommy o' Lin, a name which in the sixteenth century belonged to the hero of a further nursery song, 'Tom a lin and his wife, and his wiues mother' (q.v.). Nursery rhyme reformers have recently taken particular objection to 'Ding, dong, bell', claiming that children have been known to throw cats into ponds through the direct influence of this rhyme.

MG's Melody, c. 1765 / *GG's Garland*, 1784 / *T Tit's SB*, c. 1790 / *Infant Institutes*, 1797 / *Songs for the Nursery*, 1805 / *Vocal Harmony*, c. 1806 / *Children's Tales or Infant Prattle*, 1818, 'Tom Snout' / JOH, 1842, gives 'Dog with long snout' or 'Little Johnny Grout' as the rescuer / Ford, 1904, 'Ding dong, bell rang, Cattie's in the well, man. Fa' dang her in, man? Jean and Sandy Din, man. Fa' took her out, man? Me and Willie Cout, man. A' them that kent her When she was alive, Come to the burialie Between four and five.'

Reformed rhyme: *New Nursery Rhymes for Old*, Geoffrey Hall, 1949, 'Ding dong bell, Pussy's at the well. Who took her there? Little Johnny Hare. Who'll bring her in? Little Tommy Thin. What a jolly boy was that To get some milk for pussy cat, Who ne'er did any harm, But played with the mice in his father's barn.'

135

Dingle dingle doosey,
The cat's in the well,
The dog's away to Bellingen
To buy the bairn a bell.

'A dingle doosey (or dousie)', says Mactaggart, 'is a piece of wood burned red at one end as a toy for children. The mother will whirl round the ignited stick very fast, when the eye, by following it, seems to see a beautiful red circle. She accompanies this pleasant show to her bairns with the following rhyme:

Dingle dingle-dousie,
The cat's a' lousy:
Dingle dingle-dousie,
The dog's a' fleas.

Dingle Doosey

Dingle dingle-dousie,
Be crouse ay, be crouse ay;
Dingle dingle-dousie,
Ye'se hae a brose o' pease, &c.'

Douce MS, c. 1805 / GG's Garland, 1810 / Gallovidian Encyclopedia, J. Mactaggart, 1824 [1867] / Chambers, 1842, additional quatrain, 'Greet, greet, bairnie, And ye'll get a bell; If ye dinna greet, bairnie, I'll keep it to mysel'!' / JOH, 1842 / Ford, 1904.
    Cf. Gomme, 1898, for same game, 'Ringie, ringie, Red Belt, rides wi' the king, Nae a penny in 's purse t' buy a gold ring.'

136

There was a man, and his name was Dob,
And he had a wife, and her name was Mob,
And he had a dog, and he called it Cob,
And she had a cat, called Chitterabob.
    Cob, says Dob,
    Chitterabob, says Mob.
    Cob was Dob's dog,
    Chitterabob Mob's cat.

Tongue-twister. The earliest recording appears to be that in a scrap book dating from before 1817, reported in *Folk-Lore* (1881). In Miss Leslie's *Girl's Book of Diversions* (1835) and Chambers's *Fireside Amusements* (1850), the words are quoted as the formula for a forfeits game similar to 'Buff says Buff to all his men' (q.v.). JOH has the rhyme in his 1853 collection.

137

The little black dog ran round the house,
And set the bull a-roaring,
And drove the monkey in the boat,
Who set the oars a-rowing,
And scared the cock upon the rock,
Who cracked his throat with crowing.

Mother Goose's Quarto, c. 1825, 'The little dog turned round the wheel' / *Mother Goose's Melodies* (New York and Boston), 'copyright 1833', as text / Correspondent, 1946.

Dog

138

Bow, wow, wow,
Whose dog art thou?
Little Tom Tinker's dog,
Bow, wow, wow.

In *Mother Goose's Melody* this is titled 'Caesar's Song' and carries the facetious note, 'Tom Tinker's Dog is a very good Dog, and an honester Dog than his Master.' The version JOH knew in 1844 goes,

How d' 'e dogs, how? whose dog art thou?
Little Tom Tinker's dog! what's that to thou?
Hiss! bow, a wow, wow!

And the one Northall knew goes,

Fools must be meddling;
As you can plainly see—
I'm Mr.——dog,
Whose dog bist thee?

It seems evident that Pope had this rhyme in mind when he wrote the epigram 'engraved on the collar of a dog which I gave to his Royal Highness':

I am his Highness's dog at Kew;
Pray, tell me, sir, whose dog are you?

MG's Melody, c. 1765 / *Vocal Harmony*, c. 1806 / *Nurse Lovechild's DFN*, c. 1830 / JOH, 1844 / Northall, 1892 / Gomme, 1898, part of a rhyme for a 'Dingle doosey' game, 'Bow-ow-ow, fat dog art thou, Tam Tinker's dog, bow-ow-ow.'

139

Oh where, oh where has my little dog gone?
Oh where, oh where can he be?
With his ears cut short and his tail cut long,
Oh where, oh where is he?

A song popular today in nurseries on both sides of the Atlantic, which, although one of the most recently composed of all pieces which have become traditional, was not originally designed for the young. Its author, Septimus Winner (1826–1902) is now almost entirely forgotten. A Philadelphian, he was music publisher, critic, and arranger and composer of more

Dog

than 2,000 pieces, including 'Our Nation Calls for Peace Again', 'He's gone to the arms of Abraham', 'What is Home without a Mother', 'Our Sweethearts at Home', and other songs of the American Civil War. *Der Deitcher's Dog*, a 'Comic Ballad by Sep. Winner' was registered in 1864, and published by him at '933 Sp. Gardens St., Philadelphia'. The original words were:

> Oh where, oh where ish mine lit-tle dog gone;
> Oh where, oh where can he be...
> His ears cut short und his tail cut long:
> Oh where, oh where ish he...
>
> I loves mine la-ger' tish ve-ry goot beer,
> Oh where, oh where can he be...
> But mit no mon-ey I can-not drink here,
> Oh where, oh where ish he...
>
> A-cross the o-cean in Gar-ma-nie
> Oh where, oh where can he be...
> Der deitch-ers dog ish der best com-pan-ie
> Oh where, oh where ish he...
>
> Un sas-age ish goot, bo-lo-nie of course,
> Oh where, oh where can he be...
> Dey makes un mit dog und dey makes em mit horse,
> I guess dey makes em mit he...

At the end of the nineteenth century the song was often called for at convivial college parties, and was maintained as a speciality song, e.g. at The Players' Club, London, but through a mis-hearing it has now become 'The Dutchman's Dog'.

140

> Hark, hark,
> The dogs do bark,
> The beggars are coming to town;
> Some in rags,
> And some in jags,
> And one in a velvet gown.

It has been suggested that this rhyme contains an echo of conditions in Elizabeth's day when wandering beggars were so numerous they were becoming a menace to society. As G. M. Trevelyan says in his *English*

Dogs

Social History, 'All through the Tudor reigns, the "beggars coming to town" preyed on the fears of dwellers in lonely farms and hamlets, and exercised the minds of magistrates, Privy Councillors and Parliaments'. Popular tradition, however, has it that 'the Beggars coming to town' were the Dutchmen in the train of William III, 1688. *Beggars* is believed to have been, at that time, a common epithet for the Dutch. In this case the 'one in a velvet gown' might refer to William himself. The theory is perhaps supported by a song in *Westminster Drollery* (1672) called 'A Dialogue between a man (in Garrison) and his wife (with her company) Storming without', the first verse of which goes,

> Hark, hark, the Doggs do bark,
>   My Wife is coming in
> With Rogues and Jades,
>   And roaring blades,
> They make a devilish din.

If this song is a parody of the rhyme it disposes of the William of Orange theory, but it may well have given the idea for the rhyme to some lampoonist.

GG's Garland, 1784, 'And some in velvet gowns' / *T Thumb's SB*, 1788, and *MG's Quarto*, c. 1825, as 1784 / *Nurse Lovechild's DFN*, c. 1830 / *New Year's Gift* (J. Catnach), c. 1830 [Hindley, 1878] / *Poetic Trifles* (J. G. Rusher), c. 1840 / *Traditional Nursery Songs*, Felix Summerly, 1843, illustration by C. W. Cope / *JOH*, 1843 / *Mother Goose*, Kate Greenaway, 1881, 'Hark! hark! the dogs bark, The beggars are coming to town; Some in rags and some in tags, And some in silken gowns. Some gave them white bread, And some gave them brown, And some gave them a good horse-whip, And sent them out of the town' / *Tailor of Gloucester*, Beatrix Potter (p.p. ed.), 1902 / Kidson, 1904 / *Hark! Hark! the Dogs do Bark and other rhymes about dogs*, L. Blegvad, illus. E. Blegvad, 1974.

141

> Two little dogs
> Sat by the fire
> Over a fender of coal-dust;
> Said one little dog
> To the other little dog,
> If you don't talk, why, I must.

In 1854 a letter was written to *Notes & Queries*, on behalf of 'a very old lady in her ninetieth year', wanting to know the end of a ballad that began thus:

Dogs

Three cats sat by the fire-side
With a basket full of coal dust,
Coal dust, coal dust,
With a basket full of coal dust.

The answers were various. One said it was a joke song, for endless repetition. One volunteered a curious confection which finished, as in the folk tale, with one of the cats flying up the chimney. One gave a verse similar to our text, but applied to two dogs who were turnspits ('... "If you don't go in, I must" '). The fourth supplied an ending like the second part of our text, but concerning two cats, not dogs.

Nursery Poems (J. G. Rusher), c. 1840 / NR, *Tales and Jingles*, 1844 / *Children's Encyclopedia*, 1908, 'If Pompey won't talk, why, I must'.

142

If I had a donkey that wouldn't go,
Would I beat him? Oh no, no.
I'd put him in the barn and give him some corn,
The best little donkey that ever was born.

Jacob Beuler, author of a number of popular broadside songs, wrote a mock-costermonger's ditty which was sung to the tune of 'The White Cockade'. It was occasioned by The Prevention of Cruelty to Animals Act (1822), the bill for which had been brought in by Richard 'Humanity' Martin, one of the Founders of the R.S.P.C.A. The first of six verses went,

If I had a donkey wot wouldn't go,
D'ye think I'd wollop him? no, no, no;
By gentle means I'd try, d'ye see,
Because I hate all cruelty.
If all had been like me, in fact,
There'd ha' been no occasion for Martin's Act,
Dumb animals to prevent getting crackt
On the head.

And the chorus:

If I had a donkey wot wouldn't go
I never would wollop him—no, no, no;
I'd give him some hay and cry gee O!
And come up Neddy.

Beuler, however, did not originate the nursery rhyme; the first two lines, at least, were already traditional. Beuler with very good grace explained,

Donkey

'These two lines were given to me, to work upon by a friend, for which I return thanks; for the song has proved one of the most popular I have ever written.' The song is mentioned in Dickens's *The Old Curiosity Shop* where one of the handbills for Jarley's Wax-Work Show was 'a parody on the favourite air of "If I had a donkey"'. At about the same time it was also being parodied by *Punch*:

> Had I an ass averse to speed
> Deem'st thou I'd strike him? No, indeed!
> I'd give him hay, and cry 'Proceed!'
> And 'Go on, Edward.'

If I had a Donkey, Jacob Beuler, c. 1822, sheet music [advt. c. 1825] / *The Blackbird* (J. Catnach), c. 1830 / *Comic Songs to Popular Tunes*, J. Beuler, 1831 / *If I had a Donkey wot wouldn't go*, c. 1855, broadside ballad [Ashton, 1888] / *Harper's Young People*, Sept. 1885, 'That wonderful old woman Mother Goose, I think, found out the secret first, for, as you all remember, she says: If I had a donkey that wouldn't go, Do you think I'd whip him? Oh, no, no, I'd give him some hay, and say, Gee, haw, whoa, Get along, donkey. Why don't you go?' / *Folkspeech of S. Cheshire*, T. Darlington, 1887, 'If I had a buzzack an hey wudna go, Wudna I wollup him, oh, no, no! I'd stuff him wi' nuts, And I'd kick him i' the guts, And I'd make him go with his teal cock'd up' / Children's postcard (C. W. Faulkner), c. 1949 / Oral collection, 1949.

143

> The dove says, Coo, coo, what shall I do?
> I can scarce maintain two.
> Pooh, pooh, says the wren, I have ten,
> And keep them all like gentlemen.

A rustic rhyme which has been adopted by the nursery, possibly through JOH including it. 'What-shall-I-do? I-can-scarce-maintain-two' is how country people interpret the dove's (or pigeon's) cooing, referring to the fact that she seldom has more than two eggs in each brood. This is in contrast to the wren who rears a family of fourteen, fifteen, or sixteen.

JOH, 1853 / Northall, 1892 / Crofton MS, 1901 / *Book of NR*, Enid Marx, 1939.

144

> Leg over leg,
> As the dog went to Dover,
> When he came to a stile,
> Jump he went over.

PLATE VII

Tommy Thumb's Pretty Song Book, c. 1744. The earliest known
book of nursery rhymes. British Museum

Dover

Crofton (1901) explains that this rhyme is repeated while moving the child's legs backwards and forwards, 'Leg over, leg over, The dog went to Dover! When he came to a stile (pause) He jump't over.' Maria Edgeworth wrote from Edgeworthstown (6 Sept. 1805): 'Lady Elizabeth Pakenham has sent me a little pony, as quiet and almost as small as a dog, on which I go trit-trot, trit-trot; but I hope it will never take it into its head to add

> When we come to the stile,
> Skip we go over.'

A friend of a correspondent (1946) remembered being taught,

> Old Farmer Giles
> Walked seven miles
> With his faithful dog, old Rover;
> And old Farmer Giles
> When he came to the stiles,
> Took a run, and jumped clean over.

JOH, 1844 / JOH, 1853, 'The dog of the kill (kiln), He went to the mill To lick mill-dust: The miller he came With a stick on his back—Home, dog, home! The foot behind, The foot before: When he came to a stile, Thus he jumped o'er' / Crofton, 1901 / Correspondent, 1946 / *Housewife*, Dec. 1948.

145

> There was an old woman
> Who lived in Dundee,
> And in her back garden
> There grew a plum tree;
> The plums they grew rotten
> Before they grew ripe,
> And she sold them three farthings a pint.

County Folk-Lore, Suffolk, The Lady Eveline Gurdon, 1893.

146

> St. Dunstan, as the story goes,
> Once pulled the devil by his nose,
> With red hot tongs, which made him roar,
> That could be heard ten miles or more.

JOH, 1842 / *Mother Goose*, E. Boyd Smith, 1919.

Dyer's Door

147

As I went by a dyer's door,
I met a lusty tawnymoor;
Tawny hands, and tawny face,
Tawny petticoats,
Silver lace.

Appears in *Tommy Thumb's Pretty Song Book* (c. 1744), and, very similar, in *Tom Tit's Song Book* (c. 1790). Tawnymoor is an old word for blackamoor. The form of the rhyme is analogous to several popular riddles. The antiquary, John Bell of Newcastle, wrote down a similar verse in his interleaved copy of *Gammer Gurton's Garland* (c. 1840):

As I was going o'er Tanzy Moor
I met a little Blacky Moor
With Tanzy Hands and Tanzy Face
A Little Cock'd Hat with Silver Lace.

148

Mr. East gave a feast;
Mr. North laid the cloth;
Mr. West did his best;
Mr. South burnt his mouth
With eating a cold potato.

Children's Encyclopedia, Arthur Mee, 1908 / *Less Familiar NR*, Robert Graves, 1927 / Oral collection, 1948.

149

Eena, meena, mina, mo,
Catch a nigger by his toe;
If he squeals, let him go,
Eena, meena, mina, mo.

Eena, Meena, Mina, Mo

Undoubtedly the most popular rhyme for counting-out both in England and America until the mid-1950s; this version is Anglo-American also in origin, the first and last lines being old British, the middle two from New England. In the mid-1970s 'nigger', was being replaced by 'tigger', 'tiger', 'spider', 'beggar', etc. The rhyme is not found recorded until comparatively recently. JOH did not know it. Nor did Northall (1892) who knew fifty-six counting-out rhymes. But Bolton in America (1888) who secured one version from Scotland and one from Ireland, found it in colloquial use in almost every State in the Union. The earlier English versions, 'Catch a tinker' and 'Catch a chicken by his toe', seem to have been completely supplanted by 'Catch a nigger'. The word nigger was common in American folk-lore but is unknown in any English traditional rhyme or proverb. Charles Francis Potter (*Harper's Bazaar*, May, 1950) compares the rhyme with the French-Canadian game,

> Meeny, meeny, miney, mo,
> Cache ton poing derrière ton dos...

and suggests that the 'Catch a nigger by his toe' line is an American corruption of it about 100 years ago. The first line has more venerable parentage. It is said (*Notes & Queries*, 1855) that the following was repeated by children in New York as early as 1815:

> Hana, mana, mona, mike;
> Barcelona, bona, strike;
> Hare, ware, frown, venac;
> Harrico, warrico, we, wo, wac.

Bolton compares many similar versions with the German,

> Ene, tene, mone, mei,
> Pastor, lone, bone, strei,
> Ene, fune, herke, berke,
> Wer? Wie? Wo? Was?

And F. W. P. Jago in his *Glossary of the Cornish Dialect* gives a rhyme beginning

> Ena, mena, mona, mite,
> Basca, lora, hora, bite.

While one of the commonest Austrian counting-out formulas in the present day is,

> Eine, meine, mine, mu,
> Und draust bist du,

of which the first line sounds all but identical with the English. These words may be a memory of ancient numerals, as in the Shepherd's Score, 'Ina, mina, tethra, methera', and the distant starting-point of the nursery verse, whose dark mystery was expressed by Kipling:

> Eenee, Meenee, Mainee and Mo
> Were the first Big Four of the Long Ago.

Newell, 1883, 'Eny, meny, mony, mite, Butter, lather, bony strike, Hair cut, froth neck, Halico, balico, We, wo, wack', and three other versions / Bolton, 1888, eight versions; 'If he hollers let him go', given as the most common American wording at that time / Gomme, 1898, 'Eendy, Beendy, baniba, roe, Caught a chicken by the toe . . .' / *Dorset Field Club*, 1917, 'Ena, meena, mina, mo, Catch a tinker by his toe. If he screams, let him go, Ena meena, mina, mo. O. U. T. spells out, And out you must go. As fair as it can be' / *Counting Out*, Carl Withers, 1946, 'Eenie, meenie, minie, mo, Catch a rooster by the toe . . .' / *American Folk-Lore*, 1947, 'Eny, meny, miny, mo, Catch a nigger by his toe, If he hollers make him pay Fifty dollars every day. O-U-T spells out, and out goes she, In the middle of the deep blue sea', given as currently the most common wording in U.S.A. / Correspondent, 1949, 'Ena, dena, dina, doh, Catla, wheeler, whiler, woe, Each, peach, pear, plum, Out goes old Tom Thumb' / Noel Coward wrote a song on the rhyme for *Bitter Sweet.*

Cf. Bolton, 1888, as German quote / Oral collection, 1949, Austrian quote.

150

> Eeny, weeny, winey, wo,
> Where do all the Frenchmen go?
> To the east and to the west,
> And into the old crow's nest.

Generally employed as a counting-out formula, also used for, or related to, a running game. In Scott's *The Bride of Lammermoor* (1819) Ravenswood says, 'But all this while, Caleb, you have never told me what became of the arms and powder'. To which Caleb replies, 'Why, as for the arms, it was just like the bairns' rhyme—

> Some gaed east, and some gaed west,
> And some gaed to the craw's nest.'

As well as Frenchmen, a young man, a poor Scotsman, and sailors, are found as the subject of the rhyme, but in almost every version the arrival is to a bird's nest. The significance of this may probably be found in the realm of folk-lore. The rhyme is undoubtedly old, even apart from the early numerals preserved in the first line (see previous article).

Chatterings of the Pica, Charles Taylor, 1820, 'Hickery, pickery, pease scon, Where will this young man gang? He'll go east, he'll go west, He'll go to the crow's nest; Hickery pickery, hickery pickery.' Stated to have been obtained from J. Gaucher, an old Scottish writer, who said it was used long before his day / *Blackwood's Magazine*, 1821, 'Scotsman, Scotsman, lo! Where shall this poor Scotsman go? Send him east, or send him west, Send him to the craw's nest' / Chambers, 1842, 'My Lord Provo', my Lord Provo', Where shall this poor fellow go? Some goes east, and some goes west, And some goes to the craw's nest', and another version given as a game / *NR* (Webb Millington and Co.), c. 1850, 'Lotsman, lotsman, lo! Where shall this poor lotsman go? Let him go east', &c. / *Shropshire Folk-Lore*, C. S. Burne, 1883, 'Iram, biram, brendom, bo, Where do the sailors go? To the east and to the west, To the land which they love best'; also as text / Newell, 1883, 'Charley, barley, buck and rye, What's the way the Frenchmen fly? Some fly east, and some fly west, And some fly over the cuckoo's nest', collected in Massachusetts / Maclagan, 1901, formula for a game 'Hickety, Bickety' / Bett, 1924, 'Eena, meena, mina, mo, Where do all the Frenchmen go? To the East, to the West, To the bonny bird's nest; Apples in the garden, Fishes in the sea, If you want a pretty girl, Please choose me!', from Durham.

151

Elizabeth, Elspeth, Betsy, and Bess,
They all went together to seek a bird's nest;
They found a bird's nest with five eggs in,
They all took one, and left four in.

RIDDLE. It is argued that 'they *all* took one' should not be taken to mean 'they *each* took one'; but since Elspeth, Betsy, and Bess are diminutives of Elizabeth the riddle is more likely to be making fun of the number of diminutives there are of this name (there are quite fifteen) and the solution that only one person went bird's-nesting. The riddle is of a style common in the seventeenth century, and has been consistently popular during the past 150 years.

JOH, 1842 / N & Q, 1865 / *Pygmalion*, George Bernard Shaw, 1912, Higgins: 'Eliza, Elizabeth, Betsy and Bess, They went to the woods to get a bird's nes' '. Pickering: 'They found a nest with four eggs in it'; Higgins: 'They took one apiece, and left three in it.' / *Folk-Lore*, 1923 / Oral collection, 1946.

152

Elsie Marley is grown so fine,
She won't get up to feed the swine,
But lies in bed till eight or nine.
Lazy Elsie Marley.

Elsie Marley

This is the opening verse of a song written in the middle of the eighteenth century and first found on a slip sheet printed about 1756. Another version, entitled 'A New Song, Made on Alice Marley, An Alewife, at * * * *, near Chester', is one of the songs relating to the county of Durham collected by Ritson in *The Bishoprick Garland* (1784). Ritson later, in 1792, identified * * * * as Picktree, near Chester-le-Street. Alice Marley was a lady much fêted in the North Country, and the song is still popular there today, especially on Tyneside:

Elsie Marley is grown so fine,
She won't get up to serve her swine,
But lies in bed till eight or nine,
And surely she does take her time.

And do you ken Elsie Marley, honey,
The wife that sells the barley, honey?
She lost her pocket and all her money
Aback o' the bush i' the garden, honey.

Elsie Marley is so neat,
It is hard for one to walk the street,
But every lad and lass they meet,
Cries do you ken Elsie Marley, honey?

Elsie Marley wore a straw hat,
But now she's gotten a velvet cap,
She may thank the Lambton lads for that,
Do you ken Elsie Marley, honey?

Elsie keeps wine, gin and ale,
In her house below the dale,
Where every tradesman up and down,
Does call to spend his half-a-crown.

The farmers as they come that way,
They drink with Elsie every day,
And call the fiddler for to play
The tune of 'Elsie Marley', honey.

The pitmen and the keelmen trim,
They drink bumbo made of gin,
And for the dance they do begin
To the tune of 'Elsie Marley', honey.

The sailors they do call for flip
As soon as they come from the ship,
And then begin to dance and skip
To the tune of 'Elsie Marley', honey.

Elsie Marley

Those gentlemen that go so fine,
They'll treat her with a bottle of wine,
And freely will sit down and dine,
Along with Elsie Marley, honey.

So to conclude these lines I've penn'd,
Hoping there's none I do offend,
And thus my merry joke doth end
Concerning Elsie Marley, honey.

Judging from further verses about her, however, which were current while she was still alive, it is evident that the way she served her ale was not the entire cause of her fame, and a contemporary writer confirms that she enjoyed a certain reputation. It is possible from one source and another to learn a considerable amount about her, and she is, in fact, one of the best documented of the nursery rhyme characters. Alice Marley, known to her friends as Ailcie or Elsie, was born Alice Harrison about 1715. She was the first wife of Ralph Marley, and the attractive proprietress of The Swan at Picktree. A writer in the *Newcastle Magazine* met her in her later days, and describes her as 'a tall, slender, genteel-looking woman', who successfully kept him and his party of horsemen amused with her badinage while she served them. She had a son, Harrison Marley, whose son Ralph also left an account of her. According to him the story of his grandmother's lethargy was poetic licence. 'Elsie was an active manager, and the household affairs were entrusted to her sole control.' In illustration, he says that the 'lost pocket' incident in the chorus arose on an occasion when Elsie was going to Newcastle, with twenty guineas sewn into her pocket, to pay the brewer's bill. On Sandhill someone jostled her, and clapping her hand to her side, she exclaimed aloud, 'O honney, honney, I've lost my pocket and all my money'. According to Sir Cuthbert Sharp (1834) she had already given her name to a spirited and lively tune often called for as a dance at country fairs; and he adds that the 'Lambton Lads' were five brothers, 'all bachelors to a certain period', and all Elsie's admirers. A happy temperament and a wide circle of friends, did not, however, save Elsie from a melancholy end. In Sykes's *Local Records* under the date 5 August 1768, the death is recorded of 'the well-known Alice Marley', and it is stated that, being in a fever, she 'got out of her house and went into a field where there was an old coal-pit full of water, which she fell into and was drowned'. This date is confirmed by the Chester-le-Street Parish Register, her burial being on 7 August. According to Sharp her husband married again. Sharp further records that at the time of the '45 rebellion, Dutch troops marching northwards used the signboard of The Swan as a shooting target. It is not improbable that these troops, or their like, heard the song and turned it to their own purposes, for Chambers, in Scotland, thought it was a Scottish song, and only knew it in an anti-Jacobite vein:

Elsie Marley

Saw ye Eppie Marly, honey,
The woman that sells the barley, honey?
She's lost her pocket and a' her money,
Wi' following Jacobite Charlie, honey.

Burns knew, under the name 'Elsie Marley', what is possibly an alternative chorus:

O little wats thou o' thy daddie, hiney,
An' little wats thou o' thy daddie, hiney;
For lairds and lords hae kiss'd thy minnie,
An' little wats thou o' thy daddie, hiney.

The text rhyme, which JOH quoted in 1853 as having become a favourite in the nursery, is sometimes found as 'Nancy Dawson was so fine', and was given thus in 1842.

Alice Marley, A New Song, c. 1756, fifteen verses / *Bishoprick Garland*, Joseph Ritson, 1784, eight verses / *Rhymes of Northern Bards*, John Bell, 1812, nine verses / *The Fortunes of Nigel*, Sir Walter Scott, 1822, Moniplies, singing a verse, boasts 'I own that I, moreover, sung the good old song of Elsie Marley, so as they never heard it chaunted in their lives' / *Bishoprick Garland*, C. Sharp, 1834 / JOH, 1842, 'Nancy Dawson'; 1853, 'Elsie Marley' / Chambers, 1847 / *N & Q*, 1855, old lady's mother used to sing 'Ken ye Mysie Barley hinnie, The lass that sell't the barley hinnie, She's lost her pouch an' a' her siller, Ne'er a laud will ere come till her. Wae's me! for Mysie Barley hinnie' / *Mother Goose*, Kate Greenaway, 1881 / The tune 'Elsie Marley' is in Robert Bremner's *Reels*, 1759.

*** There was a Nancy Dawson, a dancer at Sadler's Wells, who was contemporary with Elsie Marley, being the toast of the town in the middle of the 18th century. A song about her exists which is not very dissimilar to that on Elsie and probably on occasion the names were confused.

153

Flour of England, fruit of Spain,
Met together in a shower of rain;
Put in a bag, tied round with a string;
If you'll tell me this riddle,
I'll give you a ring.

A correspondent to *Notes & Queries* in 1907 told of Christmas a half century earlier, when, in country places, after the carol singers had been invited to 'warm themselves with a sup of posset' before saying goodnight, 'the leader would ask a riddle: Flour of England, Fruit of Spain, Met together in a shower of rain. Answer—Plum-pudding.' This is the obvious and generally accepted solution, but the authoress of *The Real Personages of Mother Goose* speculates on a possible hidden significance. The rhyme, she says, was current at the time when Queen Mary was proposing to marry Philip II. In the minds of those who propounded the riddle the 'Flour of England and fruit of Spain' may have been the Queen and Philip of Spain. If this was so 'Met together in a shower of rain' would describe their first meeting which, according to a contemporary account, took place in 'downpouring rain'; and the last line might refer to the Queen's action when she publicly sent Philip a ring, which would also, of course, symbolize the marriage. The liaison with Spain was resented throughout England and caused risings among high and low, and, if this was a lampoon, one can imagine the circulation it would have.

JOH, 1844 / *Gentleman's Magazine*, 1881 / *Squirrel Nutkin*, Beatrix Potter, 1903 / *N & Q*, 1907 / *Less Familiar NR*, Robert Graves, 1927.

154

A farmer went trotting upon his grey mare,
    Bumpety, bumpety, bump!
With his daughter behind him so rosy and fair,
    Lumpety, lumpety, lump!

A raven cried, Croak! and they all tumbled down,
    Bumpety, bumpety, bump!
The mare broke her knees and the farmer his crown,
    Lumpety, lumpety, lump!

The mischievous raven flew laughing away,
    Bumpety, bumpety, bump!
And vowed he would serve them the same the next day,
    Lumpety, lumpety, lump!

This story became well known after it had been illustrated by Caldecott in 1884. Whether the unknown author of *Original Ditties* collected it, or wrote it herself, as she did all or the majority of the other pieces, is uncertain.

Original Ditties for the Nursery (J. Harris), c. 1805 [1807] / *Only True MG Melodies*, c. 1843 / *Old Nurse's Book*, Charles Bennett, 1858 / *A Farmer went Trotting upon his Grey Mare*, Randolph Caldecott, 1884.

155

My father died a month ago
And left me all his riches;
A feather bed, and a wooden leg,
And a pair of leather breeches.

He left me a teapot without a spout,
A cup without a handle,
A tobacco pipe without a lid,
And half a farthing candle.

In 1894 a correspondent sent the first verse to *Notes & Queries* (with the third line 'A stewed stool foot, an old top hat'), having remembered it from his youth. He remarked that it was not in JOH. Several variants, and the second verse, were sent in response, all very similar, including one reading,

My father died when I was young,
And left me all his riches:
His gun and volunteering-cap
Long sword and leather breeches.

These lines were believed to refer to the American War of Independence, and it is to be remarked that the wearing of leather breeches began to cease in the middle of the eighteenth century. In *Paul Pry's Merry Minstrel or Budget of New Songs*, published about 1825, they are the opening lines of a long song, 'The Bumkin's Wife; or Fashion in its Glory', the rest of the first verse being,

A bit of land at my command,
A horse both lame and blind, sir,
You'd swear he'd in a trap been catch'd
He was cropt so close behind, sir.

The succeeding verses have little to do with the opening and were probably of contemporary composition.

Paul Pry's Merry Minstrel (Orlando Hodgson), c. 1825, 'My father died the other day', otherwise as quotes, to the tune 'Merrily Danced the Quaker's Wife' / N & Q, 1894 / Rymour Club, 1912, accompanying a round game, 'My uncle died a week ago, He left me all his riches, A wooden leg, a feather bed, A pair of leather breeches, A tobacco box without a lid, A jug without a handle, A coffee pot without a spout, And half a farthing candle. I travelled east, I travelled west, I came to Alabama, I fell in love with a nice young girl, Her name was Susy Anna. I took her to the ball one night, And also to the supper, The table fell, and she fell too, And stuck her nose in the butter.' Also variant, 1915, to the tune 'The girl I left behind me' / *The Mummers' Play*, R. J. E. Tiddy, 1923, sung in Warwickshire folk-play, similar to text but penulti-

Father

mate line 'A guinea pig without a wig' / *Weekend Book*, V. and F. Meynell, 1924, 'My aunt she died a month ago' and left 'a pair of calico breeches', stated to be an 'Irish fragment' / Correspondent, 1949.

Cf. 'Willie Winkie's Testament' in Thomson's *Orpheus Caledonius*, vol. II, 1733, 'My daddy left me gear enough, a couter and an auld bean plough, a nebbed staff, a nutting tyne, a fishing wand wi' hook and line', &c.

156

My father he died, but I can't tell you how,
He left me six horses to drive in my plough:
    With a whim, wham, wabble ho!
    Jack's lost his saddle oh!
    Blossy boys, bubble oh!
    Over the brow.

I sold my six horses and bought me a cow,
I'd fain have made a fortune, but didn't know how:
    With a whim, wham, wabble ho!
    Jack's lost his saddle oh!
    Blossy boys, bubble oh!
    Over the brow.

I sold my cow and bought me a calf,
I never made a bargain but I lost the better half:
    With a whim, wham, wabble ho!
    Jack's lost his saddle oh!
    Blossy boys, bubble oh!
    Over the brow.

I sold my calf and bought me a cat,
To lie down before the fire and warm its little back:
    With a whim, wham, wabble ho!
    Jack's lost his saddle oh!
    Blossy boys, bubble oh!
    Over the brow.

I sold my cat and bought me a mouse,
But she fired her tail and burnt down my house:
    With a whim, wham, wabble ho!
    Jack's lost his saddle oh!
    Blossy boys, bubble oh!
    Over the brow.

Father

The story of a succession of increasingly bad bargains made, so it appears, with blissful indifference, is not uncommon in folk literature, e.g. Hans Christian Andersen's tale 'What the Old Man does is always right', and the Grimms's tale 'Hans in luck'.

GG's Garland, 1810, 'With my wing wang waddle oh, Jack sing saddle oh, Blowsey boys bubble oh, under the broom' / Douce MS II, c. 1820, 'With a wimmy lo! wommy lo! Jack Straw, blazey-boys! Wimmy lo! wommy lo! wob, wob, wob!' / JOH, 1842, the Douce version quoted as a political song of Richard II's time referring to Jack Straw and his 'blazey-boys!' / JOH, 1843, 'My daddy is dead...' / *Baby's Opera*, 1877 / Mason, 1877 / Baring-Gould, 1895, 'Whimma whimme wobble, O! Jigga-jiggee-joggle, O! Little boys a wobble, O! lived under the gloam'. Also 'Withamy, widy, waddle, O! Jack has sold his saddle, O! Bubble ho! pretty boy, over the brow' / Williams, 1923, 'My grandmother died and left me fifty pounds' / *The Ploughboy in Luck*, illus. Marion Rivers-Moore, c. 1946.

157

My father he left me, just as he was able,
One bowl, one bottle, one table,
Two bowls, two bottles, two tables,
Three bowls, three bottles, three tables...

'And so on *ad lib.* in one breath' says JOH (1844).

158

My father left me three acres of land,
    Sing ivy, sing ivy;
My father left me three acres of land,
    Sing holly, go whistle and ivy!

I ploughed it with a ram's horn,
    Sing ivy, sing ivy;
And sowed it all over with one peppercorn,
    Sing holly, go whistle and ivy!

I harrowed it with a bramble bush,
    Sing ivy, sing ivy;
And reaped it with my little penknife,
    Sing holly, go whistle and ivy!

I got the mice to carry it to the barn,
    Sing ivy, sing ivy;

Father

And thrashed it with a goose's quill,
    Sing holly, go whistle and ivy!

I got the cat to carry it to the mill,
    Sing ivy, sing ivy;
The miller he swore he would have her paw,
And the cat she swore she would scratch his face,
    Sing holly, go whistle and ivy!

This appears to be an offshoot of the song 'Can you make me a cambric shirt?' (q.v.), which in turn emanates from the old ballad 'The Elfin Knight', a copy of which was printed in the seventeenth century.

N & Q, 1853, 'My father gave me an acre of land, Sing green bush, holly and ivy' / JOH, 1853 / *Folk-Song*, 1901, 'My mother she gave me an acre of land, Sing Ivy, sing Ivy, My mother she gave me an acre of land, Shall I go whistling Ivy?', &c.; another version 1909 / Williams, 1923, nine verses.

159

Good morning, Father Francis.
Good morning, Mrs. Sheckleton.
What has brought you abroad so early, Mrs. Sheckleton?
I have come to confess a great sin, Father Francis.
What is it, Mrs. Sheckleton?
Your cat stole a pound of my butter, Father Francis.
O, no sin at all, Mrs. Sheckleton.
But I killed your cat for it, Father Francis.
O, a very great sin indeed, Mrs. Sheckleton, you must do penance.
What penance, Father Francis?
Kiss me three times.
Oh! but I can't!
Oh! but you must!
Oh! but I can't!
Oh! but you must!
Well, what must be must,
So kiss, kiss, kiss and away.

This mock confessional is sometimes dramatized with the two hands draped in handkerchiefs, one representing a cowled monk and the other the female penitent. As the forefingers wag alternately, each speaks in the appropriate gruff or falsetto voice. The game is also played with finger-shadows on the wall. Versions of the dialogue are very various.

Father Francis

The piece is one of those levelled at the Roman priesthood which were bandied about in the sixteenth century, and Flora Thompson tells in *Lark Rise* how, even at the end of the nineteenth century, the Oxfordshire village children would chant it when the 'Old Catholics! Old lick the cats!' passed by. The same story is found in an elongation of the well-known 'Il était une bergère', in which, after the shepherdess has killed her cat for stealing the cheese, she confesses to the priest,

> Mon père, je m'accuse,
> Eh! ron, ron, ron,
> Petit patapon;
> Mon père, je m'accuse
> D'avoir tué mon chaton,
>   Ron, ron,
> D'avoir tué mon chaton.
>
> Ma fill', pour pénitence, &c.,
> Nous nous embrasserons.
>
> La pénitence est douce, &c.,
> Nous recommencerons.

The French and English versions are sufficiently similar in detail for it to be presumed that they are not of independent origin. It would be interesting to know in which country the slander started and at what date it crossed the Channel.

JOH, 1842, two versions, including as text / *Shropshire Folk-Lore*, C. S. Burne, 1883, 'Please, Father Francis, I've come to confess' / Maclagan, 1901, 'Holy father I have come to confess. Well, daughter, well daughter, what is this? I stole a fish at the market place. Well, daughter, you must be punished for this. How many days in prison to be? Twenty days and then you'll be free' / *Lark Rise*, Flora Thompson, 1939 / Correspondent, 1948.

Cf. *Rimes et jeux de l'enfance*, E. Rolland, 1883, 'Bonjour, père François, Bonjour, sœur Jacqueline. Je suis venue me confesser. Eh bien, dites vos péchés. Je suis allée à la cohue (halle); J'ai acheté une queue de morue, Je l'ai mise sur la table; Le chat l'a emportée. Alors j'ai dit trois fois: Diable de chat; diable de chat; diable de chat! Pour ce péché-la, Il faut aller à Rome...A Rome, père François? A Rome, sœur Jacqueline, Ou bien vous m'embrasserez trois fois. Nenni, petit père François. Si fait, sœur Jacqueline. Puisqu'il faut, il faut, Puisqu'il faut, il faut, Puisqu'il faut, il faut' / *Vieilles chansons* (éditions Novos S.A.), c. 1945, as quote.

Cf. also 'The fair Penitent' in *The Tea-Table Miscellany*, vol. i, 1724.

160

Old Father Greybeard,
Without tooth or tongue,

Father Greybeard

If you'll give me your finger
I'll give you my thumb.

The significance of this, if any, is not apparent, and is not made clearer by four additional lines found in *Nancy Cock's Pretty Song Book:*

Go! you're a naughty boy,
So is your brother;
If you give him your blockhead,
He'll give you another.

That the lines may originally have had some meaning is indicated in a manuscript of about 1725 (Harley MS 7316):

I'm a Dull Senseless Blockhead 'tis true when I'm Young
And like old *Grandsire Greyberd* without tooth or tongue
But by ye kind help & Assistance of Arts
I Sometimes attain to Politeness of Parts.

A 'Greybeard', as well as being a term for an old man, is a species of large stoneware jug, bearing a venerable bearded face on its front, originally designed by the Protestant party in the Netherlands to ridicule Cardinal Bellarmine.

Nancy Cock's PSB, c. 1780 / *GG's Garland*, 1784 / *T Thumb's SB*, 1788 / *Christmas Box*, vol. iii, 1798, as c. 1780 / JOH, 1843 / *Popular Rhymes of Ireland*, J. J. Marshall, 1931, 'Grannie greybeard, without tooth or tongue; Give me your wee finger and I'll give you my thumb'.

161

Father Short came down the lane;
    Oh! I'm obliged to hammer and smite
    From four in the morning till eight at night,
For a bad master, and a worse dame.

JOH, 1846.

162

Doctor Faustus was a good man,
He whipped his scholars now and then;
When he whipped them he made them dance
Out of Scotland into France,

Faustus

Out of France into Spain,
And then he whipped them back again.

In JOH's 1842 version, given here, the legendary German magician Dr. Faustus puts in an appearance in Scotland. However, other parts of Great Britain provide their own interpretations of the doctor's name, and the starting-point of his travels. The earliest recording found is Francis Douce's counting-out rhyme—

Doctor Foster was a good man,
He whipped his scholars now and then,
And when he had done he took a dance
Out of England into France.
He had a brave beaver with a fine snout.
Stand you there out!

—for which he was 'indebted to his pretty little Sister Emily Corry, 1795'. In the American *Mother Goose's Quarto* (c. 1825) is the emigrant Irish form,

John O'Gudgeon was a wild man,
He whipt his children now and then,
When he whipt them he made them dance
Out of Ireland into France.

The original rhyming ending to the second line, 'than', now occurs only in dialect.

Douce MS, c. 1805 / *GG's Garland*, 1810 / *MG's Quarto*, c. 1825 / JOH, 1842 / Chambers, 1847 / *Baby's Opera*, 1877 / *Folk-Lore*, 1881 / Northall, 1892, 'The master is a very good man, He tries to teach us all he can, Reading, writing, arithmetic, But he never forgets to give us the stick. When he strikes, it makes us dance, Out of England into France, Out of France into Spain, Over the hills and back again' / Kidson, 1904 / *Sandy Candy*, W. and M. Montgomerie, 1948, 'John Smith's a very guid man, Teaches scholars noo and than, And whan he's dune, he taks a dance, Up tae London, doon tae France' / Correspondent, 1949, class-room rhyme 'Old Mr. Grundy is a nice man' similar to 1892.

163

I do not like thee, Doctor Fell,
The reason why I cannot tell;
But this I know, and know full well,
I do not like thee, Doctor Fell.

Fell

The story is that Dr. Fell (1625–86), Dean of Christ Church, was about to expel the satirist Tom Brown, but, in the face of urgent protestations, said he would remit the sentence if Brown could translate extempore Martial's lines,

> Non amo te, Sabidi, nec possum dicere quare;
> Hoc tantum possum dicere, Non amo te.

Tom Brown's immediate rendering is said to have been the verse above, and he was allowed to stay up. This well-known epigram, which was quoted in the House of Commons by Sheridan, and appears in Carlyle's pamphlet *Parliaments* (1850), has caused the name of Dr. Fell to be used to describe anyone who is disliked, though for no adducible reason—an undoubted aspersion on the benevolent patron of the Oxford University Press. Tom Brown, however, may not have been so original as he is made out to be. He had probably read *Faenestra in Pectore* (1660) where Thomas Forde paraphrases Martial's epigram in 'the words of a Gentleman to his wife,

> I love thee not Nel
> But why, I can't tell:
> But this I can tell,
> I love thee not Nel.'

Works, Thomas Brown, 1760, 'I do not love you, Dr. Fell, But why I cannot tell, But this I know full well, I do not love you, Dr. Fell' / *Beauties of Tom Brown*, C. H. Wilson, 1808 / *Less Familiar NR*, Robert Graves, 1927 / *Mother Goose* (T. Nelson), c. 1945 / *Big Book of Mother Goose* (James and Jonathan Co., Wisconsin), 1946 / *Home Chat*, 8 Nov. 1947, 'Almost every child learns to say "I do not like thee, Dr. Fell"'.

164

> The little priest of Felton,
> The little priest of Felton,
> He killed a mouse within his house,
> And nobody there to help him.

'Being ignorant that this old rhyme is claimed either by Herefordshire, Somersetshire, or Shropshire, I am (although without the slightest authority) induced to give our northern village the benefit of all the honours arising from the truly heroic, though not bloodless, exploit of the little warlike vicar of the olden time.' Denham (1858) was probably not incorrect in thus championing the north; half a century earlier the words had appeared in the form of a round in a collection 'Peculiar to the Counties of Newcastle upon Tyne, Northumberland, and Durham'.

Rhymes of Northern Bards, John Bell, 1812 / JOH, 1843 / Rimbault, 1846, sung to the same tune as 'Tommy Tucker' / *Folk-Lore of the N. Counties*, M. A. Denham, 1858 / *Mother Goose's NR*, L. E. Walter, 1924 / *Folk Tales of N. Country*, F. Grice, 1944.

165

The fiddler and his wife,
   The piper and his mother,
Ate three half-cakes, three whole cakes,
   And three quarters of another.

How much did each get? If the fiddler's wife was the piper's mother each received one and three quarters of a cake. It is likely that this solution has been pondered on for more than 350 years. The author of *The Riddles of Heraclitus and Democritus*, published by John Norton in 1598, was a man of literary bent; as well as inventing his own riddles he lengthened and embroidered ones which were already popular. His forty-seventh was,

The Miller, and the Millers wife,
   That they might merrie make,
Were set down with a dish of fruite,
   A cake, and half a cake,
The parson of the towne with them,
   His sister and no more:
Now haue you heard of all the guests,
   And of their bread the store.
Yet did they vse the matter with
   Such cunning, skill, and art,
That euerie one eate halfe a cake,
   Before they did depart.

On this he commented, 'the milners [*sic*] wife, was the parson's sister: and so the diuision not hard to make'.

JOH, 1849 / *Come Hither*, Walter de la Mare, 1923.

166

In a cottage in Fife
   Lived a man and his wife,
Who, believe me, were comical folk;
   For, to people's surprise,
   They both saw with their eyes,

And their tongues moved whenever they spoke!
> When quite fast asleep,
> I've been told that to keep
Their eyes open they could not contrive;
> They walked on their feet,
> And 'twas thought what they eat
Helped, with drinking, to keep them alive!

Original Ditties for the Nursery (J. Harris), c. 1805, additional lines, 'What's amazing to tell! I have heard that their smell Chiefly lay in a thing call'd their nose! And, though strange are such tales, On their fingers they'd nails, As well as on each of their toes' [1807] / *NR from the Royal Collections* (J. G. Rusher), c. 1840 / *NR, Tales and Jingles*, 1844 / *The Orchard Book of Nursery Rhymes*, Zena Sutherland, illus. Faith Jaques, 1990.
  Cf. *Description of a Wonderful Old Man*, c. 1775, slip song. '...Tis reported his tongue always mov'd when he talk'd, And he stirr'd both his legs and his arms when he walk'd', &c.

167

> I saw a fishpond all on fire
> I saw a house bow to a squire
> I saw a parson twelve feet high
> I saw a cottage near the sky
> I saw a balloon made of lead
> I saw a coffin drop down dead
> I saw two sparrows run a race
> I saw two horses making lace
> I saw a girl just like a cat
> I saw a kitten wear a hat
> I saw a man who saw these too
> And said though strange they all were true.

These lines, which are to be understood two ways, are in the manner of 'I saw a peacock with a fiery tail' (q.v.). They were orally collected by a contributor to *Folk-Lore* in 1889.

168

> Fiddle-de-dee, fiddle-de-dee,
> The fly shall marry the humble-bee.

Fly

> They went to the church, and married was she:
> The fly has married the humble-bee.

This ditty of 'The Fly and the Humble Bee' would seem to be the one (referred to as 'Fiddle-de-dee! The wasp has married the humble bee!' and 'Fiddle cum fee, the mouse has married the humble-bee') sung by the musical cat in 'The cat came fiddling out of a barn' (q.v.), a rhyme which has been traced back to 1740. If this is so the lines above, or ones very similar, must be at least as old. It seems likely that both rhymes were once part of the same song. Edward Smith Biggs set such a song to music, probably in 1803, under the title 'Fiddle-Dee-Dee! A Song for the Nursery':

> Fiddle-dee-dee! Fiddle-dee-dee!
> The Fly shall marry the Humble-bee! (bis)
> The Humble-bee was never so glad,
> As when she had met with so pretty a lad,
> As—Fiddle-dee-dee! Fiddle-dee-dee!
> The Fly shall marry the Humble-bee!
>
> As to Church they went said the Fly (said he)
> 'Will you make a kind wife my sweet Humble-bee?'
> Said the Humble-bee 'I'll sit under your wing,
> And you never shall know that I carry a sting
> But—for Fiddle-dee-dee! etc.
>
> Now when the Parson had join'd the pair,
> He bade them fly out to take the air;
> Then away flew they, to sip sweet flow'rs,
> And thus they pass'd their happy hours
> With—Fiddle-dee-dee! etc.
>
> Then the Flies did buz, and the Bells did ring,
> And the Humble-bees, their drones did sing,
> For joy, to think amongst all the Flies,
> The Humble-bee should have found such a prize
> As—Fiddle-dee-dee! etc.

Biggs may have embellished the words, but it is interesting that his first verse is like the last lines of 'The cat came fiddling' in Crane's *Baby's Bouquet* (1879), and that in the same book Crane produced a version of 'Fiddle-dee-dee' very like Biggs's, above.

Fiddle-dee-dee [Edmund Smith Biggs] (Printed and sold by Rt. Birchall, 133 New Bond Street), 1803? / JOH, 1842 / *Baby's Bouquet*, 1879.

169

> Formed long ago, yet made today,
> Employed while others sleep;
> What few would like to give away,
> Nor any wish to keep.

This riddle (*solution:* a bed) has been attributed to Charles James Fox (1749–1806). It appeared without acknowledgement in Elizabeth Newbery's riddle collection (1792) where only the second line, 'I'm most enjoyed while others sleep', differs from the modern version. Thereafter it has been a usual constituent of the riddle books.

A New Collection of Enigmas, 1791 / Peter Puzzlewell, 1792 / *Mince Pies for Christmas*, 1804 / MS collection of 'Riddles, Jokes, and Charades', c. 1810 (Opie collection) / *The Phoenix*, 1823 / *Riddle Book or Fireside Amusements* (T. Richardson), c. 1830 / JOH, 1842 / *Favourite Rhymes and Riddles*, 1892.

170

> Doctor Foster went to Gloucester
> In a shower of rain;
> He stepped in a puddle,
> Right up to his middle,
> And never went there again.

Although making a regular appearance in recent nursery-rhyme books, Doctor Foster has little traceable history and was first printed by JOH in 1844. The rhyming of middle with puddle, however, points to the old form of the word *piddle* having been originally used. Boyd Smith (1919) suggests that the rhyme describes an incident in the travels of Edward I, whose horse, the story goes, once stuck so deep in the mud of a Gloucester street that planks had to be laid on the ground before the creature could regain its footing. Edward is said to have refused ever to visit the city again. A rhyme in *Gammer Gurton's Garland* (1810) tells a different story:

> Old Dr. Foster went to Gloster,
> To preach the word of God.
> When he came there, he sat in his chair,
> And gave all the people a nod.

Fox

171

A fox jumped up one winter's night,
And begged the moon to give him light,
For he'd many miles to trot that night
Before he reached his den O!
    Den O! Den O!
For he'd many miles to trot that night
Before he reached his den O!

The first place he came to was a farmer's yard,
Where the ducks and the geese declared it hard
That their nerves should be shaken and their rest so marred
By a visit from Mr. Fox O!
    Fox O! Fox O!
That their nerves should be shaken and their rest so marred
By a visit from Mr. Fox O!

He took the grey goose by the neck,
And swung him right across his back;
The grey goose cried out, Quack, quack, quack,
With his legs hanging dangling down O!
    Down O! Down O!
The grey goose cried out, Quack, quack, quack,
With his legs hanging dangling down O!

Old Mother Slipper Slopper jumped out of bed,
And out of the window she popped her head:
Oh! John, John, John, the grey goose is gone,
And the fox is off to his den O!
    Den O! Den O!
Oh! John, John, John, the grey goose is gone,
And the fox is off to his den O!

John ran up to the top of the hill,
And blew his whistle loud and shrill;
Said the fox, That is very pretty music; still—
I'd rather be in my den O!
    Den O! Den O!
Said the fox, That is very pretty music; still—
I'd rather be in my den O!

Fox

The fox went back to his hungry den,
And his dear little foxes, eight, nine, ten;
Quoth they, Good daddy, you must go there again,
If you bring such good cheer from the farm O!
  Farm O! Farm O!
Quoth they, Good daddy, you must go there again,
If you bring such good cheer from the farm O!

The fox and his wife, without any strife,
Said they never ate a better goose in all their life:
They did very well without fork or knife,
And the little ones picked the bones O!
  Bones O! Bones O!
They did very well without fork or knife,
And the little ones picked the bones O!

This rollicking song is traditional both in England and America, the
fourth verse being a particular favourite and sometimes appearing
alone. Old Mother Slipper Slopper is also known as 'Widdle Waddle',
'Hipple-hopple', 'Chittle Chattle', 'Snipper Snapper', 'Flipper Flapper',
and 'Wig Wag'. The song has descended from a carol which was probably
already old when it happened to be written down on the flyleaf of a
manuscript, c. 1500 (Royal MS 19. B. iv). The first verse then went:

> It fell ageyns the next nyght
> the fox yede to with all his myghte,
> with-outen cole or candlelight,
> whan that he cam vnto the toowne.

Secular Lyrics of the XIVth and XVth Centuries, R. H. Robbins, 1952 / *GG's Garland*,
1810, one verse only, 'Old Mother Widdle Waddle jumpt out of bed, And out of
the casement she popt her head: Crying the house is on fire, the grey goose is
dead, and the fox he is come to the town, oh!' / Memorandum by Sir Walter
Scott on old songs he knew, c. 1826, 'Eh, quo' the Tod, it's a braw light night, The
wind's in the west, and the moon shines bright, The wind's in the west, and the
moon shines bright, And I'll away to the toun, oh' [Sharpe, 1880] / *The Opera, or
Cabinet of Song*, ed. ? James Ballantyne, 1832 / *The Fox came thro' the Town, O* (Disley),
c. 1840; (John Harkness), c. 1840, broadsides / JOH, 1842, corrupted version beginning 'The Fox and his wife they had a great strife' / *Illustrated Ditties for the Nursery*
(Dean and Son), 1851, slightly sophisticated version / *Mister Fox*, Comus [R. M. Bal-
lantyne], 1857 / Baring-Gould, 1895 / Kidson, 1904, 'A fox went out in a hungry
plight' / *Nursery Songs from the Appalachian Mountains*, Cecil Sharp, 1923 / Williams,
1923 / *Oxford Song Book*, vol. ii, Thomas Wood, 1927.
See discussion in *American Folk-Lore*, vol. 74, pp. 235–44.

172

> Put your finger in Foxy's hole,
>   Foxy's not at home;
> Foxy's at the back door
>   Picking at a bone.

A trick rhyme to please the young which seems to be best known north of the Tweed. The two first fingers of one hand are crossed over the two first fingers of the other, leaving a small opening between, and the invitation is extended to 'Put your finger in Foxy's hole'. If the child is innocent enough to comply, he gets a sharp nip from the thumb nail underneath, for the foxy has come back again. In Scotland the trap usually belongs to a 'craw', 'corbie' (carrion crow), or crab, while in Hertfordshire it is the home of 'the cob' (spider).

Chambers, 1842 / JOH, 1849 / *Folk-Lore*, 1886 / Maclagan, 1901, 'Put your finger in the crab's nest, The crab is not at home, The crab is at the back door, Picking a marrow bone' / *Scottish NR*, R. J. MacLennan, 1909 / *Shetland Traditional Lore*, J. M. E. Saxby, 1932 / Correspondents, 1948 and 1949.

173

> The King of France went up the hill
> With forty thousand men;
> The King of France came down the hill,
> And ne'er went up again.

Clearly a popular song in Charles I's time. It is found familiarly quoted in the contemporary writings of a journalist, a poet, and an anthologist; and in the succeeding reign the words were used proverbially by a noted divine. Furthermore, the origin of the song was mentioned by a future Historiographer Royal. James Howell, in a letter from Paris, 12 May 1620, wrote to his friend Sir James Crofts, 'France as all Christendom besides was in a profound peace . . . when Henry the fourth fell upon some great Martiall designe, the bottom whereof is not known to this day; . . . he levied a huge army of 40,000 men, whence came the Song, *The King of France with fourty thousand men*.' This enterprise (which came to nothing when Henry was assassinated) was in 1610. Thirty years later, also in France, the writer of a news sheet, *Pigges Corantoe, or Newes from the North*, was reminded of the song by a similar political situation, and, quoting the refrain, referred to it as 'Old Tarlton's Song'. Ned Tarlton died in 1588 and in consequence most commentators have thought that the song must date from before the jester's death. Howell's derivation, nevertheless, is probably the correct one. In the same way as today all good spoonerisms eventually get attributed to the late W. A. Spooner, during the last decade of the sixteenth century and throughout the seventeenth century many of the best jests which became current were fathered on Tarlton. Although the song of the King of France has probably been popular in oral tradition ever since it was composed, its only appearance in print during the seventeenth and eighteenth centuries seems to have been in *King Pippin's Delight* (c. 1780): 'Little King Pippin here appears Strutting beside his grenadiers, And leads his mighty valiant men, First up the hill, then down again'. In more recent times other names, such as Napoleon, have been substituted, and a probable offshoot is the well-known song of the Duke of York (q.v.). The air is old French, a version of 'Le petit tambour'.

MS Sloane 1489, c. 1630, 'The K. of France & 4000 men They drew y^{er} swords & put y^{em} up againe' / *Pigges Corantoe*, 1642, 'The King of France with forty thousand men Went up a Hill, and so came downe agen' / *Epistolae Ho-Elianae*, James Howell, 1645 / *Wandering, to see the Wonders of the West*, John Taylor (the 'Water Poet'), 1649, 'twenty thousand men' / *The Rustick's Alarm to the Rabbies*, Samuel Fisher, 1660, 'As the King of Spain and forty thousand men, Went up a Hill, and then came down agen' / *King Pippin's Delight* (G. Thompson and J. Evans), c. 1780 / JOH, 1842; other versions, 1844, 'The King of France, with twenty thousand men, Went up the hill, and then came down again; The King of Spain, with twenty thousand more, Climb'd the same hill the French had climb'd before', also 'The king of France, the king of France, with forty thousand men, Oh, they all went up the hill, and so—came back again!' as a game in which the first line is repeated until the child asks 'What next?' then comes the climax / Kidson, 1904.

174

My father was a Frenchman,
A Frenchman, a Frenchman,
My father was a Frenchman
And he bought me a fiddle.
   He cut it here,
   He cut it here,
He cut it through the middle.

One of the less restful infant amusements. The nurse holds out the child's arm and illustrates the rhyme by striking gently with the side of her hand first the wrist, then the shoulder, 'and then', says JOH, 'at the word "middle", with considerable force, on the flexor muscles of the elbow joint'. The game is also indulged in by elder brothers and sisters at school.

Frenchman

JOH, 1844 / Gomme, 1894, 'Divv ye ken aboot my father's fiddle? My father had a fiddle, an' he brook it here, an' he brook it here, an' he brook it throw the middle' / Maclagan, 1901, 'He learned me to fiddle' / Oral collection, 1946.

175

A frog he would a-wooing go,
   Heigh ho! says Rowley,
A frog he would a-wooing go,
Whether his mother would let him or no.
   With a rowley, powley, gammon and spinach,
   Heigh ho! says Anthony Rowley.

So off he set with his opera hat,
   Heigh ho! says Rowley,
So off he set with his opera hat,
And on the road he met with a rat.
   With a rowley, powley, &c.

Pray, Mister Rat, will you go with me?
   Heigh ho! says Rowley,
Pray, Mister Rat, will you go with me,
Kind Mrs. Mousey for to see?
   With a rowley, powley, &c.

They came to the door of Mousey's hall,
   Heigh ho! says Rowley,
They gave a loud knock, and they gave a loud call.
   With a rowley, powley, &c.

Pray, Mrs. Mouse, are you within?
   Heigh ho! says Rowley,
Oh yes, kind sirs, I'm sitting to spin.
   With a rowley, powley, &c.

Pray, Mrs. Mouse, will you give us some beer?
   Heigh ho! says Rowley,
For Froggy and I are fond of good cheer.
   With a rowley, powley, &c.

Pray, Mr. Frog, will you give us a song?
   Heigh ho! says Rowley,

Frog

Let it be something that's not very long.
  With a rowley, powley, &c.

Indeed, Mrs. Mouse, replied Mr. Frog,
  Heigh ho! says Rowley,
A cold has made me as hoarse as a dog.
  With a rowley, powley, &c.

Since you have a cold, Mr. Frog, Mousey said,
  Heigh ho! says Rowley,
I'll sing you a song that I have just made.
  With a rowley, powley, &c.

But while they were all a-merry-making,
  Heigh ho! says Rowley,
A cat and her kittens came tumbling in.
  With a rowley, powley, &c.

The cat she seized the rat by the crown,
  Heigh ho! says Rowley,
The kittens they pulled the little mouse down.
  With a rowley, powley, &c.

This put Mr. Frog in a terrible fright,
  Heigh ho! says Rowley,
He took up his hat and he wished them good-night.
  With a rowley, powley, &c.

But as Froggy was crossing over a brook,
  Heigh ho! says Rowley,
A lily-white duck came and gobbled him up.
  With a rowley, powley, &c.

So there was an end of one, two, three,
  Heigh ho! says Rowley,
The rat, the mouse, and the little frog-ee.
  With a rowley, powley, &c.

This version of the old song is the best known and also the most recent. It was popularized perhaps first by Grimaldi, and then by the comedian John Liston, early in the nineteenth century. It was published with tune under the title 'The Love-sick Frog' some time about 1809, when it seems to have been very popular; it is twice found parodied in that year, once when Lord Grenville became Chancellor of Oxford, and once during the 'O.P. Riots' at Covent Garden:

Frog

> John Kemble would an acting go;
>   Heigho, says Rowley.
> He raised the price which he thought too low,
> Whether the public would let him or no,
>   With his roly-poly,
>   Gammon, and spinage,
>   Heigho, says Kemble.

The 'rowley-powley' refrain is not found before the nineteenth century, either connected with earlier versions of the song, or elsewhere, and the suggestion often made that Charles II ('Old Rowley') is named seems improbable. A *Notes & Queries* correspondent remembered seeing 'rowley powley' given as a name for a plump fowl, and of this, he justly remarked, 'both gammon and spinach are posthumous connexions'. The song itself may be traced through four centuries. In *The Complaynt of Scotlande* (1549) one of the 'sueit melodius sangis' the shepherds sing is 'The frog cam to the myl dur'. This is almost certainly the same as 'A moste Strange weddinge of the ffrogge and the mowse', a ballad licensed by the Stationers to Edward White, 21 November 1580. The earliest extant text is in Ravenscroft's *Melismata* (1611) where, with tune, 'The Marriage of the Frogge and the Movse' is made up of thirteen verses, beginning,

> It was the Frogge in the well,
>   Humble-dum, humble-dum.
> And the merrie Mouse in the Mill,
>   tweedle, tweedle twino.
>
> The Frogge would a woing ride,
>   humble dum, humble dum.
> Sword and buckler by his side,
>   tweedle, tweedle twino.
>
> When he was upon his high horse set,
>   humble dum, humble dum.
> His boots they shone as black as jet,
>   tweedle, tweedle twino.

Subsequently the frog makes his proposal to the mouse, they are married by the rat, the wedding supper of 'three beanes in a pound of butter' is interrupted by the cat who catches the mouse, 'Dicke our Drake' carries off the frog, and the rat escapes up the wall. The principal variation on this story is in Kirkpatrick Sharpe's *Ballad Book* (1824), a rendering taken from recitation:

> There lived a puddy in a well,
> And a merry mouse in a mill.
> Puddy he'd a wooin' ride,
> Sword and pistol by his side.

Frog

The incidents are: the mouse's refusal to accept the frog until 'Uncle Rotten' comes home and gives consent, marriage feast, interruption by duck (who 'took Puddy and garnt him squaik') and drake, entrance of cat, capture of frog while swimming down the brook, and the attack on Lord Rotten by cat and kittens. 'But Lady Mouse baith jimp and sma', Crept into a hole beneath the wa'; "Squeak!" quo' she, "I'm weel awa'!"' In a footnote Sharpe says that the chorus '"Cuddie alone and I" &c.', is 'not worthy of insertion'. Part of an English version of this was collected by Ritson (*Gammer Gurton's Garland*, 1784) and later reproduced by JOH and Rimbault. The narrative breaks off after the mouse's refusal to give the frog an answer, and he is swallowed by a duck on his way home. The refrain runs, 'Kitty alone, kitty alone, Kitty alone and I! Cock me cary, Kitty alone, Kitty alone and I'. Despite Sharpe's derogatory footnote, the refrains are not without interest. The one in *Melismata*, going

> Humble-dum, humble-dum,
> tweedle, tweedle twino,

is similar to several known spinning refrains, and may be another of them ('Humble-dum' representing the humming of the wheel, and 'tweedle twino' the twiddling and twining of the thread). 'The Frog and Mouse' is the type of ballad which would be a favourite with 'spinsters and the knitters in the sun'—the mouse herself is found spinning in some versions—so there may be another early allusion to the story when the Earl of Surrey wrote,

> My mother's maids they do sit and spin,
> They sing a song made of a fieldish mouse.

The song seems to have been consistently popular, more so than the number of its appearances in print would suggest. Thomas Warton, for instance, born in 1728, speaks of it familiarly as a 'nursery song' in 1781, and says it had recently been sung about the streets to a fine Italian air. John Pinkerton, writing in 1783, said it had lately been sung on the stage in Edinburgh. It was also frequently parodied, not only in the nineteenth century, but in the eighteenth century as early as 1714 (D'Urfey's 'A Ditty on a High Amore at St. James').

Melismata, Thomas Ravenscroft, 1611 / Scott MS, 1630, begins 'Itt was ye frog in ye wall, Humble doune, humble doune; And ye mirrie mouse in ye mill, Tweidle, tweidle, twino' [Chambers] / *Wit and Mirth*, Tom D'Urfey, vol. v, 1714 / *GG's Garland*, 1784 / *Original Ditties for the Nursery* (J. Harris), c. 1805, 'Squire Frog's Visit', 'Heigh ho! says Brittle! With a namby, pamby, Mannikin, pannikin, Heigh! says Barnaby Brittle!' &c. [1807] / *The Love-sick Frog* (G. Walker), c. 1809, 'A Favourite Song sung by Mr. Liston, At the Theatre Royal, Covent Garden, Arranged with an Accompan[t] for the Harp or Pianoforte by My Grandmother' / *Heigh ho said Rowley* (William Walker), c. 1810 / *The Love Sick Frog* (Goulding and Co.), c. 1812, 'with original tune by C. E. H., Esq., and accompaniment by Thomas Cooke' / *Ballad Book*,

PLATE VIII

a. The forerunner of 'A frog he would a-wooing go'. 'The Marriage of the Frogge and the Movse' in *Melismata*, 1611. British Museum

b. The frontispiece of the 1816 edition of Marshall's *Mother Goose's Melody*. Opie collection

Frog

C. Kirkpatrick Sharpe, 1824 / Later, c. 1825, Scott, writing to Sharpe about the book, gave some typically Scottish varia: 'being a frog of Celtic race' he had 'dirk and pistol by his side' [1880] / *Scottish Songs*, R. Chambers, 1829, 'There was a frogge in a well, Fa, la, linkum, leerie! And a mousie in a mill, Linkum-a-leerie, linkum-a-leerie, cow-dow', &c. / *Frog in a Cock'd Hat* (Hodges), c. 1840, street broadsheet / JOH, 1842 / Rimbault, 1846 / *N & Q*, vol. ii, 1850, p. 110, refrain known c. 1790, 'Heigho, crowdie! With a howdie, crowdie', &c. / *The Frog who would a Wooing Go*, illus. Charles Bennett, c. 1865 / *N & Q*, vol. vi, 1876, pp. 212–13, refrain from c. 1750, also known to several correspondents, 'With a rigdum bonum duo coino. Coi min ero giltee caro coi minero coino, Stim stam pammediddle lara bona ringcan, Ringcan bonum duo coino' / *A Frog he would a Wooing Go*, Randolph Caldecott, 1883 / *Garland of Country Songs*, S. Baring-Gould, 1895, refrain 'Crocka-my-daisy, Kitty alone, Kitty alone and I' / *Tailor of Gloucester*, Beatrix Potter (p.p. ed.), 1902, fragment similar to 1824 version / *Folk- Song*, 1906 / *Nursery Songs from the Appalachian Mountains*, Cecil Sharp, 1921, 'A frog went a-courting, he did ride h'm, h'm, A frog went a courting he did ride. Sword and pistol by his side, &c. / Williams, 1923 / The song has become an especial favourite in U.S.A. / *Texas Folk-Lore Society*, 1926, forty versions / *Song Catcher in Southern Mountains*, Dorothy Scarborough, 1937, with biblio. / *American Folk-Lore*, 1939, biblio. of twenty-two American variants / *A Frog He Would A-Wooing Go*, picture book by William Stobbs, 1969.

176

A gaping wide-mouthed waddling frog.

Two pudding ends would choke a dog,
With a gaping wide-mouthed waddling frog.

Three monkeys tied to a clog,
Two pudding ends would choke a dog,
With a gaping wide-mouthed waddling frog.

Four horses stuck in a bog,
Three monkeys tied to a clog,
Two pudding ends would choke a dog,
With a gaping wide-mouthed waddling frog.

Five puppies by our dog Ball,
Who daily for their breakfast call;
Four horses stuck in a bog,
Three monkeys tied to a clog, &c.

Six beetles against a wall,
Close by an old woman's apple-stall;
Five puppies by our dog Ball,
Who daily for their breakfast call; &c.

Frog

Seven lobsters in a dish,
As fresh as any heart could wish;
Six beetles against a wall,
Close by an old woman's apple-stall; &c.

Eight joiners in joiner's hall,
Working with their tools and all;
Seven lobsters in a dish,
As fresh as any heart could wish; &c.

Nine peacocks in the air,
I wonder how they all came there,
I don't know, nor I don't care;
Eight joiners in joiner's hall,
Working with their tools and all; &c.

Ten comets in the sky,
Some low and some high;
Nine peacocks in the air,
I wonder how they all came there,
I don't know, nor I don't care; &c.

Eleven ships sailing o'er the main,
Some bound for France and some for Spain;
Ten comets in the sky,
Some low and some high; &c.

Twelve huntsmen with horn and hounds,
Hunting over other men's grounds;
Eleven ships sailing o'er the main,
Some bound for France and some for Spain;
Ten comets in the sky,
Some low and some high;
Nine peacocks in the air,
I wonder how they all came there,
I don't know, nor I don't care;
Eight joiners in joiner's hall,
Working with their tools and all;
Seven lobsters in a dish,
As fresh as any heart could wish;
Six beetles against a wall,
Close by an old woman's apple-stall;
Five puppies by our dog Ball,

Frog

Who daily for their breakfast call;
Four horses stuck in a bog,
Three monkeys tied to a clog,
Two pudding ends would choke a dog,
With a gaping wide-mouthed waddling frog.

This is the cumulative wording of 'The Play of the Wide-mouth waddling Frog, to amuse the Mind, and exercise The Memory', which s featured, amongst other places, in *The Top Book of All* (c. 1760). It is a family game of questions and forfeits which was popular, especially at Christmas time, up to the middle of the nineteenth century. Eckenstein compares the rhyme with 'The Twelve Days of Christmas' (q.v.), but it is unlikely that there is any special significance in the imagery, although the line 'Two pudding ends would choke a dog' is reminiscent of a line in a Mummers' play, also belonging to the Christmas season. JOH only knew the rhyme for saying in one breath, a practice confirmed by a correspondent (1951), who had recited 'The Lady's Lap Dog' thus as a child (c. 1880). Imitations of 'The Waddling Frog' include *The Frisking, Barking, Lady's Lap-Dog* (1817), *The Pretty, Playful, Tortoiseshell Cat* (1817), and *The Noble, Prancing, Cantering Horse* (1819).

Top Book, c. 1760 / *Mirth without Mischief* (C. Sheppard), c. 1780, with directions for the play / *Universal Shuttlecock* (John Marshall), c. 1786 / *The Gaping, Wide-Mouthed, Waddling Frog* (A. K. Newman & Co.), 1822; (Dean and Munday), c. 1825 / *Girl's Own Book*, Mrs. Child, 1831 [1832] *Book of Forfeits* (Hodgson and Co.), c. 1840, rewritten version 'The Feast of Industry' / JOH, 1842, versions begin 'Eleven comets in the sky' and 'Eight ships on the main', extended in some editions to 'Twelve huntsmen with horns and hounds' / *Fireside Amusements*, R. Chambers, 1850 / *A Gaping Wide-mouthed Waddling Frog*, Walter Crane, 1872 / N & Q, 1880 / Gomme, 1898.

*** Ball is an old name for a dog, e.g. Spenser's 'Indeed, thy Ball is a bold big cur'.

177

Round and round the garden
Like a teddy bear;
One step, two step,
Tickle you under there!

Infant amusement. Circles are traced round the palm of the child's hand with a forefinger, and the steps are taken up the arm to reach, with the concluding line, the ticklish armpit. Orally collected on a number of occasions 1946–50, this rhyme is probably a recent off-shoot of 'Round about there went a little hare' (q.v.). 'Teddy bears' came into vogue about 1903, after, it is said, President 'Teddy' Roosevelt was presented with one of them on his return from an unsuccessful bear-hunting trip.

178

I went into my grandmother's garden,
And there I found a farthing.
I went into my next door neighbour's;
There I bought a pipkin and a popkin,
A slipkin and a slopkin,
A nailboard, a sailboard,
And all for a farthing.

JOH (1853) gives this as a riddle, the solution, not easily come by, being a tobacco pipe. In Beatrix Potter's *The Tailor of Gloucester* (1903) the rude little mice when they heard the last four lines added 'and upon the kitchen dresser!'
    Cf. the song for swing pushing 'I went down the garden' in *Folk-Lore* (1895) and Gomme (1898).

179

If you are a gentleman,
As I suppose you be,
You'll neither laugh nor smile
At the tickling of your knee.

An infant amusement which is self-explanatory. Although not recorded until the middle of the nineteenth century, games of this type have been played from time immemorial. Rabelais (1534) listed 'A je te pince sans rire' among Gargantua's games, and 'Buff says Buff to all his men' (q.v.) is similar. A correspondent to *Notes & Queries* in 1890 said, 'I never knew it included in the stock of children's rhymes (i.e. in print). It was, however, known among young people, the meaning being not exactly decent.'

JOH, 1846, 'A good child, a good child, As I suppose you be' / '*Chimes, Rhymes, and Jingles* (New York), c. 1860, 'If you are to be a gentleman, as I suppose you to be, You'll neither laugh nor smile for a tickling of the knee' / *Folk-Lore*, 1883, as text, also 'If you are an old bachelor' and 'If you be a fair maid' / Newell, 1883, 'Tickle'e, tickle'e on the knee; If you laugh you don't love me', from Philadelphia, and two other versions / Crofton MS, 1901, 'Lady, lady, in the land Can you bear a tickly hand? If you laugh or if you smile You'll ne'er be lady in the land' / Correspondent, 1948, 'Tickly wickly, in your hand, If you laugh you'll be a man, If you smile you'll be a lady, If you cry you'll be a baby' / *Sandy Candy*, N. and W. Montgomerie, 1948, 'Leddy, leddy o the lan, Can ye bear a tickly palm? If ye laugh or if ye smile, Ye canna be a leddy' / Correspondent, 1949, had the rhyme handed down from ancestor born 1768.

Cf. *Alemannisches Kinderlied aus der Schweiz*, E. L. Rochholz, 1857, 'Ehrügeli-nägeli ûf em Dach, Wer lacht? Wer fine wîsse Zähn fürlocht, Muess Pfand, Pfand-pfand geb!' / *Chinese Mother Goose Rhymes*, I. T. Headland, 1900, rhyme entitled 'Grab the knee': 'One grab of gold, One grab of silver. Three—not smile; That's a good man!' (literal translation of the Chinese given).

Cf. also *Household Tales*, S. O. Addy, 1895, 'Can you keep a secret? I don't suppose you can. Don't laugh and don't cry Till it tickles in your hand', repeated similarly while tickling hand.

180

Wine and cakes for gentlemen,
Hay and corn for horses,
A cup of ale for good old wives,
And kisses for young lasses.

This verse appears consistently (though incongruously) in an old ballad, 'The Trooper and the Maid', when the maiden welcomes her lover and offers him hospitality (see F. J. Child, *English and Scottish Popular Ballads*, 1882–98, No. 299).

Cheerful Warbler (J. Kendrew), c. 1820 / *NR for Children* (J. Fairburn), c. 1825, 'Cheese, and bread for gentlemen' / Gomme, 1898, as part of Aberdeen version of 'Sally Waters', 'A cup of tea for a' good wives, And bonnie lads and lassies' / Crofton MS, 1901, 'Bread and cheese for farmers' boys' (collected 1873) / *Book of NR*, Enid Marx, 1939, 'Tobacco for the old wives'.

181

Georgie Porgie, pudding and pie,
Kissed the girls and made them cry;
When the boys came out to play,
Georgie Porgie ran away.

As with other of the better-known rhymes, numerous guesses have been hazarded that an historical character is portrayed. Andrew Lang says

Georgie Porgie

'George I'; Lady Maxse gives 'George Villiers, Duke of Buckingham'; popular tradition insists 'Charles II'. As usual, no evidence is vouchsafed. Although so popular today, it has not been found in any of the early nursery-rhyme literature. However, it must have been well-known when 'Quis-Quis', in *The Kentish Coronal*, 1841, used it to satirize the poetry critics of his day. 'In turning over the leaves of an ancient edition of the Doolittlean Hididdle-diddle, of child-pacifying notoriety, we discovered the heart-stirring fragment which stands at the head of this article...There are few men, we imagine...who have not at some period of their lives, been attentive perusers of the interesting work above mentioned.' He proceeds with his 'full exposition' of Georgy Peorgy, 'a celebrated character, who existed in the reign of the Emperor Charlemagne.'

JOH, 1844 / *NR Book*, Andrew Lang, 1897 / Kidson, 1904, to the air of an old country dance 'Tom and Mary', and of the song 'Tom loves Mary passing well', c. 1750 / *National Review*, Lady Maxse, Sept. 1941 / Correspondent (G. B. Shaw), 1950.

182

Gilly Silly Jarter,
She lost a garter,
   In a shower of rain.
The miller found it,
The miller ground it,
   And the miller gave it to Silly again.

Songs for the Nursery, 1805, 'Who has lost a garter' / JOH, 1842.

183

A girl in the army
She longed for a baby,
She took her father's greyhound
And laid it in the cradle.
Lullaby, Baby Bow Wow,
Long legs hast thou,
And wasn't it for thy cold snout
I would kiss thee now, now.

This was scribbled down by a child early in the nineteenth century and has been found since only in Scottish and north-country versions.

Girl

It appears to contain reference to the belief preserved in the saying,

> If you rock the cradle empty,
> You shall have babies plenty.

Pretence that a thing desired has already come about is found frequently in primitive folk-lore. That the rhyme is very old seems certain. Although JOH was unaware of an English version he gives a rhyme from Sweden the similarity of which to the present piece is remarkable.

MS addition in contemporary hand to *MG's Melody*, 1803 (Bussell collection) / Chambers, 1842, 'There was a miller's dochter, She couldna want a babie, O; She took her father's greyhound, And rowed it in a plaidie, O. Saying, Hush a ba! hush a ba! Hush a ba, my babie, O; An 'twere na for your lang beard, Oh I wad kiss your gabbie, O!' / *Folk-Lore of N. E. Scotland*, W. Gregor, 1881, 'The little lady lairdie She longt for a baby, She took her father's grey hunn An row'd it in a plaidy. Says Hishie, bishie, bow, wow, Lang leggit now ow, In't warna for yir muckle baird I wud kiss yir mou-ow' / *Rymour Club*, 1911, similar to 1881 / Correspondent, 1946, 'There once was a lady Who longed for a babby oh; She took her father's greyhound And put him in the cradle oh—Hush a bish a bee bo, Hush a bish a babby oh,—If it wasn't for your long nose Tha'd have a drop of titty oh.'

Cf. *Svenska Fornsånger*, A. J. Arwidsson, 1842, 'Gumman ville vagga Och inga barn hade hon; Då tog hon in Fölungen sin, Och lade den i vaggan sin. Vyssa, vyssa, långskånken min, Långa ben har du; Lefver du till sommaren, Blir du lik far din' [JOH, 1849] ('The old woman wanted to rock the cradle, But no child had she. So she took in her foal and laid it in her cradle. Lulla, lulla, long-shanks mine, Long legs have you. If you live till summer You shall be like your father.') Similar in *Norske Barnerim og Leikar*, B. Støylen, 1899, 'Det var ei gamal kjerring'.

184

> The girl in the lane, that couldn't speak plain,
> Cried, Gobble, gobble, gobble.
> The man on the hill, that couldn't stand still,
> Went hobble, hobble, hobble.

Songs for the Nursery, 1805 / *MG's Quarto*, c. 1825 / *Traditional Nursery Songs*, Felix Summerly, 1843 / JOH, 1844 / *New Statesman*, 18 Mar. 1922.

185

> There was a girl in our town,
> Silk an' satin was her gown,

Girl

Silk an' satin, gold an' velvet,
Guess her name, three times I've telled it.

This is a better verse than that in *The Booke of meery Riddles* (1600):

Yonder side sea there is a Bote,
The King's daughter of England, there
     she sate;
An if you tell her name no man it wot;
What is the maids name that sate in the boate?

'Solution. Her name is Anne, for in the fourth line it saith "An if ye tell
me her name". But this riddle is not to be seene on the booke, but to be
put without the booke, or else it will be soone understood' [1629]. One can
only wonder at the riddle-maker's restraint in not adding that her sur-
name was 'What'.

JOH, 1844 / Oral collection, 1945.
     Cf. 1600 version with Chambers, 1842, 'Down i' yon meadow There sails a boat,
And in that boat The king's son sat. I'm aye telling ye, And ye're never kenning,
Hoo they ca' the king's son, In yon boat sailing.'

186

There was a little girl, and she had a little curl
Right in the middle of her forehead;
When she was good, she was very, very good,
But when she was bad, she was horrid.

There is still doubt about the authorship of this rhyme. Most stories point
to it coming from Longfellow, but there are unexplained anomalies and it
has been noted that the inelegance of the words, particularly 'horrid',
contrast strongly with Longfellow's manner of composition. The problem
was very thoroughly discussed in 1946 in the *Papers of the Bibliographical
Society of America*, where it was stated that the earliest recording is on
an anonymous broadside, headed 'Wrong Side Up. A Poem.' This is
known to have been printed before 1870; but it is uncertain where.
From the standpoint of paper, typography, and format, it might equally
well have been produced on either side of the Atlantic. There are four
verses of which the fourth is headed 'Moral' and begins,

Little girls—as well as big—
If you want to run a rig.

This seems to indicate a British origin. 'To run a rig' (to play pranks) was a
phrase colloquial in nineteenth-century England, but never prevalent in

the U.S. All subsequent early recordings, however, are American and are dated. They include two local special-event papers, the *Reveille*, 'Published Daily for the Grand Army Fair' at Salem, Massachusetts (near Longfellow's country home), 21 December 1870, which gives a baby-talk version, and *Balloon Post*, edited at Boston by Susan Hale, 11 April 1871, which gives a musical setting. The earliest definite statement to the effect that the lines were Longfellow's was made by Blanche Roosevelt Tucker Macchetta in *The Home Life of Henry W. Longfellow* published two months after the poet's death in 1882. According to this somewhat flamboyant account, Longfellow acknowledged the authorship when taxed with it, his version being,

> There was a little durl,
> And she had a little curl,
> That hung in the middle of her forehead,
> When she was dood,
> She was very dood indeed,
> But when she was bad she was horrid.

The lines, it is said, were composed when his daughter Edith refused to have her hair curled. This story was never confirmed by a member of the Longfellow family until 1922 when Ernest Wadsworth Longfellow, then an old man, published a similar story in his *Random Memories*. Yet Susan Hale, the editor of *Balloon Post*, who was a member of the same house-party with Miss Tucker when the authorship is alleged to have been admitted, though a prolific writer, never mentioned the incident, and though seeking contributors with celebrated names for her paper, did not connect Longfellow with the poem. It is noteworthy, however, that the version she published agrees with the Tucker version in that there is no rhyme in the fourth and fifth lines. If Longfellow composed the poem it would have been during the late fifties. Other verses, usually two, are often found with the first, but it has never been suggested that Longfellow was responsible for more than the one, nor that it was ever more than a verse produced on the spur of the moment. It is possible that he tried to conceal his authorship. In *Table Talk* he wrote, 'When I recall my juvenile poems and prose sketches, I wish that they were forgotten entirely. They, however, cling to one's skirt with a terrible grasp.'

*** *Magic Mother Goose Melodies*, 1879, plate 9, is the earliest known recording of the lines in a nursery-rhyme book. The two additional verses, as now usually known, first appeared in *Sugar and Spice, And All That's Nice*, 1885, thus: 'One day she went upstairs, while her parents, unawares, In the kitchen down below were occupied with meals; And she stood upon her head, on her little truckle bed, And she then began hurraying with her heels. Her mother heard the noise, and thought it was the boys A-playing at a combat in the attic; But when she climbed the stair, and saw Jemima there, She took and she did whip her most emphatic.' The authorship of the rhyme has also been attributed to Thomas Bailey Aldrich (*N & Q*, 11th s.).

Girl

187

When I was a little girl,
  About seven years old,
I hadn't got a petticoat,
  To keep me from the cold.

So I went into Darlington,
  That pretty little town,
And there I bought a petticoat,
  A cloak, and a gown,

I went into the woods
  And built me a kirk,
And all the birds of the air,
  They helped me to work.

The hawk, with his long claws,
  Pulled down the stone,
The dove, with her rough bill,
  Brought me them home.

The parrot was the clergyman,
  The peacock was the clerk,
The bullfinch played the organ,
  And we made merry work.

JOH, 1853 / Chambers, 1870, 'When I was a wee thing, 'Bout six or seven year auld, I had no worth a petticoat, To keep me frae the cauld. Then I went to Edinburgh, To bonnie burrows town, And there I coft a petticoat, A kirtle, and a gown. As I cam hame again, I thought I wad big a kirk, And a' the fowls o' the air Wad help me to work. The heron, wi' her lang neb, She moupit me the stanes; The doo, wi' her rough legs, She led me them hame. The gled he was a wily thief, He rackled up the wa'; The pyat was a curst thief, She dang down a'. The hare came hirpling owre the knowe, To ring the morning bell; The hurcheon she came after, and said she wad do 't hersel. The herring was the high priest, The salmon was the clerk, The howlet read the order—They held a bonnie wark' / *Rymour Club*, vol. ii, pt. 1, 1912, from a lady of Hawick, born c. 1792 / *Scottish NR*, A. Moffat, 1933, shorter version, to the air 'Lennox love to Blantyre'.

  Cf. 'When I was a little boy I lived by myself'.

188

What God never sees;
What the king seldom sees;

God

What we see every day;
Read my riddle, I pray.

This simple but clever riddle (*solution*: an equal) has been well-documented on the Continent, and is shown to be both old and widely diffused. Despite the dearth of English recordings, it has very probably had an almost equally long life in Britain.

JOH, 1849 / *Folk-Lore*, 1923.
Cf. *Strassburger Räthselbuch*, 1505, 'Was Gott nit hab, der Babst selten vnnd der gemeyn man deglich. *Antwort*. Gott hat kein der jm gleich oder vber yn ist' [1876] / *Das deutsche Kinderbuch*, Karl Simrock, 1848, 'Gott sicht es nie, der Kaiser selten, Doch alle Tage Bauer Velten' / *Kleinere Schriften*, R. Köhler, 1900, 'Wass Gott nie nicht gesehen habe, das doch der gemeine Mann täglich siehet', from a MS of 1678. Köhler gives many other German versions, and one Hungarian / JOH, 1849, Swedish, 'Jag ser det dagligen; Kungen ser det sällan; Gud ser de aldrig' ('I see it daily; the king sees it seldom; God sees it never') / *Norske Folkeviser*, M. B. Landstag, 1853, 'Eg sér deð Du sér deð, Kongin sér deð sjelda, Guð sér deð alli' [Rolland, 1877] / *Polissoniana ou Recueil de turlupinades*, 1722, 'Qu'est-ce que Dieu ne voit jamais, un roi rarement et un paysan souvent?' [Rolland, 1877] / *Devinettes ou énigmes populaires*, 1877, as well as the French and Norwegian samples, Rolland quotes Dutch, Moravian, and further Swedish and German analogues.

189

Gray goose and gander,
Waft your wings together,
And carry the good king's daughter
Over the one-strand river.

There was some correspondence about this beautiful fragment in *The Times Literary Supplement*, October 1947. It was surmised that the 'one-strand river' is the sea, a metaphor 'suggestive of early Anglo-Saxon imagery'. The lines have been frequently reprinted since 1844, but where JOH obtained them is unknown.

JOH, 1844 / *The One Strand River*, H. F. Hall, 1903 / *London Treasury of NR*, J. Murray MacBain, 1933, given as 'A baby's rhyme—throwing up and catching'.

190

Goosey, goosey gander,
Whither shall I wander?

Goosey, Goosey Gander

Upstairs and downstairs
And in my lady's chamber.
There I met an old man
Who would not say his prayers.
I took him by the left leg
And threw him down the stairs.

The earliest record of this rhyme does not embrace the last four lines, and it is very probable that they had a separate origin. They are much the same as the lines which school-children address to the cranefly ('Daddy-long-legs'), sometimes pulling off its legs as they repeat,

Old father Long-Legs
Can't say his prayers:
Take him by the left leg,
And throw him downstairs.

A child who added the rhyme to his (or her) nursery rhyme book some 150 years ago seems to confirm the idea that two distinct pieces have been amalgamated:

Goosey Goosey Gander where shall we wander
Up stairs and down stairs and in my Lady's chamber.
Old father long legs will not say his Prayers,
Take him by the left leg and throw him downstairs.

It is certainly simpler to throw a cranefly downstairs than an old man. The earliest recording of the rhyme (1784) goes,

Goose-a, goose-a, gander,
Where shall I wander?
Up stairs, down stairs,
In my lady's chamber;
There you'll find a cup of sack
And a race of ginger.

In Hook's *Original Christmas Box* (1798) appears a verse:

Up stairs, down stairs, upon my Lady's window
There I saw a Cup of Sack, and a race of Ginger.
Apples at the Fire and nuts to crack,
A little Boy in the Cream Pot, up to his Neck.

It is possible that the original 'Goosey, goosey gander' rhyme was made up of these last two pieces. This rhyme, in fact, seems more than usually subject to divisions and additions. At the end of the last century 'In my lady's chamber' was often followed by,

CARTOONS BASED ON NURSERY RHYMES

a. 'The Genius of France nursing her darling', by Gillray, 26 November 1804
b. 'Kaiser, Kaiser-gander', by G. A. Stevens, 1914

Goosey, Goosey Gander

The parson in the pulpit
Couldn't say his prayers
He gabbled and he gabbled
Till he tumbled down stairs!
The stairs gave a crack,
And he broke his old back,
And all the congregation gave a quack,
    quack, quack.

The last three lines of this have become the accepted ending to the ordinary eight-line verse in the present day, except that it is 'all the little ducks' who go 'Quack, quack, quack!'

GG's Garland, 1784, as quote / *T Tit's SB*, c. 1790 / Contemporary MS addition to Bussell copy of *MG's Melody*, c. 1803, as second quote / *Songs for the Nursery*, 1805 / *Vocal Harmony*, c. 1806 / *GG's Garland* (Lumsden), c. 1815 / JOH, 1842 / Rimbault, 1846 / *NR and Songs* (T. Nelson), 1875, 'There I met an old man, And he had many cares, For bad boys stole his apples, And birds peck'd all his pears' / Mason, 1877, as c. 1803.

   Cranefly rhyme: Nancy Cock's PSB, c. 1780, 'Old father Long-Legs Can't say his prayers: Take him by the left leg, And throw him down stairs. And when he's at the bottom, Before he long has lain, Take him by the right leg, And throw him up again' / Crofton MS, 1901, 'Old Daddy long legs Wouldn't say his prayers' &c., described as 'in common use' / *Journal of Ecology*, 1949, 'Old Harry long legs Cannot say his prayers, Catch him by the right leg, Catch him by the left leg, And throw him downstairs', from Montgomeryshire. 'Harry-long-legs' is one of the oldest names for a cranefly.

191

Goosey, goosey gander,
Who stands yonder?
Little Jenny Baker;
Take her up and shake her.

London Jingles (J. G. Rusher), c. 1840 / *NR, Tales and Jingles*, 1844 / JOH, 1853, 'Little Betsy Baker' / *N & Q*, 1883, a ring game, 'Giddy Gaddy Gander, Who stands yonder? Little Bessie Baker, Pick her up and shake her, Give her a bit of bread and cheese And throw her over the water' / *Quentin Blake's Nursery Rhyme Book*, 1983.

192

Three wise men of Gotham,
They went to sea in a bowl,

Gotham

And if the bowl had been stronger
My song had been longer.

From the Middle Ages until about the end of the last century Gotham (a village near Nottingham) was proverbial for the stupidity of its inhabitants. In the fifteenth and sixteenth centuries many stories were told commemorating their follies, e.g. how, in order to have perpetual summer, they built a hedge around a cuckoo to prevent it flying away. The villagers today explain their reputation with a tale of King John. News had been received, they say, that John intended to pass through their fields on his way to Nottingham, and they, apprehending that the ground over which a king passed became ever after a public road, prevented him. The king, naturally, was incensed at their action, and sent servants to find out the reason for it. The villagers, knowing that they were likely to be severely punished, determined, if they could, to avert it. They resolved that when the king's men arrived they should be found engaged in idiotic pursuits, so that the king, when he heard of them, would be persuaded that it was a village of fools. In this they were successful. Thus, say the Gothamites, they are really 'The wise men of Gotham'.

The 'foles of gotyam' are mentioned in a MS of about 1450, and in *C Mery Talys*, 1526, there is a story 'Of the iii wyse men of gotham' / *Merie Tales of the mad men of Gotham*, c. 1565, ed. S. J. Kahrl, 1965 / The rhyme itself is not found before *MG's Melody*, c. 1765 / Also in *GG's Garland*, 1784; *Walks Round Nottingham*, 1835; *Men of Goshen*, E. J. Bellerby, 1884 / The Bussell copy of *MG's Melody*, 1803, has an additional couplet inscribed in a contemporary hand, 'They sat down on their botham, And the sea began to roll' / Thomas Love Peacock's poem *Seamen Three* begins, 'Seamen three! What men be ye? Gotham's three wise men we be. Whither in your bowl so free? To rake the moon from out the sea.'

*** The claim that the Gotham here referred to is near Pevensey is peculiar to Sussex local historians.

Cf. 'Little Tee Wee'.

193

Grandfa' Grig
Had a pig,
In a field of clover;
Piggie died,
Grandfa' cried,
And all the fun was over.

N & Q, 1883 / Oral collection, 1947, 'He put him in the clover'.

194

There was a man rode through our town,
Gray Grizzle was his name;
His saddle-bow was gilt and gold,
Three times I've named his name.

RIDDLE. JOH (1846) makes no comment on this rhyme, possibly considering that the solution *was* too silly to specify.

Holme MS, c. 1645, 'On yonder hill ther stand a Knight booted & spured & stands
upright gray-grisled is his horse, black is his saddle, j have tould y^u his name thrice
what is it say you. A. the mans name is His' / JOH, 1846; variant 1849, 'There was a
man went over the Wash, Grizzle grey was his horse; Bent was his saddle-bow. I've
told you his name three times, And yet you don't know!' / N & Q, 1865 / *Rymour
Club*, 1911, 'Great Greysteil'.

195

Gregory Griggs, Gregory Griggs,
Had forty-seven different wigs.
He wore them up, he wore them down,
To please the people of Boston town,
He wore them east, he wore them west,
But he never could tell which he loved the best.

In my Nursery, Laura E. Richards, 1890 / *Mother Goose*, Margaret Tarrant, 1929, 'Had
twenty seven different wigs, He wore them up, he wore them down, To please the
people of the town...' / *Big Book of Mother Goose* (James and Jonathan Co., Wisconsin), 1946 / Oral collection, 1946 / *Quentin Blake's Nursery Rhyme Book*, 1983.

196

Who comes here?
A grenadier.
What do you want?
A pot of beer.
Where's your money?
I forgot.
Get you gone,
You drunken lot.

Grenadier

Carey incorporated this in his ballad *Namby Pamby* which he wrote in 1725:

> Now he acts the *Grenadier*,
> Calling for *a Pot of Beer*:
> *Where's his Money? He's forgot*:
> *Get him gone, a Drunken Sot*.

Although the rhyme is here being quoted as a children's rhyme, and appears again as such in *Mother Goose's Melody*, it is found later in the century, with music, amongst a number of catches. If one is to judge by other pieces of this kind, the words were not first a children's verse later made into a catch, but first a catch and then a children's verse, and in all probability these words (or ones very similar to them) were first sung in Stuart ale houses soon after the first formation of Grenadier units.

Namby Pamby, Henry Carey, 1725 [1726] / *MG's Melody*, c. 1765 / Additional MS 34998 (British Museum), 1774/5, 'Catch, the Soldier and the Ale House Man. Who's there. A Granidier. What d'ye want. A pint of beer' / *GG's Garland*, 1784 / *T Tit's SB*, c. 1790 / *Christmas Box*, 1797 / *Songs for the Nursery*, 1805 / *Vocal Harmony*, c. 1806 / *Cheerful Warbler* (J. Kendrew), c. 1820 / *NR* (T. Richardson), c. 1830 / JOH, 1842 / *Who Comes Here, A Grenadier* (Dean and Co.), c. 1870, sheet music / *NR and Songs*, 1875 / *Rymour Club*, 1911 / Oral collection, 1947, 'Where's your money? In my pocket. Where's your pocket? I forgot it. Go away you silly blockhead.'

197

> There was a little guinea-pig,
> Who, being little, was not big;
> He always walked upon his feet,
> And never fasted when he eat.
>
> When from a place he ran away,
> He never at that place did stay;
> And while he ran, as I am told,
> He ne'er stood still for young or old.
>
> He often squeaked and sometimes vi'lent,
> And when he squeaked he ne'er was silent;
> Though ne'er instructed by a cat,
> He knew a mouse was not a rat.
>
> One day, as I am certified,
> He took a whim and fairly died;
> And as I'm told by men of sense,
> He never has been living since.

Guinea-pig

Printed at the end of *A Poetical Description of Beasts, with Moral Reflections for the Amusement of Children* (T. Carnan, 1773), where it is called 'A Guinea-pig Song'. The verses are not in the manner of the 'poetical descriptions' of the rest of the book, and it would appear that they have been included as a page-filler. Verse of this type was popular at the time, see 'In a cottage in Fife'.

GG's Garland, 1784 / *T Tit's SB*, c. 1790 / *Nurse Lovechild's DFN*, c. 1830 / *Nursery Poems* (J. G. Rusher), c. 1840 / JOH, 1842 / *National Rhymes of the Nursery*, George Saintsbury, 1895 / All recordings identical except in Rusher's chapbook, c. 1840, when the rhyme begins 'There was a little Rabbit sprig' obviously because the printer had not available a cut of a guinea-pig.

198

There was a little one-eyed gunner,
Who killed all the birds that died last summer.

A jeer at the expense of the indifferent or weekend sportsman that evidently goes back at least to the eighteenth century. Grose, in his *Dictionary of the Vulgar Tongue* (2nd edn., 1788), states that 'a piece of wit commonly thrown out at a person walking through a street or village near London, with a gun in his hand' was 'Peter Gunner, will kill all the birds that died last summer'. In this context the term Peter Gunner goes back to the seventeenth century, appearing both in Shirley's comedy *The Wittie Faire One* (1633), and in *The Cold Yeare, 1614*, which is a dialogue (printed 1615) between a London shopkeeper and a north-countryman:

> 'It was a shame that poore harmelesse birds could not be suffered in such pittifull cold weather to save themselves under a bush, when every lowsie beggar had the same libertie, but that every paltrie *Peter-gunner* must shoote fire and brimstone at them.'

JOH, 1844 / *Mother Goose's NR*, L. E. Walter, 1924.

199

In marble halls as white as milk,
Lined with a skin as soft as silk,
Within a fountain crystal-clear,
A golden apple doth appear.
No doors there are to this stronghold,
Yet thieves break in and steal the gold.

RIDDLE. *Solution:* an egg.

Minor's Pocket Book for 1791 / MS collection 'Riddles, Jokes, and Charades', c. 1810, begins with the more literal 'In marble walls as white as milk' (Opie collection) / JOH, 1844 / *Mother Goose* (T. Nelson), c. 1945.

200

> Clap hands, clap hands,
> Till father comes home;
> For father's got money,
> But mother's got none.

Infant amusement. 'The mother takes the infant's hands,' says a Scottish writer, 'and, clapping them, repeats the following pretty words:

> Clap, clap handies,
> Mamie's wee wee ain,
> Clap, clap handies,
> Dadie's comin hame,
> Hame till his wee bonnie wee bit laddie;
> Clap, clap handies.'

JOH, 1846 / *NR and Songs*, 1865, 'Clap hands! Daddy comes, With his pockets full of plums, And a cake for Johnny' / *Folk-Lore*, 1886, as quote / *Sandy Candy*, N. and W. Montgomerie, 1948, 'Clap, clap hannies, till daddy comes hame; Daddie's got pennies, And mammie's got nane' / Correspondent and oral, 1949, as 1865.

201

> Warm, hands, warm,
> The men are gone to plough,
> If you want to warm your hands,
> Warm your hands now.

JOH gives a version starting 'Wash, hands, wash' and says it is 'a formula for making young children submit to the operation of having their hands washed'. '*Mutatis mutandis,*' he adds, 'the lines will serve as a specific for everything of the kind, as brushing hair, &c.'

JOH, 1853 / *Baby's Opera*, 1877 / Oral collection, 1946, 'Warm, pandies, warm, Daddy's gone to plough, If you want to warm your pandies, Warm your pandies now'.

202

Handy dandy, riddledy ro,
Which hand will you have, high or low?

Infant's amusement in which a small object is juggled back and forth behind the back, the fists then being brought forward with an invitation to guess in which hand the object is concealed. The game, in its many simple variations, is common today. It is referred to by Shakespeare (*King Lear*, IV. vi), probably by William Langland in 1362, certainly by Skelton in 'Speke, Parrot' (c. 1525), and according to the authors of *Martinus Scriblerus* it dates back to classical times. The jingle itself is found in Chapman's play, *The Blinde Begger of Alexandria* (1598), where the beggar asks the lady Elimine to choose between himself and his rival, 'why loe heere we are both, I am in this hand, and hee is in that *handy dandy prickly prandy, which hand will you haue*', and in Jonson's *Bartholomew Fair* (1614), 'Handy-dandy, which hand will he have?' Four centuries later it was collected in London by Gomme:

Handy pandy, Sugary candy,
Which will you have?

The Scottish and north-country version is 'Nievie nievie nack', referred to by Alexander Montgomerie in his *Miscellaneous Poems* (c. 1585): 'Can ʒe not play at "nevie nevie nak"?', and by Scott in *St. Ronan's Well* (1824): 'I played it awa' at neevie-neevie-nick-nack.'

JOH, 1849, as text, also 'Handy-dandy, Jack-a-dandy, Which good hand will you have?' / *Cumberland Glossary*, William Dickinson, 1878, 'mode of casting lots: Neevy neevy nack, Whether hand will ta tak—'T topmer or t' lower' / *N & Q*, 1883, 'Handy dandy, Picady pandy, High Church or Low' / *Folk-Lore*, 1889 / Gomme, 1894 / *English Dialect Dictionary*, 1902, under Nimmy Nimmy Nack' / *Rymour Club*, 1911, 'Nievie, nievie, nick, nack, Which hand will ye tak'? The richt, or the rang? I'll beguile ye if I can' / *Land of NR*, Ernest Rhys, 1932, 'Nicky-nicky-nack, Which hand will ye tak; The right or the left, Or the little Boo-Jack?'
   Cf. *Deutsche Kinder-Reime*, E. Meier, 1851, 'Tire Tire Titz, In welcher Hand sitzts? In der untre oder obre!' / Newell, 1883, 'Windle, wandle, in welchem Handle, oben oder unt?' Gargantua played at 'la nicnoque', 1534 (Rabelais, Bk. I, ch. 22), which was Englished by Urquhart, 1653, as 'nivinivinack'.

203

Hannah Bantry, in the pantry,
Gnawing at a mutton bone;

Hannah Bantry

How she gnawed it,
How she clawed it,
When she found herself alone.

After much preluding Frederick sings this in Maria Edgeworth's story *The Mimic* (1796). His version started 'Violante, in the pantry'; JOH (1846) gives 'Hannah Bantry'; a correspondent (1946) 'Iolanthe'. A similar rhyme known to JOH was,

Hie, hie, says Anthony,
Puss in the pantry
Gnawing, gnawing
A mutton mutton-bone;
See now she tumbles it,
See now she mumbles it,
See how she tosses
The mutton mutton-bone.

204

Round about there
Sat a little hare,
The bow-wows came and chased him
Right up there!

Infant amusement. The above is the simplest of several versions collected 1945–9. The hare is represented by a finger which is passed round the palm of the child's hand; the 'bow-wows' then chase it up the arm to the neck, in the manner of 'Round and round the garden' (q.v.). Traditional in the Opie family is a fuller version, much like one recorded in *Folk-Song* (1938) and making play with all the fingers:

Round about, round about,
    here sits the hare,
In the corner of a cornfield
    and that's just there. (*close to thumb*)
This little dog found her, (*fingers, starting with thumb*)
This little dog ran her,
This little dog caught her,
This little dog ate her,
And this little dog said, Give me a little bit please.

Hare

This wording has extraordinary similarity with the Italian child-song which is accompanied with identical actions:

Piazza, bella piazza!	(A square, a fine square! (i.e. *palm of hand*)
Ci passò una lepre pazza.	There goes a mad hare.
Questo la chiappò,	This one caught her,
Questo l'ammazzò,	This one killed her,
Questo la cucinò,	This one cooked her,
E a questo, piccin, piccino,	And to this little one
Non gli restò nemmeno un	there was not left a scrap.)
briciolino.	

Folk-Lore, 1886, 'Roon aboot, roon aboot, Catch a wee mouse. Up a bit, up a bit, In a wee hoose' / Crofton MS, 1901, 'There was a wee mousie Which had a wee housie, And it ran, and it ran, Till it tickled up there' / Opie family traditional, as quote / *Folk-Song*, 1938, 'Roundabout, roundabout, there sits the old hare, This ran her, this caught her, this killed her, this ate her, And this one said, give me a bit, give me a bit, give me a bit' / Correspondent, 1946, 'Round about there, There lived a little hare, That broke its heart with grief and care, To see the pastures all so bare, And a little mouse ran right up there'. Stated to have been known in the family for more than a hundred years, having been originally learnt from north-country gypsies / Correspondent, 1949, 'There was a little mouse that lived just there (middle of the palm), And if anyone touched him he ran right up there (into arm pit)'; also 'There was a little hare and he ate his pasture bare, And he crept and he crept—right up there'.

Cf. *Canti popolari Toscani*, 1921, as quote [*Folk-Song*, 1938] / *Rimes et jeux de l'enfance*, E. Rolland, 1883, 'Celui-ci a vu le lièvre, Celui-ci l'a couru, Celui-ci l'a tenu, Celui-ci l'a mangé, Celui-là n'a rien eu. Il a dit à sa mère: J'n'ai pas eu, j'n'ai pas eu!'; 'Une petit' souris vert' passait par là, Et sa queue traînait par ci, Celui-là l'attrape. Celui-là la plume, Celui-là la fait cuire, Celui-là mange tout, Le p'tit n'a rien du tout; Liche le plat, mon p'tit, liche le plat'.

Cf. also 'This pig got in the barn'.

205

Oh, rare Harry Parry,
When will you marry?
When apples and pears are ripe.
I'll come to your wedding
Without any bidding,
And dance and sing all the night.

Rare—or wise—Harry Parry here reveals his sagacity by waiting to marry until after the harvest season. If his name is any indication, the scene of the rhyme is Wales. The guest who proposes to come 'without any bidding' may perhaps be an uninvited guest, but more likely he comes without a wedding present. On wedding days in Wales, until recently, a 'bidding' ceremony was held. Relations and neighbours would present the young couple with sums of money for setting up house and repay gifts received from the bridal families on similar occasions.

Nancy Cock's PSB, c. 1780, and *GG's Garland*, 1784, 'And lye with your bride all night' / *T Thumb's SB*, 1788 / *Newest Christmas Box*, c. 1797, 'and dance with your bride all night' / *Songs for the Nursery*, 1805, 'Harry come Parry...and stay with your bride all night' / JOH, 1843.

206

> The hart he loves the high wood,
> The hare she loves the hill;
> The knight he loves his bright sword,
> The lady loves her will.

This song is at least four centuries old. It is found in a late-fifteenth-century commonplace book from Broome Hall, Norfolk, thus:

> The hart loves the wood, the hare loves the hill,
> The knight loves the sword, the woodman loves his bill,
> The fool loves his folly, the wise man loves his skill,
> And what a shrewish woman loves is to have her will.

A Commonplace Book of the Fifteenth Century, L. T. Smith, 1886 / *The Pinder of Wakefield*, 1632, described as a 'catch'; last line 'the Churle loves his Bill' / Rimbault, 1846 / *Illustrated Ditties for the Nursery* (Dean and Son), c. 1851 / *Big Book of Mother Goose* (James and Jonathan Co., Wisconsin), 1946.

207

> Hector Protector was dressed all in green;
> Hector Protector was sent to the Queen.
> The Queen did not like him,
> No more did the King;
> So Hector Protector was sent back again.

Included by JOH in his 'Historical' section. A possible descendant is the school rhyme,

> Jumbo had a baby
> All dressed in green.
> Jumbo didn't like it
> Sent it to the Queen.

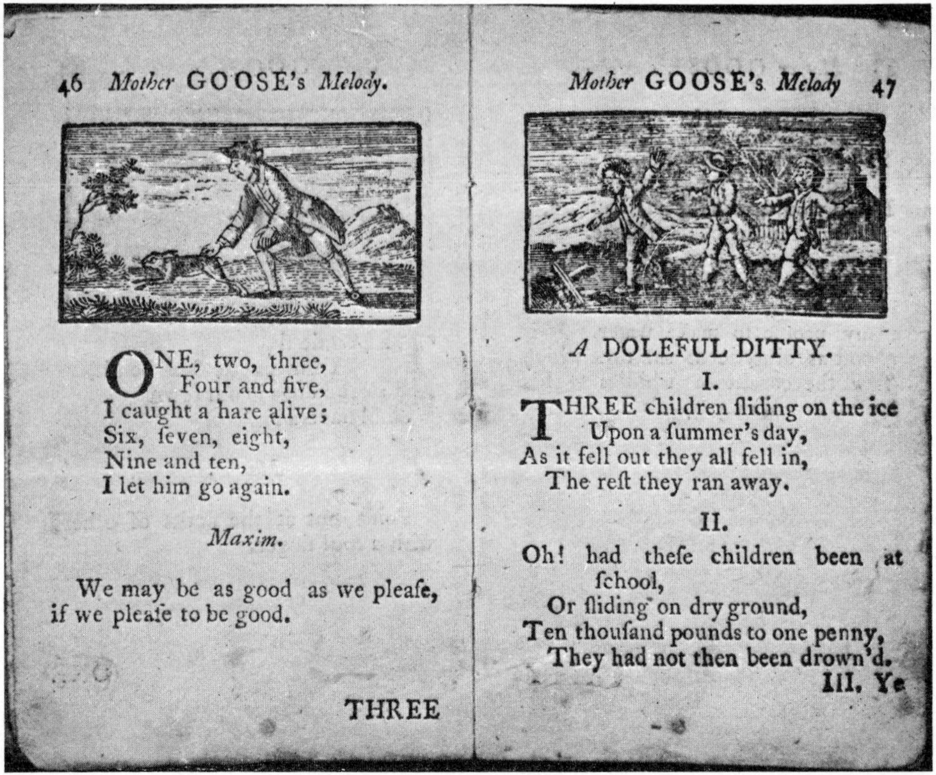

PLATE IX

The 1791 edition of *Mother Goose's Melody*. Actual size. Collection of Miss Elisabeth Ball

Hector Protector

The Queen did not like it
Because it was so fat,
Cut it up in slices
And gave it to the cat.

JOH, 1853 / *London Street Games*, Norman Douglas, 1916 / Correspondent, 1946, fairly
similar / *Hector Protector and As I Went over the Water*, Maurice Sendak (NY: Harper &
Row), 1965.

208

Heigh ho! who's above?
Nobody's here but me, my love.
Shall I come up and say how do?
Aye, marry, and thank you to.
Where's your governess? She's a-bed.
Where's the key? Under her head.
Gently trip and bring it here,
And let me in to you, my dear.
The dog will bark, I dare not stir.
Take a halter and hang the cur.
No, no. Why, why?
'Cause not for a guinea my dog should die.

This story in *Vocal Harmony* (c. 1806) throws some light on the lines in
Tommy Thumb's Pretty Song Book (c. 1744),

The Dog will bark,
I dare not to stir;
Take a Halter
And Hang up the Cur,
No, No, Why, Why,
I woud not for a Guinea
My dog should die.

The song comes from a popular 'opera' by Charles Coffey, *The Boarding-
School* (1733). One of the girls is on the verge of eloping with her lover,
the dancing master at the school. The dialogue goes:

He   Hey ho! Who's there?
She   No body here but I, my Dear.
He   Hey ho! Who's above.
She   No body here but I, my Love.
He   Shall I come up, and see how you do?

Heigh

SHE Ay, marry, and thank you too.
HE Where's your Governess?
SHE She is a-Bed.
HE Where are the Keys, my Love?
SHE Under her Head.
HE Go, go, fetch them hither,
    That you and I may be merry together.
SHE The Dog it will bark, and I dare not, I'll swear;
HE Take then a Halter, and hang up the Cur.
SHE Oh! no.
HE Why? why?
SHE I'd not for a Guinea my Dog shou'd die.
HE Then farewel, my Dear, for I must be gone.
SHE Tarry, sweet Tom, I'll be with you anon.
HE Oh! no.
SHE Why? why?
HE Your Dog is much better belov'd than I.

209

Hickety, pickety, my black hen,
She lays eggs for gentlemen;
Gentlemen come every day
To see what my black hen doth lay.
Sometimes nine and sometimes ten,
Hickety, pickety, my black hen.

This may be a version, shorn of unseemly associations, of the older 'Little blue Betty' (q.v.).

JOH, 1853, four lines / Newell, 1883, 'Mittie Mattie had a hen, She laid eggs for gentlemen, Sometimes nine and sometimes ten' / Bolton, 1888 / Gomme, 1898, 'Ticky, ticky, touchwood, my black hen...' given as formula for a game / Maclagan, 1901 / *Book of NR*, Enid Marx, 1939, 'Tiggy, tiggy, touchwood.'
    Parody: *The Face is Familiar*, Ogden Nash, 1940, 'One from One Leaves Two'.

210

I had a little hen,
    The prettiest ever seen;
She washed up the dishes,
    And kept the house clean.

Hen

She went to the mill
  To fetch me some flour,
And always got home
  In less than an hour.
She baked me my bread,
  She brewed me my ale,
She sat by the fire
  And told a fine tale.

Since, in the rest of the rhyme, there is no confirmation that the subject of it is a bird, the word 'hen' is here perhaps being used in the seven-teenth- and eighteenth-century humorous sense of 'woman' or 'dear creature'. As if in confirmation of this the version in the American *Mother Goose's Quarto* is 'I had a little doll, the prettiest ever seen' and in *Traditional Nursery Songs* 'I had a little wife'.

Songs for the Nursery, 1805 / *MG's Quarto*, c. 1825 / *Traditional Nursery Songs*, Felix Summerly, 1843 / JOH, 1853 / *Land of NR*, Ernest Rhys, 1932.

211

Chuck, chuck, chuck, chuck,
  Good morning, pretty hen.
How many chickens have you got?
  Madam, I've got ten.
Three of them are yellow,
  And three of them are brown,
And four of them are black-and-white,
  The nicest in the town.

This was, apparently, specially written (by 'Uncle James') for *The Infant's Magazine*, vol. I, No. 1 (Jan. 1866).

The Child's Illustrated Poetry Book, 1868, as above / *Word Lore*, 1927, 'Good morning, Mrs Hen . . . Four of them are yellow, And four of them are brown, And two of them are black and brown, The nicest in the town' / Correspondents, 1970s, similar to *Word Lore*, but 'And two of them are speckled red'.

212

Hey diddle diddle,
  And hey diddle dan!

239

Hey Diddle Diddle

And with a little money,
I bought an old man.
His legs were all crooked
And wrongways set on,
So what do you think
Of my little old man?

Rhyme repeated when bouncing a baby on the knee.

Crofton MS, 1901.

213

Hey diddle diddle,
The cat and the fiddle,
The cow jumped over the moon;
The little dog laughed
To see such sport,
And the dish ran away with the spoon.

Probably the best-known nonsense verse in the language, a considerable amount of nonsense has been written about it. One of the few statements which can be authenticated is that it appeared in print c. 1765. A quotation which may possibly refer to it is in *A lamentable tragedy mixed ful of pleasant mirth, conteyning the life of Cambises King of Percia*, by Thomas Preston, printed 1569,

They be at hand Sir with stick and fidle;
They can play a new dance called hey-didle-didle.

Another is in *The Cherry and the Slae* by Alexander Montgomerie, 1597,

But since ye think't an easy thing
To mount above the moon,
Of your own fidle take a spring
And dance when ye have done.

Earlier in the poem a cow had been mentioned. In his spoof *Musical Travels through England*, 1774, 'Joel Collier' (probably John Laurens Bicknell, the Elder), boasting that he was born with 'uncommon musical propensities', said that his mother could sing him to sleep whenever he was peevish, 'and that even by means of such simple melody as *Jack Sprat*, or *hey diddle diddle, the cat and the fiddle.*' 'Historical origins' abound

Hey Diddle Diddle

for this song. JOH put forward the theory that the unmeaning *Hey diddle diddle* is a corruption of Ἀδ' ἄδηλα, δῆλα δ' ᾇδε. Probably he knew he was being hoaxed when he was presented with a parallel verse in 'ancient' Greek. He omits the statement in his 1853 edition. Some other theories which may safely be discounted are (i) that it is connected with Hathor worship; (ii) that it refers to various constellations (Taurus, Canis minor, &c.); (iii) that it describes the flight from the rising of the waters in Egypt (little dog, the Dog Star, or 'Sohet'; fiddler, beetle, hence scarab; cow jumping over moon, symbol of sky, &c.); (iv) that it portrays Elizabeth, Lady Katherine Grey, and the Earls of Hertford and Leicester; (v) that it tells of Papist priests urging the labouring class to work harder; (vi) that the expression 'Cat and the fiddle' comes (*a*) from Katherine of Aragon (Katherine la Fidèle); (*b*) from Catherine, wife of Peter the Great, and (*c*) from Caton, a supposed Governor of Calais (Caton le fidèle); (vii) that it originated in the parish of Bolton Abbey soon after the dissolution of the priory in 1539, when Prior Moon had to settle down as a farmer in friendly rivalry with the local family of Heys; (viii) that it was written as a protest against Richard III's seizure of the throne, the cat being Sir William Catesby, speaker of the House of Commons. The sanest observation on this rhyme seems to have been made by Sir Henry Reid, 'I prefer to think', he says, 'that it commemorates the athletic lunacy to which the strange conspiracy of the cat and the fiddle incited the cow.'

MG's Melody, c. 1765, 'High diddle, diddle, The Cat and the Fiddle, The Cow jump'd over the Moon; The little Dog laugh'd to see such Craft, And the Dish ran away with the Spoon' / *GG's Garland*, 1784, 'Sing hey diddle, diddle' / *T Thumb's SB*, 1788 / *T Tit's SB*, c. 1790 / *The Favourite Juvenile Song of Heigh Diddle Diddle* (R. Wornum), c. 1790, 'Composed by J. Drol', sheet music, 'Heigh Diddle Diddle The Cat and the Fiddle the Cow jump'd over the Moon, Sir . . . the little Dog barked to see the sport and the Maid ran away with the Spoon, Sir' / *Infant Institutes*, 1797, 'And the dish lick't up the spoon' / *Christmas Box*, 1797 / *MG's Melody*, 1803 (appears twice) / *Songs for the Nursery*, 1805 / *Vocal Harmony*, c. 1806 / *Pretty Tales* (T. Hughes) 1808, 'High diddle, The Cat and Fiddle, The Cow leap'd o'er the Moon, The Dog he laugh'd, To see the craft, And the dish ran of[f] with the spoon' / *Blackwood's*, ? John Wilson, July 1824, 'the goats jumped over the moon . . . the cat ran away with the spoon' / *Nurse Lovechild's DFN*, c. 1830 / *The Juvenile Numerator* (D. Carvalho), c. 1830 / JOH, 1842 / *Shropshire Word-Book*, G. F. Jackson, 1881 / *Hey, Diddle, Diddle*, Randolph Caldecott, 1882.

Pantomime: *Hey Diddle Diddle or the Seven Ages of Man*, was performed at Drury Lane in 1855.

*** The rhyme is also mentioned by Haydon as being quoted by Lamb on the 'immortal evening' of 28 Dec. 1817—an evening memorable for Wordsworth's fine intonation as he quoted Milton and Virgil, Keats's inspired look, and Lamb's interjections with nursery rhymes (see under 'Diddle, diddle, dumpling, my son John').

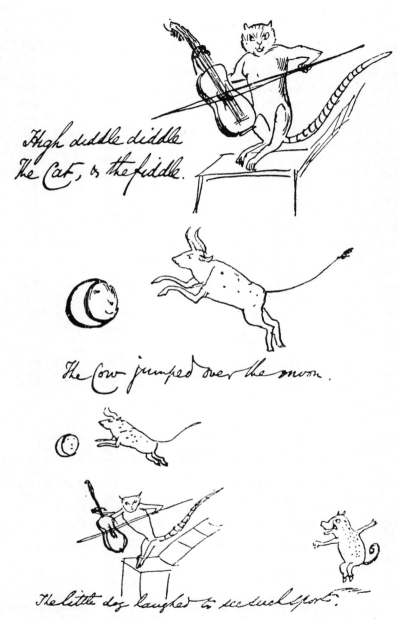

High diddle diddle
The Cat, & the fiddle.

The Cow jumped over the moon.

The little dog laughed to see such sport.

The master of nonsense depicts a nonsense masterpiece. Edward Lear's drawings for the daughter of John Addington Symonds. Collection of Angus Davidson, Esq.

214

Hey ding a ding, what shall I sing?
How many holes in a skimmer?
Four-and-twenty. My stomach is empty;
Pray, mamma, give me some dinner.

Songs for the Nursery, 1805 / JOH, 1842 / *Only True MG Melodies*, c. 1843, 'Four and twenty. I'm half starving!'

215

Hey, dorolot, dorolot!
Hey, dorolay, dorolay!
Hey, my bonny boat, bonny boat,
Hey, drag away, drag away!

JOH, 1842 / Correspondent, 1947.

216

Hick-a-more, Hack-a-more,
Hung on a kitchen door;
Nothing so long,
And nothing so strong,
As Hick-a-more, Hack-a-more,
Hung on the kitchen door.

Squirrel Nutkin, becoming more and more impertinent, 'danced up and down like a *sunbeam*', singing,

'Old Mr. B! Old Mr. B!
Hickamore, Hackamore, on the King's kitchen door;
All the King's horses, and all the King's men,
Couldn't drive Hickamore, Hackamore,
Off the King's kitchen door!'

JOH, 1846 / N & Q, 1865 / *Squirrel Nutkin*, Beatrix Potter, 1903.

217

Hickory, dickory, dock,
The mouse ran up the clock.
The clock struck one,
The mouse ran down,
Hickory, dickory, dock.

Formerly used for counting-out, the rhyme retains in the first and last lines more than a suggestion of its origin. Westmorland shepherds' telling-numbers include *Hevera* (8), *Devera* (9), and *Dick* (10), numbers which are not inappropriate in connexion with a clock. A writer in *Blackwood's Magazine* (1821) stated that the rhyme was the most frequently employed in Edinburgh 'by children to decide who is to begin a game' both then, and as far back as he could remember. And telling of the same city, John Brown recounts how Sir Walter Scott in an evening in 1810 received his frequent visitor, the child Marjorie Fleming. 'Having made the fire cheery, he sat her down in his ample chair, and standing sheepishly before her, began to say his lesson, which happened to be— "Ziccoty, diccoty, dock, the mouse ran up the clock, the clock struck wan, down the mouse ran, ziccoty, diccoty, dock".' This charming story seems likely, however, to have been a figment of Dr. Brown's imagination, and the rhyme to have been one he himself knew c. 1820 in Edinburgh (see *Scottish Historical Review*, vol. XXVI).

T Thumb's PSB, c. 1744, 'Hickere, Dickere Dock' / *MG's Melody*, c. 1765, 'Dickery, Dickery Dock' / *T Tit's SB*, c. 1790, 'Dimity, dimity, dock' / *Songs for the Nursery*, 1805 / *GG's Garland*, 1810 / Douce MS, c. 1815 / *Melincourt*, Thomas Love Peacock, 1817, 'that sublime strain of immortal genius, entitled Dickery Dock' / *Blackwood's*, 1821 / JOH, 1842 / Rimbault, 1846, two additional verses, 'The clock struck three, The mouse ran away', and 'The clock struck ten, The mouse came again' / *North British Review*, Nov. 1863, John Brown [*Horae Subsecivae*, 1882] / Mason, 1877 / *County Folk-Lore, Suffolk*, The Lady Eveline Gurdon, 1893, 'Dimmitee, Dimmitee Dot' / *Folk-Lore*, 1929, 'Ena, Dena, Dinah, Dock, Twenty mice ran up the clock, The clock strikes one, Down they run, Ena, Dena, Dinah, done!'

218

Higgledy-piggledy
Here we lie,
Picked and plucked,
And put in a pie.
My first is snapping, snarling, growling,
My second's hard-working, romping, and prowling.

Higgledy-piggledy

Higgledy-piggledy
Here we lie,
Picked and plucked,
And put in a pie.

CHARADE. *Solution:* Cur(r)-ants. The verse was the first Squirrel Nutkin song in the original manuscript of Beatrix Potter's story.

JOH, 1844 / Letter to Norah Moore, Beatrix Potter, 25 Sept. 1901

219

Higglety, pigglety, pop!
The dog has eaten the mop;
The pig's in a hurry,
The cat's in a flurry,
Higglety, pigglety, pop!

This rhyme, orally collected in England in 1945, was the invention of one who was an ardent opponent of nursery rhymes. Samuel Griswold Goodrich, an American born in 1793, and best known as the original 'Peter Parley', devoted thirty years to an endeavour to reform children's literature. He wrote, on his own reckoning, some seventy volumes of truth and instruction, and in the thirties of the last century very nearly succeeded in banishing the nursery rhyme and fairy tale from the more expensive nurseries of both England and America. In 1846, incensed by the revival of the old lore as exemplified by Halliwell's researches and 'Felix Summerley's' *Traditional Songs for the Nursery*, he wrote a skit for *Merry's Museum.* Nursery rhymes, he said, were nonsense. Anyone, even a child, could make one up. Listen!

Higglety, pigglety, pop!
The dog has eat the mop;
The pig's in a hurry,
The cat's in a flurry—
Higglety, pigglety—pop!

And because, in spite of everything, he was a bit of a genius, Goodrich had unwittingly added to the store of nursery rhyme literature. The rhyme formed the basis for Maurice Sendak's story *Higglety Pigglety Pop; or there must be more to life* (NY: Harper & Row), 1967.

Highty, Tighty, Paradighty

220

Highty, tighty, paradighty, clothed all in green,
The king could not read it, no more could the queen;
They sent for a wise man out of the East,
Who said it had horns, but was not a beast.

This verse which, as V. Sackville-West remarked (1947) 'cannot conceivably have been composed by an author in the doldrums', is said to portray the holly tree.

JOH, 1842 / N & Q, 1865, 'Itum Pāraditum all clothed in green, The King could not read it, nor Madam the Queen; They sent for the wise men out of the East, They said it had horns, but it wasn't a beast', / Rymour Club, 1912.

221

Hinx, minx, the old witch winks,
The fat begins to fry,
Nobody at home but Jumping Joan,
Father, mother and I.
Stick, stock, stone dead,
Blind man can't see,
Every knave will have a slave,
You or I must be he.

Counting-out formula from which doubtless have descended the chants of schoolchildren,

Ink, minx, pepper, drink,
Bottle full of rotten ink.

And,

Ink, pink, pen and ink,
You go out because you stink.

Archaeology of NR, J. B. Ker, 1835, beginning 'Hink, spink, the puddings stink', and subjoined to 'One-ery, two-ery, Ziccary zan' / JOH, 1843, first four lines only / New Statesman, 1922, an old favourite of 'Affable Hawk' [Desmond MacCarthy] / The Listener, 1938 / Correspondent, 1949, 'Hinx, minx, the pudding stinks, The fat begins to fry, Nobody in but Jumping Jack, Hot Pork Pie!'

Hitty Pitty

222

Hitty Pitty within the wall,
Hitty Pitty without the wall;
If you touch Hitty Pitty,
Hitty Pitty will bite you.

Squirrel Nutkin sang this riddle as he danced up and down tickling old
Mr. Brown with a *nettle*. Had he been Scottish he might have sung of
'Heg-beg', 'Hobbity-bobbity', or 'Robbie Stobbie', had he been German
'Kripple die Krapple' or 'Peter Krus', but had he lived in England three
centuries ago he would probably still have sung of 'Hitty Pitty'.

Book of merrie Riddles, 1631, 'Hitty pitty within the wall, And hitty pitty without the
wall, If you touch hitty my toy, Hitty pitty will bite the boy' / Holme MS, c. 1645, as
text / Chambers, 1842, 'Heg-beg adist the dike, and Heg-beg ayont the dike, If ye
touch Heg-beg, Heb-beg will gar you fyke' / JOH, 1849, 'Hitty-titty in-doors, Hitty-
titty out; You touch Hitty-titty, And Hitty-titty will bite you', given as a game / *Folk-
Lore of N.E. Scotland*, W. Gregor, 1881 / *Shropshire Folk-Lore*, C. S. Burne, 1883 / *Squirrel
Nutkin*, Beatrix Potter, 1903.
   Cf. *Das deutsche Rätselbuch*, Karl Simrock, 1849 / *Mecklenburgische Volksüberlieferungen*, R. Wossidlo, 1897, 'Achter'n hus' steit Peter Krus'; Wenn man em anfött,
denn bitt he'.

223

I had a little horse,
His name was Dappled Grey,
His head was made of gingerbread,
His tail was made of hay:
He could amble, he could trot,
He could carry the mustard pot,
He could amble, he could trot,
Through the old Town of Windsor.

This contains echoes of Elizabethan phraseology, e.g. in Dekker's *Satiro-
Mastix*, IV. i (1602), 'Will you amble Hobby-horse, will you trot and
amble?'

Juvenile Amusements, 1797, as text / *Songs for the Nursery*, 1805 / *Vocal Harmony*, c. 1806,
'Dobbin Grey, I bridled him, I saddled him, I gave him corn and hay. He could
amble, he could trot All around the chimney top, With a little mustard pot, Hight
gee ho!' / Chambers, 1826, first verse; in a later edition he says the rhyme is
addressed to a hobby-horse or 'a walking-cane exalted to an equestrian capacity' /

Horse

JOH, 1853, 'There was a little nobby colt, His name was Nobby Gray; His head was made of pouce straw, His tail was made of hay; He could ramble, he could trot, He could carry a mustard-pot, Round the town of Woodstock. Hey, Jenny, hey!' / *Folk-Lore*, 1901 / Correspondent, 1949, similar to 1853 but 'I had a little hobbledehoy, His name was Dapplegrey, His head was made of ginger bread . . .'.

Cf. 'I had a little pony, His name was Dapple Gray'.

224

I had a little hobby horse, it was well shod,
It carried me to London, niddety nod,
And when we got to London we heard a great shout,
Down fell my hobby horse and I cried out:
Up again, hobby horse, if thou be a beast,
When we get to our town we will have a feast,
And if there is but little, why thou shalt have some,
And dance to the bag-pipes and beating of the drum.

Newest Christmas Box, c. 1797 / JOH, 1842, 'I had a little hobby-horse, and it was well shod, It carried me to the mill-door, trod, trod, trod; When I got there I gave a great shout, Down came the hobby-horse, and I cried out. Fie upon the miller, he was a great beast, He would not come to my house, I made a little feast; I had but little, but I would give him some, For playing of his bagpipes and beating his drum' / *Mother Goose's NR*, L. E. Walter, 1924.

225

Hoddley, poddley, puddle and fogs,
Cats are to marry the poodle dogs;
Cats in blue jackets and dogs in red hats,
What will become of the mice and rats?

Hoddley Poddley, accompaniment by Paul Edmonds, 1932 / *London Treasury of NR*, J. Murray MacBain, 1933, 'Hoddley, poddley, tempests and fogs, Cats will play with the terrier dogs; Cats in blue frocks and dogs in red hats, What will become of the mice and the rats?' / *Book of NR*, Enid Marx, 1939.

226

Hoddy doddy,
With a round black body,

Hoddy Doddy

Three feet and a wooden hat.
Pray tell me what's that?

RIDDLE. *Solution:* a three-legged iron cooking pot with wooden lid (of the
kind seen suspended over fires in gipsy encampments). Hoddy-doddy:
dumpy.

Delights for Young Men and Maids (William and Cluer Dicey), c. 1745, 'Hoddy, doddy,
short Neck, round Body, 3 Feet and a wooden Hat—porridge pot' / JOH, 1849 / Eckenstein, 1906 / *Rymour Club*, 1911, 'Eetie-ottie, black bottie, Three feet and a timmer
hattie.'

227

Hokey, pokey, whisky, thum,
How d'you like potatoes done?
Boiled in whisky, boiled in rum,
Says the King of the Cannibal Islands.

Heard sung as a lullaby in 1947, and also known as a school song and
counting-out rhyme, the lines are evidently a somewhat rationalized
memory of the chorus of a popular comic song 'The King of the Cannibal
Islands' written about 1830 by A. W. Humphreys and 'Sung by him with
great applause at the London Concerts':

Oh, have you heard the news of late,
About a mighty King so great?
If you have not, 'tis in my pate—
The King of the Cannibal Islands.
He was so tall—near six feet six,
He had a head like Mister Nick's,
His palace was like Dirty Dick's,
'Twas built of mud for want of bricks,
And his name was Poonoo wingkewang,
Flibeedee-flobeedee-buskeebang;
And a lot of the Indians swore they'd hang,
The King of the Cannibal Islands.

Chorus

Hokee pokee wonkee fum,
Puttee po pee kaihula cum,
Tongaree, wongaree, ching ring wum,
The King of the Cannibal Islands.

The song is still remembered in some English and American universities.

The King of the Cannibal Islands (J. Pannell), c. 1845, broadside / Bolton, 1888, 'Hoky poky, winky wum, How do you like your 'taters done? Snip, snap, snorum, High popolorum. Kate go scratch it, You are out!' / *Folk-Lore*, 1889 / *Dorset Field Club*, 1917, 'Inky, pinky, wokey, wum, How d'ye like your teäties done? Can't ye now jest gi'e I wone? Teäties and cabbage and onions' / Oral collection, 1947 / Correspondents, 1949, 'Hokey-pokey, winky, wang, Slippery-sloppery buskey bang, A lot of Indians swore they would hang. The King of the Cannibal Islands'. Also 'How do you like your 'taties [or, praties] done? All to pieces that's the fun [or, Boiled in whisky or in rum?]'.

228

Shoe a little horse,
Shoe a little mare,
But let the little colt go bare, bare, bare.

Infant amusement in which the words are repeated while patting the soles of the feet. 'Shoe, shoe, shoe, the wild colt', a line in *The Nurse's Song*, c. 1728 (see note to No. 288), possibly refers to this game, and it may have something to do with the boys' sport 'Shoe the wild mare', referred to by Sidney (c. 1586) and commonly played at Christmas in the seventeenth century.

MG's Melody, c. 1765, 'Shoe the colt, Shoe the colt, Shoe the wild mare; Here a nail, There a nail, Yet she goes bare' / *GG's Garland*, 1784; *T Tit's SB*, c. 1790; *Vocal Harmony*, c. 1806; all as c. 1765 / *Songs for the Nursery*, 1805 / *London Jingles* (J. G. Rusher), c. 1840 / JOH, 1844, 'Pitty Patty Polt, Shoe the wild colt...' / JOH, 1849, 'Shoe the colt, shoe! Shoe the wild mare! Put a sack on her back, See if she'll bear. If she'll bear, We'll give her some grains; If she won't bear, We'll dash out her brains' / *Folk-Lore*, 1889.

229

Thirty white horses
Upon a red hill,
Now they tramp,
Now they champ,
Now they stand still.

Riddle. *Solution:* the teeth and gums. Very similar is,

Four and twenty white Bulls
sate upon a stall,

Horses

forth came the red Bull
and licked them all

of the seventeenth century. *Solution*, 'it is one's teeth and tongue'. The French have a riddle which likens the tongue and teeth to 'Une vache rouge entourée de veaux blancs'.

Holme MS, c. 1645, and *New Help to Discourse*, William Winstanley, 1669, as quote / JOH, 1842 / JOH, 1849, 'A flock of white sheep On a red hill; Here they go, there they go, Now they stand still' / N & Q, 1865, 'Four and twenty white horses on yonder hill, Gnaw they go, gnaw they go, now they stand still' / *Folk-Lore*, 1923, 'A team of white horses' / *Rocket in my Pocket*, Carl Withers, 1948, 'Thirty-two white horses, On a red hill; When you say Stop! They all stand still.'

230

A house full, a hole full,
And you cannot gather a bowl full.

RIDDLE. *Solution:* mist, or smoke, as Squirrel Nutkin knew when he sang these words through the keyhole on seeing the smoke coming from old Mr. Brown's chimney.

The Child's Weeks-work, William Ronksley, 1712, 'A House full, and a Yard full; And you cannot take up a Dish full' / Chambers, 1842, 'Banks fou, braes fou, Gather ye a' the day, ye'll no gather your nieves [hands] fou' / JOH, 1849, 'A hill full, a hole full, Ye cannot catch a bowl full' / N & Q, 1865 / *Squirrel Nutkin*, Beatrix Potter, 1903 / *American Folk-Lore*, 1935, from Tennessee 'House full, yard full, Can't catch a spoonful'.

231

Higher than a house,
Higher than a tree;
Oh, whatever can that be?

One of the vague type of riddle beloved in Tudor days. *Solution:* 'It is a starre in the skie.'

Booke of meery Riddles, 1600, 'What is it that is higher then a house, and yet seemes much lesser then a mouse' [1629] / *New Booke of Merry Riddles*, 1665 / *Delights for Young Men and Maids* (William and Cluer Dicey), c. 1745 / *Royal Riddle Book*, 1820, 'Much higher than the trees I am, My bulk exceeds a house; And yet I seem unto most men, No larger than a mouse' / JOH, 1846, as text.

Cf. variations of 'As soft as silk'.

Mr. Hubbard

232

What's in the cupboard?
Says Mr. Hubbard.
A knuckle of veal,
Says Mr. Beal.
Is that all?
Says Mr. Ball.
And enough too,
Says Mr. Glue;
And away they all flew.

Sent to *Notes & Queries* (1887) by a reader who had learnt it from his old nurse.

233

Humpty Dumpty sat on a wall,
Humpty Dumpty had a great fall.
　All the king's horses,
　And all the king's men,
Couldn't put Humpty together again.

Humpty Dumpty has become so popular a nursery figure and is pictured so frequently that few people today think of the verse as containing a riddle. The reason the king's men could not put him together again is known to everyone. 'It's very provoking to be called an egg—very', as Humpty admits in *Through the Looking-Glass*, but such common knowledge cannot be gainsaid. What is not so certain is for how long the riddle has been known. It does not appear in early riddle books, but this may be because it was already too well-known. Students of linguistics believe that it is one of those pieces the antiquity of which 'is to be measured in thousands of years, or rather it is so great that it cannot be measured at all' (Bett). Humpty Dumpty of England is elsewhere known as 'Boule, boule' (France), 'Thille Lille' (Sweden), 'Lille-Trille' (Denmark), 'Hillerin-Lillerin' (Finland), 'Annebadadeli' (Switzerland), and 'Trille Trölle', 'Etje-Papetje', 'Wirgele-Wargele', 'Gigele-Gagele', 'Rüntzelken-Püntzelken', and 'Hümpelken-Pümpelken' (different parts of Germany). The riddles have the same form and motif, and it seems undeniable that they are connected with the English rhyme. The word *Humpty-dumpty* is given in the *OED* for a boiled ale-and-brandy drink from the end of the

'To show you I'm not
proud, you may shake hands
with me.'
Tenniel's Humpty Dumpty in
Through the Looking-Glass, 1872.

'Oranges and lemons' in Mrs. Valentine's *Games for Family
Parties*, 1869

Humpty Dumpty

seventeenth century. The earliest reference to Humpty Dumpty as a squat, comical little person appears in the caption to an engraving with the title 'A Lilliputian Prize Fighting' in *The Lilliputian Riding School*, published by John Bowles & Son sometime between 1754 and 1764. Part of the caption reads:

> Sir Humpty Dumpty fierce as Turk,
> At Captain Doodle runs his fork.

There is a girls' game called 'Humpty Dumpty', described by Newell (1883) and other American writers, and apparently referred to in *Blackwood's Magazine* for July 1848. In this game the players sit down holding their skirts tightly about their feet. At an agreed signal they throw themselves backwards and must recover their balance without letting go their skirts. Eckenstein thinks the game may be older than the rhyme. Perhaps the rhyme was not originally a riddle. Eggs do not sit on walls; but the verse becomes intelligible if it describes human beings who are personating eggs. E. G. Withycombe (*Oxford Dictionary of Christian Names*) associates a human being with the name, suggesting that it echoes the pet forms of *Humphrey*, which were *Dumphry* and *Dump*; Robert L. Ripley, 'Believe it or Not', stated that the original Humpty was Richard III (1452–85); and Professor David Daube, in one of a series of spoof nursery-rhyme histories for *The Oxford Magazine* (1956), put forward the ingenious idea that Humpty Dumpty was a siege machine in the Civil War.

Juvenile Amusements, 1797, as text, but last two lines 'Four-score Men, and Four-score more Could not make Humpty Dumpty where he was before' / MS addition to Bussell copy of *MG's Melody*, c. 1803, as text but last line 'Could not set Humpty Dumpty up again' / *GG's Garland*, 1810, 'Humpty Dumpty sate on a wall, Humpti Dumpti [*sic*] had a great fall; Threescore men and threescore more, Cannot place Humpty Dumpty as he was before' / *Nurse Lovechild's DFN*, c. 1830 / *Girl's Book of Diversions*, Miss Leslie, 1835, 'Rowly bowly sat on a wall' / *The Real History of Humpty Dumty* (Cowan and Slandring), c. 1840 [Gumuchian] / *Humpty Dumpty* (D. Bogue), 1843, an unfolding panorama / JOH, 1846, 'Humpty Dumpty lay in a beck, With all his sinews round his neck; Forty doctors and forty wrights Couldn't put Humpty Dumpty to rights!' / *Through the Looking-Glass*, Lewis Carroll, 1872, last line 'Couldn't put Humpty Dumpty in his place again' which, as Alice remarked, 'is much too long for the poetry' / *Humpty-Dumpty and other nursery rhymes*, illus. J. Tenniel, &c., 1890 / *The (Eggs)traordinary Adventures of the Humpty Dumpty Family*, 1903 / *Squirrel Nutkin*, Beatrix Potter, 1903, as 1846 / *Humpty Dumpty and Belinda*, Enid Blyton, 1949.

Cf. *Danske Folkesagn*, J. M. Thiele, 1820–3, 'Lille Trille Laae paa Hylde; Lille Trille Faldt ned af Hylde. Ingen Mand I hele Land Lille Trille curere kan' (Little Trille Lay on a shelf: Little Trille Thence pitch'd himself: Not all the men In our land, I ken, Can put Little Trille right again) [JOH] / JOH, 1849, 'Thille Lille Satt på take'; Thille Lille Trilla' ner; Ingen läkare i hela verlden Thille Lille laga kan' (Thille Lille On the roof-tree sat; Thille Lille Down fell flat; Never a leech the world can show That Thille Lille can heal, I trow); also 'Lille Bulle Trilla' ner å skulle; Ingen man i detta lan' Lille Bulle laga kan' (Little Bulle fell from the shelf; No man in the whole world can restore Little Bulle) / *Deutsche Kinder-Reime*, E. Meier, 1851, 'Wirgele-Wargele, auf der Bank, Fällt es 'runter, ist es krank, Ist kein Doktor im ganzen Land, Der dem Wirgele-Wargele helfen kann' / *Germanische Mythen*, W. Mannhardt, 1858, 'Hümpelken-Pümpelken sat op de Bank, Hümpelken-Pümpelken fêl von de Bank; Do is kên Dokter in Engelland De Hümpelken-Pümpelken kuräre kann', and other versions / *Deutsches Kinderlied*, F. M. Böhme, 1897, 'Trille, Trölle uf'm Bank, Wenn's Trillele, Trälle na fällt, Ka ihm kein Doktor me helfa' [1924] / *American Folk-Lore*, 1906, Pennsylvania German, 'Hobberti Bob uf der Bank, Hobberti Bob unich der Bank, Es is ken Mann im ganse Land, Das die Hobberti Bob fange kan' / *Rimes et Jeux de l'enfance*, E. Rolland, 1883, 'Boule, boule su l'keyere, Boule, boule par terre. Y n'a nuz homme ein Angleterre Pou l'erfaire—L'œuf.' / Rudyard Kipling wrote to the American children's magazine *St. Nicholas*, 1893, with an Indian version beginning 'Hamti-Damti chargya chhutt!', remarking 'That's how we sing Humpty Dumpty in the East, when we are small'.

234

I had a little husband,
　No bigger than my thumb;
I put him in a pint-pot
　And there I bade him drum.
I bought a little horse
　That galloped up and down;
I bridled him, and saddled him
　And sent him out of town.
I gave him some garters
　To garter up his hose,
And a little silk handkerchief
　To wipe his pretty nose.

JOH suggests (1842) that this commemorates a part of Tom Thumb's history, 'extant in a little Danish work, treating of "Swain Tomling, a man no bigger than a thumb, who would be married to a woman three ells and three quarters long"'. This idea had jocularly been put forward by Sir Francis Palgrave in the *Quarterly Review* (1819) but there seems no reason why the rhyme should commemorate this particular gentleman or any of the others whose candidature has been put forward. The attractive Scottish version quoted by Chambers varies slightly in that the thumb is the little man's steed,

　　I got a little manikin, I set him on my thoomiken;
　　I saddled him, I bridled him, I sent him to the tooniken:
　　I coffed a pair o' garters to tie his little hosiken;
　　I coffed a pocket-napkin to dight his little nosiken;

Husband

I sent him to the garden to fetch a pund o' sage
And fand him in the kitchen-neuk kissing little Madge.

Songs about impossibly small husbands are also popular in France.

Nancy Cock's PSB, c. 1780, similar to text / *GG's Garland*, 1784, lacks middle four lines
/ *Infant Institutes*, 1797, four lines only / *Newest Christmas Box*, c. 1797 / *Songs for the Nursery*, 1805, as 1784 and most hereafter / *Vocal Harmony*, c. 1806 / *Pretty Tales*, 1808 /
Nursery Songs (G. Ross), c. 1812 / *Cheerful Warbler* (J. Kendrew), c. 1820 / *Grandmamma's NR* (J. Fairburn), c. 1825 / Chambers, 1842, as quote / JOH, 1842 / *Folk-Lore*, 1901,
'I had a little nabby colt No bigger than my finger. I bridled him and saddled him,
And sent him to town. I sent him to the garden To pick a little sage, He popped into
the kitchen And kissed the pretty maids' / *Rocket in my Pocket*, Carl Withers, 1948, 'I
had a little brother, no bigger than my thumb; I put him in the coffee pot—He
rattled like a drum.'

Cf. *Chansonnier de Société*, 1812, 'Le Petit Mari', in which the tiny husband gets lost
in the marital bed, roasted in the cinders, and eaten by the cat / *Chants du Langue-doc*, L. Lambert, II, 1906, three versions in which the husbands have various Tom
Thumb-like adventures.

Cf. 'I had a little horse', c. 1806, quoted p. 247.

235

Hyder iddle diddle dell,
A yard of pudding's not an ell;
Not forgetting tweedle-dye,
A tailor's goose will never fly.

'Who does not remember "A yard of pudding is not an ell"', wrote a cor-respondent to *Notes & Queries* in 1850, wondering where the rhyme came
from. Halliwell (1844) likewise only knew it as a homeless nursery rhyme.
But George Bernard Shaw, whose memory nearly stretched to this period,
recollected that the couplet he used to repeat in his youth,

Hunkydorum titherum tie
A tailor's goose it cannot fly,

was followed by a string of similar lines, of which one was 'Ham sand-wiches aren't made of tin'. From a slip-sheet preserved by Francis Douce
it may be seen that the lines form the refrain of a comic song 'A Bundle of
Truths',

Right fol de riddle del,
A yard of pudding's not an ell,
Not forgetting didderum hi,
A taylor's goose can never fly.

Hyder Iddle

The first four lines of the song, beginning 'Barney Bodkin broke his nose' (q.v.) are also maintained in the nursery. Douce dated the song-slip '1812 June'.

236

I'm called by the name of a man,
Yet am as little as a mouse;
When winter comes I love to be
With my red target near the house.

RIDDLE. *Solution:* 'A bird called Robin-Red brest.'

Book of merrie Riddles, 1631, 'I am cald by name of man, Yet am as litle as the mouse: When winter comes, I loue to be with my red gorget neere the house' / Holme MS, c. 1645, as text / *New Help to Discourse*, William Winstanley, 1669 / *Puzzling-Cap* (F. Newbery), advert 1771 (E. Newbery), 1786 / *Pleasant Exercises for Little Minds* (T. Batchelar), c. 1815 / *Royal Riddle Book*, 1820 / *Amusing Riddle Book*, c. 1830 [1903] / *New Riddles* (Henry Mozley and Sons), c. 1830, 'In winter I am often seen with red vest near the house.'

237

I'm in everyone's way,
But no one I stop;
My four horns every day
In every way play,
And my head is nailed on at the top.

RIDDLE. *Solution:* a turnstile.

Peter Puzzlewell, 1792, 'I'm in ev'ry one's way, yet no Christian I stop, My four horns ev'ry day, Horizontally play, And my head is nailed down at the top' / *Girl's Book of Diversions*, Miss Leslie, 1835 / JOH, 1849.

238

I would, if I could,
If I couldn't how could I?
I couldn't, without I could, could I?

I

Could you, without you could, could ye?
　　Could ye? could ye?
Could you, without you could, could ye?

Titled 'A Logical Song; or the Conjuror's Reason for not getting Money', the words appear in *Mother Goose's Melody*, with the facetious note, 'This is a new Way of handling an old Argument, said to have been invented by a famous Senator; but it has something in it of Gothick Construction—Sanderson'. The lines may originally have been the refrain of a ballad and are found as such in the 19th century. In Playford's *English Dancing Master* (1651) there is a dance named 'Faine I would if I could' and in *The Second Book of the Compleat Country Dancing Master* (1719) 'She would if she could'.

MG's Melody, c. 1765 / *I Would if I Could* (John Harkness), c. 1840, broadside ballad; the verse appears as a refrain to spoken intermissions, e.g. 'Lord, Dolly, said I, thou doesn't mean to be rumbustical, dost thee, can't thee fancy I? no says she but—I would, &c.' / JOH, 1846.

239

As I looked out of my chamber window,
　　I heard something fall;
I sent my maid to pick it up,
　　But she couldn't pick it all.

RIDDLE. *Solution:* snuff.

JOH, 1846 / *Mother Goose's NR*, L. E. Walter, 1924.

240

As I walked by myself
And talked to myself,
　　Myself said unto me,
Look to thyself,
Take care of thyself,
　　For nobody cares for thee.

I answered myself,
And said to myself
　　In the self-same repartee,

I

Look to thyself,
Or not to thyself,
The self-same thing will be.

In a commonplace book of about 1720 the subject of this song is given as
William III. Subsequently it appeared in early nineteenth-century gar-
lands, and then in poetry anthologies extended to seventeen verses,
entitled 'A Colloquy with Myself' and attributed to Bernard Barton, 'the
Quaker Poet' (1780–1840). Sir Walter Scott quoted it on the title-page of
his journal,

As I walked by myself
I talked to myself
And thus myself said to me.
            Old Song.

JOH (1849) remarked that the lines were not yet obsolete in the nursery.

Harley MS 7316, c. 1720 / Herd MS, 1776, 'Tune: Greensleeves' / *Pleasures of Human
Life*, 1807 / *Garland of New Songs* (J. Marshall, Newcastle), c. 1810 / *Readings in Poetry*,
1847 [N & Q] / JOH, 1849 / N & Q, 1918 / A Scottish Tune 'As I walk'd by myself' is in
the McFarlan MS, 1740 [Glen, *Early Scottish Melodies*].

241

As I was going along,
        long, long,
A-singing a comical song,
        song, song,
The lane that I went was so
        long, long, long,
And the song that I sung
        was as long, long, long,
And so I went singing along.

JOH, 1853 / *Big Book of Mother Goose* (James and Jonathan Co., Wisconsin), 1946.

242

As I was going to sell my eggs,
I met a man with bandy legs;

I

Bandy legs and crooked toes,
I tripped up his heels and he fell on his nose.

Songs for the Nursery, 1805 / *GG's Garland*, 1810 / *Grandmamma's NR* (J. Fairburn)
c. 1825 / *MG's Quarto*, c. 1825 / JOH, 1842 / *Old Nursery Songs* (Ward Lock), c. 1870.

243

As I was walking in a field of wheat,
I picked up something good to eat;
Neither fish, flesh, fowl, nor bone,
I kept it till it ran alone.

RIDDLE. *Solution:* an egg.

Peter Puzzlewell, 1792 / *Anthony Askabout's Pleasant Exercises for Little Minds* (T.
Batchelar), c. 1820 / *Fireside Amusements*, R. Chambers, 1850 / *N & Q*, 1865 / *Rocket
in my Pocket*, Carl Withers, 1948, 'in twenty-one days it walked alone'.

244

As I went over the water,
    The water went over me.
I saw two little blackbirds
    Sitting on a tree;
One called me a rascal,
    And one called me a thief,
I took up my little black stick
    And knocked out all their teeth.

JOH included this in his 1853 edition. In his edition of ten years earlier he
had printed four lines of what is probably another verse of the song:

> As I went over the water,
>   The water went over me,
> I heard an old woman crying,
>   Will you buy some furmity?

The remaining lines of this verse are given by Ker in his *Essay on the
Archaeology of Nursery Rhymes* (1834), and are of questionable humour.
Maurice Sendak illustrated the text rhyme in *Hector Protector and As I
Went over the Water* (NY: Harper & Row), 1965.

245

Now I lay me down to sleep,
I pray the Lord my soul to keep;
And if I die before I wake,
I pray the Lord my soul to take.

During its existence this bedtime verse has been revised by prayer writers and flowered by poets, but the early version remains the best remembered. Its widespread dissemination during the eighteenth century, particularly in the United States (Merle Johnson in 1935 included it in his *Most Quoted Verses in American Poetry*) was probably due to its inclusion in almost all editions of *The New-England Primer* subsequent to 1737. The circulation of this publication was perhaps unequalled in colonial days. The rhyme usually appeared with two other pieces under the heading 'Verses for Children', or, occasionally, as a 'Prayer for Lying Down'.

New-England Primer (T. Fleet, Boston), 1737, begins 'Now I lay me down to take my sleep' [1897] / *New-England Primer Improved* (John Green, Boston), 1750, exactly as text; (Alex Weir, Paisley), 1781, first British appearance [1897] / *London Jingles* (J. G. Rusher), c. 1840, 'I lay me down to rest me, I pray to God to bless me: If I should sleep and never wake, I pray the Lord my soul to take' / *NR, Tales, and Jingles*, 1844, as c. 1840 / *Study of Folk-Songs*, E. Martinengo-Cesaresco, 1886, 'no more to wake' / *N & Q*, 1909 / *Rocket in my Pocket*, Carl Withers, 1948, American side-walk rhyme 'Now I lay me down to sleep, A bag of peanuts at my feet, If I should die before I wake, Give them to my sister Kate.'

Revised version: 'Now I lay me down to sleep, I pray Thee, Lord, my soul to keep; When in the morning light I wake, Lead Thou my feet, that I may take The path of love for Thy dear sake.'

Grenville Kleiser's version: 'I lay me down in peace and sleep, For thou, dear Lord, my soul will keep. And as I rest, this prayer I make; To do thy will when I awake' [Stevenson's *Quotations*, 1935].

246

Oh that I were where I would be,
Then would I be where I am not;
But where I am there I must be,
And where I would be I can not.

The only nursery rhyme to obtain entry into *The Oxford Book of English Verse*. Entitled 'Suspiria' it was included among the anonymous ballads and songs in the 1939 edition. These same lines form the chorus of an American folk song, 'Katy Cruel'.

GG's Garland, 1784 / JOH, 1842 / *Only True MG Melodies*, c. 1843 / *Nursery Playmate*, 1864 / *Oxford Book of English Verse*, Sir Arthur Quiller-Couch, 1939, 'O would I were where I would be! There would I be where I am not: For where I am would I not be, And where I would be I can not' / *Folk Songs of Old New England*, E. H. Linscott, 1939.

247

Mr. Ibister, and Betsy his sister,
Resolved upon giving a treat;
   So letters they write,
   Their friends to invite,
To their house in Great Camomile Street.

Collected by L. Edna Walter in *Mother Goose's Nursery Rhymes* (1924) this is a memory of the first verse of *The Dandies' Ball; or, High Life in the City*, published by John Marshall with illustrations by Robert Cruikshank. The original wording was,

Mr. Pillblister,
And Betsy his sister,
Determin'd on giving a treat;
   Gay Dandies they call,
   To a supper and ball,
At their house in Great Camomile Street.

The Dandies' Ball was issued in 1819 and became immensely popular. The second edition appeared in 1820, and the third in 1821.

248

Ickle ockle, blue bockle,
   Fishes in the sea,
If you want a pretty maid,
   Please choose me.

The Only Child, J. Kirkup, from childhood in South Shields, c. 1927, 'Ickle Ockle, black bockle' / *Folk Tales of the N. Country*, F. Grice, 1944.

249

In fir tar is,
In oak none is,
In mud eels are,
In clay none are.
Goat eat ivy;
Mare eat oats.

A catch which, when said quickly, appears to be in Latin. The joke may be traced back 500 years to a medical manuscript of Henry VI's time,

'Is thy pott enty, Colelent? Is gote eate yvy. Mare eate ootys. Is thy cocke lyke owrs?'

The last two lines of the catch form the basis of 'Mairzy Doats', a swing song contagious in Britain and America in 1943, the words of which were claimed as original.

Sloane MS 4, medical collectanea by William Wyrcestre, c. 1450 (*Reliquae Antiquae*) / Chambers, 1842, 'Infir taris, inoknonis, Inmudeelsis, in claynonis, Canamaretots?' / JOH, 1843 / *Moorland Cottage*, Mrs. Gaskell, 1850, 'Infir dealis, inoak noneis; inmud eelis, inclay noneis' / *Book of NR*, Paul Woodroffe, 1896 / *Mairzy Doats*, Milton Drake, Al Hoffman, and Jerry Livingston, 1943, 'Mairzy doats and dozy doats and liddle lamzy divey. A kiddley divey too, wouldn't you?' Oral collection, 1945.

250

As black as ink and isn't ink,
As white as milk and isn't milk,
As soft as silk and isn't silk,
And hops about like a filly-foal.

In the 400-year-old *Booke of meery Riddles* the solution is 'It is a Pye that hoppeth in the street, for part of her feathers be white, and part be blacke'. The rhyme seems to have survived chiefly in dialect and was not heard by JOH, although he knew 'As soft as silk' (q.v.). It has parallels in German and French.

Booke of meery Riddles, 1600, 'What is that: as white as milke, as soft as silke, as blacke as a coale, and hops in the street like a steed foale' [1629] / *Chatterings of the Pica*, Charles Taylor, 1820, 'As 'tis the case With the Magpie 'Twill change its place But not its cry, "As white as milk, As black as coal; a long tail has This skirling fowl"' / *Lindsay Folk-speech*, Mabel Peacock, 1886 / *Rymour Club*, 1911, 'As white as the mune, as black's the coal, A lang tail and a pumpin' hole'.

Ink

Cf. *Volkslieder der Deutschen*, 'What is greener than clover? What is whiter than snow? What is blacker than coal? And trips about more than a foal?' [*N & Q*, 7th s.] / *Devinettes ou énigmes populaires*, E. Rolland, 1877, 'Qui est-ce qui est noir et blanc, Qui sautille à travers champs Et qui ressemble à monsieur le curé, Quand il est en train de chanter?'

251

Inter, mitzy, titzy, tool,
Ira, dira, dominu,
Oker, poker, dominoker,
Out goes you.

Counting-out formula. Bolton collected thirty jingles in England and America which seem to have a common origin with this, although some are much corrupted.

Bolton, 1888, examples: 'Inty, minty, tipsy, toe, Alabama, domino; Outcha, poutcha, dominoutcha, Hon, pon, tusk'; 'Eenie, meenie, tipsy, toe; Olla, bolla, domino; Okka, pocha, dominocha, Hy, pon, tush'; 'Elaka, nelaka, tipakenee, Ilaka, nolaka, domicanee, Ocheke, pochake, domicanochake, Out goes she!' All these from U.S.A. / Text verse orally collected, England, 1946 / *Children's Games*, I. & P. Opie, 1969, 'Inty, minty, tipsy, tee, I-la, dila, dominee, Occapusha, dominusha, Hi, tom, tush'.

252

Intery, mintery, cutery, corn,
Apple seed and briar thorn;
Wire, briar, limber lock,
Five geese in a flock,
Sit and sing by a spring,
O-U-T, and in again.

Counting-out formula. Fourteen versions were collected by Bolton. The oldest, given as from Massachusetts, 1806, has the lines 'As I went up the Brandy Hill' (q.v.) attached to it, another, 'Nova Scotia, 1815', has 'My little old man and I fell out' (q.v.) subjoined.

MG's Melody (Jesse Cochran, Windsor, Vt.), 1814 [Rosenbach] / *Girl's Own Book*, Mrs. Child, 1831 [1832] / JOH, 1842 / Newell, 1883 / Bolton, 1888 / Crofton MS, 1901 / *Tailor of Gloucester*, Beatrix Potter (p.p. ed.), 1902, two lines / *American Folk-Lore*, 1941, commencing 'Higher, brier, limberlock' / *Counting-Out*, Carl Withers, 1946.

253

Jack and Gye
 Went out in the rye,
And they found a little boy with one black eye.
Come, says Jack, let's knock him on the head.
No, says Gye, let's buy him some bread;
You buy one loaf and I'll buy two,
And we'll bring him up as other folk do.

A correspondent quoted this in *Notes & Queries* (1901). It used to be repeated to him, when a baby, by his mother who came from the south of England. The rhyme was used by Maurice Sendak for the ending of *We Are All in the Dumps with Jack and Guy* (HarperCollins), 1993.

254

Jack and Jill went up the hill
 To fetch a pail of water;
Jack fell down and broke his crown,
 And Jill came tumbling after.

Up Jack got, and home did trot,
 As fast as he could caper,
To old Dame Dob, who patched his nob
 With vinegar and brown paper.

This nursery rhyme, on account of its romantic possibilities, has vied with the fairy tales as a favourite for pantomime performances, e.g. *Harlequin Jack and Jill; or Mother Goose at Home Once More* at the Adelphi, 1855; *Jack and Jill* at His Majesty's, 1942. From the beginning of the nineteenth century it formed one of the chapbook series, the story being extended to fifteen verses. The second verse, above, is probably a legacy of this extension and not so old as the first which alone appears in the eighteenth-century recordings. The rhyming of water with after (*wahter* and *ahter*) in the first verse may be an indication that it dates from the first half of the seventeenth century. Claims that traces of antiquity and mystery may be seen in the rhyme have received undue notice. An origin theory put forward by the Rev. S. Baring-Gould in *Curious Myths of the Middle Ages* (1866) has been curiously often accepted. 'This verse', he said, 'which to us seems at first sight to be nonsense, I have no hesitation in saying has a high antiquity, and refers to the Eddaic Hjuki and Bil. The names

JACK AND JILL,

OLD DAME GILL.

Read it who will,
They'll laugh their fill

YORK :
Printed and Sold by J. Kendrew, Colliergate.

Jack and Jill
Went up the hill,
To fetch a pail of water
Jack fell down,
And broke his crown,
And Jill came tumbling after.

A a   B b   C c   D d

Then up Jack got,
And home did trot,
As fast as he could caper ;
Dame Gill did the job,
To plaster his nob
With vinegar and brown paper.

Then Jill came in,
And she did grin,
To see Jack's paper plaster ;
Her mother whipt her,
Across her knee,
For laughing at Jack's disaster.

Pages, actual size, from the chapbook printed by James Kendrew
of York, c. 1820

indicate as much. Hjuki, in Norse, would be pronounced Juki, which would readily become Jack; and Bil, for the sake of euphony, and in order to give a female name to one of the children, would become Jill.' Previously it had been explained that in a Scandinavian myth accounting for the markings on the moon, Mani, the moon, captured two children Hjuki and Bil, while they were drawing water. When the moon is full the children can be seen with the bucket on a pole between them. According to Lewis Spence (*Myth and Ritual*, 1947) some ancient mystic ceremony might be traced in the rhyme, if only in that 'no one in the folk-lore sense climbs to the top of a hill for water unless that water has special significance'—dew water, for instance. Spence also recalls the eighteenth-century merriment in which boys and girls rolled down Greenwich Hill on Whit-Monday. From a quotation in the Towneley Mysteries (iii. 336) Eckenstein considered that Jack and Jill were once known as superhuman beings; this inference may be doubted. Nor is it likely that the comedy *Jack and Jill*, mentioned in the Revels Accounts as having been played at court in 1567–8 refers to the nursery rhyme characters. Most early quotations coupling *Jack* and *Jill* use the names in the general sense of *lad* and *lass*, e.g. Shakespeare's 'Jack shall have Jill; Nought shall go ill', the proverb 'A good Jack makes a good Jill', and the nursery rhyme 'I won't be my father's Jack' (q.v.).

MG's Melody, c. 1765, 'Jack and Gill' (woodcut depicts two boys) / *GG's Garland*, 1784 / *Jack and Jill went up the Hill* (A. Bland and Weller), c. 1795, sheet music / *Jack and Jill and Old Dame Gill* (J. Evans), c. 1800 / Printers of other many-verse editions include G. Martin, c. 1820, with coloured illustrations and, after the first stanza, a bizarre text of its own; J. Kendrew, c. 1820; W. Walker and Son, c. 1835, panorama. The third verse is 'When Jill came in how she did grin To see Jack's paper plaster; Dame Gill (Dame Dob, or Mother) vexed, did whip her next For causing Jack's disaster' / *Songs for the Nursery*, 1805 / *Vocal Harmony*, c. 1806 / *Sugar Plum* (J. Roberts), c. 1825 / *Nurse Lovechild's DFN*, c. 1830 / JOH, 1843 / Correspondent, 1948, second verse, '. . . Jill put him to bed and plastered his head With vinegar and brown paper.'

255

Jack be nimble,
Jack be quick,
Jack jump over
The candle stick.

Candle-leaping both as a sport and as a form of fortune-telling was practised in England for some centuries and possibly engendered this rhyme. It is reported, for instance, from Wendover in Buckinghamshire, that St. Catherine's Day was formerly celebrated with many curious observances by the lace-makers there, the festivities being brought to a conclusion by 'jumping the candlestick for luck'. A candlestick with a lighted candle was placed on the floor and if, when jumping over it, the light was not extinguished, good luck was supposed to follow during the coming year. From several accounts in Ginette Dunn's *Fellowship of Song* (1980), it seems clear that 'the candlestick dance' was still popular in Suffolk pubs, at least, in the early years of the twentieth century; a contributor remembered that, especially at Christmas time, they 'used to have a lighted candle on the floor and two of the old girls used to . . . pull their skirts up and do "Jack be nimble, Jack be quick, Jack be over the candle-stick".'

Douce MS, c. 1815 / JOH, 1844 / *Mother Goose*, Arthur Rackham, 1913 / *British Calendar Customs*, 1940, 'Kit be nimble, Kit be quick' / Oral collection, 1949.
   Cf. 'The Tailor of Bisiter'.

256

Jack is alive, and likely to live,
If he dies in your hand you've a forfeit to give.

This couplet belongs to a game of forfeits. A spill which has been set alight but on which only a spark remains is passed from player to player. The rhyme has to be repeated while in charge of the spark. If the spark goes out before the lines have been completed a forfeit is demanded. Some versions also name the punishment which must be endured, such as *back-saddling*, when the unlucky player has to lie down and have chairs and other furniture piled on him. The game is also known in France, Germany (mentioned in Grimm's *Deutsche Mythologie*), Denmark, and Russia. Sir Edward Tylor in *Primitive Culture* (1871) suggests that this was the game which John of Osun, Patriarch of Armenia (c. A.D. 700) accused the Paulicians of playing, but with a live baby.

Letter from Thomas Jefferson to Dr. Cooper, 16 Jan. 1814, 'Prudent men must be on their guard in this game of *Robin's alive*, and take care that the spark does not extinguish in their hands' [*N & Q*, 10th ser., XII] / *Anecdotes*, Lætitia-Matilda Hawkins, 1822, ? travesty 'Jack's alive in my hand: if he dies in your hand smutted you shall be' / *Scottish Dictionary*, J. Jamieson, 1825, 'Jack's alive, he'se no die in my hand' / JOH, 1849, 'Jack's alive and in very good health, If he dies in your hand you must look to yourself' / Newell, 1883, 'The bird is alive, and alive like to be, If it dies in my hand you may back-saddle me'; 'Robin's alive, and alive he shall be; if he dies in my hand, my mouth shall be bridled, my back shall be saddled, and I be sent home to the King's Whitehall' / *Sheffield Glossary*, S. O. Addy, 1888 / Gomme, 1894, quotes several similar formulas / *Shetland Traditional Lore*, J. M. E. Saxby, 1932, 'Jockie-be-laund' played with a 'lowan taund' (blazing peat).

Jack

Cf. *Jeux et exercices des jeunes filles*, Mme de Chabreul, 1860, 'Petit bonhomme
vit encore, car il n'est pas mort' / *Volks- und Kinder-Spiel aus Schleswig-Holstein*, H.
Handelmann, 1874 / *Svyatochnoia Pyesni*, A. Mozarowski, 1873 [Newell] / *Children's
Games throughout the Year*, L. Daiken, 1949, Gaelic version, 'Trom! trom, cad ta os
do chionn?—A live spit, a dead spit, If my spit dies between your hands The
forfeit will be on you', &c.

257

I won't be my father's Jack,
I won't be my mother's Jill,
I will be the fiddler's wife
And have music when I will.
T'other little tune, t'other little tune,
Prithee, love, play me t'other little tune.

MG's Melody, c. 1765, 'I won't be my Father's Gill' / *GG's Garland*, 1784 / *Vocal Harmony*, c. 1806 / JOH, 1842 / *Less Familiar Nursery Rhymes*, Robert Graves, 1927, 'Won't,
won't, won't, won't, I won't be my father's Jack...And have music when I will,
will, will, will.'

258

This is the house that Jack built.

This is the malt
That lay in the house that Jack built.

This is the rat,
That ate the malt
That lay in the house that Jack built.

This is the cat,
That killed the rat,
That ate the malt
That lay in the house that Jack built.

This is the dog,
That worried the cat,
That killed the rat,
That ate the malt
That lay in the house that Jack built.

'This is the House that Jack Built' as pictured in Harris's edition of the story, originally published c. 1820 (*top*), and in Kendrew's edition, c. 1820

Jack

This is the cow with the crumpled horn,
That tossed the dog,
That worried the cat,
That killed the rat,
That ate the malt
That lay in the house that Jack built.

This is the maiden all forlorn,
That milked the cow with the crumpled horn,
That tossed the dog,
That worried the cat,
That killed the rat,
That ate the malt
That lay in the house that Jack built.

This is the man all tattered and torn,
That kissed the maiden all forlorn,
That milked the cow with the crumpled horn,
That tossed the dog,
That worried the cat,
That killed the rat,
That ate the malt
That lay in the house that Jack built.

This is the priest all shaven and shorn,
That married the man all tattered and torn,
That kissed the maiden all forlorn,
That milked the cow with the crumpled horn,
That tossed the dog,
That worried the cat,
That killed the rat,
That ate the malt
That lay in the house that Jack built.

This is the cock that crowed in the morn,
That waked the priest all shaven and shorn,
That married the man all tattered and torn,
That kissed the maiden all forlorn,
That milked the cow with the crumpled horn,
That tossed the dog,
That worried the cat,
That killed the rat,

Jack

That ate the malt
That lay in the house that Jack built.

This is the farmer sowing his corn,
That kept the cock that crowed in the morn,
That waked the priest all shaven and shorn,
That married the man all tattered and torn,
That kissed the maiden all forlorn,
That milked the cow with the crumpled horn,
That tossed the dog,
That worried the cat,
That killed the rat,
That ate the malt
That lay in the house that Jack built.

An accumulative rhyme which has had immense popularity for more than 200 years, and has probably been more parodied than any other nursery story, e.g. William Hone's *The Political House that Jack Built*, published 1819, illustrated by Cruikshank, which went into fifty-four editions; *The House that Austin Reed Built*, advertisement displayed in London Undergrounds in 1946. The rhyme has attracted the attention of both scholars and cranks, and at least two whole publications have been devoted to its significance. Facts to go on, however, are meagre. Whitmore suggests that the story is referred to in the *Boston News Letter*, 12 April 1739, in which the reviewer of a psalm book fears that one of the psalms 'may make our Children think of the Line of their vulgar Play Song, so much like it, *This is the Man all forlorn*, &c.' The rhyme is first found in *Nurse Truelove's New-Year's-Gift: or, the Book of Books for Children*, printed for John Newbery c. 1750. It has often been presumed that the original of 'The House that Jack built' is a Jewish chant, 'Had Gadya', which was first printed in 1590 in a Prague edition of the *Haggadah*. The chant, a fine early example of the accumulative story, bears comparison with an English folktale, 'The Old Woman and her Pig', but a stretch of imagination is needed to connect the subject-matter (kid, cat, dog, staff, fire, water, ox, butcher, angel of death) with the nuptials of the tattered man and forlorn milkmaid. This is not to disprove the antiquity of the English rhyme which, as JOH points out, 'is probably very old, as may be inferred from the mention of the priest all shaven and shorn'. More substantial evidence of its age, however, is shown by the equivalents to the rhyme in European languages.

Nurse Truelove's New-Year's-Gift (J. Newbery), c. 1750 [c. 1770] / *The House that Jack Built...A diverting Story for Children of all Ages* (Aldermary Church-Yard, ? R. Marshall), c. 1770 / Other early editions: J. Marshall, advt. 1780; T. Saint, c. 1780, illus. Bewick brothers; R. Christopher, with *Cock Robin*, c. 1782; Isaiah Thomas, Worcester,

Jack

Mass., c. 1786 [Worcester biblio.]; H. G. Mozley, 1800; T. Evans, c. 1800; Broadbent, c. 1800; Lincoln and Gleason, Hartford, 1806 [Rosenbach]; T. Wilson and R. Spence, 1806 [Hugo]; J. Evans and Son, 1809; T. Batchelar, c. 1810; Johnson and Warner, Philadelphia, 1812 [Rosenbach]; G. Ross, 1813; T. Brandard, c. 1815; F. Houlston, c. 1818 / *Companion for the Nursery* (J. Hodson), c. 1795 / *This is the House that Jack Built* (A. Bland and Weller), advt. 1798, sheet music / *History of the House that Jack Built* (Harris and Son), 1820, extended version, 'This is Sir John Barley-corn that treated the Boy that every morn, swept the Stable snug and warm, that was made for the Horse of a beautiful form, that carried Jack with his Hound and Horn, that caught the Fox that lived under the Thorn, that stole the Cock that crowed in the morn, that waked the Priest', &c. / Other coloured editions: J. Marshall, 1821; Dean and Munday, c. 1825; D. Carvalho, c. 1825 / Other small chapbook editions: J. Kendrew, c. 1820, ? illus. T. Bewick; T. Richardson, c. 1830; J. G. Rusher, c. 1835; J. S. Publishing, c. 1840; 'For the booksellers', c. 1840 / Special editions: Addey and Co., c. 1853; Darton and Co., c. 1860; illus. Walter Crane, 1870 [Massé biblio.]; illus. Randolph Caldecott, 1878; illus. E. Morant Cox, 1888; illus. Arnrid Johnstone, 1944.

Pantomimes: *Harlequin and Poor Robin; or The House that Jack Built*, performed at Covent Garden, 1823 / *The House that Jack Built; or Old Mother Hubbard*, by E. L. Blanchard, performed at Drury Lane, 1861.

Cf. *Danske Folkesagen*, J. M. Thiele, 1820–3, 'Der har du det Huus som Jacob bygde' [JOH, 1849] / *Das deutsche Kinderbuch*, Karl Simrock, 1848, 'Ist alles verloren' / *Chants et chansons du Cambrésis*, A. Durieux et A. Bruyelles, 1864, 'Ce jeu si connu "Voici la maison que Pierre a bâtie"' / Eckenstein and Bett quote further verses similar in form.

Parodies, political, &c., separate publications: *The Political House that Jack Built*, W. Hone, illus. G. Cruikshank, 1819 / *The Real or Constitutional House that Jack Built* (J. Asperne), 1819 / *The Financial House that Jack Built* (J. M. Richardson), 1819 / *The Theatrical House that Jack Built* (J. Grove), 1819, on management of Covent Garden Theatre / *The Loyalist House that Jack Built*, c. 1819 / *The True Political House that Jack Built, being a Parody on 'The Political...'*, 1820 / *The Royal House that Jack Built*, 1820, satire on Queen Caroline / *The Political Queen that Jack Loves*, W. Hone, illus. G. Cruikshank, 1820 / *The Christian House that Jack built by Truth on a Rock*, 1820 / Also about 1820 appeared: *The Queen that Jack Found; The Queen and Magna Charta, or the Thing that Jack Signed; The Dorchester Guide, or the House that Jack Built / The Palace that N—h built*, A parody on an old English Poem, I. Hume, c. 1830, satire on Nash / *The New House that Jack Built; a Ministerial Chaunt for Whig Nurseries*, 1837 / *The Crystal Palace that Fox Built* (David Bogue), illus. John Gilbert, 1851 / *The House that Jack Built*, George Cruikshank, 1853.

Parodies, separate juvenile publications: *Juvenile Reduplications: or, the New House that Jack Built*, J. Bisset, 1800 / *The Oak of Boscobel; a New and Ingenious Parody on the House that Jack Built* (J. Harris), 1813 / *The Coach that Nap Ran From* (Juvenile Library), 1816, on Napoleon / *The Barn that Tom Built* (J. Marshall), 1817 / *The House that Paxton Built, being a Peep at the Crystal Palace* (Darton and Co.), c. 1855.

Parodies, poetic: The best known, beginning 'Behold the mansion reared by Daedal Jack' is sometimes attributed to Pope. It first appeared, however, c. 1870, and is merely an improvement of 'Behold the mansion swift upreared for Jack!' by E. L. Blanchard, 1861. The one beginning 'And this reft house is that the which he built' is, on his own admission, by Samuel Taylor Coleridge. The one beginning 'This is the domiciliary edifice erected by John' headed 'The School Board version' first appeared c. 1885.

Curiosa: *A Kid, a Kid, Or the Jewish Origin of the Celebrated Legend The House that Jack Built* (Mahlon Day, N.Y.), 1835 / *An Attempt to Show That Our Nursery Rhyme, The House that Jack Built, is an Historical Allegory*, Henry George, M.R.C.S., 1862.

273

259

Handy spandy, Jack-a-Dandy,
Loves plum cake and sugar candy;
He bought some at a grocer's shop,
And out he came, hop, hop, hop, hop.

It is interesting that a version remembered today begins 'Namby-pamby,
Jack-a-Dandy' for 'Namby Pamby' was the nickname Pope and Carey
bestowed on Ambrose Philips. The soft and sickly style of Philips's verse
was ridiculed by Carey in *Namby Pamby or a Panegyric on the New Versification*
which had as its headpiece,

Nauty Pauty, Jack-a-Dandy
Stole a Piece of Sugar-Candy
From the Grocer's Shoppy-shop,
And away did Hoppy-hop.

It is not suggested, however, that this was the origin of these lines, and, in
fact, in an anonymous poem *The Heaven-Drivers* (1701) there appears to be
an earlier reference to the rhyme,

You Saucy Jack a dandy
Nurs'd up with tea and sugar candy.

Carey's ballad introduces a number of traditional nursery pieces (e.g.
'Little Jack Horner') and he is undoubtedly using a rhyme already well
known, the point of his ballad being that Philips's verses were no better
than the old common-place jingles sung by children.

Namby Pamby, Henry Carey, 1725 [1726] / *T Thumb's PSB*, c. 1744, 'Nauty Pauty' /
Jacky Dandy's Delight (J. Marshall), advt. 1780; (Isaiah Thomas, Worcester), 1788
[Rosenbach]; (J. Ferraby), c. 1810; (G. Ross), c. 1815; (J. Kendrew), c. 1820; (J.
Roberts), c. 1825 / *T Thumb's SB*, 1788 / *Songs for the Nursery*, 1805 / JOH, 1844 / Oral
collection, 1945, 'Namby pamby, Jack-a-Dandy'.
  Cf. 'Charlie, Charlie, stole the barley'.

260

I'll tell you a story
About Jack a Nory,
And now my story's begun;
I'll tell you another
Of Jack and his brother,
And now my story is done.

Jack a Nory

Sometimes used to put off children's demands for a story. 'Jack a Nory' is found under other names, 'Mother Morey' (c. 1825), 'Peg Amo-re' (c. 1840), 'Jack a Manory' (1865), 'Jacopo Minore' (1890), 'Jack a minory' (1913), and 'Jock o' Binnorie', as in Robert Graves's lines, in the library of the Queen's Dolls' House:

> Old friends are best, the monarch cried,
>   And stories told again,
> Tell me the story of Jock o' Binnorie
>   Every night of my reign.

In the Answers to Knot V of *A Tangled Tale*, Lewis Carroll says that one of his correspondent's answers is so meagre that, like the nursery tale of 'Jack-a-Minory', it is scarcely to be distinguished from 'zero'.

Jacky Nory's Story Book for all Little Masters and Misses, Nurse Lovechild [advertised Dec. 1745], 'I'll tell you a Story of Jackey Nory, Will you have it now or anon; I'll tell you another of Jack and his Brother, And now my Story's done' / *GG's Garland*, 1784 / *MG's Quarto*, c. 1825 / *New Year's Gift* (J. Catnach), c. 1830 / *Nursery Poems* (J. G. Rusher), c. 1840 / JOH, 1842 / *Our Mutual Friend*, Charles Dickens, 1864–5, 'The children's narrative... Get on, and get it over' / *N & Q*, 1890 / *Folk-Lore*, 1913 / *Wiltshire Magazine*, 1942.

    Cf. JOH, 1846, 'I'll tell you a story about Joll McRory; He went to the wood and shot a tory; Then he came back and told his brother, And went to the wood and shot another'.

261

> Little Jack Dandy-prat was my first suitor;
> He had a dish and a spoon, and he'd some pewter;
> He'd linen and woollen, and woollen and linen,
> A little pig on a string cost him five shilling.

Dandiprat: an old, derisive word for a small boy.

Douce MS, c. 1805, 'Little Tom Dandy Was my first shooter, He had a spoon and dish And a little Pewter' / *GG's Garland*, 1810 / JOH, 1844.

262

> Little Jack Horner
> Sat in the corner,
> Eating a Christmas pie;
> He put in his thumb,

THE
HISTORY
OF
JACK HORNER.

Containing,

The Witty Pranks he play'd,

From his YOUTH to his RIPER Years,

Being pleaſant for Winter Evenings.

*Printed and Sold in Aldermary Church
Yvrd, Bow Lane, London.*

A chapbook *History of Jack Horner*, printed c. 1770.
British Museum

Jack Horner

And pulled out a plum,
And said, What a good boy am I!

The legend which has gained currency during the past century is that the original Jack Horner was steward to Richard Whiting, last of the abbots of Glastonbury. The story goes that at the time of the Dissolution the abbot, perhaps hoping to appease Henry VIII, sent his steward to London with a Christmas gift: a pie in which were hidden the title deeds of twelve manors. On the journey Jack Horner is said to have opened the pie and extracted the deeds of the Manor of Mells. However this may be, it is a fact that one Thomas Horner took up residence at Mells soon after the Dissolution and his descendants live there to this day. What the Horner family say is that their ancestor bought the manor (together with several other manors and neighbouring farms) for £1,831. 9s. 1¾d. They point out that John Leland confirms that 'Mr. Horner hath boute the lordship of the king', in his *Itinerary* (1543). Furthermore they say that the rhyme has nothing to do with their ancestor; it is part of a long merriment called *The History of Jack Horner Containing The Witty Pranks he Play'd. From his Youth to his riper Years, Being pleasant for Winter Evenings.* Not only was their ancestor's name Tom, not Jack, but the character who sits in the corner is here specifically described as being only 13 inches high and as living near London. This *History of Jack Horner* formed one of the favourite productions of the chapbook printers in the latter half of the eighteenth century, the earliest dated copy found being issued in 1764. This metrical tale, divided into six chapters, begins,

> Jack Horner was a pretty lad,
> near London he did dwell,
> His father's heart he made full glad,
> his mother lov'd him well.

From line 21, still in the first chapter, it proceeds,

> When friends they did together meet,
> To pass away the time,
> Why little Jack be sure would eat
> his Christmas pye in rhyme.
> And said, Jack-Horner, in the corner,
> eats good Christmas-pye:
> And with his thumbs pulls out the plumbs
> and said Good boy am I.

It will be noted that the traditional lines are exceedingly awkward; they fit even more awkwardly into the piece as a whole, having no bearing on the story, and, in fact, they impede the narrative. It seems clear that they have been dragged in, probably as a peg on which to hang the tale. This is in the

Jack Horner

tradition of chapbook literature. A number of the more popular nursery rhymes have been similarly extended (e.g. 'Jack Sprat'). Indeed the traditional rhyme is found several decades earlier than the chapbook history, it being quoted in 1725 by Henry Carey in his *Namby Pamby* ballad:

> Now he sings of *Jacky Horner*
> *Sitting in the Chimney-corner*
> *Eating of a Christmas-Pie,*
> *Putting in his Thumb*, Oh fie!
> Putting in, Oh fie! *his Thumb*
> *Pulling out*, Oh, Strange! *a Plum.*

On comparing these words (the italics are Carey's) with *The History* it appears that Carey was not quoting from the chapbook version, but from a rhyme similar if not identical to the one known today. The chapbook story is, in fact, apart from the pie incident, taken from the old tale of *The Fryer and the Boy* (*ante* 1520) which in turn emanates from the more ancient *Jak & his Stepdame*, and includes (as chapter vi) a part of the *Tale of a Basyn* (c. 1340). It may be added that, from the historical angle, there is no objection to the short rhyme having originally referred to the Horner ancestor. Glastonbury, at the beginning of 1539, was the only religious house in Somerset left untouched, and it was the richest abbey in the kingdom. When Abbot Whiting was on trial for his life, Thomas Horner was a member of the complaisant jury which condemned him. It is admitted that Horner benefited by being a King's man, and the local people may well have had their own ideas about how he acquired his estates. A distich, still current in Somersetshire, which was put on record as early as 1680, runs,

> Hopton, Horner, Smyth, and Thynne,
> When abbots went out, they came in.

Horner's name, it is true, was Thomas, but, then as now, anybody might be called Jack, particularly if he was believed to be a knave. It is on record, also, that in the relevant period Whiting several times sent Christmas gifts to the king, and the story of a special presentation being concealed under a pie-crust is not so preposterous as it may seem. In the sixteenth century some surprising things found their way into pies (*vide* 'Sing a Song of Sixpence'). It may be stressed, however, that the legend which has now become so firmly attached to the rhyme has not been found in print before the nineteenth century.

Namby Pamby, Henry Carey, 1725 [1726] / [*The History of*] *Jack Horner*, advertised by William and Cluer Dicey, 1754; (Bow Church Yard), purchased by Boswell, 1763; (Glasgow), 1764; (Aldermary Church Yard), c. 1770; Patrick Mair, c. 1785; &c. / *MG's Melody*, c. 1765 / *GG's Garland*, 1784 / *T Thumb's SB*, 1788 / *T Tit's SB*, c. 1790 / *Christmas Box*, c. 1797 / *Little Jack Horner*, 'A Favourite Duett or Trio' (J. Dale), c. 1800, sheet

Jack Horner

music / *Songs for the Nursery*, 1805 / *Memoirs of Little Jack Horner* (W. Darton), 1806 / *Vocal Harmony*, c. 1806 / *Pretty Tales*, 1808, 'With his two thumbs he took two plums' / *Jack Horner's Pretty Toy* (J. E. Evans), c. 1820 / In *The Grub Street Opera*, 1731, the finale is directed to be sung to the tune 'Little Jack Horner' [*N & Q*, 5th s.] / W. Osborne and others, c. 1800, published *Little Jack Horner, Tales and Stories*, by Solomon Winlove, the contents of which (prose tales) were first issued by F. Newbery, c. 1770.

Pantomime: *Harlequin Horner or the Christmas Pie* was performed at the Theatre Royal, Drury Lane, in 1816, and, according to Gumuchian, a juvenile book of it was published by J. and E. Wallis.

*** The figure of Jack Horner has frequently been used metaphorically, as by Swift in 'A Christmas Box', by Byron in *Don Juan*, by the Member for Farnham in the House of Commons, 22 Apr. 1947. Charles Lamb put the rhyme into Latin in a letter 30 Apr. 1831, 'Horner quidam Johannulus in angulo sedebat, artocreas quasdam deglutiens. Inseruit pollices, pruna nana evellens, et magnâ voce exclamavit Dii boni, quàm bonus puer fio!' [1905], and Thomas Love Peacock (*Melincourt*, 1817) described the rhyme as 'one of the most splendid examples on record of the admirable practical doctrine of "taking care of number one"'.

263

> Now what do you think
> Of little Jack Jingle?
> Before he was married
> He used to live single.

These lines are part of the eighth verse of the fifteen-verse story of *Jacky Jingle and Sucky Shingle* which appears in the chapbook series. The remaining lines of the verse are,

> But after he married,
> To alter his life,
> He left off living single,
> And lived with his wife.

Jacky Jingle, etc. (T. Evans), c. 1800; (T. Batchelar), c. 1810; (J. Kendrew), c. 1825; (D. Carvalho), c. 1830 / *Nurse Love-Child's Legacy* (J. Catnach), c. 1830 / JOH, 1842, 'Little Jack Jingle, He used to live single: But when he got tired of this kind of life, He left off being single, and liv'd with his wife'.

Cf. 'Here's Sulky Sue'.

*** In J. Marshall's *The House that Jack built* (advertised c. 1780) there is appended 'some account of Jack Jingle', but it is a prose tale.

264

> Jack Sprat could eat no fat,
> His wife could eat no lean,

Jack Sprat

And so between them both, you see,
They licked the platter clean.

There seems to be an allusion to this rhyme in *The Marriage of Witte and Science* (c. 1570): 'Ye are but Jack Sprot to mee.—Haue houlde heare is a morsell for thee to eate.' In the seventeenth century it was a familiar proverbial rhyme, appearing twice in John Clarke's proverb collection:

Jack will eat no fat, and Jill doth love no leane.
Yet betwixt them both they lick the dishes cleane.

The name Jack Sprat also appears, but in a different context. Twenty years later the rhyme is found in James Howell's collection of proverbs but with an archdeacon as the central figure:

Archdeacon Pratt would eat no fatt,
His wife would eat no lean;
Twixt Archdeacon Pratt, and Joan his wife,
The meat was eat up clean.

In the sixteenth and seventeenth centuries 'Jack Sprat' was a term for a dwarf, and an earlier form was 'Jack Prat'. Conceivably Howell's rhyme was used against a contemporary cleric of small proportions. The verse was first recorded as it is known today by John Ray in 1670.

Paroemiologia Anglo-Latina, John Clarke, 1639, second appearance is of the first line only / *Proverbs, or old Sayed Sawes & Adages*, James Howell, 1659 / *English Proverbs*, John Ray, 1670, 'Jack Sprat he loved no fat, and his wife she lov'd no lean: And yet betwixt them both, they lick't the platters clean' / *MG's Melody*, c. 1765 / *Nancy Cock's PSB*, c. 1780 / *Life of Jack Sprat and his Wife and Cat* (J. Evans), c. 1795; (T. Evans), c. 1800; (T. Batchelar), c. 1810; (J. E. Evans), c. 1815; (J. Kendrew), c. 1820 / *GG's Garland*, 1810, 'Jack Sprat would eat no fat, His wife would eat no lean; Now was not this a pretty trick, To make the platter clean' / *Nursery Songs* (G. Ross), c. 1812 / *Jack Sprat and his Cat* (D. Carvalho), c. 1830 / *Life of Jack Sprat* (J. G. Rusher), c. 1840 / JOH, 1842 / *Only True MG Melodies*, c. 1843, 'So 'twixt them both they cleared the cloth, and lick'd the platter clean' / *Story of Little Jack Sprat*, 1904 / *Mother Goose*, Arthur Rackham, 1913 / *Popular Rhymes of Ireland*, J. J. Marshall, 1931, 'Jack Spratt could eat no fat, His wife could eat no lean, So between them both, Poor Paddy was left behind'.

265

Jack Sprat
Had a cat,
It had but one ear;
It went to buy butter
When butter was dear.

Jack Sprat

In the chapbook series the tale of Jack Sprat, which opens with the well-known lines of the previous rhyme, continues by describing the exploits of his wife Joan Cole and his 'poor one-ear'd cat'. On the title-page of *The Delightful Adventures of Honest John Cole* (1732) stands an unpleasant four-line verse beginning,

> Jack Sprat's Black-Cat
> had but one Ear,

and continuing about Joan Cole. A further indelicate version appears, also independently, in the children's garland *Tom Tit's Song Book* (c. 1790). This verse may emanate from the chapbook history, but more probably it was already known, and the idea of the one-eared cat was seized upon by the chapbook writer when he had to extend 'Jack Sprat could eat no fat' to fill the chapbook's sixteen pages. He used a number of other nursery rhymes (e.g. 'Betty Pringle's pig').

Delightful Adventures of Honest John Cole, Tipling Philosopher of the Royal Society [William Oldisworth], 1732 / T Tit's SB, c. 1790, as quote / JOH, 1843 / *Tailor of Gloucester*, Beatrix Potter (p.p. ed.), 1902 / For *Life of Jack Sprat* chapbooks see previous bibliography.

266

> As I was going up the hill,
>   I met with Jack the piper;
> And all the tune that he could play
>   Was, 'Tie up your petticoats tighter'.
>
> I tied them once, I tied them twice,
>   I tied them three times over;
> And all the song that he could sing
>   Was, 'Carry me safe to Dover'.

JOH, 1853 / *Mother Goose's NR*, L. E. Walter, 1924 / *Cakes and Custard*, Brian Alderson, illus. Helen Oxenbury, 1974.

267

> Jacky, come give me thy fiddle,
>   If ever you mean to thrive.
> Nay, I'll not give my fiddle
>   To any man alive.

Jacky

If I should give my fiddle,
   They'll think that I'm gone mad,
For many a joyful day
   My fiddle and I have had.

Burns recovered for his friend Johnson, who compiled *The Scots Musical Museum*, a song about the ancient border minstrel, Rattlin' Roarin' Willie:

O, Rattlin, roarin Willie,
   O, he held to the fair,
An' for to sell his fiddle
   And buy some other ware;
But parting wi' his fiddle,
   The saut tear blin't his e'e;
And Rattlin, roarin Willie,
   Ye're welcome hame to me.

O Willie, come sell your fiddle,
   O, sell your fiddle sae fine;
O Willie, come sell your fiddle
   And buy a pint o' wine.
If I should sell my fiddle
   The warld would think I was mad,
For mony a rantin day
   My fiddle and I hae had.

As I cam by Crochallan,
   I cannily keekit ben,
Rattlin, roarin Willie
   Was sitting at yon boord-en',
Sitting at yon boord en',
   And amang guid companie;
Rattlin, roarin Willie,
   Ye're welcome hame to me.

Burns explained that the last stanza was his own, 'composed out of compliment to one of the worthiest fellows in the world, William Dunbar, Esq.'; and the first stanza also, although not attributed to him, seems to bear his mark. The other, however, had possibly been alive on the breath of tradition for a century before the days of Burns. Scott alludes to Rattlin' Roarin' Willie (as 'the jovial harper') in *The Lay of the Last Minstrel*, and adds a note that he was a real person. Tradition says that he lived in the seventeenth century, a roaring, ranting boy, who did business in the Hawick and Langholm districts, until, having had the misfortune to murder a brother in trade who passed by the name of 'Sweet Milk', he was executed at Jedburgh. The original air which Burns collected is in Atkinson's

Jacky

MS (1694) and is cited in Ramsay's *Miscellany* (1725). It was a great favourite, and often mentioned in the eighteenth and nineteenth centuries. In *Gammer Gurton's Garland* (1784) Ritson collected a four-line verse which appears to belong to the same song:

> John, come sell thy fiddle,
> And buy thy wife a gown.
> No, I'll not sell my fiddle,
> For ne'er a wife in town.

GG's Garland, 1784 / *Musical Museum*, James Johnson, 1788 / *Songs for the Nursery*, 1805 / *GG's Garland* (Lumsden), c. 1815 / JOH, 1843 / N & Q, 1858, 'O' Willie you'll sell youre fiddle, And buy some other thing: O' Willie you'll sell youre fiddle, And buy some cradle or string. If I would sell my fiddle, The folk wid think I war mad; For monna a canty nicht My fiddle and I hae had' / *Songs of Scotland*, R. Chambers, 1863 / *Past and Present of Aberdeenshire*, Rev. W. Paul, 1881 / Kidson, 1904 / *New Statesman*, 18 Mar. 1922.

268

> When Jacky's a good boy,
> He shall have cakes and custard;
> But when he does nothing but cry,
> He shall have nothing but mustard.

Douce MS, c. 1815 / JOH, 1844 / *Cakes and Custard*, Brian Alderson, illus. Helen Oxenbury, 1974.

269

> There was a poor man of Jamaica,
> He opened a shop as a baker:
> The nice biscuits he made
> Procured him much trade
> With the little black boys of Jamaica.

The story of the poor man of Jamaica comes from *Anecdotes and Adventures of Fifteen Gentlemen*, a toy book attributed to R. S. Sharpe, published by John Marshall about 1821, with hand-coloured illustrations probably by Robert Cruikshank. (*Vide* 'As a little fat man of Bombay'.)

270

Brave news is come to town,
　Brave news is carried;
Brave news is come to town,
　Jemmy Dawson's married.

First he got a porridge-pot,
　Then he bought a ladle;
Then he got a wife and child,
　And then he bought a cradle.

One 'Jemmy Dawson', a Manchester rebel who supported the Young Pretender, was hung, drawn, and quartered on Kennington Common in 1746. He was made the hero of a ballad by Shenstone. In *The European Magazine* for January 1801 a contributor writes, apropos of Jemmy Dawson, 'A ballad is said to have been cried about the streets different from Shenstone's, which we should be glad to see, if it is in existence'. It is possible that the present verses are the ones in question. On the other hand, they seem to date from the previous century. The writer of a broadside ballad *The Unconstant Maiden* (c. 1690) seems to be incorporating or parodying verses already known to him, when in the third stanza he has the lines,

　Bad news is come to Town, bad news is carry'd;
　Bad news is come to Town, my Love is Marry'd.

Similar lines occur in the folk-song 'A blacksmith courted me'.

Chambers, 1842, second verse, 'First she gat the frying-pan, Syne she gat the ladle, Syne she gat the young man, Dancing on the table', repeated by children round the fireside, one of them being named in the first verse / JOH, 1846.

271

Jenny Wren fell sick
　Upon a merry time,
In came Robin Redbreast
　And brought her sops and wine.

Eat well of the sop, Jenny,
　Drink well of the wine.
Thank you, Robin, kindly,
　You shall be mine.

Jenny Wren

Jenny Wren got well,
    And stood upon her feet;
And told Robin plainly,
    She loved him not a bit.

Robin he got angry,
    And hopped upon a twig,
Saying, Out upon you, fie upon you!
    Bold faced jig!

This appears in Part I of T. Evans's *Life and Death of Jenny Wren* first published about 1800. The story is traditional. David Herd collected a song 'The Wren, or Lennox's Love to Blantyre' in 1776. Unfortunately, he was not able to recover every verse.

The wren scho lyes in care's bed,
    In care's bed, in care's bed,
The wren scho lyes in care's bed,
    In mickle dule and pyne O,
Quhen in cam Robbin Redbreist,
    Redbreist, Redbreist
Quhen in cam Robbin Redbreist,
    Wi' succar-saps and wyn O.

Now, maiden, will ye taste o' this,
    Taste o' this, taste o' this,
Now, maiden, will ye taste o' this?
    It's succar-saps and wyn O.
Na, ne'er a drap, Robin,
    Robin, Robin.
Na, ne'er a drap, Robin,
    Gin it was ne'er so fyn O.

*   *   *   *

And quhere's the ring that I gied ye,
    That I gied ye, that I gied ye?
And quhere's the ring that I gied ye,
    Ye little cutty quyn O?
I gied it till a soger,
    A soger, a soger,
I gied it till a soger,
    A kynd sweet-heart o' myn O.

These with two other verses (possibly his own) are given by Buchan (British Museum Adds. MS 29408). The tune 'Lennox love to Blanter' occurs in Margaret Sinkler's *Musick-Book* (1710).

Jenny Wren

The Life and Death of Jenny Wren (T. Evans), c. 1800; (T. Batchelar), c. 1810; (J. Evans and Son), 1813; (J. Kendrew), c. 1820; (D. Carvalho), c. 1830. Douce MS II, c. 1820 / *The White Mouse* (J. Bailey), c. 1820 / *History of Jenny Wren* (London), c. 1830 / *Cock Robin and Jenny Wren* (J.S. Publishing), c. 1840 / JOH, 1842, slight varia / *Life of Jenny Wren*, illus. Harrison Weir, 1853 / *Word Lore*, 1927, Somerset song, slight varia, 'When Jenny Wren was sick And in a deep decline', &c. / Correspondents, 1946 and 1967.

272

> Jeremiah, blow the fire,
> Puff, puff, puff!
> First you blow it gently,
> Then you blow it rough.

These lines apparently come from the chorus of 'Jeremiah, blow the fire (puff, puff, puff)' written and composed by John Stamford, and published 21 July 1877. The song was one of 'The Great Macdermott's' music-hall successes. 'Jeremiah, blow the fire' seems to have been a catch-phrase in the middle of the nineteenth century, as appears from a caption to a paragraph in *Punch* (30 August 1851), 'Jeremiah, You needn't blow the Fire'. An extension of the verse was popular in Scotland until about 1910, sometimes being used for ball-bouncing:

> Jeremiah, Obadiah, puff, puff, puff,
> When she goes her messages she snuffs, snuffs, snuffs,
> When she goes to school by day she roars, roars, roars,
> When she goes to bed at night she snores, snores, snores.
> When she goes to Christmas treat she eats plum-duff,
> Jeremiah, Obadiah, puff, puff, puff.

Mother Goose's NR, L. E. Walter, 1924 / *London Treasury of NR*, J. Murray MacBain, 1933 / Oral collection, 1946, 'Jeremiah, blow the fire, Puff, puff, puff! Stick a pin in Jerry's chin And blow the fire up' / Correspondent, 1949.

273

> Jerry Hall,
> He is so small,
> A rat could eat him,
> Hat and all.

Jerry Hall

Mother Goose's NR, L. E. Walter, 1924 / *Big Book of Mother Goose* (James and Jonathan Co., Wisconsin), 1946.

274

Twist about, turn about, jump Jim Crow;
Every time I wheel about I do just so.

The American comedian Thomas D. Rice is said to have heard a negro stage-driver singing this couplet in 1830. He determined to devise a new act and, with face blackened and wearing a wig of moss, he sang it as the chorus of a song he composed, 'Jump Jim Crow'. His success was immediate; he and his song became the rage in America, audiences recalling him fifteen and twenty times in an evening, and it was in this act, incidentally, that Joseph Jefferson, then aged four, made his first appearance on any stage, being carried on by Rice in a valise, from which he emerged as a 'miniature Jim Crow' and joined Rice in the song and dance. In 1836 Thomas Rice came to the Surrey Theatre, London, later moving to the Adelphi where he played for twenty-one weeks on end, a run then considered extraordinary. 'Jump Jim Crow' which, it was calculated, he sang 1,260 times in the period, was on everyone's lips, and it is believed that through this song 'Jim Crow' became the generic name for the negro in the United States. Rice, while always retaining the original refrain, constantly revised his song to meet new circumstances or refer to passing events. When he opened at the Surrey Theatre the first verse went,

> How are you massa gemmen,
>   An de ladies in a row,
> All for to tell you whar I'm from,
>   I'se going for to go!
> For I wheel about an turn about, an do just so,
> An ebery time I turn about, I jump Jim Crow.

It was later said that 'No collection of songs ever gained more popularity than those sung by Mr. Rice'. According to a contemporary ballad there was 'Jim Crow rum, Jim Crow gin, Jim Crow needle, Jim Crow pin...Jim Crow pipe, Jim Crow hat, Jim Crow this and Jim Crow that'. 'In the fashionable colonnade, in the filthiest street, in the naked damp cellar, and the luxuriantly carpeted drawing-room, the words and the tune of Jim Crow are constantly to be heard', goes another account. The story is told that the original Jim Crow was a runaway slave of American-Indian parentage who earned a precarious living as a street entertainer. He is said to have composed his own songs, notably autobiographical ones, and later to have become so successful that he was able to buy a farm of his own in Virginia where he settled until his death in 1809. According to Harry Reynolds (*Minstrel Memoirs*, 1928) his tombstone can still be seen bearing the inscription,

> Here lies poor Jim, who never more will sing
> His Jump Jim Crow or tune the fiddle string,
> Unless above, he chance to shake a toe,
> And please his friends by jumping his Jim Crow.

Bernard Shaw, one of whose nursery recollections was this song, told us: 'Jump Jim Crow was an arduous performance as you had to wheel about and turn about and jump your highest when singing it. Barry Sullivan, the greatest English-Irish tragedian of the last century, used to do this in private to amuse his friends at the height of his fame.'

Humorous Adventures of Jump Jim Crow, c. 1836 / *Fairburn's Brilliant Song Book for* 1837 / *Jim Crow's Vagaries*, 1860 / *Word Lore*, 1926, 'the nursery jingle' / *N & Q*, 1928 / Oral collection, 1946; also 1949, in the Punch and Judy show at Chessington Zoo / Correspondent (G. B. Shaw), 1950.

*** Attempts have been made to connect the traditional refrain with the hanging either in 1718 of a man named Crow, 'supposed to be the man that beheaded King Charles', or in 1727 of James Crow, a man later proved to be innocent, but there is no evidence to support an English origin.

275

> Diddle, diddle, dumpling, my son John,
> Went to bed with his trousers on;
> One shoe off, and one shoe on,
> Diddle, diddle, dumpling, my son John.

This rhyme is the centre of a choice anecdote about Charles Lamb. Robert Haydon tells in his diary of a party, held on 28 December 1817, to Wordsworth, Keats, Lamb, Monkhouse, and others, including an intrusive Comptroller of Stamps. Haydon, who was host, in introducing the comptroller to Wordsworth forgot to say who he was. After a little time the comptroller said to Wordsworth, 'Don't you think, sir, Milton was a great genius?' Lamb who was dozing by the fire turned round and said, 'Pray, sir, did you say Milton was a great genius?' 'No, sir,' replied the comptroller, 'I asked Mr. Wordsworth if he were not.' 'Oh', said Lamb, 'then you are a silly fellow.' After an awful pause the comptroller said, 'Don't you think Newton a great genius?' Haydon continues, 'I could not stand it any longer. Keats put his head into my books. Ritchie squeezed in a laugh. Wordsworth seemed asking himself, 'Who is this?' Lamb got up, and taking a candle, said, 'Sir, will you allow me to look at your phrenological development?' He then turned his back on the poor man, and at every question of the comptroller he chanted—

> Diddle diddle dumpling, my son John
> Went to bed with his breeches on.'

The rhyme seems to have been a favourite of Lamb's. Fourteen years later he returned to it in a letter to Bernard Barton. Keats alludes to it in 'The Cap and Bells', the comic fairy poem he began writing in 1819 but never finished:

> He always comes down backwards, with one shoe'—
> Returned the porter—'off, and one shoe on,
> Like, saving shoe for sock or stocking, my man John.

'Diddle, diddle, dumpling' may have been very well known at the time or possibly (an intriguing thought), Keats learned the verse from Lamb on that memorable occasion at Haydon's house.

Newest Christmas Box, c. 1797 / Contemporary MS addition to Bussell copy of *MG's Melody*, 1803, 'My son John He went to bed with his Breeches on. One shoe off and one shoe on, These were the deeds of my son John' / *Songs for the Nursery*, 1805 / Douce MS, c. 1815 / Letter to Bernard Barton from Charles Lamb, 30 Apr. 1831, 'Diddle-diddle-dumkins! meus unicus filius Johannes cubitum ivit, integris braceis, caligâ unâ tantum, inductus. Diddle-diddle, &c.' [1905] / *NR from the Royal Collections* (J. G. Rusher), c. 1840 / JOH, 1842 / *Autobiography of Benjamin Robert Haydon*, ed. Tom Taylor, 1853 / *Folk-Lore of N. E. Scotland*, W. Gregor, 1881, 'When the child was being undressed for bed the nurse kept repeating "Hey diddle dumplin', my son John"'.

***'Diddle, diddle, diddle Dumpling' was the cry of the hot-dumpling sellers.

276

> John Cook had a little grey mare,
>> He, haw, hum!
> Her back stood up and her bones were bare,
>> He, haw, hum!
>
> John Cook was riding up Shuter's Bank,
>> He, haw, hum!
> And there his nag did kick and prank,
>> He, haw, hum!

John Cook

John Cook was riding up Shuter's Hill,
    He, haw, hum!
His mare fell down and she made her will,
    He, haw, hum!

The bridle and saddle he laid on the shelf,
    He, haw, hum!
If you want any more you may sing it yourself,
    He, haw, hum!

This excellent song, now rarely heard beyond the four walls of the nursery, may already have been old when Queen Elizabeth came to the throne. The last verse is quoted in a medley by the simpleton in 'a very mery and Pythie Commedie', *The longer thou livest, the more foole thou art*, written by Wager about 1559:

I layd my Bridle upon the shelfe,
If you will any more sing it your selfe.

When the singer is asked if he is not ashamed 'thus vainly the time to spend' with such songs, he defends himself, saying, 'My Mother, as I war wont in her lappe to sit she taught me these'. The lines are, however, used as a conclusion to many other old folksongs.

The longer thou livest, William Wager, printed c. 1569 / *GG's Garland*, 1810 / JOH, 1842 / Rimbault, 1846 / *March's Nursery Tales*, c. 1860 / *Songs of Norfolk*, W. Rye, 1897, 'Robin Cook's wife she had a grey mare' / *Big Book of Mother Goose* (James and Jonathan Co., Wisconsin), 1946.

277

Little John Jiggy Jag,
He rode a penny nag,
    And went to Wigan to woo:
When he came to a beck,
He fell and broke his neck,
    Johnny, how dost thou now?

I made him a hat,
Of my coat lap,
    And stockings of pearly blue;
A hat and a feather,

John Jiggy Jag

To keep out cold weather,
So, Johnny, how dost thou now?

JOH, 1844 / *Mother Goose's NR*, L. E. Walter, 1924.

278

Is John Smith within?
Yes, that he is.
Can he set a shoe?
Aye, marry, two;
Here a nail and there a nail,
Tick, tack, too.

This rhyme appeared about 1765 in *Mother Goose's Melody*, with the maxim, 'Knowledge is a Treasure, but practice is the Key to it', and in *Gammer Gurton's Garland* (1784). It is repeated while tapping the soles of a baby's feet, being an alternative verse to 'Robert Barnes, fellow fine' (q.v.).

279

Pretty John Watts,
We are troubled with rats,
Will you drive them out of the house?
We have mice, too, in plenty,
That feast in the pantry;
But let them stay,
And nibble away:
What harm is a little brown mouse?

Songs for the Nursery, 1805 / *MG's Quarto*, c. 1825 / JOH, 1853 / *Quentin Blake's Nursery Rhyme Book, 1983*.

280

Johnny shall have a new bonnet,
And Johnny shall go to the fair,

Johnny

And Johnny shall have a blue ribbon
  To tie up his bonny brown hair.

And why may not I love Johnny?
  And why may not Johnny love me?
And why may not I love Johnny
  As well as another body?

And here's a leg for a stocking,
  And here's a leg for a shoe,
And he has a kiss for his daddy,
  And two for his mammy, I trow.

And why may not I love Johnny?
  And why may not Johnny love me?
And why may not I love Johnny
  As well as another body?

This is the nursery, and possibly original, version of the popular song 'Oh dear, what can the matter be', itself a favourite with young nursemaids of romantic disposition, and hence with their charges and confidants:

O dear, what can the matter be?
Dear, dear, what can the matter be?
O dear, what can the matter be?
Johnny's so long at the fair.

He promised he'd buy me a fairing should please me,
And then for a kiss, oh! he vowed he would tease me,
He promised he'd bring me a bunch of blue ribbons
To tie up my bonny brown hair.

And it's O dear, what can the matter be?
Dear, dear, what can the matter be?
O dear, what can the matter be?
Johnny's so long at the fair.

He promised to buy me a pair of sleeve buttons,
A pair of new garters that cost him but two pence,
He promised he'd bring me a bunch of blue ribbons
To tie up my bonny brown hair.

And it's O dear, what can the matter be?
Dear, dear, what can the matter be?
O dear, what can the matter be?
Johnny's so long at the fair.

Johnny

He promised he'd bring me a basket of posies,
A garland of lilies, a garland of roses,
A little straw hat, to set off the blue ribbons
That tie up my bonny brown hair.

It has the lilt and light-heartedness of a folk-song, but has long been thought to have been written towards the close of the eighteenth century (c. 1792) when it first appeared in print, and came into public favour, Chappell says, through being sung as a duet at Harrison's concerts. However, in the Mansfield MS, a collection of Scots songs, compiled probably by Elizabeth St. Clair between 1770 and 1780, there appears an earlier version of the song as follows:

> O what can the matter be
> And what can the matter be
> O what can the matter be
> Johnny bydes lang at the fair
>
> He'll buy me a twopenny whistle
> He'll buy me a threepenny fair
> He'll buy me a Bunch o' Blue Ribbons
> To tye up my bonny Broun Hair
>
> O saw ye him coming
> And saw ye him coming
> O saw ye him coming
> Hame frae the Newcastle fair

Nursery version: *Songs for the Nursery*, 1805 / *MG's Quarto*, c. 1825 / JOH, 1853 / *Mother Goose*, Kate Greenaway, 1881 / *Past and Present of Aberdeenshire*, W. Paul, 1881 / *Mother Goose*, Arthur Rackham, 1913.

Popular song: Mansfield MS, c. 1775 [1935] / *O! dear what can the matter be?* (J. Dale), c. 1792, sheet music 'engraved from the Original Manuscript'; (R. Birchall), c. 1792 / *The British Lyre, or Muses Repository*, Jan. 1793, 'a favourite duet' / *O dear, what can the matter be?* (Stewart and Co., Edinburgh), c. 1795, sheet music / *Musical Museum*, 1799 / N & Q, 1906–7 / Williams, 1923, 'He promised to buy me a basket of linen, A little straw hat and a bunch of blue ribbon, Before he had spent his very last shilling' / *Come Hither*, Walter de la Mare, 1923 / *Mother Goose's NR*, L. E. Walter, 1924.

Frequently parodied, e.g. at the time of George IV's coronation, 'Oh! dear, what can the matter be? Caroline's come, lack-a-day'; and during Crimean War, 'O dear, what can the matter be? England and France they're going to shatter me; O dear, what can the matter be? Pity poor Nicholas the Bear.'

281

Ride away, ride away,
Johnny shall ride,

Johnny

He shall have a pussy cat
Tied to one side;
He shall have a little dog
Tied to the other,
And Johnny shall ride
To see his grandmother.

Denham (1858) says that the Scottish version, in which Johnny rides to Berwick, is a fragment of the 'good old border song "Go to Berwick, Johnny"'. One of the surviving stanzas, collected by Denham from an old woman born c. 1750, runs,

Go to Berwick, Johnny,
On yer braid sword bind ye;
Wi' a' my graith upon me,
I'll be close behind ye.
Ye'll ride on the colt
And I'll ride on the filly;
Saddle horse and mare,
And we'll to Berwick, Billy.

Ritson (1794) knew a less ornate version beginning:

Go, go, go,
Go to Berwick, Johnny,
Thou shalt have the horse,
And I shall have the poney.

He said he had heard that it was made up during one of the marauding expeditions of Sir William Wallace, the Scottish hero; and that the person thus addressed was 'no other than his *fidus Achates*, Sir John Graham'. This was ridiculed by David Laing (1839) who said he 'never heard such an assertion from the lips of any Scotsman.... The silly old verses are usually chanted by nurses to divert their little ones, and have not the smallest allusion either to Wallace or Graham.'

Vocal Harmony, c. 1806, 'High a cock horse, my baby shall ride' / JOH, 1842, 'Ride, baby, ride, Pretty baby shall ride, And have little puppy-dog tied to her side, And little pussy-cat tied to the other, And away she shall ride to see her grandmother'; also 'Highty cock O! To London we go, To York we ride; And Edward has pussy-cat tied to his side; He shall have little dog tied to the other, and then he goes trid trod to see his grandmother' / *Children's Encyclopedia*, 1908 / Correspondent, 1946, 'Off we go to London, to London we shall ride, Little dog and Chitty-cat tied to a side. Little dog on one side, Chitty on the other, And away we shall go, to see Grandmother.'

282

Johnny Armstrong killed a calf,
Peter Henderson got half,
Willy Wilkinson got the head,
Ring the bell, the calf is dead.

Possibly refers to the famous freebooter of the Border country, John Armstrong, who was captured by James V and hanged in 1528. A number of songs and ballads were written about him. Izaak Walton mentions one, and another is in *Wit Restor'd* (1658). An early eighteenth-century chapbook gives a detailed prose account of the outlaw's adventures.

New Year's Gift (J. Catnach), c. 1830 [Hindley, 1878] / JOH, 1844.

283

Little Johnny Morgan,
Gentleman of Wales,
Came riding on a nanny-goat,
Selling of pigs' tails.

Knee song. 'Shon [John] ap Morgan' was a common stereotypical name for a Welshman in the seventeenth and eighteenth centuries, and probably before. Eighteenth century woodcuts making fun of Welshmen often showed them riding on goats (see *Words with Pictures: Welsh Images and Images of Wales in the Popular Press, 1640–1860*, Peter Lord, 1995, pp. 46–9).

JOH, 1849, 'Little Shon a Morgan' / *Favourite NR* (Juvenile Productions), c. 1942.

284

Here am I,
Little Jumping Joan;
When nobody's with me
I'm all alone.

This is probably a bawdy quip from Stuart times. JOH infers from Beaumont and Fletcher that *jumping Joan* was a cant term for a lady of little reputation. This would seem to be borne out by a catch in Playford's *Catch that Catch can* (1685):

> Joan, Joan, for your part,
> you love kissing with all your Heart,
> I marry do I, says jumping Joan;
> and therefore to thee I make my moan.

In a manuscript *Livre de Contredance*, by André Lorin (probably 1688), there is a country dance called 'Jeanne la Sauteusse'. Lorin says he went to England in 1684 to learn dances. In a manuscript of about 1725 (Harley 7316) a poet regrets that in a large roomful of people there was 'never a one that could whistle Moll Peatly or sing Jumping Joan'. The lines are reminiscent of the manner in which the mummers used to introduce themselves.

Adventures of Jumping Joan (T. Hughes), advt. 1808 / *Jumping Joan* (J. E. Evans), c. 1820, first of sixteen verses; (J. Catnach), c. 1820 / *Little Jumping Joan with her Cat, Dog, and Parrot* (G. Martin), c. 1820 / *The Diverting History of Jumping Joan* (W. Walker), c. 1825; (J. S. Publishing), c. 1840 / Letter to Bernard Barton from Charles Lamb, 30 Apr. 1831, 'Hic adsum saltans Joannula. Cum nemo adsit mihi, semper resto sola' [1905] / JOH, 1842 / *Mother Goose*, Kate Greenaway, 1881 / Oral collection, c. 1945.

285

> There was a king, and he had three daughters,
> And they all lived in a basin of water;
> The basin bended,
> My story's ended.
> If the basin had been stronger,
> My story would have been longer.

JOH, 1844.
   Cf. 'Three wise men of Gotham'.

286

> There was a king met a king
> In a narrow lane;
> Said the king to the king,
> Where have you been?

a

b

c

JUMPING JOAN.

→►►◄◄—

Here am I, little

Jumping Joan,

When nobody's with me,

I'm always alone.

e

d

f

g

Woodcuts from (*a* & *b*) Catnach's *Nursery Rhymes*, c. 1830; (*c* & *f*) *The Waggon Load of Money*, c. 1825; (*d*) *The Top Book of All*, c. 1760; (*e*) J. E. Evans's *Jumping Joan*, c. 1820; (*g*) Kendrew's *Jack Sprat*, c. 1820

King

I have been a hunting
  The buck and the doe.
Will you lend me your dog?
  Yes, I will do so;
Call upon him, call upon him.
  What is his name?
I have told you twice
  And won't tell you again.

RIDDLE. *Solution:* 'the mens names were King & the dogs name was Bin.' This is one of the riddles collected by Randle Holme in the seventeenth century which, in spite of the paucity of its wit, is still heard today.

Holme MS, c. 1645 / *Nurse Lovechild's DFN*, c. 1830 / JOH, 1844, last verse, 'There's the dog, *take* the dog'. 'What's the dog's name?' 'I've told you already.' 'Pray tell me again' / N & Q, 1866, 'Says the body to a body, where has't thou a-*ben*? I've ben in my wood A-hunting me some roe', &c. / *Folk-Lore*, 1889 / *Rymour Club*, 1913 / Oral collection, 1945 / Correspondent, 1949, 'My nurse had another version "There were three knights going over the water. Saith the knight to the knight call the dog after. Saith the knight to the knight what shall I call him. Saith the knight to the knight thrice have I named him." Dog's name was *Seth*. My invariable answer was *After*, which was coldly received.'

Cf. *Germanische Mythen*, W. Mannhardt, 1858, p. 332, many German equivalents, beginning 'There was a dog in "Engelland" [or "Pömelland"]', the dog's name being 'was'; also a Swedish version, p. 331.

287

I'm the king of the castle,
Get down you dirty rascal.

Game and challenge in which a player jumps atop a sandcastle or other height and dares all comers to pull him down. 'It is necessary for the king to be thus emphatic', says a nineteenth-century American children's book, 'for he has no trumpeter, no bodyguard, and no assistance whatever to aid him to retain his position, whereas he is assailed on all sides by the other players.' Once the king has been pulled down he who causes the downfall takes the royal position. But 'it is always to be remembered that only pulls and pushes at the king are allowed: pulling at his clothes is distinctly forbidden under penalty of exclusion from the game'. The game, with its authoritarian couplet, may be exceedingly old; Horace (20 B.C.) quotes the rhyme (*puerorum nenia*) in his *Epistulae* I. I. 59–60, and the scholium gives a fuller version of the Roman children's words:

King of the Castle

Rex erit qui recte faciet;
Qui non faciet, non erit.

A similar children's catchword seems to be referred to in his *Ars Poetica* (417).

More evidence of the game comes from France. In *Les Trente-six figures contenant tous les jeux* (1587), boys defending a small hill are playing 'le roy despouillé'. In a copy of Jacques Stella's *Jeux et plaisirs de l'enfance* (1657), the English names for the games have been written on the plates in a contemporary hand. On the plate 'L'Assaut de Chasteau' has been written 'Keep of My Castle'. As if in confirmation, Cromek (1810) says that in England the game used to be called 'Keep the Castle'. A Scottish version of the rhyme was apparently well known in the seventeenth century:

> I William of the Wastle
> Am now in my Castle,
> And awe the Dogs in the Town
> Shan't gar me gang down.

On the authority of one Henry Fletcher, who was living at the time, when the Roundhead commander Fenwick demanded the surrender of Hume Castle in 1651, Thomas Cockburn, the governor, sent these words as his reply, whereupon 'Col. Fenwick having placed a Battery against the Castle, returns him Heroick Verse for his resolute Rhymes'.

Brand's Popular Antiquities, ed. W. C. Hazlitt, 1870 / *Plays and Games for Little Folks*, Josephine Pollard, 1889 / *Boy's Modern Playmate*, J. G. Wood, 1890 / Gomme, 1894, 'I'm the King of the Castle, An' nane can ding me doon'. The rhyme is very common in the present day.

'Willie Wastle' version: *The Perfect Politician*, H. Fletcher, 1680 / *Memorials of the English Affairs*, Bulstrode Whitelocke, 1682 / *Scotch Presbyterian Eloquence Display'd*, John Curate [Gilbert Crokatt and John Monroe], 1692 / *Gentleman's Magazine*, 1822 / Chambers, 1842 / *Oliver Cromwell*, Thomas Carlyle, 1845 / N & Q, 1859 / It is still known in the north: *Scottish Nursery Rhymes*, R. J. MacLennan, 1906 / *Sandy Candy*, N. and W. Montgomerie 1948 / In America it is rendered 'Hally, hally, hastle, Get off my new castle'.

Cf. *Epistulae*, Quintus Horatius Flaccus, 20 B.C. [1892] / *Jeux des adolescents*, G. Belèze, 1873, 'Le Roi détrôné' / *Volks-und Kinder-Spiele aus Schleswig-Holstein*, H. Handelmann, 1874, 'Die Katzen von dem Berge'.

288

Hey, my kitten, my kitten,
And hey my kitten, my deary!

Kitten

Such a sweet pet as this
    There is not far nor neary.
Here we go up, up, up,
    Here we go down, down, downy;
Here we go backwards and forwards,
    And here we go round, round, roundy.

In the fourth volume (1740) of Allan Ramsay's *Tea-Table Miscellany* this stands as the first of five verses in 'The Nurse's Song' sung to the tune 'Yellow Stockings'. This song is stated in a letter dated 1765 (quoted *Notes & Queries*, 6th s.) to be by Swift. David Laing (1839) also believed it to be by Swift, and Chappell refers to it as 'Dean Swift's Song' adding that it was written to the tune of 'The Virgin Mary' which is in the 1703 edition of *The Dancing Master*. In *The Trader's Garland* (c. 1785) the song is called 'A new Song for young mothers and nurses' and is set beside two other songs 'The answer from the B—— to the D——' and 'The D—— Reply to the B——'. These two pieces, beginning respectively,

O my sweet Jonathan, Jonathan,
    O my sweet Jonathan Swifty,

and,

O my sweet F——y, sweet F——,
    And O my sweet F——y D'Lany

appear to be lines written in derision of Swift and Patrick Delany, and are clearly a parody of 'The Nurse's Song'. When first printed (c. 1728) these parodies were 'to the Tune of the Nurses Ballad' and called *A Lullaby For the D—n of St P—ks; Or, The D—n fed with his own Spoon*. The first verse of 'The Nurse's Song' (as text) appears with an abridgement of the others in *Tommy Thumb's Pretty Song Book* (c. 1744) and is probably traditional, being merely the tag on which the author hung his ballad (cf. Carey's *Namby Pamby*). The tune is a 9/8 dance (a jig) and no doubt the verse began life like this. The succeeding four verses are distinct in character, and also possess interest since they embody lines from several nursery rhymes (e.g. 'This pig went to market'), and JOH quotes (1844) two quatrains independently:

Where was a sugar and fretty?
    And where was jewel and spicy?
Hush-a-bye, babe in a cradle,
    And we'll go away in a tricy!

and,

Give me a blow, and I'll beat 'em,
    Why did they vex my baby?

Kitten

Kissy, kiss, kissy, my honey,
    And cuddle your nurse, my deary.

Together these two pieces appear to be a memory of the third verse. Harold Williams, the Swiftian authority, does not think that there is any likelihood that 'The Nurse's Song' is by Swift.

Tea-Table Miscellany, vol. iv, 1740 / *T Thumb's PSB*, c. 1744, with part of other verses / *FT Thumb's LSB*, c. 1760 / *MG's Melody*, c. 1765 / *Nancy Cock's PSB*, c. 1780, complete song / *Cobwebs to Catch Flies*, Lady Fenn, c. 1783, 'In another part of the fair the boys saw some children tossing about [on a type of swing]. They were singing merrily the old nurse's ditty. "Now we go up, up, up, Now we go down, down, down; Now we go backward and forward, Now we go round, round, round"' / *Trader's Garland*, c. 1785 / *Pretty Little Poems for Pretty Little Children* (H. Mozley), c. 1785, 'A Nursing Song' [Gumuchian] / *T Thumb's SB*, 1788 / *Musical Museum*, 1803 / *Songs for the Nursery*, 1805 / *Vocal Harmony*, c. 1806 / *Pretty Tales* (T. Hughes), 1808 / *Old Dame Margery's Hush-A-Bye*, 1814, 'Oh! my chicken, my chicken' / *Sugar Plum* (J. Roberts), c. 1825 / *Waggon Load of Money* (J. Kendrew), c. 1825, second four lines only / JOH, 1843 / *Only True MG's Melody*, c. 1843, with part of other verse / Rimbault, 1846 / *Folk-Lore of the N. of Scotland*, Rev. W. Gregor, 1881, 'Hey me kitten, ma kitten, Hey ma kitten, ma dearie; Sic a fit as this Wis na far nor nearie. Here we gae up, up, up; Here we gae doon, doon doonie; Here we gae back and fore; Here we gae roon and roonie; Here's a leg for a stockin, And here's a fit for a shoeie' / Crofton, 1901.

Frequently parodied, e.g. in *Muse's Mirrour*, 1778, 'O My Yankee, my Yankee, And O my Yankee, my sweet-ee, And was its nurse North asham'd Because such a bantling hath beat-ee?'

289

Three little kittens they lost their mittens,
    And they began to cry,
Oh, mother dear, we sadly fear
    That we have lost our mittens.
What! lost your mittens, you naughty kittens!
    Then you shall have no pie.
    Mee-ow, mee-ow, mee-ow.
    No, you shall have no pie.

The three little kittens they found their mittens,
    And they began to cry,
Oh, mother dear, see here, see here,
    For we have found our mittens.

Put on your mittens, you silly kittens,
    And you shall have some pie.

Kittens

Purr-r, purr-r, purr-r,
Oh, let us have some pie.

The three little kittens put on their mittens,
    And soon ate up the pie;
Oh, mother dear, we greatly fear
    That we have soiled our mittens.
What! soiled your mittens, you naughty kittens!
    Then they began to sigh.
    Mee-ow, mee-ow, mee-ow.
    Then they began to sigh.

The three little kittens they washed their mittens,
    And hung them out to dry;
Oh! mother dear, do you not hear
    That we have washed our mittens?
What! washed your mittens, then you're good kittens,
    But I smell a rat close by.
    Mee-ow, mee-ow, mee-ow.
    We smell a rat close by.

These verses are sometimes ascribed to Eliza Follen (1787–1860) a New England writer of children's books. They appear at the end of her *New Nursery Songs for All Good Children* and are there described as 'traditional'. It seems that the verses were added by the English publisher, Addey, from his *Charm Almanack for Boys and Girls . . . 1853*, which he will have published the previous year. The tune is a variant of 'The Seven Joys of Mary'.

New Nursery Songs, Eliza Follen, 1853 / *Only True MG Melodies*, c. 1860, apparently copied from previous / *The Three Little Kittens*, 1857, with prose commentary by Comus [R. M. Ballantyne] / *The story of the Cat and the Mouse and The Three Little Kittens*, illus. John Absolon and Harrison Weir, c. 1859 / *The Three Little Kittens* (T. Nelson and Sons), c. 1869; (Dean and Son), 1881 / *D'Alcorn's Little Songs for Little Singers*, c. 1870, sheet music / *Baby's Bouquet*, 1879, short version beginning 'There were three little kittens Put on their mittens To eat some Christmas pie' / *The Three Little Kittens* (Tiny Tuck Book), c. 1948 / *Mittens for Kittens and other rhymes about cats*, L. Blegvad, illus. E. Blegvad, 1974.
    *** The line 'O, mither dear, I 'gin to fear' is the first of a song in Herd's *Scottish Songs*, 1776.

290

This is the way the ladies ride,
    Nimble, nimble, nimble, nimble;

Ladies

This is the way the gentlemen ride,
  A gallop a trot, a gallop a trot;

This is the way the farmers ride,
  Jiggety jog, jiggety jog;
And when they come to a hedge—they jump over!
And when they come to a slippery place—they scramble,
  scramble,
      Tumble-down Dick!

'Sung', says Crofton, 'while jumping a child up and down on one's crossed legs. The child faces one, and is held by the two hands.' On the last line 'let the child slip down over one's toes to the ground'.

JOH, 1842, 'To market ride the gentlemen, So do we, so do we; Then come's the country clown, Hobbledy gee, Hobbledy gee!' / Chambers, 1842, 'This is the way the ladies ride, Jimp and sma', jimp and sma'! This is the way the gentlemen ride, Trotting a', trotting a'! This is the way the cadgers ride, Creels and a'! creels and a'! creels and a'!' / *Only True MG Melodies*, c. 1843, 'This is the way the ladies ride, Prim, prim, prim; This is the way the gentlemen ride, Trim, trim, trim. Presently come the country-folks, Hobbledy gee, hobbledy gee' / JOH, 1849, similar to text / N & Q, 1869, remembered from Lowland Scotland seventy-five years previously, as Chambers 1842 / *Folk-Lore*, 1886, thirteen Scottish variations including one which introduces a romantic aspect 'This is the way the ladies ride...when they go to see the gentlemen' / Crofton MS, 1901 / *American Folk-Lore*, 1941, 'This is the way the ladies ride, Tree, tree, tree', &c. / Correspondent 1950, 'This is the way the ladies go, Nim, nim, nim...the gentlemen go, A-canter...the butcher boy goes, Trot ...the huntsman goes, A-gallop, a-gallop, right into the ditch'.

Cf. 'Here goes my lord.' Also *Rimes et jeux de l'enfance*, E. Rolland, 1883, 'Quande madame va en campagne, Elle va au pas, au pas, au pas; Quande le fils va en campagne, Il va au trot, au trot, au trot; Quande le monsieur va en campagne, Il va au galop, au galop, au galop' / *Das deutsche Kinderbuch*, Karl Simrock, 1848, 'So reiten die Herren Auf ihren stolzen Pferden: Zuck zuck, zuck zuck, zuck zuck. So reiten die Düfferchen Mit ihren spitzen Tüffelchen: Tripp trapp, tripp trapp, tripp trapp. So reiten die Bauern, Die Bauern, Die Humpels, Die Pumpels: Truf truf, truf truf, truf truf! So reiten die Husaren: Klabaster, klabaster, klabaster, Reit Junker, reit Junker, zuck zuck'; / *Deutsche Kinder-Reime*, Ernst Meier, 1851, 'So riten die Herren, So riten die Bauern, So riten die Frauen, So riten die Jungfern'.

291

Every lady in this land
Has twenty nails upon each hand
Five and twenty on hands and feet
All this is true without deceit.

Lady

As 'Mr. Stops' says in *Punctuation Personified*, this is 'a riddle repeated, to shew WITHOUT STOPS, how the ear may be cheated'.

Puzzling-Cap (F. Newbery, advert 1771), (E. Newbery), 1786 / *A New Collection of Enigmas*, 1791, 'Ev'ry lady in ev'ry land' / *Mince Pies for Christmas* 'By an Old Friend' (Tabart and Co.), 1804 / *Punctuation Personified* (J. Harris), 1824; (J. and B. Turnbull, Steubenville), 1831 [Rosenbach] / JOH, 1843 / *Favourite Rhymes and Riddles*, 1892.

292

I have been to market, my lady, my lady;
Then you've not been to the fair, says pussy, says pussy;
I bought me a rabbit, my lady, my lady;
Then you did not buy a hare, says pussy, says pussy;
I roasted it, my lady, my lady;
Then you did not boil it, says pussy, says pussy;
I eat it, my lady, my lady;
And I'll eat you, says pussy, says pussy.

This dialogue given by JOH (1853) is the middle portion of a ten-verse ballad. The ballad was collected from oral tradition by Chambers in the first half of the nineteenth century, and the scene of the conversation and the ability of the cat to eat her companion is immediately apparent:

> The cattie sits in the kiln-ring,
>   Spinning, spinning;
> And by came a little wee mousie,
>   Rinning, rinning.
>
> Oh, what's that you're spinning, my loesome,
>   Loesome lady?
> I'm spinning a sark to my young son,
>   Said she, said she.
>
> Weel mot he brook it, my loesome,
>   Loesome lady.
> Gif he dinna brook it weel, he may brook it ill,
>   Said she, said she.
>
> I soopit my house, my loesome,
>   Loesome lady.
> 'Twas a sign ye didna sit amang dirt then,
>   Said she, said she.

Lady

I fand twall pennies, my winsome,
  Winsome lady.
'Twas a sign ye warna sillerless,
  Said she, said she.

I gaed to the market, my loesome,
  Loesome lady.
'Twas a sign ye didna sit at hame then,
  Said she, said she.

I coft a sheepie's head, my winsome,
  Winsome lady.
'Twas a sign ye warna kitchenless,
  Said she, said she.

I put it in my pottie to boil, my loesome,
  Loesome lady.
'Twas a sign ye didna eat it raw,
  Said she, said she.

I put it in my winnock to cool, my winsome,
  Winsome lady.
'Twas a sign ye didna burn your chafts then,
  Said she, said she.

By came a cattie, and ate it a' up, my loesome,
  Loesome lady.
And sae will I you—worrie, worrie—guash, guash,
  Said she, said she.

The narrator of the above added, 'The old nurse's imitation of the *guash, guash* (which she played off upon the youngest urchin laying in her lap) was electric!' The earliest notice of this ballad is in Leyden's commentary (1801) on *The Complaynt of Scotland*, where he gives a specimen of the 'many confused and obscure rhymes' which tenaciously retain their hold of the memories of nurses and children in Scotland,

> The cat sat in the mill-door, spin, spin, spinning,
> When by came the little mouse, rin, rin, rinning.

'The mouse', he says, 'proposes to join her in spinning, and inquires,

> But where will I get a spindle, fair lady mine?'

and the cat desires it to take ' "The old mill lewer" or lever'.

The Complaynt of Scotland, ed. John Leyden, 1801 / Chambers, 1842 / JOH, 1853, as text / *Scottish Nursery Rhymes*, R. J. Maclennan, 1909 / *Mother Goose's NR*, L. E. Walter, 1924, first four lines only.

Lady

293

There was a lady all skin and bone,
Sure such a lady was never known:
It happened upon a certain day,
This lady went to church to pray.

When she came to the church stile,
There she did rest a little while;
When she came to the church yard,
There the bells so loud she heard.

When she came to the church door,
She stopped to rest a little more;
When she came the church within,
The parson prayed 'gainst pride and sin.

On looking up, on looking down,
She saw a dead man on the ground;
And from his nose unto his chin,
The worms crawled out, the worms crawled in.

Then she unto the parson said,
Shall I be so when I am dead?
O yes! O yes, the parson said,
You will be so when you are dead.

'O yes! O yes, the parson said, You will be so when you are dead. *Here the lady screams*', notes the editor of *Gammer Gurton's Garland*, and ever since the story was first told, her experience has been bringing terror to the listeners in the nursery. Southey, in tears, used to beg his family not to proceed. An essayist, in 1863, recalled his 'suppressed anticipation' as the story 'drew near its terribly personal ending'; a correspondent in 1946 said that these verses in Rimbault's book 'scared us so much as children, we fastened the leaves together'. The lady, the title says, was a 'gay' lady before the event, and therefore undoubtedly wanting in virtue. Perhaps the macabre moralist who wrote the tale had in mind the paintings of bodies corrupting in the grave at one time hung in churches.

GG's Garland, 1810 / JOH, 1842, slightly different version / Rimbault, 1846 / *N & Q*, 1873 / *Ancient Music of Ireland*, G. Petrie, 1855 / Oral collection, 1945 / Correspondents, 1946.

Lady

294

There was a lady loved a swine,
    Honey, quoth she,
Pig-hog wilt thou be mine?
    Hoogh, quoth he.

I'll build thee a silver sty,
    Honey, quoth she,
And in it thou shalt lie.
    Hoogh, quoth he.

Pinned with a silver pin,
    Honey, quoth she,
That thou may go out and in.
    Hoogh, quoth he.

Wilt thou have me now,
    Honey? quoth she.
Speak or my heart will break.
    Hoogh, quoth he.

In an unpublished play of James I's time, *Grobiana's Nuptialls*, probably written by students for the Twelfth Night revels at St. John's College, Oxford, this is introduced as a song so well known, it would seem, that it was not necessary to write it out in full. 'Wood I might heare a songe', says Grobiana, and another character responds, 'I will singe on.

> There was a Lady lov'd a hogge, hony quoth shee.
> Woo't thou lie with me tonight? ogh, quoth he, &c.'

The song seems to have remained popular in society throughout the seventeenth century. It is introduced, for instance, in Brome's comedy *The English Moor* (1658), where Millicent sings,

> There was a Lady lov'd a swine. Honey, quoth she,
> And wilt thou be true love mine. Hoogh, quoth he.

Upon which her uncle exclaims, appropriately enough, 'Do you hear gentlewoman; are you i' the wits?'

Bodley MS 30, c. 1620 / *English Moor*, Richard Brome, 1658 / *Rehearsal Transpros'd*, Andrew Marvell, 1673, an 'Ancient Distich', 'Thou shouldest have had a Silver Stye, And she her self have pigg'd thee by' / *London Cuckolds*, Edward Ravenscroft, 1682, 'There was a Lady lov'd a Swine, hunny quoth she. Pig-hog wilt thou be mine—Hunh—quoth he—' / *Nancy Cock's PSB*, c. 1780, two verses, the second being, 'Thou shalt have a silver stye With a door of ivory; And clean straw whereon to lie, Hunk! quoth he' / *GG's Garland*, 1784, last verse, 'Wilt thou have me now,

Honey? quoth she. Hoogh, hoogh, hoogh, quoth he. And went his way' / *Nurse Lovechild's DFN*, c. 1830 / JOH, 1842 / Rimbault, 1846 / *Old Nursery Rhymes with Chimes* (Bell & Daldy), 1863, 6 verses, '"I'll buy my love a silver dish, Honey!" said she; "And thou shalt eat buttered fish." "Hunc," said he.' / Kidson, 1904 / *Singing Together*, Herbert Wiseman, 1947.

295

Here are the lady's knives and forks,
Here is the lady's table,
Here is the lady's looking-glass,
And here is the baby's cradle.

An infant amusement known in most families. The hands are placed back to back, the fingers pointing upwards and interlaced represent the knives and forks. With the fingers still interlaced the hands are turned over, the backs of the fingers forming the table. The two little fingers are then raised to make a looking-glass, and the index fingers are raised as well to complete the picture of an old-fashioned cradle.

Chambers, 1842 / Maclagan, 1901, with two additional lines, 'Rock rock, Bubby Jock, O'er the seas and far away' / *Scottish NR*, R. J. MacLennan, 1909, associated with a cat's-cradle game / *Folk-Lore*, 1913.

296

Ladybird, ladybird,
    Fly away home,
Your house is on fire
    And your children all gone;

All except one
    And that's little Ann
And she has crept under
    The warming pan.

Child's warning to the ladybird. Traditionally the insect is set on a finger before being addressed. This is what the present writers used to do, and what a woodcut of the reign of George II depicts. When the warning has been recited (and the ladybird blown upon once), it nearly always happens that the seemingly earthbound little beetle produces wings and flies away. The names by which it is popularly known in this and other countries show that it has always had sacred associations: 'Ladybird' (from Our Lady's bird), 'Marygold', 'God's Little Cow', 'Bishop that burneth'; the German 'Marienkäfer' and 'Himmelsküchlichen'; the Swedish 'Marias Nyckelpiga', the Russian 'Bózhia koróvka', the French 'Bête à bon Dieu', the Spanish 'Vaquilla de Dios', and the Hindu 'Indragôpa.' The rhyme is undoubtedly a relic of something once possessed of an awful significance. It is closely matched by incantations known in France, Germany, Switzerland, Denmark, and Sweden, sometimes even to the detail of the name Ann:

> Goldchäber, flüg uf, uf dine hoche Tanne,
> Zue diner Muetter Anne.
> Si git dir Chäs und Brod,
> 's isch besser as der bitter Tod.

Another German version is:

> Himmelsküchlichen, flieg aus!
> Dein Haus brennt,
> Deine Kinder weinen alle miteinander.

And in France, where the words are also addressed to the cockchafer:

> Vole au firmament bleu,
> Ton nid est en feu,
> Les Turcs avec leur épée
> Vont te tuer ta couvée.
> Hanneton, vole, vole,
> Hanneton, vole.

Varieties of the *Coccinella* are found in most parts of the world, and are almost everywhere regarded as friendly. To kill one is unlucky. This would seem to rule out the hypothesis that a witch or evil spirit is represented and that the rhyme is a form of exorcism. (A much-practised method of ridding oneself of witches was to tell them that their dwelling was on fire.) A theory in Germany is that the rhyme originated as a charm to speed the sun across the dangers of sunset, the house on fire symbolizing the red evening sky. In *The Rosicrucians* the beetle is compared with the Egyptian scarab and the rhyme thought to be a remnant of beliefs associated with Isis. It has also been pronounced to be a relic of Freya worship. In England country children also employ the insect for divination.

T Thumb's PSB, c. 1744, 'Lady Bird, Lady Bird, Fly away home, Your house is on fire, your children will burn' / *Nancy Cock's PSB*, c. 1780, ends 'Your children are gone' / Similar in *GG's Garland*, 1784; *T Tit's SB*, c. 1790; *Newest Christmas Box*, c. 1797; *Songs for the Nursery*, 1805; *Vocal Harmony*, c. 1806; *Northern Antiquities*, 1814; *Nurse Lovechild's DFN*, c. 1830; *Boy's Week-Day Book*, 1833. Full version appears in *Poetic Trifles*

Ladybird

(J. G. Rusher), c. 1840. Numerous variants are given by Chambers, 1847; Northall, 1892; Eckenstein, 1906 (who quotes foreign equivalents). Also in *N & Q*; *Folk-Lore*, especially 1938; *I saw Esau*, I. and P. Opie, 1947. Emily Brontë (c. 1840) based a poem on the rhyme.

Cf. *Das deutsche Kinderbuch*, Karl Simrock, 1848, 'Marienkäferchen, fliege weg! Dein Häuschen brennt, Dein Mutterchen flennt, Dein Vater sitzt auf der Schwelle: Flieg in Himmel aus der Hölle', and other variations / *Deutsche Kinder-Reime*, Ernst Meier, 1851, 'Maikäfer, flieg! Dein Vater ist im Krieg, Deine Mutter ist in Pommerland, Pommerland ist abgebrannt' / *Deutsche Mythologie*, Jacob Grimm, 1854 / *Germanische Mythen*, W. Mannhardt, 1858, 'Maikäfer fliege fort, Dein Häuschen brennt, Dein Kreischen brennt, Die Jungen sitzen drinnen Und spinnen, Und wenn sie ihre Zahl (10 Schock) nicht haben, Können sie nicht spazieren gan', and many variations / *Deutsches Kinderlied*, F. M. Böhme, 1897 [1924] / *Faune populaire de la France*, E. Rolland, 1881, 'Petite manivole, Vole, vole, vole! Ton père est à l'école, Vole, vole, vole! Il t'achète une belle robe, Vole, vole, vole, Si tu ne voles pas Tu n'en auras pas' / *Chinese Mother Goose Rhymes*, I. T. Headland [1900], 'Lady-bug, lady-bug, Fly away, do, Fly to the mountain, And feed upon dew, Feed upon dew And sleep on a rug, And then run away Like a good little bug' (original Chinese given) / *Finnisch-ugrische Forschungen*, 1937 [*American Folk-Lore*].

297

Young lambs to sell! Young lambs to sell!
I never would cry young lambs to sell,
If I'd as much money as I could tell,
I never would cry young lambs to sell.

For a century the cry 'Young lambs to sell' brought children running into the street with their pennies and halfpennies. The toy lambs had white cotton wool fleeces spangled with Dutch gilt, heads of flour paste, horns and legs of tin, and collars of pink tape. In Hone's *Table Book* (1827) there is an engraving of one of the best-known vendors, William Liston, who turned to the manufacture of toy lambs in 1799, after he had lost an arm and a leg in the wars in Holland. Liston travelled the length and breadth of the country; and his basket of lambs, and cry,

Young lambs to sell! young lambs to sell!
If I'd as much money as I could tell,
I'd not come here with lambs to sell!
Dolly and Molly, Richard and Nell,
Buy my young lambs and I'll use you well!

were introduced into the Christmas pantomime at Covent Garden in 1826. Liston sold his lambs at a penny each, although the disabled sailor who is said to have originated the trade in the eighteenth century used to

Lambs

offer, 'Young lambs to sell! Two for a penny young lambs to sell!' Until recently there were people who recalled the sale of these toys, and Walter de la Mare remembered hearing in the streets the singing cry of their vendors.

London Cries (T. Evans), c. 1805, 'Get ready your money and come to me, I sell a young lamb for a penny, Young lambs to sell' &c. / *Letters Written from London*, 1808, has description of toy lamb seller, probably Liston, and gives his cry / *Cries of York, for the amusement of Young Children* (J. Kendrew), c. 1820, 'If I'd as much money as I could tell, I never would cry young lambs to sell' / *Table Book*, William Hone, 1827 / *Nurse Lovechild's DFN*, c. 1830, 'Young lambs to sell With fine gilt fleece, You can buy from me At a penny a piece' / JOH, 1853 / *Folk-Song*, 1910, second two lines 'Two for a penny, eight for a grawt (groat) The finest young lambs that ever were bought', with tune; further version 1919 / *Come Hither*, Walter de la Mare, 1923, 'Young lambs to sell, white lambs to sell; If I'd as much money as I could tell I wouldn't be crying, Young lambs to sell!' / *Less Familiar NR*, Robert Graves, 1927.

Cf. 'Old Chairs to mend'.

298

It's once I courted as pretty a lass,
　　As ever your eyes did see;
But now she's come to such a pass,
　　She never will do for me.
She invited me to her own house,
　　Where oft I'd been before,
And she tumbled me into the hog-tub,
　　And I'll never go there any more.

JOH, 1846 / Williams, 1923, 'Once I courted as pretty a girl As ever your eyes did see, And then she got so very fine, She didn't care a pin about me; She invited me to her own home—'Twas what she never did before; She bundled me into the hog-tub, And I won't go there any more', with chorus and second verse.

299

Lavender's blue, diddle, diddle,
　　Lavender's green;
When I am king, diddle, diddle,
　　You shall be queen.

Lavender

Call up your men, diddle, diddle,
    Set them to work,
Some to the plough, diddle, diddle,
    Some to the cart.

Some to make hay, diddle, diddle,
    Some to thresh corn,
Whilst you and I, diddle, diddle,
    Keep ourselves warm.

Once a playful love song, possessing its own tune. It was remembered almost solely in the nursery until 1948–9 when a dance version, popularly called 'The dilly dilly song', swept America and Britain. The source, titled *Diddle Diddle, Or, The Kind Country Lovers*, was printed sometimes between 1672 and 1685 on a black-letter broadside:

Lavenders green, Diddle diddle,
    Lavenders blue
You must love me, diddle diddle,
    cause I love you,
I heard one say, diddle diddle,
    since I came hither,
That you and I, diddle diddle,
    must lie together.

My hosttess maid, diddle diddle,
    her name was *Nell*,
She was a lass, diddle diddle,
    that I loved well,
But if she dye, diddle diddle,
    by some mishap,
Then she shall lie, diddle diddle,
    under the Tap.

That she may drink, Diddle diddle,
    when she's a dry,
Because she lov'd, Diddle diddle,
    my dog & I,
Coll up your Maids, Diddle diddle,
    set them to work,
Some to make hay, Diddle diddle,
    some to the Rock.

Some to make hay, Diddle diddle,
    some to the Corn,
Whilst you and I, Diddle, diddle,
    keep the bed warm,

PLATE X

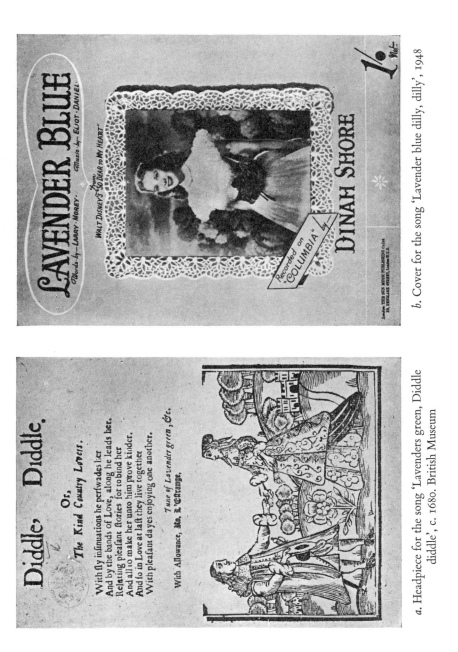

b. Cover for the song 'Lavender blue dilly, dilly', 1948

a. Headpiece for the song 'Lavenders green, Diddle diddle', c. 1680. British Museum

Lavender

Let the birds sing, Diddle, diddle,
and the Lambs play,
We shall be safe, Diddle, diddle
out of harms way.

There were ten verses in all. Over a century later the lay emerged in abbreviated form in *Songs for the Nursery* (1805):

Lavender blue and Rosemary green,
When I am king you shall be queen;
Call up my maids at four o'clock,
Some to the wheel and some to the rock;
Some to make hay and some to shear corn,
And you and I will keep the bed warm.

Several similar versions occur in nineteenth-century children's literature
with such titles as 'The Lady's Song in Leap Year' (1810) and 'The Entertainment of My Dog and I' (c. 1820).

Diddle Diddle (J. Wright, &c.), c. 1680 / *Songs for the Nursery*, 1805 / *GG's Garland*,
1810, 'Roses are red, diddle, diddle, Lavender's blue: If you will have me, diddle,
diddle, I will have you' / *Comedy of Billy and Betty* (T. Batchelar), c. 1820 / *MG's
Quarto*, c. 1825 / JOH, 1849, '. . . you shall be queen. Who told you so, dilly, dilly,
who told you so? 'Twas mine own heart, dilly, dilly, that told me so', &c. / *Baby's
Opera*, 1877 / *Lavender Blue*, Larry Morey and Eliot Daniel, 1948, sheet music,
'Lavender blue dilly, dilly, Lavender green. If I were king, dilly, dilly, I'd need a
queen. Who told me so, dilly, dilly, who told me so? I told myself, dilly, dilly, I
told myself.'
    Cf. a popular rhyme for St. Valentine's Day 'Lillies are white Rosemary's
green; When you are king I will be queen. Roses are red Lavender's blue; If you
will have me, I will have you.' Also the old song 'My dog and I, we have a trick'
sung by Oliver Proudfute, the bonnet maker, in *The Fair Maid of Perth*, a song
that was listed amongst 'Old Ballads' in William and Cluer Dicey's catalogue of
1754.

300

There was an old woman of Leeds
Who spent all her time in good deeds;
She worked for the poor
Till her fingers were sore,
This pious old woman of Leeds.

'The old woman of Leeds' comes from the first-known book of limericks, *The History of Sixteen Wonderful Old Women*, published by J. Harris in 1820. (*Vide* 'As a little
fat man of Bombay'.)

Legs

301

Long legs and short thighs,
Little head and no eyes.

Riddle. *Solution:* a pair of tongs.

Pleasant Exercises for Little Minds (T. Batchelar), c. 1815 / JOH, 1842, 'crooked thighs' /
N & Q, 1865 / *Shropshire Folk-Lore*, C. S. Burne, 1883 / *Folk-Lore*, 1889 and 1923,
described as 'common'.

302

Two legs sat upon three legs
With one leg in his lap;
In comes four legs
And runs away with one leg;
Up jumps two legs,
Catches up three legs,
Throws it after four legs,
And makes him bring back one leg.

One of the most popular riddles of past times, and still commonly found
in nursery books, the solution being delightful to illustrate. A man sits on
a three-legged stool with a leg of mutton in his lap. A dog snatches the leg
of mutton and runs off with it. Up jumps the man and throws the stool at
the dog who brings back the leg of mutton. The germ of this may be seen
in Bede's *Flores* 'Vidi bipedem super tripodem sedentem: cecidit bipes,
corruit tripes.' The riddle is the first in the *Booke of meery Riddles* (1600)
and there is another of the same type included. Leg riddles, which are
universal, are as old as the Riddle of the Sphinx.

Booke of meery Riddles, 1600 [1629] / *Book of merrie Riddles*, 1631 / Holme MS, c. 1645 /
Girl's Book of Diversions, Miss Leslie, 1835 / A scrapbook of the Opie family, c. 1840,
MS entry / JOH, 1842 / *N & Q*, 1865 / *National Rhymes of the Nursery*, George Saintsbury, 1895 / *Mother Goose*, Arthur Rackham, 1913.
    Cf. *Das deutsche Kinderbuch*, Karl Simrock, 1848, 'Zweibein sass auf Dreibein und
ass Ein Bein, Da nahm Vierbein Zweibein Ein Bein, Da nahm Zweibein Dreibein
und schmiss Vierbein, Dass Vierbein Ein Bein fallen liess. (Mensch, Dreistuhl, Kno-
chen, Hund)' / *Deutsche Kinder-Reime*, Ernst Meier, 1851, 'Es war einmal ein Zweifuss,
Der sass auf einem Dreifuss; Da kam ein Vierfuss, Der brachte einen Kühfuss. Da
nahm der Zweifuss den Dreifuss Und schlug damit den Vierfuss, Dass er den Kühfuss fallen liess' / *Mecklenburgische Volksüberlieferungen*, R. Wossidlo, 1897, 'Tweebeen
seet up dreebeen un hadd eenbeen up'n schoot; dunn kümmt vierbeen un spüng

up vierbeen un wull sik keenbeen hahlen. Tweebeen fohrt to, dreebeen föllt üm, eenbeen flücht vierbeen an'n kopp, dat he von vierbeen run föllt; dunn ett tweebeen keenbeen up.'

303

I lost my mare in Lincoln Lane,
   And couldn't tell where to find her,
Till she came home both lame and blind,
   With never a tail behind her.

Newest Christmas Box, c. 1797 / JOH, 1844.
   Cf. 'Little Bo-peep'.

304

The lion and the unicorn
   Were fighting for the crown;
The lion beat the unicorn
   All round about the town.

Some gave them white bread,
   And some gave them brown;
Some gave them plum cake
   And drummed them out of town.

The antagonism, reflected in this rhyme, between the lion and the unicorn has been legendary in many countries through many ages. It is mentioned in the earliest English natural history books, and may be depicted on a coin of Akanthos; but some supposed unicorn images are of two-horned animals misleadingly shown in profile. It has been said that the golden-bearded lion symbolizes the invariable triumph of summer over the unicorn or white horse, representing spring. The popular tradition is that the rhyme tells the story of the amalgamation of the Royal Arms of Scotland with those of England when James VI of Scotland was crowned James I of England. Two unicorns were supporters of the Scottish Royal Arms and, with a lion on the other side, one of them became a supporter of the English shield. The appearance of the new coat of arms could readily have given rise to the feeling that the lion, who wore a crown, was in conflict with the unicorn who was merely 'armed'; and this may have been felt to be the more so in the years immediately prior to the Union (1707). In *Through the Looking-Glass* Lewis Carroll refers to 'the words of the old song', and a song it seems at one time to have been, containing many verses now mostly lost. A second verse is found in a chapbook published about 1806:

> And when he had beat him out,
>   He beat him in again;
> He beat him three times over,
>   His power to maintain.

This is probably older than the second verse usually remembered today. The definite statement that the lion beat the unicorn 'three times over, his power to maintain' gives the impression that a particular battle or series of battles is being referred to.

MS inscription dated 1691 beside a woodcut of the royal arms *with supporters* in a copy of *The Holy Bible*, 1638 (Opie Collection), 'the unicorn & the lyon fiteing for the Crown and the lyon beat the unicorn Round About the town' / *Useful Transactions in Philosophy*, William King, 1708–9, 'The Lyon and the Unicorn fighting for the Crown, The Lyon beat the Unicorn round about the Town' / *T Thumb's SB*, 1788 / *The Golden Present* (W. Appleton), c. 1790 / *Songs for the Nursery*, 1805, with second verse, 'Some gave them white bread', &c. / *Vocal Harmony*, c. 1806, see quote / *MG's Quarto*, c. 1825 / *Nursery Songs* (Alfred Miller), c. 1830 / *Nurse Lovechild's Legacy* (J. Catnach), c. 1830 / JOH, 1842 / Chambers, 1842, 'Up starts the little dog, And knocked them both down'; he suggests 'the little dog' may be the small 'Lion sejant' on top of the crown / Kidson, 1904 / N & Q, 1908 / *Man in the Moon*, L. Leslie Brooke, 1913.

***In N & Q, 1908, it is stated that in the palace on the Isola Bella in Lago Maggiore there are two large tapestries, one representing a lion and a unicorn fighting for a crown which is lying between them, the other showing the lion chasing the unicorn round a medieval town. This is a traveller's tale. In the renowned Serie del Liocorno tapestries of the sixteenth century, the only ones in the palace showing the fight, there is no crown and the action has an Arcadian setting.

305

> Hey diddle dinkety, poppety, pet,
> The merchants of London they wear scarlet;
> Silk in the collar and gold in the hem,
> So merrily march the merchant men.

The little mice who were helping the tailor of Gloucester clicked their thimbles to mark the time as they sung this song.

JOH, 1844 / *Tailor of Gloucester*, Beatrix Potter, 1903 / *Less Familiar NR*, Robert Graves, 1927 / *Book of NR*, Enid Marx, 1939.

London Bridge

London Bridge is broken down,
    Broken down, broken down,
London Bridge is broken down,
    My fair lady.

Build it up with wood and clay,
    Wood and clay, wood and clay,
Build it up with wood and clay,
    My fair lady.

Wood and clay will wash away,
    Wash away, wash away,
Wood and clay will wash away,
    My fair lady.

Build it up with bricks and mortar,
    Bricks and mortar, bricks and mortar,
Build it up with bricks and mortar,
    My fair lady.

Bricks and mortar will not stay,
    Will not stay, will not stay,
Bricks and mortar will not stay,
    My fair lady.

Build it up with iron and steel,
    Iron and steel, iron and steel,
Build it up with iron and steel,
    My fair lady.

Iron and steel will bend and bow,
    Bend and bow, bend and bow,
Iron and steel will bend and bow,
    My fair lady.

Build it up with silver and gold,
    Silver and gold, silver and gold,
Build it up with silver and gold,
    My fair lady.

Silver and gold will be stolen away,
    Stolen away, stolen away,

London Bridge

Silver and gold will be stolen away,
  My fair lady.

Set a man to watch all night,
  Watch all night, watch all night,
Set a man to watch all night,
  My fair lady.

Suppose the man should fall asleep,
  Fall asleep, fall asleep,
Suppose the man should fall asleep?
  My fair lady.

Give him a pipe to smoke all night,
  Smoke all night, smoke all night,
Give him a pipe to smoke all night,
  My fair lady.

Few songs stir the imagination more deeply, evoking pictures both of a mysterious bridge which must ceaselessly be rebuilt, and of children singing lightheartedly as they play a game upon which there still rests an element of fear. The words, however, are now often separated from the play, and are known to even the smallest in the nursery; 'London Bridge is falling down' has become a popular nursery recitation. It is one of the few, perhaps the only one, in which there is justification for suggesting that it preserves the memory of a dark and terrible rite of past times; and the literary history of the song does not frustrate the idea of its antiquity. In *The London Chaunticleres*, a 'Witty Comoedy' printed 1659, appears the dialogue:

Heath. '. . . thou sha't be the Lady o' the Town.'
Curds. 'I have been one in my daies, when we kept the Whitson-Ale, where we daunc't the building of London-Bridge upon woolpacks and the hay upon a Grasse-plat, and when we were a weary with dauncing hard, we alwaies went to the Cushion daunce.'

The dance 'London Bridge' figures in Playford's *Dancing Master* (1718), and again in *The Second Book of the Compleat Dancing Master* (1719). No words are given in these books, and the tune is not that associated with the words today, but it is certain that the verses were already sung. Indeed by 1725 they were already thought of as belonging to children, for Carey quoted the refrain in his nursery satire *Namby Pamby*:

  Namby Pamby is no Clown,
  London-Bridge is broken down:

319

London Bridge

Now he *courts the gay Ladee*,
Dancing o'er The Lady-Lee.

'London Bridge is broken down' is mentioned again in *The Fashionable Lady, or, Harlequin's Opera* (1730); and in *Tommy Thumb's Pretty Song Book* (c. 1744) appears the earliest text:

London Bridge
Is Broken down,
Dance over my Lady Lee.
London Bridge
Is Broken down
With a gay Lady.

How shall we build
It up again,
Dance over my Lady Lee, &c.

Build it up with
Gravel, and Stone,
Dance over my Lady Lee, &c.

Gravel, and Stone,
Will wash a away,
Dance over my Lady Lee, &c.

Build it up with
Iron, and Steel,
Dance over my Lady Lee, &c.

Iron and Steel,
Will bend, and Bow,
Dance over my Lady Lee, &c.

Build it up with
Silver, and Gold,
Dance over my Lady Lee, &c.

Silver, and Gold
Will be stolen away,
Dance over my Lady Lee, &c.

Then we'l set
A man to Watch,
Dance over my Lady Lee.
Then we'l set
A Man to Watch
With a gay Lady.

London Bridge

This unsophisticated rendering, not having been previously transcribed, has escaped comment. It agrees in some important particulars with a record which appeared in the *Gentleman's Magazine* for September, 1823. A correspondent there wrote, 'The projected demolition of London Bridge recalls to my mind the introductory lines of an old Ballad, which more than 70 years ago I heard plaintively warbled by a lady who was born in the reign of Charles the Second, and who lived till nearly the end of that of George the Second...

> London Bridge is broken down,
> *Dance over the Lady Lea;*
> London Bridge is broken down,
> *With a gay lady* (la-dee).
>
> Then we must build it up again.
> What shall we build it up withal?
> Build it up with iron and steel,
> Iron and steel will bend and break.
> Build it up with wood and stone,
> Wood and stone will fall away.
> Build it up with silver and gold,
> Silver and gold will be stolen away.
> Then we must set a man to watch,
> Suppose the man should fall asleep?
> Then we must put a pipe in his mouth,
> Suppose the pipe should fall and break?
> Then we must set a dog to watch,
> Suppose the dog should run away?
> Then we must chain him to a post.

'The two lines in italic are regularly repeated after each line.' Since this again takes the words back in England no further than the seventeenth century, it is necessary to examine the continental parallels. Urquhart (1653) in his translation of *Gargantua* lists 'the fallen bridges' as one of the games played. Rabelais in the original French (1534) lists 'pont chus', and, in parenthesis, it may be noted that this does not invalidate the English reference, Urquhart's *Gargantua* being a transmutation rather than a translation of Rabelais's text; all the games Urquhart lists were ones known in seventeenth-century England. With the English title 'fallen bridges' may be compared the Scottish wording recorded by Maclagan (1901),

> Broken bridges falling down, falling down, falling down,
> Broken bridges falling down, my fair ladies.

The French may be compared with 'Le Pont-Levis' (in *Manuel complet des jeux de société*, 1830), played in a similar manner to the English game,

London Bridge

> Trois fois passera,
> La dernière, la dernière;
> Trois fois passera,
> La dernière y restera.

Bett compares this with practically the same game, 'La porte du Gloria', and another variant, 'Olivé Beauvé',

> Que tu as de jolies filles!
> Olivé Beauvé;
> Que tu as de jolies filles!
> Sur le pont-chevalier,

ending,

> Je la donne, si tu l'attrapes,
> Olivé Beauvé;
> Je la donne, si tu l'attrapes,
> Sur le pont-chevalier.

In fact, knowledge of the game is so widespread that any doubt about its early origin can be dispelled. In Denmark it is 'Brö, Brö, Brille'. In Italy it is 'Le porte', and Newell considered it to be the game 'Coda Romana' described as being played by Florentine children in 1328. In Spain they play a similar game. In Germany there are numerous versions, for instance 'Die Magdeburger Brück':

> Ich wollte gern über die Magdeburger Brück':
> Die ist zerbrochen.
> Wer hat sie zerbrochen?
> Der Goldschmied, der Goldschmied,
> Mit seiner jüngsten Tochter.
> Laßt sie doch wieder bauen.
> Mit was denn? mit was denn?
> Mit Ketten und mit Stangen.
> Kriegt Alle durch, kriegt Alle durch,
> Den letzten wollen wir fangen.

And 'Die goldene Brücke', which ends in an equally sinister manner:

> Ich werde sie wieder machen lassen.
> Womit?
> Mit Perlenring und goldenem Stein,
> Was giebst du mir zum Pfande?
> Den hintesten, den du kriegen kannst.

I. V. Zingerle (*Das deutsche Kinderspiel in Mittelalter*) states that the game was known in the Middle Ages to Meister Altswert ('zwei spilten der fuln brucken'). Fischart knew it under the names 'der faulen Brucken'

London Bridge

and 'auf der Brucken suppern in glorie'. Geiler von Kaisersberg knew the game when he wrote, 'es wird ihnen nichts mehr, dann dass sie wie im Spiel der faulen Brucken einmal die Händ zusammenschlagen und jauchzen und alsdann wieder herabspringen, ritschen und burzeln'. Mannhardt, the great German folk-lorist, collected versions in Slavic, Hungarian, and Scandinavian. The game is also known in Pennsylvania German ('Die Holländisch Brück'). From what can be ascertained the main features of the play are everywhere similar. Two players form a bridge with uplifted arms; the others pass through in a line, each holding onto the one in front and hurrying, fearful that they may be caught by the descending arms of the first two players. In America the game often ends with a tug of war as in 'Oranges and Lemons' (q.v.), but in England this is not common. The end verses, sometimes heard, in which a prisoner who stole a watch and chain cannot pay a ransom, do not figure in eighteenth-century records and may be apocryphal; they appear to have been attached from an independent game 'Hark the Robbers' (Gomme, i. 192). Tommy Thumb's 250-year-old version stops significantly when it has been decided to set a man to watch. The builders have had to meet what has every appearance of being supernatural opposition. The bridge cannot be made to stand by ordinary means. Even stone will be washed away. So a 'watchman' is required. Somehow, it is felt, this watchman can protect the bridge even against the malicious forces of nature. (Only when it is proposed that the edifice be made of 'silver and gold', possibly a later interpolation, is there a suggestion of human sabotage.) Clearly the watchman himself has special powers. It is on record that in 1872 when the Hooghly Bridge was being built across the Ganges the native population feared that to placate the river each structure would have to be founded on a layer of children's skulls. Frazer in *The Golden Bough* quotes examples of living people being built into the foundations of walls and gates to serve as guardian spirits; and all over the world stories of human sacrifice are associated with bridges, to the erection of which the rivers are supposed to have an especial antipathy. In Germany as recently as 1843, when a new bridge was to be built at Halle, the notion was abroad among the people that a child was wanted to be built into the foundation. When the Bridge Gate at Bremen was demolished in the last century the skeleton of a child was found embedded in the foundations. The bridge of Aryte in Greece is said to have kept falling down until they walled in the wife of the master-mason. The building of the bridge of Rosporden in Brittany is another case where legend has it that all attempts were unsuccessful until a four-year-old boy was immured at the foot of it. Further, the legend goes, the little boy was buried with a candle in one hand and a piece of bread in the other. Food and light was given so that the guardian might keep alive and watchful, which immediately recalls the words of the old Stuart lady:

London Bridge

Suppose the man should fall asleep?
Then we must put a pipe in his mouth.

In similar verses, handed down in oral tradition, the man is given a bag of
nuts to crack, a dog which will bark all night, and a horse on which he
can gallop around. At Stoneleigh Park, the seat of the Leigh family in
Warwickshire, the story is maintained that one or more human victims
lie buried under the foundations, and attempts have been made to connect the name of Leigh with the refrain 'Dance over my Lady Lea'.
Another suggestion is that 'my Lady Lea' is the river Lea, which loses its
identity in the river Thames. And London Bridge itself is not without a
tainted reputation, for there is in the capital a tradition that the stones
of this great bridge, too, were once bespattered with the blood of little
children.

Namby Pamby, Henry Carey, 1725 [1726] / *T Thumb's PSB*, c. 1744 / *GG's Garland*, 1784,
similar to 1744 but verse 2 'How shall we build it up again?' followed by 'silver and
gold', 'iron and steel', 'wood and clay'. Final verse 'Build it up with stone so strong,
Dance o'er my lady lee, Huzza! 'twill last for ages long, With a gay lady' / *T Thumb's
SB*, 1788, 'Charleston Bridge is broken down', otherwise as c. 1744; 1814 English ed.
'London Bridge' / *T Tit's SB*, c. 1790, as 1784 / *Songs for the Nursery*, 1805 / *Gentleman's
Magazine*, Sept. and Nov. 1823 / *Mirror*, Nov. 1823 / *Blackwoods*, ? Professor Wilson,
July 1824 / *MG's Quarto*, c. 1825. (Hereafter a common constituent of *NR* collections.)
Archaeology of NR, J. B. Ker, 1835 / JOH, 1843, from *GG's Garland* / Rimbault, 1846 /
The Critic, Jan. and Feb. 1857 / *Shropshire Folklore*, C. S. Burne and G. F. Jackson,
1883, 'Build it up with lime and sand, Lime and sand will wash away, Build it up
with penny loaves, Penny loaves'll get stole. O, what has my poor prisoner done?
Robbed a house and killed a man. What will you have to set her free? Fourteen
pounds and a wedding gown. Stamp your foot and let her go!' / Newell, 1883 /
Northall, 1892, 'Over London bridge we go, Gay ladies, gay' then similar to previous, but it is a different (a ring) game / Gomme, 1894 and 1898, collected eleven
contemporary variants, four of them suggest building with penny loaves, as 1883,
which will 'mould', 'melt', or 'get stole' away; two suggest pins and needles
which 'break' or 'rust and bend'. Most are of the 'What has this poor prisoner
done?' variety. Two have endings of interest to cf. with 1823; 'Suppose the man
should fall asleep? Give him a pipe of tobacco to smoke. Suppose the pipe should
fall and break? We'll give him a bag of nuts to crack. Suppose the nuts were rotten
and bad? We'll give him a horse to gallop around', and 'If the man should fall
asleep? Set a dog to bark all night. If the dog should meet a bone? Set a cock to
crow all night. If the cock should meet a hen? Here comes my lord Duke, let everyone pass by but the very last one' / *Study of Man*, A. C. Haddon, 1898 / Maclagan,
1901 / Kidson, 1904 / *Come Hither*, Walter de la Mare, 1923 / *American Folk Lore*,
1947 / *London Bridge is Falling Down*, illus. Peter Spier, 1967.

    Cf. *Manuel complet des jeux de société*, M. Celnart, 1830 / *Jeux des jeunes filles*, M. de
Chabreul, 1860 / *Rimes et jeux de l'enfance*, E. Rolland, 1883 / *Chants et chansons populaires de Languedoc*, L. Lambert, 1906, 'Le pont est tombé, ma petite dame (*bis*) Il faudra l'arranger. Nous n'avons point d'argent. Nous irons en voler. Que fait-on aux
voleurs? On les pend par le cou' / *Rimas infantiles*, F. R. Marin, 1882 / *Giuochi Pop.
Veneziani*, G. Bernoni, 1874 / *Das deutsche Kinderbuch*, Karl Simrock, 1848 / *Deutsche
Kinder-Reime*, E. Meier, 1851, 'Die goldige Brücke . . . Mit Steinerlei, Mit Beinerlei,

London Bridge

Mit Silber und mit Gold beschlagen, Der letzte muss bezahlen' / *Germanische Mythen*, W. Mannhardt, 1858 / *Svenska Fornsångar*, A. I. Arwiddson, 1842 / *Danmarks Sanglege*, S. Tvermose Thyregod, 1931, many references to continental parallels.

307

> As I was going o'er London Bridge,
> And peeped through a nick,
> I saw four and twenty ladies
> Riding on a stick.

RIDDLE: *Solution:* sparks.

JOH, 1846 / *N & Q*, 1865, 'As I were going over London Brig, I pipp't into a winder; And I saw four and twenty ladies Dancing on a cinder.'

308

> As I was going o'er London Bridge,
> I heard something crack;
> Not a man in all England
> Can mend that!

RIDDLE. *Solution:* ice. Before 1750 the Thames froze fairly often owing to it not being as canalized as it is today.

Chambers, 1842, 'As I gaed owre Bottle-brig, Bottle-brig brak; Though ye guess a' day, Ye winna guess that' / JOH, 1849 / *Sandy Candy*, N. & W. Montgomerie, 1948, 'As I gaed ower Glesca brig, Glesca brig brak; And a the men in Glesca toon Cudna mend that'.

309

> See-saw, sacradown,
> Which is the way to London town?
> One foot up and the other foot down,
> That is the way to London town.

To Henry Carey (1725) this was the song which commonly accompanied a play on the see-saw:

London Town

Now on Cock-horse does he ride;
And anon on Timber stride,
See-and-Saw and Sacch'ry-down,
London is a gallant Town.

And the author of 'The Nurse's Song' (c. 1728) probably had the same verse in mind:

Chicky, cockow, my lily cock;
See, see, sic a downy;
Gallop a trot, trot, trot,
And hey for Dublin towny.

Various editors have altered the name of the town to suit their locality. One version, with a pleasant *amor urbis* addition, appears in the Massachusetts *Mother Goose's Quarto*:

See, saw, sacradown, sacradown,
Which is the way to Boston town?
One foot up the other foot down,
That is the way to Boston town.
Boston town's chang'd into a city,
But I've no time to change my ditty.

Boston received her charter in 1822.

Namby Pamby, Henry Carey, 1725 [1726] / *MG's Melody*, c. 1765 / *GG's Garland*, 1784 / *Christmas Box*, 1797 / *Vocal Harmony*, c. 1806 / *MG's Quarto*, c. 1825 / *Poetic Trifles* (J. G. Rusher), c. 1840, 'Sing see-saw, Jack thatching the ridge, Which is the way to Banbury-bridge?' / JOH, 1842, 'See saw, Jack in a hedge, Which is the way to London bridge?...' / *Mother Goose*, Kate Greenaway, 1881, as 1842, two lines only / *Mother Goose's NR*, L. E. Walter, 1924, as 1881, then 'Put on your shoes, and away you trudge, that is the way to London Bridge'. For further on *sacradown* see 'Margery Daw'.

310

Here goes my lord,
  A trot, a trot, a trot, a trot...
Here goes my lady,
  A canter, a canter, a canter, a canter...
Here goes my young master,
  Jockey-hitch, jockey-hitch, jockey-hitch, jockey-hitch...
Here goes my young miss,
  An amble, an amble, an amble, an amble...
The footman lags behind to tipple ale and wine,
And goes a gallop, a gallop, a gallop, to make up his time.

Lord

Knee song. A ditty beginning 'A nimble, an amble! a nimble, an amble!' possibly based on the song appears in Harris's *Original Ditties for the Nursery* (c. 1805). And a variation of great charm was sent by a correspondent in 1946:

> Here comes my lady with her little baby,
>   A nim, a nim, a nim.
> Here comes my lord with his trusty sword,
>   Trot, trot, trot.
> Here comes old Jack with a broken pack,
>   A gallop, a gallop, a gallop.

JOH, 1849, where compared with 'This is the way the ladies ride' (q.v.) and the Swedish 'Hvem är det som rider? Det är en fröken som rider: Det går i sakta traf, I sakta traf!' ('And pray, who now is riding? A lady it is that's riding: And she goes with a gentle trot, a gentle trot.') In the two succeeding verses a galloping gentleman and a jog-along farmer are described / Correspondents, 1946; and 1949, 'Here comes an old woman, Nimble namble, Here comes a lord, Trot, trot, Here comes Jack, With his black hat, Gallopy, gallopy, gallopy....' / Informant, 1990, 'Here comes mother, nurse, and the baby, Jiggedy-jog, jiggedy-jog, Here comes John with the butter and eggs, Trit-trot, trit-trot, Here comes the Lord with his shining sword, Gallopa, gallopa, gallopa—Down in the mire!'.

311

> Here sits the Lord Mayor,
> Here sit his men,
> Here sits the cockadoodle,
> Here sits the hen,
> Here sit the little chickens,
> Here they run in,
> Chin chopper, chin chopper, chin chopper, chin.

Infant amusement, in which the 'face-tapper' touches successively the forehead, eyes, right cheek, left cheek, tip of nose, mouth, and then chucks under the chin. The game is brought to life by James Joyce in *Ulysses*, 1922 (1960, p. 459): 'She tickled the tiny tot's two cheeks to make him forget and played here's the lord mayor, here's his two horses, here's his gingerbread carriage and here he walks in, chinchopper, chinchopper, chinchopper chin.'

JOH, 1846 and 1849, two very similar versions / *Come Hither*, Walter de la Mare, 1923 / Correspondent, 1953, from Ireland, 'Here is the king, Here are his two min, Here's the post office, Here's the way to go in'.

312

> Lucy Locket lost her pocket,
> Kitty Fisher found it;
> Not a penny was there in it,
> Only ribbon round it.

Statements which have been made about the identity of these two ladies are purely suppositional. JOH says they were 'two celebrated courtesans of the time of Charles II'. He possibly had the idea from his confrère Dr. Rimbault who persisted with unscholastic statements about 'Lydia Fisher's Jig', a song believed to have been popular in the seventeenth century. This was supposed to have embraced the above lines, but no copy has been found. In the eighteenth century there was another Kitty Fisher, also of negligent virtue, with whom attempts have been made to associate the rhyme. This second professional beauty (her portrait by Reynolds is at Petworth House) was at the height of her fame about 1759 and has a right to be considered if only because she was the subject of many other verses. There is an air named 'Kitty Fisher' in Thomson's *Country Dances* (1760). Gay's Lucy Lockit in *The Beggar's Opera* might also be one of the originals; on the other hand Gay may well have been employing a traditional name. All that is known for certain is that the lines were being repeated in nurseries during the first half of the nineteenth century both in England and America, sung to the same tune as 'Yankee Doodle' (q.v.). A writer in *Notes & Queries* (1908) stated that he knew an allusion to the lines in 1832, and another writer (1865) had been informed that the verse was current some fifty years previously in Hampshire girls' schools. This is the earliest notice except for the unsupported assertion of a New England lady (reported by O. G. Sonneck) who claimed to remember that the words were sung as 'a favourite jig' before the Revolution. However, in a version of 'Yankee Doodle' published in London in 1777, and apparently written some years earlier, four lines appear to be a take off of 'Lucy Locket lost her pocket', or anyway show awareness of a verse very similar to it:

> Dolly Bushel let a Fart,
> Jenny Jones she found it,
> Ambrose carried it to Mill,
> Where Doctor Warren ground it.

JOH, 1842, 'Nothing in it, nothing in it, But the binding round it' / Rimbault, 1846 / N & Q, 1865 and 1908 / *Baby's Bouquet*, 1879 / Bolton, 1888, for counting-out; also a corruption, 'Lady Fisher lost her pocket, Lady Parker found it. Lady Fisher thanked her friend, And said her cow was drownded' / *Report on the Star-Spangled Banner*, O. G. Sonneck, 1909 / *Mother Goose* (T. Nelson), c. 1945 / *Yankee Doodle*, S. Foster Damon, 1959.

Maid

313

Little maid, pretty maid, whither goest thou?
    Down in the forest to milk my cow.
Shall I go with thee? No, not now.
    When I send for thee then come thou.

This dialogue may not be so inconsequential as it appears. In some parts of England to ask a girl if one might go milking with her was considered tantamount to a proposal of marriage. The situation occurs again in 'Where are you going to my pretty maid?' (q.v.).

GG's Garland, 1810 / JOH, 1843 / *Mother Goose*, Kate Greenaway, 1881, 'Down to the meadow'.
    Cf. British Museum MS Add. 31922, c. 1511, a song said to have been sung by Henry VIII, beginning, 'Hey, troly, loly, lo; made, whether go you? I go to the medowe to mylke my cowe.' The gallant here has no honourable intentions, however.

314

There was a little maid, and she was afraid
    That her sweetheart would come unto her;
So she went to bed, and covered up her head,
    And fastened the door with a skewer.

JOH, 1844 / *Nursery Rhymes for Certain Times*, Elinor Darwin, 1946.

315

Rowsty dowt,
My fire is out,
My little maid's not at home!
I'll saddle my cock,
And bridle my hen,
And fetch my little maid home.
Home she came,
Tritty trot,
She asked for the porridge she left in the pot;
Some she ate,
And some she shod,

Maid

And some she gave to the truckler's dog;
She took up the ladle and knocked its head,
And now poor Dapsy dog is dead!

Possibly this is an extract from a folk-play though the context has not been identified. The idiom is much in the manner of the mummers, and clearly the rhyme is either very old or has been recited in dialect. 'Rowsty dowt' is probably the same as 'rousty toust', from 'rouse, touse', meaning bustle. 'Shod' is the old past tense for shed, hence split: so the porridge appears to have been pease-porridge. Truckler is a word for a pedlar. The saddled hog in some versions of this rhyme is reminiscent of 'The sow came in with the saddle' (q.v.).

GG's Garland, 1784, short version, 'I doubt, I doubt, My fire is out, My little dame an't at home, Come, bridle my hog, And saddle my dog, And fetch my little dame home' / *NR from the Royal Collections* (J. G. Rusher), c. 1840, short version, 'Hey, diddle dout, my candle's out, My little maid's not at home; Saddle the hog, bridle the dog, And fetch my little maid home' / JOH, 1842 / Chambers, 1842 / *Mr. Sponge's Sporting Tour*, R. S. Surtees, 1849, 'Diddle, diddle, doubt, My candle's out, My 'ittle dame's not at 'ome—So saddle my hog, and bridle my dog, And bring my 'ittle dame 'ome.'

316

Dingty diddlety,
　My mammy's maid,
She stole oranges,
　I am afraid;
Some in her pocket,
　Some in her sleeve,
She stole oranges,
　I do believe.

Songs for the Nursery, 1805 / *MG's Quarto*, c. 1825 / JOH, 1842 / *Tom Tiddler's Ground*, Walter de la Mare, 1932 / *Mother Goose Comes to Cable Street*, R. Stones and A. Mann, illus. Dan Jones, 1977.

317

Where are you going to, my pretty maid?
I'm going a-milking, sir, she said,

Maid

Sir, she said, sir, she said,
I'm going a-milking, sir, she said.

May I go with you, my pretty maid?
You're kindly welcome, sir, she said.

Say, will you marry me, my pretty maid?
Yes, if you please, kind sir, she said.

What is your father, my pretty maid?
My father's a farmer, sir, she said.

What is your fortune, my pretty maid?
My face is my fortune, sir, she said.

Then I can't marry you, my pretty maid.
Nobody asked you, sir, she said.

This is a nineteenth-century, carefully rewritten version of a folk-song which had long been popular, and which survived in isolated places into the present century. Thomas Tonkin, a Cornish antiquary, heard it sung at Cardew in 1698, the words (quoted by William Pryce in 1790) being,

Whither are you going pretty fair maid, said he,
With your white face and your yellow hair?

I am going to the well, sweet Sir, she said,
For strawberry leaves make maidens fair.

Shall I go with thee pretty fair maid, he said, &c.

Do if you will, sweet Sir, she said, &c.

What if I do lay you down on the ground, &c.

I will rise up again, sweet Sir, she said, &c.

What if I do bring you with child, &c.

I will bear it, sweet Sir, she said, &c.

Who will you have for father for your child, &c.

You shall be his father, sweet Sir, she said, &c.

What will you do for whittles for your child, &c.

His father shall be a taylor, sweet Sir, she said, &c.

In one of the earlier broadsides in the Pepys collection 'Strawberry leaves make maidens fair' is given as the tune to 'A mery new Jigge', so the song

331

PLATE XI

One of Caldecott's hand-
coloured proofs for
The Milkmaid, 1882,
with his instructions to
the engraver.
Opie collection

Maid

would seem to have been known in the reign of James I. Alternative refrains are 'It's rolling in the dew makes the milk-maids fair' (on a broadside) and 'It's dabbling in the dew where you'll find me' (1846), references to the belief that dew water is good for the complexion. Cecil Sharp collected a sea-chanty version in Somerset (1909) entitled 'Heave away, my Johnny' with the recurring line 'All in the month of May':

> As I was walking out one fine morning
> All in the month of May,
> I overtook a fair pretty maid,
> And unto her did say:
> O where are you going to, my pretty maid?
> I unto her did say.
> I'm going a milking, sir, she said,
> All in the month of May....

It is possible that this version preserves the original introduction to the song. C. B. Lewis (*Folk-Lore*, 1935) pointed out that if it did it belonged to a recognized type of poem, a genre that is met with elsewhere, especially in France. In the oldest *pastourelle* extant, the poem written by Troubadour Marcabrun about the year 1150, the knight and the shepherdess address each other, as in the English song, as 'Sir' and 'Pretty maiden', mention is made of the occupation of the father who is also a farmer, and the knight's love is eventually refused. Of the origin of the *pastourelle* itself much has been written and little concluded. Dr. Lewis, however, remarks on the similarity of the theme to the *Song of Solomon*, if the modern interpretation is adopted. (Cf. also 'Little maid, pretty maid, whither goest thou?')

Archaeologia Cornu-Britannica, William Pryce, 1790 / Laing MS II, 210–11, Robert Burns, c. 1795, collected by Burns 'from a country girl's voice', to the air 'The Posie': 'There was a pretty May and a-milkin' she went, Wi' her red, rosy cheeks and her coal-black hair: And she has met a young man a-comin' o'er the bent; With a double and adieu to thee fair May. O whare are ye goin', my ain pretty May...Unto the yowes a-milkin', kind Sir, she says...What if I gang alang wi' thee, my ain pretty May, Wad I be aught the warse o' that, kind Sir, she says...&c.' / *Where are you going to my pretty maid?* (Rt. Birchell), c. 1800, accompaniment by E. S. Biggs / JOH, 1846, 'Oh, where are you going, My pretty maiden fair, With your red rosy cheeks, And your coal-black hair? I'm going a-milking, Kind sir, says she; And it's dabbling in the dew, Where you'll find me', five verses / JOH, 1849, three additional verses similar in vein to 1790 / JOH, 1853, 'Will you be constant, my pretty maid? That I can't promise you, sir, she said' / N & Q, 1870, quoting old Bristol broadside, 'Where are you going to, my pretty maid, With your sweet looks and your yellow hair? Going a milking, kind master, she said, And it's rolling in the dew makes the milk-maids fair' / *Baby's Opera*, 1877 / *The Milkmaid*, Randolph Caldecott, 1882 / Kidson, 1904, stated it had been sung on the stage by Mrs. Jordan some 100 years previously / *Folk Songs from Somerset*, Cecil Sharp, 1905, verses collected given as 'quite unsuitable for publication'; fifth series, 1909, as quote / *Folk-Song*, 1913, several versions with tunes noted by Cecil

Sharp and Vaughan Williams, including the refrain 'For roving in the dew makes milk-maids fair', and the final verse 'I wish you guid morning, my pretty fair maid', to which she replies 'Thank you for going, kind sir' / *Folk-Lore*, 1935.

Cf. Herd MS, 1776, 'Kind Hearted Nancy' / *Folk-Song*, 1901, 1905, and 1918, 'Seventeen come Sunday' / *Folk Songs from Somerset*, 1904–9, 'Earl Richard', 'As I walked through the meadows', 'Green Bushes', and 'Sweet lovely Joan'. Earlier versions of some of these ballads are to be found in the Roxburghe collection. *Provenzalische Chrestomathie*, C. Appel, 1920, No. 64, by Marcabrun, beginning 'L'autrier iost' una sebissa, trobey pastora mestissa, de ioy e de sen massissa'; ninety lines.

318

A man in the wilderness asked me,
How many strawberries grow in the sea?
I answered him, as I thought good,
As many as red herrings grow in the wood.

In the early seventeenth century, two versions of this were written in a catalogue of arms, by one Thomas Renshall. The longer version goes,

> A man of the forrist demanded of mee
> how manie Strebearies groo on the se
> and I answard againe as I though best
> aske how manie hearing weare in forrest

> But here I am on well discuse this doubte
> That both se and forrest are quite wth oute
> yet both have plentie, questian is good
> Strebearies to land, and fishes to flood

Bodleian MS Top. gen. c. 51, and see *N & Q*, New Ser. vol. xxiii, 1976 / MS addition to church records of St. Andrews, Yardley-Hastings, Northants, 1716, 'A man in the wilderness asked of me How many strawberries grow in the sea? I answered him as I thought good As many red herrings as swim in the wood' / *Waggon Load of Money* (R. Moffet), c. 1800; (J. Kendrew), c. 1825 / *Songs for the Nursery*, 1805 / *GG's Garland*, illus. T. Bewick, c. 1814 / JOH, 1843 / Chambers, 1847, a similar Scottish rhyme, 'I met a man who speer'ed at me, Grow there berries in the sea? I answered him by speering again, Is there skate on Clochnaben?' Clochnaben is a hill in Aberdeenshire / *Macclesfield Courier*, 14 Oct. 1882, in a report of a court case, the prisoner performed many antics and sang, 'The man in the moon one morning did say, How many oak trees are there in the sea? I answered him and said, When I'm understood, As many red herrings as there are in the wood' [*Folk-Lore*, 1883] / Crofton MS, 1901, two variants / *Squirrel Nutkin*, Beatrix Potter, 1903 / *Folk-Song*, 1940, 'The men of yon forest they askit of me How many strawberries grew in the saut sea? But I askit them back wi' a tear in my e'e—How many ships sail in the forest?' given as extension of a Shetland version of the song 'The Week before Easter', which is preserved on a broadsheet of the reign of James II.

319

If a man who turnips cries,
Cry not when his father dies,
It is proof that he would rather
Have a turnip than his father.

Dr. Johnson's contribution to the nursery: a burlesque of the quatrain,

Se acquien los leones vence
Vence una muger hermosa
O el de flaco averguençe
O ella di ser más furiosa.

Mrs. Thrale tells how one day when she praised Lope de Vega's lines to the Doctor more than he thought they deserved, he retorted that they were 'a mere play of words', and spontaneously produced this epigram about a turnip-seller, saying that it was certainly no worse.

Anecdotes of the late Samuel Johnson, Mrs. Piozzi, 1786 / JOH, 1846, apparently orally collected / Commonly appears in modern nursery books.
　***Boswell had commented, 'He could condescend to trifle with namby pamby rhymes to please Mrs. Thrale and her daughter'.

320

There was a man and he had nought,
　And robbers came to rob him;
He crept up to the chimney top,
　And then they thought they had him.

But he got down on the other side,
　And then they could not find him;
He ran fourteen miles in fifteen days,
　And never looked behind him.

This seems to have evolved from a verse in a manuscript of c. 1475:

There was a man that hadde nought;
There come thevys & robbed hym, & toke nought:
He ranne owte, and cryde nought.
Why shoulde he crye? he loste nought.
Here ys a tale of ryght nought.

Man

BM MS Egerton 1995, ed. Furnivall, 1903 / *Songs for the Nursery*, 1805 / *GG's Garland*, 1810, 'There was an old woman had nothing, And there came thieves to rob her; When she cried out she made no noise, But all the whole country heard her' / *GG's Garland* (Lumsden), c. 1815 / JOH, 1843 / *Folk-Lore*, 1901, 'There was an old woman lived under a hill, and three thieves came to rob her, She cried out, And made a great rout, For the thieves had a mind to stab her. She ran fourteen miles in fifteen days. And never looked behind her. She got in a wood, And there she stood, And the thieves could never find her' / *Man in the Moon*, L. Leslie Brooke, 1913 / Correspondent, 1947, '...He gained the roof by a gutter spout...He ran fifteen miles within the hour.'

321

There was a man, he went mad,
He jumped into a paper bag;
The paper bag was too narrow,
He jumped into a wheelbarrow;
The wheelbarrow took on fire,
He jumped into a cow byre;
The cow byre was too nasty,
He jumped into an apple pasty;
The apple pasty was too sweet,
He jumped into Chester-le-Street;
Chester-le-Street was full of stones,
He fell down and broke his bones.

Collection of NR (Oliver and Boyd), c. 1830, 'Little wee laddie, Wha's your daddie? I came out o' a busket lady. A busket lady's owre fine; I cam out o' a bottle o' wine. A bottle o' wine's owre dear; I cam out o' a bottle o' beer. A bottle o' beer's owre thick; I cam out o' a gauger's stick. A gauger's stick's but and ben; I cam out o' a peacock hen.' JOH, 1846, 'There was a man and he was mad', he jumped into a pea-swad which was over-full; subsequently he jumped into an over-fat roaring bull, an over-fine gentleman's hat, an over-dear bottle of wine, an over-thick bottle of beer, an over-narrow club-stick, a wheelbarrow which began to crack, so he jumped into a hay-stack which began to blaze, so he did 'nothing but cough and sneeze!' / *Household Tales*, S. O. Addy, 1895, 'There was a man who had a lad; He put him in a pea swad. The pea swad it was so green; He put him in a silver pin'; subsequently in a good glass of wine, a thick log of wood, a nasty candlestick, a hot apple pasty, a wide porridge pot, and an old house side, 'And there he lived and there he died, And nobody either laughed or cried' / *Folk-Lore*, 1909, sequence collected c. 1893: over-full pea swad, over-fat roaring bull, over-fine gentleman's hat, over-red bottle of wine, over-hard crust of bread, over-little half crown, over-narrow weaver's sickle, 'the wheelbarrow gave a crack and there was the end of poor Jack' / *Street Games of N. Shields Children*, M. and R. King, 1930 / *Folk Tales of the N. Country*, F. Grice, 1944 / *Sandy Candy*, N. and W. Montgomerie, 1948, Scottish version 'Little Tammie Tyrie'.

Man

322

There was a man of double deed
Sowed his garden full of seed.
When the seed began to grow,
'Twas like a garden full of snow;
When the snow began to melt,
'Twas like a ship without a belt;
When the ship began to sail,
'Twas like a bird without a tail;
When the bird began to fly,
'Twas like an eagle in the sky;
When the sky began to roar,
'Twas like a lion at the door;
When the door began to crack,
'Twas like a stick across my back;
When my back began to smart,
'Twas like a penknife in my heart;
When my heart began to bleed,
'Twas death and death and death indeed.

A rhyme of strange fascination; many people have recalled the awe-inspiring effect it had on them when children, and yet how they continued to want it repeated to them. In *Gammer Gurton's Garland* (1784) the rhyme starts:

A man of words and not of deeds
Is like a garden full of weeds.

This couplet in various forms appears to have been proverbial; it is found in several proverb collections, e.g. in James Howell's collection (1659), where is also included 'Good words without deeds are rushes without weeds'. Similar sentiments occur in Harley MS, 1927, of the time of James I, Harley MS 6580, and Sloane MS 406. JOH (1849) recorded a version which he said was a burlesque song on the battle of Culloden:

Double Dee Double Day,
Set a garden full of seeds;
When the seeds began to grow,
It's like a garden full of snow.
When the snow began to melt,
Like a ship without a belt.
When the ship began to sail,
Like a bird without a tail.

337

Man

When the bird began to fly,
Like an eagle in the sky.
When the sky began to roar,
Like a lion at the door.
When the door began to crack,
Like a stick laid o'er my back.
When my back began to smart,
Like a penknife in my heart.
When my heart began to bleed,
Like a needleful of thread.
When the thread began to rot,
Like a turnip in the pot.
When the pot began to boil,
Like a bottle full of oil.
When the oil began to settle,
Like our Geordie's bloody battle.

This is very similar to a ball-bouncing song sent by a correspondent in 1946. The rhyme is apparently also known as a riddle, for in 1948 a *John o' London's* reader sought the solution to similar lines beginning 'Riddle me, riddle me, Ready O, My father gave me seeds to sow'.

GG's Garland, 1784, sixteen lines / *Nurse Lovechild's DFN*, c. 1830, as 1784 but 'It's like a thorn stuck in your heart' instead of penknife / JOH, 1842 / *Girl's Own Book*, Mrs. Child, 1844, 'A girl of words' / *Street Games of N. Shields Children*, M. and R. King, 1930 / Correspondents, 1946–9, several versions including 'Adam and Eve Saved some seed; When the seed began to grow, Like a garden full of snow...Like a diamond in the sky...Like potatoes in the pot...When the oil began to settle King George's soldiers went out to battle, battle, battle'. Repeated while bouncing a ball, four bounces to a line, and 'battle' repeated until ball is missed / *John o' London's*, 1948.

323

There was a man who had no eyes,
He went abroad to view the skies;
He saw a tree with apples on it,
He took no apples off, yet left no apples on it.

RIDDLE. The traditional solution is that the man had one eye, there were two apples on the tree, he took one and left one. The illustrator of a modern nursery book neatly solved the problem by drawing the tree with a board nailed to it marked APPLES.

JOH, 1844 / *N & Q*, 1872, 'A man without eyes saw plums on a tree, Neither took plums nor left plums; pray how can that be?' / *Mother Goose's NR*, L. E. Walter, 1924.

THE MALIGNED MATRON

There was an old woman who lived in a shoe.
She had dozens of children—adopted ones too;
She nursed them and taught them and said they might go;
But did they say 'Thank you'? Not all of them—no.

a. Cartoon by Illingworth in *Punch*, 5 February 1947

b. Election Day cartoon, *Daily Express*, 23 February 1950

c. Advertisement of Arthur Guinness, Son & Co., Ltd.

Cf. *Booke of meery Riddles*, 1600, 'I came to a tree where were Apples; I eat no apples, I gaue away no apples, nor I left no apples behinde me. And yet I eat, gaue away, and left behinde me', and Holme MS, c. 1645.

Cf. also *Das deutsche Kinderbuch*, Karl Simrock, 1848, 'Ein Mann der keine Augen hatte, sah Aepfel auf einem Baume hangen. Er warf darnach, da fielen keine herab und blieben keine hangen.'

324

There was a crooked man, and he walked a crooked mile,
He found a crooked sixpence against a crooked stile;
He bought a crooked cat, which caught a crooked mouse,
And they all lived together in a little crooked house.

JOH, 1842 / Maclagan, 1901 / *Mother Goose*, Arthur Rackham, 1913 / In *Less Familiar NR*, 1927, Robert Graves improved on his memory with a second couplet: 'He brought it crooked back To his crooked wife Joan, And cut a crooked snippet From the crooked ham-bone.'

325

There was a little man, and he had a little gun,
    And his bullets were made of lead, lead, lead;
He went to the brook, and shot a little duck,
    Right through the middle of the head, head, head.

He carried it home to his old wife Joan,
    And bade her a fire for to make, make, make,
To roast the little duck he had shot in the brook,
    And he'd go and fetch her the drake, drake, drake.

A fanciful explanation given by Kathleen Thomas in *The Real Personages of Mother Goose* is that Philip of Spain, Mary Tudor, and Sir Francis Drake are depicted.

T Thumb's PSB, c. 1744, rhyme words not triplicated, as also in *Top Book*, c. 1760 / *Songs for the Nursery*, 1805, 'There was a little man and he had a little gun, And his gun was made of lead; He shot John Sprig thro' the middle of his wig, And knock'd it off his head' / *Vocal Harmony*, c. 1806 / *Whole Particulars of that Renowned Sportsman Sam and his Gun... with a description of his Wife Joan* (Didier & Tebbett), 1808, gives an elongated story based on the rhyme / *GG's Garland*, 1810, rhyme words triplicated / *Nurse Love-Child's Legacy* (J. Catnach), c. 1830 / JOH, 1842, with reduplications and third verse 'The drake was a swimming, With his curly tail; The little man made it his mark, mark, mark! He let off his gun, But he fir'd too soon, And the

Man

drake flew away with a quack, quack, quack' / Rimbault, 1846 / *Little Man & his Little Gun*, Marcus Ward, c. 1875 / Williams, 1923 / The rhyme is incorporated in chapbooks of *The Life of Jack Sprat* (q.v.).

Parodies: the best of many is Lewis Carroll's 'In stature the Manlet was dwarfish', in *Sylvie and Bruno*, 1889.

Cf. 'The Little Man who woo'd a Little Maid'.

326

There was a little man,
And he wooed a little maid,
And he said, Little maid, will you wed, wed, wed?
    I have little more to say,
    Than will you, yea or nay?
For the least said is soonest mended, ded, ded.

Then this little maid she said,
Little sir, you've little said,
To induce a little maid for to wed, wed, wed;
    You must say a little more,
    And produce a little ore,
Ere I to the church will be led, led, led.

Then the little man replied,
If you'll be my little bride,
I will raise my love notes a little higher, higher, higher;
    Though I little love to prate
    Yet you'll find my heart is great,
With the little God of Love all on fire, fire, fire.

Then the little maid replied,
If I should be your bride,
Pray, what must we have for to eat, eat, eat?
    Will the flames that you're so rich in
    Make a fire in the kitchen,
And the little God of Love turn the spit, spit, spit?

Then the little man he sighed,
And some say a little cried,
And his little heart was big with sorrow, sorrow, sorrow;
    I'll be your little slave,
    And if the little that I have,
Be too little, little dear, I will borrow, borrow, borrow.

Man

Then the little man so gent,
Made the little maid relent,
And set her little soul a-thinking, king, king;
Though his little was but small,
Yet she had his little all,
And could have of a cat but her skin, skin, skin.

Horace Walpole entered in his Journal of the Printing-Office at Strawberry Hill, 31 May 1764, 'Printed some copies of a ballad by S^r Ch. Sidley, beginning, "There was a little man"'. Whether this was Sir Charles Sedley (properly Sidley), c. 1639–1701, the Restoration wit, or his great-grandson Sir Charles Sedley, c. 1721–78, is still open. In the Strawberry Hill version the lines are headed simply 'A Song'. In the otherwise earliest known appearance, in *The Fairing, or a Golden Toy for Children*, published by Newbery, 1 January 1765, the heading is, 'A New Love Song By the Poets of Great Britain'. Although the great-grandson was a fellow-member of White's with Walpole, it is more likely that the first Sir Charles was the author. He wrote many songs. The version in *The Fairing* (as in *Mother Goose's Melody*) differs from the broadside in that the rhyme-words are repeated. This verse form appears also in an 1810 rendering of 'There was a little man, and he had a little gun' (q.v.), first recorded c. 1744, and in a song *The Dumb Maid*, extant on a broadside (Roxburghe Collection) c. 1678:

All you that pass along,
give ear unto my Song,
Concerning a Youth that was young, young, young;
And of a Maiden fair,
few with her might compare,
But alack, and alas! she was dumb, dumb, dumb.

The words of 'There was a little man, and he woo'd a little maid' are believed to have been sung to the tune 'I am the Duke of Norfolk; or, Paul's Steeple' given in Playford's *Dancing Master* (1685) and a passage, curious when compared with the 'Little Man', appears in Mrs. Centlivre's play *Artifice*, printed in 1723, 'Now in the Summer of our Love, little Cares would not offend us: But when the Glowing of the Passion's over, and pinching Cold of winter follows, will amorous Sighs supply the Want of Fire? Or kind Looks and Kisses keep off Hunger?'

A Song (Strawberry Hill broadside) 1764, second verse ends, 'E'er I make a little print in your bed'; fourth verse begins, 'Then the little Maid she said, your fire may warm the bed' / *The Fairing* (J. Newbery), 1765 [1767] / *MG's Melody*, c. 1765 / *Scots Nightingale*, 1778 [A. T. Hazen, 1942] / *The Charmer*, 1782 [A. T. Hazen, 1942] / *The Golden Toy* (no imprint), c. 1800 / *Vocal Harmony*, c. 1806 / *Memoirs of the little Man and the little Maid, with some interesting particulars of their lives* (B. Tabart),

1807, 12 stanzas, differing substantially from text, with music by Dr. Calcott; (Wm. Charles, Philadelphia), 1811; (E. Wallis), ? 1830 / *The Cheerful Warbler* (J. Kendrew), c. 1820, two verses / JOH, 1842 / Rimbault, 1846 / *The Courtship and Wedding of the Little Man and the Little Maid*, illus. John Absolon (Grant & Griffith), 1850, 34 3-line stanzas differing substantially from foregoing / *Harlequin Cock Robin and Jenny Wren*, W. S. Gilbert, 1866, 'We will manage as we can Said this foolish little man, And what we haven't got we will borrow', verses 1, 2, and 5 only [*Pantomime Pageant*, 1946] / *Baby's Bouquet*, 1879 / Kidson, 1904 / In *Melincourt* (1817) Thomas Love Peacock refers to it as the 'very admirable ballad'; and Sir Walter Scott in his *Journal* refers to it twice (14 Mar. and 25 Nov. 1827). In *A Catalogue of Books printed at Strawberry Hill* (1813) J. McCreery attributed the authorship to Silvester Harding.

327

There was a mad man and he had a mad wife,
    And they lived in a mad town:
And they had children three at a birth,
    And mad they were every one.

The father was mad, the mother was mad,
    And the children mad beside;
And they all got on a mad horse,
    And madly they did ride.

They rode by night and they rode by day,
    Yet never a one of them fell;
They rode so madly all the way,
    Till they came to the gates of hell.

Old Nick was glad to see them so mad,
    And gladly let them in:
But he soon grew sorry to see them so merry,
    And let them out again.

Benjamin Franklin wrote to Peter Collinson from Philadelphia (26 June 1755): 'The Assembly ride restive; and the Governor, tho' he spurs with both Heels, at the same time reins-in with both Hands, so that the Publick Business can never move forward, and he remains like St. George in the Sign, always a Horseback, and never going on. Did you never hear this old Catch?

There was a mad Man, He had a mad Wife,
    And three mad Sons beside;

Man

And they all got upon a mad Horse
And madly they did ride.

'Tis a Compendium of our Proceedings and may save you the Trouble of reading them.' According to some sheet music (c. 1780) a version of this entitled *The Mad Family* was 'sung by Mrs. Massey with great Applause in *The Devil to Pay*'. It was not, however, a part of Coffey's original production, as published in 1731.

T Thumb's PSB, c. 1744, first two verses only; the cut, however, shows the children falling off the horse / *A Little Play-Book*, c. 1746, as previous / *Top Book*, c. 1760 / *The Mad Family* (printed at the little a), c. 1780, 'There was a Mad Man he had a Mad Wife, And they lived in a Mad Lane, Sir, They had Ten children to bring up, And they were mad the same, Sir', succeeding verses in same vein, last verse, 'The Devil was glad to see them all Mad And rose to let them in, Sir, But when he found them more mad than himself He turn'd them out again, Sir' / *GG's Garland*, 1810 / *MG's Quarto*, c. 1825 / JOH, 1842 / *The Lovely Ambition*, M. E. Chase, 1960, recited by Suffolk schoolchildren in grandfather's day, with two extra verses, 'Then God came down . . .'.

328

There was an old man,
And he had a calf,
And that's half;
He took him out of the stall,
And put him on the wall,
And that's all.

As JOH says, this is 'a composition apparently of little interest or curiosity', yet it was recorded in England over 200 years ago, and a Swede, in the last century, unacquainted with the English rhyme, repeated a lullaby current in Sweden which bears far too striking a similarity to the above to have had a separate origin.

MG's Melody, c. 1765 / *GG's Garland*, 1784 / JOH, 1842, 'There was an old woman sat spinning, And that's the first beginning; She had a calf, and that's half; She took it by the tail, and threw it over the wall, and that's all' / *NR from the Royal Collections* (J. G. Rusher), c. 1840 / JOH, 1853, 'I had a little cow; Hey-diddle, ho diddle! I had a little cow, and it had a little calf; Hey-diddle, ho-diddle; and there's my song half. I had a little cow; Hey-diddle, ho-diddle! I had a little cow, and I drove it to the stall; Hey-diddle, ho-diddle; and there's my song all!'.
Cf. *Svenska Fornsånger*, A. I. Arwidsson, 1842, 'Gubben och gumman hade en kalf, Och nu är visan half! Och begge sä körde de kalfven i vall, Och nu är visan all!' (Gaffer and gammer had a calf, And now that's half of the song. And both of them drove the calf into the meadow. And now that's all.)

329

There was an old man in a velvet coat,
He kissed a maid and gave her a groat;
The groat was cracked and would not go,
Ah, old man, do you serve me so?

'If the coat be ever so fine that a Fool wears, it is still but a Fool's Coat', remarks the editor of *Mother Goose's Melody*.

MG's Melody, c. 1765 / *GG's Garland*, 1784 / JOH, 1842.

330

My little old man and I fell out,
How shall we bring this matter about?
Bring it about as well as you can,
And get you gone, you little old man!

'Down inside the woodpecker's tree', tells the author of *The Tale of Timmy Tiptoes*, 'a fat squirrel voice and a thin squirrel voice sang this together'. J. R. Prior, writing to Hone's *Every-Day Book* (1827), said that in June 1826 he had seen a company of Morris dancers in Clerkenwell, dancing to the tune 'Moll in the wad and I fell out, And what d'ye think it was about?' 'This may be remembered,' he added, 'as one of the once popular street songs of the late Charles Dibdin's composition.'

GG's Garland, 1784 / Chambers, 1842, for 'chapping out', 'My grandfather's man and me coost out, How will we bring the matter about? We'll bring it about as weel as we can, And a' for the sake o' my grandfather's man' / JOH, 1843, 'My little old man and I fell out. I'll tell you what 'twas all about: I had money, and he had none, And that's the way the row begun' / N & Q, 1866, words 'chaunted by soldiers in barrack': 'Moll-in-the-wad and I fell out, What do you think it was about? I gave her a shilling, she swore it was bad; "It's an old soldier's button," says Moll-in-the-wad,' and three other versions / *Mother Goose's Melodies*, G. A. R., 1872, 'Mollie, my sister and I fell out, And what do you think it was all about? She loved coffee, and I loved tea, And that was the reason we couldn't agree' / Bolton, 1888, part of a longer rhyme, given as from Nova Scotia, 1815 / Maclagan, 1900, 'Me an' the minister's wife cast out, And guess ye what it was about? Black puddin', dish clout, Eiri orie, you're out' / *Timmy Tiptoes*, Beatrix Potter, 1911 / *Counting Out*, Carl Withers, 1946, similar to 1843.

Man in the Moon

331

The man in the moon
Came down too soon,
And asked his way to Norwich;
He went by the south,
And burnt his mouth
With supping cold plum porridge.

'I know less of his life', said Mrs. Micawber of her husband, 'than I do of the man of the south, connected with whose mouth the thoughtless children repeat an idle tale respecting cold plum porridge.' The rhyme was certainly common in the nineteenth century, though it is not likely, as has been suggested, to have been associated with the nineteenth-century 'man in the moon' who used to negotiate bribes at election time, for it was current earlier. The term 'man in the moon' has had many applications. In Martin Parker's ballad 'When the King enjoys his own again' (c. 1647), the lines,

The Man in the Moon
May wear out his shoon
By running after Charles his wain,

refer to a royalist almanack-maker. In another ballad, beginning,

The man o' the moon for ever!

the reference seems to be to King Charles. While in his *Jacobite Relics* Hogg prints a Scottish song,

There was a man came from the moon
And landed in our town, sir,
And he has sworn a solemn oath
That all but knaves must down, sir.

In 1884 the rhyme was the subject of a letter in *Notes & Queries* when it was pointed out that if 'plum porridge' was the true wording, the rhyme was likely to date from the time before modern cloth had converted plum porridge into plum pudding. The melody, says Kidson, is an old English air of the sixteenth or seventeenth century entitled 'Thomas I cannot'.

GG's Garland, 1784, 'with supping hot pease porridge' / Songs for the Nursery, 1805, '...The man in the South He burnt his mouth, With eating cold plum-porridge' / Spectator, 4 July 1840 / N & Q, 1884 / Kidson, 1904 / The Man in the Moon, L. Leslie Brooke, 1913 / Eastern Daily Press, Sept. 1946.

PLATE XII

a. 'The man in the moon' in Darton's *Songs for the Nursery*, 1818.
British Museum

b. The round 'Three blinde Mice' in *Deuteromelia*, 1609. British Museum

Man in the Moon

332

The man in the moon drinks claret,
But he is a dull jack-a-dandy;
Would he know a sheep's head from a carrot
He should learn to drink cider and brandy.

JOH gave this as the first stanza of a traditional Somersetshire song. It appears to be stemmed from, or part quoted in, a ballad printed in *Le Prince d'Amour* (1660). This was reprinted about 1673 on a broadside, and again two years later (registered 1 Mar. 1675) when it was titled:

New Mad Tom of Bedlam

OR

The Man in the Moon drinks Clarret,
With Powder-beef, Turnep and Carret.

Tune is, Grays Inn Mask.

The ballad ends,

The man in the Moon drinks Clarret;
With Powder-beef, Turnep and Carret,
A Cup of old Malago Sack
Will fire his bush at his back.

The tune 'Graies Inne Maske' is given in Playford's *English Dancing Master* (1651) called in the 1670 edition 'Grays Inne Maske, or Mad Tom'. The song was frequently reprinted or referred to in seventeenth- and eighteenth-century catch books, e.g. under the title 'Tom of Bedlam' in *The 2nd Book of the Pleasant Musical Companion* (1686), where it is quoted as 'sung at the Theater—For Bass alone'. In *Catch that Catch can* (1658) appears a song for four voices arranged by William Laws:

'Ha we to the other world, where 'tis thought they very merry be, there the man in the moon drinks claret, a health to thee and me.'

The ballad may well be earlier than any recording of it extant. Its penultimate verse goes:

Poor naked Tom is very dry—
A little drink for charity!
Hark! I hear Actæon's hounds!
The huntsmen whoop and hallowe;
Ringwood, Royster, Bowman, Jowler,
All the chase now follow.

This appears to have been known to Shakespeare. In *The Merry Wives of Windsor* (II. i) Pistol says,

Man in the Moon

Prevent, or go thou,
Like Sir Actæon he, with Ringwood at thy heels.

Pistol's words are more likely to be an allusion to the above verse in the ballad than to Golding's translation of *The Metamorphoses*. The 'Tom of Bedlam' referred to by Piscator in *The Compleat Angler* (1653) as having been 'lately made at my request by Mr. William Basse' was probably one of several songs of a similar title which were current at the time.

Ballad: *Le Prince d'Amour*, 1660 / *Covent Garden Drollery*, 1672 / *Man in the Moon drinks Claret* (W. Gilbertson, &c.), c. 1673, 'as it was lately sung at the Curtain, Hollywell' / *Choice Songs*, 1673 / *Choice Ayres*, 1676 / *New Mad Tom of Bedlam*, 1675 / *Pleasant Musical Companion*, 1686 / *Theatre of Complements*, 1688 / Song: *Midsummer Night's Dream*, JOH, 1841 / Nursery rhyme: Douce MS II, c. 1820, 'The man in the moon loves claret, Powder-beef, mutton, and carrot' / JOH, 1842 / *Mother Goose's NR*, L. E. Walter, 1924.

333

The Man in the Moon was caught in a trap
For stealing the thorns from another man's gap.
If he had gone by, and let the thorns lie,
He'd never been Man in the Moon so high.

This rhyme, heard by a contributor to *Folk-Lore* (1913) gives the traditional picture of the Man in the Moon who is identified by his lantern and bush of thorns (as in *A Midsummer Night's Dream*). The legend is that the man was banished to the moon for strewing a church path with thorns to hinder the people attending mass.

334

Will you lend me your mare to ride a mile?
No, she is lame leaping over a stile.
Alack! and I must go to the fair,
I'll give you good money for lending your mare.
Oh, oh! say you so?
Money will make the mare to go.

This catch has long been a favourite, particularly in the seventeenth century when it appeared in song books above the name of Edmund Nelham (who became a gentleman of the Chapel Royal in 1617). The earliest recording is probably the manuscript addition to the British Museum copy of *Deuteromelia or The Seconde part of Musicks melodie* (1609):

> Wilt thou lend me thy mare to ride but a mile?
> No, she's lame goinge over a stile;
> but if thou wilt her to me spare,
> thou shalt have mony for thy mare.
> ho ho say you soe
> mony shall make my mare to goe.

In some song books of the second half of the century a reply is quoted:

> Your mare is lame she halts downe right
> Then shall we not get to *London* tonight:
> You'd cry'd ho, ho, mony made her go,
> But now I well perceive it is not so
> You must spur her up, and put her to 't
> Though mony will not make her goe, your spurs will do 't.

MS addition to B.M. copy of *Deuteromelia*, Thomas Ravenscroft, 1609 / *Catch that Catch can*, collected by John Hilton, 1652 / *Antidote against Melancholy*, 1661, with 'The Answer' / *Catch that Catch Can*, 1667, with 'Reply' / *The Musical Companion* (John Playford), 1672 / *The Catch Club, or Merry Companion* (I. Walsh), 1762, with 'Reply' / JOH, 1846 / Williams, 1923, orally collected as a catch / *Mother Goose* (T. Nelson), c. 1945. The proverb 'Money makes the gray mare to go' is included in Howell's proverb collection (1659).

335

> See-saw, Margery Daw,
> Jacky shall have a new master;
> Jacky shall have but a penny a day,
> Because he can't work any faster.

It is possible that this rhyme, and the one succeeding, repeated as they are by children when playing on the see-saw, were originally sung by sawyers to keep the rhythm of the two-handled saw. Brome in *The Antipodes* (1640) connects sawyers with the phrase *see saw sacke a downe*. 'Let me not see you act now, In your Scholasticke way, you brought to towne wi' yee, With see saw sacke a downe, like a Sawyer.' This phrase is also preserved in the rhyme, 'See-saw, sacradown, Which is the way to London town' (q.v.) which probably has the same origin. According to *OED* the game of see-saw itself is not mentioned before 1821, whereas the word, as we have seen, is earlier. The game is one likely to be played where wood sawing is in progress, and the theory that the rhyme originally belonged to sawyers might explain the lines 'Jacky must have but a penny a day, Because he can't work any faster'. (For note on *Margery Daw* see succeeding article.)

MG's Melody, c. 1765 / *T Thumb's SB*, 1788 / *Songs for the Nursery*, 1805 / *Blackwood's*, ? John Wilson; July 1824, 'See, Say, a penny a-day, Tommy must have a new master —Why must he have but a penny a-day? Because he can work no faster' / *Rhymes for the Fireside* (Thomas Richardson), c. 1828 / *Favourite Rhymes for the Nursery*, 1892 / Oral collection, 1947.

336

See-saw, Margery Daw,
Sold her bed and lay upon straw;
Was not she a dirty slut
To sell her bed and lie in the dirt.

Daw is given in *OED* as 'a lazy person, sluggard', and in Scotland as 'an untidy woman, slut, slattern'. The name Margery, in the eighteenth and nineteenth centuries, was used almost exclusively by poor country people. The picture given by this rhyme sustains the idea that an appellation for a slut was *Margery Daw*. An extended version of the rhyme, quoted in 1886 as coming from Cornwall, is one of the very few instances of a fairy being mentioned in an English nursery rhyme:

See-saw, Margery Daw,
Sold her bed and lay upon straw;
Sold her bed and lay upon hay,
And pisky came and carried her away.
For wasn't she a dirty slut
To sell her bed and lie in the dirt?

De Quincy, in *Confessions of an English Opium Eater* (1821) [1856], retreats once more into 'the same opium lull. To and fro, up and down, did I tilt upon these mountainous seas, for year after year. "See-saw, like Margery Daw, that sold her bed and lay on straw".' Kipling quotes Mrs. Buzgago as singing the verse in *The Hill of Illusion*. After hearing it Captain Congleton says, 'I'm going to alter that to "flirt". It sounds better.'

GG's Garland, 1784 / *T Thumb's SB*, 1788 / *Christmas Box*, 1797 / MS addition in contemporary hand to Bussell copy of *MG's Melody*, 1803 / JOH, 1842, 'See-saw, jack a daw, What is the craw to do wi' her; She has not a stocking to put on her, And the craw has not one for to gi' her' / *Only True MG Melodies*, c. 1843 / Rimbault, 1846 / Mason, 1877 / *Baby's Bouquet*, 1879 / *Folk-Lore*, 1886, as quote / *See-saw, Margery Daw: or, Harlequin Ups and Downs* was the Christmas production at Drury Lane, 1857 / Kidson, 1901, states that there is a parody found dating from the time of Charles II.

337

See-saw, Margery Daw,
The old hen flew over the malt house;
She counted her chickens one by one,
Still she missed the little white one,
And this is it, this is it, this is it.

Toe rhyme.

JOH, 1853 / *Mother Goose's NR*, L. E. Walter, 1924 / *Texas and Southwestern Lore*, vol. vi,
1927, from woman born before 1830, 'See, saw, saddle the old goose, The old hen
jumped over the punkin house, And called her chickens one by one, And left the
poor little black-headed one' / Girl, 15, letter to 'Blue Peter' TV BBC, 1988, 'My
grandfather has many a time told me a nursery rhyme that has been passed down
through our family, in Dorset, "See-Saw, Margery Dawe, Coupie flew over the Malt
mill, Caught her chickies one by one, And lost the little whitey one".'

338

Margery Mutton-pie and Johnny Bo-peep,
They met together in Gracechurch Street;
In and out, in and out, over the way,
Oh, said Johnny, it's chop-nose day.

*The Merry History of Miss Margery Mutton Pye, and Bobby Bo-peep. Now first
published from a Lilliputian Manuscript* (London: Printed for H. Roberts, at
No. 56, almost opposite Great Turnstile) was published on the 17th of
January, 1776; but there is no rhyme or anything about the rhyme in it.

JOH, 1853 / *Old Nurse's Book*, Charles H. Bennett, 1858 / *London Treasury of NR*, J.
Murray MacBain, 1933.
  Cf. 'My mother and your mother'.

339

To market, to market,
To buy a plum bun:
Home again, home again,
Market is done.

Market

Knee rhyme. In 1598 John Florio published his dictionary *A Worlde of Wordes, or Most Copious, and exact Dictionarie in Italian and English*. The word *Abomba* is defined as 'a man's home or resting place: home againe, home againe'. In the augmented edition published in 1611 the definition is expanded, '*Abomba*, is properly the place where children playing hide themselves.... Also as we use to say Home againe home againe, market is done.' Florio may have known the rhyme in his childhood fifty years previously, but it does not appear to have been written down again until the nineteenth century. A common variation in the present day is,

> To market, to market, to buy a fat pig,
> Home again, home again, jiggety-jig;
> To market, to market, to buy a fat hog,
> Home again, home again, jiggety-jog.

Worlde of Wordes, 1598 and 1611 / *Songs for the Nursery*, 1805, 'To market, to market, to buy a penny bun, Home again, home again, market is done' / Douce MS, c. 1815 / *MG's Quarto*, c. 1825 / *Nursery Poems* (J. G. Rusher), c. 1840, as quote / JOH, 1842, 'Ride to the market to buy a fat pig' / JOH, 1853, 'To market, to market, To buy a plum cake; Home again, home again, Ne'er a one baked; The baker is dead and all his men, And we must go to market again' / *Mother Goose*, Kate Greenaway, 1881, 'market is late' / *Man in the Moon*, Leslie Brooke, 1913.

340

> To market, to market, a gallop, a trot,
> To buy some meat to put in the pot;
> Three pence a quarter, a groat a side,
> If it hadn't been killed it must have died.

JOH, 1844 / *Riddles and Rhymes* (T. Nelson), 1892, 'Upon my cock horse to market I'll trot, To buy a pig to boil in the pot. A shilling a quarter, half-a-crown a side, If it had not been killed, it would surely have died' / *Mother Goose's NR*, L. E. Walter, 1924.

341

> Mary had a little lamb,
> Its fleece was white as snow;
> And everywhere that Mary went
> The lamb was sure to go.

Mary

It followed her to school one day,
   That was against the rule;
It made the children laugh and play
   To see a lamb at school.

And so the teacher turned it out,
   But still it lingered near,
And waited patiently about
   Till Mary did appear.

Why does the lamb love Mary so?
   The eager children cry;
Why, Mary loves the lamb, you know,
   The teacher did reply.

E. V. Lucas came to the conclusion that these were the best-known four-line verses in the English language. They were written by Mrs. Sarah Josepha Hale (1788–1879) of Boston, 'early in the year 1830' about an incident which was 'partly true'. They were published in September 1830 over her initials in the *Juvenile Miscellany*, a periodical edited by Mrs. L. M. Child, and later in the year appeared in a volume of her work, *Poems for Our Children*. The verses have been claimed for several other authors including her son, Horatio Hale, Jane Burls, and for John Roulstone by a Mrs. Tyler. This last claim has gained a wide circulation, Mrs. Tyler, née Mary Sawyer, of Sudbury, Massachusetts, believing herself to be the original Mary; Henry Ford collected 'two hundred documents' to prove it and he restored the old schoolhouse at Sudbury as a memorial. The claim, however, was refuted both by Mrs. Hale in a letter written shortly before her death (*The Lady of Godey's*, R. E. Finley, 1931) and by her son a while after (*Boston Transcript*, 10 Apr. 1889). The Welsh claim, that Mary Hughes, née Thomas, was Mrs. Hale's original in 1847 (as appears on her tombstone) is precluded by the first date of publication. As Mrs. Hale herself pointed out, the incident of an adopted lamb following a child to school has probably occurred many times. One example pre-dating the Hale verses is a children's story written by Dorothy Wordsworth, c. 1805, about a Lakeland child called Mary and her pet lamb (MS printed in *Dorothy Wordsworth and Romanticism*, Susan Levin, 1989). 'Mary had a little lamb' was the first utterance recorded on Edison's talking machine or phonograph (1877).

Juvenile Miscellany, Sept.-Oct., 1830, three eight-line stanzas / *Poems for Our Children: Designed for Families, Sabbath Schools, and Infant Schools...by Mrs. Sarah J. Hale, 1830* / *Juvenile Lyre: or, Hymns and Songs* 'Set to Appropriate Music' (Boston), 1831, appears anonymously, music probably by Lowell Mason / *The School Song Book*, Mrs. Sarah J. Hale, 1834, words set to music by Mr. Mason / *McGuffey's Second Reader*, 1857, anonymous and in quatrains; its appearance in this reader, for fifty years a standard text book in America's common schools, probably established its fame / *Songs for the Little Ones at Home* (Joseph Cundall), 1860, illus. Birket Foster, given as from *Songs for Children* / *Little Songs for me to Sing*, 1865, illus. Sir John Millais / It was reprinted by Mrs. Hale in her *Godey's Lady's Book*, 1875.

Curiosa: *The Story of Mary's Little Lamb as told by Mary and her Neighbors and Friends* . . . published by Mr. and Mrs. Henry Ford, Dearborn, Michigan, 1928.

342

Mary, Mary, quite contrary,
    How does your garden grow?
With silver bells and cockle shells,
    And pretty maids all in a row.

It is possible (as has been frequently stated) that this rhyme has a religious background; that it is 'a word-picture of Our Lady's convent' has been suggested, the bells being the sanctus bells, the cockleshells the badges of the pilgrims, the pretty maids the nuns 'rank behind rank at office'. But there is disagreement as to the significance of the piece as a whole. Catholic writers feel it to be a lament for the persecution of the Roman Church; Protestant writers declare it is a lament at the reinstatement of the Roman Church. Popular tradition has it that the original Mary was Mary, Queen of Scots, who with her gay, French, and Popish inclinations much displeased the dour John Knox. In this case 'the pretty maids' might be the renowned 'Four Marys', her ladies-in-waiting, and it has even been stated that the 'cockleshells' were the decorations upon a particular dress she was given by the Dauphin. Such assertions are, of course, the work of the 'happy guessers'. No proof has been found that the rhyme was known before the eighteenth century. It is to be remarked, however, that a lost ballad 'Cuckolds all a row' was registered in June 1637, and that there is a tune 'Cuckolds all a row' in the 1651 edition of Playford's *Dancing Master*. The last line of the 1780 version of the rhyme goes 'Sing cuckolds all on a row' and it could well be sung to the tune in *The Dancing Master*. 'When cockle shells turn silver bells' is a folk phrase for 'never'.

T Thumb's PSB, c. 1744, 'Mistress Mary, Quite contrary, How does your Garden grow? With Silver Bells, And Cockle Shells, And so my Garden grows' / *Nancy Cock's PSB*, c. 1780, 'Mrs. Mary, Quite contrary, How does your garden grow? With silver bells, And cockle shells: Sing cuckolds all on a row' / *GG's Garland*, 1784, 'Cowslips all arow' / *T Thumb's SB*, 1788 / *T Tit's SB*, c. 1790, 'With lady bells all in a row' / *Infant Institutes*, 1797, 'And cuckolds all in a row' / *Christmas Box*, 1797, 'How does my Lady's garden grow?' / Letter to Bernard Barton from Charles Lamb, 30 Apr. 1831, 'O Maria, Maria, valdè contraria, quomodo crescit hortulus tuus?' [1905] / *Poetic Trifles* (J. G. Rusher), c. 1840, 'And Columbines in a row' / JOH, 1842, 'And cowslips all a row' alternatively, 'muscles all in a row' / *Mother Goose*, Kate Greenaway, 1881.

343

My maid Mary
She minds her dairy,
While I go a-hoeing and mowing each morn;
Merrily run the reel,
And the little spinning-wheel,
Whilst I am singing and mowing my corn.

This popular little rhyme comes from *The Happy Husbandman: Or, Country Innocence*, a black-letter broadside ballad sung 'To a pleasant new Court Tune':

My young Mary do's mind the Dairy,
   while I go a Howing, and Mowing each Morn;
Then hey the little Spinning-Wheel
Merrily round do's Reel
   while I am singing amidst the Corn:
Cream and Kisses both are my Delight,
She gives me them, and the Joys of Night;
   She's soft as the Air,
   As Morning fair,
Is not such a Maid a most pleasing sight?

It was licensed by R. P. (Richard Pocock) so it must have been printed between August 1685 and December 1688. When referred to in 'A New-Made Medley', 1688–9, the first line was quoted, 'There's my maid Mary, she does mind her Dairy', and it is notable that this wording is very similar to the version which JOH collected 170 years later. The tune of 'My Maid Mary' is in Charles Coffey's *The Merry Cobler* (1733); later in the century the song appeared as sheet music (British Library).

The Happy Husbandman (P. Brooksby), c. 1687 / JOH, 1853, as text / *This Little Piggy* (Juvenile Productions), c. 1945.

344

Mrs. Mason broke a bason,
Mrs. Frost asked her how much it cost,
Mrs. Brown said half-a-crown,
Mrs. Flory said what a story.

Shropshire Folk-Lore, C. S. Burne, 1883, 'Mrs Mason broke her bason How much will it be? Half-a-crown says Mr. Brown, Out goes she!' / *County Folk-Lore, Suffolk*, The Lady

Mrs. Mason

Eveline Gurdon, 1893, as text. / *Rymour Club*, 1911, 'Katty Mason broke a bason, How much had she to gi'e? Half a crown, lay it down, And out goes she' / Enfield school-child, 1952, 'Mrs Mason bought a basin. Mrs Tyson said, "What a nice 'un". "What did it cost?" said Mrs Frost. "Half a crown," said Mrs Brown. "Did it indeed," said Mrs Reed. "It did for certain," said Mrs Burton. Then Mrs Nix, up to her tricks, Threw the basin on the bricks.'

345

Master I have, and I am his man,
Gallop a dreary dun;
Master I have, and I am his man,
And I'll get a wife as fast as I can;
With a heighly gaily, gambo raily,
Higgledy piggledy, niggledy, niggledy,
Gallop a dreary dun.

This, which JOH included in his 1844 edition (collected apparently from oral tradition), is the first of six verses of a song written by O'Keeffe for his comic opera *The Castle of Andalusia* (1782). The rendering there is,

A master I have, and I am his man,
Galloping dreary dun,
And he'll get a wife as fast as he can,
With a haily
Gaily
Gambo raily,
Gigg'ling,
Nigg'ling
Galloping galloway, draggle tail, dreary dun.

It was popular at glee clubs in the early nineteenth century and appears in such song collections as *The Universal Songster* (1825) and *The Nightingale* (1831).

346

Matthew, Mark, Luke, and John,
Bless the bed that I lie on.
Four corners to my bed,
Four angels round my head;
One to watch and one to pray
And two to bear my soul away.

Matthew

A nursery prayer, frequently known as the 'White Paternoster'. Thomas Ady writing in 1656 said 'An old Woman in Essex who was living in my time, she had lived also in Queen Maries time, had learned thence many Popish Charms, one whereof was this; every night when she lay down to sleep she charmed her Bed, saying:

> Matthew, Mark, Luke and John,
> The Bed be blest that I lye on.

And this would she repeat three times, reposing great confidence therein, because (as she said) she had been taught it, when she was a young Maid, by the Church-men of those times.' James Sinclair in 1685, quoting Ady's story, tells of a witch 'much addicted to Nonsensical Rhymes' and gives her Black Paternoster which, clearly, is a distortion of the 'White':

> Four newks in this house, for haly Angels,
> A post in the midst, that's Christ Jesus,
> Lucas, Marcus, Matthew, Joannes,
> God be into this house, and all that belangs us.

The prayer is again recorded in the following year. In more recent times the prayer, which in fact amounts to a night-spell, has been found throughout England, and more than one authority during the past century has complained that in country places the blessing was almost the only prayer known to children, and was more often repeated than the Lord's Prayer. Some versions are lengthy, as that collected by the Rev. Sabine Baring-Gould from a woman in the workhouse in Tavistock, of which,

> Matthew, Mark, Luke, and John,
> Bless this bed that I lie on;
> Four angels to my bed,
> Two to pillow, two to head,
> Two to hear me when I pray,
> Two to bear my soul away,

is the first of four verses. In *The Miller's Tale* (c. 1387) Chaucer refers to a White Paternoster, possibly the same prayer. Certainly its beginning lies centuries deep, and it is a part of the living traditional matter in most European countries, often being particularly associated with children. Johannes Agricola (b. 1492), for instance, tells how he used to know the German version as a child: 'Uns kinder lernten unsere eltern also beten, wenn wir schlafen giengen,

> Ich will heint schlafen gehen,
> Zwölf engel sollen mit mir gehen,
> Zwen zur haupten,
> Zwen zur seiten,

Matthew

Zwen zun Füssen,
Zwen die mich decken,
Zwen die mich wecken,
Zwen die mich weisen,
Zů dem himlischen paradeise. Amen.'

It will be noticed that the angels are here set in pairs as in many versions of the English rhyme. It will also be seen that they are placed at head, side, and feet. This form of invocation (known as 'lorica' because, like armour, it protects from all directions) can be traced to Celtic half-magic, half-Christian, charms and, according to Dr. Barb in his thesis 'Animula Vagula Blandula', through these to Jewish cabbalistic prayers against the 'terrors that threaten by night' ('At my right Michael, at my left Gabriel, before me Uriel, behind me Raphael'), and so to ancient Babylonian incantations ('Shamash before me, behind me Sin, Nergal at my right, Ninib at my left').

A Candle in the Dark, or, a treatise concerning the nature of witches and witchcraft, Thomas Ady, 1656, as quote [1661] / *Satan's Invisible World Discovered,* George Sinclair, 1685 / Lansdowne MS 231, John Aubrey, 1686-7, 'A prayer used when they went to Bed: Matthew, Mark, Luke, and John, Bless the bed that I lye on. And blessed Guardian-Angel keep Me safe from danger whilst I sleep' / *Diocese of Worcester Report,* 1841 / JOH, 1842 / Chambers, 1847 / *Lancashire Folk-lore,* J. Harland, &c., 1867, '... There are four corners to my bed, And four angels overspread, Two at the feet, two at the head. If any ill thing me betide, Beneath your wings my body hide. Matthew, Mark, Luke, and John, Bless the bed that I lie on. Amen' / 'Chaucer's Night-Spell', W. Thoms, *Folk-Lore,* 1878 / *Songs of the West,* S. Baring-Gould, 1891, as quote / Northall, 1892, thirteen versions, also similar prayers / *Brand's Popular Antiquities,* ed. H. Ellis, 1893, 'Matthew, Mark, Luke, and John, God bless the bed that I lie on; If anything appear to me, Sweet Christ arise and comfort me' / *Denham Tracts,* 1895 / Crofton, 1901, as 1867, version Crofton knew as a boy / *N & Q,* 1909, variations including, 'One to sing and one to pray'; 'And two to drive the devil away'; 'I pray the Lord my soul to keep, If I should die whilst in my sleep' / *Folk-Lore,* 1910, variations including, 'Four posts around my bed, Four angels have it spread, Matthew, Mark, Luke and John, Keep me, O God, till day shall dawn' / *Lark Rise,* Flora Thompson, 1939 / *Matthew Mark Luke and John* (S.P.C.K.), illus. N. S. Unwin, c. 1945 / Baring-Gould MSS, *Folk Songs of the West Country,* G. Hitchcock, 1974.

Cf. *Enchiridion Papae Leonis,* 1633 (from the Latin of 1532), 'Au soir, m'allant coucher, je trouvis trois anges à mon lit couchés, un aux pieds, deux au chevet, la bonne Vierge Marie du milieu, qui me dit que je couchis, que rien ne doutis' / *Les Misérables,* Victor Hugo, 1862, 'Au-dessus de la porte du réfectoire etait ecrite en grosses lettres noires cette prière qu'on appelait la Patenôtre blanche... "Petite patenôtre blanche, que Dieu fit, que Dieu dit, que Dieu mit en paradis. Au soir, m'allant coucher, je trouvis trois anges à mon lit couchés, un aux pieds, deux aux chevet, la bonne vierge Marie aux milieu... Sant Jean, Sant Luc, Sant Marc, Sant Mathiou, Les quatre Evangelistes de Diou, Sieguetz toujours ben eme iou, Coumo eme toutes les mious..." En 1827, cette oraison caractéristique avait disparu du mur sous triple couche de badigeon. Elle achève à cette heure de s'effacer dans la mémoire de quelques jeunes filles d'alors, vieilles femmes aujourd'hui' / *La Revue des traditions populaires,* 1889, 'Saint Luc, Saint Marc, et Saint Mathieu, Evangelistes du bon Dieu; Gardez les quatres coins de mon lit Pendant toute cette nuit. Ainsi soit-il' / *Das deutsche Kinderbuch*, Karl Simrock, 1848, 'Abends wenn ich schlafen geh, Vierzehn Engel bei mir stehn, Zwei zu meiner Rechten, Zwei zu meiner Linken, Zwei zu meinen Häupten, Zwei zu meinen Füssen, Zwei die mich decken, Zwei die mich wecken, Zwei die mich weisen In das himmlische Paradeischen'. This version also features in Humperdinck's opera *Hänsel und Gretel* (1893) as the evening prayer of the two children / *Kleinere Schriften*, Reinhold Köhler, 1900, 'Johannes, Lucas, Mattheus, Marcus, die vier evangelisten, Die müssen unser end fristen', from 14th-century MS. Also Dutch, Swedish, Norwegian, Spanish, and Swiss versions / *Study of Folk-Songs*, E. Martinengo-Cesaresco, 1886, 'Quatro pirondelitas Tiene mi cama; Quatro angelitos Me la acompāna. La madre de dios Esta en medio, Dicendome: Duerme y reposa, Que no te sucedera Ninguna mala cosa' (from Spain); 'Au lieche de Diou Me couche iou, Sept anges n'en trouve iou, Tres es peds, Quatre au capet (caput); La Buoeno Mero es au mitan Uno roso blanco à la man' (from Provence); 'Su letto meo est de battor cantones, Et battor anghelos si bie ponen; Duos in pes, et duos in cabitta, Nostra Segnora a costazu m'ista' (from Sardinia, early poetical rendering) / *Gamle Danske Folkebønner*, F. Ohrt, 1928, 'Hvar Awten a til Senge gaar, fjauten Guds Engle om mœ staar, tau ve mi Hoiem, tau ve mi Fojem, tau ve mi hyver Sie, tau ve mi venster Sie; tau mœ vœk, tau mœ dœk, tau mœ Vej viis' te den evige Paridis' / 'Animula Vagula Blandula', A. A. Barb, paper read to the English Folk-Lore Society, 16 Nov. 1949.

347

Matthew, Mark, Luke and John,
Hold the horse till I get on;
When I got on I could not ride,
I fell off and broke my side.

Chambers says that boys in Scotland chant this 'in the course of their rollicking sports'. It is in the nature of being a hobby-horse rhyme, with the invocation borrowed from the nursery prayer, of which improper versions have so frequently been a joy to schoolchildren. JOH said he was at a loss to explain it, unless it was written by the Puritans to ridicule the prayer.

Chambers, 1842, 'Matthew, Mark, Luke, John. Haud the horse till I loup on; Haud it fast, and haud it sure, Till I get owre the misty muir' / JOH, 1849 / Maclagan, 1900 / *Encyclopedia Americana*, 'Matthew, Mark, Luke, and John, Saddle the horse and I'll get on . . .' / *I Saw Esau*, I. and P. Opie, 1947.

348

Three blind mice, see how they run!
They all ran after the farmer's wife,

Mice

> Who cut off their tails with a carving knife,
> Did you ever see such a thing in your life,
> As three blind mice?

This is probably the best-known round in the world. A version of it, as follows, was included among the 'Pleasant Roundelaies' in *Deuteromelia or The Seconde part of Musicks melodie* (1609):

> Three blinde Mice, three blinde Mice,
> Dame Iulian, Dame Iulian,
> the Miller and his merry olde Wife,
> shee scrapte her tripe licke thou the knife.

The editor and probable part author of this collection was Thomas Ravenscroft, a young man still in his teens, lately a chorister at St. Paul's. 'Three Blind Mice' continued to be popular. On 14 March 1763, according to his London journal, James Boswell twitted the indolent Lord Eglinton about his offer of help: 'I believe you intend to do what you say, but perhaps the song of *Three blind mice* comes across you and prevents you from thinking of it.' (Lord Eglinton was an enthusiastic member of the Catch Club.) It was JOH who brought the song into the nursery. As far as has been ascertained the words make no appearance in children's literature prior to 1842, and JOH, at first, only knew three lines of it. Rimbault probably assisted its nursery popularity by including the tune in his 1846 collection.

Deuteromelia, Thomas Ravenscroft, 1609 / *Catch that Catch can*, John Hilton, 1658, and *Catch Club*, 1762, as 1609 / British Museum MS Additional 34126, c. 1789 / JOH, 1842; fourth line, 1843, 'Did you ever see such fools in your life' / Rimbault, 1846 / *N & Q*, 1890, version going back three generations, 'Three blind mice, See how they run, A farmer married an ugly wife, And she cut her throat with a carving knife, Did you ever see such a fool in your life, Three blind mice'.

349

> Six little mice sat down to spin;
> Pussy passed by and she peeped in.
> What are you doing, my little men?
> Weaving coats for gentlemen.
> Shall I come in and cut off your threads?
> No, no, Mistress Pussy, you'd bite off our heads.
> Oh, no, I'll not; I'll help you to spin.
> That may be so, but you don't come in.

Mice

' "Mew! Mew!" interrupted Simpkin (the Tailor of Gloucester's cat) and he scratched at the door'—But the little mice in Beatrix Potter's tale only laughed, and sang this tune.

NR from the Royal Collections (J. G. Rusher), c. 1840, 'Ten mice', thus third line 'What are you at my jolly ten?', three couplets / JOH, 1842, first and third couplets / JOH, 1844, version starting 'As titty mouse sat in the witty to spin' / *Tailor of Gloucester*, Beatrix Potter, 1903 / Kidson, 1904, 'Three mice went into a hole to spin' / *Mother Goose's NR*, L. E. Walter, 1924, additional verse, 'Says Puss: You look so wondrous wise, I like your whiskers and bright black eyes; Your house is the nicest house I see, I think there is room for you and for me. The mice were so pleased that they opened the door, And pussy soon laid them all dead on the floor.'

350

There was an old man who lived in Middle Row,
He had five hens and a name for them, oh!
Bill and Ned and Battock,
Cut-her-foot and Pattock,
Chuck, my lady Pattock,
Go to thy nest and lay.

Middle Row was a common name for a line of houses down the centre of a broad street. Stratford-upon-Avon's Middle Row lay down the centre of Bridge Street, and was spelt 'Middulrewe' in a MS of c. 1275.

Songs for the Nursery, 2nd series (Darton & Co.), c. 1847 / JOH, 1853 / Oral collection, 1949. / Probably a verse of a folk-song.

351

O the little rusty dusty miller,
Dusty was his coat,
Dusty was his colour,
Dusty was the kiss I got from the miller;
If I had my pockets
Full of gold and siller,
I would give it all
To my dusty miller.

The tune 'Dusty Miller' is contained in the first volume of Walsh's *Compleat Country Dancing Master* (1708), and also in his *The Lady's Banquet*. It was apparently well known throughout the century, often being referred to, as in *The Fortunate Miller's Garland* (c. 1770) where a song is given simply 'To the tune of, The Dusty Miller'. Burns founded his charming scherzando on a fragment in Herd's MS (1776) and it was first printed, unsigned, in *The Scots Musical Museum* in 1788:

> Hey, the dusty Miller
> And his dusty coat,
> He will win a shilling,
> Or he spend a groat.
> Dusty was the coat,
> Dusty was the colour,
> Dusty was the kiss
> That I gat frae the Miller!
>
> Hey, the dusty Miller
> And his dusty sack;
> Leeze me on the calling
> Fills the dusty peck:
> Fills the dusty peck,
> Brings the dusty siller;
> I wad gie my coatie
> For the dusty Miller.

Herd MS, 1776, 'O the Dusty Miller, O the Dusty Miller, Dusty was his coat, Dusty was his cullour, Dusty was the kiss I got frae the miller! O the Dusty Miller with the Dusty Coat, He will spend a shilling ere he win a groat' / *Musical Museum*, 1788, contribution by Burns with tune / Douce MS, c. 1805, and *GG's Garland*, 1810, 'O the little rusty, dusty, rusty miller! I'll not change my wife for either gold or siller' / *Lyric Poetry*, William Stenhouse, 1839, according to C. K. Sharpe the old words were 'Dusty was his coat, Dusty was his colour, Dusty was the kiss, That I gat frae the miller. Chorus: Hey the dusty, &c.' [1853] / JOH, 1844, with the inappropriate variation 'He'll earn a shilling Or he'll spend a groat'; 1853, song begins 'Margaret wrote a letter, Seal'd it with her finger, Threw it in the dam For the dusty miller' / *Song Book*, J. Hullah, 1866, version from *Scottish Minstrel* / *Folk-Song*, 1940, additional couplets, 'She has wrote a letter with a Pen of siller, Sealed it up and sent it to the Dusty Miller. O the dusty miller, O the jovial carrier, First he came to woo her, Then he came to marry her', quoted from fiddlers' MS Song Books (c. 1820).

352

> There was a jolly miller once,
> Lived on the river Dee;
> He worked and sang from morn till night,
> No lark more blithe than he.

And this the burden of his song
Forever used to be,
I care for nobody, no! not I,
If nobody cares for me.

This song, a general favourite in Scotland, and of Sir Walter Scott in particular, became well known after it was sung by John Beard in Bickerstaffe's *Love in a Village*. The music of this successful opera, performed at Covent Garden in 1762, was arranged and largely composed by Arne. The tune of 'The Miller' was an old one which had appeared in ballad operas from 1728 onwards, and the words, too, were probably traditional. The old Dee mill at Chester, where the legendary miller of Dee is supposed to have plied his trade, was burned down in May, 1895. It stood on the Dee bridge, where there had been a mill since the eleventh century. The last descendant of the jolly miller, whose independence is said in Charles Mackay's ballad to have provoked the envy of Henry VIII, died the year before the mill was destroyed. The song's popularity among the Scottish may be due to the patriotic conclusion that it refers to their own river.

Love in a Village, Isaac Bickerstaffe, 1762 (it went to seven editions within the year) / Herd MS, 1776, with three additional verses / *Convivial Songster*, 1783 / *Calliope*, 1788 / *T Tit's SB*, c. 1790 / *Journal*, Sir Walter Scott, 10 Mar. 1826 / *Universal Songster*, 1828 / *Scottish Songs*, R. Chambers, 1829, from an old MS copy / *The Nightingale*, 1831 / JOH, 1844 / *Baby's Opera*, 1877 / Mackay's version, 'The Miller of the Dee', was collected in his *Songs for Music*, 1856. It had already gained broadside popularity (e.g. printed by H. Such, c. 1850), It begins 'There dwelt a miller hale and bold, Beside the river Dee; He wrought and sang from morn to night No lark more blithe than he; And this the burden of his song For ever used to be,—I envy nobody, no, not I, And nobody envies me! Thou'rt wrong, my friend! said old King Hal, Thou'rt wrong as wrong can be; For could my heart be light as thine, I'd gladly change with thee....' This version was orally collected by Williams in 1923.

Cf. the conclusion of 'I hae a Wife o' my ain' said to have been written by Burns a few days after his marriage, and printed in *The Musical Museum* (1792): 'I'll be merry and free, I'll be sad for naebody; Naebody cares for me, I care for naebody.'

353

Monday's child is fair of face,
Tuesday's child is full of grace,
Wednesday's child is full of woe,
Thursday's child has far to go,
Friday's child is loving and giving,
Saturday's child works hard for his living,

Monday's Child

> And the child that is born on the Sabbath day
> Is bonny and blithe, and good and gay.

When the First Lord of the Admiralty (Viscount Hall) moved in the House of Lords, 16 November 1948, that an humble Address be presented to His Majesty to congratulate the Royal Family on the birth of a son to Princess Elizabeth, he concluded 'The baby Prince...has come amongst us as a Sunday's child, and we remember the good omen of the age-old saying:

> The child that is born on the Sabbath day
> Is fair and wise, and good and gay.

My Lords, the occasion needs no further words from me.' To which the Lord Bishop of London responded 'I would like to add to the graceful couplet which the noble Viscount gave us in his speech in moving the humble Address. In our English way we put it simply that,

> Sunday's child is full of grace.'

This started practically a national controversy on what was the correct wording of the rhyme. Many newspapers and readers took pleasure in saying that both of their Lordships were incorrect, the Scottish 'bonny and blithe' being the favourite epithet for a Sunday's child. As may be seen there are numerous versions of the rhyme, though none of the recordings is very old.

Traditions of Devonshire, A. E. Bray, 1838, and JOH, 1849, instead of Sabbath day 'And a child that's born on Christmas day Is fair and wise, good and gay' / N & Q, 1850, 'Born of a Monday, Fair in face; Born of a Tuesday, Full of God's grace; Born of a Wednesday, Merry and glad; Born of a Thursday, Sour and sad; Born of a Friday, Godly given; Born of a Saturday, Work for your living; Born of a Sunday, Never shall we want; So there ends the week, And there's an end on't' / N & Q, 1877, 'The child of Sunday and Christmas Day, Is good and fair, and wise and gay' / *Popular Romances of the West of England*, R. Hunt, 1872, 'Sunday's child is full of grace, Monday's child is full in the face, Tuesday's child is solemn and sad, Wednesday's child is merry and glad, Thursday's child is inclined to thieving, Friday's child is free in giving, And Saturday's child works hard for a living' / Newell, 1883, as 1849 but 'Friday's child is full of sin, Saturday's child is pure within; The child that is born on the Sabbath day, To heaven its steps shall tend alway'.

***In all cases the prediction for 'Sunday's child' is a favourable one, reflecting a belief which is as old as the Middle Ages.

354

> Little General Monk
> Sat upon a trunk,
> Eating a crust of bread;

Monk

There fell a hot coal
And burnt in his clothes a hole,
Now little General Monk is dead.

Although the only historically authenticated fact in this verse is that General Monk is dead, there is no particular reason to suppose that it was not a contemporary squib on the great Cromwellian soldier who died in 1669.

History of Master Friendly (G. Swindells), c. 1795, 'And burnt his toes' / *Nursery Songs* (G. Ross), c. 1812 / *Collection of NR* (Oliver and Boyd), c. 1830 / JOH, 1842, additional lines, 'Keep always from the fire: If it catch your attire, You too, like Monk, will be dead.'
   Cf. 'Little Miss Muffet'.

355

There was a monkey climbed a tree,
When he fell down, then down fell he.

There was a crow sat on a stone,
When he was gone, then there was none.

There was an old wife did eat an apple,
When she ate two, she ate a couple.

There was a horse going to the mill,
When he went on, he stood not still.

There was a butcher cut his thumb,
When it did bleed, then blood did come.

There was a lackey ran a race,
When he ran fast, he ran apace.

There was a cobbler clouting shoon,
When they were mended, they were done.

There was a chandler making candle,
When he them stripped, he did them handle.

There was a navy went to Spain,
When it returned, it came again.

In a letter to Sir Martin Stuteville (1 July 1626), in which he complained about the Duke of Buckingham's faction, the Rev. Joseph Mead (fellow

Monkey

of Christ's College, Cambridge) enclosed without comment the following verses:

> There was a Crow sate on a stone
>   he flew away & there was none.
> There was a man that ran a race
>   when he ran fast, he ran apace.
> There was a mayd that eate an apple
>   when she eate two, she eat a couple.
> There was an ape sate on a tree
>   when he fell downe then downe fell hee.
> There was a Fleet that went to Spaine
>   when it return'd, it came againe.

It is generally supposed that these lines refer to the failure of the expedition against Cadiz in 1625. A second, longer and less restrained version of the rhyme is found in another MS of the same period. The first couplet, and the form of the verses, bear comparison with another nursery piece,

> There was Two Craws sat on a stane,
> Ane flew awa & there remain'd ane. (q.v.)

It may be hazarded that 'There was a Munkye climbe a tree', 'There was a Crow sate on a stone', &c., were already well-known joke-verses when Charles I came to the throne, and that after Buckingham's mismanagement of the Spanish expedition the final couplet was added: 'There was a fleet...' or, as the other contemporary record has it,

> There was a Navye went into Spayne
> When it returned it came againe.

Harley MS 390, Joseph Mead, 1 July 1626 / Sloane MS 1489, c. 1630. Possibly entered the nursery through JOH, 1843, whence commonly copied for subsequent collections.

356

> I see the moon,
>   And the moon sees me;
> God bless the moon,
>   And God bless me.

The English nursery is on friendly terms with the moon. Little children bow to it when it is new, see a man in it when it is eight days old, and cry when they can't have it. Yorkshire nurses say: 'Moon penny bright

Moon

as silver, come and play with little childer.' The lads and lassies of Lancashire say: 'I see the moon, and the moon sees me; God bless the priest that christened me.' And when the moon shines into the bedrooms of trawlermen's children, they say: 'I see the moon, and the moon sees me, God bless the sailors on the sea.'

GG's Garland, 1784 / JOH, 1842 / *Whitby Glossary*, F. K. Robinson, 1855 / *Lancashire Legends*, J. Harland, 1867 / Baring-Gould, 1895 / *Come Hither*, Walter de la Mare, 1923 / Oral collection, 1946. American children are similarly fanciful, cf. *Rocket in my Pocket*, Carl Withers, 1948, 'I see the moon, the moon sees me, The moon sees somebody I want to see'.

357

As I was walking o'er little Moorfields,
I saw St. Paul's a-running on wheels,
　　With a fee, fo, fum.
Then for further frolics I'll go to France,
While Jack shall sing and his wife shall dance,
　　With a fee, fo, fum.

This seems to come from the ballad *Tom Tell-Truth*, a copy of which, printed in black-letter, is in the Roxburghe collection:

I see Paul's steeple run upon wheels, fal la, &c.
I see Paul's steeple run upon wheels and in the middle of all Moor-fields,
　With a fa la, fa la la la, fa la la la la la.

Another version of the ballad, collected by a contributor to *Folk-Song* (1918) has been preserved in oral tradition. It was known to a lady who learnt it when a child, about 1835–40, and has seven verses, beginning:

A shoulder of mutton jumped over from France,
　Fal lal, lal-de-ro-lee.
A shoulder of mutton jumped over from France,
And the music did play and the people did dance.
　With a fal lal, lal-de-ro-lee.

As I was a-walking along in the fields,
　Fal lal, lal-de-ro-lee.
As I was a-walking along in the fields,
I saw St. Paul's Steeple a-running on wheels.
　With a fal lal, lal-de-ro-lee.

On the top of the Steeple, O what should I see
　Fal lal, lal-de-ro-lee.

Moorfields

On the top of the Steeple, O what should I see
But a fine young sapling codling tree.
   With a fal lal, lal-de-ro-lee.

When the codlings were ripe they began to fall;
   Fal lal, lal-de-ro-lee.
When the codlings were ripe they began to fall;
They killed six thousand people and all.
   With a fal lal, lal-de-ro-lee.

The fifth verse tells how 'they killed a man when he was dead', the sixth how in his head they found 'a spring and twenty live salmon a-swimming within', and the seventh that 'each salmon was as big as an elf'. The precise locality of these strange happenings is here lost, but it is probable that it was Moorfields as in the broadside edition and in the nursery rhyme. This would be an appropriate setting for a nonsense song, for in 1675 the Old Bethlem Hospital was moved to Moorfields from Bishops Gate Without. An associated verse, also preserved in the nursery is 'Upon Paul's steeple stands a tree' (q.v.).

Tom Tell-Truth (W. Thackeray, &c.), c. 1676 [this dating is independent of the Bethlem Hospital move] / Douce MS II, c. 1820 / JOH, 1842 / *Folk-Song*, 1918 / '*As I was walking o'er little Moorfields*', accompaniment by Roy Thompson, 1935, sheet music.

358

I had a little moppet,
I kept it in my pocket
And fed it on corn and hay;
Then came a proud beggar
And said he would wed her,
And stole my little moppet away.

GG's Garland, 1784 / *History of Master Friendly* (G. Swindells), c. 1795 / JOH, 1842, gives the rhyme as for a game (undescribed) / Mason, 1877, additional lines, 'And through the wood she ran, ran, ran, ran, And through the wood she ran. And all the long winter she followed the hunter, And never was heard of again' / *Cumberland Glossary*, William Dickinson, 1878, 'I had a laal moppet I pot in my pocket, And fed it wi' corn and hay; There com a Scotch pedder and swore he wad wed her, And stole my laal moppet away. Through the kirk yard she ran, she ran, O'er the broad watter she swam, she swam; And o' the last winter I lost my laal twinter [two-year-old sheep], And than she com hèamm wi' lamb, wi' lamb.'
  *** *Moppet*, an 18th-century term for a baby or doll, which has recently been coming into use again.

Morning

359

One misty, moisty, morning,
When cloudy was the weather,
There I met an old man
Clothed all in leather;
Clothed all in leather,
With cap under his chin.
How do you do, and how do you do,
And how do you do again?

This is the first of the fifteen stanzas of *The Wiltshire Wedding*, 'Between Daniel Do-well and Doll the Dairy-Maid. With the Consent of her old Father Leather-Coat, and her dear and tender Mother Plodwell', a broadside ballad printed about 1680. The first four stanzas are:

All in a misty Morning
  So cloudy was the Weather,
I meeting with an old Man,
  Who was cloathed all in Leather,
With ne'er a Shirt unto his Back,
  But Woollen to his Skin.
With how do you do, and how do you do,
  And how do you do again?

The Rustic was a Thresher,
  And on the Way he hy'd,
And with a Leather Bottle
  Fast buckled to his Side;
And with a Cap of Woollen,
  That cover'd Cheek and Chin.
With how do you do, &c.

I went a little farther,
  And there I met a Maid,
Was going then a Milking,
  A Milking, Sir, she said.
Then I began to compliment,
  And she began to sing.
With how do you do, &c.

This Maiden's Name was Dolly,
  Cloathed in a Gown of Grey.
I being somewhat jolly,
  Persuaded her to stay;

Morning

> Then straight I fell to courting her,
> In hopes her love to win.
> With -
> *And how do you do again?*

The Wiltshire Wedding was sung to the tune 'The Fryar and the Nun' (in Playford's *Dancing Master*, 1651) which is mentioned in the *Apophthegmes* of Erasmus. The Air 'All in a misty morning' is No. 23 in *The Beggar's Opera* (1728).

Pills to Purge Melancholy, 1700, as *Wiltshire Wedding*, above / *Songs for the Nursery*, 1805, as text / JOH, 1842 / Rimbault, 1846 / *Baby's Bouquet*, 1879 / *Less Familiar NR*, Robert Graves, 1927, 'Misty-moisty was the morn, Chilly was the weather...' / *Real Personages of Mother Goose*, K. E. Thomas, 1930, 'He began to compliment And I began to grin' / Correspondent, 1948, 'With strap below his chin'.

360

> Mother may I go and bathe?
> Yes, my darling daughter.
> Hang your clothes on yonder tree,
> But don't go near the water.

'Holiday tasks', remarks Letitia's uncle in Walter de la Mare's *The Scarecrow* (1945), '...always remind me, my dear, of the young lady who wanted to go out to swim:

> Mother may I go out to swim?
> Yes, my darling daughter.
> Fold your clothes up neat and trim,
> And don't go near the water.'

'The rhyme *I* know', said Letitia, 'is, Hang your clothes on a hickory limb.' 'That's all very well', said her uncle, 'but just you show me one!'

The rhyme, though not often found in print, seems to be familiar in many households (in America more than in England), and may have been the inspiration of the dance song of the late 1940s 'Mother may I go out dancing?'

Midwest Folklore, winter 1951, W. L. McAtee, Indiana in the 1890s, 'Mother, may I go out to swim? Yes, my darling daughter, Hang your clothes on a hickory limb But don't go near the water' / Correspondent, 1960, from Birmingham c. 1900, 'Hang your clothes on a gooseberry bush'.

Mother

361

My mother and your mother
Went over the way;
Said my mother to your mother,
It's chop-a-nose day.

Infant amusement in which the child's nose is held between finger and thumb and chopped off smartly with the other hand.

NR (J. Catnach), c. 1830 [Hindley, 1881] / JOH, 1849 / *Mother Goose*, Kate Greenaway, 1881 / Oral collection, 1946; and 1955, 'My father and your father Went down the waggon way; My father said to your father—It's Nippy Nose Day'.

362

My mother said that I never should
Play with the gypsies in the wood;
If I did, she would say,
Naughty girl to disobey.

These words may have well have been sung to the polka, a dance which was a sensation when it arrived in London in 1842, and whose popularity did not diminish throughout the nineteenth century. The first definite sighting of the song is in the Revd Francis Kilvert's diary, 3 June 1870, when he mentions that 'Teddy Evans was singing "My Mother said that I never should, Play with the gipsies in the wood, etc."'. The tune is identical with the first part of 'The King Pippen Polka' (c. 1870); and has also been recognized in a gypsy dance in Smetana's *The Bartered Bride*—not surprisingly, since Smetana and the polka were both Bohemian. Polkas very often had unofficial words, and, bearing in mind the Kilvert quote, it seems that 'My mother said' was sung to 'The King Pippen Polka' from the very earliest days of its popularity. Other lines were added, such as:

The wood is dark, the grass is green,
Here comes Sally with a tambourine,

and a song recorded in the *Rymour Club*, 1913:

Hey Cocky doo, how d' you do,
Sailing about in your best o' blue,
An alpaca frock, a green silk shawl,
A white straw bonnet and a pink parasol.

The Scottish equivalent to 'My mother said I never should' was:

Mother

My mother said I must go
With my father's dinner O,
Chappit tatties, beef and steak,
Twa red herrin' and a bawbee cake,

often followed by:

I came to a river and I couldn't get across,
I paid five shillings for an old blind horse;
I jumped on its back, its bones gave a crack,
And we all played the fiddle till the boat came back.

'I came to a river' has had a long life as a make-weight verse in American play-party and minstrel songs. It is first noted in 'Clare de Kitchen, or Old Virginia Never Tire' (c. 1838).

Less Familiar NR, Robert Graves, 1927, 'My mother said, I never should Play with the gipsies in the wood. If I did, she would say, You naughty girl to disobey. Your hair shan't curl and your shoes shan't shine, You gipsy girl, you shan't be mine. And my father said that if I did He'd rap my head with the tea-pot lid' / *Street Games of N. Shields Children*, M. and R. King, 1930 / *N & Q*, 1931 and 1934, known to correspondents sixty and seventy years previously; first recording of 'The wood was dark' lines, c. 1890 / Oral collection, 1945 and correspondents 1947–9, many *varia*, often traced to mid-19th century / *The Singing Game*, I. and P. Opie, 1985, as clapping song.
    Parody: Advertisement for Guinness, 1946, 'My mother said that I never should Miss my Guinness—As if I would!'

363

Cackle, cackle, Mother Goose,
Have you any feathers loose?
Truly have I, pretty fellow,
Half enough to fill a pillow.
Here are quills, take one or two,
And down to make a bed for you.

Mother Goose's NR, L. E. Walter, 1924, slight variations ending, 'And here are quills, take one or ten, And make from each, pop-gun or pen' / Oral collection, 1945.

364

Old Mother Goose,
When she wanted to wander,

Mother Goose

Would ride through the air
On a very fine gander.

This is the first verse of the chapbook story of the goose which laid the golden eggs.

Old Mother Goose or, The Golden Egg (T. Batchelar), c. 1815; (J. E. Evans), c. 1820: first of fifteen verses / *Nurse Lovechild's DFN*, c. 1830 / JOH, 1853 / *Mother Goose* (T. Nelson), c. 1945 / *Old Mother Goose and the Golden Egg*, picture book by William Stobbs (15 stanzas), 1977.

365

Old Mother Hubbard
Went to the cupboard,
To fetch her poor dog a bone;
But when she came there
The cupboard was bare
And so the poor dog had none.

She went to the baker's
To buy him some bread;
But when she came back
The poor dog was dead.

She went to the undertaker's
To buy him a coffin;
But when she came back
The poor dog was laughing.

She took a clean dish
To get him some tripe;
But when she came back
He was smoking a pipe.

She went to the alehouse
To get him some beer;
But when she came back
The dog sat in a chair.

She went to the tavern
For white wine and red;
But when she came back
The dog stood on his head.

a. Cover of chapbook printed by G. Ingram, c. 1840. *b.* 'Round about, round about, Maggoty pie', from Davison's halfpenny *Nursery Rhymes for Children*, c. 1830. *c.* Mrs. Mary's 'cuckolds all on a row', from *Nancy Cock's Pretty Song Book*, c. 1780. *d. & e.* Woodcuts from Kendrew's *Simple Simon* and *Cock Robin*, c. 1820. All actual size

Mother Hubbard

She went to the fruiterer's
　To buy him some fruit;
But when she came back
　He was playing the flute.

She went to the tailor's
　To buy him a coat;
But when she came back
　He was riding a goat.

She went to the hatter's
　To buy him a hat;
But when she came back
　He was feeding the cat.

She went to the barber's
　To buy him a wig;
But when she came back
　He was dancing a jig.

She went to the cobbler's
　To buy him some shoes;
But when she came back
　He was reading the news.

She went to the seamstress
　To buy him some linen;
But when she came back
　The dog was a-spinning.

She went to the hosier's
　To buy him some hose;
But when she came back
　He was dressed in his clothes.

The dame made a curtsy,
　The dog made a bow;
The dame said, Your servant,
　The dog said, Bow-wow.

The above verses were published in a toy book, *The Comic Adventures of Old Mother Hubbard and Her Dog*, 'Publish'd June 1—1805, by J. Harris, Succeser to E. Newbery, Corner of St. Pauls Church Yard'. In the booklet appear the words 'To J...B...Esq....M.P. County of...at

Mother Hubbard

whose suggestion and at whose House these Notable Sketches were design'd this Volume is with all suitable deference Dedicated by his Humble Servant S. M. C.' (amended in the 2nd edition to S. C. M.). The success of the publication was instantaneous. Harris said that 'upwards of ten thousand copies' were distributed in a few months. He reprinted it the following year, and also brought out a continuation and a sequel. Indeed, it was so successful that in 1806 'Peter Pindar' (the poet John Wolcot) was moved to protest at the way the public doted on the story. Pirated editions by the chapbook publishers were to be found everywhere, and it rapidly established itself as one of their stock productions. 'Old Mother Hubbard' has taken a leading place among the nursery rhyme characters; in 1950 the British Museum catalogue listed twenty-six titles under her name. 'S. C. M.' was Sarah Catherine Martin (1768–1826). She was the daughter of Sir Henry Martin, and an early love of Prince William Henry (afterwards William IV). Her original manuscript was discovered in 1936 and exhibited at the Bodleian Library. A collotype reproduction was made of it by the Oxford University Press. From this it appears that Miss Martin wrote the rhyme in 1804 while staying with her future brother-in-law, John Pollexfen Bastard, M.P., of Kitley, Devon. According to a tradition handed down in the Bastard family she was a woman of a vivacious nature, and one day, continuing to chatter while her host was writing, he told her to 'run away and write one of your stupid little rhymes'. A further tradition, inscribed in the copy of *The Comic Adventures* which Miss Martin afterwards gave her brother-in-law, is that the original Mother Hubbard was housekeeper at Kitley. There is evidence, though, that the public believed it to be a political squib, and this may, in part, account for it having so immediate a success. JOH, although he knew of the Harris publication, considered that the first three verses must be of some antiquity, 'were we merely to judge of the rhyme *laughing* to *coffin* in the third verse'. *Loffe* is an old English word used by Shakespeare. It is now clear that the first three verses of Sarah Catherine Martin's 'Old Mother Hubbard' were taken from tradition, and that her contribution was to write eleven more verses, and to illustrate the whole. The first three verses had appeared in sheet-music form as one of Dr. Samuel Arnold's *Juvenile Amusements* (1797), and were certainly not new then:

> Old Mother Hubbard went to the Cupboard
> to give the poor Children a bone
> And when she came there the Cupboard was bare,
> and so the poor Children had none.
> She went to the Bakers to buy them some bread,
> and when she return'd she found them all dead,
> She went to the Mans to bespeak them a Coffin,
> and when she return'd she found them all laughing.

PLATE XIII

a. Title-page of the dedication copy of *The Comic Adventures of Old Mother Hubbard and Her Dog*, 1805, presented by Sarah Catherine Martin to John Pollexfen Bastard, M.P., 'at whose House these Notable Sketches were design'd'. Possession of Colonel Reginald Bastard, D.S.O.

b. Sarah Catherine Martin (1768–1826)

Mother Hubbard

The words are curiously intertwined with the *Infant Institutes* (1797), version of 'The old woman who lived in a shoe' (q.v.); ludicrously so, since children do not usually enjoy gnawing bones. Perhaps more of an influence on 'S.C.M.'s' script, was *Old Dame Trot, and Her Comical Cat*, published by T. Evans in 1803:

> Old Dame Trot
> Some cold fish had got,
> Which for pussy,
> She kept in Store,
> When she looked there was none
> The cold fish had gone,
> For puss had been there before.
>
> She went to the butcher's
> To buy her some meat,
> When she came back
> She lay dead at her feet.
>
> She went to the undertaker's
> For a coffin and Shroud,
> When she came back,
> Puss sat up and mewed.

The eleven succeeding verses continue in the same style. It should also be noted that the 1808 edition of *Pretty Tales* and the 1810 edition of *GG's Garland* include only the first verse of 'Old Mother Hubbard', as if no others were known; and that in *Songs for the Nursery*, published by Tabart the same year as *The Comic Adventures*, only three verses are included, whereas in Darton's edition, published in 1818, all fourteen verses of the story are given. It seems that a traditional version of 'Old Mother Hubbard' was firmly established at around the time 'S.C.M.' wrote her toy book, and may have been in print before. *Vocal Harmony*, which prints the basic six-line Mother Hubbard verse with a commentary beginning, 'Poor fellow! it was a sad disappointment for him', has previously been dated 'c. 1806' in deference to Sarah Catherine Martin, but having no imprint could well have appeared earlier than 1805.

The Comic Adventures... (J. Harris), 1 June 1805; 2nd ed. 1 May 1806 / *Songs for the Nursery*, 1805 / *Vocal Harmony*, c. 1806 / *Pretty Tales*, 1808 / *GG's Garland*, 1810 / Publishers of early chapbook editions include John Evans, c. 1805; Wm Charles (New York), 1807; J. Marshall, c. 1810; T. Batchelar, c. 1812; G. Ross, 1813; J. Kendrew, c. 1820 or earlier; J. Fairburn, c. 1820; J. Lumsden, c. 1820; J. G. Rusher, c. 1820 and c. 1840; West and Coldwells, c. 1820; F. Houlston, c. 1820; J. Catnach, c. 1830; T. Richardson, c. 1830; J.S. Publishing, c. 1830; S. and J. Keys, c. 1830. Larger editions with coloured plates include: Dean and Munday, 1822, illus. George Cruikshank; J. Innes, c. 1825; Morgan and Yeager, Philadelphia, c. 1825, reprint of Harris [Rosenbach]; D. Carvalho, c. 1825; John Bysh, c. 1830; W. Walker, c. 1840. Other notable editions, now with stiff covers: Grant and Griffiths, 1847; J. Cundall, illus. T. Webster, R.A.; Addey and Co., illus. Harrison Weir, 1853; Darton and Co., 'Moveable' also 'Indestructible' editions; Ward Lock 'Aunt Affable', c. 1860 / *Mother Hubbard's Picture Book*, Walter Crane, 1873. *Mother Hubbard* (Augener and Co.), by 'Marion', c. 1880, sheet music, with introductory verse. There has probably been a new edition of Mother Hubbard published somewhere every year since 1805.

Cf. *Old Dame Trot, and Her Comical Cat* (T. Evans), 1803. Also the 1784, second verse of 'There was an old woman and what do you think?'; the 1797 version and the JOH Scottish version of 'There was an old woman who lived in a shoe'; the 1887 'What's in the cupboard, says Mr. Hubbard'.

A Continuation of the Comic Adventures of Old Mother Hubbard and Her Dog, by S. C. M., was published by Harris, 1 Jan. 1806, and *A Sequel to the Comic Adventures of Old Mother Hubbard and Her Dog*, 'by another Hand' (W. F.), was published by Harris, 1 Mar. 1806 / *The Adventures of Old Mother Hubbard's Dog*, John Yeoman, illus. Quentin Blake, 1989.

Early rival imitation: *The Comic Adventures of Old Mother Lantry and her Wonderful Goat* (John Marshall), 1819.

Translation: *Komische Abentheuer der Frau Hubbard mit ihrem Hunde*, Joseph Scholz (Mainz), c. 1830.

Pantomime: *Old Mother Hubbard and her Dog; or, Harlequin and Tales of the Nursery*, performed at the Theatre Royal, Covent Garden, 1833.

Parody: The Prime Minister, Clement Attlee, in election speech, 16 Feb. 1950, 'Old Mother Hubbard went to the cupboard For something to quench her thirst, But when she went there the cupboard was bare: Mr. Hubbard had been there first.'

Curiosa: Gramophone record, *Nursery Rhymes Selection* (Regal-Zonophone MR 3804), Leslie Douglas and The Skymasters, 1948, 'Hubb-hubba Old Mother Hubbard in a Rubber Dinghy... press on regardless!'

366

Old Mother Niddity Nod swore by the pudding-bag,
    She would go to Stoken Church fair;
Then old Father Peter, said he would meet her,
    Before she got half-way there.

Stokenchurch is on the Oxon.-Bucks. border.

GG's Garland, 1810 / JOH, 1842.

367

Old Mother Shuttle
Lived in a coal-scuttle
Along with her dog and her cat;

Mother Shuttle

What they ate I can't tell,
But 'tis known very well
That not one of the party was fat.

Old Mother Shuttle
Scoured out her coal-scuttle,
And washed both her dog and her cat;
The cat scratched her nose,
So they came to hard blows,
And who was the gainer by that?

Mother Shuttle, through her introduction in the influential Boston
Mother Goose's Quarto (c. 1825), is better known in America than her native
England. In the New World, it will be noted, she has acquired a Gaelic
patronymic prefix.

Original Ditties for the Nursery (J. Harris), c. 1805 [1807] / *MG's Quarto*, c. 1825, 'Old
Mistress M'Shuttle' / *Big Book of Mother Goose* (James and Jonathan Co., Wisconsin),
1946, 'McShuttle'.

368

Old Mother Twitchett has but one eye,
And a long tail which she can let fly,
And every time she goes over a gap,
She leaves a bit of her tail in a trap.

This is an elaboration of a time-honoured enigma. Among the 'meery
riddles' printed in 1600 appears,

What is it goes through thicke and thin
and drawes his guts after him?

Solution: 'It is an Needle that goeth through thicke and thin cloth,
drawing the thred after it, which is taken for the guts.' Rolland quotes
four European equivalents, and Tylor in *Primitive Culture* notes an Aztec
specimen.

JOH, 1843 / *Rymour Club*, 1911 / *Rhyme a Riddle*, Paul Henning, 1946.
Cf. *Devinettes ou énigmes populaires*, E. Rolland, 1877, especially the Flemish:
'Juteko peerdeken Met ze vlassche steerdeken Hoe zeerder dat ze peerdeken liep,
Hoe korter dat ze steerdeken wierd.'

Little Miss Muffet
Sat on a tuffet,
Eating her curds and whey;
There came a big spider,
Who sat down beside her
And frightened Miss Muffet away.

This rhyme provides entertaining material for speculation. The suggestion has been put forward that Miss Muffet was Patience, the daughter of the entomologist Dr. Thomas Muffet (*d.* 1604) a man 'whose admiration for spiders has never been surpassed'. Since Dr. Muffet (or Moffett or Moufet) was the author of *The Silkwormes and their flies* 'lively described in verse', it may be seen how easily the rhyme can be attributed to him. But as only Dr. Muffet could describe his verse as 'lively', and no record of the epigram has been found earlier than 1805, any estimation must be cautious. Also it subsequently appears with material variations, 'Little Mary Ester sat upon a tester' (1812), and 'Little Miss Mopsey, Sat in the shopsey' (1842). It has, however, noticeable similarity to 'Little Polly Flinders', 'Little Poll Parrot', 'Little Tommy Tacket', 'Little General Monk', and 'Little Jack Horner' (qq.v.). The last-named jingle is known to have been current in 1720, and is probably earlier, as also the lampoon 'Little General Monk'. Eckenstein compares these verses with the singing game 'Little Polly Sanders' or 'Little Alice Sander' who 'sat upon a cinder' (recorded by Gomme), hence with the Cushion Dance called 'Joan Saunderson' (described in 1686) which may be a variation of 'Sally Waters'. The Cushion Dance is said to preserve 'the association with weddings and with the May-Day festival which at one time was the occasion for mating and marriage'. The inference is that the *form* of the rhyme, a person sitting and waiting and something important arriving, dates to heathen times. It is possible that most of these rhymes are parodies of whichever is the earliest of them. An analysis of the children's books published in 1945–6 showed that of all the nursery verses 'Miss Muffet' figures the most frequently, perhaps because the subject lends itself to illustration. Millais painted the picture 'Little Miss Muffet' in 1884.

Songs for the Nursery, 1805; 1812 edition, 'Little Mary Ester' / JOH, 1842, 'Little Miss Mopsey' / *Traditional Nursery Songs*, Felix Summerly, 1843 / *Mother Goose*, Kate Greenaway, 1881 / *OED*, 1888, 'sat on a buffet' / *Man in the Moon*, Leslie Brooke, 1913.

*** Miss Muffet probably sat on a grassy hillock, though *tuffet* has also been described as a 'three-legged-stool'. When she sits on a *buffet* she is certainly on a stool, and may come from the north country. Whether Mary Ester perched on a sixpence, a bed canopy, or a piece of armour for the head is a moot point.

Nail

370

For want of a nail the shoe was lost,
For want of a shoe the horse was lost,
For want of a horse the rider was lost,
For want of a rider the battle was lost,
For want of a battle the kingdom was lost,
And all for the want of a horseshoe nail.

The full-grown version of this rhyme, now bringing wisdom to nursery warriors, appears to be comparatively recent. The first three lines, however, may be seen in the seventeenth century, and *The Oxford Dictionary of English Proverbs* compares them with a sentiment in John Gower's *Confessio Amantis* (c. 1390):

> For sparinge of a litel cost
> Ful ofte time a man hath lost
> The largë cotë for the hod.

Thomas Adams, in one of his *Sermons* (collected 1629), said 'The Frenchmen have a military proverb: "The loss of a nail, the loss of an army"', and continued 'The want of a nail loseth the shoe, the loss of a shoe troubles the horse, the horse endangereth the rider, the rider breaking his rank molests the company so far as to hazard the whole army'. By 1640, when Herbert's *Outlandish Proverbs* was published, the sentiment had become formalized:

For want of a naile The shoe is lost; for want of a shoe the horse is lost; for want of a horse the rider is lost.

This was repeated by Ray (1670), and other collectors. In the care of the nursery, 'the well-known catastrophe', as Samuel Smiles called it, has grown in size and favour, and it was probably from a nursery book that it was copied when it was framed and kept on the wall of Anglo-American Supply Headquarters in London during the Second World War.

Outlandish Proverbs, George Herbert, 1640, as quote / *English Proverbs*, John Ray, 1670, as 1640 / *Poor Richard's Almanack*, Benjamin Franklin, 1758, 'A little neglect may breed mischief... For want of a nail the shoe was lost, For want of a shoe the horse was lost; and for want of a horse the rider was lost; being overtaken and slain by the enemy, all for want of care about a horse-shoe nail' / *Mother Goose*, Arthur Rackham, 1913 / *Puffin Rhymes*, John Harwood, 1944.
Cf. Freydank's *Proverbia eloquentia*, 1500, 'ich hore sagen die wisen, ein nagel behalte ein isen...' [I hear wise folks say That a nail may save a horse-shoe—A shoe a horse; a horse a man; A man who can fight,—a fortress; A fortress may compel a land to sue for mercy. The nail therefore is well spent Which helped the shoe, the horse, man, fortress and land to such honour, So its name should stand high]; Spanish proverb, 'Por un punto se pierde un zapato' (For want of a stitch a

shoe is lost); modern Greek proverb, 'διὰ τὸν ἧλον χαύει τὸ πέταλον' (For the nail he looseth the shoe).

371

Little pretty Nancy girl,
  She sat upon the green,
Scouring of her candlesticks,
  They were not very clean.
Her cupboard that was musty,
  Her table that was dusty;
And pretty little Nancy girl,
  She was not very lusty.

Collected from an old woman by a contributor to *Folk-Lore* (1901).

372

Up hill and down dale,
Butter is made in every vale,
And if that Nancy Cock
Is a good girl
She shall have a spouse
And make butter anon,
Before her old grandmother
Grows a young man.

This was part-quoted by Henry Carey (1725) whose wording indicates that, as he knew it, line four (which above is out of rhyme) contained an indelicacy. Nancy Cock seems to have been an accepted nursery figure. At the end of *Nancy Cock's Pretty Song Book* John Marshall printed 'Some account of Nancy-Cock, and our good Friend Nurse Love-child'. According to this, young readers were to believe that Nancy Cock, although she did not come from the richest house, was the best girl in the village. She 'would not tell a fib could she have got her belly full of custards by it'. She was so obliging and dutiful that Nurse Love-child, who was tired of looking after naughty children, made her the collection of songs and verses published in her book.

Nancy cock

Namby-Pamby, Henry Carey, 1725 [1726] / *Nancy Cock's PSB*, c. 1780, additional lines 'Then let us sing merrily, Merrily now, We'll live on the custards that come from the cow' / *GG's Garland*, 1784 / JOH, 1842 / Baring-Gould, 1895.

373

Little Nancy Etticoat,
With a white petticoat,
And a red nose;
She has no feet or hands,
The longer she stands
The shorter she grows.

The answer to this riddle, which has been posed for at least three centuries, is 'a lighted candle'. Nancy Etticoat has been called Old Nancy Netty Cote, Nanny Goat, and Little Miss Hetty Cote. 'I have a little boy in a whit cote The biger he is the leser he goes', appears in the Holme MS. The riddle is also known in Germany, 'Lütt Johann Öölken'.

Holme MS, c. 1645 / *Royal Riddle Book*, 1820, without fourth line / *Sir Gregory Guess's Present* (T. Batchelar), c. 1820, 'Hittery hetty coat' / *Girl's Book of Diversions*, Miss Leslie, 1835 / JOH, 1842, without third and fourth lines / *NR, Tales and Jingles*, 1844 / *Fireside Amusements*, R. Chambers, 1850, fullest version / *N & Q*, 1865 and 1909 / *Weardale*, J. J. Graham, 1939, 'Little nannie neetie coat Stands in a white petticoat . . .' / *Rhyme a Riddle*, Paul Henning, 1946.

Cf. *Mecklenburgische Volksüberlieferungen*, R. Wossidlo, 1897, 'Lütt Johann Öölken satt up sien stöhlken, je länger he satt, je lutter he ward, plumps fölt he hen.'

374

I need not your needles, they're needless to me;
For kneading of needles were needless, you see;
But did my neat trousers but need to be kneed,
I then should have need of your needles indeed.

Tongue twister entitled 'The Baker's reply to the Needle Pedlar', which appears in Margaret Tarrant's *Mother Goose* (1929). The needle pedlar was a familiar figure in the first half of the nineteenth century. He could be seen with a piece of flannel on his left arm stuck all over with his wares of various sorts and sizes, which he sold for three a penny.

Neighbour

375

What's the news of the day,
Good neighbour, I pray?
They say the balloon
Is gone up to the moon.

This rhyme seems likely to be contemporary with the start of hot-air ballooning (the first ascent was in 1783). It appears as a conversational caption to two portraits in an engraved sheet issued by Bowles and Carver, London (c. 1790), and is as text, except for the third line, 'Why they say the Balloon'.

Songs for the Nursery, 1805 / *MG's Quarto*, c. 1825 / *NR for Children* (J. Fairburn), c. 1825 / *Nurse Love-Child's Legacy* (J. Catnach), c. 1830 / JOH, 1843 / *Puffin Rhymes*, John Harwood, 1944, 'Good fellow, now pray What's the news of the day? I'm told a balloon Has gone up past the moon.'

376

Ten little nigger boys went out to dine;
One choked his little self, and then there were nine.

Nine little nigger boys sat up very late;
One overslept himself, and then there were eight.

Eight little nigger boys travelling in Devon;
One said he'd stay there, and then there were seven.

Seven little nigger boys chopping up sticks;
One chopped himself in half, and then there were six.

Six little nigger boys playing with a hive;
A bumble-bee stung one; and then there were five.

Five little nigger boys going in for law;
One got in chancery, and then there were four.

Four little nigger boys going out to sea;
A red herring swallowed one, and then there were three.

Three little nigger boys walking in the Zoo;
A big bear hugged one, and then there were two.

386

Nigger Boys

Two little nigger boys sitting in the sun;
One got frizzled up, and then there was one.

One little nigger boy living all alone;
He got married, and then there were none.

This song was written by Frank Green, either at the beginning of 1869 or
the end of the previous year. It was undoubtedly inspired by the American Septimus Winner's 'Ten Little Injuns', published in England a short
while earlier, and still remembered in American nurseries:

Ten little Injuns standin' in a line,
One toddled home and then there were nine;
Nine little Injuns swingin' on a gate,
One tumbled off and then there were eight.

One little, two little, three little, four little, five little Injun boys,
Six little, seven little, eight little, nine little, ten little Injun boys.

Eight little Injuns gayest under heav'n,
One went to sleep and then there were seven;
Seven little Injuns cutting up their tricks,
One broke his neck and then there were six.

Six little Injuns kickin' all alive,
One kick'd the bucket and then there were five;
Five little Injuns on a cellar door,
One tumbled in and then there were four.

Four little Injuns up on a spree,
One he got fuddled and then there were three;
Three little Injuns out in a canoe,
One tumbled overboard and then there were two.

Two little Injuns foolin' with a gun,
One shot t'other and then there was one;
One little Injun livin' all alone,
He got married and then there were none.

Adaptations of this were immensely popular at nigger minstrel shows,
and version followed version in quick succession, written for the rival
troupes. Frank Green wrote his words for G. W. ('Pony') Moore, a broad-
humoured tenor of the Christy Minstrels, whose performances were
given at St. James's Hall in Piccadilly. Five years later the song was still
popular, being said not to lack patronage at 'Social Gatherings, Penny
Readings, & Musical Societies', and it had already become 'a great favourite with young people, to whom it affords a fund of amusement'. Early

versions have a happy-ending verse in which the last little nigger boy with his little wife soon raised a family of ten more, but oral tradition has discarded this as unnecessarily sentimental.

Ten Little Injuns, comic song and chorus, S. Winner, published London, July 1868 / *Ten Little Niggers*, the celebrated serio comic song, Frank Green, music by Mark Mason, Feb. 1869, varies from text in second and third couplets, 'Nine little niggers crying at his fate, One cried himself away, and then there were eight. Eight little niggers slept until eleven, One over-slept himself then there were seven' / *Ten Little Negroes*, D. Tucker, Mar. 1869, begins 'Ten little Negroes climbing up a pine, One fell and broke his neck and then there were nine' / *Ten Little Darkies*, T. Kennick, arranged W. Notley, June 1869, begins 'Ten little Darkies stood all in a line, One ran away and then there were nine' / *The Ten Youthful Africans*, W. Shepherd, Sept. 1869, begins 'Ten youthful Africans sailing up the Rhine, One tumbled over board and then there were nine' / *Ten Little Darkies*, D. Tucker, c. 1870, begins 'Ten little Negroes sitting on a line, One tumbled on his head and then there were nine' / *Ten Little Niggers*, street broadside no imprint, c. 1870 / *Ten Little Negro Boys*, Julius Crow, Dec. 1874, begins 'Ten little Negroes drinking Sherry wine, One swallowed glass and all then there were nine' / *Ten Little Niggers*, Aunt Louisa's Toy Books series, [1874] / *Ten Little Niggers and Other NR* (Day-Dawn Library), 1890 / *Heart Songs dear to the American People*, c. 1909 / *Mother Goose's NR*, L. E. Walter, 1924 / *American Mountain Songs*, c. 1927 / *Counting Rhymes* (Simon and Schuster, New York), 1947, Winner's version.

Early parody: *Ten Undergraduates*, A. Graduate, May 1869, begins, 'Ten Undergraduates going out to wine, One got proctorized then there were nine'.

377

I went to Noke,
But nobody spoke;
I went to Thame,
It was just the same;
Burford and Brill
Were silent and still,
But I went to Beckley
And they spoke directly.

Another local rhyme which has been adopted by the nursery. All the villages are grouped fairly closely together to the east of Oxford, except Burford which lies to the west. Burford may perhaps be a mis-hearing of 'Boarstall'.

Less Familiar NR, Robert Graves, 1927 / *Look! The Sun*, Edith Sitwell, 1941 / Oral collection, 1944 / *I went to Noke*, J. E. Lloyd, 1946.
Cf. 'At Brill on the hill'.

378

There was an old woman of Norwich,
Who lived upon nothing but porridge;
    Parading the town,
    She turned cloak into gown,
The thrifty old woman of Norwich.

'The old woman of Norwich' comes from the first-known book of limericks, *The History of Sixteen Wonderful Old Women*, published by J. Harris in 1820. (*Vide* 'As a little fat man of Bombay'.)

379

Nose, nose, jolly red nose,
And what gave thee that jolly red nose?
Nutmeg and ginger, cinnamon and cloves,
That's what gave me this jolly red nose.

These lines form the burden of one of King Henry's Mirth or Freemen's Songs printed in *Deuteromelia* (1609). In the same year Beaumont and Fletcher introduced it into *The Knight of the Burning Pestle* where old Merrythought sings it, at which his wife retorts 'If you would consider your state, you would have little lust to sing, I wist'. But Merrythought emphasizes the nutmegs and ginger, cinnamon and cloves, because, of course, the spice deserved the blame, not the liquor. The catch was still being sung in appropriate settings (e.g. at the Johnson in Fleet Street) two centuries later; and when well sung, as Woodfall Ebsworth recalls, there is a suggestive lingering over the first syllable of 'ginger'. Bearing in mind other inappropriate pieces which entered early nursery collections it is perhaps not strange that this one should have been included; what is delightful is that it is still sometimes retained. JOH did not include it except as an end note to 'Of all the gay birds that e'er I did see' (q.v.).

Deuteromelia, Thomas Ravenscroft, 1609, 'Te whit, to whom drinks thou, this song is well sung, I make you a vow, and he is a knave that drinketh now, Nose, nose, nose, nose, and who gave mee This jolly red nose? Sinamont, and Ginger, Nutmegs and Cloves, and that gave mee my jolly red nose' / *Knight of the Burning Pestle*, F. Beaumont and J. Fletcher, 1609 (printed 1613), 'Nose, nose, jolly red nose, And who gave thee this jolly red nose? Nutmegs and ginger, cinnamon and cloves, And they gave me this jolly red nose' [1884] / *Book of merrie Riddles*, 1631, '...then Ale-Knights should To sing this song not be so bold, Nutmegs, Ginger, Cinamon and Cloves, They gave us this jolly red nose' / *The Pinder of Wakefield*, 1632 / *Antidote against*

Melancholy, 1661 / *Windsor Drollery*, 1672 / *Songs for the Nursery*, 1805 / *MG's Quarto*, c. 1825 / *NR, Tales and Jingles*, 1844 / Williams, 1923, whole song / *Less Familiar NR*, Robert Graves, 1927 / *Big Book of Mother Goose* (James and Jonathan Co., Wisconsin), 1946 / *Mother Goose NR* (W. Collins and Sons), 1949.

380

There was an old woman called Nothing-at-all,
Who lived in a dwelling exceedingly small;
A man stretched his mouth to its utmost extent,
And down at one gulp house and old woman went.

JOH, 1843 / *NR*, V. Sackville-West, 1947 / *Cakes and Custard*, Brian Alderson, illus. Helen Oxenbury, 1974.

381

I had a little nut tree,
 Nothing would it bear
But a silver nutmeg
 And a golden pear;

The King of Spain's daughter
 Came to visit me,
And all for the sake
 Of my little nut tree.

The beginnings of 'I had a little nut tree' can be seen in Sloane MS 2593, a collection of songs and carols made (c. 1440). The first three verses are:

I haue a newe gardyn,
 & newe is be-gunne;
swych an-oþer gardyn
 know I not vnder sunne.

In þe myddis of my garden
 is a peryr set,
& it wele non per bern
 but a per Ienet.

þe fayrest mayde of þis toun
 preyid me,
for to gryffyn her a gryf [graft her a graft]
 of myn pery tre.

Nut Tree

The fruit of the grafting was born twenty weeks later. It is not known when the King of Spain's daughter first made her appearance, but she seems to have been a stock figure in romantic song (see *Bulletin de la Société d'Études Folkloriques du Centre-Ouest*, III:2). JOH suggested that Juana of Castile is here celebrated, and this may have inspired Edith Sitwell in *Fanfare for Elizabeth* (1946) to picture Lady Bryane, governess-in-ordinary to the young Princess Mary and then to Elizabeth, singing this song to her charges, and remembering a black and terrible shadow, the shadow of Juana of Castile the mad 'King of Spain's daughter', who visited the court of Henry VII in 1506. The rhyme is said to have been the favourite recitation of the Shakespearian actress Dame Sybil Thorndike.

Newest Christmas Box, c. 1797, additional couplet 'I skipp'd over water I danc'd over Sea and all the birds in the Air cou'd not catch me' / JOH, 1843 / *NR* (Webb Millington and Co.), c. 1850, 'I had a silver nettle-tree, Nothing could it ever be, But a silver nettle' / *Baby's Opera*, 1877 / *Folk-Lore*, 1883, for counting-out / *N & Q*, 1885, second couplet 'The Queen of France's daughter gave it unto me, That I might go a nutting upon that little nut tree' / Gomme, 1894 / *Tailor of Gloucester*, Beatrix Potter (p.p. ed.), 1902 / *Street Games of N. Shields Children*, M. and R. King, 1930.

382

> One I love, two I love,
>   Three I love, I say,
> Four I love with all my heart,
>   Five I cast away;
> Six he loves, seven she loves, eight both love.
>   Nine he comes, ten he tarries,
> Eleven he courts, twelve he marries.

Child's divination rhyme usually recited when plucking daisy petals, counting the seeds of couch grass, or extracting pips from an apple core. A variant common among older children is:

> He loves me,
>   He don't,
> He'll have me,
>   He won't,
> He would if he could,
> But he can't
>   So he don't.

This is also repeated when skipping, and the first letter of the lover's name is discovered by jumping through the alphabet until the feet are caught in the rope. Such divination formulas are probably old. The transliteration of a poem by Walther von der Vogelweide (1170–1230), quoted by Newell, goes:

> A spire of grass hath made me gay;
> It saith, I shall find mercy mild.
> I measured in the selfsame way
> I have seen practiced by a child.
> Come look and listen if she really does:
> She does, does not, she does, does not, she does.
> Each time I try, the end so augureth.
> That comforts me—'tis right that we have faith.

Our Year, Mrs. Craik, 1860, 'Children pluck this flower [the Moon-Daisy] petal by petal, saying, "You love me—you love me not," alternately: the last petal being supposed to tell the truth' / Newell, 1883, known in New England at beginning of the 19th century, with addition 'Thirteen wishes, Fourteen kisses, All the rest little witches'; also 'He loves me, longs for me, desires me, wishes me well, wishes me ill, does not care' / Bolton, 1888 / *N & Q*, 1943 / Oral collection, 1947 / *American Folk-Lore*, 1947, 'Thirteen, they quarrel, fourteen, they part; Fifteen, they die of a broken heart'.

Cf. *The Edwardians*, V. Sackville-West, 1930, 'Elle m'aime, un peu, beaucoup, Passionnément, pas du tout' / *Deutsche Kinder-Reime*, Ernst Meier, 1851, 'Er liebt mich, von Herzen, mit Schmerzen, e kleins bisle, oder gar nit' / *Deutsche Kinderlied*, F. M. Böhme, 1897. Also Gretchen's flower game in Goethe's *Faust*, 'Er liebt mich, er liebt mich nicht; er—liebt—mich'.

383

> One's none;
> Two's some;
> Three's many;
> Four's a penny;
> Five's a little hundred.

Variously employed for infantile mathematics, for counting the hits at shuttlecock, and for underlining generosity when presenting sweets to a small companion.

JOH, 1842 / Chambers, 1842, 'Ane's nane, Twa's some, Three's a pickle, Four's a curn, Five's a horse-lade, Six'll gar his back bow, Seven'll vex his breath, Aught'll bear him to the grund, And nine'll be his death' / *Leicestershire Words*, A. B. and S. Evans, 1881, as text but 'Four's a plenty', 'a flush', or 'a mort' / *Laugh and Learn*, Jennet Humphreys, 1890 / Maclagan, 1901, 'One's nane, two's some, Three's a pickle, four's a pund, Five's a dainty, Six is plenty, Seven's a horse's meal' / *Rymour Club*, 1911, 'Ane's nane, twa's some; Three's a pistol, four's a gun, Five's the laird o' Bougie's son, An' six is curlie dougie'.

One

384

One to make ready,
And two to prepare;
Good luck to the rider,
And away goes the mare.

For race-starting.

JOH, 1853 / Newell, 1883, the common schoolboy verse 'One to make ready, Two to prepare, Three to *go slambang*, Right-down-there', and also gives the 'older English rhyme' (as text) / Bolton, 1888, 'One for the money, two for the show, Three to make ready, and four to go!'
   Cf. 'Bell horses'.

385

One, two,
Buckle my shoe;
Three, four,
Knock at the door;
Five, six,
Pick up sticks;
Seven, eight,
Lay them straight;
Nine, ten,
A big fat hen;
Eleven, twelve,
Dig and delve;
Thirteen, fourteen,
Maids a-courting;
Fifteen, sixteen,
Maids in the kitchen;
Seventeen, eighteen,
Maids in waiting;
Nineteen, twenty,
My plate's empty.

Bolton quotes a version which originally, he believed, went up to thirty, 'make a kerchy'; 'Eleven, twelve, bake it well; Thirteen, fourteen, go a courtin'; Fifteen, sixteen, go to milkin'; Seventeen, eighteen, do the bakin'; Nineteen, twenty, the mill is empty; Twenty-one, charge the gun; Twenty-two, the partridge flew; Twenty-three, she lit on a tree; Twenty-four she lit down lower', and 'Twenty-nine, the game is mine'. This was said to be 'Used in Wrentham, Massachusetts, as early as 1780'. The form of the rhyme is common in Germany, France, Holland, and Turkey.

Songs for the Nursery, 1805, 'Thirteen, fourteen, draw the curtain, Fifteen, sixteen, the maid's in the kitchen...she's in waiting...my stomach's empty, Please Ma'am to give me some dinner' / *Peter Prim's Profitable Present* (J. Harris), 1809, 'One, Two, Come Buckle my Shoe, You lazy Elf! Pray do it yourself' / *GG's Garland*, 1810, 'Three, four, Lay down lower...Eleven, twelve, Who will delve...Fifteen, sixteen, Maids a-kissing...Nineteen, twenty, My belly's empty' / *Jack Horner's Pretty Toy* (J. E. Evans), c. 1820 / *Juvenile Numerator* (D. Carvalho), c. 1825 / *London Jingles* (J. G. Rusher), c. 1840, 'Eleven, twelve, roast her well' / JOH, 1842 / *One, Two, Buckle my Shoe*, Walter Crane, 1867 / Bolton, 1888, also gives sequence for 'Nine, ten' onwards, 'a good fat hen; roast her well; boys a courtin'; girls a fixin'; maids a bakin'; weddings plenty' / *Rymour Club*, 1911, sequence 'buckle my shoe; ne'er gae owre; break sticks; lay them straight; a gude fat hen; gang tae the wal; gang tae the fair; what tae dae there; buy a young mear; she's far owre dear; One-and-twenty, two-and-twenty, yoke her in the pleuch; Three-and-twenty, four-and-twenty, she'll dae weel enuch' / *A Rocket in my Pocket*, Carl Withers, 1948, 'One, two, tie your shoe' for skipping / Correspondent, 1948, 'Fifteen, sixteen, maids in the miskin'.

386

One, two, three,
I love coffee,
And Billy loves tea,
How good you be,
One, two, three,
I love coffee,
And Billy loves tea.

New Year's Gift (J. Catnach), c. 1830 [Hindley, 1878] / JOH, 1842.

387

One, two, three, four,
Mary at the cottage door,
Five, six, seven, eight,
Eating cherries off a plate.

Sometimes used for counting-out.

Nursery Calculations (W. Belch), c. 1815, with additional couplet, 'Nine, Ten, Eleven, Twelve, Peasants oft in ditches delve' / *Mill Hill Magazine*, 1877, 'One, two, three, four, Little Freddy at the door Picking cherries off the floor. One, two, three, four' / Newell, 1883, '. . . Mary at the kitchen door. . . Mary at the garden gate', said to have been known in Massachusetts in 1820 / *Dorset Field Club*, 1917, with introductory couplet, 'Monkeys, monkeys, draw the beer, How many monkeys have you here?'

388

One, two, three, four, five,
Once I caught a fish alive,
Six, seven, eight, nine, ten,
Then I let it go again.

Why did you let it go?
Because it bit my finger so.
Which finger did it bite?
This little finger on the right.

Primarily a counting-out rhyme, it has been adapted to many purposes, as at the Baptist Mission, London S.E. 1, where (according to *Picture Post*, 21 December 1946) the Wednesday children's meeting 'flutters the tarpaulin off the blitzed roof' with the opening tune:

> One, two, three, four, five,
> Jesus Christ is still alive.
> Six, seven, eight, nine, ten,
> He will come back again.

MG's Melody, c. 1765, four lines only, 'One, two, three, Four and five, I caught a hare alive; Six, seven, eight, Nine and ten, I let him go again'. All quotes up to 1888 are similar / Letter to Joseph Frank from Joseph Ritson, 23 Jan. 1782 [1833] / *GG's Garland*, 1784 / *T Tit's SB*, c. 1790 / *Nurse Lovechild's DFN*, c. 1830 / JOH, 1842 / *Traditional Nursery Songs*, Felix Summerly, 1843, illustration by John Linnell / Bolton, 1888, three American versions / Crofton MS, 1901 / *London Street Games*, Norman Douglas, 1916 / *Word Lore*, 1927 / *Housewife*, Dec. 1948, given as a finger-game at nursery schools.

389

Miss One, Two, and Three
Could never agree

One

While they gossipped around
A tea-caddy.

Douce MS II, c. 1820 / JOH, 1842.

390

One-ery, two-ery, ickery, Ann,
Phillisy, phollisy, Nicholas John,
Quever, quaver, Irish Mary,
Stickeram, stackeram, buck.

A counting-out formula (15 counts) the origin of which should probably be sought in antiquity. It has been noted on numerous occasions both in England and America during the past 180 years; and, everything considered, the deviations from the text version (which appears to be the basic form) are remarkably slight. Bolton compares it with,

'Ekkeri, akai-ri, you kair-an,
Fillisin, follasy, Nicholas ja'n:
Kivi, kavi, Irishman,
Stini, stani, buck,

which according to C.G. Leland is virtually a gypsy spell. This, however, may be questioned. Although the word *stàni* is Anglo-Romani for 'stag' or 'deer'; *filishin* Romani for 'castle, house, mansion'; *jan* Romani for 'go'; *kavi* 'this one', or corrupt for *kekkavi* 'kettle'; and *kair-an* could be from the Romani *ker* 'to do', the resemblances are probably fortuitous. It is more likely that gypsies, who are notorious borrowers, picked it up from their English neighbours.

Douce MS, c. 1815, 'Onery, ooery, ickery, an, Hops in vinegar, Little Sir Ian. Queevy, quavy, Deevy dawvey, Stinkerum stankerum Buck' / *MG's Quarto*, c. 1825, 'One-ery, you-ery, ekery, Ann, Phillisy, follysy, Nicholas, John, Quee-bee, quaw-bee, Irish Mary, Stinkle-em, stankle-em, buck' / JOH, 1842, similar to text / Bolton, 1888, thirty-one variations / *Longman's Magazine*, 1889, P. H. Gosse (written 1869, remembered from c. 1820), 'One-ry, oo-ry, ick-ry, an; Bipsy, bopsy Little Sir Jan [or Solomon san]; Queery, quaury, Virgin Mary, Nick, tick, tolomon tick, O, U, T, out. Rotten, totten, dish-clout, Out jumps-He' / *American Mother Goose*, Ray Wood, 1938, gathered from the 'peckerwood' people, 'Eerie oarie, eekerie, Ann, Fillison, follison, Nicholas, John, Queavy, quavy, English navy, Sticklum, stacklum, Buck' / *Counting Out*, Carl Withers, 1946, 'One's all, two's all, zig-a-zall zan; Bobtail nanny-goat, tittle tall tan. Harum, scarum, merchant marum, Sinctum, sanctum, Buck'; and similar to 1938 / Correspondent, 1949, 'Iggory, oggory, iggory, amm, Filsy, folsy, filsy famm, Heeby, coby, Virgin Mary, Sprinkle, sprinkle, block'.

391

> One-ery, two-ery, tickery, seven,
> Hallibo, crackibo, ten and eleven,
> Spin, span, muskidan,
> Twiddle-um, twaddle-um, twenty-one.

Counting-out formula (? 21 counts) probably of an age equal to the previous example, and the centre of John Brown's pleasant anecdote about Sir Walter Scott and the seven-year-old Marjorie Fleming. 'She (Marjorie) gave him his new lesson, gravely and slowly, timing it upon her small fingers—he saying it after her—

> Wonery, twoery, tickery, seven;
> Alibi, crackaby, ten, and eleven;
> Pin, pan, musky, dan;
> Tweedle-um, twoddle-um, twenty-wan;
> Eeerie, orie, ourie,
> You, are, out.

He pretended to great difficulty, and she rebuked him with most comical gravity, treating him as a child. He used to say that when he came to Alibi Crackaby he broke down, and Pin-Pan, Musky-Dan, Tweedle-um Twoddle-um made him roar with laughter. He said Musky-Dan especially was beyond endurance, bringing up an Irishman and his hat fresh from the Spice Islands and odoriferous Ind; she getting quite bitter in her displeasure at his ill behaviour and stupidness.' The story, however, is apocryphal, and the rhyme must be one Dr. Brown remembered from his own childhood in Edinburgh (c. 1820) (see *Scottish Historical Review*, vol. xxvi).

GG's Garland, 1810, 'One-ery, two-ery, Ziccary zan; Hollow bone, crack a bone, Ninery ten: Spittery spot, It must be done; Twiddleum twaddleum Twenty ONE' with eight more lines / *Chatterings of the Pica*, Charles Taylor, 1820, 'One-ery, two-ery, duckery, seven, Alama, crack, ten am eleven. Peem, pom, it must be done; Come teetle, come total, Come twenty-one' / *Blackwood's Magazine*, 1821, 'Anery, twäery, tickery, seven, Aliby crackiby, ten or eleven; Pin-pan, muskidan, Tweedlum, twodlum, twenty-one' / *MG's Quarto*, c. 1825, 'One-ery, you-ery, ekery, haven, Hollow-bone, tollow-bone, ten or eleven, Spin, spun, must be done, Hollow-bone, tollow-bone, twenty-one' / JOH, 1849, similar to text / *North British Review*, Nov. 1863, John Brown [*Horae Subsecivae*, 1882] / Newell, 1883, eight *varia* / Bolton, 1888, thirty variations / *NR Book*, Andrew Lang, 1897, 'Onery, twoery, tickery, tin, alamacrack, tenamalin, pin, pan, musky dan, tweedlum, twiddlum, twenty-one, black fish, white trout, eery, ory, you are out' / *John O' London's*, Mar. 1947, 'Onery, twoery, tickery, seven: onaba, crackaba, ten and eleven' / Correspondents, 1949, 'Eema, deema, dima, dell, Potla, wheelum, whilum, wem, Pot, pan, master Dan, Dallogly, cockoly, twenty-one. One, two, three, Out goes she'; and 'One-ery, Two-ery, Dickery, Davy, Alabon, Crackabon, Discum, Dan'.

One-ery

Cf. *Deutsche Kinder-Reime*, Ernst Meier, 1851, 'Ehne Dehne du, Kappernelle wu, Isa-belle, Pempernelle, Ibille, Pibille, Geh weg!'

392

Oranges and lemons,
Say the bells of St. Clement's.

You owe me five farthings,
Say the bells of St. Martin's.

When will you pay me?
Say the bells of Old Bailey.

When I grow rich,
Say the bells of Shoreditch.

When will that be?
Say the bells of Stepney.

I'm sure I don't know,
Says the great bell at Bow.

Here comes a candle to light you to bed,
Here comes a chopper to chop off your head.

This renowned song is known to young children even when they have never played the game which accompanies it. In the game (played in the manner of 'London Bridge' and 'Through the needle e'e, boys') two of the bigger players determine in secret which of them shall be an 'orange' and which a 'lemon'; they then form an arch by joining hands, and sing the song while the others in a line troop underneath. When the two players who form the arch approach, with quickening tempo, the climax of their recitation,

Here comes a candle to light you to bed,
Here comes a chopper to chop off your head,

they repeat ominously 'Chop, chop, chop, chop, *chop*!' and on the last CHOP they bring their arms down around whichever child is at that moment passing under the arch. The captured player is asked privately whether he will be an 'orange' or a 'lemon' (alternatively a 'plum pud-ding' or 'roast beef'; 'tart' or 'cheesecake'; a 'sack of corn' or 'sack of coals') and he goes to the back of the player he finds he has chosen, and the game and singing recommence. As now usually played, the end

Oranges and Lemons

comes when every child has been lined up on one or other side of the arch, whereupon there is a tug of war to test whether the 'oranges' or the 'lemons' are the stronger. The execution formula has been seen by some folk-lorists as a relic of the gory past, and origins of the nature of those linked with 'London Bridge is falling down' have been suggested. The days of public executions have been cited, when the condemned were led along the street to the accompaniment of the tolling of bells. It has also been suggested that the words refer to Henry VIII's many marriages and the speedy demise of some of his wives. Whether or not the terminating lines have special significance, they do not appear in the song's earliest recording (c. 1744):

> Two Sticks and Apple,
> Ring y^e Bells at Whitechapple,
> Old Father Bald Pate,
> Ring y^e Bells Aldgate,
> Maids in white Aprons,
> Ring y^e Bells a S$^t\cdot$ Catherines,
> Oranges and Lemmons,
> Ring y^e Bells at S$^t\cdot$ Clemens,
> When will you pay me,
> Ring y^e Bells at y^e Old Bailey,
> When I am Rich,
> Ring y^e Bells at Fleetditch,
> When will that be,
> Ring y^e Bells at Stepney,
> When I am Old,
> Ring y^e Bells at Pauls.

In the previous century 'Oringes and Lemons' was the name of a square-for-eight dance, published in the third edition of Playford's *Dancing Master* (1665). It is a common practice to give words to the chimes of bells and there are a number of local rhymes similar to 'Oranges and Lemons'. In Shropshire there is an old and lengthy jingle beginning,

> A knut and a kernel
> Say the bells of Acton Burnell.

In Northamptonshire they repeat similar words, and in Derby they used to say,

> Pancakes and fritters,
> Say All Saints' and Peter's;
> When will the ball come?
> Says the bell of St. Alkum;
> At two will they throw,
> Says Saint Warabo;

Oranges and Lemons

O very well,
Says little Michael.

All Saints' and Peter's, &c., are ancient churches in the town of Derby (St. Warabo is St. Werburgh), and the words were chanted on Shrove Tuesday when the great game of football was played in the streets with a very large ball, half the town against the other half of the town. The province of 'Oranges and Lemons' appears to be the City of London. In fact the long version in *Gammer Gurton's Garland* (1810) begins,

Gay go up and gay go down,
To ring the bells of London Town.

Edward Everett Hale described (1905) the thrill an American visitor feels as he reaches the City and hears the names of the churches he has known only in song spoken of familiarly. St. Martin's probably refers to St. Martin's Lane in the City, where the moneylenders used to live; Old Bailey is near the Fleet Prison where debtors were sent; Shoreditch, where an old church once stood, is just outside the city walls; Stepney, nearby, is also without the city; Bow must be St. Mary-le-Bow in Cheapside, whose bells told Dick Whittington to 'Turn again'. Which church peals 'oranges and lemons' is the subject of contention. Claims have been made both for St. Clement's, Eastcheap, and for St. Clement Danes. The former is situated near the Thames Street wharves at the foot of London Bridge, where the berths for landing citrus fruit from the Mediterranean used to be situated. The latter, on behalf of which there has lately been strenuous propaganda, and a special service held each 31 March, is similarly placed. Sir Frank Lockwood in *Law and Lawyers in Pickwick* (1893) describes how in past times the tenants at Clement's Inn used to receive a toll for allowing the porters to carry oranges and lemons through to nearby Clare Market. The subject has, however, been given undue importance. In the second and fourth earliest versions of the song (c. 1760 and 1805) the 'oranges and lemons' couplet does not even appear.

T Thumb's PSB, c. 1744, as quote / *Top Book*, c. 1760, similar to previous, but 'You owe me ten Shillings, Say the Bells at St. Hellens' instead of 'oranges and lemons', 'Shoreditch' instead of 'Fleetditch', and ends 'I do not know, Says the great Bell at Bow' / *T Thumb's SB*, 1788, as c. 1744, but 'Ring the Great Bells at Paul's' / *Songs for the Nursery*, 1805, 'You owe me five shillings, Say the bells of St. Helen's. When will you pay me? Say the bells of Old Bailey. When I grow rich, Say the bells of Shoreditch. When will that be? Say the bells of Stepney. I do not know, Says the great Bell of Bow, Two sticks in an apple, Ring the bells of Whitechapel. Halfpence and farthings, Say the bells of St. Martin's. Kettles and pans, Say the bells of St. Ann's. Brickbats and tiles, Say the bells of St. Giles. Old shoes and slippers, Say the bells of St. Peter's. Pokers and tongs, Say the bells of St. John's' / *GG's Garland*, 1810, begins as quote, then 'Bull's eyes and targets, Say the bells of St. Marg'ret's', followed by the bells of St. Giles', St. Martin's, St. Clement's, St. Peter's ('Pancakes and fritters'), Whitechapel, Aldgate, St. Helen's, Old Bailey, Shoreditch, Stepney, Bow / *MG's*

400

Oranges and Lemons

Quarto, c. 1825, as 1805 / JOH, 1844, as 1810 with addition of St. John's, St. Ann's, and 'Here comes a candle' etc. / Rimbault, 1846 / *Old Nurse's Book*, Charles Bennett, 1858, as text but 'And here comes a chopper to chop-off-the-last-man's-head' / *Baby's Opera*, 1877 / Gomme, 1898, sixteen versions principally similar to text / *Mother Goose*, Arthur Rackham, 1913 / In George Orwell's *Nineteen Eighty-Four*, 1949, the quotation of the forgotten song 'Oranges and Lemons' is used to symbolize the unattainable and desirable past.

393

There was an owl lived in an oak,
    Wisky, wasky, weedle;
And every word he ever spoke
    Was, Fiddle, faddle, feedle.

A gunner chanced to come that way,
    Wisky, wasky, weedle;
Says he, I'll shoot you, silly bird.
    Fiddle, faddle, feedle.

The above two verses collected by JOH are probably closer to the original song than any of the four verses in *Original Ditties for the Nursery* (c. 1805):

In an oak there liv'd an owl,
    Frisky, whisky, wheedle!
She thought herself a clever fowl;
    Fiddle, faddle, feedle.

Her face alone her wisdom shew,
    Frisky, whisky, wheedle!
For all she said was, Whit te whoo!
    Fiddle, faddle, feedle.

Her silly note a gunner heard,
    Frisky, whisky, wheedle!
Says he, I'll shoot you, stupid bird!
    Fiddle, faddle, feedle.

Now if he had not heard her hoot,
    Frisky, whisky, wheedle,
He had not found her out to shoot,
    Fiddle, faddle, feedle.

Original Ditties (J. Harris), c. 1805 [1807] / JOH, 1853 / *Mother Goose's Melodies* (Houghton, Osgood and Co.), 1879.

PLATE XIV

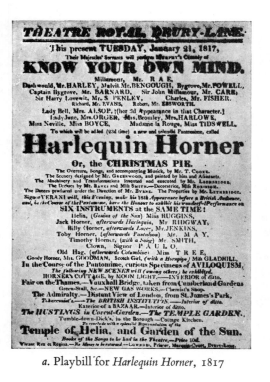

b. Tommy Tucker

a. Playbill for *Harlequin Horner*, 1817

c

b. Tommy Tucker in Skelt's toy-theatre production, c. 1850

c. Pat Kirkwood as Tommy Tucker at the London Casino, 1949–50

d. Frederick Vokes in *Harlequin Humpty Dumpty* at the Lyceum, 1869

NURSERY RHYME PANTOMIMES

Owl

394

A wise old owl lived in an oak;
The more he saw the less he spoke;
The less he spoke the more he heard.
Why can't we all be like that wise old bird?

In *Punch* (10 April 1875), the following appeared as one of a series of 'Nursery Rhymes New Set For the Times':

There was an owl liv'd in an oak,
The more he heard, the less he spoke,
The less he spoke, the more he heard -
O, if men were all like that wise bird.

Since the other rhymes in this series only bear initial resemblance to the traditional verses, it looks as if this is the first appearance of the rhyme, now repeated in its own right, and that it was inspired by 'There was an owl lived in an oak, wisky, wasky, weedle' (q.v.). This is an example of a parody being a better rhyme and becoming better known than its original.

395

High diddle ding, did you hear the bells ring?
The parliament soldiers are gone to the king!
Some they did laugh, and some they did cry,
To see the parliament soldiers go by.

It is suggested that this refers not to the Parliamentarians fetching Charles I for execution, but to those approaching Charles II with the offer of the crown. This theory is supported by a version recorded in 1810:

High ding a ding, and ho ding a ding,
The Parliament soldiers are gone to the king;
Some with new beavers, some with new bands,
The parliament soldiers are all to be hang'd.

Christmas Box, vol. ii, 1798, 'High ding a ding, I heard a bird sing' / *GG's Garland*, 1810, as quote / *MG's Quarto*, c. 1825 / JOH, 1843 / *Folk-Lore*, 1916.

396

Pat-a-cake, pat-a-cake, baker's man,
Bake me a cake as fast as you can;
Pat it and prick it, and mark it with B,
Put it in the oven for baby and me.

This was portrayed as an infants' ditty as early as 1698. In D'Urfey's comedy *The Campaigners* the 'affected tattling nurse' murmurs endearments as she suckles her charge:

'Ah Doddy blesse dat pitty face of myn Sylds, and his pitty, pitty hands, and his pitty, pitty foots, and all his pitty things, and pat a cake, pat a cake Bakers man, so I will master as I can, and prick it, and prick it, and prick it, and prick it, and prick it, and throw't into the Oven.'

The verse often accompanies a game. Mrs. Child, in the nineteenth century, instructed, 'Clap the hands together, saying "Pat a cake, pat a cake, baker's man; that I will, master, as fast as I can"; then rub the hands together, saying, "Roll it, and roll it"; then peck the palm of the left hand with the forefinger of the right, saying, "Prick it, and prick it"; then throw up both hands saying, "Toss it in the oven and bake it"'. More usually today the words punctuate the excellent hand-warming exercise also associated with 'Pease porridge hot' (q.v.).

The Campaigners, Tom D'Urfey, 1698 / *MG's Melody*, c. 1765, 'Patty Cake, Patty Cake. Baker's Man; That I will Master, As fast as I can; Prick it and prick it, And mark it with a T, And there will be enough for Jackey and me' / *GG's Garland*, 1784 / *T Thumb's SB*, 1788 / *T Tit's SB*, c. 1790 / *Christmas Box*, 1797, 'Make a Cake, Make a Cake Bakerman' / Douce MS, c. 1805, 'Batt the cake' / *Songs for the Nursery*, 1805 / *Vocal Harmony*, c. 1806 / *Pretty Tales*, 1808 / *Girl's Own Book*, Mrs. Child, 1831 [1832] / JOH, 1842.

Pantomime: *Pat-a-Cake, Pat-a-Cake, Baker's Man; or, Harlequin Baa Baa Black Sheep*, performed at The Strand Theatre, 1865.

Parody by James Robinson Planché on the publication of *The Nursery Rhymes of England*, 1842, by his friend Halliwell, 'Halliwell-Halliwell, My pretty man, Make me a book as fast as you can; Write it and print it, And mark it with P., And send it by Parcels Deliverye'.

397

Upon Paul's steeple stands a tree
As full of apples as may be;
The little boys of London town
They run with hooks to pull them down:

Paul's Steeple

And then they go from hedge to hedge
Until they come to London Bridge.

An apple tree on the steeple of St. Paul's seems to have been an old joke or popular imagery. In a ballad *Tom Tell-Truth* printed about 1676 appears,

Atop of Paul's steeple there did I see
a delicate, dainty, fine Apple-Tree.
The Apples were ripe, and ready to fall,
and kill'd seven hundred men on a stall.

St Paul's steeple was destroyed by lightning on 4 June 1571, and never rebuilt. However, 'steeple' and 'tower' seem to have been interchangeable in seventeenth-century parlance, and during the reconstruction following the Great Fire, Pepys could write (26 August 1668), 'It is strange to see with what speed the people imployed do pull down Paul's steeple—and with what ease'. Thus a seventeenth-century origin is possible for the song. On the other hand it was the sixteenth century that saw some curious events on the steeple. Strutt in his *Sports and Pastimes* (1801) describes rope dancing on the steeple battlements (1553), a Dutchman standing on one foot on the weathercock (1546), and an acrobat being killed while sliding down (1554).

Rimbault, 1846 / *Baby's Opera*, 1877 / N & Q, 1924, given as 'still current in some households'.
Cf. 'As I was walking o'er little Moorfields'.

398

I saw a peacock with a fiery tail
I saw a blazing comet drop down hail
I saw a cloud with ivy circled round
I saw a sturdy oak creep on the ground
I saw a pismire swallow up a whale
I saw a raging sea brim full of ale
I saw a Venice glass sixteen foot deep
I saw a well full of men's tears that weep
I saw their eyes all in a flame of fire
I saw a house as big as the moon and higher
I saw the sun even in the midst of night
I saw the man that saw this wondrous sight.

'So may the omission of a few commas effect a wonder in the imagination' says the poet-guide of *Come Hither*. These lines are perhaps now best known to readers of adult anthologies, though around 1855 they were said to be 'still a favourite with schoolboys'. The recording in *Westminster Drollery* (1671) has been accepted as the original it seems to be, but the lines also appear in a Caroline commonplace book in our possession, and this particular entry may precede the *Drollery*. It is not unlikely that in the mid-seventeenth century the piece was already known widely; several similar compositions have been found in this period.

A Commonplace Book, c. 1665, as text but 'I saw ye Brackish sea brimful of Ale' / *Westminster Drollery, or A Choice Collection Of the Newest Songs & Poems both at Court and Theatres*, by a Person of Quality, 1671, as text / *A Little Book for Little Children*, T. W., c. 1705, minor variations, e.g. 'I saw the Sun Red even at midnight, I saw the man that saw this dreadful sight' / *The Puzzling Cap* (E. Newbery), 1786 [and advertised F. Newbery 1771] / *Girl's Book of Diversions*, Miss Leslie, 1835 / Chambers, 1842 / *Come Hither*, Walter de la Mare, 1923.

399

Twelve pears hanging high,
Twelve knights riding by;
Each knight took a pear,
And yet left eleven there.

Riddle. JOH (1843) wisely refrained from trying to solve this. Readers of *John o' London's* and *Notes & Queries* have been less cautious. Their suggestions include: that there were eleven pairs of pears and one pear; that eleven knights took a pear and one took a pair; that each knight took the same pear; and that Eachknight was the name of the knight who took the pear. Improbable as this last solution might seem, it has French support. In *Les Adeuineaux amoureux*, printed at Bruges about 1478, appears,

'Trois moines passoient
Trois poires pendoient
Chascun en prist une
Et s'en demoura deux.

L'explication—L'un des moines avoit nom Chascun' [1831].

400

Pease porridge hot,
Pease porridge cold,

a.

Chapbook illustrations, actual size.

a. Printed c. 1825. The rest printed c. 1830 in Richardson of Derby's *Nursery Rhymes*.

b. 'A carrion crow sat on an oak.'

c. 'I had a little pony.'

d. 'Who comes here? A grenadier.'

e. 'When I was a little boy, I had but little wit.'

b.

c.

d.

e.

Pease Porridge

Pease porridge in the pot
Nine days old.

Some like it hot,
Some like it cold,
Some like it in the pot
Nine days old.

As often happens, this rhyme makes fun of a street cry. 'Pease porridge hot.' was cried by the hawkers at Bartholomew's Fair in the eighteenth century, as appears in G. A. Stevens's description (1762):

> Here's Punch's whole play of the gunpowder-plot, Sir,
> With beasts all alive, and pease-porridge hot, Sir.

It is now an infant amusement, also employed by schoolchildren on cold days for hand-warming. Two players, standing opposite each other, clap their own hands together on the first word, their right hands with each other on the second, their own hands together again on the third, and with succeeding words their left hands with each other, their own hands together, and both hands with each other. They immediately restart the sequence, saying the rhyme faster and faster until one of the players breaks the sequence through addleheadedness or exhaustion. Another such formula is 'Pat-a-cake, pat-a-cake' (q.v.).

Newest Christmas Box, c. 1797 / JOH, 1844, 'Pease-pudding hot' / Newell, 1883 / Oral collection, 1945.

*** The query may be raised whether there is significance in the unvarying and reoccurring 'nine days old'. Compare the street cry 'Mince pies hot, mince pies cold, mince pies in addition nine days old', and the parodies of it in the folk plays:

> Mince pies hot, mince pies cold,
> I'll send you to the devil till he's nine days old.

401

Pease porridge hot,
Pease porridge cold,
Pease porridge in the pot
Nine days old.
Spell me that without a P,
And a clever scholar you will be.

'I will, THAT', said the editor of *Mother Goose's Melody*. This is a riddle and a clapping-game in one.

Pease Porridge

MG's Melody, c. 1765, 'Spell me that in four letters' instead of last couplet / *NR* (T. Richardson), c. 1830, similar to previous / Chambers, 1842 / JOH, 1842 / *Rymour Club*, 1906, 'Cauld kail cauld, Nine days auld, Boiled in a pat and sottert in a pan; Spell "that" wi' four letters if you can' / *Street Games of N. Shields Children*, M. and R. King, 1926.
  Cf. previous rhyme.

402

I have a little sister, they call her Peep-Peep,
She wades the waters, deep, deep, deep;
She climbs the mountains high, high, high;
Poor little creature she has but one eye.

RIDDLE. *Solution:* a star.

Chambers, 1842 / JOH, 1842, 'Poor little creature she wanted an eye' / *Aunt Judy's Magazine*, 1868 / *Rymour Club*, 1919.

403

There was an old woman, her name it was Peg;
Her head was of wood and she wore a cork leg.
The neighbours all pitched her into the water,
Her leg was drowned first, and her head followed after.

JOH, 1842, 'Peg, Peg, with a wooden leg, Her father was a miller: He tossed the dumpling at her head, And said he could not kill her' / JOH, 1844, as text.

404

Little Peg a Ramsey,
With the yellow hair,
Double ruff around her neck
And ne'er a shirt to wear.

The writer who contributed this rhyme to *Notes & Queries* (1884) said it used to be repeated by an aged servant. The name Peg a Ramsay is old

Peg

(e.g. Shakespeare's 'Malvolio's a Peg-a-Ramsay'), and there was a song called 'Peggy Ramsay', witty, but indelicate, beginning,

> Bonny Peggy Ramsay,
> As ony man may see,
> Has a bonny sweet face,
> And a gleg glintin ee.

A rewritten copy of this is in the third volume of Henry Playford's *Pills to Purge Melancholy* (1704).

Correspondent, 1951, from c. 1850, 'Blow the fire, blacksmith, Make a lovely light, Here comes a little girl All dressed in white, Lovely shoes and stockings, Lovely curly hair, Ruffle muffle round her neck, And no shirt to wear' / Correspondent, 1988, from grandfather, 'Blow a fire, blacksmith...White shoes and stockings, And fair curly hair, A ruffle, ruffle round her neck, And not a shirt to wear' / 'Blacksmith' version much used for skipping, 1950s and 1960s.

405

> Peter, Peter, pumpkin eater,
> Had a wife and couldn't keep her;
> He put her in a pumpkin shell
> And there he kept her very well.
>
> Peter, Peter, pumpkin eater,
> Had another, and didn't love her;
> Peter learned to read and spell,
> And then he loved her very well.

Infant Institutes, 1797 / *MG's Quarto*, c. 1825 / *Aberdeen and its Folk*, 1868, 'Peter, my neeper, Had a wife, And he couldna' keep her, He pat her i' the wa', And lat a' the mice eat her' / *N & Q*, 1918, 'Had another, didn't love her, causing instantaneous bother' / Oral collection, 1945.

406

> Peter Piper picked a peck of pickled pepper;
> A peck of pickled pepper Peter Piper picked;
> If Peter Piper picked a peck of pickled pepper,
> Where's the peck of pickled pepper Peter Piper picked?

These tongue-tripping lines are regularly given to the pupils of R.A.D.A. and other dramatic schools as an exercise in articulation. Sometimes the task is aggravated by the addition of 'off a pewter plate' at the end of each line. The practice is not new. In *Literary Leisure, or the Recreations of Solomon Saunter* (1802), the satirist Hewson Clarke (b. 1787) said that 'Peter Piper', 'in my younger days a particular favourite with me', should be rehearsed 'three times without drawing breath', which 'renders it an useful lesson in the art of elocution'. The words he knew were 'Peter Piper pick'd a peck of pepper; If Peter Piper pick'd a peck of pepper, Where's the peck of pepper Peter Piper pick'd?'. In *Our Village*, vol. ii, Mary Russell Mitford remembered that the French mistress at her London school, in 1798, 'insisted on translating our old forfeits game of "Peter Piper" ... into their Gallic counterpart'.

Peter Piper's Practical Principles of Plain and Perfect Pronunciation (J. Harris), 1813, with tongue-twisters for every letter of the alphabet; (Carter Andrews and Co., Lancaster), c. 1830 [Rosenbach]; (Grant and Griffiths), c. 1845; ed. E. V. Lucas, 1897; pictured by A. Wyndham Payne, 1926 / *MG's Quarto*, c. 1825 / *Girl's Own Book*, Mrs. Child, 1831 [1832] / *Girl's Book of Diversions*, Miss Leslie, 1835, 'A peacock pick'd a peck of pepper: Did he pick a peck of pepper? Yes, he pick'd a peck of pepper: Pick pecker peacock' / JOH, 1842 / *Folk-Lore*, 1878.

Parody: *Itma Rhymes*, Dorothy Worsley, 1946, 'If Peter Geekie pack'd a pile of picture papers...'

407

Peter White will ne'er go right;
Would you know the reason why?
He follows his nose wherever he goes,
And that stands all awry.

In *The Second Book of the Pleasant Musical Companion* (1701) this is described as a catch for three voices written and composed by Mr. Richard Brown. The lines were familiarly quoted by the Rector of Oxburgh, Charles Parkin, in 1748, and in two children's books of the same century, but JOH (1842) said he was not aware that the lines were still current. They are, however, well known in the present day both in England and America.

Pleasant Musical Companion (Henry Playford), 1701, 'Peter White that never goes right, would you know the reason why. He follows his Nose where ever he goes, and that stands all a wry'; (John Young), 1720 / *Catch Club* (I. Walsh), 1733, 'A Catch on a Man with a Wry Nose' / *A Reply to the ... Malevolent Objections brought by Dr. Stukeley in his Origines Roystonianae*, No. 2, Charles Parkin, 1748, as text / *Six-Pennyworth of Wit* (J. Newbery), c. 1767 / *T Tit's SB*, c. 1790, 'Mary White will ne'er go right' / JOH, 1842 / *Mother Goose*, E. Boyd Smith, 1919 / *Cakes and Custard*, Brian Alderson, illus. Helen Oxenbury, 1974.

Pettitoes

408

The pettitoes are little feet,
        And the little feet not big;
Great feet belong to the grunting hog,
        And the pettitoes to the little pig.

In one of Coleridge's notebooks (August 1804) is an effusion supposed to be spoken by a 'Dr Paolo Cesareo': 'Mon charmant, prenez garde—Mind what your Signior begs, Ven you wash, don't scrub so harda—you may rub my shirt to rags. While you make the water hotter, un solo I compose. Put in the Pot the nice Sheep's Trotter, and de little Pettitoes. De Petty Toes are leetle feet. The leetle feet not big great feet Belong to this grunting Hog. The petty feet of the leetle Pig'.

Notebooks of Samuel Taylor Coleridge, ed. K. Coburn, vol. II, 1804-8, note 2178 / JOH, 1853 / *Mother Goose's NR*, L. E. Walter, 1924.

409

Up at Piccadilly oh!
    The coachman takes his stand,
And when he meets a pretty girl,
    He takes her by the hand;
        Whip away for ever oh!
        Drive away so clever oh!
        All the way to Bristol oh!
    He drives her four-in-hand.

'The Jolly Bristol Coachman' was 'Printed and Sold by W. Collard, Bridewell Lane, & Hotwell-Road' between 1818 and 1835. It begins 'Come all you country lasses, and listen to my song, 'Tis of a country Coachman who drives them four in hand', and the chorus and second verse run:

> With his whip away for ever O,
> Drive away so clever O,
> All the way to Bristol
> He drives them four in hand.

> 'Tis up at Piccadilly,
>   this coachman takes his stand,
> And if he meets a pretty girl,
>   he takes her by the hand.

Piccadilly

Instead of the coachman seducing the 'pretty girl', it is the 'pretty girl' who tricks the coachman; her husband turns up at the appropriate moment and demands forty pounds, 'And if the money you don't find, the Coach and all must go'.

410

> This pig got in the barn,
> This ate all the corn,
> This said he wasn't well,
> This said he would go and tell,
> And this said—weke, weke, weke,
> Can't get over the barn door sill.

Infant amusement, similar to the better-known 'This little pig went to market' (q.v.) with which it probably has a common origin.

Scottish Dictionary Suppl., J. Jamieson, vol. II, 1825, 'There's the thief that brak the barn, There's the ane that steal'd the corn; There's the ane that tell'd a'; And puir pirliewinkie paid for a'', and second version, 'Here's Break-bam...Steal-corn... Hand-Watch...Rinn-awa', and little wee, wee Cronachie pays for a'' / JOH, 1844, 'Thimbikin, Thimbikin, broke the barn, Pinnikin, Pinnikin, stole the corn; Long-backed Gray Carried it away; Old Mid-man sat and saw, But Peesy-weesy paid for a'' / *Shropshire Folk-Lore*, C. S. Burne, 1883 / *Folk-Lore*, 1913 / *Shetland Traditional Lore*, J. M. E. Saxby, 1932, 'Dis is da een 'at brük da barn, Dis is da een 'at stül da corn, Dis is da een 'at ran awa', Dis is da een 'at telled it a', And dis is da peerie, weerie, winkie een 'at fell idda burn wi' da hollow o' straw, and peyed for a'' / *N & Q*, 1943, 'Black Barney Lope Dake Steel Corney Runaway And Little Canny Wanny who Pays All (Black Barney loups the dyke, steals the corn, runs away, and little Canny Wanny—who had nothing to do with it—has to face the racket)'.

Cf. *Rimes et jeux de l'enfance*, E. Rolland, 1883, 'Celui-ci a vu le lièvre, Celui-ci l'a couru, Celui-ci l'a tenu, Celui-ci l'a mangé, Celui-là n'a rien eu. Il a dit à sa mère; J'n'ai pas eu, j'n'ai pas eu!' / *Das deutsche Kinderbuch*, Karl Simrock, 1848, 'Das ist der Daumen, Der schüttelt Pflaumen, Der liest sie, Der isst sie, Und der sagt: wart, ich wills der Mutter sagen' / *Come giuocano i fanciulli d'Italia*, S. La Sorsa, 1937, 'Quistu dice: ca vole lu pane, Quistu dice: ca non ci n'ane, Quistu dice: sciamu cu lu cattamu, sciamu cu lu rubbamu, Quistu dice: zicchili, zicchili!' / *Chinese Mother Goose Rhymes*, I. T. Headland, 1900, 'This one's old, This one's young, This one has no meat, This one's gone To buy some hay, And this one's gone to the village' (original Chinese given).

Pig

411

Let's go to the wood, says this pig,
What to do there? says that pig,
To look for my mother, says this pig,
What to do with her? says that pig,
Kiss her to death, says this pig.

Infant amusement. This 'Song for Five Toes' (1805) seems to be an off-spring of the marriage between 'We will go to the wood, says Robin to Bobbin' and 'This little pig went to market' (qq.v.).

Songs for the Nursery, 1805 / *Grandmama's NR* (J. Fairburn), c. 1825 / JOH, 1842 / *Cries of Banbury and London* (J. G. Rusher), c. 1843, 'She's gone for my father, says that pig, They'll come home to dinner, said this pig'.

412

This little pig went to market,
This little pig stayed at home,
This little pig had roast beef,
This little pig had none,
And this little pig cried, Wee-wee-wee-wee-wee,
I can't find my way home.

The first line of this infant amusement is quoted in a medley, 'The Nurse's Song', written about 1728 and included by Ramsay in the fourth volume of *The Tea-Table Miscellany* (1740). It is the most common toe or finger rhyme in the present day, and has been so for more than a century.

FT Thumb's LSB, c. 1760 / *MG's Melody*, c. 1765, 'This Pig went to Market, That Pig staid at Home; This Pig had roast Meat, That Pig had none; This Pig went to the Barn Door, And cry'd Week, Week, for more' / *Songs for the Nursery*, 1805 / *Vocal Harmony*, c. 1806 / *Nurse Lovechild's DFN*, c. 1830 / *Girl's Own Book*, Mrs. Child, 1831 [1832] / *This Little Pig Went to Market*, Walter Crane, 1869 / *N & Q*, 1890, 3rd finger 'This little pig had bread and butter'; 1891, 'This little pig said, Me a bit, me a bit, me a bit, before it all be gone' / *Pigling Bland*, Beatrix Potter, 1913 / *This Little Pig Went to Market*, L. Leslie Brooke, 1922.

Cf. preceding rhyme, lines from which are sometimes found incorporated in versions of this one.

Pigs

413

Whose little pigs are these, these, these?
Whose little pigs are these?
They are Roger the Cook's
I know by their looks;
I found them among my peas.
Go pound them, go pound them.
I dare not on my life,
For though I love not Roger the Cook
I dearly love his wife.

This song has been jingling at the back of popular memory for more than three centuries. It was rescued in 1877 by Miss Mason for her *Nursery Rhymes and Country Songs* together with a traditional tune, and noted a second time by a correspondent to *Notes & Queries* in 1903. Unknown to either, it had been recorded in the reign of Charles I:

Whose three Hogs are these, are these,
  whose three Hogs are these:
They are John Cookes, I know them by their lookes,
  I found them in the Pease;
Goe pound them, goe pound them, I dare not for my life, my life,
  I dare not for my life;
No, for once thou knewest John Cooke very well,
  but better thou know'st his wife.

Described as a 'catch', it was sung to the tune 'Iohn come kisse me now'.

The Pinder of Wakefield: being the merry history of George a Greene, 1632 / Mason, 1877 / *N & Q*, 1903, 'Johnny Coke' / Correspondent, 1949, 'For though I do not fear Roger the Cook, I greatly fear his wife'.

414

I had two pigeons bright and gay,
They flew from me the other day;
What was the reason they did go?
I cannot tell for I do not know.

The Golden Present (W. Appleton), c. 1790, 'Here is two pigeons fine and gay, Which flew from me the other day But now I've got them back secure, I hope they go from me no more' / JOH, 1853 / *Land of NR*, Ernest Rhys, 1932.

Piper

415

Doodledy, doodledy, doodledy, dan;
I'll have a piper to be my good-man;
And if I get less meat, I shall have game,
Doodledy, doodledy, doodledy, dan.

Another rhyme which portrays the apparent light-heartedness of life with a musician—though again questioning his financial stability. A snatch of it was collected in Scotland in 1776:

I'll hae a Piper, a Piper, a Piper,
I'll hae a Piper to be my Goodman.

Herd MS, 1776 / *Songs for the Nursery*, 1805 / JOH, 1842.
Cf. 'I won't be my father's Jack'.

416

There was a piper had a cow,
And he had nought to give her.
He pulled out his pipes and played her a tune,
And bade the cow consider.

The cow considered very well
And gave the piper a penny,
And bade him play the other tune,
'Corn rigs are bonny'.

Part of an old ballad, 'The tune the old cow died of'. The version printed in *Fraser's Magazine*, Dec. 1833, was rather different from the above:

There was a piper had a cow,
And he had nought to give her;
He took his pipes, and played a spring,
And bade the cow consider.

The cow considered wi' hersel
That mirth would ne'er fill her;
'Gie me a pickle peastrae,
And sell your wind for siller.'

Thomas Carlyle quoted this in letters to his family in 1834, and two further copies of the verse exist among his papers. Either he had been much taken by the song when he saw it in *Fraser's*, or more probably, since he was a frequent contributor, he had sent it himself. Fuller, in an anti-Caledonian mood, explained (1732) that the tune the old cow died of was the 'old Tune upon the Bag-Pipe'. The cow, however, understood very well that a jig was no substitute for a rig.

History of Master Friendly (G. Swindells), c. 1795 / *Songs for the Nursery*, 1805 / *MG's Quarto*, c. 1825 / Letter, Lady Granville, 1836, 'Jack Whaley had a cow, And he had nought to feed her; He took a pipe and played a tune, And bid the cow consider' [1907] / JOH, 1844, slightly different version / N & Q, 1856, 'This isn't the time for the grass to grow, Consider, good cow, consider' / *Less Familiar NR*, Robert Graves, 1927 / *Cakes and Custard*, Brian Alderson, illus. Helen Oxenbury, 1974.

*** The song 'Corn Riggs are bonny' is described as having been popular a few years previously in *An Answer to the Scotch Presbyterian Eloquence*, 1693. Burns refers to it, and quotes the chorus, 'O corn rigs and rye rigs, O corn rigs is bonie'.

417

As I was going up Pippen Hill,
    Pippen Hill was dirty.
There I met a pretty miss
    And she dropt me a curtsey.

Little miss, pretty miss,
    Blessings light upon you!
If I had half a crown a day,
    I'd spend it all upon you.

GG's Garland, 1810 / *Nursery Poems* (J. G. Rusher), c. 1840, second verse only / JOH, 1842 / *Mother Goose*, Kate Greenaway, 1881, first verse only.

418

Little King Pippin he built a fine hall,
Pie-crust and pastry-crust that was the wall;
The windows were made of black pudding and white,
And slated with pancakes, you ne'er saw the like.

This rhyme is part of an age-old tradition of lands 'flowing with milk and honey', where the dwellings are built of delectable foodstuffs all ready to be eaten. In the Utopian Land of Cockayne, far out in the sea to the west of Spain, there was, according to a manuscript of c. 1300–25 (MS Harley 913. f. 3a) a 'fair abbey of white monks and of grey' where:

Ther beeth cloisters, bowres and halles:
Al of pasteyes beeth the walles,
Of flesh, of fishe and riche mete,
The likfullest that man may ete;
Flouren cakes beeth the shingles alle
Of cherche, cloister, bowr and halle;
The pinnes beeth fat puddings,
Riche mete to princes and kinges.

The name of King Pippin of France probably became familiar to the English nursery through the tale of Valentine and Orson (*ante* 1489), which was printed in translation times without number. This would be before 1775, when Francis Newbery considered the name well enough known to advertise a moral booklet for children with the title of *The History of Little King Pippin*. The cartoonist Gillray must also have seen King Pippin as a familiar nursery figure, for (26 Nov. 1804), he captioned a picture of the self-proclaimed French Emperor Bonaparte with a parody of 'Hey my kitten' (q.v.):

There's a little King Pippin
He shall have a Rattle & Crown.
Bless thy five Wits, my Baby
Mind it dont throw itself down!

Songs for the Nursery, 1805, 'Little King Boggen' / *MG's Quarto*, c. 1825 / *NR from the Royal Collections* (J. G. Rusher), c. 1840 / JOH, 1853 / *Harper's Young People*, Dec. 1884, 'Little King Bobbin'.

419

Little Poll Parrot
Sat in his garret
Eating toast and tea;
A little brown mouse,
Jumped into the house,
And stole it all away.

This is one of the songs the sparrows sang in the first (privately printed) version of Beatrix Potter's *The Tailor of Gloucester*.

Poll Parrot

JOH, 1853 / *Book of Nursery Songs*, S. Baring-Gould, 1895 / *Tailor of Gloucester*, Beatrix Potter (p.p. ed.), 1902 / *Mother Goose's NR*, illus. Mabel Lucy Attwell, c. 1925.
    Cf. 'Little Miss Muffet'.
    *** *Tea* is here rhymed with *away* as in 'Polly put the kettle on' (q.v.).

420

Polly put the kettle on,
Polly put the kettle on,
Polly put the kettle on,
   We'll all have tea.

Sukey take it off again,
Sukey take it off again,
Sukey take it off again,
   They've all gone away.

This was sung to the old tune of 'Jenny's Bawbee', which was mentioned by Herd in 1776, and given in Joshua Campbell's *Collection* of 1778. The tune was published under the title *Jenny's Baubie or Jenny Put the Kettle On* by McDonnell, Dublin, (c. 1790–1810), as *Molly put the Kettle On* by Paff, New York City (c. 1803–7), and as *Molly Put the Kettle On or Jenny's Baubie* by Dale (c. 1809–10). Around 1810 the song was clearly the rage in London. It appeared in the songsters as 'Molly Put the Kettle On', and had six verses of a rambling and mildly bawdy nature. In *The Vocal Museum, containing Twenty-one of the Newest Songs Sung at Vauxhall, the Theatres, and Convivial Societies* (c. 1810), it begins:

Molly put the kettle on, Molly put the kettle on,
Molly put the kettle on, we'll all have tea.
Suckey take it off again, Suckey take it off again,
Suckey take it off again, they've run away.

O what did Jenny do, O what did Jenny do,
O what did Jenny do, for a bawbee,
She turned up her peticoat, her blue fring'd peticoat
She turned up her peticoat, above her knee.

Then a sailor returns from sea, and a dancing party ensues during which Jenny declares 'it is no sin for girls to have a drop of gin' and the song ends clumsily, 'Molly put the kettle on, we shall have a drop of gin'. Obviously 'Molly put the kettle on' was already a well-known verse. The first appearance of 'Polly' in print is in *Barnaby Rudge*, when Grip the raven becomes very excited and cries, 'Hurray! Polly put the ket-tle on,

Polly

we'll all have tea; Polly put the ket-tle on, we'll all have tea. Hurrah! hurrah! hurrah!'.

Barnaby Rudge, Charles Dickens, 1841 / JOH, 1853 / *Old Nurse's Book*, Charles Bennett, 1858, 'Sukey take it off again, It will all boil away', and additional verse 'Blow the fire and make the toast, Put the muffins down to roast, Blow the fire and make the toast, We'll all have tea' / *Baby's Bouquet*, 1879 / Newell, 1883, 'Kittie put the kettle on' / *Sheffield Glossary*, S. O. Addy, 1888, 'Come Betty, set the kettle on, Let's have a cup of tay; Sukey take it off again We'll have no more today'.

421

Little Polly Flinders
Sat among the cinders,
Warming her pretty little toes;
Her mother came and caught her,
And whipped her little daughter
For spoiling her nice new clothes.

Original Ditties for the Nursery (J. Harris), c. 1805, 'Little Jenny Flinders . . . for dirtying her clothes' [1807] / JOH, 1846 / *Favourite Rhymes* (Dean and Son), c. 1945.

422

What is the rhyme for porringer?
What is the rhyme for porringer?
The king he had a daughter fair
And gave the Prince of Orange her.

This is the subdued part of a ranting Jacobite song (c. 1689) threatening the life of William, Prince of Orange, after he had 'ta'en the crown' from his father-in-law, James II. The seeming difficulty to the unenlightened of finding a rhyme for the word porringer has since frequently attracted attention, and may already have been a joke before the Jacobite protest (see 1865 quote, 'a noble lad'). Money has been won and lost by those who, boasting of their rhyming abilities, have been challenged with the word. A neat answer given extempore by an old gardener to win a guinea was,

The second James a daughter had,
He gave the Prince of Orange her;
And now I think I've won the prize
In making rhyme to porringer.

Porringer

Jacobite Relics, James Hogg, 1819, 'O what's the rhyme to porringer? Ken ye the rhyme to porringer? King James the Seventh had ae dochter, And he ga'e her to an Oranger', with twelve more lines / *Jacobite Minstrelsy*, 1829 / JOH, 1842 / *N & Q*, 1865, 'Our noble king a daughter had. Too fine to lick a porringer, He sought her out a noble lad, And gave the prince of Orange her'.

423

Punch and Judy
   Fought for a pie;
Punch gave Judy
   A knock in the eye.

Says Punch to Judy
   Will you have any more?
Says Judy to Punch,
   My eye is sore.

There is a reference to puppet-plays in Bale's *King John* (c. 1550), but the character 'Punch' almost certainly comes from Italy, Punch being a shortened form of *Punchinello*, a name which much amused the English at the time of its introduction (the Restoration) and gave rise to the old riddle, 'Oh, Mother I shall be married to Mr. Punch, Mr. Joe, Mr. Nell, Mr. Lo' (q.v.). Pepys in the 1660's records having seen 'Polichinello' at fairs, which 'pleased him mightily'. 'Punch and his Wife' are spoken of together from 1707 onwards, the scolding shrew sometimes being called Joan. She does not appear to have acquired the name Judy until the end of the century.

JOH, 1844 / Oral collection, 1945.

424

Oh, mother, I shall be married to
Mr. Punchinello,
   To Mr. Punch,
     To Mr. Joe,
      To Mr. Nell,
       To Mr. Lo,
   Mr. Punch, Mr. Joe,
   Mr. Nell, Mr. Lo,
   To Mr. Punchinello.

Punchinello

JOH, 1844 / *Less Familiar NR*, Robert Graves, 1927, 'to Mr. Neele, to Mr. Lowe' / *Cakes and Custard*, Brian Alderson, illus. Helen Oxenbury, 1974. For further see previous article.

Cf. *Rimes et jeux de l'enfance*, E. Rolland, 1883. 'Arlequin fit sa boutique Sur les marches du palais. Il enseigne la musique A tous ces petits valets, A monsieur Po, à monsieur li, A monsieur chi, à monsieur nelle, A monsieur Polichinelle.' Rolland adds the footnote, 'Cette formulette, souvent chantée dans les Guignols de la capitale, est connue de tous les enfants.'

425

Purple, yellow, red, and green,
The king cannot reach it, nor yet the queen;
Nor can Old Noll, whose power's so great:
Tell me this riddle while I count eight.

RIDDLE. *Solution:* a rainbow. 'Old Noll' was the Royalists' nickname for Oliver Cromwell and a reasonable guess may be made at the exact year in which the rhyme was composed. The king and queen are here mentioned, without qualification, in the present tense, so it is unlikely that Charles had yet been executed (Jan. 1649). On the other hand Cromwell, to a Royalist, would scarcely have been considered a figure of power—comparable, that is to say, with the king—until he began to represent the Army (June 1647). If the year 1648 be considered, when the king was a refugee, real poignancy can be read in the words 'whose power is so great'.

JOH, 1842 / *Mother Goose* (T. Nelson), c. 1945 / *Rocket in my Pocket*, Carl Withers, 1948, 'Red and blue and delicate green; The king can't catch it and neither can the queen. Pull it in the room and you can catch it soon. Answer this riddle by tomorrow at noon.'

426

Pussicat, wussicat, with a white foot,
When is your wedding, and I'll come to it.
The beer's to brew, the bread's to bake,
Pussy cat, pussy cat, don't be too late!

JOH, 1842 / Crofton MS, 1901, 'Pussy Cat, Pussy Cat, with a white foot; She went from home and the door was shut. She'd cakes to bake and ale to brew, What is poor Pussy Cat to do?' / *Michael Foreman's Mother Goose*, 1991.

427

I love little pussy,
Her coat is so warm,
And if I don't hurt her
She'll do me no harm.
So I'll not pull her tail,
Nor drive her away,
But pussy and I
Very gently will play.

This is first found in *Hints for the formation of Infant Schools, with an account of the apparatus, and a selection of hymns and verses, adapted to these schools*, Lindfield: Printed by C. Green, at the Schools of Industry, for Harvey and Darton; sold also by William Darton and Edmund Fry, London; and at the Liberty Infant School, Dublin (1829). Such a pleasantly improving little verse was soon adopted in America. It appeared the following year in *The Child's Song Book* and *The Juvenile Miscellany*, where it had a second verse:

I'll pat pretty Pussy, and then she will purr;
And thus show her thanks for my kindness to her.
But I'll not pinch her ears, nor tread on her paw,
Least I should provoke her to use her sharp claw.
I never will vex her nor make her displeased:
For Pussy don't like to be worried and teaz'd.

The song has often been attributed to Jane Taylor, as has so much other unclaimed verse, but evidence for this is wanting.

Hints for the formation of Infant Schools, 1829, 'I like little pussy... And she'll love me because I am gentle and good' / *The Child's Song Book* (Boston), 1830 / *Juvenile Miscellany* (Boston), July 1830 / *Only True MG Melodies*, c. 1843, 'I like little pussy' / *Verses and Hymns* (W. Foster), c. 1843 / JOH, 1853 / *Songs for the Little Ones at Home* (Joseph Cundall), 1863, described as from *Amusing Songs / Infant Amusements; or, How to Make a Nursery Happy*, W. H. G. Kingston, 1867, given to the air 'Love's Ritornella' / *Here we come a'piping*, Rose Fyleman, 1936.

428

Pussy cat, pussy cat, where have you been?
I've been to London to look at the queen.

Pussy Cat

Pussy cat, pussy cat, what did you there?
I frightened a little mouse under her chair.

Lord Ernle tells of an occasion when, invited to Osborne by Queen Victoria, he asked his little daughter whether she had any message for the queen. 'Oh, yes', she said, 'ask her to give me the little mouse that lives under the chair.' After dinner, knowing the queen's love for the odd sayings of children, Lord Ernle delivered his daughter's message. Queen Victoria, he says, was highly amused. She called up several of the guests and insisted on him retelling the story for their benefit. The last to be summoned, recalls Lord Ernle, was an elderly peer, who evidently did not see the point of the story. The queen turned upon him almost with indignation, and said: 'What! Lord——, don't you know,

Pussy cat, pussy cat, where have you been?
I've been to London to see the great Queen.
Pussy cat, pussy cat, what saw you there?
I saw a little mouse under her chair.'

A rather similar incident occurred in 1949 when Queen Elizabeth was visiting the families of men on a Royal Air Force station. A little boy stopped her and asked critically, 'Where's the pussy cat?' It was explained to the queen that the child had been repeating the rhyme all day; whereupon Her Majesty apologized to the little boy for not bringing her cat. It is more often believed, however, that the queen referred to in the nursery rhyme is the Tudor Queen Elizabeth. When the lines are illustrated it is usually she who is depicted, and there is a widespread folk tradition, mentioned by a number of writers, that the words tell of an actual happening in her reign. P. B. Green (*A History of Nursery Rhymes*, 1899) gives them as 'a dialogue between a ward nurse of Elizabeth's time and a truant Tom'. Lady Maxse, nevertheless (*National Review*, 1941), gives space to the idea that the verse is a skit on the democratic parties held by the unfortunate Queen Caroline.

Songs for the Nursery, 1805 / *New Year's Gift* (J. Catnach), c. 1830 [Hindley, 1878] / *Poetic Trifles* (J. G. Rusher), c. 1840 / Chambers, 1842, 'Poussie, poussie, baudrons, Where hae ye been? I've been at London Seein' the king! Poussie, poussie, baudrons, What got ye there? I got a wee mousie, Rinnin' up a stair! Poussie, poussie, baudrons, What did ye do wi't? I put it in my meal-pock, To eat it to my bread!' (Poussie baudrons: pussy cat) / JOH, 1844, 'Little girl, little girl, where have you been? Gathering roses to give to the queen. Little girl, little girl, what gave she you? She gave me a diamond as big as my shoe' / Rimbault, 1846 / Chambers, 1870, differs from previous edition in that poussie sees the queen and catches 'a guid fat mousikie' / N & Q, 1890, 'Pussycat, pussycat, where have you been? I've been to see grandmother over the green! What did she give you? Milk in a can. What did you say for it? Thank you, Grandam!' / Kidson, 1901 / Correspondent, 1949, as 1890.

424

Pussy Cat

429

Pussy cat sits beside the fire,
So pretty and so fair.
In walks the little dog,
Ah, Pussy, are you there?
How do you do, Mistress Pussy?
Mistress Pussy, how do you do?
I thank you kindly, little dog,
I'm very well just now.

Versions very similar appear in *Songs for the Nursery*, 1805; *Little Rhymes for Little Folks* (J. Harris), 1823; *Nursery Poems* (J. G. Rusher), c. 1840 / *Puss in Boots* (Henry Mozley and Sons), c. 1825, 'As Pussy stept out of the house, To take the nice fresh air, A pretty looking Dog came by, Ah, Pussy, are you there?' &c. / JOH, 1846, as text / *Pie and the Patty-Pan*, Beatrix Potter, 1905 / Oral collection, 1947 / *Hilda Boswell's Treasury of Nursery Rhymes*, 1960, 'How should she be fair? . . . I fare as well as you.'

430

Who's that ringing at my door bell?
A little pussy cat that isn't very well.
Rub its little nose with a little mutton fat,
For that's the best cure for a little pussy cat.

The original of this is by D'Arcy Wentworth Thompson, and appeared in his *Nursery Nonsense* (1864):

Who's that ringing at our door-bell?
I'm a little black cat, and I'm not very well.
Then rub your little nose with a little mutton-fat,
And that's the best cure for a little pussy-cat.

Oral collection, 1945 / Correspondent, 1949, childhood memory of an old lady, materially as above but 'front door' and 'tallow fat'.

431

Pussy cat Mole jumped over a coal
And in her best petticoat burnt a great hole.
Poor pussy's weeping, she'll have no more milk
Until her best petticoat's mended with silk.

Pussy Cat

Douce MS, c. 1815, 'Pussy cat Miaw' / JOH, 1844 / *Stories for my children*, E. H. Knatchbull-Hugersen, 1869, 'Every child knows the sweet nursery rhyme of "Pussy-cat Mew"'.

432

The Quaker's wife got up to bake,
Her children all about her,
She gave them every one a cake,
And the miller wants his moulter.

Moulter, payment for grinding corn. Scott in his novel *Redgauntlet*, which is set in about the year 1765, etches in a plausible detail when he makes the blind fiddler Wandering Willie strike up the 'well-known and popular measure,

Merrily danced the Quaker's wife,
And merrily danced the Quaker.'

The tune 'So merrily danc'd the Quaker' had appeared in Oswald's *Pocket Companion for the Guittar* printed about 1755, and has had fairly constant popularity in Scotland and the North Country ever since, sometimes as a reel, and usually under the title 'The Quaker's Wife'. It was a favourite air of Burns's under the title 'Leiger m'chose, my bonie wee lass', and he variously affirmed that he had been taught the old chorus of this name by an antiquarian gentleman, a grand aunt, and his old mother.

Songs for the Nursery, 1805 / *Scottish Songs*, R. Chambers, 1829, from an Edinburgh MS 1770–80, 'The quaker's wife sat down to bake, And a' her bairns about her; Ilk ane got their quarter cake, The miller got his mou'ter. Merrily, merrily, merrily, merrily, Merrily danced the quaker's wife, And merrily danced the quakers' / JOH, 1842 / Mason, 1877, 'The baker's wife sat doon to bake' / Kidson, 1904 / *Rymour Club*, 1914.

433

A tailor, who sailed from Quebec,
In a storm ventured once upon deck;
But the waves of the sea
Were as strong as could be,
And he tumbled in up to his neck.

Quebec

The story of the tailor of Quebec comes from *Anecdotes and Adventures of Fifteen Gentlemen*, a toy book attributed to R. S. Sharpe, published by John Marshall about 1821. (*Vide* 'As a little fat man of Bombay'.)

434

The Queen of Hearts
She made some tarts,
All on a summer's day;
The Knave of Hearts
He stole the tarts,
And took them clean away.

The King of Hearts
Called for the tarts,
And beat the knave full sore;
The Knave of Hearts
Brought back the tarts,
And vowed he'd steal no more.

In a feature called 'The Hive, A Collection of Scraps' in *The European Magazine* for April 1782, there are four twelve-line stanzas of which the above is the first. The succeeding three deal with the kings, queens and knaves of the other suits. It would seem that this was the original setting of the now well-known lines, were it not that the three succeeding stanzas fall short of the first in story and simplicity. Also, only five years later, the first stanza alone was used by Canning as the basis of a satire on poetic criticism, and no indication is given of his being aware of any continuation. Furthermore, although the rhyme is not specifically mentioned as being a children's piece, it is used to represent the quintessence of trivial verse, and the point of the satire would be lost if the author were not sure that the words he was quoting were familiar to all his readers. Indeed, that it was already a children's rhyme would seem to be certain, for Lamb, in 1805, made it the basis of his first nursery book. The rhyme, however, does not appear in the early collections, nor was it found by JOH until preparing his third edition, and, curiously, he omits it in later editions. It may be that there is some subterranean mockery, probably political, in the rhyme or its attached stanzas. Four stanzas mentioning king, queen, knave, and Thomas Burke, identical in form to those in *The European Magazine* and apparently of about the same date, were quoted in *Notes & Queries* (1862) from an eighteenth-century manuscript.

Queen of Hearts

European Magazine, 1782 / *Queen of Hearts* (W. Bailey), c. 1785, sheet music, song adapted to the air of 'In Infancy our hopes and fears' from Arne's *Artaxerxes*, 'The Queen of Hearts she made some Tarts upon a Summer's day, The Knave of Hearts he saw those Tarts and stole them all away; and stole them all away; The King of Hearts heard of those Tarts, and to the Knave did say; You Knave of Hearts restore the Tarts, or else for them you Pay; or else for them you Pay' / *The Microcosm*, 1787 / *King and Queen of Hearts: with the Rogueries of the Knave who stole the Queen's Pies*, Charles Lamb, illus. William Mulready, 1805 / JOH, 1844 / *Changing Panoramic Toy Book* (Dean and Son), 1880 / *Queen of Hearts*, Randolph Caldecott, 1881. In *The New Story of the Queen of Hearts*, illus. George Cruikshank, c. 1860, the text is based on the traditional story. Lewis Carroll introduces the rhyme-characters in *Alice in Wonderland*, 1865.

435

> Rain, rain, go away,
> Come again another day.

'Little children', said Aubrey in 1687, 'have a custome when it raines to sing, or charme away the Raine; thus they all joine in a chorus and sing thus, viz.

> Raine, raine, goe away,
> Come againe a Saterday.

I have a conceit that this childish custom is of Great Antiquity, y^t it is derived from ye Gentiles.' Aubrey's notion about the age of the custom is not unreasonable. Children in ancient Greece seem to have had similar practices. According to Strattis (c. 409–375 B.C.) when a cloud obscured the sun they called out ἔξεχ᾿ ὦ φίλ ἥλιε ('Come forth, beloved sun!'). In England in the present day the call takes many forms. Some are diversional and final, as,

> Rain, rain, go to Spain,
> Never show your face again.

Some only provisional,

> Rain, rain, go away,
> Come again on April day,
> [Midsummer day,
> Washing day,]

or,

> Don't come back till Christmas day.
> Little Arthur wants to play.

Some egotistical,

> Rain on the green grass, and rain on the tree,
> And rain on the housetop, but not on me.

Rain

Some municipal,

> Rain, rain, pour down,
> But not a drop on our town.

Some practical,

> Rain, rain, come down and pour,
> Then you'll only last an hour.

Some deferential,

> And when I brew, and when I bake
> I'll give you a figgy cake.

And some mystical,

> Rain, rain, go away,
> Come on Martha's wedding day,

apparently malevolently linked with the superstition that 'Happy is the bride that the sun shines on, and the corpse that the rain rains on'.

Proverbs, James Howell, 1659, 'Raine, raine, goe to Spain: faire weather come againe' / Lansdowne MS 231, 1686–7 / *Songs for the Nursery*, 1805, and *MG's Quarto*, c. 1825, 'Rain, rain, Go away, Come again April day; Little Johnny Wants to play'. Other versions mostly obtained from oral collection and correspondents. Also in JOH, 1842 / *Proverbs*, M. A. Denham, 1846 / Chambers, 1847 / N & Q, 1853 / *Household Tales*, S. O. Addy, 1895.

Cf. Oral collection (Russian), 1947, 'Dozhdik, dozhdik perestan' Mȳ poedem na Iordan' (Rain, rain, stop; we are travelling to the Jordan).

Parody: *The Times*, 8 Jan. 1948, 'In our own day the conjoint influences of old patriotism and New Verse adapted this to "Rain, rain, Go to Germany, And remain there permanently"'.

436

> There was a rat, for want of stairs,
> Went down a rope to say his prayers.

JOH, 1844 / *Rymour Club*, 1914, as Lothian counting-out rhyme / *A Rocket in my Pocket*, Carl Withers, 1948, American children, 'There was a rabbit Who had no stairs; He went down a rope To say his prayers'.

437

> Three young rats with black felt hats,
> Three young ducks with white straw flats,

Rats

Three young dogs with curling tails,
Three young cats with demi-veils,
Went out to walk with two young pigs
In satin vests and sorrel wigs.
But suddenly it chanced to rain
And so they all went home again.

Collected orally by Enid Marx (1939) and traced back for two generations.
'Flats' were, in nineteenth-century America, broad-brimmed, low-crowned straw hats.

Land of NR, Ernest Rhys, 1932 / *Oxford Book of Light Verse*, W. H. Auden, 1938 / *Book of NR*, Enid Marx, 1939 / *Big Book of Mother Goose* (James and Jonathan Co., Wisconsin), 1946.

438

Red within and red without,
Four corners round about.

RIDDLE. *Solution:* a brick (*Notes & Queries*, 1865). Riddles sometimes fall into small groups, and it is likely that the solver of one riddle would reply with a quibbling counterpart. Thus:

Black within and red without,
Four corners round about.

Solution: a chimney (JOH, 1846).

Black within and black without,
Four corners round about.

Solution: an oven (*Notes & Queries*, 1865).

Black within and black without,
Three legs and an iron cap.

Solution: a porridge pot (*Notes & Queries*, 1865).

'Tis black without and black within,
and hath foure corners, as I win.

Solution: A dry turfe (*Booke of merrie Riddles*, 1631).

Richard Dick

439

Richard Dick upon a stick,
Sampson on a sow,
We'll ride away to Colley Fair
To buy a horse to plough.

The Scottish version is perhaps better known, even in England:

Cripple Dick upon a stick
Sandy on a soo,
Ride away to Galloway,
To buy a pund o' woo'.

This is considered an excellent jingle when astride a hobby horse, the ride to Galloway being equivalent to the Sassenach journey to Banbury Cross. Galloway has long been as renowned for its wool as Banbury is for its cakes. The suggestion has been made that the rhyme originally referred to border raiding.

Chambers, 1826, and JOH, 1842, as quote / Maclagan, 1900, '...Sawney on a sow, Ride awa' to Campbelton' / *Word Lore*, 1927.

Cf. *Word Lore*, 1927, from Suffolk, 'Dicky Death rode on an ass, Job Nunn he rode a sow. They are off to Bungay Fair To buy a calf and cow.' A nurse used to sing 'Thomas Rous has left his house With his good wife Ellene. They are off to Bungay Town, To be ground young again.' (A Suffolk saying is 'Go to Bungay and be ground young again'.)

440

A riddle, a riddle,
As I suppose;
A hundred eyes,
And never a nose.

RIDDLE. *Solution:* a sieve, or perhaps (if a pun is intended) a riddle.

JOH, 1842 / N & Q, 1865, 'Fifty eyes' / *Shropshire Folk-Lore*, C. S. Burne, 1883, 'Forty eyes' / *London Treasury of NR*, J. Murray MacBain, 1933, 'Full of eyes'.

441

Riddle me, riddle me ree,
A hawk sat up in a tree;

Riddle Me

And he says to himself, says he,
Lord! what a fine bird I be!

JOH, 1844 / *Mother Goose's NR*, L. E. Walter, 1924, slight variations.

442

Riddle me, riddle me ree,
A little man in a tree;
A stick in his hand,
A stone in his throat,
If you read me this riddle
I'll give you a groat.

Squirrel Nutkin in Beatrix Potter's tale 'bobbed up and down like a red *cherry*, singing,

Riddle me, riddle me, rot-tot-tote!
A little wee man, in a red red coat!
A staff in his hand, and a stone in his throat;
If you tell me this riddle, I'll give you a groat.'

A number of riddles have been based on the imagery of 'a stick in his hand, a stone in his throat', the solution being also given (1923) as the hawthorn berry. *Riddle me, riddle me ree:* expound my riddle rightly.

Holme MS, c. 1645, 'Hurble purple hath a red gurdle a stone in his belly a stake throw his a—& yet hurble purple is neur the worse' / Chambers, 1842 / JOH, 1842, 'As I went through the garden gap, Who should I meet but Dick Red-cap! A stick in his hand, a stone in his throat. If you'll tell me this riddle, I'll give you a groat' / N & Q, 1865 / Maclagan, 1901, 'Wee Willie red, wi' the red red coat, A staff in his hand, and a stone in his throat, Come a riddle, come a riddle, come a rot tot tot, Run boys run, run, fire at the gun' as formula for a running game / *Squirrel Nutkin*, 1903 / *Rymour Club*, 1911 / *Folk-Lore*, 1923, 'Down in the meadow there sits Pat, With a red petticoat and a black hat, A stick in his hand and a stone in his throat, You tell me this riddle I'll give you a groat' / Correspondent, 1949, 'Round the rick, Round the rick, There I met my Uncle Dick, A stick in his bum A stone in his belly, If you tell me his name I will give you a cherry.'
    Cf. The cherry motif is also found in Germany. *Das deutsche Kinderbuch*, Karl Simrock, 1848, 'Es sass eine Jungfrau auf dem Baum Hat ein rothes Röcklein an. Im Herzen war ein Stein: Rath, was mag das sein? (Kirsche)' / *Mecklenburgische Volksüberlieferungen*, R. Wossidlo, 1897.

Ring o' Roses

443

Ring-a-ring o' roses,
A pocket full of posies,
A-tishoo! A-tishoo!
We all fall down.

The words of this little ring-song seem to be becoming standardized though this was not so a hundred years ago when Lady Gomme was collecting (*ante* 1898). Of the twelve versions she gathered only one was similar to the above. Although 'Ring-a-ring o' roses' is now one of the most popular nursery games—the song which instantly rises from the lips of small children whenever they join hands in a circle—the words were not known to Halliwell, and have not been found in children's literature before 1881. Newell, however, says that,

Ring a ring a rosie,
A bottle full of posie,
All the girls in our town,
Ring for little Josie,

was current to the familiar tune in New Bedford, Massachusetts, about 1790. The 'A-tishoo' is notably absent here, as it is also in other versions he gives, in which the players squat or stoop rather than fall down:

Round the ring of roses,
Pots full of posies,
The one who stoops last
Shall tell whom she loves best.

The invariable sneezing and falling down in modern English versions has given would-be origin finders the opportunity to say that the rhyme dates back to the days of the Great Plague. A rosy rash, they allege, was a symptom of the plague, posies of herbs were carried as protection, sneezing was a final fatal symptom, and 'all fall down' was exactly what happened. It would be more delightful to recall the old belief that gifted children had the power to laugh roses (Grimm's *Deutsche Mythologie*). The foreign and nineteenth-century versions seem to show that the fall was originally a curtsy or other gracious movement of a ring game (see I. and P. Opie, *The Singing Game*). A sequel rhyme which enabled the players to rise to their feet again was in vogue in the 1940s:

The cows are in the meadow
Lying fast asleep,
A-tishoo! A-tishoo!
We all get up again.

PLATE XV

a. Kate Greenaway's *Mother Goose*, 1881

b. 'One, Two, Buckle my shoe', in Carvalho's *Juvenile Numerator*, c. 1825. Opie collection

Ring o' Roses

Lines similar to these last are also known to the Irish Celts.

Mother Goose, Kate Greenaway, 1881, 'Hush! hush! hush! hush! We're all tumbled down' / *Shropshire Folk-Lore*, C. S. Burne, 1883, 'One for Jack, and one for Jim, and one for little Moses—A-tisha! a-tisha! a-tisha!' also varia ending 'A curchey in, and a curchey out, And a curchey all together' / Newell, 1883, as quotes / *Sheffield Glossary*, S. O. Addy, 1888, varia / Gomme, 1898, varia including 'Ring a ring o' roses, A pocket-full o' posies; One for me, and one for you, And one for little Moses— Hasher, Hasher, Hasher, all fall down' / *Mother Goose*, Arthur Rackham, 1913 / *What the Children Sing*, Alfred Moffat, 1915, 'A ring, a ring o' roses, A pocket full of posies, Ash-a! Ash-a! All stand still. The King has sent his daughter To fetch a pail of water, Ash-a! Ash-a! All bow down. The bird above the steeple Sits high above the people, Ash-a! Ash-a! All kneel down. The wedding bells are ringing, And boys and girls are singing, Ash-a! Ash-a! All fall down' / Oral collection, 1947, as quote.

Cf. *Folk-lore*, 1882, 'Here we go round by ring, by ring, As ladies do in Yorkshire; A curtsey here, a curtsey there, A curtsey to the ground, sir' / *Das deutsche Kinderbuch*, Karl Simrock, 1848, 'Ringel, Ringel Reihe! Sind der Kinder dreie. Sitzen auf dem Holderbusch, Schreien alle musch musch musch: Sitzt nieder! Sitzt ne Frau im Ringelein, Mit sieben kleinen Kinderlein. Was essens gerne? Fischlein. Was trinkens gerne? Rothen Wein. Sitzt nieder!', also rhyme beginning 'Ringel Ringel Rosenkranz' / *Alemannisches Kinderlied*, E. L. Rochholz, 1857 / *Reime der Kinder in Oesterreich*, T. Vernaleben, 1873 / *Chants Populaire du Languedoc*, L. Lambert, 1906, 'Branle, calandre, La Fille d'Alexandre, La pêche bien mûre, La figue bien mûre, Le rosier tout fleuri, Coucou toupi!—En disant "coucou toupi", tous les enfants, qui forment la ronde, s'accroupissent' / *American Folk Lore*, 1897, Swiss, 'Randin, picotin, La Marie a fait son pain, Pas plus gros que son levain. Pugh! dans l'eau.' Last one down is *it* / *Children's Games throughout the Year*, L. Daiken, 1949, from County Donegal, 'Here we go round the Jingo Ring, Jingo Ring, Jingo Ring, Here we go round the Jingo Ring And the last pops down!' Also cf. the Gaelic 'Bulla! Bulla! Baisín, Ta'n bo sa gùirdín. Síos libh! !Síos libh! Éirigidh anois, Éirigidh! Déanam arís é. (Clap! Clap! Hands, The cow is in the garden. Down ye go! Down ye go! Get up now, get up! Let's do it again.)'

Parody: *The Observer*, 9 Jan. 1949, 'Ring-a-ring-o'-geranium, A pocket full of uranium, Hiro, shima, All fall down!'

444

Robert Barnes, fellow fine,
Can you shoe this horse of mine?
Yes, good sir, that I can,
As well as any other man.
There's a nail, and there's a prod,
And now, good sir, your horse is shod.

This rhyme is heard particularly in Scotland and the north country. A prod is an iron pin used in making patterns. A version recorded in 1881 gives details about the nails:

Robert Barnes

Pit a bit upo' the tae,
T' gar the horsie clim' the brae;
Pit a bit upo' the brod,
T' gar the horsie clim' the road;
Pit a bit upo' the heel,
T' gar the horsie trot weel.

More than twenty variants were collected in *Folk-Lore* (1884 and 1886), the name 'John Smith' (q.v.) being a frequent alternative. One writer said it was 'generally repeated to children who resisted having their clogs put on'. It is also used for knee-bouncing and for a game with the feet, and Bolton says that in Georgia it is used for counting-out. JOH (1849) gives a Danish version which is somewhat akin.

T Thumb's PSB, c. 1744, 'Blow Bobby Blow, Can you make a Horshoe Yes Master that I can, As well as any Little Man' / *Songs for the Nursery*, 1805 / *Vocal Harmony*, c. 1806 / *Poetic Trifles* (J. G. Rusher), c. 1840, 'Is John Smith within? Yes, Mister Griffin' / Chambers, 1842 / *Only True MG Melodies*, c. 1843, 'Robert Barnes, fellow fine, Can you shoe this horse of mine, So that I may cut a shine?...' / *Folk-Lore of N.E. Scotland*, W. Gregor, 1881 / *Folk-Lore*, 1884 and 1886 / Bolton, 1888, 'Blacksmith very fine, Can you shoe this horse of mine? Yes, master, that I can, As well as any other man. Bring the mare before the stall, One nail drives all. Whip Jack, spur Tom, Blow the bellows good old man' / *Tailor of Gloucester*, Beatrix Potter (p.p. ed.), 1902 / Correspondents, 1946, several variants.

Cf. JOH, 1849, 'Skoe min hest! Hvem kan bedst? Det kan vor Praest! Nei maen kan han ej! For det kan vor smed, Som boer ved Leed.' (Shoe my horse! Who can best? Why, our priest! Not he, indeed! But our smith can, He lives at Leed.)

445

Robert Rowley rolled a round roll round,
A round roll Robert Rowley rolled round;
Where rolled the round roll Robert Rowley rolled round?

Tongue twister. Also, in past times, considered to be a remedy for hiccups when repeated thrice in one breath.

Girl's Own Book, Mrs. Child, 1831 [1832] / *NR from the Royal Collections* (J. G. Rusher), c. 1840 / JOH, 1842 / *Games for Family Parties*, Mrs. Valentine, 1869, for repeating as a forfeit.

446

Robin and Richard
Were two pretty men,

Robin

They lay in bed
   Till the clock struck ten
Then up starts Robin
   And looks at the sky,
Oh, brother Richard,
   The sun's very high.
You go before
   With the bottle and bag,
And I will come after
   On little Jack Nag.

In *Mr. Sponge's Sporting Tour* (1849) this was one of Gustavus James's rhymes, to which the unfortunate Mr. Sponge had to listen. At Mrs. Jogglebury's behest the child recited:

Obin and Ichard, two pretty men,
Lay in bed till 'e clock struck ten;
Up starts Obin, and looks at the sky—

And then the brat stopped.

'"Very beautiful!" exclaimed Mr. Sponge; "very beautiful! One of Moore's, isn't it? Thank you, my little dear, thank you," added he, chucking him under the chin, and putting on his hat to be off.'

'"O, but stop, Mr. Sponge!" exclaimed Mrs. Jogglebury, "you haven't heard it all—there's more yet." '

MG's Melody, c. 1765 / *GG's Garland*, 1784 / *Christmas Box*, vol. iii, 1798 / *Songs for the Nursery*, 1805; 1818, 'Alfred and Richard' / *Nurse Lovechild's DFN*, c. 1830, 'Robin and Richard were two lazy men' / JOH, 1842, additional couplet, 'You go first, and open the gate, And I'll come after and break your pate' / *Mr. Sponge's Sporting Tour*, R. S. Surtees, 1849.

447

We will go to the wood, says Robin to Bobbin,
We will go to the wood, says Richard to Robin,
We will go to the wood, says John all alone,
We will go to the wood, says everyone.

What to do there? says Robin to Bobbin,
What to do there? says Richard to Robin,
What to do there? says John all alone,
What to do there? says everyone.

Robin

We'll shoot at a wren, says Robin to Bobbin,
We'll shoot at a wren, says Richard to Robin,
We'll shoot at a wren, says John all alone,
We'll shoot at a wren, says everyone.

She's down, she's down, says Robin to Bobbin,
She's down, she's down, says Richard to Robin,
She's down, she's down, says John all alone,
She's down, she's down, says everyone.

Then pounce, then pounce, says Robin to Bobbin,
Then pounce, then pounce, says Richard to Robin,
Then pounce, then pounce, says John all alone,
Then pounce, then pounce, says everyone.

She is dead, she is dead, says Robin to Bobbin,
She is dead, she is dead, says Richard to Robin,
She is dead, she is dead, says John all alone,
She is dead, she is dead, says everyone.

How get her home? says Robin to Bobbin,
How get her home? says Richard to Robin,
How get her home? says John all alone,
How get her home? says everyone.

In a cart with six horses, says Robin to Bobbin,
In a cart with six horses, says Richard to Robin,
In a cart with six horses, says John all alone,
In a cart with six horses, says everyone.

Then hoist, boys, hoist, says Robin to Bobbin,
Then hoist, boys, hoist, says Richard to Robin,
Then hoist, boys, hoist, says John all alone,
Then hoist, boys, hoist, says everyone.

How shall we dress her? says Robin to Bobbin,
How shall we dress her? says Richard to Robin,
How shall we dress her? says John all alone,
How shall we dress her? says everyone.

We'll hire seven cooks, says Robin to Bobbin,
We'll hire seven cooks, says Richard to Robin,
We'll hire seven cooks, says John all alone,
We'll hire seven cooks, says everyone.

Robin

How shall we boil her? says Robin to Bobbin,
How shall we boil her? says Richard to Robin,
How shall we boil her? says John all alone,
How shall we boil her? says everyone.

In the brewer's big pan, says Robin to Bobbin,
In the brewer's big pan, says Richard to Robin,
In the brewer's big pan, says John all alone.
In the brewer's big pan, says everyone.

A folk-chant of considerable curiosity, which was embodied in nursery
rhyme books at an early date. It appears to be indigenous to all four kingdoms, and is likely to be exceptionally old. In Ireland the characters have
been recorded as 'O, Andhra Roe, Brothers-in-Three, and the Kriggera-
wee'; in Wales, 'Dibyn, Dobyn, Risiart, Robin, John, a y tri'; in Scotland,
'Fozie Mozie, Johnie Rednosie, Foslin 'ene, and brither and kin'. A point
common to all accounts of the hunt is the vast size of the quarry, doubts
are expressed about the adequacy of the weapons, bows and arrows 'will
not do', it must be 'great guns and cannon' (1927); there is a conference
about how to bring the body home, and after a cart has been obtained,
the lowland Scots ask 'What way will ye get her in?' They needs must
'drive down the door-cheeks' (1776). The dinner that the little bird's car-
cass will provide is such that the Manx would invite 'King and Queen'
and yet have enough over to give 'eyes to the blind, legs to the lame,
and pluck to the poor'; while in some versions of the rhyme methods of
disposing of the bones also engage discussion. The hunting of the wren
on Christmas morning (latterly on St. Stephen's Day) has been described
by many folk-lore writers, from the time of Aubrey (1696), who tells of 'a
whole Parish running like madmen from Hedg to Hedg a Wren-hunting',
down to modern times (*The Times*, 24 December 1963). The rhyme was
chanted in the ceremonial procession after the kill had been made. Stories
differ about why it should be the wren which is singled out for slaughter.
Those legends having purely local significance may be disregarded. The
wren has been looked upon as the king of birds in many countries, and
the Druids are said to have represented it as such. The story, quoted in *Collectanea de rebus Hibernicis* (1786), that the first Christian missionaries took
offence at the respect shown to the wren, and commanded that it be
hunted and killed on Christmas Day, has certainly a long tradition. Sir
James Frazer, however, suggests looking even deeper than this (*Golden
Bough*, pt. V). On the other hand the song may be part of a European tradition of comic songs about hunting a ridiculously small quarry. There is
an accumulative song on the partition of a wren in Luzel's *Chansons populaires de la Basse-Bretagne*, and another in *Chants et Chansons du Languedoc*,
L. Lambert, vol. i ('The king's son has gone hunting, He has killed a great
bird, It took six to lift it up, It took at least seven to carry it, It took at least

Robin

eight to pluck it, It took at least nine to prepare it, Twelve men to eat it. The cat came and took it away...'). In Flanders and the Netherlands the hunters go down to the sea to catch a mole, from which a purse is made, in which money is kept, to buy a child, who is sent to school to learn his ABC (C. E. Coussemaker, *Chants populaires des Flamands de France*; *Kinderspel in Zuid-Nederland*, A. De Cock & I. Teirlinck, vol. ii).

T Thumb's PSB, c. 1744, verses 1, 3, 4, 7, 8 ('We will hire a cart'), 9, and 'She's up, she's up' / Herd MS, 1776, eight verses (as Scottish quotes) / *GG's Garland*, 1784, commences 'We'll go a shooting... What shall we kill... We'll shoot at the wren', eight verses in all / *T Thumb's SB*, 1788, as c. 1744 / *T Tit's SB*, c. 1790, as 1784 / *Songs for the Nursery*, 1805, verses, 1, 2, 3, 5, 6, 7, 8, 10, and 11 / British Museum MS Adds. 29408, Peter Buchan, c. 1828, 'Where are ye gain? quoth Hose to Mose... Johnny Rednose... bretheren three, To shoot the wren, quo' Wise Willie', three verses. Other versions appear in JOH, 1842 (English and Manx); Mason, 1877; *Oriau'r Haf*, Ceiriog (Englished by Jennett Humphreys in *Old Welsh Knee Songs*, 1894); *Viking Society Miscellany*, 1908, given as an Orkney lullaby, tune recognized as dating at least from 1567 [Gosset]; *Welsh Folk Song Society*, 1911; *Folk-Song*, 1914; Williams, 1923, 'Richat, Robet, Bobet and John in the Long'; *Word-Lore*, 1927 and 1928, 'Robin the Bobbin' (cf. No. 449), also 'Milder and Malder, Fested and Fose, and John the Red Nose' from South Wales / Several correspondents, 1946, including Yorkshire and Irish versions.

448

Pit, pat, well-a-day,
Little Robin flew away;
Where can little Robin be?
Gone into the cherry tree.

JOH, 1846.

449

Robin-a-bobbin
He bent his bow,
Shot at a pigeon
And killed a crow;
Shot at another
And killed his own brother,
Did Robin-a-bobbin
Who bent his bow.

Interest attaches particularly to a version collected in 1892 which mentions a wren. Here again is the association of 'Robin a Bobbin', 'Robin

Robin-a-bobbin

the Bobbin' or 'Robin and Bobbin' (qq.v.) with the bird and with hunting. 'To shoot at a pigeon and kill a crow' is an expression dating at least from 1639 and still in use (e.g. the Home Secretary in the House of Commons, 24 January 1946, and Winston Churchill, 17 November 1949).

New Year's Gift (J. Catnach), c. 1830, four lines, 'All of a row, Bend the bow, Shot at a pigeon And killed a crow' [Hindley, 1878]; as also *London Jingles* (J. G. Rusher), c. 1840 / *NR, Tales and Jingles*, 1844 / JOH, 1853, 'Robbin-a-Bobbin bent his bow, And shot at a woodcock and kill'd a yowe: The yowe cried ba, and he ran away, But never came back 'till midsummer-day', also as text / Northall, 1892, 'All of a row, a bendy bow, Shoot at a pigeon, and kill a crow, Shoot at another, and kill his brother, Shoot again, and kill a wren, And that will do for gentlemen'. Given as chant for a follow-my-leader game.

450

Robin Hood, Robin Hood,
Is in the mickle wood;
Little John, Little John,
He to the town is gone.

Robin Hood, Robin Hood,
Is telling his beads,
All in the green wood,
Among the green weeds.

Little John, Little John,
If he comes no more,
Robin Hood, Robin Hood,
He will fret full sore.

Probably a fragment of one of the multitude of ballads and songs there have been telling of the heroic deeds of Robin Hood and his merry men. The circulation of Robin Hood 'rymes' is attested by William Langland in 1377.

JOH, 1842 / *Land of NR*, Ernest Rhys, 1932 / *Big Book of Mother Goose* (James and Jonathan Co., Wisconsin), 1946.

451

Little Robin Redbreast
Came to visit me;

Robin Redbreast

This is what he whistled,
Thank you for my tea.

Oral collection, 1947.

452

Little Robin Redbreast
Sat upon a rail;
Niddle noddle went his head,
Wiggle waggle went his tail.

Early recordings show that this rhyme was originally a rude little jest. Latterday editors have shown ingenuity in making it suitable for their collections.

T Thumb's PSB, c. 1744, 'Little Robin red breast, Sitting on a pole, Niddle, Noddle, Went his head. And Poop went his Hole' / Similarly in *Death and Burial of Cock Robin* (R. Marshall), c. 1770; *Nancy Cock's PSB*, c. 1780 / *T Thumb's SB*, 1788; *T Tit's SB*, c. 1790 / *Newest Christmas Box*, c. 1797 / *Death and Burial*...(M. Morgan), c. 1797, 'wag went his tail' / *Cock Robin* (G. Ross), 1815, 'Little Robin Red-breast, Sat upon a pole, Wiggle waggle went his tail Which made him look quite droll' / *Death and Burial*...(T. Richardson), c. 1830, 'Little Robin Redbreast Sat upon a tree; He noddl'd with his head, And warbl'd merrily' / JOH, 1843, as text / JOH, 1853, 'Little Robin Redbreast, Sat upon a hirdle; With a pair of speckled legs, And a green girdle' / Correspondent, 1950, an interesting survival of the 18th-century version learnt from a nanny, 'Little Robin Red-breast sat upon a pole, Wiggle waggle went his tail, pop! through the hole'.

453

Little Robin Redbreast sat upon a tree,
Up went pussy cat, and down went he;
Down came pussy, and away Robin ran;
Says little Robin Redbreast, Catch me if you can.
Little Robin Redbreast jumped upon a wall,
Pussy cat jumped after him, and almost got a fall;
Little Robin chirped and sang, and what did pussy say?
Pussy cat said, Mew, and Robin jumped away.

Robin Redbreast

Little Robin Redbreast sat upon a tree, 'A Song for the Nursery with an accompaniment for the Pianoforte by Robert Birchell' (Musical Circulating Library), c. 1800, sheet music, as text but with repetitive lines / *Songs for the Nursery*, 1805 / *London Jingles* (J. G. Rusher), c. 1840, less third couplet / *Traditional Nursery Songs*, Felix Summerly, 1843 / *Nursery Ditties* (J. T. Wood), c. 1850 / JOH, 1853 / Correspondent, 1946 / *Little Robin Redbreast*, illus. Shari Halpern, 1994.

454

Robin the Bobbin, the big-bellied Ben,
He ate more meat than fourscore men;
He ate a cow, he ate a calf,
He ate a butcher and a half,
He ate a church, he ate a steeple,
He ate the priest and all the people!
   A cow and a calf,
   An ox and a half,
   A church and a steeple,
   And all the good people,
And yet he complained that his stomach wasn't full.

A correspondent to *Notes & Queries* (1904), remembering the rhyme from sixty years before, recalled that it was popularly supposed to have reference to the 'rapacious nature of Henry VIII in seizing on Church estates'. This belief has been expressed several times (e.g. by Kathleen Thomas in *Real Personages of Mother Goose*) but the fact that in some of the versions two characters are named tends to weigh against it. Eckenstein compares the rhyme with 'We will go to the wood, says Robin to Bobbin' (q.v.) and there may be connexion in that a great stomach capacity would be essential for devouring a wren so gigantic that a cart had to be hired to bring it home.

T Thumb's PSB, c. 1744, first two lines only, 'Robin and Bobbin, Two great belly'd men, They ate more victuals Than threescore men' / *Nancy Cock's PSB*, c. 1780, begins 'Robbin-a-bobbin, A-Bilberry-hen' / *GG's Garland*, 1784, begins 'Robin the Robin the big bellied hen' / *T Thumb's SB*, 1788 / *T Tit's SB*, c. 1790 / *Christmas Box*, vol. ii, 1798, as c. 1780 / *Songs for the Nursery*, 1805 / *Vocal Harmony*, c. 1806 / NR (T. Richardson), c. 1830 / JOH, 1842 / Maclagan, 1901, 'Robert the Parbet, the big-bellied man, Could eat as much as three score and ten; He ate the cow, he ate the calf, He ate the minister off his staff, He licked the ladle, he swallowed the spune, And wasna fu' when a' was done' / *Rymour Club*, 1911, 'Andrew, ca'ed Anro, The laird o' Kinap, Suppit his sowans out o' his caup. He swallowed the Kirk, he swallowed the Queir, He swallowed the minister's auld grey mear.'

455

Poor old Robinson Crusoe!
Poor old Robinson Crusoe!
They made him a coat,
Of an old nanny goat,
   I wonder how they could do so!
With a ring a ting tang,
And a ring a ting tang,
   Poor old Robinson Crusoe!

Jack Cussans, vagabond and singer of the late eighteenth century, wrote the following version for his own use to a tune from *Robinson Crusoe, or Harlequin Friday* which was staged at Drury Lane in 1781:

When I was a lad,
I had cause to be sad,
My grandfather I did lose O;
I'll bet you a can
You've heard of the man,
His name it was Robinson Crusoe.

There were nine more verses, each with the refrain,

O Robinson Crusoe,
O poor Robinson Crusoe!
Tink a tink tang,
Tink a tink tang,
O poor Robinson Crusoe!

It was later (c. 1809) sung by Russell in the character of Jerry Sneak, in the revival of Foote's farce, *The Mayor of Garret.*

Oh, poor Robinson Crusoe, 'A favourite Comic Chaunt written and sung by Mr. Cussans at the Royal Circus and Sadler's Wells with universal applause' (E. Bates), 1797, sheet music [*N & Q*, 1869] / *No. III of the Newcastle Songster; or Tyne Minstrel* (David Bass), 1806 / *The Songster's Multum in Parvo* (John Fairburn), 1809 / *Universal Songster,* 1825 / *Robinson Crusoe* (no imprint) n.d. [*Massachusetts Broadsides,* 1922] / JOH, 1842 / *Our Familiar Songs,* H. K. Johnson, 1881 / Kidson, 1904 / *Mother Goose,* Arthur Rackham, 1913.

456

Young Roger came tapping at Dolly's window,
Thumpaty, thumpaty, thump.

Roger

He begged for admittance, she answered him, No,
    Glumpaty, glumpaty, glump.
My Dolly, my dear, your true love is here,
    Dumpaty, dumpaty, dump.
No, no, Roger, no, as you come you may go,
    Stumpaty, stumpaty, stump.

In Daniel Bellamy's farce *The Rival Priests: or, the Female politician* (1739), the fifth song, beginning 'Ah! turn, my dear Nacky, and see your poor Slave, Mumpetey, mumpety, mump', was directed to be sung to the air 'Roger's Courtship'. The song must already have been well known at that time.

Tea-table Miscellany, Allan Ramsay, 1740, version continues 'Oh what is the reason, dear Dolly, he cry'd, Humpaty &c., That thus I'm cast off, and unkindly deny'd, Trumpaty, &c. Some rival more dear, I guess has been here, Crumpaty, &c. Suppose there's been two, Sir, pray what's that to you? Numpaty, &c.' Upon which (in two more verses) Roger jumps into a brook and Dolly dies an old maid / *Philomel* (M. Cooper), 1744 / *The Robin*, 1749 / JOH, 1844.
    Cf. the rhythm of 'A farmer went trotting upon his grey mare'.

457

The rose is red, the grass is green,
Serve Queen Bess our noble queen!
    Kitty the spinner
    Will sit down to dinner,
And eat the leg of a frog:
    All you good people
    Look over the steeple,
And see the cat play with the dog.

'The rose is red, the leaves are green, God save Elizabeth our Queen' was a favourite couplet in the days of the first Queen Elizabeth. Throughout the pages of his copy of *Caesar* (now in Brasenose College Library, Oxford) a Westminster schoolboy wrote, in 1589, a long verse of ownership which ends: 'The rose is redd—the leves—are grene, God save—Elizabeth—our noble—Quene.' The couplet also appears round the rim of a plate dated 1600 in the London Museum. JOH says the tune may be found in the *English Dancing Master* (1651), but the title 'The rose is white, the rose is red' may equally refer to several other songs. Abbreviated versions of the rhyme are sometimes addressed to the spider, or, as 'Jenny good spinner', to the daddy-long-legs.

Douce MS, c. 1805, 'Serve King George our noble king'. Douce says 'I am indebted [for this] to my pretty little Sister Emily Corry, 1795' / *GG's Garland*, 1810 / *Cinderella* (Henry Mozley and Sons), c. 1825, short version beginning 'Jenny, good spinner' / Chambers, 1842, part of a conglomeration, 'The rose is red, the leaves are green, The days are past that I have seen! Jenny, good spinner, Come down to your dinner, And taste the leg of a roasted frog! I pray ye, good people, Look owre the kirk-steeple, And see the cat play wi' the dog!' / JOH, 1842 / *Cries of Banbury and London* (J. G. Rusher), c. 1843, short version 'Come, Jenny, good spinner, Come down, to your dinner, And taste the leg of a fly; Then all you good people Look near the church steeple, And see a good boy who don't cry' / Bolton, 1888, two corrupted versions / *Siamsa an Geimridh*, O'Flaherty, 1892, 'Mrs. Fitzhenry, I invite you to dinner, To eat a piece of roasted frog . . .' [L. Daiken, 1949].

458

The rose is red, the violet blue,
The gillyflower sweet, and so are you.
These are the words you bade me say
For a pair of new gloves on Easter day.

One of several pleasant Valentine rhymes remembered in the nursery. Gloves, which have always possessed a strong social significance, were a customary compliment or 'forfeit' gift between lovers. Claudio sent Hero a pair of perfumed gloves in *Much Ado About Nothing*. Gay, in *The Shepherd's Week*, and Scott, in *The Fair Maid of Perth*, tell how the maiden who ventures to kiss a sleeping man wins from him a pair of gloves.

GG's Garland, 1784, 'The rose is red, the violet's blue, The honey's sweet, and so are you. Thou art my love and I am thine; I drew thee to my Valentine: The lot was cast and then I drew, And fortune said it shou'd be you' / *Songs for the Nursery*, 1805 / *MG's Quarto*, c. 1825 / JOH, 1849, 'Sugar is sweet' / Crofton MS, 1901, 'The Rose is red, the Rose is white, The Rose is in my garden, I would not part with my sweetheart, For tuppence ha'penny farden.' Also sung as part of a May Song, Oxford, 1886 / *New Yorker*, 13 Nov. 1937, sidewalk rhymes of New York children, 'Roses are red, violets are blue, I like pecans, Nuts to you.'

459

Round about, round about,
Maggotty pie;
My father loves good ale,
And so do I.

Round About

MG's Melody, c. 1765 / *GG's Garland*, 1784 / *T Thumb's SB*, 1788 / *Vocal Harmony*, c. 1806 / *Nursery Songs* (G. Ross), c. 1812, 'My father loves strong beer' / *GG's Garland* (Lumsden), c. 1815 / *Chatterings of the Pica*, Charles Taylor, 1820, 'Here we go, there we go, Maggoty pie'; 'This is said while they [children] join each other's hands, and go round about as if they were dancing steps in a reel' / Douce MS II, c. 1820 / *MG's Quarto*, c. 1825, 'Round about, round about, Gooseberry Pie' / *NR for Children* (J. Fairburn), c. 1825 / JOH, 1842 / *Mill Hill Magazine*, 1877 / Correspondents, 1946 and 1949, 'Round about, round about, applety pie, Baby loves good ale and so do I. Up! mother, up! and fill us a cup, And baby and I will sup it all up.'

*** *Maggotty pie*, 16th- and 17th-century word for magpie, now retained only in dialect.

460

> Rub-a-dub-dub,
> Three men in a tub,
> And how do you think they got there?
> The butcher, the baker,
> The candlestick-maker,
> They all jumped out of a rotten potato,
> 'Twas enough to make a man stare.

It is questionable whether the harmless antics currently attributed to these three characters are the original. In the earliest recordings the rhyme goes:

> Hey! rub-a-dub, ho! rub-a-dub, three maids in a tub,
> And who do you think were there?
> The butcher, the baker, the candlestick-maker,
> And all of them gone to the fair.

This shows the three tradesmen in a very different light. Apparently they have been found in a place where no respectable townsfolk should be found, watching a dubious side-show at the local fair.

Christmas Box, vol. ii, 1798, similar to quote / *MG's Quarto*, c. 1825, as quote / *Nurse Lovechild's DFN*, c. 1830, 'The Brewer, the Baker, The Candle-stick maker, All fell out of a mealy potato' / JOH, 1842 / *Cries of Banbury and London* (J. G. Rusher), c. 1843 / *NR, Tales and Jingles*, 1844 / JOH, 1846, 'And who do you think they be . . . Turn 'em out, knaves all three' / *Mill Hill Magazine*, 1877.

Cf. Northall, 1892, for swinging, 'Rub-a-dub-dub. Three men in a tub, The brewer, the baker, the candlestick-maker, They all sprung out of a rotten potato. An apple for the king, a pear for the queen, And a good toss over the bowling-green. The bowling-green it was so high, It nearly toss'd me over the sky, Sky—sky—Let the cat die.'

461

Rumpty-iddity, row, row, row,
If I had a good supper, I could eat it now.

This rousing ditty has been in existence for some time. It is found as the chorus to Queen Dollalolla's drinking song, in the version of Fielding's burlesque drama *Tom Thumb* 'now performed at the Theatres Royal, Hay-market and Covent-Garden' (1810) (*Fairburn's Complete Edition*): 'Rum ti iddity, row, row, row, If we'd a good sup, we'd take it now.'

JOH, 1844.

462

As I was going to St. Ives,
I met a man with seven wives,
Each wife had seven sacks,
Each sack had seven cats,
Each cat had seven kits:
Kits, cats, sacks, and wives,
How many were there going to St. Ives?

CATCH. The solution is 'one' or 'none' according to how the question is read. If the question is as plainly put as it was by a writer more than 200 years ago, 'Qu: How many Wives, Sacs, Cats and Kittens went to St. Ives?' the answer is clearly 'none'. The formula seems to have been, in ancient times, a straightforward mathematical exercise. When the 'Rhind Mathematical Papyrus' of c. 1600–1800 BC was deciphered in the early 1920s it was found to contain some familiar phraseology: 'In a village there are seven houses, and each house has seven cats, and each cat kills seven mice, and each mouse would have eaten seven grains of corn, and each grain of corn would have produced seven hekats. What is the total of all these?' In a Latin version of c. 1200, the *Liber Abacus* of Leonardo Pisano, seven men went to Rome: each man had seven donkeys, each donkey carried seven sacks, each sack contained seven loaves of bread, in each loaf were seven knives, and each knife had seven sheaths. See *Folklore* (summer 1975).

Harley MS 7316, c. 1730, 'As I went to St. Ives I met Nine Wives And every Wife had nine Sacs And every Sac had nine Cats And every Cat had Nine Kittens' / *Child's New Play-thing*, 4th edn., 1745 / *Mother Chit-Chat's Curious Tales and Puzzles*, 1798 / *MG's Quarto*, c. 1825 / *Girl's Book of Diversions*, Miss Leslie, c. 1835 / JOH, 1842 / *N & Q*, 1865 and 1866 / *Nicola Bayley's Book of Nursery Rhymes*, 1975.

St. Ives

Cf. *Mecklenburgische Volksüberlieferungen*, R. Wossidlo, 1897, 'Güng'n mann na Teterow, dor begegneten em nägen wiwer, jedes wief hadd'n sack up'n nacken, in jeden sack wiren nägen katten, jede katt hadd nägen jungen, wöval güngen na Teterow?—Blos de mann' / *American Folk-Lore*, 1906, Pennsylvania German, 'En Mühl hat sieve Ecke, Im jederem Eck stehne sieve Säck, Uf jederm Säck hocke sieve Katze, Un jeder Katz hat sieve junge. Dann komm der Müller un sie Frau noch in die Mühl. Wei veil Füss sin noh drim?—Vier Füss, es anner sin Dobe.'

463

> When I went up Sandy-Hill,
> I met a sandy-boy;
> I cut his throat, I sucked his blood,
> And left his skin a-hanging-o.

RIDDLE. JOH (1842) volunteered no solution, but when orally collected in 1947 (last line 'And threw his body by') the solution was, 'of course', an orange. The actions of killing a person, drinking his blood, and throwing away his body are applicable to all kinds of fruit; see A. Taylor, *English Riddles* (pp. 293–7).

464

> On Saturday night shall be my care
> To powder my locks and curl my hair;
> On Sunday morning my love will come in,
> When he will marry me with a gold ring.

In Mrs. Centlivre's comedy *The Platonick Lady* (1707), Mrs. Dowdy sings 'A Country Song':

> As I walk'd forth one May Morning,
> I heard a pretty Maid sweetly Sing
> As she sat under the Cow a Milking,
>   Sing I shall be Marry'd a *Tuesday*;
>   I mun look Smug upon *Tuesday*.
>
> I prithee Sweet-heart what makes thee to Marry,
> Is your Maiden-hood grown a Burthen to carry?
> Or are you afraid that you shall Miscarry?
>   I prithee now tarry till *Wednesday*.
>
> I pray good Sir, don't wish me such ill,
> I have kept it these Seven Years against my own Will;

449

Saturday Night

I have made a Vow, and I will it fulfil,
  That I will be Marry'd on *Tuesday*,
  So I mun look Smug upon *Tuesday*.

A Tuesday Morn it will be all my care,
To pouder my Locks and to curl up my Hair,
And two pretty Maids for to wait on me there;
  So I mun look Smug upon *Tuesday*,
  So Fine and so Smug upon *Tuesday*.

Then two Young Men to the Church will me bring,
Where my Husband will give me a gay Gold Ring;
But at Night he will give me a far better thing;
  So I mun look Smug upon *Tuesday*,
  So Fine and so Smug upon *Tuesday*.

'Smug' meant 'smart' at that time. Cecil Sharp collected recognizably the same song, with all five verses, in Somerset in 1903. A tune named 'I mun be marry'd a Tuesday' appeared in Walsh's *Twenty-four New Country Dances* for 1708, and again in *The Second Book of the Country Dancing Master* (1719). In *The Village Opera* (1729) the air is entitled 'I mun snug up on Tuesday, &c.'

Songs for the Nursery, 1805 / *MG's Quarto*, c. 1825, 'Saturday night shall be my whole care' / JOH, 1844 / *I shall be married on Monday morning* (Williamson), c. 1850 / *Folk-Lore of Women*, T. Thistleton Dyer, 1905 / *Folk-Song*, 1905, as quote, and 1931.

465

A diller, a dollar,
A ten o'clock scholar,
What makes you come so soon?
You used to come at ten o'clock,
But now you come at noon.

Exactly what 'a diller, a dollar' signifies is undetermined. Crofton suggests diller and dollar are shortened forms of dilatory and dullard. It may be that they are connected with dilly-dally. Or again, diller is a Yorkshire word for a school-boy who is dull and stupid at learning.

GG's Garland, 1784 / *Nurse Lovechild's DFN*, c. 1830 / *Boy's Country Book*, William Howitt, 1839 / JOH, 1842 / *Mother Goose*, Kate Greenaway, 1881 / *Jolly Jump-Ups* (McLoughlin Bros., Springfield, Mass.), c. 1947.

Sea

466

If all the seas were one sea,
What a *great* sea that would be!
If all the trees were one tree,
What a *great* tree that would be!
And if all the axes were one axe,
What a *great* axe that would be!
And if all the men were one man,
What a *great* man that would be!
And if the *great* man took the *great* axe,
And cut down the *great* tree,
And let it fall into the *great* sea,
What a splish-splash that would be!

It is said of Rowland Hill (1744–1833), the great preacher, that two strangers passing the church in which he was preaching, entered, walked up the aisle, and finding no seat, stood for a while and listened to the sermon. Presently they turned to walk out. Before they reached the door the preacher said, 'But I will tell you a story'. This arrested the strangers, and they paused, turned again and listened. 'Once there was a man,' said the speaker, 'who said that if he had all the axes in the world made into one great axe, and all the trees in the world were made into one great tree, and he could wield the axe and cut down the tree, he would make it into one great whip to thrash those ungodly men who turn their backs upon the Gospel, and stop to hear a story.'

JOH, 1842 / *Leicestershire Words*, A. B. and S. Evans, 1881, 'a rebuke to fanciful folk: If all the trees were wan tree, And this here tree was to fall into that there sea, Moy, surs! what a splish-splosh there'd be!'

467

See, see! what shall I see?
A horse's head where his tail should be.

This enigma becomes clearer when seen in its original context:

There was a sight near Charing-Cross,
A Creature almost like a Horse;
But when I came this Beast to see,
The Head was where the Tail should be.

See, See!

Answer: 'It was a Mare with her Tail ty'd to the Manger.' For a long time 'The Wonderful Horse, With His Head Where His Tail Ought To Be' was a popular side-show at fairs. Those who paid their money to see the wonder do not seem to have resented the trick, but to have persuaded their friends to see it too.

Child's Weeks-work, William Ronksley, 1712, and *True Trial of Understanding*, S. M., c. 1765, old version / JOH, 1842 / *Mother Goose* (T. Nelson), c. 1945 / Correspondent, 1956, There was a man who went to the fair, He bought three horses and one was a mare; One was blind and one couldn't see, And t'other had its head where its tail should be.

468

See-saw, down in my lap,
　Up again on to her feet;
Little girl lost her white cap,
　Blown away in the street.

Apparently an energetic knee rhyme.

MG's Quarto, c. 1825.

469

Thirty days hath September,
April, June, and November;
All the rest have thirty-one,
Excepting February alone,
And that has twenty-eight days clear
And twenty-nine in each leap year.

The best-known mnemonic rhyme in the language—probably through its inclusion in the canons of the nursery. It appears in most nursery rhyme books subsequent to 1825. Versions of this 'rule to knowe how many dayes euery moneth in the yere hath' are cited by several Elizabethan writers, and, as JOH says, 'our own reminiscences of such matters, and those of Shakespeare, may thus have been identical'. Concerning its origin, Arthur Hopton, 'the miracle of his age for learning', writing in 1612, says the 'ordination of yᵉ moneths, and position of dayes, is vsed to this present time, according to these verses:

September

Sep. No. Iun. Ap. dato triginta: reliquis magis vno:
Ni sit bissextus, februus minor esto duobus.

Which is:

> Thirtie daies hath September,
> Aprill, June, and November;
> The rest haue thirty and one,
> Saue February alone.
> Which moneth hath but eight and twenty meere,
> Saue when it is Bissextile or Leape-yeare.'

William Harrison (1577) gives,

> Thirty dayes hath Nouember,
> Aprill, Iune and September;
> Twentie and eyght hath February alone,
> And all the rest thirty and one,
> But in the leape you must adde one.

as an English version of the Latin hexameters,

> Iunius, Aprilis, Septemq;, Nouemq; tricenos
> vnū plus reliqui, Febru' tenet octo vicenos;
> At si bissextus fuerit super additur vnus.

Whether or not the Latin is older than the French poem *De Computo*, written in the thirteenth century, is impossible to say:

> En avril, en juing, en septembre
> A .xxx. jours et en novembre:
> Tout li autre ont .xxxj. jour,
> Fors fevriers qi est li plus cour,
> En soi que .xxviij. jors n'a,
> Ne plus ne meins n'i avra ja
> Fors en l'an qe bissextres vient,
> Adont en a, einsi avient,
> .xxix., de tant est creüs,
> L'an que bixestres est cheüs.

Another juvenile way of discovering the number of days in a month is along the knuckles of the hand.

Stevins MS, c. 1555, similar to Harrison [*N & Q*, 1871, A. E. Brae] / *Abridgement of the Chronicles of England*, 1570, and *A litle treatise, conteyning many proper Tables*, 1572, both by Rychard Grafton / *The description of England*, William Harrison, 1577 / *The Retvrne from Pernassvs*, 1606 / *A Concordancy of Yeares*, Arthur Hopton, 1612 / *Cambridge Almanac*, 1635, 'Aprill, June, and September, Thirty daies have as November: Ech month else doth never vary From thirty-one, save February; Wich twenty-eight doth still confine, Save on Leap-yeare, then twenty-nine' [*Rara Mathematica*] / *New*

September

Help to Discourse, William Winstanley, 1669 / *Instructions for Children*, B. Keach, 4th edn., 1696 / *The Young Man's Companion*, c. 1703 [Northall] / *The Young Clerks Assistant* (Richard Ware), 1733 / *The Tutor's Guide*, C. Vyse, 1771 / *The Children's Magazine* (Marshall), 1799 / *The Scholar's Arithmetic*, J. Willett, 4th edn., 1822, Quaker version, USA, 'The fourth, eleventh, ninth, and sixth, Have thirty days to each affixed; And every other thirty-one, Except the second month alone, Which has but twenty-eight in fine, Till leap-year gives it twenty-nine' / *A Peep at the Stars; or an Introduction to Astrology* (John Harris), 1825 / *MG's Quarto*, c. 1825 / JOH, 1849 / *Old Nurse's Book*, Charles Bennett, 1858 / *Mother Goose*, Arthur Rackham, 1913.

Cf. *La Société des anciens textes français*, 13th-century quote [N & Q, 1884] / French MS book of Hours, 15th century, four lines beginning 'Trente Jours a Novembre' [N & Q, 1874].

Parody: Tom Hood, 'Dirty days hath September, April, June, and November, From January up to May The rain it raineth every day. February hath twenty-eight alone, And all the rest have thirty-one. If any of them had two and thirty they'd be just as wet and dirty.'

470

I saw a ship a-sailing,
  A-sailing on the sea,
And oh but it was laden
  With pretty things for thee.

There were comfits in the cabin,
  And apples in the hold;
The sails were made of silk,
  And the masts were all of gold.

The four-and-twenty sailors,
  That stood between the decks,
Were four-and-twenty white mice
  With chains about their necks.

The captain was a duck
  With a packet on his back,
And when the ship began to move
  The captain said Quack! Quack!

These lines, with some variations, were copied into an album of family verse, dated 1815, by Mrs. Elizabeth Susannah Graham, better known as 'Theresa Tidy', author of *Eighteen Maxims of Neatness and Order*. None of the verses in the album seem to be copyings from print or settings-down from oral tradition; on the other hand, none has the imaginative quality of the above. It is noticeable that early recordings differ, and that Walter Crane's version, recorded in 1870, with the cargo of almonds and raisins and the mice with rings about their necks, is nearer to Mrs Graham's version than is Halliwell's in 1846.

Family album, 1815, 'There was a ship...laden with pretty things for me...And twenty little sailors were skipping on the deck And they were little white mice with rings about their neck. The captain was a duck With a jacket on his back And when the ship begun [sic] to sail the Captain cried "Quack"' / JOH, 1846 / *Illustrated Ditties of the Olden Time* (Dean and Son), c. 1851, kisses in the hold / *The Fairy Ship*, Walter Crane, 1870, 'it was deeply laden...raisins in the cabin, And almonds in the hold' / *Revue Celtique*, 1880, correspondent who had never heard it before saw children singing it as they danced in a ring imitating ducks / *Songs everyone should know*, C. Johnson, 1908 / *Mother Goose*, Arthur Rackham, 1913 / Correspondent, 1946.

471

I saw three ships come sailing by,
   Come sailing by, come sailing by,
I saw three ships come sailing by,
   On New-Year's day in the morning.

And what do you think was in them then,
   Was in them then, was in them then?
And what do you think was in them then,
   On New-Year's day in the morning?

Three pretty girls were in them then,
   Were in them then, were in them then,
Three pretty girls were in them then,
   On New-Year's day in the morning.

One could whistle, and one could sing,
   And one could play on the violin;
Such joy there was at my wedding,
   On New-Year's day in the morning.

This is the nursery version of the traditional carol, 'As I sat on a sunny bank', which has the refrain 'On Christmas Day in the morning'. It continues, 'I spied three ships come sailing by...And who should be with those three ships But Joseph and his fair lady! O he did whistle and she did sing...And all the bells on earth did ring...For joy that our Saviour

he was born, On Christmas Day in the morning.' There is an early version
in Forbes's *Cantus* (Aberdeen), 1666:

> There comes a ship far sailing then,
> Saint Michel was the stieres-man:
> Saint Iohn sate in the horn:
> Our Lord harped, our Lady sang,
> And all the bells of heaven they rang,
> On Christs Sunday at morn,
> On Christs Sonday at morn.

Bishoprick Garland, Sir Cuthbert Sharp, 1834, given as second verse of 'Dame get up
and bake your pies' (q.v.), 'See the ships all sailing by, Sailing by, sailing by, See the
ships all sailing by, On Christmas day in the Morning' / Rimbault, 1846 / *Baby's
Opera*, 1877 / Baring-Gould, 1895.

472

> Hob, shoe, hob,
> Hob, shoe, hob,
> Here a nail,
> And there a nail,
> And that's well shod.

This verse shot into popularity in Britain in the spring of 1950 when it was
broadcast day after day in the BBC's newly introduced programme for
children under five, 'Listen with Mother'. The hammering tune to
which the words are chanted was composed by Miss Ann Driver. She
had collected the verse some years previously from a friend whose grandfather used to recite it, and found it much amused young children. The
words have not been traced in print but are probably an off-shoot of
'Is John Smith within?' (q.v.). The Revd Addison Crofton noted the following version when he was a curate at Walmersley, Lancs, in 1872:
'Shoe pat, shoe! Shoe pat, shoe! Here a nail and there a nail And shoe it
well too!'

473

> A shoemaker makes shoes without leather,
> With all the four elements put together,

Shoemaker

Fire, Water, Earth, Air,
And every customer takes two pair.

RIDDLE. *Solution:* the blacksmith.

Book of merrie Riddles, 1631, 'There dwels a shoomaker neere the hall that makes his shooes without a nawle; though men of them doe not were, yet they of them have many a paire' / *New Collection of Enigmas*, 1791, 'Yonder lives a shoemaker, who works without leather, And, strange! employs all the four elements together; Of fire he makes use, of water, earth, and air, And for ev'ry customer makes a double pair' / Peter Puzzlewell, 1792 / JOH, 1843 / *Rymour Club*, 1911 / *Junior Mirror*, schoolboy's letter, 1 Jan. 1956, 'What shoe-maker makes shoes without leather? A horseshoe maker'.

474

As soft as silk,
As white as milk,
As bitter as gall;
A thick wall,
And a green coat covers me all.

RIDDLE. *Solution:* a walnut on a tree.

Booke of meery Riddles, 1600, 'What is that as high as a hall, as bitter as gall, as soft as silke, as white as milke?' [1629] / *Book of merrie Riddles*, 1631, 'As bitter as gall, as sweet as milke, as high as hall and hard withall', and 'I am within as white as snow, without as greene as hearbs that grow; I am higher then a house, And yet am lesser than a mouse' / Holme MS, c. 1645, 'As sweet as milk as greene as a leefe as bitter as galle as high as a hall & yet as litt: as a mouse' / *Delights for Young Men and Maids* (William and Cluer Dicey), c. 1745 / JOH, 1853 / N & Q, 1891, 'As white as milk, As soft as silk, As high as a wall, As bitter as gall'.

Cf. 'As black as ink', and 'Higher than a house', with the 17th-century versions, and JOH, 1849, 'There was a little green house, And in the little green house There was a little brown house And in the little brown house There was a little yellow house, And in the little yellow house There was a little white house, And in the little white house There was a little heart'—a walnut.

Cf. also *Strassburger Räthselbuch*, 1505, 'Es stat hoch ob dem haus, hat die gröss als ein mauss, ist weiss wie der schne und bräun wie der klee, auch gryn wie das grass, sag gutter freündt was ist das?' [1876] *Das deutsche Kinderbuch*, Karl Simrock, 1848, 'Hoch ob dem Haus, Gross wie 'ne Maus, Weiss wie der Schnee, Braun wie der Klee, Dazu grün wie das Gras, Rath was ist das? (Baumnuss)' / *Devinettes ou enigmes populaires*, E. Rolland, 1877, 'Vert comme pré, Blanc comme neige, Amer comme fiel, Doux comme miel' / *American Folk-Lore*, 1906, Pennsylvania German, 'So hoch ass en Haus, So nidder ass en Maus, So rauh ass en Riegel, So glatt ass en Spiegel, So bitter ass Gall, Un is gut fer uns all'.

475

Old Sir Simon the king,
And young Sir Simon the squire,
And old Mrs. Hickabout
Kicked Mrs. Kickabout
Round about our coal fire.

The tune 'Old Simon the King' with its refrain,

Sayes old simon the King, sayes old Simon the King,
with his ale-dropt hose, & his malmesy nose,
with a hey ding, ding a ding, ding,

was popular throughout the seventeenth century and was later a favourite of Fielding's Squire Weston. Furnivall deduced, solely on account of its
burden, that this was the song 'Hey ding a ding' listed by Laneham in
1575. 'Old Sir Simon', however, is commonly supposed to be Simon
Wadloe, 'a witty butt of a man, much such another as honest Jack Fal-
staffe', who kept the Devil Tavern in Fleet Street and died in the year
1627. Gomme (1898) gives,

Old Simon, the king, young Simon the squire,
Old Simon, the king, sat round a nice warm fire,

as the introductory lines to a version of Looby Loo, the old ring dance.

JOH, 1844 / Gomme, 1898 / *Rymour Club*, 1911, 'There's auld Sir Simon the priest, And
young Sir Simon the square; The cat's a comical beast, It's a' clad owre wi' hair.'

476

Simple Simon met a pieman,
Going to the fair;
Says Simple Simon to the pieman,
Let me taste your ware.

Says the pieman to Simple Simon,
Show me first your penny;
Says Simple Simon to the pieman,
Indeed I have not any.

Simple Simon went a-fishing,
For to catch a whale;

Simple Simon

All the water he had got
Was in his mother's pail.

Simple Simon went to look
If plums grew on a thistle;
He pricked his finger very much,
Which made poor Simon whistle.

These are the four verses generally heard in the nursery and are part of the tale of Simple Simon in the chapbook history. For *Simple Simon*, the OED quotes Grose's *Dictionary* (1785) 'a natural, a silly fellow', and suggests the term comes from the nursery rhyme. Simon, however, may have been a name for a simpleton for several centuries (*vide Notes & Queries*, 8th s.), perhaps arising from the stories of Simon Peter. Boyd Smith (*Mother Goose*, 1919) repeats the statement that a tale of Simple Simon formed one of the chapbooks of the Elizabethan era. A ballad, *Simple Simon's Misfortunes and his Wife Margery's Cruelty*, earlier known as *Dead and Alive*, dates at least from c. 1685, and a tune 'Simple Simon' is included in the third edition of Playford's *The Dancing Master* (1665). The tune Kidson gives for the song is the old Welsh air 'Ar hyd y nos'.

Simple Simon, chapbook advt. by Cluer Dicey and Richard Marshall, 1764. Other editions: T. Batchelar, c. 1810; J. Kendrew, c. 1820; A. Park, c. 1840 / *Nicola Bayley's Book of Nursery Rhymes*, 1975.

477

Sing jigmijole, the pudding bowl,
The table and the frame;
My master he did cudgel me,
For kissing of my dame.

'Jigmajole', usually 'jig by jole', i.e. 'cheek by jowl', means 'together in a friendly way'.

Infant Institutes, 1797 / Douce MS, c. 1805 / *GG's Garland*, 1810 / JOH, 1842 (in later editions bowdlerized to 'For speaking of my dame').

478

I have four sisters beyond the sea,
Perrie, Merrie, Dixie, Dominie;

Sisters

And they each sent a present to me,
  Petrum, Partrum, Paradisi, Temporie,
  Perrie, Merrie, Dixie, Dominie.

The first sent a chicken, without e'er a bone,
  Perrie, Merrie, Dixie, Dominie;
The second a cherry, without e'er a stone,
  Petrum, Partrum, Paradisi, Temporie,
  Perrie, Merrie, Dixie, Dominie.

The third sent a book which no man could read,
  Perrie, Merrie, Dixie, Dominie;
The fourth sent a blanket, without e'er a thread,
  Petrum, Partrum, Paradisi, Temporie,
  Perrie, Merrie, Dixie, Dominie.

How can there be a chicken without e'er a bone?
  Perrie, Merrie, Dixie, Dominie;
How can there be a cherry without e'er a stone?
  Petrum, Partrum, Paradisi, Temporie,
  Perrie, Merrie, Dixie, Dominie.

How can there be a book which no man can read?
  Perrie, Merrie, Dixie, Dominie;
How can there be a blanket without e'er a thread?
  Petrum, Partrum, Paradisi, Temporie,
  Perrie, Merrie, Dixie, Dominie.

When the chicken's in the egg-shell there is no bone,
  Perrie, Merrie, Dixie, Dominie;
When the cherry's in the bud, there is no stone,
  Petrum, Partrum, Paradisi, Temporie,
  Perrie, Merrie, Dixie, Dominie.

When the book's in the press, no man it can read,
  Perrie, Merrie, Dixie, Dominie;
When the blanket's in the fleece there is no thread,
  Petrum, Partrum, Paradisi, Temporie,
  Perrie, Merrie, Dixie, Dominie.

This has been thought of as a children's song for nearly 200 years. Dauney in 1838 knew it through a friend's very ancient relative to whom it was sung when a child. A correspondent to *Notes & Queries* in 1866 remembered hearing 'this old nursery rhyme' many years previ-

Sisters

ously, and in 1946 a septuagenarian correspondent to the *Sunday Times* reported that she had learnt it in her youth from her nurse. The survival of the song is remarkable. For more than 500 years it has been carried in the wallet of popular memory, and for four of these centuries successfully evaded exposure on the printed page. In a small manuscript collection of songs and carols made in the first half of the fifteenth century appears:

> I haue a ȝong suster fer beȝondyn the se,
> Many be the drowryis that che sente me.
> Che sente me the cherye withoutyn ony ston;
> And so che dede dowe withoutyn ony bon;
> Sche sente me the brere withoutyn ony rynde;
> Sche bad me loue my lemman withoute longgyng.
> How xuld ony cherye be withoute ston?
> And how xuld ony dowe ben withoute bon?
> How xuld ony brere ben withoute rynde?
> How xuld y loue myn lemman without longyng?
> Quan the cherye was a flour: than hadde it non ston;
> Quan the dowe was an ey: than hadde it non bon;
> Quan the brere was onbred: than hadde it non rynd;
> Quan the maydyn haȝt that che louit: che is without longyng.

The song may well have been old when this was written down. It has points in common with the traditional ballad 'Captain Wedderburn's Courtship', but whether the ballad is older, or whether, as seems more probable, the song became incorporated, or was the partial inspiration of it, is uncertain. In the ballad story, Captain Wedderburn, a servant of the king, meets Lord Roslin's daughter and immediately wishes to marry her. He speaks highly of her (and also of himself) and takes her to Edinburgh. The maiden nevertheless still says,

> O haud awa frae me, kind sir, I pray ye lat me be,
> For I'll na lie in your bed till I get dishes three;
> Dishes three maun be dressd for me, gif I should eat them a',
> Before I lie in your bed, at either stock or wa'.
>
> 'Tis I maun hae to my supper a chicken without a bane;
> And I maun hae to my supper a cherry without a stane;
> And I maun hae to my supper a bird without a gaw,
> Before I lie in your bed, at either stock or wa'.

Captain Wedderburn, however, answers these and other of her riddles, 'and now' ends the ballad 'she's Mrs. Wedderburn, and she lies at the wa''. The 'Perrie, Merrie, Dixie' refrain appears only in the song. Dauney believed that it was a relic of the times when Romish hymns were adapted to secular purposes; alternatively it may be a corruption of a Latin exorcism (cf. the refrain of 'Can you make me a cambric shirt'). The tune is a variant of 'Go no more a rushing, maids, in May'.

Sloane MS 2593, c. 1440 / *Ancient Scottish Melodies*, W. Dauney, 1838, 'I have a true love beyond the sea Para mee dicksa do mee nee; And mony a love-token he sends to me With a rattum, pattum, Para mee dicksa do mee nee.' / JOH, 1849 / JOH, 1853, 'My true love lives far from me' / *Macmillan's Magazine*, 1862, in 'The Ashen Faggot' by Thomas Hughes / N & Q, 1866 / Mason, 1877, two versions / *Baby's Bouquet*, 1879, 'I had four brothers over the sea' / Baring-Gould, 1895 / *Sunday Times*, 1946.

Cf. 'Captain Wedderburn's Courtship' in Herd MS 1776; *Popular Ballads*, R. Jamieson, 1806, said to be 'quite familiar to him in early youth'; Kinloch MS, c. 1826; Buchan MS, c. 1828; N & Q, 1857; *English and Scottish Ballads*, F. J. Child, 1883–98.

Cf. also *The Riddle*, song sheet printed by J. Pitts, c. 1830, and *Folk-Song*, 1907, 'I will give my love an apple without e'er a core; I will give my love a house without e'er a door; I will give my love a palace wherein she may be, And she may unlock it without e'er a key', four verses.

479

There were three sisters in a hall,
There came a knight amongst them all;
Good morrow, aunt, to the one,
Good morrow, aunt, to the other,
Good morrow, gentlewoman, to the third,
    If you were aunt,
        As the other two be,
    I would say good morrow,
        Then, aunts, all three.

This riddle is found jotted down in a commonplace book of the seventeenth century, and is another in the style of 'The fiddler and his wife' (q.v.).

Sloane MS 1489, c. 1630 / JOH, 1843.

480

I love sixpence, jolly little sixpence,
    I love sixpence better than my life;
I spent a penny of it, I lent a penny of it,
    And I took fourpence home to my wife.

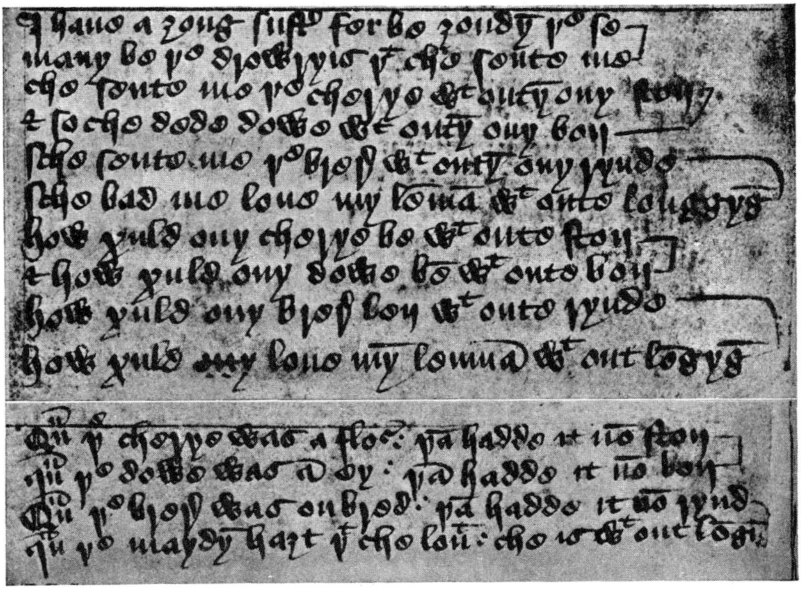
I haue a yong suster fer beyondyn þe se
many be þe druryis þat che sente me
che sente me þe cherye wtoutyn ony ston
& so che dede þe dowe wtoutyn ony bon
sche sente me þe brer wtoutyn ony rynde
sche bad me loue my lemman wtoute longgyng
how xuld ony cherye be wtoute ston
& how xuld ony dowe ben wtoute bon
how xuld ony brer ben wtoute rynde
how xuld y loue myn lemman wtout longyng
Quan þe cherye was a flour: þan hadde it non ston
Quan þe dowe was an ey: þan hadde it non bon
Quan þe brer was onbred: þan hadde it non rynd
Quan þe maydyn hayt þat che louit: che is wtout longyng

a. 'I have four sisters beyond the sea' as it was written in the first half of the 15th century. British Museum, Sloane MS 2593

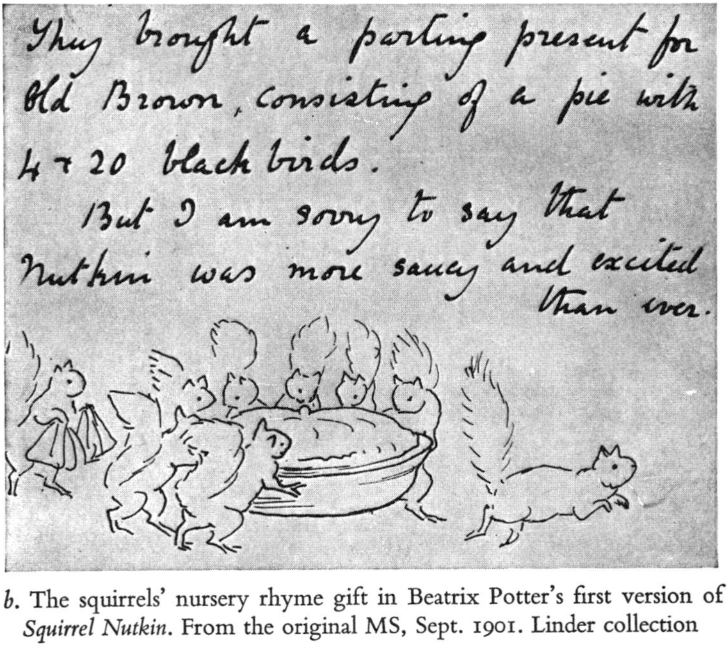
They brought a parting present for Old Brown, consisting of a pie with 4 & 20 black birds.
But I am sorry to say that Nutkin was more saucy and excited than ever.

b. The squirrels' nursery rhyme gift in Beatrix Potter's first version of *Squirrel Nutkin*. From the original MS, Sept. 1901. Linder collection

Sixpence

Oh, my little fourpence, jolly little fourpence,
   I love fourpence better than my life;
I spent a penny of it, I lent a penny of it,
   And I took twopence home to my wife.

Oh, my little twopence, jolly little twopence,
   I love twopence better than my life;
I spent a penny of it, I lent a penny of it,
   And I took nothing home to my wife.

Oh, my little nothing, jolly little nothing,
   What will nothing buy for my wife?
I have nothing, I spend nothing,
   I love nothing better than my wife.

An old song which was recently given new life by Tin Pan Alley. Some versions begin with 'twelvepence', as Rimbault's alternative reading:

O dear twelvepence, I've got twelvepence,
   I love twelvepence as I love my life;
I'll grind a penny on't, I'll spend another,
   And I'll carry tenpence home to my wife.

And Williams's picaresque 'Jolly Shilling':

I have a jolly shilling a lovely jolly shilling,
I love my jolly shilling as I do love my life;
I've a penny for to spend, another for to lend,
And a jolly, jolly tenpence to carry home to my wife.

Chorus

There's neither pins nor quarts shall grieve me,
Nor this wide world shall deceive me,
But bring me the girl that will keep me,
While I go fambling about.

Garland, 1810 / *Don Giovanni in London*, W. T. Moncrieff, 1817 / JOH, 1842 / Splt, 1846 / Mason, 1877 / *Baby's Bouquet*, 1879 / *Traditional Tunes*, Frank Kidson, The Jolly Shilling chorus A pint nor a quart won't grieve me, Nor false, young believe me; Here's to my wife, who will kiss me When I come rolling home' / Baring-1895 / *Mother Goose*, Arthur Backham, 1913 / Williams, 1923 / *Folf-Song*, 1930. *I've got Sixpence*, 'Words and music by Box, Cox and Hall', 1941, 'I've got sixpence, I've six pence, I've got sixpence to last me all my life, I've got tuppence to spend and to lend And tuppence to send unto my wife'.

Sleepy-head

481

Come, let's to bed,
Says Sleepy-head;
Tarry a while, says Slow;
Put on the pot,
Says Greedy-gut,
We'll sup before we go.

GG's Garland, 1784, 'Sit up a while, says Slow; Hang on the pot...' / *Infant Institutes*, 1797 / *Songs for the Nursery*, 1805 / *Traditional Nursery Songs*, Felix Summerly, 1843, illustration by John Linnell / JOH, 1843 / N & Q, 1872, 'I was taught it as a child thus: To bed, to bed, says Drowsy-head; Not so fast, says Slow; Put on the pot, says Greedy-gut, We'll sup before we go' / Crofton MS, 1901, 'Put on the pot, says Greedy Sot', 'Put on the pan, Said Greedy Nan' or 'Greedy Dan' / *Less Familiar NR*, Robert Graves, 1927, additional verse, 'To bed, to bed, cried Sleepy head, But all the rest said, No! It is morning now; you must milk the cow, And tomorrow to bed we go' / *Daily Express*, James Agate, 18 Apr. 1947.

482

Snail, snail,
Come out of your hole,
Or else I'll beat you
As black as coal.

Snail, snail,
Put out your horns,
I'll give you bread
And barley corns.

This chant is comparable to 'Ladybird, ladybird, fly away home' (q.v.) in its inexplicableness and probable antiquity. The rhyme was said, or sung, or sometimes the snail was held at arm's length and swung round. Douce says (c. 1805), 'It was probably the custom, on repeating these lines, to hold the snail to a candle, in order to make it quit the shell. In Normandy it was the practice at Christmas for boys to run round fruit-trees, with lighted torches, singing these lines:

Taupes et mulots,
Sortez de vos clos,
Sinon vous brulerai et la barbe et les os.'

Snail

This conjuration of field-mice and moles was still employed in France in the present century, the summons sometimes being lengthier:

> Taupe et mulot,
> Sors de mon clos,
> Ou je te casse les os;
> Barbassione! Si tu viens dans mon clos,
> Je te brûle la barbe jusqu'aux os.

On the first Sunday in Lent (*la Fête des Brandons ou des Bures*) the peasants walked through the fields and orchards with lighted torches of twisted straw, accompanying their threats with discordant tin horns and cat-calls, in order to be rid of the pests. A similar motive may have provoked the threat to the snail. Chambers (1842) remarks, 'In England, the snail scoops out hollows, little rotund chambers, in limestone, for its resid-ence. This habit of the animal is so important in its effects, as to have attracted the attention of geologists, one of the most distinguished of whom (Dr. Buckland) alluded to it at the meeting of the British Associa-tion at Plymouth in 1841. The...rhyme is a boy's invocation to the snail to come out of such holes.' Chambers adds that in Scotland good weather is prognosticated by the creature appearing to obey the injunction,

> Snailie, snailie, shoot out your horn,
> And tell us if it will be a bonny day the morn.

Whatever is the significance of the snail to engender such invocations, it must lie deep in the history of the world. The diversity of languages in which the rhyme is found is almost unparalleled. JOH quotes equivalents from Denmark and Germany; a writer in *Notes & Queries* (1851) from Naples and Silesia. Countess Evelyn Martinengo-Cesaresco (1886) adds verses from France, Tuscany, Russia, Roumania, and China. The call is also known in Spain. The English rhyme is found in print from 1744 onwards, and may have been referred to by Shakespeare. In *The Merry Wives of Windsor* (iv. ii) Mistress Page tells how Mr. Ford, considering himself a cuckold, 'buffets himself on the forehead crying, "Peer out, peer out"', meaning, appear horns. A version of the rhyme still known is,

> Peer out, peer out, peer out of your hole,
> Or else I'll beat you as black as a coal.

T Thumb's PSB, c. 1744 / *A Little Play-Book*, c. 1746 / *Songs for the Nursery*, 1805, second couplet 'Snail, Snail, put out your horns, Here comes a thief to pull down your walls' / Douce MS, c. 1805 / *MG's Quarto*, c. 1825 / *New Year's Gift* (J. Catnach), c. 1830 [Hindley, 1878] / Chambers, 1842, 'Willie, my buck, shoot out your horn, And you'll get milk and bread the morn' / JOH, 1842 / *Only True MG Melodies*, c. 1843, '...Snail, Snail, put out your head, Or else I'll beat you till you're dead' / JOH, 1844, 'Sneel, snaul, Robbers are coming to pull down your wall; Sneel, snaul, put out your horn, Robbers are coming to steal your corn, Coming at four o'clock in the morn' / *Folk-Lore of N. Counties*, W. Henderson, 1879, 'Snail, snail, put out your horn, Tell me what's the day t'morn; Today's the morn to shear the corn, Blaw bil buck thorn' / *West Somerset Word-book*, F. T. Elworthy, 1886, 'Snarley-'orn, put out your corn, Father and mother's dead; Zister'n brither's out to back door, Bakin' o' barley bread' / *County Folk-Lore, Suffolk*, The Lady Eveline Gurdon, 1893, 'Hod-ma-Dod, Hod-ma-Dod, Stick out your horns, Here comes an old beggar To cut off your corns' / Maclagan, 1901, 'Buckie, buckie, snail, cock out your horn, And I'll give you bread and butter the morn' (said while lifting the snail and throwing over left shoulder) / *Word Lore*, 1926 / *Popular Rhymes of Ireland*, J. J. Marshall, 1931, 'Shell a muddy, shell a muddy, Put out your horns, For the king's daughter is coming to town With a red petticoat and a green gown.' There are also many varia in *N & Q* and *Folk-Lore*.

Cf. Douce MS, c. 1805, Norman version as quote / *Danske Folkesagn*, J. M. Thiele, 1820–3, 'Snegl! snegl! kom herud! Her er en Mand, som vil kjöbe dit Huus, For en Skjaeppe Penge!' ('Snail, snail, come out here! Here is a man thy house will buy, For a measure of white money') [JOH] / *Household Words*, R. C. Horne, 20 Sept. 1851, 'Chiocciola, chiocciola marinella, Butta fuori le tu' cornella' (Tuscan) / *N & Q*, 1851, 'Schnecke, schnecke, schnürre! Zeig mir dein viere, Wenn mir dein viere nicht zeigst, Schmeisz ich dich in den Graben, Fressen dich die Raben' (Silesian); 'Jesce, jesce, corna; Ça mammata te scorna, Te scorna 'ncoppa lastrico, Che fa lo figlio mascolo' (Neapolitan) / *Faune populaire de la France*, E. Rolland, 1881 and 1909, numerous versions including 'Colimaçon borgne, Montre-moi tes cornes; Si tu ne les montres pas Je te couperai la gorge avec un couteau de Saint-Georges.' 'C'est la forme sous laquelle cette formulette est le plus connue.' Also quotes Italian formula from Nathanael Duez's dictionary, 1678, 'Lumaca lumachella Cavar fuor le tuè cornilla' / *Study of Folk-Songs*, E. Martinengo-Cesaresco, 1886, 'Colimaçon borgne! Montre-moi tes cornes; Je te dirai où ta mère est morte, Elle est morte à Paris, à Rouen, Où l'on sonne les cloches. Bi, bim, bom, Bi, bim, bom, Bi, bim, bom'; 'Chiocciola, chiocciola, vien da me, Ti darò i' pan d' i' re; E dell' ova affrittellate Corni secchi e brucherate' (Tuscan); 'Culbecu, culbecu, Scóte corne boeresci Si te du la Dunăre Si bé apă tulbure' (Roumanian); 'Ulitka, ulitka, Vypusti roga, Ya tebé dam piroga (Russian, 'Snail, snail, put forth thy horns, I will give thee cakes'); the Chinese is rendered 'Snail, snail, come here to be fed, Put out your horns and lift up your head; Father and mother will give you to eat, Good boiled mutton shall be your meat' / *Das deutsche Kinderbuch*, Karl Simrock, 1848, 'Schneck im haus, Komm heraus. Kommen zwei mit Spiessen, Wollen dich erschiessen; Kommen zwei mit Stecken, Wollen dich erschrecken' (this version also orally collected 1949) / *Deutsche Kinderlied*, F. M. Böhme, 1897 (1924) / *Folklore infantile de Espana*, V. Serra Boldú, 1931, 'Caracol, caracol, Saca los cuernos al sol; Que tu padre y tu madre También los sacó.' (Snail, snail, put out your horns to the sun, For your father and mother both did the same.)

483

Solomon Grundy,
Born on a Monday,
Christened on Tuesday,
Married on Wednesday,

PLATE XVII

a. The happy ending to *Aunt Louisa's Sing a Song of Six-pence*, 1866. Opie collection

b. John Linnell's illustration of 'The cat sat asleep by the side of the fire' in *Traditional Nursery Songs*, 1843. London Library

Solomon Grundy

Took ill on Thursday,
Worse on Friday,
Died on Saturday,
Buried on Sunday.
This is the end
Of Solomon Grundy.

Frequently reprinted since it was set down by JOH in 1842, this rhyme was sufficiently well known in Britain in 1945 to be parodied in an advertisement issued by the National Savings Committee. A similar jingle, attributed to 'a facetious Jacobite, on the occasion of the early death of some infant princess of the reigning house', appeared in the *Bristol Observer* (c. Apr. 1881), according to a writer in *Notes & Queries* (6th s.):

Little Goody Tidy
Was born on a Friday,
Was christened on a Saturday,
Ate roast beef on Sunday,
Was very well on Monday,
Was taken ill on Tuesday,
Sent for the doctor on Wednesday,
Died on Thursday,
So there's an end to little Goody Tidy.

Cf. 'Tom married a wife on Sunday'.

484

I'll sing you a song,
Nine verses long,
   For a pin;
Three and three are six,
And three are nine;
You are a fool,
   And the pin is mine.

Douce MS, c. 1805 / *GG's Garland*, 1810 / JOH, 1842.

485

I'll sing you a song,
The days are long,

Song

The woodcock and the sparrow;
The little dog has burnt his tail,
And he must be hanged tomorrow.

Since this rhyme dates at least from the eighteenth century, the statement in the last line that the dog must be hanged on the morrow may be based on more than poetic fancy. The trial of animals and the judicial hanging of dogs, although uncommon, appears at one time to have been considered reasonable. On 25 May 1595, at Leyden, a dog, 'Troeveetie' by name, was hung by means of a string on the gallows in punishment after proper trial in the Domstool (public Court of Justice) for accidentally inflicting a fatal injury on a child's finger. In 1714 Addison in *The Spectator* (11 Aug.) refers to the hanging of all the mastiffs of Syracuse because they had attacked a priest. And as late as 1771 a dog belonging to a Farmer Carpenter was on trial at Chichester. However, hanging appears to have been the customary method of killing old or unwanted dogs until as recently as the beginning of this century. No doubt from this practice come the phrases 'a hang-dog look', 'give a dog a bad name and hang him', and 'there are more ways of killing a dog than by hanging'. See also the nursery song, 'Barnaby Bright'.

GG's Garland, 1784 / *Infant Institutes*, 1797, 'of two days long... and bids his dame good-morrow' / *Come Sing a Song*, c. 1797, 'a glee for three voices composed by F. Ball', 'The cuckoo and the sparrow, The little dog has lost his clog' / *Songs for the Nursery*, 1805 / *Vocal Harmony*, c. 1806 / *Squire Summerton's Picture Gallery* (T. Batchelar), c. 1832 / JOH, 1842, 'Ding, dong, darrow, The cat and the sparrow...' / Gomme, 1898, 'Wingy, wongy, Days are longy, Cuckoo and the sparrow; Little dog has lost his tail, And he shall be hung tomorrow', given as swinging rhyme / *County Folk-Lore, Lincolnshire*, Mabel Peacock, 1908, 'I'll tell you a tale Of a jack of ale, A hen, a cock, and a sparrow, My little dog has burnt his tail, And won't get home tomorrow' / *Word Lore*, 1927.

486

Sing a song of sixpence,
A pocket full of rye;
Four and twenty blackbirds,
Baked in a pie.

When the pie was opened,
The birds began to sing;
Was not that a dainty dish,
To set before the king?

Song of Sixpence

The king was in his counting-house,
    Counting out his money;
The queen was in the parlour,
    Eating bread and honey.

The maid was in the garden,
    Hanging out the clothes,
There came a little blackbird,
    And snapped off her nose.

When Henry James Pye was appointed Poet Laureate in 1790 his first ode, a very poor one, was in honour of the king's birthday and was full of allusions to the 'vocal groves and the feathered choir'. George Steevens immediately punned, 'And when the PYE was opened the birds began to sing; Was not that a dainty dish to set before the king?' This witty story, told in *DNB* without attribution, had a long life in oral tradition; Lamb recounted it to Mary Lamb's nurse, Sarah James, in a letter (April 1829). Less entertaining are the stories giving the rhyme allegorical significance. Theories upon which too much ink has been expended are (i) that the twenty-four blackbirds are the hours of the day; the king, the sun; the queen the moon, &c.; (ii) that the blackbirds are the choirs of about-to-be-dissolved monasteries making a dainty pie for Henry; the queen, Katherine; the maid, Anne Boleyn, &c.; (iii) that the king, again, is Henry VIII; the rye, tribute in kind; the birds, twenty-four manorial title-deeds presented under a crust, &c.; (iv) that the maid is a sinner; the blackbird, the demon snapping off the maid's nose to reach her soul, &c.; (v) that the printing of the English Bible is celebrated, blackbirds being the letters of the alphabet which were 'baked in a pie' when set up by the printers in pica form, &c. Supposed references to the rhyme have been seen in *Twelfth Night* ('Come on, there is sixpence for you; let's have a song'), and in Beaumont and Fletcher's *Bonduca*, 1614 ('Whoa, here's a stir now! Sing a song o' sixpence!'). If any particular explanation is required of the rhyme the straightforward one that it is a description of a familiar entertainment is the most probable. In an Italian cookery book, *Epulario, quale tratta del modo de cucinare ogni carne . . .* (1549; translated 1598, *Epulario, or, the Italian Banquet*), there is a recipe 'to make pies so that the birds may be alive in them and flie out when it is cut up'. This dish is further referred to (1723) by John Nott, cook to the Duke of Bolton, as a practice of former days, the purpose of the birds being to put out the candles and so cause a 'diverting Hurley-Burley amongst the Guests in the Dark'. It is well known that in the sixteenth century surprising things were inserted in pies, as in the legend which attaches itself to the rhyme 'Jack Horner' (q.v.). The mention of a 'counting-house', much referred to in *The Merry Wives of Windsor*, also helps to indicate that the

Song of Sixpence

rhyme may be traced to the sixteenth century, and the 'pocket full of rye' might be the specific 'pocket' sack-measurement of that grain. Kidson says that the air to which the words are generally sung is the old Scottish dance tune 'Calder Fair'.

T Thumb's PSB, c. 1744, one verse, 'Sing a Song of Sixpence, A bag full of Rye, Four and twenty Naughty boys, Bak'd in a Pye' / *Nancy Cock's PSB*, c. 1780, two verses / *GG's Garland*, 1784, ending 'Up came a magpie and bit off her nose' / *T Thumb's SB*, 1788 / *T Tit's SB*, c. 1790 / *Christmas Box*, vol. ii, 1798 / *Songs for the Nursery*, 1805 / *Vocal Harmony*, c. 1806, 'I'll sing a song of sixpence' / *Pretty Tales*, 1808 / *Chatterings of the Pica*, Charles Taylor, 1820 / *MG's Quarto*, c. 1825 / Charles Lamb, letter to Miss Sarah James, ?Apr. 1829 / JOH, 1842, additional verse 'Jenny was so mad, She didn't know what to do; She put her finger in her ear, And crackt it right in two' / *Traditional Nursery Songs*, Felix Summerly, 1843, illustration by J. C. Horsley / *The Song of Sixpence*, Walter Crane, 1865 [Massé biblio.] / *Aunt Louisa's Sing a Song of Sixpence*, 1866, further verse, 'They sent for the King's doctor, who sewed it on again, He sewed it on so neatly, the seam was never seen; and the jackdaw for his naughtiness deservedly was slain' / *Sing a Song for Sixpence*, Randolph Caldecott, 1880, additional couplet 'But there came a Jenny Wren and popped it on again' / Kidson, 1904 / BBC programme, 'Listen with Mother', Ann Driver, 1950, happy ending, 'They made such a commotion that little Jenny Wren Flew down into the garden And popped it on again' / *Sing a Song of Sixpence*, illus. Tracey Campbell Pearson, 1985.

Parody: In *The Memoirs of the Duke of Windsor*, 1951, H.R.H. tells that the information he brought back from his American tour in 1919 which most pleased George V was the doggerel picked up in a Canadian border town, 'Four and twenty Yankees, feeling very dry, Went across the border to get a drink of Rye. When the Rye was opened, the Yanks began to sing "God bless America, but God save the King!"'

487

The sow came in with the saddle,
The little pig rocked the cradle,
    The dish jumped up on the table,
    To see the pot swallow the ladle.
The spit that stood behind the door
Threw the pudding-stick on the floor.
    Odd's-bobs! says the gridiron,
      Can't you agree?
    I'm the head constable,
      Bring them to me.

This nonsense tale undoubtedly originated in the recitations of the mummers. In the Robin Hood play traditionally enacted at Kempsford, in Gloucestershire, and taken down in 1868, Tom Pinny says,

Sow

Last Xmas day I turned the spit
I burnt my fingers and felt it hit—
The spark jumped over the table
And the frying pan beat the ladle,
Aye aye says the gridiron
What can't you two agree.
Bring 'em to me. I'm the Justice of Peace
And I'll make 'em agree.

All these lines are remembered in the nursery. While the last three couplets are related to the present rhyme, the first couplet, together with
another version of the second, form the nursery rhyme, 'On Christmas
Eve I turned the spit' (q.v.). It is interesting that as early as 1760 children
had parted these lines from their context, for their versions, recorded in
the reign of George III, were not very seemly. It is probable that nursery
literature here reflects the old vernacular of the mummers' plays more
accurately than the texts, orally collected in the nineteenth century,
which had to accommodate themselves to a more polite age.

FT Thumb's LSB, c. 1760, '...The spit that stood behind the door, Call'd the dish-
clout dirty whore. Odsplut, says the gridiron, Can't you agree? I'm the head constable, Bring 'em to me' / *Top Book*, c. 1760, as previous / *MG's Melody*, c. 1765,
'...To see the Pot wash the Ladle. The Spit that stood behind a Bench, Call'd the
Dishclout dirty Wench' / MS version headed 'MR BLAKE'S NURSERY RHYME',
laid loose in Blake's own copy of *Songs of Innocence*, 1789, 'The sow came in with
the saddle...The old pot behind the door Called the kettle a blackamoor...' /
MG's Melody, 1803, 'The spit that stood behind the door, Call'd the dishclout dirty
o'er and o'er' / *Vocal Harmony*, c. 1806, as c. 1765 / *Pretty Tales*, 1808, four lines only /
Nursery Songs (G. Ross), c. 1812, 'The spit...called the dish-clout dirty boor' / *Nurse
Lovechild's DFN*, c. 1830, 'The broom behind the butt Call'd the dish-clout a nasty
slut. Odds-plud, says the gridiron...' / JOH, 1842 / *Only True MG Melodies*, c. 1843,
similar to text / JOH, 1853, 'Oh! Oh! says the gridiron...' / *Mummers' Play*, R. J. E.
Tiddy, 1923, as quote, also the Weston-sub-Edge text 'The sparks flew over the
table, The pot-lid kicked the ladle, Up jumped spit jack Like a mansion man
Swore he'd fight the dripping pan With his long tail, Swore he'd send them all to
jail. In comes the grid iron, if you can't agree I'm the justice, bring 'um to me' / *Second Manx Scrapbook*, W. W. Gill, 1932, given as part of 'an Irish wren-song', 'A [little]
cock-sparrow flew over the table, The dish began to fight with the ladle, The spit
got up like a naked man And swore he'd fight with the dripping pan, The pan got
up and cocked his tail, And swore he'd send them all to jail.'

488

Four stiff-standers,
Four dilly-danders,
Two lookers, two crookers,
And a wig-wag.

Stiff-standers

This terse but picturesque description of a cow has been called a 'world riddle', and is of immense antiquity. In one of the earlier Icelandic sagas, the *Saga of King Heidrek the Wise* (trans. C. Tolkien, 1960) Odin, in disguise, asks King Heidrek a number of riddles, one of which is:

> Four are hanging,
> four are walking,
> two point the way out,
> two ward the dogs off,
> one ever dirty
> dangles behind it.

'Your riddle is good,' said the king; 'I have guessed it. That is the cow.'

The riddle has numerous analogues in European languages. As well as a French version, Rolland quotes three Italian, one German, two Alsatian, one Norwegian, one Moravian, and one Lithuanian.

Royal Riddle Book, 1820, 'Two lookers, two crookers, Four hangers, four gangers, And a flap to scar the flies away' / *N & Q*, 1865 / *Rymour Club*, 1912, 'Foure redrootres, foure upstanders, Twa lookie-oots, twa crookit boots, Twa leatherin' cloots, and a waggie' / *Folk-Lore*, 1932, 'Two lookers, two hookers, two snookers' / *American Mother Goose*, Ray Wood, 1938, gathered from the peckerwood people, 'Two lookers, Two crookers Four stiff-standers And a fly-flooker' / *Wesdale*, J. J. Graham, 1939 / *A Rocket in My Pocket*, Carl Withers, 1948, 'Four pusher-uppers, Four puller-downers, Two lookers, Two hookers, And a swishy-wishy.'

Cf. *Devinettes ou énigmes populaires*, E. Rolland, 1877, 'Quatre allants, Quatre à lait, Deux voyants, Deux fichets, La queue faite comme un balai'; 'Do lusenti, Do punzenti, Quatro mazzoche E un bon scovoloto'; 'Vier lamble Vier bamble Vier lueghe d'r Himmel a', &c. / *Faune populaire*, E. Rolland, 1882, 'Cuatro andantes, Cuatro mamantes, Un quita-moscas, Y dos apuntantes' / *Mecklenburgische Volksüberlieferungen*, R. Wossidlo, 1897 / *Shetland Traditional Lore*, J. M. E. Saxby, 1932, 'Four hang and four go, Two stand firm and fast; Two shine like the Lift (sky), and een comes last', translated from 'faulty Norse and obscure dialect'.

489

> Twinkle, twinkle, little star,
> How I wonder what you are!
> Up above the world so high,
> Like a diamond in the sky.
>
> When the blazing sun is gone,
> When he nothing shines upon,
> Then you show your little light,
> Twinkle, twinkle, all the night.

Star

Then the traveller in the dark,
Thanks you for your tiny spark,
He could not see which way to go,
If you did not twinkle so.

In the dark blue sky you keep,
And often through my curtains peep,
For you never shut your eye,
Till the sun is in the sky.

As your bright and tiny spark,
Lights the traveller in the dark,—
Though I know not what you are,
Twinkle, twinkle, little star.

One of the best-known poems in the English language, this was written
by Jane Taylor (1783–1824). Entitled 'The Star', it appeared in *Rhymes for
the Nursery*, published by Darton and Harvey in 1806. This volume was a
joint work with her sister Ann, and met with considerable success (27th
edn., 1835). 'The Star' had not, at first, the popularity of Ann's earlier
poem, 'My Mother', which, however, never really entered oral tradition.
Like much else of the Taylors' work 'The Star' has been frequently parodied, an example being the Mad Hatter's,

Twinkle, twinkle, little bat!
How I wonder what you're at!
Up above the world you fly,
Like a tea-tray in the sky.

Rhymes for the Nursery, A. and J. Taylor, 1806 [1810] / *The Little Star*, tune by J. Green,
c. 1860, sheet music / *Little Songs for me to Sing*, illus. Sir John Millais, 1865.
    Pantomime: *Twinkle, Twinkle, Little Star; or, Harlequin Jack Frost, And Little Tom
Tucker who sang for his Supper* performed at the Prince of Wales Theatre, Birmingham, c. 1870.

490

He that lies at the stock,
Shall have a gold rock;
He that lies at the wall,
Shall have a gold ball;
He that lies in the middle,
Shall have a gold fiddle.

Stock

Rhyme for inducing children to settle down for the night in the days when everybody from king to kitchenmaid slept more than one to a bed. The stock is the outer rail of the bedstead. Goldsmith said that the stock was considered the place of honour. In the old ballad of 'Captain Wedderburn's Courtship' the lady demands that various riddles be solved,

> Before I lie in your bed,
> Either at stock or wa'.

And when these have been solved she still says to the Captain, 'thou's lie next the wa''.

JOH, 1849 / *Mother Goose's NR*, L. E. Walter, 1924 / *Housewife*, Nov. 1949.

491

> Here's Sulky Sue;
> What shall we do?
> Turn her face to the wall
> Till she comes to.

In chapbooks titled *Jacky Jingle and Sucky Shingle* (T. Evans, c. 1800; J. Kendrew, c. 1825; &c.) these lines comprise the first half of the second verse; the remaining lines are,

> If that should fail,
> A smart touch with the cane,
> Will soon make her good,
> When she feels the pain.

Cf. 'Little Jack Jingle'.

492

> There was an old woman of Surrey,
> Who was morn, noon, and night in a hurry;
> Called her husband a fool,
> Drove her children to school,
> The worrying old woman of Surrey.

'The old woman of Surrey' comes from the first known book of limericks, *The History of Sixteen Wonderful Old Women*, published by J. Harris in 1820. (See under 'As a little fat man of Bombay'.)

493

Swan swam over the sea,
Swim, swan, swim!
Swan swam back again,
Well swum swan!

JOH, 1842 / Well known in the present day.

494

Taffy was a Welshman, Taffy was a thief,
Taffy came to my house and stole a piece of beef;
I went to Taffy's house, Taffy wasn't in,
I jumped upon his Sunday hat, and poked it with a pin.

Taffy was a Welshman, Taffy was a sham,
Taffy came to my house and stole a leg of lamb;
I went to Taffy's house, Taffy was away,
I stuffed his socks with sawdust and filled his shoes with clay.

Taffy was a Welshman, Taffy was a cheat,
Taffy came to my house and stole a piece of meat;
I went to Taffy's house, Taffy was not there,
I hung his coat and trousers to roast before a fire.

JOH says this was sung on the first of March on the Welsh borders and
other parts of England. Baiting the Welsh was certainly customary in London on St. David's Day. On 1 March 1667 Pepys observed 'the picture of a
man dressed like a Welchman, hanging by the neck upon one of the poles
that stand out at the top of one of the merchant's houses, in full propor-
tion and very handsomely done'. In an early eighteenth-century chapbook, *Taffy's Progress to London*, it is narrated 'how Despiseable the poor
Welshmen alias Britains were made in England on Saint Tafy's day, by
the Rabbles hanging out of a Bundle of Rags in representation of a Welshman mounted on a red Herring with a Leek in his Hat'. In *Tommy
Thumb's Pretty Song Book* (c. 1744) appears another rhyme, apparently ridi-
culing those from across the border:

Taffy was born
On a Moon Shiny Night,
His head in the Pipkin,
His Heels upright.

PLATE XVIII

Taffy was a Welshman. A music title-page by Alfred Concanen, c. 1865.
Collection of A. Hyatt King, Esq.

Taffy

The accompanying cut shows a child with his head in a cooking pot. 'Taffy' is a corruption of 'Dafydd', Welsh for 'David'.

Nancy Cock's PSB, c. 1780, first couplet and 'I went to Taffy's house, Taffy wasn't home, Taffy came to my house And stole a marrow-bone'. Similar to 1780 are *GG's Garland,* 1784; *Newest Christmas Box,* c. 1797; *Songs for the Nursery,* 1805 (ends 'I went to Taffy's house, Taffy was in bed, I took the marrow bone and beat about his head'); *Vocal Harmony,* c. 1806; *Nursery Songs* (G. Ross), c. 1812; *Sugar Plum* (J. Roberts), c. 1825 / JOH, 1842, slight variations / *Taffy was a Welshman,* c. 1865, music sheet / N & Q, 1889 / *Word Lore,* 1927.

495

Four and twenty tailors
   Went to kill a snail,
The best man among them
   Durst not touch her tail;
She put out her horns
   Like a little Kyloe cow,
Run, tailors, run,
   Or she'll kill you all e'en now.

It has been pleaded (and not only by the outfitting trade) that in the proverb 'Nine tailors make but one man' the word *tailor* is a facetious transformation of *teller,* a *teller* being a stroke on the bell at a funeral: three for a child, six for a woman, and *nine* for a *man.* Alternatively, it has been put forward that nine tailors are the number needed to make one man's suit of clothes; or that this is the number necessary to 'make a man' because it is his clothes that make him; whilst James Kelly (1721), recording the proverb 'Four and twenty tailors cannot make a man', says 'The jest is in the word *make,* for though one tailor can shew himself a man, yet no number of them can frame one'. It must be acknowledged, however, that the occupation of tailoring (or of weaving, see 1871 quote) does not make for sturdiness. The joke is too old to be gainsaid. Butler refers to it in *Hudibras* (1663); and the incongruity of seeing a tailor at the sign of a lion is observed in *The Spectator* (No. 28). Together with the evidence in this rhyme the aspersion on thread and thimble cannot lightly be dispelled.

GG's Garland, 1784 / JOH, 1844, ' 'Twas the twenty-ninth of May, 'twas a holiday, Four and twenty tailors set out to hunt a snail; The snail put forth his horns, and roared like a bull, Away ran the tailors, and catch the snail who wull' / N & Q, 1871, 'Four and twenty weavers went out to kill a snail, The bravest man among them trod upon his tail; The snail turned round with horns like a cow—God bless us, said the weavers, we're dead men now' / *Tailor of Gloucester,* Beatrix Potter, 1903 /

Tailors

Rymour Club, 1911, 'Five and twenty tailors, Ridin' on a snail, Says the foremost to the hindmost, We'll a' be owre the tail; The snail put oot her horns. Like ony hummil coo, Says the hindmost to the foremost, We'll a' be stickit noo!'

Cf. *Calliope: or The Musical Miscellany* (C. Elliott and T. Kay), 1788 '... upon us' / *Slovenske Narodne Pesmi*, K. Strekelj, 'Enkrat so bli znidarji trije o joj! So polza na korajzo klicali' etc ('Once there were three tailors, They called a snail to show his courage. Before the tailors go to war, They get their weapons ready. The tailors stand against the snail, They hold a needle in their hands as a weapon. The snail shows his horns, The tailors lay down their weapons. The snail starts to foam, The trousers of all the tailors start to smell. The apprentice says: I don't go, The assistant says: I don't dare. The master shouted so, That he made it in his trousers. Go away you monster from hell, You have no power over us. Help us, oh you Turkish god, Out of this misery and trouble').

496

Little Tee-Wee,
He went to sea,
In an open boat;
And while afloat,
The little boat bended.
My story's ended.

Douce MS, c. 1815 / JOH, 1844.
Cf. 'There was a king, and he had three daughters'.

497

There was a man of Thessaly,
  And he was wondrous wise,
He jumped into a bramble bush
  And scratched out both his eyes.
And when he saw his eyes were out,
  With all his might and main
He jumped into another bush
  And scratched them in again.

As well as Thessaly, the home-town of this curious gentleman has variously been designated Thessary (c. 1760), Thistleworth (c. 1760), Nineveh (1828), Newington (c. 1830), and Babylon (1842), this last giving rise to the suggestion that there is a reference to the rhyme in *Twelfth Night* ('There dwelt a man in Babylon'). It is more likely, however, that Sir Toby is quoting a ballad *The godly and constante wyse Susanna* (printed 1562–3) which has the same first line. Mrs Thrale called it an 'old Song' in a letter (17 May 1781), and gave the following words:

> There was a Man in Switzerland, in Switzerland,
> in Switzerland,
> There was a Man in Switzerland
> And he was wondrous wise;
> He jump'd into a Quickset Hedge, a Quickset Hedge,
> a Quickset Hedge,
> He jump'd into a Quickset hedge
> And scratch'd out both his Eyes:
> But when he *saw* his Eyes were out, his Eyes were out,
> his Eyes were out,
> But when he saw his Eyes were out
> with all his might & Main,
> He jump'd into another hedge
> And scratch'd them in again.

T Thumb's PSB, c. 1744, 'There was a Man so Wise, He jumpt into A Bramble Bush, And scratcht out both his Eyes. And when he saw, His eyes where out, And reason to Complain, He jumpt into a Quickset Hedge And Scratcht them in again' / *FT Thumb's LSB*, c. 1760 / *Top Book*, c. 1760 / *MG's Melody*, c. 1765, 'Thessaly' / *Songs for the Nursery*, 1805, 'our town' / *Ancient Ballads and Songs*, Peter Buchan, 1828 / *Nurse Lovechild's DFN*, c. 1830 / *Nursery Songs* (Alfred Miller), c. 1830 / JOH, 1842 / Kidson, 1904 / Oral collection, 1946.

498

> There was a thing a full month old
> When Adam was no more;
> Before the thing was five weeks old
> Adam was years four score.

RIDDLE. *Solution:* the moon. In *Love's Labour's Lost* (IV. ii), probably first produced in 1593, Dull the constable asks what was a month old at Cain's birth that is not five weeks old yet; and, after some witticicms have been exchanged, Holofernes replies, 'The moon was a month old when Adam was no more, And raught not to five weeks when he came to five-score'.

Ashmole MS 36, Elias Ashmole, 1643, 'On the Man in the Moone—Tis strange! yet true; He's but a Month old Man: And yet hath livd, since the World began' / *Food for the Mind* (J. Newbery), advert. 1757, 1758 / *Puzzling Cap* (F. Newbery), advert. 1771, (E. Newbery), 1786 / *Child's New Year Gift* (L. Thompson), c. 1790 / *New Collection of*

Thing

Enigmas, 1791 / Peter Puzzlewell, 1792 / *Mince Pies for Christmas*, 1804 / *Guess Book* (W. Davison), c. 1825 / *Fireside Amusements*, R. Chambers, 1850 / *Folk-Lore*, 1889.

499

Thomas a Tattamus took two tees,
To tie two tups to two tall trees,
To frighten the terrible Thomas a Tattamus!
Tell me how many T's there are in that.

CATCH. *Answer:* two. *Tees:* ties; *Tups:* rams.

JOH, 1844 / *American Folk-Lore*, 1897, from Shropshire, England, 'Timothy Titus took two ties To tie two tups to two tall trees, To terrify the terrible Thomas a Tullamees', for counting-out / Crofton MS, 1901, 'Tommy Tottery took two tees'.

500

Dance, Thumbkin, dance,
Dance, ye merry men, every one:
But Thumbkin, he can dance alone,
Thumbkin, he can dance alone.

Dance, Foreman, dance,
Dance, ye merry men, every one:
But Foreman, he can dance alone,
Foreman, he can dance alone.

Dance, Longman, dance,
Dance, ye merry men, every one:
But Longman, he can dance alone,
Longman, he can dance alone.

Dance, Ringman, dance,
Dance, ye merry men, every one:
But Ringman, he can dance alone,
Ringman, he can dance alone.

Dance, Littleman, dance,
Dance, ye merry men, every one:
But Littleman, he can dance alone,
Littleman, he can dance alone.

Thumbkin

Infant amusement conducted with the fingers, solos being executed by the 'Thumbkin' (or 'Bumpkin'), then the 'Foreman', then the 'Longman', then the 'Ringman', and finally the 'Littleman'. A correspondent to *Notes & Queries* (1850), describing the game as a 'valuable and still popular nursery classic', protested against this formula, arguing that it should be 'Thumbkin *cannot* dance alone, So dance ye merry men every one', &c. The correspondent had learnt it thus from a nurse who died in 1796.

Girl's Own Book, Mrs. Child, 1831 [1832] / JOH, 1842, 'Littleman *cannot* dance alone' / Chambers, 1842, 'Dance my wee man, ring man, foreman, foreman, Dance, dance, for thoomiken canna weel dance his lane' / Rimbault, 1846 / N & Q, 1850.

501

> Tinker,
> Tailor,
> Soldier,
> Sailor,
> Rich man,
> Poor man,
> Beggarman,
> Thief.

Small children's fortune-telling rhyme used when counting cherry stones, waistcoat buttons, daisy petals, or the seeds of the Timothy grass. Edward Moor says, in *Suffolk Words* (1823), under *Soldier*: 'On a first appearance with a new coat or waistcoat, a comrade predicts your fate by your buttons, thus:—Sowja, sailor, tinker, tailor, gentleman, apothecary, plowboy, thief—beginning at top, and touching a button, like dropping a bead at each epithet... Another *reading* gives this course—tinker, tailor, sowja, sailor, richman, poorman, plow-boy, poticarry, thief.'

Professor Skeat has pointed out that in Caxton's *The Game and Playe of the Chesse* (c. 1475) each pawn is shown to have an individuality of its own. 'The pawns were the Labourer, Smith, Clerk (or Notary), Merchant, Physician, Taverner, Guard and Ribald', so the rhyme enumerates the eight conditions. 'The thief is the Ribald; the ploughboy, the Labourer; the apothecary, the Physician; the soldier, the Guard; the tailor, the Merchant; the tinker, the Smith. Only two are changed.' (*N & Q*, 1943.) The first four professions in the rhyme are found linked together in a song in Congreve's *Love for Love* (1695):

> A Soldier and a Sailor, a Tinker and a Taylor,
> Had once a doubtful strife, sir.

Needless to say the strife was for a maiden's favour.

Tinker, Tailor

JOH, 1849, 'My belief—A captain, a colonel, a cow-boy, a thief' / *Folk-Lore in N. England*, M. A. Denham, 1858, '... A priest, a parson, A ploughman or a thief' / Newell, 1883, 'Rich man, poor man, beggar-man, thief, Doctor, lawyer, Indian (or merchant) chief' / Bolton, 1888, 'Gentleman, apothecary, Ploughboy, thief' / Gomme, 1898, 'Potter's boy, flour boy, thief' and others / Crofton MS, 1901, '... Prodigal, thief' / Ford, 1904, 'A laird, a lord, A richman, a thief, A tailor, a drummer, A stealer o' beef' / *Rymour Club*, 1911 / Oral collection, 1945–9, 'Army, Navy, Peerage, Trade, Doctor, Divinity, Law'; 'Army, Navy, Medicine, Church, Architect, Lawyer, Left in the lurch'; 'Army, Navy, Church, Law, Medicine, Business, Nothing at all'; and 'Soldier brave, Sailor true, Skilled physician, Oxford blue; Learned lawyer (or Gouty nobleman), Squire so hale, Dashing airman, Curate pale.'

Poetical versions. *Tinker Tailor*, A. P. Herbert, 1922; *Now We are Six*, A. A. Milne, 1927, 'Cherry Stones', '... And what about a Cowboy, Policeman, Jailor, Enginedriver, Or Pirate Chief?'; *Cherry Stones*, John Jerome, 1949, popular dance song.

Cf. *Alemannisches Kinderlied aus der Schweiz*, E. L. Rochholz, 1857, 'Edelmann, Bettelmann, Bû'r, Soldat, Student', two versions / *Das deutsche Kinderbuch*, Karl Simrock, 1857, 'Kaufmann, Laufmann, Docter, Majur, Scheper, Schinner, Besenbinner' / *Deutsche Kinderlied*, F. M. Böhme, 1897, 'Ädelmann, Bädelmann, Doctor, Pastor, Buur, Backer, Kramer, Major', three versions / Oral collection, 1949, 'Kaiser, König, Edelmann, Bürger, Bauer, Bettelmann' / *I Componimenti Minori della Letteratura Pop. Ital.*, F. Corazzini, 1877 [Newell] / Bolton, 1888, from Holland, 'Edelman, Bedelman, Dokter, Pastoor, Roadshur, Nelaatshur, Notaris, Majoor'.

502

As I was going o'er Tipple Tine,
I met a flock of bonny swine;
Some yellow necked,
Some yellow backed,
They were the very bonniest swine
That ever went over Tipple Tine.

RIDDLE. Mactaggart (1824) explains 'There are three kinds of humble bees in Scotland—the black, the *brawnet*, and the brown.... In an old riddle the three kinds are thus specified:—

As I cam ower the tap o' Tyne,
I met a drove o' Highlan' swine;
Some o'm black, some o'm brown,
Some o'm rigget owre the crown;
Sic a drove o' Highlan' swine,
I ne'er met on the tap o' Tyne.'

Gallovidian Encyclopedia, J. Mactaggart, 1824 [1876] / Chambers, 1842 / JOH, 1846 / *Squirrel Nutkin*, Beatrix Potter, 1903 / *Rymour Club*, 1911, 'As I went owre the Hill o' Hoos, I met a bonny flock o' doos; They were a' nick nackit, They were a' brown-backit; Sic a bonnie flock o' doos, Commin' owre the Hill o' Hoos' / *Less Familiar NR*, Robert Graves, 1927.

503

Tit, tat, toe,
My first go,
Three jolly butcher boys all in a row.
Stick one up, stick one down,
Stick one in the old man's crown.

This was at one time used as a formula for a lottery game, of which Gomme gives a detailed description, and was also declaimed by the winner after a game of Noughts and Crosses. In a rhymed account of *Bluebeard*, of the early nineteenth century, appear the lines:

'Tis not a game of tit-tat-to,
And three jolly butcher boys all in a row,
But a double game of tit-tat-to,
And six dead women all of a row.

And in Anne Manning's *The Old Chelsea Bun-house, a tale of the last century* (1855) a character says 'I played at Tit-tat-to with Joe, and posed him with hard riddles'.

Douce MS II, c. 1820, 'Tick, tack, toe, Three little gentlemen all in a row' / Gomme, 1898 / Ford, 1904, 'Tit tat toe, Here I go, And if I miss, I pitch on this' / *Mother Goose*, Arthur Rackham, 1913 / Correspondent, 1948, 'Tit, tat, toe, My first go, Three jolly bully-boys all in a row, Stick one up, stick one down, Stick one in the old man's burying ground' / Correspondents, 1949 and 1950.

504

Titty cum tawtay,
The ducks in the water:
Titty cum tawtay,
The geese follow after.

Game rhyme. Edward Moor, *Suffolk Words* (1823), describes it as 'a song of appropriate cadence' while playing see-saw. JOH had it from Moor, and altered the spelling. The rhyming of *water* with *after* is as in 'Jack and Jill'.

505

I went to the toad that lies under the wall,
I charmed him out, and he came at my call;
I scratched out the eyes of the owl before,
I tore the bat's wing: what would you have more?

It may be presumed that JOH gathered this from oral tradition, since, when he included it in his first nursery rhyme collection, he was apparently unaware that it was the song of the eleventh hag in Ben Jonson's *The Masque of Queens*. Jonson himself annotated this verse for Queen Elizabeth, saying of toads, owls' eyes, and bats' wings, 'These also, both by the confessions of Witches, and testemonye of writers, are of principal vse in they[r] witch-craft.'

Masque of Queens, Ben Jonson, 1609 / JOH, 1842 / *Mother Goose's NR*, L. E. Walter, 1924.

506

There was an old man of Tobago,
Who lived on rice, gruel, and sago;
　　Till, much to his bliss,
　　His physician said this—
To a leg, sir, of mutton you may go.

This rhyme was instrumental in popularizing a new verse form through being the direct inspiration of Lear's limericks. It stands, almost as above, in *Anecdotes and Adventures of Fifteen Gentlemen*, published by John Marshall about 1822. The author of this book may have been R. S. Sharpe, grocer, amateur poet, and author of several other books for children. In the original introduction of *More Nonsense*, Lear wrote: 'Long years ago, in the days when much of my time was passed in a country house, where children and mirth abounded, the lines beginning, "There was an Old Man of Tobago", were suggested to me by a valued friend, as a form of verse lending itself to limitless variety for Rhymes and Pictures; and thenceforth the greater part of the original drawings and verses for the first *Book of Nonsense* were struck off.' When the term 'limerick' first came to be applied to this type of verse, and where it comes from, is obscure. The description does not appear in the *Adventures of Fifteen Gentlemen*, nor in any of the books of limerick-form verse published about the same time by Harris (*vide* 'There was an old woman of

PLATE XIX

There was a sick man of Tobago

Liv'd long on rice-gruel and sago;

But at last, to his bliss,

The physician said this---

"To a roast leg of mutton you

may go."

The rhyme which started Lear making limericks. 'There was a sick man of Tobago' in Marshall's *Anecdotes and Adventures of Fifteen Gentlemen*, c. 1822, probably illustrated by Robert Cruikshank. Opie collection

Surrey', &c.). It is not on record that Lear ever employed the word, and the earliest that the Supplement to *OED* knows of it is in 1896, eight years after his death. The story that the term comes from the chorus 'We'll all come up, come up to Limerick', sung after extempore verses at convivial parties, has not been substantiated; it is not believed that the limerick type of verse was ever employed at these gatherings; indeed it would be more appropriate to say that the original form of the word was 'learick'. JOH printed 'There was an old man of Tobago', without comment, as a nursery rhyme in 1853; and Dickens apparently thought of it as such eleven years later. When Eugene, in *Our Mutual Friend* (1864), recalled the Man of Tobago as, 'our friend who long lived on rice-pudding and isinglass, till at length to his something or other, his physician said something else, and a leg of mutton somehow ended in daygo', Lady Tippins complained he was 'pretending that he can't remember his nursery rhymes!'

Another rhyme from *Adventures of Fifteen Gentlemen* is 'There was a fat man of Bombay' (q.v.).

507

Tom, he was a piper's son,
He learnt to play when he was young,
And all the tune that he could play
Was, 'Over the hills and far away';
Over the hills and a great way off,
The wind shall blow my top-knot off.

Tom with his pipe made such a noise,
That he pleased both the girls and boys,
And they all stopped to hear him play,
'Over the hills and far away'.

Tom with his pipe did play with such skill
That those who heard him could never keep still;
As soon as he played they began for to dance,
Even pigs on their hind legs would after him prance.

As Dolly was milking her cow one day,
Tom took his pipe and began for to play;
So Doll and the cow danced 'The Cheshire Round',
Till the pail was broken and the milk ran on the ground.

Tom

He met old Dame Trot with a basket of eggs,
He used his pipe and she used her legs;
She danced about till the eggs were all broke,
She began for to fret, but he laughed at the joke.

Tom saw a cross fellow was beating an ass,
Heavy laden with pots, pans, dishes, and glass;
He took out his pipe and he played them a tune,
And the poor donkey's load was lightened full soon.

These verses make up the second part of chapbooks titled *Tom, The Piper's Son* and appear to form a version of the old metrical tale, 'The Friar and the Boy', the nearest British approach to the story of the Pied Piper of Hamelin. The first part of the chapbook includes the rhyme, 'Tom, Tom, the piper's son' (q.v.) with which the present song is sometimes confused, as by Pigling Bland, in Beatrix Potter's story, who went off to market singing,

Tom, Tom the piper's son, stole a pig and away he ran!
But all the tune that he could play, was, 'Over the hills and far away!'

The verse 'Tom, he was a piper's son' is recognizable in a song, 'The Distracted Jockey's Lamentation', in *Wit and Mirth: or Pills to Purge Melancholy* (1706):

> Jockey was a Piper's Son,
> And fell in love when he was young;
> But all the Tunes that he could play,
> Was, o'er the Hills, and far away,
> And 'Tis o'er the Hills, and far away,
> 'Tis o'er the Hills, and far away,
> 'Tis o'er the Hills, and far away,
> The Wind has blown my Plad away. [1709]

According to J. W. Ebsworth (*Roxburghe Ballads*) this was written by P. A. Motteux for D'Urfey's comedy, *The Campaigners*, 1698, but it is not in the published version of the play. By 1705 it had been imitated in a song, 'The Recruiting Officer; or, The Merry Volunteers' for Marlborough's campaign. The tenth stanza, which became well known through Farquhar's *The Recruiting Officer* (1706), names the hero Tom:

> Our Prentice Tom may now refuse
> To wipe his scoundrel Master's Shoes;
> For now he's free to sing and play,
> Over the Hills and far away.

'Tom' has, apparently, long been the familiar name for pipers. Spenser, in 1579, says 'Tom Piper makes us better melodie', and Drayton, a few years

PLATE XX

'A New yeares guift for Shrews',
c. 1620, a precursor of 'Tom
married a wife on Sunday'.
British Museum

PLATE XXI

a. Frieze from Walter Crane's *The Baby's Opera*, with the pig as conventionally
pictured today

THE PIG PYE MAN.

b. Hawker, offering for sale the kind of pig
Tom originally stole

c

d

e

c, *d*, and *e*. Woodcuts from
Kendrew's edition of *Tom, the
Piper's Son*, c. 1820, which em-
braces (*e*) the story of the pipe-
playing Tom (p. 408)

later, 'Tom Piper is gone out, and mirth bewails'. The refrain 'Over the hills and far away' has been used by poets and song writers on numerous occasions, and was already old in Motteux's time. It appears in a black-letter ballad, *The Wind hath blown my Plaid away, or, A Discourse betwixt a young Woman and the Elphin Knight* (c. 1670):

> My plaid awa, my plaid awa,
> And ore the hill and far awa,
> And far awa to Norrowa,
> My plaid shall not be blown awa,

a ballad which was possibly alluded to in 1549. The earliest appearance of the tune 'Over the hills and far away' is in the Atkinson MS in Newcastle University Library, pp. 102 and 261. ('Henry Atkinson, his book 1694/5' is written on the front.)

For list of *Tom, The Piper's Son* chapbooks see rhyme No. 509.

508

> Tom married a wife on Sunday,
> Beat her well on Monday,
> Bad was she on Tuesday,
> Middling was she on Wednesday,
> Worse was she on Thursday,
> Dead was she on Friday;
> Glad was Tom on Saturday night,
> To bury his wife on Sunday.

This is a long-lived type of jest. A print of about James I's time, titled 'A New yeares guift for Shrews', carries the advice:

> Who marieth a Wife vppon a Moneday.
> If she will not be good vppon a Tewesday.
> Lett him go to ye wood vppon a Wensday
> And cutt him a cudgell upon the Thursday.
> And pay her soundly uppon a Fryday.
> And she mend not, ye Diuil take her a Saterday.
> Then may he eate his meate in peace on the Sonday.

A similar marriage is reported by 'Poor Robin' in *An Almanack of Old and New Fashion* (1693), and again in a seven-verse folk song ('On Monday morning I married a wife') collected by Vaughan Williams in 1909. In the nineteenth century the common nursery version seems to have been,

Tom

Tom, Tom, of Islington,
Married a wife on Sunday,
Brought her home on Monday,
Bought a stick on Tuesday,
Beat her well on Wednesday,
Sick was she on Thursday,
Dead was she on Friday,
Glad was Tom on Saturday night
To bury his wife on Sunday.

This was the wording known to Charles Lamb, who sent Latin renderings of the verse ('A domestic Iliad! A cycle of calamity! A seven-days' Tragedy!') in letters to two friends in 1831.

Newest Christmas Box, c. 1797, 'I married a Wife on Sunday, She began to scold on Monday...' / *Songs for the Nursery*, 1805, and *MG's Quarto*, c. 1825, as quote / MS addition by Ralph Speerman (c. 1747–1823) to John Bell's interleaved *GG's Garland*, 1810, 'I married A wife upon Sunday She made me A Cuckold on Monday I bought a good stick on Tuesday and I beat my Wife on Wednesday She Sicken'd soar [? sore] on Thursday She gave her last Puff on Friday I buried her on the Saturday then Who was so happy on Sunday. Variation: so I married Another on Sunday' / Letter to Bernard Barton from Charles Lamb, 30 Apr. 1831, 'Thomas, Thomas, de Islington, uxorem duxit die nuperâ Dominicâ. Reduxit domum posterâ. Succedenti baculum emit. Postridiè ferit illam. Ægrescit illa subsequenti. Proximâ (nempe Veneris) est Mortua. Plurimum gestiit Thomas, quòd appropinquanti Sabbato efferenda sit' [1905] / JOH, 1842 / N & Q, 1881 / *Roxburghe Ballads*, vol. vii, J. W. Ebsworth, 1893.
Cf. 'Solomon Grundy'.

509

Tom, Tom, the piper's son,
Stole a pig and away he run;
   The pig was eat
   And Tom was beat,
And Tom went howling down the street.

Children are often concerned about the stolen pig being straightway eaten; modern illustrators, however, depict the scene incorrectly. The pig was not a live one but a sweetmeat model sold by a street hawker, as is narrated in the chapbooks. 'This man makes pigs of paste and fills their bellies with currants and places two little currants in their heads for eyes.' Vendors of such pigs were common in the eighteenth century; their street cry, still remembered in some nurseries, being,

Tom

A long tail'd Pig,
Or a short tail'd Pig,
Or a Pig without any tail,
A Boar Pig, or a Sow Pig,
Or a Pig with a curly tail.
Take hold of the Tail and eat off his head;
And then you'll be sure the Pig hog is dead.

The only live pigs with which Tom had anything to do are in the quite separate song (No. 507) in which Tom's musical ability is said to be such that 'Even pigs on their hind legs would after him prance'.

Tom, The Piper's Son (J. Evans), c. 1795; (T. Evans), c. 1800; (J. E. Evans), c. 1803; (J. Kendrew), c. 1820 / *Songs for the Nursery*, 1805 / *GG's Garland*, 1810, 'Tom Thumb the piper's son' / *Adventures of Tom, The Piper's Son* (D. Carvalho), c. 1830 / *Tom the Piper's Son* (W. Walker and Son), c. 1835, panorama / JOH, 1842 / *Baby's Opera*, 1877 / *County Folk-Lore, Lincolnshire*, Mabel Peacock, 1908, 'Tom, Tom, the baker's son, Stole a wig (small cake) and away he run'.

510

Go to bed, Tom,
Go to bed, Tom,
Tired or not, Tom,
Go to bed, Tom.

Crofton says that in The Warwickshire Regiment the nickname for Tattoo was 'Go to bed Tom', and the above verse, chanted on one note, was accompanied by drumming with the fists. A military song it may originally have been. In *The Battle of Prague*, a musical composition printed about 1800, the commentary runs 'Word of Command'... 'flying bullets'... 'Light Dragoons advancing'... 'Trumpet of Recall'... and after 'Finale'—'Go to bed home'. In *Nancy Cock's Pretty Song Book* (c. 1780) the verse is well suited to barrack room voices:

Drunk or sober, go to-bed Tom,
Go to-bed Tom,
Go to-bed Tom,
Drunk or sober, go to-bed Tom,
T' other pipe,
And t'other pot;
Then to-bed, Tom,
Then to-bed, Tom,
Drunk or sober, go to-bed Tom.

Tom

This is illustrated with a cut of Tom with pipe and pint pot, and a drummer boy drumming by his side.

Nancy Cock's PSB, c. 1780, as quote / *Songs for the Nursery*, 1805 / *Vocal Harmony*, c. 1806, as c. 1780 / *Nursery Songs* (G. Ross), c. 1812 / *Cheerful Warbler* (J. Kendrew), c. 1820 / *Sugar Plum* (J. Roberts), c. 1825 / JOH, 1843 / *Only True MG Melodies*, c. 1843, final rhyme in book, 'Go to bed, Tom, go to bed, Tom—Merry or sober, go to bed, Tom' / Crofton, 1901 / Correspondent, 1949, 'Go to bed, Tom, Go to bed, Tom, Get up in the morning I beat the big drum'.

511

Tom Brown's two little Indian boys;
One ran away,
The other wouldn't stay,
Tom Brown's two little Indian boys.

Given by JOH (1842) as a game, undescribed; it is probably an infant amusement similar to 'Two little dicky birds sitting on a wall' (q.v.).

T Thumb's PSB, c. 1744, 'Tom Brown's Two little Indians, Two little Indians, One would not play, The other would not stay, Tom Brown's two Little Indian Boys' / *Vocal Harmony*, c. 1806 / *GG's Garland*, 1810 / JOH, 1842 / *Only True MG Melodies*, c. 1843.

512

Tommy kept a chandler's shop,
Richard went to buy a mop;
Tommy gave him such a whop,
That sent him out of the chandler's shop.

Known only from JOH (1846), and by correspondent (1960), who said it was used as an election rhyme in Carlton, Nottingham (c. 1898):

Godfrey kept a butcher's shop,
Blackburn went to buy a chop;
Godfrey got behind the door
And knocked old Blackburn on the floor.

513

Tommy o'Lin, and his wife, and wife's mother,
They all went over a bridge together:
The bridge broke down, and they all tumbled in,
What a precious concern, quoth Tommy o'Lin.

Four lines which are part of an old song, probably that ('Thom of lyn') mentioned in the *Complaynt of Scotlande* (1549), and perhaps the same as the 'ballett of Thomalyn' licensed to master John Wallye and mistress Toye in 1557–8. However this may be, in a play, *The longer thou livest, the more foole thou art*, registered 1569, the verse is quoted in full:

> Tom a lin and his wife, and his wiues mother
> They went ouer a bridge all three together,
> The bridge was broken, and they fell in,
> The Deuil go with all quoth Tom a lin.

Moros, the clown, 'synging the foote of many Songes, as fooles were wont' explains that he learnt the pieces from his mother, 'as I war wont in her lappe to sit', so the song must have been an old memory to the audience of more than four hundred years ago. In the next century (1632) a rather ribald rendering of ten verses was sung, beginning,

> Tom a Lin was a Swelch man borne,
> His head was pold, his beard was shorne,
> His cloathes were ragged, his shirt was thin,
> Whoeuer saw any like Tom a Lin.

Since then the song has been printed many times, the familiar lines most often appearing at the end, as in *The Distracted Sailor's Garland* (c. 1765):

> Tommy Linn is a Scotchman born,
> His head is bald, and his beard is shorn,
> He has a cap made of hare skin,
> An elderman is Tommy Linn.
>
> Tommy Linn has no boots to put on,
> But two calf skins, and the hair it was on,
> They are open at the side and the water goes in,
> Unwholesome boots says Tommy Linn.
>
> Tommy Linn has a mare of the gray,
> Lam'd of all fours as I hear say,
> It has the farcy all over the skin,
> Its a running yade, says Tommy Linn.

Tommy o'Lin

Tommy Linn no bridle had to put on,
But two mouses tails that he put on,
Tommy Linn had no saddle to put on,
But two urchin skins, and them he put on.

Tommy Linn went to yonder hall,
Went hipping and skipping among them all,
They ask'd what made him come so boldly in,
I am come a wooing, says Tommy Linn.

Tommy Linn went to the church to be wed,
The bride followed after hanging down her head,
She hung down her cheeks, she hung down her chin,
This is a glooming queen, says Tommy Linn.

Tommy Linn's daughter sat on the stairs,
Oh, dear father, gin I be no fair,
The stairs they broke, and she fell in,
You are fair enough now, says Tommy Linn.

Tommy Linn's daughter sat on the bridge,
Oh, dear father, gin I be not trig,
The bridge it broke, and she fell in,
You are trig enough now, says Tommy Linn.

Tommy Linn and his wife, and his wife's mother
They all fell into the fire together,
They that lay undermost got a hot skin,
We are not enough, says Tommy Linn.

The name of the hero is variously given as 'Tom Bolin' (c. 1815), 'Tom o' the Lin' (1829), 'Bryan o'Lin' (1842), 'Harry Trewin' (1891), and 'Bryan O'Flynn' (oral collection). He is often confused with young Tamlane of the fairy ballad, though no connexion exists between them. Professor Child (*English and Scottish Popular Ballads*) assumed that the references in the *Complaynt of Scotlande*, and in the Stationers' *Register* were to the ballad. In the *Complaynt* there are two references, 'Thom of lyn' is listed among the tunes; 'the tayl of the ȝong tamlene' among the tales. Only the second of these might refer to the ballad, and even this is doubtful. In the *Register* the term 'ballett' is without significance, for the word had not then acquired its present specialized application. The entry is more likely to refer to a song of the type of Tom o'Lin, which is known to have been current at the time. It is possible, further, that the song was an English one (as are several others in the *Complaynt of Scotlande*). A correspondent to *Folk-Song* (1929) collected a version beginning,

> Brian O'Lynn was a gentleman born,
> He lived at a time when no clothes were worn.

This lends weight to the theory that the song was composed by a man of the South in derision of the rude habits and scanty clothing of the Celt. A contributor to *N & Q* (June 1962), gives reasons for thinking that 'Tomliu-lin' in *Greenes farewell to Folly* (1591) refers to 'Tom o'Lin'.

The longer thou livest, William Wager, 1569, written about nine years earlier / *The Pinder of Wakefield*, 1632 / *Distracted Sailor's Garland*, c. 1765 / *North Country Chorister*, J. Ritson, 1802, quoting a 'Bishoprick Ballad-singer', 1792 / *Minstrelsy of Scottish Border*, Sir Walter Scott, 1802, 'A burlesque ballad, beginning, Tom o' the Linn was a Scotsman born, is still well known.' (Scott set down the words he knew some twenty years later in a letter to Kirkpatrick Sharpe, the stanza of consequence being 'Tam o' the Linn and his wife's mither, Fa la linkum, feedledum, They fell baith in the fire thegither, Fa la linkum, feedledum, Tam being undermost gat a brunt skin, Take turn about, mither, 'quo Tam o' the Linn' [1880]) / *Tom Bolin*, c. 1815, a fifteen-verse ballad printed at Boston, Mass. [*N & Q*, 13th s.] / *MG's Melody*, c. 1825, 'Kit and Kitterit and Kitterit's mother' / *Scottish Songs*, R. Chambers, 1829, 'Tom o' the Lin, and a' his bairns, Fa la, fa la, fa lillie! Fell i' the fire in other's arms; Fa la, fa la, fa lillie! Oh! quo the bunemost, I've got a het skin! It's hetter below! quo Tom o' the Lin. Sing lindly tindly, fa la lindly, Fa la, fa la, fa lillie' / Kinloch MSS, c. 1830, and Campbell MSS, c. 1830, 'Tam o Lin' [cited by Child] / JOH, 1842, 'The bridge was loose, and they all tumbled in, What a precious concern! cried Bryan O'Lin' / JOH, 1849 / *Legends of Ireland*, Samuel Lover, 1860, 'Briann o Lynn' / Song sheet, c. 1860, 'The Bridge it broke down, they all tumbled in, We'll find ground at the bottom, said Bryan O'Lynn' [*N & Q*, 12th s.] / *Songs of the West*, S. Baring-Gould, 1891. (In 1895 Gould remarked that there were similar songs sung in Gascony, Languedoc, and French Canada.) Williams, 1923, 'Oh, we'll go home by boats, says Bryan O'Lynn' / *Come Hither*, Walter de la Mare, 1923 / *Folk-Song*, 1929 / *American Folklore*, 1941 / *Big Book of Mother Goose* (James and Jonathan Co., Wisconsin), 1946, 'The two gray kits, And the gray kits' mother, All went over The bridge together. The bridge broke down, They all fell in; May the rats go with you, Says Tom Bolin' / Oral collection, 1949.

514

As Tommy Snooks and Bessy Brooks
Were walking out one Sunday,
Says Tommy Snooks to Bessy Brooks,
Tomorrow will be Monday.

JOH, 1842 / *Mother Goose*, Kate Greenaway, 1881.

515

Little Tommy Tacket
Sits upon his cracket;

Tommy Tacket

Half a yard of cloth
Will make him coat and jacket;
Make him coat and jacket,
Breeches to the knee,
And if you will not have him,
You may let him be.

The Scottish version of this is the little ditty, now apparently forgotten,

> Wee Totum Fogg,
> Sits upon a creepie;
> Half an ell o' gray
> Wad be his coat and breekie.

Burns must have had it in mind when he wrote his nursery song,

> Wee Willie Gray, and his leather wallet,
> Peal a willow wand to be him boots and jacket...

which was published in the *Scots Musical Museum* (1803), to the tune of 'Wee Totem Fogg'. Laing said that this lively old tune, like 'The Dusty Miller' and 'Go to Berwick, Johnny' (qq.v.) had been played in Scotland time out of mind as a particular species of 'the double hornpipe'; and that James Allan, piper to the Duke of Northumberland, had assured him that this peculiar measure originated in the borders of England and Scotland. JOH's version, being a North country one, tends to confirm this.

Lyric Poetry, W. Stenhouse and D. Laing, 1839, Scottish version [1853] / *London Jingles* (J. G. Rusher), c. 1840. 'A fine young man is he' / JOH, 1842, explains cracket, 'A little three-legged stool seen by the ingle of every cottage in the north of England' / *The Only Child*, J. Kirkup, 1925, 'Little Tommy Tacket, Sits on his cracket. The "cracket" was a part of every Tyneside home'.

516

Little Tommy Tittlemouse
Lived in a little house;
He caught fishes
In other men's ditches.

JOH, 1844 / JOH, 1853, 'Little Tom Tittlemouse, Lived in a bell-house; The bell-house broke, And Tom Tittlemouse woke' / *Mother Goose*, Kate Greenaway, 1881.

517

Tommy Trot, a man of law,
Sold his bed and lay upon straw;
Sold the straw and slept on grass,
To buy his wife a looking-glass.

Douce MS II, c. 1820 / JOH, 1842 / *American Mother Goose*, Ray Wood, 1938, gathered from the 'peckerwood' people.
  Cf. 'Margery Daw'.

518

Little Tommy Tucker,
  Sings for his supper:
What shall we give him?
  White bread and butter.
How shall he cut it
  Without a knife?
How will he be married
  Without a wife?

'To be married without a wife is a terrible Thing', says the editor of *Mother Goose's Melody* in a mock-scholastic note. Unfortunately nothing is known about this would-be bridegroom. A Thomas Tucker, Bachelor of Arts, was appointed 'Prince or Lorde of the Revells' at St. John's College, Oxford, in 1607, and a 'Tom Tuck' is featured in one of Herrick's epigrams in *Witt's Recreations* (1640). In 'An excellent new Medley', printed about 1620, in which each line represented a current song or ballad, one of the lines is 'Tom would eat meat but wants a knife'. The phrase, 'To sing for one's supper', has long been proverbial, as in *The Knight of the Burning Pestle* (1613), 'No, Michael...let him stay at home and sing for his supper'.

T *Thumb's PSB*, c. 1744, 'Little Tom Tucker' (four lines) / *MG's Melody*, c. 1765 / *GG's Garland*, 1784 / T *Tit's SB*, 1790 / *Christmas Box*, vol. ii, 1798 / *Little Tom Tucker* (T. Evans), c. 1800 / *Songs for the Nursery*, 1805, 'Little Johnny Stutter' / *Vocal Harmony*, c. 1806 / *Pretty Tales*, 1808 / *The History of Tom Tucker* (J. Kendrew), c. 1820; similar titles printed by T. Batchelar, c. 1820; J. Catnach, c. 1830; T. Richardson, c. 1830; G. Walker and Son, c. 1835 / JOH, 1843 / Rimbault, 1846 / Crofton MS, 1901, given as rhyme on the name Tommy.
  Curiosa: *Friar Bacon's Miracle!* 'By the World Renowned Thom Tucker. Published by the Far Famed Jack Horner', 1867.

519

Trip upon trenchers, and dance upon dishes,
My mother sent me for some barm, some barm;
She bid me tread lightly, and come again quickly,
For fear the young men should do me some harm.
   Yet didn't you see, yet didn't you see,
   What naughty tricks they put upon me:
     They broke my pitcher,
     And spilt the water,
     And huffed my mother,
     And chid her daughter,
   And kissed my sister instead of me.

A fragment in the Herd MS suggests that this was a ribald song:

   I'll Trip upon Trenchers, I'll dance upon dishes;
   My mither sent me for barm, for barm!
   And thro' the kirk yard I met wi' the laird,
   The silly poor body could do me no harm.
   But down i' the park, I met with the clerk,
   And he gied me my barm, my barm!

Herd titled the song 'Barm, or cushen-dance'. The cushion dance, once popular at weddings, was mentioned by Heywood in 1607.

MG's Melody, c. 1765 / Herd MS, 1776 / *GG's Garland*, 1784 / *Vocal Harmony*, c. 1806 / *Heart of Midlothian*, Sir Walter Scott, 1818, a snatch is sung by Effie / *MG's Quarto*, c. 1825, 'My mother sent me for some yeast, some yeast' / JOH, 1842.

520

Tweedledum and Tweedledee
   Agreed to have a battle,
For Tweedledum said Tweedledee
   Had spoiled his nice new rattle.
Just then flew by a monstrous crow,
   As big as a tar-barrel,
Which frightened both the heroes so,
   They quite forgot their quarrel.

Alice, in *Through the Looking-Glass*, could not help recalling the words of the old song when she met the two characters marked 'DUM' and 'DEE'.

Tweedledum and Tweedledee

In 1725 a bitter feud arose between Bononcini and Handel in which, according to the onlookers, it was difficult to distinguish what difference there was between the opposing parties. John Byrom wrote:

> Some say, compar'd to Bononcini,
> That Mynheer Handel's but a Ninny;
> Others aver, that he to Handel
> Is scarcely fit to hold a Candle:
> Strange all this Difference should be
> 'Twixt Tweedle-dum and Tweedle-dee!

Byrom is said to have coined the words 'Tweedledum' and 'Tweedledee'. However, the last couplet is also attributed to Swift and to Pope. The nursery rhyme is not found in print till eighty years later, but it may originally have described the feud, or, be earlier, and have given Byrom the idea for his verse.

Original Ditties for the Nursery (J. Harris), c. 1805, 'Agreed to fight a battle ... As black as a tar barrel' [1807] / JOH, 1853 / *Through the Looking-Glass*, Lewis Carroll, 1865, 'Just then flew down a monstrous crow, As black as a tar barrel.'

521

> When a Twister a-twisting will twist him a twist,
> For the twisting of his twist, he three twines doth intwist;
> But if one of the twines of the twist do untwist,
> The twine that untwisteth, untwisteth the twist.
>
> Untwirling the twine that untwisteth between,
> He twirls, with his twister, the two in a twine;
> Then, twice having twisted the twines of the twine,
> He twitcheth, the twice he had twined, in twain.
>
> The twain that, in twining, before in the twine
> As twines were intwisted; he now doth untwine;
> Twixt the twain inter-twisting a twine more between,
> He, twirling his twister, makes a twist of the twine.

This gruelling tongue-twister comes from *Grammatica Linguae Anglicanae* (1674) by Dr. John Wallis, the mathematician and grammarian. It appears to be a rendering he himself made of a verse told him by a Frenchman in 1653:

> Quand un Cordier, cordant, veult corder une corde;
> Pour sa corde corder, trois cordons il accorde:

Twister

Mais, si un des cordons de la corde descorde,
Le cordon descordant fait descorder la corde.

The lines were written by Alain Chartier, *Œuvres* (1529).

Grammatica Linguae Anglicanae, J. Wallis, 1674 / *MG's Quarto*, c. 1825 / *Girl's Own Book*, Mrs. Child, 1831, both in English and French [1832] / *Girl's Book of Diversions*, Miss Leslie, 1835 / JOH, 1842 / Crofton, 1901 / *Dorsetshire Folk-Lore*, J. S. Udal, 1922, given as a forfeit in a Christmastide game.

522

We are all in the dumps,
For diamonds are trumps;
The kittens are gone to St. Paul's!
The babies are bit,
The moon's in a fit,
And the houses are built without walls.

Blackwood's, ? John Wilson, July 1824 / JOH, 1843 / *Mother Goose* (T. Nelson), c. 1945. / *We Are All in the Dumps with Jack and Guy*, Maurice Sendak (NY: HarperCollins), 1993.

523

We're all dry with drinking on't,
We're all dry with drinking on't,
The piper kissed the fiddler's wife,
And I can't sleep for thinking on't.

This song fragment, which has become renowned through being adopted by Robert Burns, and was, before him, twice displayed as Scottish ware, so that its northern origin has never been doubted, had all the while quietly been residing in the English nursery, where it appeared about 1744. Burns wrote his song 'My Love, she's but a Lassie yet' for the third volume of Johnson's *Scots Musical Museum:*

My love, she's but a lassie yet,
My love, she's but a lassie yet,
We'll let her stand a year or twa,
She'll no be half sae saucy yet.

We

I rue the day I sought her O,
I rue the day I sought her O,
Wha gets her need na say he's woo'd,
But he may say he's bought her O.

Come draw a drap o' the best o't yet,
Come draw a drap o' the best o't yet:
Gae seek for pleasure whare ye will,
But here I never misst it yet.

We're a' dry wi' drinking o't,
We're a' dry wi' drinking o't,
The minister kisst the fidler's wife:
He could na preach for thinkin o't.

He doubtless received his inspiration from Herd's MS (1776) with which he was very familiar:

We're a' dry wi' drinking o't,
We're a' dry wi' drinking o't,
The parson kist the fidler's wife,
And he cou'd na preach for thinking o't.

According to Henley and Henderson a still earlier version of the song is 'The Cowgate Garland, or the Drinking O't' in a chapbook in the Mother-well collection:

My wife and me we did agree,
When married I was thinking o't,
Her daughter Kate she angered me.
Then I began the drinking o't.
O weary fa' the drinking o't:
O weary fa' the drinking o't:
An ye begin as I did then
Your purse will loose the clinking o't.

We're a' dry at the drinking o't,
We're a' dry at the drinking o't;
Our punch was toom or we had done,
And this began the thinking o't.

Compare also some familiar lines in 'Daniel Cooper, Or, The High-land Laddy', a mock-Scottish ballad 'printed for P. Brooksby at the Golden-Ball' (1638):

The fidler kist the Piper's Wife,
the Blind-man sat and saw her,
She lift up her Holland smock
and Daniel Cooper claw'd her.

Burns also borrowed the title 'My Love, she's but a Lassie yet'. The tune appears in Walsh's *Caledonian Country Dances* (c. 1740), and in Johnson's *Twelve Country Dances* (1749) under the title 'Foot's Vagaries', as well as in the *Museum*.

T Thumb's PSB, c. 1744, as text / *A Little Play-Book*, c. 1746 / Herd MS, 1776 / *GG's Garland*, 1784 / *Musical Museum*, 1790, contribution by Burns / *Nurse Lovechild's DFN*, c. 1830 / JOH, 1842 / *The Poetry of Robert Burns*, W. E. Henley and T. F. Henderson, 1897.

524

There were three jovial Welshmen,
    As I have heard men say,
And they would go a-hunting
    Upon St. David's Day.

All the day they hunted
    And nothing could they find,
But a ship a-sailing,
    A-sailing with the wind.

One said it was a ship,
    The other he said, Nay;
The third said it was a house,
    With the chimney blown away.

And all the night they hunted
    And nothing could they find,
But the moon a-gliding,
    A-gliding with the wind.

One said it was the moon,
    The other he said, Nay;
The third said it was a cheese,
    And half of it cut away.

And all the day they hunted
    And nothing could they find,
But a hedgehog in a bramble bush,
    And that they left behind.

The first said it was a hedgehog,
    The second he said, Nay;
The third said it was a pincushion,
    And the pins stuck in wrong way.

Welshmen

And all the night they hunted
    And nothing could they find,
But a hare in a turnip field,
    And that they left behind.

The first said it was a hare,
    The second he said, Nay;
The third said it was a calf,
    And the cow had run away.

And all the day they hunted
    And nothing could they find,
But an owl in a holly tree,
    And that they left behind.

One said it was an owl,
    The other he said, Nay;
The third said 'twas an old man,
    And his beard growing grey.

This well-known song was embodied in a black-letter broadside ballad, *Choice of Inuentions, Or Seuerall sorts of the figure of three*, entered in the Stationers' register 2 January 1632:

There were three men of Gotam,
    as I haue heard men say,
That needs would ride a hunting
    vpon Saint Dauids day,
Though all the day they hunting were,
    yet no sport could they see,
Untill they spide an Owle
    as she sate in a tree:
The first man said it twas a Goose,
    the second man said nay,
The third man said it was a Hawke,
    but his Bels were falne away.

The song, it appears, was already old, for in Fletcher and Shakespeare's joint work, *The Two Noble Kinsmen*, which may be dated 1613, the jailor's daughter sings (III. v),

There were three fooles, fell out about an howlet
    The one sed it was an owle
    The other he said nay,
The third he sed it was a hawke, and her bels were cut away.

506

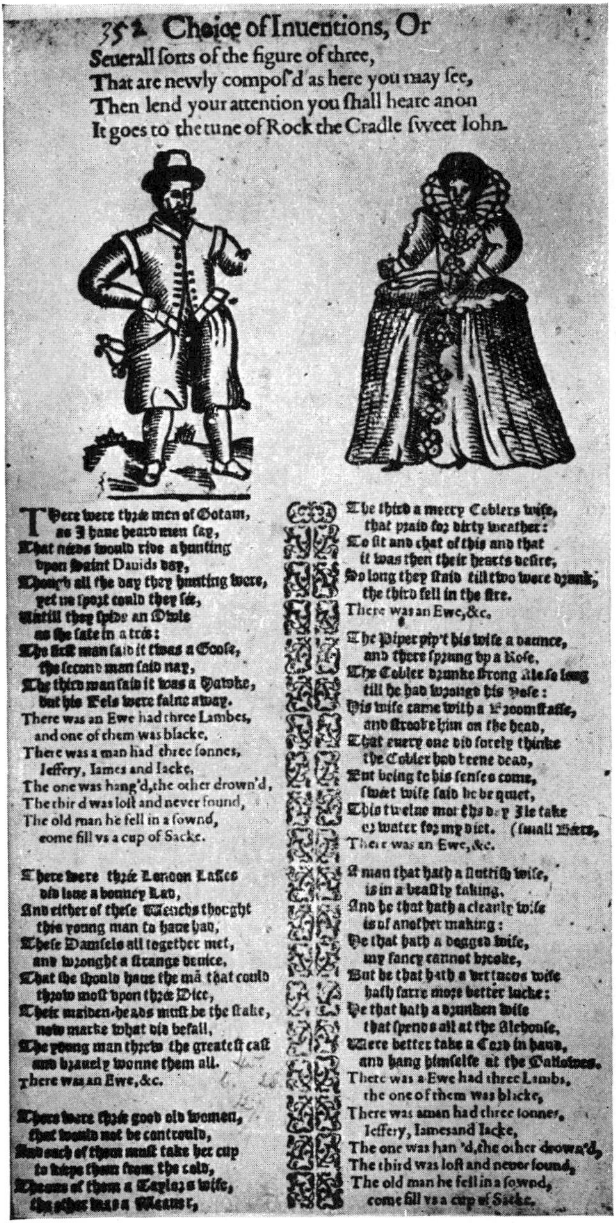

PLATE XXII

Choice of Inuentions, a broadside ballad, registered 2 January 1632, which contains lines still remembered in the nursery. British Museum. Cf. Plate XXIII

PLATE XXIII

a. 'Three wise men of Go-tham', by L. Leslie Brooke in *The Nursery Rhyme Book,* 1897

b. The Three Jovial Huntsmen, by Randolph Caldecott, 1880

c. The Old Woman and Her Three Sons, 1815. British Museum

'SEUERALL SORTS OF THE FIGURE OF THREE'
(Cf. Plate XXII)

Welshmen

The first five verses, in their present state, 'For Little Masters and Misses', are found as early as 1760 in *The Top Book of All*. These were known to JOH in 1842, and he was later able to add the rest of the story. In 1880 Randolph Caldecott further popularized the song with his illustrations to a delightful Lancashire dialect version, *The Three Jovial Huntsmen*, beginning,

> It's of three jovial huntsmen, an' a hunting they did go;
> An' they hunted, an' they hollo'd, an' they blew their horns also.
> > Look ye there!
> An' one said, Mind yo'r e'en, an' keep yo'r noses reet i' th' wind,
> An' then, by scent or seet, we'll leet o' summat to our mind.
> > Look ye there!
>
> They hunted, an' they hollo'd, an' the first thing they did find
> Was a tatter't boggart, in a field, an' that they left behind.
> > Look ye there!
> One said it was a boggart, an' another he said, Nay;
> It's just a ge'man-farmer, that has gone an' lost his way.
> > Look ye there!

A song comparative with this, which has also entered nursery collections, was possibly also old when it appeared in some sheet music about 1725:

> There was 3 Jovial Welshmen, & they w$^{d.}$ hunt y^e Fox;
> And where sh$^{d.}$ they find bold Reynolds, but among y^e Woods & Rocks.
> Wth a gibble, gibble, gibble, all in a merry tone,
> Wth a hoop, hoop, hoop & hallow, & so cry'd 'ery one.

Six verses follow. Entitled 'The Pursuit of Reynard', this is found again, with fairly similar words, in *The Woody Choristers* (c. 1770). It was also collected by Baring-Gould for *A Book of Nursery Songs and Rhymes* (1895) and by Alfred Williams in *Folk Songs of the Upper Thames* (1923). A tune is given in *Rhymes, Jingles, and Songs* (1862) [c. 1865].

525

> I am a pretty wench,
> And I come a great way hence,
> And sweethearts I can get none:
> But every dirty sow
> Can get sweethearts enough,
> And I pretty wench can get none.

GG's Garland, 1784 / *T Thumb's SB*, 1788 / *Vocal Harmony*, c. 1806 / JOH, 1842 / *Folk-Song*, 1906, first of five verses 'It's of a pretty wench, That came running 'long a trench, And sweet-heart she could not get one, When there's many dirty sow a sweetheart has got now, And I a pretty wench can't get one'; collected by R. Vaughan Williams who compared the tune with the 18th-century 'There was a pretty Lass, and a Tenant o my own' / Williams, 1923, 'I am a pretty wench, And I came a long way hence, But for sweethearts I can get none, none, none. If it had not been for one, I should have married, long and gone, To a weaver that weaves at his loom, loom, loom'; with four further verses. *Enough* originally *enow*. Cf. Williams with 'There was a little man and he wooed a little maid'.

526

As I was a-walking on Westminster Bridge,
I met with a Westminster scholar;
He pulled off his cap, an' drew off his gloves,
Now what was the name of this scholar?

RIDDLE. *Solution:* Andrew.

Holme MS, c. 1645, 'As j went by the way j met wth a boy j tooke him my freind for to bee he took of his hat & draw of his gloues & so saluted mee' / JOH, 1843 / N & Q, 1865 / *Rymour Club*, 1911. Also well known to schoolchildren.

527

Did you see my wife, did you see, did you see,
Did you see my wife looking for me?
She wears a straw bonnet, with white ribbands on it,
And dimity petticoats over her knee.

JOH, 1853 / Mason, 1877, 'Have you seen my love, my love, my love? Have you seen my love waiting for me?' / *Garland of Country Songs*, F. H. Sheppard and S. Baring-Gould, 1895, 'O did you see my man, my man, my man, Did you see my man looking for me? He wore a red jacket, a pair of blue stockings, A hump on his back, and was blind in one eye'; words and tune learnt from nurse about sixty-five years before / *Less Familiar NR*, Robert Graves, 1927.

528

William and Mary, George and Anne,
Four such children had never a man:

William and Mary

They put their father to flight and shame,
And called their brother a shocking bad name.

Undoubtedly refers to the daughters and sons-in-law of James II, and their brother, the Old Pretender. An equally disrespectful rhyme about the first couple, 'What is the rhyme for porringer' (q.v.), is also remembered in the nursery.

JOH, 1842.
Cf. a ballad, *The True Protestant's Triumph*, c. 1690, 'Come, let's sing to the Honour and Praise of William and Mary, George and Anne.'

529

Wee Willie Winkie runs through the town,
Upstairs and downstairs in his night-gown,
Rapping at the window, crying through the lock,
Are the children all in bed, for now it's eight o'clock?

The author of the following 'hamely clinky' personifying sleep was William Miller (1810–72), 'the Laureate of the Nursery'. It appears above his name in *Whistle-Binkie; a Collection of Songs for the Social Circle*, published by David Robertson in 1841:

Wee Willie Winkie rins through the town,
Up stairs and doon stairs in his nicht-gown,
Tirling at the window, crying at the lock,
Are the weans in their bed, for it's now ten o'clock?

Hey, Willie Winkie, are ye coming ben?
The cat's singing grey thrums to the sleeping hen,
The dog's spelder'd on the floor, and disna gi'e a cheep,
But here's a waukrife laddie! that winna fa' asleep.

Onything but sleep, you rogue! glow'ring like the moon,
Rattling in an airn jug wi' an airn spoon,
Rumbling, tumbling round about, crawing like a cock,
Skirling like a kenna-what, wauk'ning sleeping fock.

Hey, Willie Winkie—the wean's in a creel!
Wambling aff a bodie's knee like a very eel,
Rugging at the cat's lug, and raveling a' her thrums—
Hey, Willie Winkie—see, there he comes!

Wearied is the mither that has a stoorie wean,
A wee stumpie stoussie, that canna rin his lane,

511

Willie Winkie

That has a battle aye wi' sleep before he'll close an ee—
But a kiss frae aff his rosy lips gi'es strength anew to me.

It seems likely that, as so often happened, Miller used a traditional rhyme as his starting point and added other verses. The first verse is found in *Nursery Rhymes, Tales and Jingles* (1844), and in Rusher's *The Cries of Banbury and London*, which seems to have appeared earlier. Chambers in 1842 includes all Miller's verses among his antiquities while acknowledging their appearance the previous year. 'Willie Winkie', as may be seen in Jacobite songs, was a nickname for William III (d. 1702), and according to Robert L. Ripley the rhyme refers to that king.

Cries of Banbury and London (J. G. Rusher), c. 1840 / *Whistle-Binkie* (David Robertson), 1841 / Chambers, 1842 / *Cries of Banbury and London* (J. G. Rusher), c. 1840 / *Only True MG Melodies*, c. 1843 / *Songs for the Nursery* (David Robertson), 1844, 'Air—"Jim along Josey"' / *NR, Tales and Jingles* (J. Burns), 1844. A MS in Miller's autograph, 'Willie Winkie—The Scottish Nursery Morpheus', Oct. 1846, was one of several reported to be in the possession of readers of the *Glasgow Herald*, Jan. 1947. Some sheet music, *Wee Willie Winkie*, 'A nursery Song, by William Miller. Air by Rev. W. B. Published for the benefit of William Miller, by William Mitchison, Glasgow', appeared c. 1860. Miller's collected work, *Scottish Nursery Songs*, appeared 1863. The rhyme has been translated and is a favourite in Germany, 'Der kleine Villee Vinkee.'

530

Willy boy, Willy boy, where are you going?
I will go with you, if that I may.
I'm going to the meadow to see them a-mowing,
I am going to help them to make the hay.

Songs for the Nursery, 1805 / JOH, 1843 / *Only True MG Melodies*, c. 1843, 'Willie boy, Willie boy, Where are you going? O let us go with you this sunshiny day, I'm going to the meadow, To see them a mowing, I'm going to help the girls Turn the new hay' / *Mother Goose*, Kate Greenaway, 1881 / *Willy Boy, Willy Boy*, accompaniment by Paul Edmonds, 1936, sheet music.

531

Blow, wind, blow! and go, mill, go!
That the miller may grind his corn;
That the baker may take it,
And into bread make it,
And bring us a loaf in the morn.

Wind

Little Rhymes for Little Folks (J. Harris), 1823; 'And send us some hot in the morn' / JOH, 1844 / *My Grandmother's Budget*, F. F. Broderip, 1863 / *Mother Goose* (T. Nelson), c. 1945.

532

The north wind doth blow,
And we shall have snow,
And what will poor robin do then?
    Poor thing.
He'll sit in a barn,
And keep himself warm,
And hide his head under his wing.
    Poor thing.

Songs for the Nursery, 1805 / *MG's Quarto*, c. 1825 / *Grandmamma's NR* (J. Fairburn), c. 1825 / *A Collection of NR* (Orlando Hodgson), c. 1830 / *Nurse Lovechild's DFN*, c. 1830 / *Cries of Banbury and London* (J. G. Rusher), c. 1840 / JOH, 1844 / *The Children's Hour*, set to music by Mrs. G. Herbert Curteis, 1863, five verses / *Baby's Bouquet*, 1879 / Kidson, 1904 / *Mother Goose*, Arthur Rackham, 1913.

533

If wishes were horses
Beggars would ride;
If turnips were watches
I would wear one by my side.

Sometimes said to those who indulge in too much supposition, it comes from an old proverb whose several variations, 'If wishes were butter-cakes beggars might bite', 'If wishes were thrushes, then beggars would eat birds', 'If wishes would bide, beggars would ride', date back to the seventeenth century. The verse form was first noted by JOH in 1846. Cf. also the proverb, 'If ifs and an's were pots and pans, there'd be no work for tinkers' hands', and the French 'Si soutraits furent vrais, pastoureaux seroient rois' which dates from the fifteenth century.

534

There was a little woman,
As I have heard tell,

Woman

She went to market
  Her eggs for to sell;
She went to market
  All on a market day,
And she fell asleep
  On the king's highway.

There came by a pedlar,
  His name was Stout,
He cut her petticoats
  All round about;
He cut her petticoats
  Up to her knees;
Which made the little woman
  To shiver and sneeze.

When this little woman
  Began to awake,
She began to shiver,
  And she began to shake;
She began to shake,
  And she began to cry,
Lawk a mercy on me,
  This is none of I!

But if this be I,
  As I do hope it be,
I have a little dog at home
  And he knows me;
If it be I,
  He'll wag his little tail,
And if it be not I
  He'll loudly bark and wail!

Home went the little woman
  All in the dark,
Up starts the little dog,
  And he began to bark;
He began to bark,
  And she began to cry,
Lawk a mercy on me,
  This is none of I!

Woman

Equivalents of the story of 'The Little Woman and the Pedlar' are found in several European languages. One of them is in Grimms' *Fairy Tales*, where it forms a sequel to 'Kluge Else'. JOH says that another, a Norwegian version, is in Asbjörnsen og Moe's *Norske Folkeeventyr* (1843). The very human reason why the little woman went to sleep on the highway is given in *The Scots Musical Museum* (1797):

> There was a wee bit wiffikie And she held to the fair;
> She got a little drappikie, that cost her meikle care;
> It gaed about the wiffie's heart, and she began to speu;
> O quo' the wee bit wiffikie I wish I be na fu'.
> I wish I be na fu' quo' she, I wish I be na fu',
> Oh! quo' the wee bit wiffikie I wish I be na fu'.
>
> If Johnnie find me Barrel-sick, I'm sure he'll claw my skin;
> But I'll lye down and take a Nap before that I gae in.
> Sitting at the Dyke-side, and taking at her Nap
> By came a merchant wi' a little Pack.
> Wi' a little pack, quo' she, wi' a little pack,
> By came a merchant wi' a little pack.

Eight equally hilarious verses follow. According to Laing this version was written by the Rev. Alexander Geddes (1737–1802), a catholic priest, and projector of a new translation of the bible. Southey, who devoted a chapter to the 'lay' in his miscellany *The Doctor*, while admitting that the little lady may have drunk 'a peg lower in the cup than she generally allowed herself to do', gallantly wished to obviate the suspicion that she must have been in liquor.

Mansfield MS, c. 1775, 'There was a wee wifie as I hear tell', ending 'When the wifie went hame the night it was dark The Dogie did nae see her & it begud to bark The Dog begud to bark & the wifie to flee I was sure quo' the auld wifie this is no me' [1935]. / *The Little Market Woman*, song sheet, 'Tune. *Round about the Maypole, &c.*' (J. Wallis), 1784, 'There was a little Woman as I heard tell, Fol, lol, lol de lol, de, re' / *There Was a Little Woman. A Favorite Comic Song. Introduced & Sung By Mr Fawcett in Crochet Lodge* (G. Goulding), c. 1795, 'There was a little Woman as I've heard tell, Fal de ral lal lal lal lal de dee' / *Musical Museum*, 1797 / *Little Woman and her dog* (T. Hodgkins), 1805, illus. William Mulready, later advertised (1809) by M. J. Godwin as *The Little Woman and the Pedlar* (T. Hodgkins), 1805, illus. probably by William Mulready. (New York: Porcupine Office), 1810 / *Little Woman and the Pedlar* (Joseph Roberts), c. 1825, with happy ending, 'The dog ceases to bark, The woman then did cry, Goodness, mercy on me Now I know that it is I' / *Adventures of the Little Woman, her Dog and the Pedlar* (J. L. Marks), c. 1830 [Gumuchian] / *Woman and Pedlar* (W. Walker and Son), c. 1840, panorama / JOH, 1842 / Rimbault, 1846 / *The Little Market Woman*, Marcus Ward, c. 1875 / Mason, 1877 / *Baby's Bouquet*, 1879 / Kidson, 1904, tune given as one popular for dancing in mid-18th century, then called 'A Trip to the Laundry'; the words sung on the stage to this tune c. 1765 / *Mother Goose*, Arthur Rackham, 1913 / *Old Woman and the Pedlar*, Richard Chopping, 1944 / Oral collection, 1945.

535

Old woman, old woman, shall we go a-shearing?
Speak a little louder, sir, I'm very thick of hearing.
Old woman, old woman, shall I love you dearly?
Thank you very kindly, sir, now I hear you clearly.

Herd MS, 1776, 'Auld wife, Auld wife, Will you go a shearing? Speak a little louder
Sir, I'm unkadull o' hearing. Auld wife, Auld wife, Shall I come & Kiss ye? I think
I hear some better Sir, the Lord in Heaven bless ye' / Douce MS, c. 1805 / GG's Garland, 1810 / JOH, 1843 / Chambers, 1847 / N & Q, 1868, four verses, second, 'Old
woman! old woman! wilt thee gang a gleanin'? Speak a little louder! I canna tell
the meanin''; third, 'Old woman! old woman! wilt thee gang a walkin'? Speak a
little louder, or what's the use o' tawkin'?' The writer said that in the nursery the
final verse, 'wilt thee let me kiss thee?' was followed by 'a kiss all round' / Lincolnshire Glossary, Edward Peacock, 1877 / Nursery Songs from the Appalachian Mountains,
Cecil Sharp, 1923, 'Old woman, old woman, are you fond of smoking? Speak a little
louder, sir, I'm rather hard of hearing. Old woman, are you fond of carding? . . . I'm
rather hard of hearing. Will you let me court you? . . . I just begin to hear you. Don't
you want to marry me? Lord have mercy on my soul, I think that now I hear you' /
Correspondent, 1946, . . . 'Shall I kiss you dearly? Thank you kind Sir, I hear QUITE
clearly.' The fun of these lines is increased if the last question is asked very softly.

536

The old woman must stand at the tub, tub, tub,
The dirty clothes to rub, rub, rub;
But when they are clean, and fit to be seen,
She'll dress like a lady, and dance on the green.

Mother Goose's NR, L. E. Walter, 1924 / Big Book of Mother Goose (James and Jonathan
Co., Wisconsin), 1946.

537

There was an old woman
And nothing she had,
And so this old woman
Was said to be mad.
She'd nothing to eat
She'd nothing to wear,

Woman

She'd nothing to lose,
  She'd nothing to fear,
She'd nothing to ask,
  And nothing to give,
And when she did die
  She'd nothing to leave.

JOH, 1844 / *Land of NR*, Ernest Rhys, 1932 / *Nursery Rhymes for Certain Times*, Elinor Darwin, 1946.
  Cf. *The cries of London, for the instruction of good children* (London: printed and sold by all booksellers in town and country), c. 1775, 'There was an old woman, as I have heard tell; Who when she was sick, was not very well Two eyes she had got, and between them a nose, To see and to smell with as most folks suppose', with 7 more stanzas.

538

There was an old woman, and what do you think?
She lived upon nothing but victuals and drink:
Victuals and drink were the chief of her diet,
And yet this old woman could never keep quiet.

She went to the baker, to buy her some bread,
And when she came home, her old husband was dead;
She went to the clerk to toll the bell,
And when she came back her old husband was well.

The second verse, which figures in *Gammer Gurton's Garland* (1784) but not in *Tom Tit's Song Book* or *Songs for the Nursery*, seems to be a spurious addition, but has considerable interest in its similarity to 'Old Mother Hubbard' (q.v.).

GG's Garland, 1784, 'And tho' victuals and drink were the chief of her diet, This plaguey old woman could never be quiet' / *T Tit's SB*, c. 1790 / *Songs for the Nursery*, 1805 / JOH, 1842 / Rimbault, 1846 / Kidson, 1904.

539

There was an old woman had three cows,
  Rosy and Colin and Dun.
Rosy and Colin were sold at the fair,

Woman

And Dun broke her heart in a fit of despair,
So there was an end of her three cows,
Rosy and Colin and Dun.

This is similar to the seventh verse in Harris's toy book, *The Old Woman and Her Three Sons* (25 June 1815), the text of which has been traced back to a song printed nearly 200 years earlier. See succeeding note.

540

There was an old woman had three sons,
Jerry and James and John.
Jerry was hung and James was drowned,
John was lost and never was found,
So there was an end of her three sons,
Jerry and James and John.

This is the first of fourteen verses in *The Old Woman and Her Three Sons*, a toy book with coloured illustrations published by John Harris in 1815. It is a verse which was certainly current in the reign of Charles I, and may go back to Elizabeth's time. In a ballad, *Choice of Inuentions, Or Seuerall sorts of the figure of three*, sung to the tune 'Rock the Cradle sweet Iohn', and registered 2 January 1632, the burden goes:

There was an Ewe had three Lambes,
and one of them was blacke,
There was a man had three sonnes,
Ieffery, Iames and Iacke,
The one was hang'd, the other drown'd,
The third was lost and never found,
The old man he fell in a sownd,
come fill vs a cup of Sacke.

In *As You Like It* (I. ii), Le Beau, starting to tell about the wrestlers, says 'There comes an old man and his three sons,—' and Celia remarks, 'I could match this beginning with an old tale.' It is very possible that she is referring to this verse, and, although at the time (c. 1599) the burden may have had an independent existence, Shakespeare was probably also familiar with the narrative part of the ballad (see under 'There were three jovial Welshmen'). The verse appears on its own in *A New Academy of Compliments* (4th edn., 1715), described as 'A merry Catch':

Woman

There was an old Man had three Sons,
Had three Sons, had three Sons,
There was an old Man had three Sons,
 Jeffery, James and Jack:
Jeffery was hang'd, and James was drown'd;
And Jack was lost, and could not be found,
And the old Man fell into a Swoon;
 Come, fill's t'other Glass of Sack.

This was still being sung in glee clubs in the nineteenth century, and is featured in Hickman's 'Success to the Whistle and Wig'. Some other verses from Harris's toy book are also found independently in present-day children's books, notably, 'There was an old woman had three cows' (q.v.) and 'A famous old lady had three sticks, Ivory, ebon and gold' (in Robert Graves's *Less Familiar Nursery Rhymes*).

Choice of Inuentions, 1632 / *New Academy of Compliments*, 1715 / *The Old Woman and Her Three Sons* (J. Harris), 1815 / *Universal Songster*, 1825 / JOH, 1842 / *Old Nurse's Book*, Charles Bennett, 1858 / *Big Book of Mother Goose* (James and Jonathan Co., Wisconsin), 1946.

 Pantomime: The first E. L. Blanchard wrote, when a youth of seventeen, was *The Old Woman and Her Three Sons; or, Harlequin and The Wizard of Wookey Hole*, 1837.

541

There was an old woman
Lived under a hill,
And if she's not gone
She lives there still.

This type of fun, the 'self evident proposition, which is the very Essence of Truth', appealed to the seventeenth- and eighteenth-century mind, and many instances of it are found, e.g. in the 1810 edition of *Gammer Gurton's Garland*,

 Pillycock, pillycock, sate on a hill,
 If he's not gone—he sits there still.

This particular rhyme has been suppressed, being too indelicate for latter-day repetition, though it had already undergone treatment, and the broadness of the joke been lost. What clearly was the first line is repeated by Edgar in *King Lear* (iii. iv).

Academy of Complements, 1714, 'part of an old catch' [JOH] / *T Thumb's PSB*, c. 1744 / *MG's Melody*, c. 1765 / *T Thumb's SB*, 1788 / *Christmas Box*, vol. ii, 1798 / *Songs for the*

Woman

Nursery, 1805 / *Vocal Harmony*, c. 1806 / *History of Little King Pippin* (F. Newbery, advert. 1775), (E. Newbery), c. 1786, 'Peter Pippin was the son of Gaffer and Gammer Pippin, Who lived in the ivy house Under the hill; And if they are not gone, They live there still' [1814] / JOH, 1843 / *Only True MG Melodies*, c. 1843, additional couplet, 'Baked Apples she sold, and cranberry pies, And she's the old woman that never told lies'.

*** The title 'There was an old woman lived under a hill' in *Pills to Purge Melancholy* is probably of another song ('Green and Airy Around').

542

There was an old woman
   Lived under a hill,
She put a mouse in a bag,
   And sent it to the mill.
The miller did swear
   By the point of his knife,
He never took toll
   Of a mouse in his life.

MG's Melody, c. 1765 / *GG's Garland*, 1784 / *Vocal Harmony*, c. 1806 / *Nurse Lovechild's DFN*, c. 1830 / JOH, 1842.

543

There was an old woman
   Sold puddings and pies;
She went to the mill
   And dust blew in her eyes.
She has hot pies
   And cold pies to sell;
Wherever she goes
   You may follow her by the smell.

The above lines stand as the opening verse of *The Old Pudding-pye Woman set forth in her colours*, a ballad, printed in black-letter on a broadside, registered 1 March 1675. It is much in the vein of another of the period, *The Rag-man*, by John Lookes, and may have come from the same pen. Of somewhat schoolboy humour, the ballad appears to have been popular. It is referred to thirteen years later in 'A New-made Medley, compos'd of Sundry Songs', sung in 1689. In the succeeding eleven verses the old woman is described as having nauseous personal habits, and a warning at the end of the ballad against buying her 'pudding-pyes' (custard pies) might be thought to have been redundant.

Old Pudding-pye Woman (F. Coles, &c.), 1675 / *T Thumb's PSB*, c. 1744 / *MG's Melody*, c. 1765 / *Nancy Cock's PSB*, c. 1780, 'Wherever she goes, if you have a good nose, You may follow her by the smell' / *GG's Garland*, 1784 / *T Thumb's SB*, 1788 / *Vocal Harmony*, c. 1806 / *Rhymes for the Fireside* (Thomas Richardson), c. 1828 / JOH, 1842 / *Only True MG's Melodies*, c. 1843 / *Mother Goose's NR*, L. E. Walter, 1924.

544

There was an old woman tossed up in a basket,
Seventeen times as high as the moon;
Where she was going I couldn't but ask it,
For in her hand she carried a broom.
Old woman, old woman, old woman, quoth I,
Where are you going to up so high?
To brush the cobwebs off the sky!
May I go with you?
Aye, by-and-by.

Rimbault says this song is supposed to allude to James II. Possibly he was influenced by the fact that its usual tune is the famous 'Lilliburlero', a tune which 'danced James II out of three kingdoms'. The various assertions, however, of JOH, Kidson, and Bett, to the effect that 'Lilliburlero' is entitled 'Lilliburlero or Old Woman whither so high' in *Musick's Handmaid* (1689) have not been substantiated. The tune is first given in Robert Carr's *The Delightful Companion* (2nd edn., 1686), where it is untitled. In the preface of *Mother Goose's Melody* (c. 1765) the editor says that the old woman was Henry V, and that the words were written—to a tune the king had composed—by opponents of his war in France. This is probably a Goldsmithian jest (see p. 34). The song was a favourite of Goldsmith's. Johnson told Mrs. Thrale how Goldsmith made a point of singing 'the Song of the Old Woman toss'd in a Blanket' the night his play *The Good Natur'd Man* was produced in 1768. Williams (1923) describes the song as 'a favourite old morris piece', and adds that it was 'popular at the pastime of step-dancing, when the tune was played by fiddlers'. In spite of the rhyming, the original wording was probably 'tossed up in a *blanket Ninety-nine* times as high as the moon', as in the William and Mary ballad, *The Jacobite tossed up in a blanket*.

MG's Melody, c. 1765 / *GG's Garland*, 1784 / *Infant Institutes*, 1797, 'Nineteen times as high as the moon' / *Christmas Box*, vol. iii, 1798, 'ten times' / *Songs for the Nursery*, 1805, 'Seventy times' / *New Year's Gift* (J. Catnach), c. 1830 / *London Jingles* (J. G. Rusher), c. 1840 / JOH, 1842 / Chambers, 1842, 'There was a wee wifie row't up in a blanket, Nineteen times as hie as the moon; And what did she there I canna declare, For in her oxter she bure the sun. Wee wifie, wee wifie, wee wifie, quo' I, Oh, what are ye doin' up there sae hie? I'm blawin the cauld cluds out o' the lift: Weel dune, weel dune, wee wifie! quo' I' / *Traditional Nursery Songs*, Felix Summerly, 1843, illustration by John Linnell / *Flight of the Old Woman* (D. Bogue), 1844, an unfolding panorama / Rimbault, 1846, two tunes / Mason, 1877, 'fifty times' / *Baby's Bouquet*, 1879 / N & Q, 1886, version sung in Sussex to the tune 'Lilliburlero' as a harvest song / Williams, 1923. Snatches of the 'nursery song' or 'child's rhyme' appear in Southey's *The Doctor*, 1835; and in Dickens's *Bleak House*, 1852, 'Little old woman, and whither so high?—To sweep the cobwebs out of the sky.' The Christmas production at the City of London, 1847, was *The Old Woman Tossed in a Blanket*. Chambers, 1842 gives the tune for 'There was a wee wifie row't up in a blanket' as 'The Rock and the wee pickle Tow', which can be found in *The Caledonian Pocket Companion*, 7 vols, ?1750–60.'

545

> There was an old woman who lived in a shoe,
> She had so many children she didn't know what to do;
> She gave them some broth without any bread;
> She whipped them all soundly and put them to bed.

The celebrated inhabitant of a shoe has been identified with several ladies for little reason other than the size of their families, e.g. Caroline, wife of George II, who had eight children, and Elizabeth Vergoose of Boston who had six of her own, and ten stepchildren. It is surprising that nobody has suggested the mother of Edward Lear who had twenty-one children. That the rhyme is old may be assumed from the version in *Infant Institutes* (1797):

> There was a little old woman, and she liv'd in a shoe,
> She had so many children, she didn't know what to do.
> She crumm'd 'em some porridge without any bread;
> And she borrow'd a beetle, and she knocked 'em all o' the head.
> Then out went th' old woman to bespeak 'em a coffin,
> And when she came back, she found 'em all a-loffeing.

This is remarkable for the Shakespearian word at the end, and its similarity to 'Old Mother Hubbard' (q.v.). If the rhyme is very old, it may be wondered whether it has folk-lore significance. The shoe has long been symbolic of what is personal to a woman until marriage. Casting a shoe

PLATE XXIV

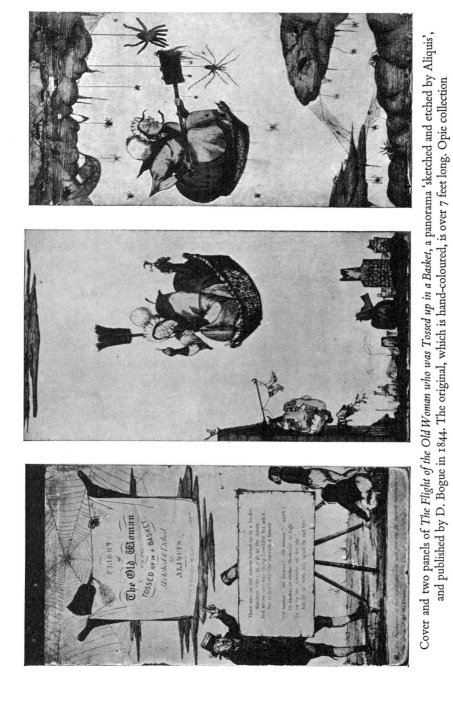

Cover and two panels of *The Flight of the Old Woman who was Tossed up in a Basket*, a panorama 'sketched and etched by Aliquis', and published by D. Bogue in 1844. The original, which is hand-coloured, is over 7 feet long. Opie collection

after the bride when she goes off on her honeymoon is possibly a relic of this, symbolizing the wish that the union shall be fruitful. This is consistent with the many children belonging to a woman who actually lived in a shoe.

GG's Garland, 1784 / *Infant Institutes*, 1797 / *Songs for the Nursery*, 1805 / *Vocal Harmony*, c. 1806 / *Nurse Lovechild's DFN*, c. 1830 / JOH, 1842, 'There was a wee bit wifie, Who lived in a shoe; She had so many bairns, She kenn'd na what to do. She gaed to the market To buy a sheep-head; When she came back They were a' lying dead. She went to the wright To get them a coffin; When she came back They were a' lying laughing. She gaed up the stair, To ring the bell; The bell-rope broke, And down she fell' / *Little Old Woman who Lived in a Shoe* (Aunt Mavor's Little Library), 1858 / *Rymour Club*, 1913, 'There was an auld wife that lived in a shoe, She had first twins, syne twins, and twice twins too; She whippit them all soundly, and sent them to bed, And when she went in she found them all dead. She went to the vricht's to get a coffin made, She thocht to the bairns, but it was hersel' instead; She gaed up the stair to ring the bell, But slipp'd her fit and doon she fell, And got the coffin to hersel', And was buried in the aise-hole' / *Appley Dapply's Nursery Rhymes*, Beatrix Potter, 1918, 'You know the old woman who lived in a shoe? And had so many children She didn't know what to do? I think if she lived in a little shoe-house—That little old woman was surely a mouse!'

A political satire, *The Old Woman who lived in a shoe; and how she fared with her many children*, etc., was published in 1871.

546

> I went to the wood and I got it;
> I sat me down, and I sought it;
> I kept it still against my will
> And so by force home I brought it.

This long-lived riddle (*solution:* 'It was a man had a thorn in his foot') is on the lines of that which baffled Homer, "Όσσ' έλομεν λιπόμεσθ', όσσ' ούχ έλομεν φερόμεσθα (All that we caught, we left behind, and carried away all that we did not catch). According to tradition, Homer was so distressed at not being able to find the solution that he died of shame. The problem no doubt will always perplex the uninitiated. A version of 'I went to the wood' was heard in a radio quiz in 1946, and had no takers.

Booke of meery Riddles, 1600 [1629] / Holme MS, c. 1645 / *New Help to Discourse*, William Winstanley, 1669 / *Little Book for Little Children*, T. W., c. 1712 / Peter Puzzlewell, 1792 / *Royal Riddle Book*, 1820 / JOH, 1853 / *N & Q*, 1864, 'I went to the wood and I caught it: Then I sate me down and I sought it: The longer I sought, For what I had caught, The less worth catching I thought it. I would rather have sold it than bought it. And when I had sought Without finding aught, Home in my hand I brought it' / *Rymour Club*, 1911, 'I gaed it and I got it, I sat it and I socht it, And when I couldna find it, I brocht it hame.'

World

547

> If all the world were paper,
> And all the sea were ink,
> If all the trees were bread and cheese,
> What should we have to drink?

This seems to have been well known in Charles I's reign. It stands as the first of six verses in *Witt's Recreations*, a book of 'ingenious conceites' and 'merrie medecines', published in 1641:

> If all the world were Paper,
> And all the sea were Ink;
> If all the trees were bread and cheese,
> How should we doe for drink.
>
> If all the world were sand'o,
> Oh then what should we lack'o;
> If as they say there were no clay;
> How should we take Tobacco?
>
> If all our vessels ran'a,
> If none but had a crack'a;
> If Spanish Apes eate all the Grapes,
> How should we doe for Sack'a.
>
> If Fryers had no bald pates,
> Nor Nuns had no dark Cloysters;
> If all the Seas were Beanes and Pease,
> How should we doe for Oysters.
>
> If there had beene no projects,
> Nor none that did great wrongs.
> If Fiddlers shall turne Players all,
> How should we doe for songs?
>
> If all things were eternall,
> And nothing their end bringing;
> If this should be, then how should we,
> Here make an end of singing.

An extra verse, not found elsewhere, and succeeded by the fourth verse of the above, appears in a manuscript miscellany by Ashmole (MS. 36) of about the same date,

> If all the World were men,
> And men lived all in trenches,

World

And there were none but we alone
How should we doe for Wenches.

The tune 'If all the World were Paper' was printed in Playford's *English Dancing Master* (1651). The verses are undoubtedly a parody of the extravagant language in ancient Jewish and Medieval Adoration. The translation, by Rabbi Mayir ben Isaac (who flourished in the eleventh-twelfth centuries), of a Chaldee ode sung in synagogues during the first day of the Feast of Pentecost goes, in part,

> Could we with ink the ocean fill...
> And were the skies of parchment made...
> To tell the love of God alone
> Would drain the ocean dry...

Such phrasing occurs elsewhere. 'Si totum celum esset pergamenum et totum mare incaustum omnes stelle essent magistri Parisienses et omnia stramina penna' appears in the German manuscript of a sermon of the Middle Ages (*Folk-Song*, 1932). The Rabbi Jochanan ben Zacchai, who lived in the first century A.D. is reported to have said of himself 'If all Heavens were parchment and all sons of men writers and all trees of the forest pens, they could not write what I have learned.' Sayings intended to illustrate the inexhaustible fullness of the Law appear in the Talmud:

> If all seas were ink and all rushes pens
> and the whole Heaven parchment and all sons
> of men writers, they would not be enough
> to describe the depth of the Mind of the Lord.

The Canticles *Schir ha Schirim Rabba* quote similar sayings of Rabbi Eliezer and Rabbi Joshua (both second century). The Koran contains passages using the same imagery:

> And were the trees that are in the earth pens,
> and the sea ink with seven more seas to swell its tide,
> the words of God would not be spent.

And a similar expression of praise may be found in St. John (xxi. 25). The imagery has entered the traditional lore of many European countries. It has been recorded in the folk-songs of Germany, Serbia, and Albania. In Italian and Corsican folk-songs the paper is thought of, as in England, not as heaven but as earth:

> Vorave che qu'i albori parlasse,
> Le folgie che xe in cima fusse lengue
> L'aqua che xe nel mar el fusse ingiostro,
> La tera fusse carta...

World

'I wish that the trees could speak, that the leaves on top were tongues, that the sea would turn to ink, the earth to paper.' An English traveller in Greece at the beginning of the last century, Edward Dodwell, heard the song of an Athenian lover lamenting,

> Νὰ ἤταν ὁ οὐρανὸς χαρτὴ καὶ ἡ θάλασσα μελαίνη,
> Διὰ νὰ γράφειν τοὺς πόνους μου ἄπομι δὲν ἔφθαινε.

'If heaven were paper and the sea ink, it would not suffice to describe my grief', a sentiment which Dodwell thought 'singularly hyperbolical and ridiculous'. Yet centuries earlier an Englishman, John Lydgate, had written in 'A balade warning men to beware of deceitful women' (c. 1430),

> In soth to saie, though all the yerth so wanne
> Wer parchiment smoth, white and scribabell,
> And the gret se, that called is the Ocean,
> Were tournid into ynke blackir than sabell,
> Eche sticke a pen, eche man a scrivener abel,
> Not coud thei writin woman's trechirie,
> Beware therefore, the blind eteth many' a flie.

John Lyly, in the sixteenth century, has it thus:

> If all the earth were paper white,
> And all the sea were ink
> 'Twere not enough for me to write
> As my poor heart doth think.

The translation of Mayir ben Isaac's ode had also entered English oral tradition. It is recounted in *The Torrington Diaries* and also in Francis Grose's *Olio* how there was found a man, almost an idiot, at Cirencester in 1779, who uttered these words which 'may be, almost, supposed the work of inspiration':

> Cou'd we with Ink the Ocean Fill;
> Was the whole Earth of Parchment made;
> Was every single stick A Quill;
> Was every Man A Scribe by Trade;
> To write the Love of God alone
> Would drain the Ocean dry;
> Nor wou'd the Scroll contain the Whole,
> Though Stretch'd from Sky to Sky.

Northall, at the close of the nineteenth century, reported the remarkable fact that the lines of the nursery rhyme were still employed for derisive purposes. In some country places a handkerchief was placed lightly over the thumb and forefinger to make them look like a gowned parson, and the words repeated:

World

If all the food was paving-stones,
And all the seas were ink,
What should we poor mortals do
For victuals and for drink?

It's enough to make a man like me,
Scratch his head and think.

This would seem to be a rustic survival from the Stuart period.

Witt's Recreations, 1641 / *GG's Garland*, 1810, 'If all the world were apple pie...' /
JOH, 1843 / Rimbault, 1846 / *Harry's Ladder to Learning* (Bogue), c. 1850, as *GG's Garland*, 1810, with additional couplet, 'It's enough to make an old man, Scratch his head and think' / Northall, 1892 / Baring-Gould, 1895.

Cf. many parallels in *Kleinere Schriften*, Reinhold Köhler, 1900; *Folk-Song*, 1932 and 1938. A late fifteenth-century Welsh version in praise of the Virgin by Hywel ap Dafydd ap Ieuan ap Rhys of Raglan is discussed by Andrew Breeze in *Bulletin of Board of Celtic Studies*, vol. 30, 1983; he cites twelfth and fourteenth-century parallels and many others. Cf. also 'If all the seas were one sea'.

548

Yankee Doodle came to town,
  Riding on a pony;
He stuck a feather in his cap
  And called it macaroni.

The tune 'Yankee Doodle', to which these words are still sometimes sung, is by way of being a national air in America. It is often stated to have been composed by Dr. Shuckburgh, a surgeon in Lord Amherst's army at Albany in 1758, but this is now discredited. In fact so many conflicting statements about its origin were made during the nineteenth century (e.g. that it was an anti-Cromwellian ditty; that it was an old Dutch folk song) that in 1909 Dr. O. G. Sonneck made a report on it for the Library of Congress. This failed to establish the origin either of the words or the tune; the only circumstance taken for granted was that the words originated in America. Recent research has tended to substantiate this. The earliest reference is in an American comic opera by Andrew Barton, *The Disappointment: or, The Force of Credulity* (New York, 1767), in which 'Yankee Doodle' is one verse of words with the direction at the end 'Exit, singing the chorus, yankee doodle. etc.' References to 'Yankee doodle' proliferate thereafter. In 1768 the Boston *Journal of the Times* for 29 September mentioned 'the Yankee Doodle Song' as being 'the capital piece in the band of music'. Subsequently, at the outbreak of the War of

Yankee Doodle

Independence, the tune was adopted by the British troops. A contemporary diarist (26 Apr. 1775) calls it 'a song composed in derision of the New Englanders'. *The Pennsylvania Evening Post* (22 July 1775) has it that 'General Gage's troops are much dispirited... and...disposed to leave off dancing any more to the tune of Yankey Doodle'. While two years later (1777) a British officer having told in a letter how the soldiers at Boston had used the term Yankee as a reproach, continued:

'but after... the affair at Bunker's Hill, the Americans gloried in it. Yankee Doodle is now their paean, a favourite of favourites, played in their army, esteemed as warlike as the Grenadiers' March—it is the lover's spell, the nurse's lullaby. After our rapid successes, we held the Yankees in great contempt, but it was not a little mortifying to hear them play this tune, when their army marched down to our surrender.'

The earliest printing of the tune may be that in Aird's *Selection of Scotch, English, Irish and Foreign Airs* (Glasgow, 1782); or may have been the sheet music entitled *Yankee Doodle* published by 'Sk:' (London: Thomas Skillern), with words; though it did not appear in Skillern's catalogue issued in 1782. Frank Kidson (*Musical Quarterly*, 1917) believed that the tune was originally evolved, without words, on the flute or fife. To 'deedle' or 'doodle' was a way of singing a tune; a not dissimilar word is 'tootle' which eighteenth-century music tutors instructed their pupils to pronounce when 'double tongueing' on the flute. In support of this, it seems that a 'doodling' chorus existed earlier in the eighteenth century. In London a satirical print entitled 'The Motion' was published (Feb. 1741), with verses underneath beginning:

> Who he dat de box do sit on?
> 'Tis John, the hero of North Briton,
> Who, out of place, does place-men spit on,
> Doodle, &c.

A political song published by T. Cooper in 1741 had for chorus '*Doodle*, &c'; and a caricature appeared, advertised 13 September 1762, entitled 'The Congress; or, a device to lower the Land Tax, to the tune of Doodle, doodle, do.' It is not inconceivable that in America a 'doodle' chorus might be named 'Yankee doodle'. Kidson quoted one of the early choruses (attributed by Edward Everett Hale to Edward Bangs, c. 1775), which lends itself to this theory:

> Yankee Doodle keep it up,
> Yankee doodle dandy;
> Mind the music and the step,
> And with the girls be handy,

as also do the words to 'Yankee Doodle' in Barton's comic opera of 1767, *The Disappointment*, mentioned above:

Yankee Doodle

O! how joyful shall I be,
  When I get the money,
I will bring it all to dee
  O! my diddling honey.

(Exit, singing the chorus, yankee doodle, etc.)

On the other hand, the name Yankee Doodle may be no more than a straight-forward nickname, formed in the same way as 'Tom-a-doodle' of the same century. The verses, it seems, followed later, dictated by fancy or the current political situation, and there were many verses as well as the familiar quatrain. Jonathan, in Tyler's play, *The Contrast* (1787), says he knows only 180 verses, although 'our Tabitha at home can sing it all'. In the supplement to *The Bath Chronicle* (21 Nov. 1776) appear what are probably some of these verses. They are headed 'A New Song. To the Tune *Yankey Doodle*', and appended is the note, 'We have been favoured by a gentleman, just arrived from Newfoundland, with the following copy of verses, written at Quebec soon after the late siege thereof'. Since these are far the earliest verses found and have not previously been reprinted, they are given here in full.

Arnold is as brave a man
  As ever dealt in horses,
And now commands a numerous clan
  Of New-England Jack-asses.
    Yankey Doodle, &c.

With sword and spear he vows and swears
  That Quebec shall be taken;
But if he'd be advised by me,
  He'd fly to save his bacon.

But th' other day he did assay
  To do some execution;
But he thought fit to run away,
  For want of resolution.

The next came in was Colonel Green,
  A blacksmith by his trade, Sir;
As great a black as e'er was seen,
  Tho' he's a Colonel made, Sir.

The Congress, who're a noted set
  Of very honest fellows,
And being upon business met,
  Told Green to sell his bellows.

He took the hint—away he went,
  And all his hammers sold, Sir;

Yankee Doodle

And for to fight was his intent,
    Like to a hero bold, Sir.

In order for to prove the same,
    (Believe me, it is true, Sir,)
When others into action came,
    He to a cellar flew, Sir.

Next Bigalow, of Vulcan race,
    Hearing of Green's success, Sir;
Resolved was to get a place,
    So went to the Congress, Sir.

A sword made of an iron hoop,
    (An emblem of his trade, Sir,)
To Philadelphia he took up,
    To show his rusty blade, Sir.

They gave him a commission straight,
    And bid him not abuse it;
Told him his rusty sword to whet,
    And sent him here to use it.

Then butcher Jophen he step'd in,
    And wished he might not thrive, Sir,
If he would spare one single skin,
    He'd flea us all alive, Sir.

Well said, says tanner Ogden strait,
    If you'll by that abide, Sir,
The villains all shall share one fate;
    I'll surely tan their hide, Sir.

Then Gullege swore, by all his shoes,
    Alive he would not leave us;
That nothing should our fault excuse,
    And Captain Thayer should shave us.

'Tis thus, my friends, we are beset,
    By all those d——n'd invaders;
No greater villains ever met,
    Than are those Yankey leaders.
        Yankey Doodle, &c.

Arnold, Green, and the other soldiers mentioned were among the Revolutionary leaders in 1775. It may be noted that the tune is referred to familiarly, and the implication of the chorus 'Yankey Doodle, &c.' is that words, too, were already known in Britain. The following verses have been recorded, all independently, the first as a nursery rhyme in *Gammer Gurton's Garland* (1810), the other three in America, c. 1830,

> Yankee Doodle came to town,
> How d'you think they serv'd him?
> One took his bag, another his scrip,
> The quicker for to starve him.

> Yankee Doodle came to town,
> Put on his strip'd trowse's;
> And vow'd he couldn't see the place
> There was so many houses.

> Yankee Doodle came to town
> For to buy a firelock:
> We will tar and feather him
> And so we will John Hancock.

> Madam Hancock dreamt a dream;
> She dreamt she wanted something;
> She dreamt she wanted a Yankee King,
> To crown him with a pumpkin.

John Hancock was the revolutionary leader renowned as the first to sign the Declaration of Independence (1776). JOH included the *Gammer Gurton* verse in his 1842 collection without comment. The tune 'Yankee Doodle' is also often associated with the nursery rhyme 'Lucy Locket' (q.v.). The word 'macaroni' in the text verse has often puzzled children. Young dandies, who had been on the Tour, wore fantastical clothes, and affected Continental habits, were dubbed 'Macaronis'; there was, indeed, a Macaroni Club flourishing in 1764.

As a nursery rhyme: *GG's Garland*, 1810 / Douce MS II, c. 1820, and JOH, 1842, 'Yankee Doodle came to town Upon a Kentish poney, Stuck a feather in his hat, And called him Macaroni' / Rimbault, 1846, the 'How d'you think they serv'd him' verse / *Land of NR*, Ernest Rhys, 1932, 'Yankee Doodle's come to town, On a speckled pony; They stuck a feather in his crown, And called him Macaroni' / Correspondent, 1948, learnt in nursery, 'Yankee Doodle borrowed money, Yankee Doodle spent it; He then began to ridicule The silly fools who lent it.'

549

> Oh, the brave old Duke of York,
> He had ten thousand men;
> He marched them up to the top of the hill,
> And he marched them down again.

York

And when they were up, they were up,
  And when they were down, they were down,
  And when they were only half-way up,
    They were neither up nor down.

'The name of Frederick Duke of York has only been preserved from oblivion by a cruel and senseless jingle' writes Colonel Burne in his biography. 'Not only Macaulay's schoolboy but the veriest office-boy of the present day knows this of the Noble Duke of York, that he marched his army up a hill and then reversed the operation.... I have been at pains to discover the origin of this jingle, and to locate the hill, if such exists. I have failed. The name of the author seems to be "sunk without trace". As for the hill, Mount Cassel in Belgium is sometimes pointed to as the spot, but there can be no substance in this; the nearest the Duke ever got to Mount Cassel was over ten miles away. Nor is there any event in his military career that remotely resembles the operation described in the jingle. Most of the country over which he operated, whether in the Flanders or Helder campaigns, is, as everyone knows, flat; there are no hills worthy of the name. Further south, in the vicinity of Cambrai, the ground is undulating, but cannot be described as hilly.' Colonel Burne compares the lampoon with the old rhyme, 'The King of France went up the hill with forty thousand men' (q.v.), and concludes, probably correctly, that some nimble-witted detractor of the Duke unscrupulously adapted the old lines to the new subject. Historians, even of recent date, have continued to malign the 'brave old Duke'. He was, however, always popular with his troops, and the latest evidence to come to light seems to establish his ability as commander-in-chief.

Northall, 1892, 'In Warwickshire, juveniles say: 'O, the mighty King of France (or Duke of York), With his twenty thousand men, He marched them up a very high hill, And he marched them down again'; &c. / Gomme, 1894 / *Golspie*, E. W. B. Nicholson, 1897, 'Napoleon was a general, he had ten thousand men', &c. / *Eighty Singing Games*, F. Kidson, 1907, two versions, one beginning 'Oh the famous Duke of York, He marched his men to war, But none of them got to the battle-field Because it was so far' / *Mother Goose*, Arthur Rackham, 1913 / *Less Familiar NR*, Robert Graves, 1927, 'The Duke of Cumberland' / *Mother Goose* (T. Nelson), c. 1945, 'O, the grand old Duke o' York, He had ten thousand men; He marched them up the hill, my boys, Then marched them down again! So when you're up, you're up', &c. / *This Little Puffin...Finger plays and nursery games*, E. Matterson, illus. Claudio Muñoz, as marching game with additional stanzas, 'They beat their drums... played their pipes...banged their guns to the top of the hill.'

An Index of Notable Figures

ASSOCIATED WITH THE INVENTION, DIFFUSION,
OR ILLUSTRATION OF NURSERY RHYMES

An Index of Notable Figures

Carnan, Thomas, 32

Carroll, Lewis, see Dodgson, C. L

Catnach, James, printer and publisher, *Nursery Rhymes* (c. 1830), reproductions, 297; *Nurse Love-Child's Legacy* (c. 1830); *New Year's Gift* (c. 1830); also, 56, 124, 181, 296, 379, 500

Catnach, John, 54, 155

Centlivre, Susannah, 449

Chambers, Sir Edmund, 64; also referred to, 17

Chambers, Robert, editor, *Popular Rhymes of Scotland* (1826, 1842, 1847, and 1870); also 23, 38, 90, 176, 211, 213, 215, 260, 283, 364, 385, 426, 482, 498

Chapman, George, 16, 232

Chappell, William, 157, 293, 300

Chesterton, G. K., 2

Child, Professor F. J., 90, 127, 128, 217, 497; also referred to, 462

Child, Mrs. L. M., 122, 173, 215, 264, 338, 404, 411, 414, 436, 483, 503

Clare, John, 90

Clarke, John, 121, 147, 280

Cockburn, Thomas, 43, 299

Coffey, Charles, 237, 356

Cole, Sir Henry ('Felix Summerly'), editor, *Traditional Nursery Songs* (1843)

Coleridge, Samuel Taylor, 411

Collier, J. P., 68, 69; also referred to, 38

Collins, Benjamin, part-publisher, *The Famous Tommy Thumb's Little Story-Book* (c. 1760), and *The Top Book of All* (c. 1760), esp. 30; reproductions, 252, plate II; also, 33, 38, 39

Comus, see Ballantyne, R. M

Concanen, Alfred, illustrator, *A Singing Quadrille* (1877); also, plate XVIII

Cooper, Mary, publisher, *Tommy Thumb's Pretty Song Book* (c. 1744), esp. 30 and plate VII; also, 53, 56, 138, 445

Cope, C. W., 179

Coward, Noel, 186

Cox, E. Morant, 155, 273

Crane, Walter, illustrator, *The Absurd A.B.C.* (c. 1873); *Baby's Own Alphabet* (1874), esp. plate I; *Alphabet of Old Friends* (1875); *Baby's Opera* (1877), esp. plate XXI; *The Baby's Bouquet* (1879); part-illustrator, *Mother Goose's Nursery Rhymes* (1877); also, 155, 215, 273, 380, 394, 414, 455, 472

Crokatt, Gilbert, 299

Crowder, Stanley, part-publisher, *The Famous Tommy Thumb's Little Story-Book* (c. 1760), and *The Top Book of All* (c. 1760), esp. 30; reproductions, 297, plate II

Crowquill, Alfred, see Forrester, A. H

Cruikshank, George, 54, 272, 273, 379, 428

Cruikshank, Robert, 262, 283; plate XIX

Cundall, Joseph, publisher, *Traditional Nursery Songs* (1843); also, 355, 380, 423

Cunningham, Allan, 23, 84, 128

Curate, John, see Crokatt, Gilbert, and Monroe, John

Cussans, Jack, 4, 22, 444

Dalziel, E., E. G., and T., engravers and part-illustrators, *National Nursery Rhymes* (1870)

Darlow, Biddy, illustrator, *Fifteen Old Nursery Rhymes* (1935)

Darton, William (Senior and/or Junior), publisher, 1818 edn. *Songs for the Nursery*, esp. 35, plate XII; also, 123, 124, 155, 279, 475; plate VI; also referred to, 423

Dauney, William, 136, 460, 461–2

De la Mare, Walter, 2, 143, 200, 293, 311, 324, 327, 330, 368, 371, 406, 498

De Quincey, Thomas, 351

Dibdin, Charles, 132

Dicey, William and/or Cluer, 249, 251, 278, 457, 459

Dickens, Charles, 134, 181, 275, 346, 419–20, 488, 522

Dodgson, C. L. ('Lewis Carroll'), 254, 275, 317, 428, 475, 502

Douce, Francis, Douce MS. (c. 1805–c. 1815); contributor to 1810 edn. *Gammer Gurton's Garland*, esp. 35; also, 31, 256

Douglas, Norman, 237, 395

D'Urfey, Thomas, 1, 211, 404, 489

Eachard, Rev. John, 53

Edgeworth, Maria, 159, 183, 233

An Index of Notable Figures

An Index of Notable Figures

Haslewood, Constance, illustrator, *Young England's Nursery Rhymes* (c. 1887); *The Dear Old Nursery Rhymes* (1896)

Haslewood, Joseph, 35

Hassall, Joan, illustrator, *Scottish Children's Rhymes and Lullabies* (1948)

Hawkins, Lætitia-Matilda, 33, 124, 173, 268

Haydon, Benjamin Robert, 241, 288

Hazlitt, W. C., 121, 299

Henley, W. E., 2; also referred to, 504

Herbert, Sir A. P., 484

Herbert, Rev. George, 383

Herd, David, esp. 23; also 86–7, 92, 98, 111, 138, 158, 259, 285, 363, 364, 416, 440, 501, 505, 516; also referred to, 302, 334, 419, 462

Hill, Rowland, 451

Hilton, John, 158, 350, 361

Hogg, James, 23, 61, 421; also referred to, 346

Holme, ? Randle, esp. 15; also, 63, 95, 228, 247, 251, 257, 298, 315, 340, 385, 432, 457, 510, 524

Hone, William, 54, 121, 273, 310; also referred to, 78

Hood, Tom, 454

Hook, James, composer, *Christmas Box* (1797–8)

Hopton, Arthur, 452

Horatius Flaccus, Quintus (Horace), 6, 298

Horne, R. C., 467

Horsley, J. C., 472

Houghton, Arthur Boyd, part-illustrator, *National Nursery Rhymes* (1870)

Howell, James, 28, 159, 206, 265, 429; also referred to, 337, 350

Howitt, Mary, 5

Howitt, William, 96, 450

Hughes, Arthur, part-illustrator, *National Nursery Rhymes* (1870)

Hughes, Thomas, 462

Hugo, Victor, 357

Humperdinck, Engelbert, 366

Humphreys, A. W., 249

Hutton, Clarke, illustrator, *15 Nursery Rhymes* (1941)

Irving, Sir Henry, 108

James I of Scotland, 127

Jamieson, John, 268

Jamieson, Robert, 9, 89–90; also referred to, 462

Jefferson, Joseph, 287

Johnson, James, 23, 157, 282, 503

Johnson, Richard, 115

Johnson, Samuel, 4, 34, 113, 335, 521; also referred to, 106

Jones, Giles, 34

Jonson, Ben, 21, 103, 486; also referred to, 5, 17, 100

Jordan, Mrs., 333

Joyce, James, 327

Jullian Philippe, illustrator, *Nursery Rhymes* (1950)

Keats, John, 289

Kelly, James, 159; also referred to, 479

Ker, John Bellenden, author, *Essay on the Archaeology of Nursery Rhymes* (1834, 1837, and 1840), esp. 26–7

Kidson, Frank, editor, *75 British Nursery Rhymes* (1904); *Children's Songs of Long Ago* (c. 1905); also, 23, 74, 128, 464, 529, 533

King, Dr. William, esp. 29; also, 25–6, 116, 157, 317

Kingsley, Charles, 98

Kingston, W. H. G., 423

Kinloch, G. R., 90, 128, 171, 498; also referred to, 462

Kipling, Rudyard, 13, 74, 101, 186, 255, 351

Kircher, Athanasius, 93–4

Kirkwood, Pat, plate XIV

Kleiser, Grenville, 261

Lamb, Charles, 58, 133, 134, 241, 279, 288–9, 296, 355, 428, 471, 493; plate IV; also referred to, 65

Lang, Andrew, editor, *The Nursery Rhyme Book* (1897), esp. plate XXIII

Lant, John, 174–5

Le Mair, H. Willebeek, illustrator, *Our Old Nursery Rhymes* (1912); *Little Songs of Long Ago* (1913); *Old Dutch Nursery Rhymes* (1917)

Lear, Edward, 5, 104, 486; reproductions, 242; also referred to, plate XIX.

An Index of Notable Figures

An Index of Notable Figures

An Index of Notable Figures

An Index of Notable Figures

Index of First Lines

Index of First Lines

Index of First Lines

Index of First Lines

Index of First Lines

Index of First Lines

Index of First Lines

Index of First Lines

Index of First Lines

Index of First Lines

Index of First Lines

Index of First Lines

Index of First Lines

Index of First Lines

Index of First Lines

Index of First Lines

Index of First Lines